KU-060-601

This book is dedicated to Miss Williams and Lilac Four. They are . . . Zack, Kiran, George H., George, Kareem, Simon, Michael, Filipp, Alek, Laurence, Tim S., Henry, Fangze, Tim W., Megan, Anna, Lily, Lottie, Lubna, Clara, Charlie, Elsie, Lola and Jessica.

I also owe a big thank you to Anna Johnson for typing out the entire text and putting it onto disk so that I could edit it properly.

boom!

(or 70,000 light years)

mark haddon

David Fickling Books

OXFORD · NEW YORK

31 Beaumont Street
Oxford OX1 2NP, UK

boom!

A DAVID FICKLING BOOK 978 1 849 92013 1

Originally published as Gridzbi Spudvetch!
by Walker Books in 1992

Published in Great Britain by David Fickling Books,
a division of Random House Children's Books
A Random House Group Company

Hardback edition published 2009
This edition published 2010

5 7 9 10 8 6

Text and illustrations copyright © Mark Haddon, 2009

The right of Mark Haddon to be identified as the
author and illustrator of this work has been asserted
in accordance with the Copyright, Designs and
Patents Act 1988.

All rights reserved. No part of this publication may be reproduced,
stored in a retrieval system, or transmitted in any form or by any
means, electronic, mechanical, photocopying, recording or
otherwise, without the prior permission of the publishers.

The Random House Group Limited supports The Forest Stewardship
Council (FSC®), the leading international forest certification organisation.
Our books carrying the FSC label are printed on FSC® certified paper. FSC
is the only forest certification scheme endorsed by the leading
environmental organisations, including Greenpeace. Our paper
procurement policy can be found at www.randomhouse.co.uk/environment

MIX
Paper from
responsible sources
FSC
www.fsc.org   FSC® C016897

Typeset in Helvetica
by Falcon Oast Graphic Art Ltd

DAVID FICKLING BOOKS
31 Beaumont Street, Oxford, OX1 2NP

www.kidsatrandomhouse.co.uk

Addresses for companies within The Random House Group Limited
can be found at: www.randomhouse.co.uk/offices.htm

THE RANDOM HOUSE GROUP Limited Reg. No. 954009

A CIP catalogue record for this book is available from the British Library.

Printed and bound by CPI Group (UK) Ltd, Croydon, CR0 4YY

foreword

*T*his book was first published in 1992 under the title Gridzbi Spudvetch! *It was a ridiculous thing to call a book. No one knew how to pronounce it. And no one knew what it meant until they'd read the story. As a result only twenty-three people bought the book. Actually, that's an exaggeration, but not much. It rapidly went out of print.*

It would have stayed out of print, but over the years a string of people got in touch to say how much they loved the book. On several occasions my publishers asked whether I wanted to update it for a new edition.

It certainly needed updating. It was full of references to floppy disks and Walkmans and cassette players. But it needed more than that. There were numerous little holes in the plot. Much of the writing was clumsy. And I couldn't read it without thinking Ouch! on almost every page. A new edition would need major rewriting. Rewriting takes time, however. And I didn't have much.

Towards the end of 2007 I got a letter from SS Philip and James Primary School (aka Phil and Jim's) in Oxford. Alison Williams said that she had been reading the book to her pupils for years and it was always guaranteed to entertain them. To prove her point she included a sheaf of letters from her Lilac Four class, and they were kind and funny and very complimentary.

I was finally persuaded. I put aside some time and returned to Gridzbi Spudvetch! armed with a scalpel and a red pencil. I cut large sections and added new ones. By the end of the process I'd changed pretty much every sentence in the book one way or another.

I'd also come up with a new title. It means something even if you haven't read the story. And everyone can pronounce it.

1

helicopter sandwich

I was on the balcony eating a sandwich. Red Leicester and gooseberry jam. I took a mouthful and chewed. It was good but not a patch on strawberry jam and Cheddar. That was my best yet.

I spent a lot of time on the balcony. The flat was tiny. Sometimes it felt like living in a submarine. But the balcony was amazing. The wind. The sky. The light. You could see the 747s circling slowly in the stack, waiting for a space on the runway at Heathrow. You could watch police cars weaving their way through the tiny streets like toys, their sirens whooping.

You could see the park too. And on this particular morning you could see, in the middle of the huge expanse of grass, a solitary man holding a metal box in his hands. Buzzing high above his head you could just make out a model helicopter, banking and swerving like a dragonfly.

Dad has always been crazy about models. Trains,

1

planes, tanks, vintage cars. But after he lost his job at the car factory it became the biggest thing in his life. To be fair, he was brilliant. Give him a brick and a rubber band and he'd have it looping the loop before you could say, 'Chocks away!' But it didn't seem right somehow. It was a hobby for little boys and weird blokes who still lived with their mums.

A flock of pigeons clattered past and I heard the sound of a familiar motorbike engine. I looked down and saw Craterface's large black Moto Guzzi turn into the estate car park. My darling sister, Becky, was on the seat behind him, a grimy leather jacket over her school uniform.

She was sixteen. I could remember the time, only a couple of years back, when she tied her hair in bunches and had pony posters on her bedroom wall. Then something went badly wrong in her brain. She started listening to death metal and stopped washing her armpits.

She met Craterface at a gig six months ago. He was nineteen. He had long greasy hair and enormous sideburns with bits of breakfast stuck in them. When he was younger he had spots. They'd gone now, but they'd left these holes behind. Hence the nickname. His face looked like the surface of the moon.

He had the brain of a toilet brush. Mum, Dad and I were in complete agreement about this. Becky, however, thought he was God's Gift to Women. Why she fancied him, I haven't a clue. Perhaps he was the only person who could stand her armpits.

The bike rumbled to a halt ten storeys below and I experienced a moment of utter madness. Without thinking, I peeled off half my sandwich, leaned out and let go. I realized almost immediately that I had done a very, very stupid thing. If it hit them I would be murdered.

The slice wobbled and flipped and veered left and veered right. Craterface turned off the engine, got off the bike, removed his helmet and looked up towards the flat. I felt sick.

The slice hit him in the face and stuck, jammy side down. For a couple of seconds Craterface just stood there, absolutely motionless, the slice of bread sitting there like a face pack. Becky was standing beside him, looking up at me. She was not a happy bunny.

Now, normally you can't hear much from the balcony, on account of the traffic. But when Craterface tore the sandwich off and roared, I think they probably heard him in Japan.

He stormed towards the doors but Becky grabbed his wrist and dragged him to a halt. She wasn't worried about me. She'd have quite liked him to kill me. Just not in the flat. Because that would get her into trouble.

Craterface finally saw sense. He waved his fist and shouted, 'You're dead, scum!' climbed onto the Moto Guzzi and thundered away in a gust of dirty grey fumes.

Becky turned and strode towards the door. I looked down at the rest of my sandwich and realized that I no longer felt very hungry. There was no one in the car park now so I dropped this half too, and watched it wobble and flip and veer and land neatly beside the first slice.

At which point the balcony door was kicked open. I said, 'It was an accident,' but Becky screamed, 'You little toad!' and hit me really hard on the side of the head, which hurt quite a lot.

For a couple of seconds everything went double. I could see two Beckys and two balconies and two rubber plants. I didn't cry, because if I cried Becky would call me a baby, which was worse than being hit. So I hung onto

4

the rail until the pain died down and there was only one Becky again.

'What did you do that for?' I asked. 'It didn't land on you. It landed on Craterface.'

She narrowed her eyes. 'You are so lucky he didn't come up here and hit you himself.'

She was right, really. Craterface had a black belt in kung fu. He could kill people with his ears.

'And another thing,' she hissed. 'His name is Terry.'

'Actually, I've heard his name is Florian. He just pretends to be called Terry.' I stepped backwards to avoid the second punch but it never came. Instead, Becky went very quiet, leaned against the railing and nodded slowly. 'That reminds me,' she said, in a sinisterly pleasant way. 'There's something I've been meaning to tell you.'

'What?'

'Amy and I were in the staff room the other day, talking to Mrs Cottingham.' Becky took a packet of cigarettes from the pocket of her leather jacket and lit one very slowly, as if she were in a black and white film.

'Smoking's bad for you,' I said.

'Shut your ugly mouth and listen.' She sucked in a lungful of smoke. 'We overheard Mr Kidd talking about you.'

'What was he saying?'

'Bad things, Jimbo. Bad things.' This had to be a

wind-up. But she wasn't smiling. And it didn't sound like a wind-up.

'What bad things?' I pulled nervously at the rubber plant and one of the leaves came off in my hand.

'That you're lazy. That you're a nuisance.'

'You're lying.' I slid the leaf of the rubber plant down the back of the deckchair.

'According to Mr Kidd your work is rubbish. According to Mr Kidd – and this is the really good bit – they're thinking of sending you to that school in Fenham. You know, that special place for kids with problems.' She blew a smoke ring.

'That's not true.' I felt giddy. 'They can't do that.'

'Apparently they can.' She nodded. 'Jodie's brother got sent there.' She stubbed out her cigarette in one of the plant pots and flicked it over the railing. 'Jodie said it's like a zoo. You know, bars on the windows, kids howling all the time.'

The glass door slid open and Mum stepped out onto the balcony holding one of her shoes in her hand.

'Hello, you two,' she said, wiping the sole of the shoe with a wet cloth. 'Honestly, the mess on this estate. I just trod on a half-eaten sandwich, of all things.'

I turned round so that Mum couldn't see my face, and as I did so I saw, in the distance, Dad's helicopter clip the top of a tree, burst into flames, spiral downwards and land in the gravel of the dog toilet, scaring the living daylights out of a large Dalmatian.

Dad threw the control box to the ground and lay face down on the grass, hammering it with his fists.

2
bad things

The atmosphere over supper was not good.

Becky told Mum it was my sandwich. Mum tore me off a strip for wasting good food. Becky said wasting food wasn't the point. The point was dropping it on Craterface. So Mum said you could drop a piano on Craterface and it wouldn't make much difference. At this point Becky swore and stomped off to her room.

To make matters worse, Dad had forgotten to take the chicken out of the freezer. He'd forgotten to buy more washing-up liquid. And he was sulking about his helicopter, which was now lying in the hall, burned, broken and covered with bits of gravel and dog-do.

'It's only a toy,' insisted Mum, halfway through yesterday's left-over lasagne.

'It. Is. Not. A. Toy!' shouted Dad.

It got very noisy at this point, so I slipped off to the kitchen and earned some Brownie points by doing the washing up. Unfortunately I had to use the lemon-flavoured soap from the bathroom, which made everything taste funny for the next few days.

When I'd finished I went out onto the balcony for some peace and quiet. Dad joined me five minutes later. He leaned on the railings beside me and gazed out into the darkness.

'Life's a cowpat sandwich, Jimbo,' he sighed, 'with very thin bread and a lot of filling.'

'You can mend the helicopter,' I reassured him.

'Yeah,' he said, 'I know.' Then he went all sad and silent. I knew what was going to happen. We were going to have one of those conversations about how he didn't feel like a real man any more. I wouldn't know what to say. He'd tell me to work hard at school, because I needed good exam results so I could get a job because there was nothing worse than being unemployed.

I didn't want one of those conversations. Not now. I particularly didn't want to think about school and exam results and jobs.

'I don't know how you lot put up with me,' he ploughed on mournfully. 'I can't cook. I can't clean. I forget the shopping and I mope around the house all day.'

'You'll get another job,' I said. 'And anyway, I think lasagne's much nicer than chicken.'

He laughed and we stared out into the dark. After a

minute or two I found myself thinking about the school thing. Mr Kidd and Fenham and the bars on the windows and the howling. 'Dad?' I asked.

'What?'

I wanted to tell him how worried I was. But it didn't seem fair. He had enough on his plate. And the possibility that I was going to be expelled wasn't going to cheer him up.

'Oh, nothing,' I said vaguely. 'Look, I've got to go and do some stuff.'

'Sure.' He ruffled my hair. 'Catch you later, pardner.'

I grabbed my jacket, slipped out of the front door and headed down the stairs.

Becky had to be lying. If she was telling the truth then she was being helpful. Warning me what was going on. Giving me a chance to pull my socks up. And Becky had never been helpful to me in her entire life.

Plus, she had a Nobel Prize in winding people up. Last year I went into hospital to have a squint in my eye put right. Before I went in, she kept telling me about all the things that could go wrong. The anaesthetic might not work. I'd be lying there, wide awake, unable to move, watching them cutting my eye open. They might give me too little oxygen and damage my brain. They might mix me up with someone else and amputate my leg.

I was so terrified that I was wheeled into the operating theatre holding a large piece of paper on which I'd written: PLEASE MAKE SURE I AM PROPERLY ASLEEP. The nurses thought it was hilarious.

On the other hand, I did muck about in class. I was in detention every other week. And I was not Albert Einstein.

In fact, getting chucked out of school would be pretty much par for the course. Everything seemed to have gone wrong over the past six months. It wasn't just Dad losing his job. It was Mum getting a job that paid double what he'd ever earned at the car plant. She did a part-time business course at the College of Further Education, came top and ended up with a job at Perkins and Thingamy in town.

So, while Dad slouched around all day feeling sorry for himself, circling job adverts in the paper and gluing bits of balsa wood together, Mum zipped back and forth in her new red Volkswagen, dressed in natty suits and carrying a briefcase with a combination lock.

Some days it seemed as if the whole world had been turned upside down.

boom!

In ten minutes I was standing in front of Charlie's house. It was a big posh job, four storeys, garage, an actual drive. Dr Brooks, Charlie's dad, was a short, wiry man with monumental eyebrows, who spoke as little as possible. He worked as a police surgeon. He was the guy you see on the TV, standing over the dead body, saying, 'He was killed by a blow to the head with a crowbar at approximately four a.m.'

Mrs Brooks, Charlie's mum, was completely different. She was a professional cook who did wedding receptions and conference banquets. She had a kitchen the size of an aircraft hangar and a fridge the size of our flat. She had a temper like a flame-thrower and talked pretty much constantly.

I walked through the gate and up to the front door, wondering why someone had ripped up the flower-bed in front of the lounge window. I was about to ring the bell when I heard a fake owl-hoot from above my head. I looked up and saw Charlie leaning out of his bedroom window. He pressed his finger to his lips and pointed round the side of the house. I kept

12

my trap shut and followed the direction of his finger.

As I stood in the dark passage next to the garage, Charlie's other window creaked open and I saw a rope ladder falling towards me. 'Come up,' whispered Charlie. I started to climb, trying very hard not to fall off or put my foot through a window.

'What's all this about?' I asked, sitting on his bed and getting my breath back.

'I'm grounded,' he explained, rolling the rope ladder back up again. 'Level Ten. No going out. No friends round. No TV. Nothing.'

'What for?'

'I decided it was time I learned to drive,' he said.

'Why?'

'Driving is a very useful skill to have, Jimbo,' he said, turning on the radio to cover the sound of our conversation. 'It seemed like a good idea to start early. So I took the keys from the fruit bowl and got Mum's car out of the garage while she was at the hairdresser's. Did a bit of first gear and reverse up and down the drive. Then it all went a bit pear-shaped.'

'Let me guess,' I said. 'You drove into the flowerbed.'

'Smashed a headlight too,' said Charlie. 'I am seriously not in Mum's good books at the moment.'

boom!

We lay around for half an hour, reading old copies of *Police Surgeon's Weekly* that Charlie had nicked from his dad's study, looking for pictures of really bad industrial accidents. Then I finally got round to telling Charlie what had been bugging me all evening.

'I'm in trouble.'

'Join the club,' he said.

'No,' I insisted. 'I mean *big* trouble.'

'Tell me.'

So I told him. He was always the right person to talk to about stuff like this. He listened properly and thought hard and when he said something it was usually pretty sensible.

Charlie looked like a Victorian chimney sweep – pointy face, beady eyes, hair going in all directions, clothes a couple of sizes too large. Not that you'd really notice him. He didn't say much in class and he avoided fights in the playground. He was the person who is always leaning against a wall somewhere in the background, keeping his eye on things.

'You know something, Jimbo,' he said when I'd finished my story.

'What?'

'You are one gullible prat. If your sister told you that the sky was going to fall down, you'd go round wearing a crash helmet.'

'But . . .' I was feeling embarrassed now. 'It could be true, couldn't it? I mean, it's possible, right?'

'Well,' he said, 'there's only one thing to do. We have to find out what the teachers really think of you.' He wandered over to the far side of the room, shoved the bed aside, lifted a loose floorboard and extracted a small black object from the hole.

'What's that?' I asked.

'A walkie-talkie,' he replied. 'And it's going to solve this problem once and for all.'

'How?' I asked.

Charlie flicked a switch on the walkie-talkie and I heard his mum's voice crackling out of the speaker: '. . . I don't care what you say, that boy has got to learn his lesson. This week he's trying to drive the car. Next week he'll be burning the house down. Now, what do you fancy for supper? I've got some of the trout left over from the Kenyons' wedding. I could rustle up some new potatoes and green beans—'

Charlie flicked the switch off. 'The other one's in the

kitchen, on top of the dresser.' He put the walkie-talkie back under the floorboards. 'I use it to keep in touch with what's going on down there in Parentland. Good, eh?'

'Brilliant,' I said. 'But how is it going to help me?'

'Use your brain, Jimbo,' said Charlie, tapping his forehead. 'We put one in the staff room.'

'Isn't that a bit risky?' I said nervously. Things were bad enough already. If the teachers found me bugging their private conversations I'd be marched out of the school gates and banged up in Fenham before tea time.

'Course it's risky,' said Charlie, shrugging his shoulders. 'It wouldn't be any fun if it wasn't risky.'

I was halfway down the rope ladder when a light came on. There was an ominous thump and I looked up to see Charlie's mum looming out of the staircase window.

She was carrying the secateurs she used for clipping her roses. 'Good evening, Jim.' She smiled down at me. 'And what a pleasant evening it is.'

'Er, yes,' I croaked. 'Very pleasant.'

'Especially for climbing into people's houses uninvited,' she tutted. 'Why, Jim, I might have thought you were a burglar, mightn't I? And if I'd thought you were a burglar, heaven knows what might have happened.'

I clambered down the ladder as fast as I could. It wasn't fast enough. And this is what I mean about the flame-thrower temper. I've seen Charlie's mum throw a breadboard across the kitchen during an argument. She just doesn't operate according to the normal rules of being a grown-up.

I was couple of metres off the ground when she cut through one of the ropes of the ladder. I lost my footing and found myself dangling upside down. Then she cut the other rope and I hit the gravel, tearing the sleeve of my shirt and scraping the skin off my elbows.

As I ran for the front gate, I could hear her bellowing, 'Charlie . . . ! You get down here right now!' I just hoped she wasn't holding the breadboard.

3
walkie-talkie

Charlie had the plan worked out like a bank heist.

He'd pop into the staff room at break and hide the walkie-talkie under a chair. The weekly teachers' meeting began just after the end of school. When the playground was empty we'd slip into the athletics shed and tune in using the second walkie-talkie.

If they said nothing, I was in the clear and we'd fill Becky's bike helmet with mayonnaise. If they mentioned my removal to Fenham, it was time to start doing three hours of homework a night and buying presents for all my teachers.

There were flaws in the plan, obviously. They might have more important things to talk about than me. They might have discussed my removal to Fenham last week. To be honest, I think Charlie was more interested in bugging the staff room than putting my mind at ease.

Worst of all we might be found by the caretaker. When Mr McLennan caught the Patterson twins in the athletics shed last year he simply pretended he hadn't seen them and locked them in overnight. He was very nearly sacked but the headmistress reckoned it would help cut down vandalism if everyone knew there was a dangerous lunatic looking after the school buildings.

On the other hand, what else could I do? I had no brilliant plan of my own and at least I was doing something positive. Doing something positive, as Mum was always saying, is a jolly good thing. Much better than sitting around all day moping. Like a certain member of our family.

Besides, two people wanted to kill me. A secateur-wielding cook and a kung-fu death metal biker. One lived at Charlie's house and the other spent a great deal of time at our flat. In the greater scheme of things the athletics shed was probably the safest place to be.

I met up with Charlie the following morning at the school gates just before assembly. His right hand was wrapped in a large white bandage, with faint bloodstains seeping through it. A hideous image flashed through my mind.

'Oh my God!' I said. 'She cut your fingers off.'

'What?'

'With the secateurs.'

'No, no, no,' Charlie laughed, shaking his head. 'She's crazy, but she's not that crazy. I tried to escape. I jumped over the window ledge and scrambled down the ladder. I thought I'd come back when she'd cooled off.'

'But she cut the ladder in half.'

'As I discovered.' He held up his wounded hands. 'I landed on a pile of old plant pots.'

'Nasty.'

'It could have been worse,' he said. 'There was a box of garden tools next to the pots.'

We began the morning doing physics with Mr Kosinsky. Mr Kosinsky thought he was very funny. We thought he was a stick insect with weird socks. You could always see his socks because his trousers were too short. This morning they had little pictures of snowmen all over them.

'Ah, you lot,' he said, whisking his jacket off and slipping it over the back of his chair. 'What a treat. Now, what were we doing last time? Was it, by any chance, the role of quarks and gluons in quantum field theory?'

'Gravity, sir,' said Mehmet. 'We were doing gravity.'

'Ah yes, my mistake,' said Mr Kosinsky, easing his lanky body into his seat. 'Now, who can give me a quick résumé of what we were doing on Monday?'

Dennis stuck his hand in the air and started telling everyone about Isaac Newton and escape velocity and why it was so difficult going to the loo in a space-ship.

I looked into Mr Kosinsky's eyes. Did he think I was a brainless nuisance? Had he decided that he couldn't bear teaching me any longer? Was he the sort of man who would want to expel someone?

I glanced over at Megan Shotts. She was sitting in the back row, as per usual, carving chunks out of her desk with a penknife. Megan beat up small boys in the playground. She knocked the wing mirrors off Mrs Benton's car. Last summer she let out the locusts from the biology lab. I found one in my packed lunch. I could be a pain at times, even I knew that. But I couldn't hold a candle to Megan.

boom!

I glanced in the other direction. Barry Griffin. He'd answered a couple of questions last year, got them wrong, then gone into permanent hibernation. He spent every lesson staring into the distance, motionless and vacant, like someone listening to music on earphones. Except that he didn't have any earphones. What he did have was short legs and very long arms. He looked like prehistoric man. Barry made me look like a guy from NASA.

Why should I get sent to a special school instead of those two? Becky had to be lying.

'Earth calling Jim.'

I looked up to see Mr Kosinsky standing next to my desk.

'Yes?' I said.

'The tides, Jim. What causes the tides?'

'Well . . .' I said, floundering.

Mr Kosinsky bent down and looked into my ear. 'Astonishing. I can see all the way through and out the other side.'

People started to laugh.

'What causes the tides, Jim?' he asked for a second time. 'Is it perhaps the gravitational pull of the sun?'

'It might be,' I said gingerly.

'Or is it perhaps a very large fish called Brian?'

'Probably not,' I said.

'Jim,' he sighed, walking back to the front of the room, 'I sometimes wonder why you bother coming to school at all.'

My heart sank. Perhaps Becky was right after all.

After lunch I lingered by the school secretary's door and watched Charlie do the drop. With the walkie-talkie tucked snugly inside his jacket pocket, he knocked on the door of the staff room. The door opened and Mr Kidd appeared with a mouth full of sausage roll and copy of *What Car?* in his hand.

Mr Kidd taught art. He wasn't really meant to be a teacher. He looked like he'd wandered into a school some years ago and never quite managed to get out. His tie was always undone, his shirtsleeves were always rolled up and he always had a slightly depressed look on his face. I think he really wanted to be at home watching Sky Sports with a can of lager. On the other hand, he could draw a really good picture of a horse. And horses are seriously difficult.

23

boom!

'Excuse me, sir,' said Charlie. 'Do you mind if I come in and have a word?'

'Can't you . . .' Mr Kidd swallowed his mouthful of sausage roll. 'Can't you tell me out here?'

'It's kind of a personal problem,' said Charlie.

'Oh, all right, all right,' agreed Mr Kidd, wafting him inside with his magazine.

A few minutes later Charlie re-emerged into the corridor and grinned at me.

'Did you do it?' I asked.

He slapped an arm round my shoulder as we walked away. 'Sometimes I am so cool I even amaze myself.'

'So what was the personal problem?'

But at this moment the bell rang.

'I'll tell you later,' said Charlie, and we headed back to the classroom.

In the afternoon we did the Industrial Revolution with Mrs Pearce. The spinning jenny. Watt's steam engine. Children being sent down mines. Or rather, that's what everyone else did. Me, I just sat at the back of the class thinking about getting sent to Fenham and being murdered by Craterface and how going down a mine sounded preferable to both.

At the end of school we hung about for ten minutes or so, then slipped into the athletics shed. Charlie took the second walkie-talkie from his bag and turned it on, and suddenly we were spying on our teachers.

For a couple of minutes it was one of the most exciting things I'd ever done. Over the next quarter of an hour, however, it rapidly became one of the most tedious things I'd ever done. They talked about the £400 they were going to spend on new books for the library. They talked about the fire safety drill. They talked about which contractors they were going to use to re-tarmac the playground. They talked about the secretary leaving to have a baby. They talked about the staff toilet and how it didn't flush properly.

I began to understand why Mr Kosinsky wore weird socks. Choosing what to put on his feet every morning was probably the most thrilling part of his day.

boom!

'By the way,' said the crackly voice of Mr Kidd over the walkie-talkie, 'Charlie Brooks came to see me at lunch today. You probably saw his bandages.'

There were murmurs around the room.

'Hey, they're talking about you,' I hissed at Charlie.

'Shhhh!' he hissed back.

'Apparently,' continued Mr Kidd, 'he was attacked by the neighbour's dog. Bit of a vicious brute, it seems. The poor boy very nearly lost his fingers. His parents had to rush him to hospital.'

'You what?' I spluttered at Charlie.

Charlie looked very smug indeed.

'So, go easy on him over the next few days,' said Mr Kidd. 'He sounded pretty shaken by the whole affair.'

Grunts of agreement came out of the little black speaker.

I glanced over at Charlie. 'Now that was clever.'

Charlie just smiled at me and said, 'Well, it looks like you're in the clear too.'

'Maybe not,' I said.

'Which is more important?' said Charlie. 'You geting expelled, or the staff toilet not flushing properly? If you were going to be expelled, I think they'd have mentioned it.'

'You're probably right,' I agreed.

'So,' said Charlie, 'when do we put the mayonnaise in Becky's helmet?'

'Now that I think about it, I'm not sure that's a terribly good plan.' I stood up. 'I don't want to wind Craterface up even more.'

In the staff room teachers were scraping their chairs back from the table, filling their briefcases and heading home.

'Give them five minutes to get away,' said Charlie, stretching his legs and yawning. 'Then the coast'll be clear and we can split.'

It was at this point that something very odd happened. I'd picked up the walkie-talkie and was about to turn the thing off when it said, 'Bretnick,' in a woman's voice.

I shook it, thinking one of the wires had come loose.

'Toller bandol venting,' said a man's voice.

'Charlie,' I whispered. 'Listen to this.'

He walked over and crouched down in time to hear the woman's voice say, 'Loy. Loy garting dendle. Nets?'

Our jaws dropped and our eyes widened.

'Zorner.'

'Zorner ment. Cruss mo plug.'

'Bo. Bo. Tractor bonting dross.'

'Are you hearing what I'm hearing?' asked Charlie.

27

'I am. But who is it?'

Charlie listened carefully. 'That's Mrs Pearce.'

'Wendo bill. Slap freedo gandy hump,' said Mrs Pearce.

'God, you're right. But who's the other one?' I turned the volume up and concentrated.

'Zecky?' said the man's voice. 'Spleeno ken mondermill.'

'It's Mr Kidd,' I said.

'I think my head is about to explode,' said Charlie.

'Wait . . .' I fiddled with every knob on the walkie-talkie. I took the batteries out and put them in again. There was no getting away from it. Our art teacher and our history teacher were standing in the empty staff room saying 'Tractor bonting dross,' and 'Slap freedo gandy hump,' to each other like it was the most natural thing in the world.

'Gasty pencil,' said Mrs Pearce.

'Spudvetch!' said Mr Kidd.

'Spudvetch!' Mrs Pearce repeated.

Two chairs scraped back, four shoes clicked across the floor, the door opened, the door closed and then there was silence.

Charlie and I looked at each other and raised our eyebrows in unison. We didn't say anything. We didn't need to. We were thinking the same thing.

Forget Fenham. There was an adventure on its way, a nuclear-powered, one-hundred-ton adventure with reclining seats and a snack trolley. And it was pulling into the station right now.

4

doing it the simple way

When I got home I had plenty of time to think about what Charlie and I had heard, on account of being locked in the bathroom for an hour and a half.

I strode into the flat, threw my school bag into my bedroom and headed to the kitchen to grab a hot chocolate. Unfortunately, the kitchen was already occupied by my sister and Craterface.

'Howdy!' I chirruped.

My head was so full of Mr Kidd and Mrs Pearce and 'Tractor bonting dross' that I had completely forgotten about the flying sandwich and the death threat until Craterface lunged at me, shouting, 'Come here, you little snotrag!' – at which point it all came flooding back.

I squealed and leaped out of grabbing range. I sprinted into the hallway, skidded into the bathroom and turned round. I saw a hideous flash of sideburns and flying fists, then I slammed the door and locked it.

'Come out and be killed!' he shouted, battering the flimsy plywood.

I wasn't stupid. I picked up the bottle of bleach, took the top off, pointed the nozzle towards the door and waited. The hinges strained but didn't give way.

Moments later I heard Dad wander out of his bedroom and mutter, 'What's all this then?'

Craterface replied that he was going to kill me. Becky said he didn't mean it. And Craterface said he did mean it.

I waited for Dad to kick Craterface out of the flat or knock him unconscious with a blow to the head. But he just ummed and erred and said, 'I'm going to the shop. If you're not gone when I'm back, there'll be trouble.'

I was beginning to see what Dad meant when he said that he wasn't a real man any more.

When the flat door banged behind him, Craterface laughed, hammered on the bathroom door a bit more, got bored and returned to the kitchen. Keeping the bleach to hand, I sat down on the fluffy blue bathmat and did some thinking.

And what I thought was this . . . They weren't talking nonsense. They weren't the sort of people who talked nonsense. Ever. Mrs Pearce was eighty-five, or thereabouts, and Mr Kidd had no sense of humour. No. What they were saying sounded exactly like a real conversation. It was just that you couldn't understand a word of it.

So they were talking a foreign language. Perhaps they used to live in Burkina Faso or the Philippines. Perhaps they'd gone on holiday to Greenland or Vietnam. Perhaps they went to Mongolian evening classes together.

In which case, why did we never see them talking at any other time? I couldn't remember them exchanging a single word in all the years I'd been at the school.

And if they spoke a foreign language, why hadn't they told us? They were teachers. Teachers loved showing off. Only last week Mr Kidd had been reminding us yet again of how he once played cricket for Somerset under-nineteens. And Mrs Pearce liked nothing better than sitting down at the piano during assembly and adding extra twiddly bits to the hymn music that weren't meant to be there. If they could speak Mongolian, you could bet your bottom dollar they'd tell us about it.

They'd waited until everyone was out of the room. They had a secret. And it was a big one. A really big one. A secret they didn't want us to know about. A secret they didn't want any of the other teachers knowing about.

And we were going to find out what that secret was.

I waited for an hour and a half and Mum finally came home from work. I stood up and pressed my ear to the door.

'Where's Jimbo?' she asked Becky.

Once again, I heard Craterface explaining that he was going to kill me. A nanosecond after that I heard a loud crunch. I later found out that this was the sound of Craterface being hit on the side of the head by a briefcase with a combination lock.

He yelped in pain. 'Wotcha do that for?'

'Out!' barked Mum, so loudly that even I jumped. 'Get your greasy backside out of this flat now, or I'm calling the police.'

'Take it easy, missus,' grumbled Craterface.

'Keep your hair on, Mum,' whined Becky.

'And less of your lip,' snapped Mum.

The sound of heavy boots was followed by a loud slam. Then Mum rapped quietly on the bathroom door.

'You can come out now, Jimbo. That oaf is gone.'

33

boom!

I came out and shook Mum's hand. 'That was classy.'

At least there was one real man in the family.

After all the commotion it turned into a surprisingly pleasant evening. Dad spent so long in the shop, for fear of coming back and finding Craterface still in residence, that he'd done enough shopping for three weeks. Toilet rolls, J-cloths, washing-up liquid, scouring powder, the works.

So Mum was happy. And Dad was happy that Mum was happy. And I was happy that Mum and Dad were happy with each other. Plus, Becky was really unhappy, which always cheered me up. And anyway, she just stayed in her room, sulking, so we had a very nice time indeed.

After I'd washed up I decided to go to bed and plan tomorrow's investigations. I got my hot chocolate and walked up to Dad, who was sitting in front of the TV, watching *Police, Camera, Action!*

'Spudvetch!' I said, catching his eye.

He looked at me in a puzzled way for a few seconds. Then he grinned and said, 'Spudvetch!' and gave me the OK sign.

I grinned back and headed off down the hall.

Charlie and I were in complete agreement. We couldn't ask them straight out. We had to be subtle. They had a secret, and they weren't going to give it away to any Tom, Dick or Harry who wanted to share it.

However, there were plenty of other things we could get away with asking. And, since I'd lost the toss, it was me who got to ask first.

My target was Mr Kidd. We trailed him over the lunch hour and followed him into the school library, where we found him browsing the Arsenal supporters' website on one of the computers.

I grabbed a book on Spain from the shelves, opened it, put my head down and bumped into him. 'Sorry, sir,' I said, stepping backwards.

boom!

'That's all right,' he replied, rapidly swivelling the monitor through ninety degrees.

'Sir . . . ?' I asked, trying to force his eyes off the page.

'What, John?'

'It's Jim, sir.' I took a deep breath. 'I was thinking of learning some Spanish.'

'Really?' he said, looking at me rather oddly, as if I had food all over my face or a dangling bogey.

'We're going on holiday there, sir. Do you speak Spanish?'

'No,' he said warily. 'Why are you asking me these questions?'

'I was wondering how quickly I could learn a foreign language. Just the basics, I mean. If I really tried.' I took a second deep breath. 'Do you speak any other languages, sir?'

'Languages aren't really my strong point,' he sighed. 'I'm a pictures bloke, really. Now they stick in my head. But languages . . . Well, it's in one ear and out the other. I tried learning a bit of French in Brittany last year, but I sounded like an idiot. And if I'm going to sound like an idiot I'd prefer to do it in my own language.'

Charlie's target was Mrs Pearce.

He got his first chance three days later when the subject of explorers came up. Scott losing the race to the North Pole and dying on the way, Livingstone trekking up the Zambezi River, Captain Cook sailing to Australia and eating biscuits with weevils in.

'Have you ever explored anywhere, Mrs Pearce?'

It was Charlie's voice. I twisted round in my seat. There was a small, bandaged hand sticking up in the air.

'Of course not,' replied Mrs Pearce, smiling and shaking her head.

She was right. It was a pretty stupid question. With her tweed suit and her handbag, I couldn't imagine Mrs Pearce exploring anything more dangerous than the freezer cabinet in Sainsbury's.

'I mean, haven't you been anywhere exciting?' Charlie soldiered on. 'Like Africa or India or someplace?'

It all sounded a bit heavy-handed to me. Charlie had

never shown much interest in history before. But she was delighted by his question.

'I'm afraid not,' she said, taking off her glasses and polishing them with her handkerchief. 'I've never actually been abroad. I go to Scotland most summers, but I don't think that counts as exploring.'

I was waiting for Charlie at the school gates, wondering what on earth we did now. If they had a secret, they were covering their tracks extremely well. So well that I was beginning to wonder if the conversation we overheard was nothing more than a very vivid dream.

'Jimbo,' panted Charlie as he ran up to me. 'Sorry I'm late. Had to get the walkie-talkie out of the staff room.'

'And what story did you tell this time?'

'Got the headmistress to sign me off sport for a month. You know' – he held up his bandaged hand – 'told her it was doctor's orders.'

'So what happens when the headmistress talks to your mum at the next parents' evening?'

Charlie shook his head. 'She never gets a word in edgeways.'

'So,' I said, getting back to the important subject, 'what do we do now?'

'We should have recorded them,' said Charlie. 'If we could play the conversation back then maybe—' He stopped mid-sentence and looked back towards the school. 'I've had an idea.'

I turned and saw Mr Kidd walking across the play-ground towards us, juggling his briefcase in one hand and his car keys in the other.

'All this suspense is driving me up the wall,' said Charlie. 'Let's do this the simple way.'

'What do you mean?' I asked, feeling slightly panicky.

Charlie stepped out into Mr Kidd's path. He waited until Kidd came to a halt in front of him, then said, in a cheery voice, 'Spudvetch!'

Mr Kidd froze for a second. Then his briefcase slid out of his hand and fell to the ground. He didn't seem to notice. His jaw started to move up and down but he was obviously having trouble getting any words out.

I started to feel a bit ill.

'But you're not—' said Mr Kidd. Then he stopped himself.

His fingers clenched and his back stiffened like an angry cat's. And then something happened to his eyes. If Charlie hadn't seen it too, I might have thought I was imagining it. But I wasn't imagining it. For the briefest of moments there was a fluorescent blue light flickering behind his pupils, just like the eyes on Charlie's robot piggy bank. Except that Mr Kidd wasn't a robot piggy bank. He was our art teacher.

I was about to turn and run when, as suddenly as it had begun, it was all over. His eyes returned to normal. Slowly and deliberately he put his right hand over his left wrist, as if calming himself down. He breathed deeply and said, 'You off home, boys?'

I tried to say, 'Yes,' but it came out as a strangled squeak.

Charlie was on his knees, refilling Mr Kidd's briefcase. He stood up and handed it back.

'Thank you.' Mr Kidd smiled. 'I'll see you tomorrow, then. Have a good evening, boys.'

We stood and watched him walk into the car park. He pressed his key fob and the indicator lights on his battered Fiat winked back with a little *boop-boop* noise.

'Crikey,' said Charlie.

A swarm of fizzy white lights started floating across my field of vision. The sky started to spin round, my knees went wobbly and I had to sit on the wall to stop myself fainting.

5
burglary

I woke up in the middle of the night, thinking that Mr Kidd was standing over my bed holding a bread knife, grinning broadly and saying, 'Have a good evening. Have a good evening. Have a good evening,' as the fluorescent blue light flickered in his eyes.

I checked inside the wardrobe. I checked under the bed. I checked the balcony and the bathroom and behind the sofa. And I still couldn't get back to sleep. So I found a packet of garibaldi biscuits and watched *Star Wars* until everyone else started waking up. Then I went into my room and pressed my forehead against the radiator for five minutes.

I came out and told everyone I had a sore throat and diarrhoea and it was clearly a very bad idea for me to go to school. Obviously I couldn't say at home for ever. But for the time being I felt a lot safer lying on the sofa under a rug watching *The Empire Strikes Back* and *Return of the Jedi*.

'You poorly, poorly thing,' sighed Becky, who could read me like a book. 'I think we ought to call an ambulance, don't you? Shall I ring for one now?'

'Mum?' I said. 'I think I've got a temperature. Here. Feel.'

But Mum was too busy, whirling round the flat putting lipstick on and grabbing presentation folders. 'Get Dad to feel it, darling,' she said, checking her hair in the glass front of the cooker. 'I'm late already.'

'I'm ringing the hospital now,' announced Becky, picking up the phone.

'Act your age and not your shoe size,' snapped Mum, taking the receiver from her, slamming it back down and scooting through the door in a cloud of perfume.

Dad wasn't much help either. 'School is important,' he said, lying on the sofa, wearing his pyjamas and watching breakfast TV. 'Every day counts. You need education. You need exam results.'

'But, Dad. Feel my head. Quickly.' My forehead was cooling off. The radiator was painful and I didn't fancy doing it a second time.

'You need qualifications,' he said, giving me his top-grade, serious-father look. 'Qualifications are what stop you ending up sitting on the sofa in your pyjamas watching breakfast television while everybody else goes off to work.'

'But . . .'

'Jimbo' – he pointed his toast at me – 'you can still walk. You can still talk. You're not coughing blood and none of your bones are broken. Go to school.'

I thought about telling him the truth. The walkie-talkie. Spleeno ken mondermill. The robot-piggy-bank eyes. But it sounded crazy. And the last thing I needed was a weekly session with the school psychologist.

I went to get dressed, then picked up my bags and slouched out of the front door to the lift.

As it happened, there was nothing to worry about. We weren't bundled into the back of a van. We weren't strangled in the toilets by men in black balaclavas. Mr Kidd nodded a polite hello to us in the corridor and Mrs Pearce did the Boer War without batting an eyelid.

By lunch time I had convinced myself that it was nothing. Mr Kidd wore strange contact lenses. Or we'd seen the blue light of a police car reflected in his eyes.

He and Mrs Pearce were members of an Esperanto club, or sharing some obscure joke. I didn't care what. I just wanted to forget the whole thing and stop being scared.

Of course, Charlie wasn't going to let that happen. 'Come on, Jimbo,' he said. 'This is hot stuff. Tell me the last time anything this exciting ever happened to either of us.'

The answer was 'never'. I didn't say it.

He soldiered on. 'Perhaps there's a boring explanation. Perhaps there isn't. Perhaps Kidd and Pearce are bank robbers talking in code. Perhaps they're drug dealers. Perhaps they're spies.'

I mumbled incoherently.

'I'm going to follow them,' said Charlie. 'I want to know what they do after school. I want to know where they go and who they speak to. Because they're up to something. I know it. And I'm going to find out what it is. So . . . are you in? Or not?'

'Charlie,' I said, 'I just need to get some sleep.'

'Suit yourself.'

boom!

I got home to one of Dad's classic dinners. It was called shepherd's pie, apparently. Though it wasn't like any other shepherd's pie I'd ever tasted. I think Dad just arranged a pile of meat and potatoes in a large baking dish, then attacked it with a blowtorch. It looked like something pulled out of a house fire.

I took a mouthful, then gave up. Becky took a mouthful, then gave up. Mum told us to stop being so fussy. Then she took a mouthful, retched visibly and used a word that parents really shouldn't use in front of children. And we all had a double helping of pears and custard to make up for the lack of main course.

Craterface turned up at the door after supper but Mum told him that he wasn't allowed into the flat until he'd apologized to me. Apologizing was not really his thing so he and Becky departed in a monstrous huff. Mum then went off to do some paperwork in the bedroom and Dad and I sat down to watch *The Phantom Menace*. It felt good sitting next to Dad. It was like being little again. All in all I had pretty good parents, I reckoned. Dad might occasionally try to poison me, but he never attacked me with secateurs.

I fell asleep just after Darth Maul tries to assassinate Qui-Gon Jinn. Dad must then have carried me to the bedroom because the next thing I knew I was waking up after eight hours' quality sleep, feeling a good deal better.

Charlie was a bit stand-offish at school. I'd offended him by not wanting to be involved in Phase Two of the plan. But I'd made up my mind. I'd had enough stress over the last few days. I didn't want to be caught stalking a teacher. I told myself to be patient. Charlie would get bored soon. Or he'd be caught and hauled in front of the headmistress and given a string of detentions. Either way the result would be the same. Life would return to normal.

We met up at the gates after school, like we did most days, and I asked if he wanted to come round to the flat.

He didn't. 'Things to do. People to watch,' he said, patting his pocket mysteriously and heading off to the bus stop.

So I wandered into town on my own, went to Waterstone's and bought a copy of *500 Recipes for Beginners*. I splashed out on gift wrapping then made my way home.

Dad didn't know whether to be deeply touched or

slightly offended. I told him I'd spent a large chunk of my pocket money, so he'd better use it. I didn't want my parents getting divorced. And if that meant Dad learning how to make a proper shepherd's pie, then he had to learn how to make a proper shepherd's pie.

'It's like building a model aircraft,' I said. 'You just follow the instructions.'

I was wrong about Charlie. He wasn't getting bored. And he hadn't been caught. Every time I bumped into him he said, 'Sorry, Jimbo. On a job. Can't stop.'

I was getting lonely. And bored. And irritated.

On Sunday morning, however, I was sitting on the wall of the park opposite the flats trying to remember what I used to do with myself before Charlie came along and wondering which of my non-best friends I should ring. Suddenly Charlie materialized next to me.

'God, you made me jump.'

Using his unbandaged hand he slid an orange notebook out of his pocket. The word *Spudvetch!* was written across the cover.

'What's this?'

'Open it,' said Charlie.

I opened it. It was Mr Kidd's diary. Except that it wasn't written by Mr Kidd. It was written by Charlie.

FRIDAY

6.30   Sainsbury's (sausages, bran flakes, shampoo, milk, broccoli, carrots and orange juice).

8.00   Arsenal v. Everton on TV.

10.00 Takes rubbish out.

'Hang on,' I said. 'How do you know what he's watching on TV?'

'He didn't shut the curtains,' said Charlie.

'Yeah, but—'

'I was standing in his garden,' said Charlie. 'There's a gap in the fence.'

'You're crazy.'

I returned to the book. There was a map. And there were photographs.

The second half of the notebook was devoted to Mrs Pearce. Diary. Map. Photographs. There was even a photocopy of her library card. It was the kind of notebook you find in a psychopath's bedside table. Next to the voodoo dolls and automatic weapons. I began to wonder whether Charlie was losing his mind.

boom!

'They live like monks,' he said. 'They don't go to the pub. They don't visit friends. They do their shopping. They weed the garden. They clean the car.' He looked at me. 'Don't you think that's suspicious?'

'No,' I said. 'Suspicious is when you have a bunker under the house, Charlie. Suspicious is when you leave home wearing a false beard. Suspicious is when you visit a deserted warehouse with a hundred thousand pounds in a suitcase.'

He wasn't listening. 'I'm going to have to get inside one of their houses. Mrs Pearce's probably. Better access. Thursday evening. During the teachers' meeting. I need to have a poke around.'

'No,' I said. 'No, no, no, no, no. Have you any idea what will happen if you get caught? The police. The headmistress. Your parents . . .'

It was a stupid, insane, suicidal idea. Which makes it quite hard to explain why I decided to help. I guess it boils down to this. Charlie was my best friend. I missed him. And I couldn't think of anything better to do. Really stupid reasons which were never going to impress the police, the headmistress or my parents.

Looking back, I reckon this was the moment when my whole life started to go pear-shaped.

burglary

On Thursday evening we jumped onto a number 45 bus, got off at Canning Road and went into the park at the bottom of Mrs Pearce's garden. Ideally we would have gone in after dark, but Mrs Pearce never left her house after dark so we had no choice.

We waited for a small group of boys to disappear from round the swings, then headed over to the fence. And it was only then that a really important question occurred to me.

'Charlie?'

'What?'

'How are we going to get in?'

He smiled and extracted a key from his pocket.

'You stole her house key?' I couldn't believe it.

'No, Jimbo,' said Charlie. 'I borrowed it. Last week. She puts it under the flowerpot when she goes out. I popped into town and got a copy made.'

I didn't know whether to be impressed or horrified. Still, I reasoned, if you were going to break into someone's house it was probably better to let yourself in through the door, rather than smashing a window.

'We don't have much time,' said Charlie. 'Let's go.'

51

boom!

Once we were inside I began to see what Charlie meant. The house wasn't just ordinary. It was super-ordinary. Creepy ordinary. Like a film set. Floral china. A tea tray. The *Radio Times*. A little silver carriage clock on the mantelpiece. A tartan shopping trolley by the front door. It really *did* look suspicious.

We opened drawers. We looked in cupboards. We looked under the sofa. Quite what we were looking for I had no idea. On the other hand, if were acting logically we wouldn't have been in the house in the first place.

With every passing minute a cold hand was starting to close around my heart, and when the clock struck five I gripped Charlie's arm so hard I left nail-marks.

Upstairs was just as characterless as down. There was a travel guide to Scotland. But that was the only piece of evidence that a real, living, breathing human being lived here.

'Right,' I said. 'Let's get out.'

'We haven't done the loft,' said Charlie.

'Are you out of your tiny mind?' I whispered.

He was. On the other hand, I didn't want to leave the

house on my own. If I was going to bump into Mrs Pearce I wanted to do it with company.

Charlie climbed onto the banisters, lifted the square white hatch and moved it to one side.

'Please, Charlie,' I said. 'Don't do this.'

But Charlie wasn't taking advice. He grabbed the side of the hatch and hoisted himself up into the darkness. He vanished briefly, then his head reappeared. 'Now you. Climb onto the banisters.'

I climbed onto the banisters and he reached down and pulled me up. When I was inside the loft Charlie took a torch from his back pocket with his working hand and I followed the oval of light as it swept over the joists.

There was a box of Christmas decorations. There were some old floor tiles. There was an empty suitcase. There was a spider the size of a gerbil.

'There's nothing here,' I said. 'Please, Charlie. I want to go home now.'

But he was making his way over to the hot-water tank and the pile of elderly cardboard boxes sitting around it. One by one he started to open them and investigate the contents. I crouched next to him and started to help so we could get this over and done with as quickly as possible.

It was me who found it. A metal biscuit tin pushed into

the recess beneath the tank. I pulled it out, blew the dust off, held it in the beam of Charlie's torch and popped the lid open. Inside were seven brass wristbands, an Ordnance Survey map of somewhere in Scotland and a piece of paper. Except that it wasn't paper. At least, not any kind of paper I'd ever seen. It was like tin foil, but smoother and softer. Yet when I unfolded it I could feel that it was as strong as leather. On it was printed:

Trezzit/Pearce/4300785

Fardal, rifco ba neddrit tonz bis pan-pan a donk bassoo dit venter. Pralio pralio doff nekterim gut vund Coruisk (NG 487196) bagnut leelo ren barnal ropper donk gastro ung dit.

Monta,

Bantid Vantresillion

'We have hit the jackpot, baby,' said Charlie.

And that was the exact moment when we heard Mrs Pearce come in through the front door downstairs.

'Don't move,' said Charlie.

He stepped round me and slid the square panel back over the hatch, shutting us both into the attic, and for a couple of seconds I thought I might be sick, which would not have been helpful.

'Charlie?' I whispered. 'What the hell are you doing?'

He tiptoed back round me and picked up the piece of stuff that wasn't quite paper.

'Charlie?'

'Shhh!'

He slipped the orange *Spudvetch!* notebook out of one pocket and a pen out of the other. Putting the torch in his mouth and holding the notebook open with the bandaged paw of his right hand, he began to copy the incomprehensible message.

I sat with my face in my hands and breathed deeply and counted slowly to calm myself down. It didn't work. Through the ceiling I could hear Mrs Pearce moving about, opening doors, rattling the cutlery drawer, filling the kettle. It occurred to me that we might very well be stuck in the loft until she left for school in the morning. And then it occurred to me that I would need to go to the toilet sometime between now and tomorrow morning. And then it occurred to me that I was going to be arrested for weeing through the bedroom ceiling of my history teacher.

'Done,' said Charlie, sliding the notebook back into his pocket and putting the message back into the biscuit tin. He pushed it under the water tank and repositioned the rest of the boxes. 'Now, let's make our getaway.'

'How, precisely, are we going to do that?' I asked.

He got to his feet, cracked his knuckles and said, 'Rev your engine, Jimbo.'

He put his hands against the roof, jiggled it and wiggled it, and after a minute or so a slate came free. He pushed his arm further through the hole and frisbee'd the slate out into the night. There was a second's silence, then the slate hit a greenhouse with an almighty shattering of glass.

'Now,' said Charlie. 'Listen.'

We waited for the sound of the back door being opened, then Charlie said, 'Go, go, go.'

I lifted the hatch, slid it to one side and lowered myself onto the banisters. Charlie did the same and slotted the hatch back into place. We'd just begun to go downstairs when Mrs Pearce walked into the hallway below us. We froze. She hadn't seen us yet, but it was surely only a matter of seconds before she turned round.

She was standing very still, staring at the front door, watching something or listening for something. I felt a single drop of sweat make its way down my spine.

And then she did something we'd seen Mr Kidd do in the playground, just after his eyes went blue. Carefully, she placed her right hand over her left wrist and lifted her head for a few seconds. We couldn't see her face, we couldn't see her eyes, but something about the gesture gave me the willies.

Then it was over. Her arms dropped to her sides, she picked up her keys from beside the telephone, took her coat from the rack, opened the front door and stepped outside, shutting it behind her.

We sprinted down the stairs, along the corridor and through the kitchen. We unbolted the back door, ran across the garden and vaulted the fence before you could say, 'Barnal ropper donk.'

We didn't stop until we'd left the park and run for five or six streets. We finally came to a halt at a bus stop on the main road. I was petrified. I was out of breath. I looked at my hands and I could see them actually shaking.

'God,' said Charlie, 'that was fantastic.'

'Next time, Charlie,' I said, 'you're doing it on your own.'

I got home expecting a grilling. About where I'd been. And why I'd been there so long. And why I hadn't told anyone beforehand. But Mum was working late, Becky was out with Craterface and Dad was so engrossed in his cooking that he wouldn't have noticed me bringing a cow

boom!

into the flat. I dumped my bag and sat down. He took a spoonful of something from the pan on the cooker and carried it carefully over to me. 'Try this.'

So I tried it. And it was really very good indeed.

'Tomato and orange soup,' said Dad, 'with basil and cream and a dash of cognac.'

'Wow,' I said. 'Mum definitely won't divorce you now.'

6

captain chicken

Charlie's bandages came off a couple of days later. To celebrate the occasion his mum decided that I should be allowed back into the house. He'd suffered enough, apparently. And learned his lesson. Clearly she knew absolutely nothing about her son.

On the other hand, it did give us the opportunity to show the secret message to Charlie's dad. Obviously we didn't want him leafing through the *Spudvetch!* notebook and finding out that Charlie had been following teachers around Sainsbury's. So we made a second copy on a clean sheet of paper and handed it to him over supper.

'What do you make of this?' asked Charlie.

Charlie's dad was, in our opinion, the brainiest person we knew. So if anyone could help us translate the mystery language, it was him.

Dr Brooks cleaned his lips with the corner of his

napkin, ferreted in his pocket for his reading glasses, eased them behind his ears and squinted hard. 'A code. Gosh, how delightfully old-fashioned.' He smiled quietly to himself. 'I thought kids these days just went around shoplifting and playing computer games. Where did this come from?'

'Confidential,' said Charlie.

'My, my,' replied his dad, winking at us. 'What fun.'

'So . . . ?' pestered Charlie.

Dr Brooks shook his head. 'It's all Greek to me, I'm afraid.'

'Greek?' I said excitedly.

Charlie's dad looked over the rim of his glasses. 'It's a phrase, Jim. All Greek to me. Double Dutch. Nonsense. Gibberish.'

'Ah,' I said, blushing slightly.

'Mind you . . .' he continued, popping the last new potato into his mouth and chewing contentedly. 'Coruisk. Now that rings a bell. I mean, it may just be a coincidence, but I think I've heard that word somewhere before. Coruisk, Coruisk, Coruisk . . . Do I get some sort of prize for working this out? Bottle of whisky? Book token?'

'I think we could manage something along those lines,' replied Charlie.

But the conversation was interrupted by Dr Brooks's

bleeper. He took the little black thingamajig from his belt and examined it. 'That's the hospital, I'm afraid. No rest for the wicked.'

'See you later,' said Charlie.

'And I shall have a jolly good think about that word.' He smiled, standing and taking his jacket from the back of the chair. 'But right now I must go and have a poke around with a dead body.'

On my way out of the Brooks's house, Charlie's mum stopped me and told me to wait for a minute. I thought I was about to get a lecture about keeping her ill-behaved son on the straight and narrow, but she returned after a minute or so carrying a large, metal, fish-shaped object.

'I very nearly forgot,' she said. 'This is for your father. He rang earlier to ask whether he could borrow my salmon mousse mould. Now, Jim, I am sure your father is a very trustworthy chap, but will you try and make sure he actually cooks with this? I don't want it welded into a scaled-down Wellington fighter-bomber.'

'I will.'

boom!

I got home to find Dad with his sleeves rolled up, wearing a stripy apron and cutting a large aubergine into thin circular slices.

'Stir those onions, will you, Jimbo?' He pointed to a pan on the stove.

I dropped my bag, took off my tie and dutifully whisked the onions round a bit.

'What happened to the planes, Dad?' I asked.

'Planes, Jimbo?' He started dipping the aubergine slices in little bowls of egg and flour. 'I can do planes. I can do helicopters. I can do radio control. I can do aileron wiring and stall cut-outs. I need a challenge. You've got to progress. Turn the gas on under the frying pan. Thanks. You've got to learn new things. Keep yourself sharp.'

'Stops you sitting on the sofa in your pyjamas watching breakfast television while everybody else goes off to work.'

'Indeed,' said Dad.

Mum thought the Aubergine Parmesan was delicious. I had to agree. Even Becky liked it. 'It's all right,' she said glumly, which is high praise from a teenage death metal fan.

Dad grinned stupidly all through supper as if he'd just won an Oscar. And Mum grinned back at him like she'd just met him for the first time and fallen madly in love. At one point they were holding hands at the table. All of which made me a bit queasy, though I guess I couldn't complain.

The only sour moment was when Becky went to the cupboard to fetch a bottle of ketchup. Dad told her ketchup was an insult to good food. For a moment I thought there might be actual fisticuffs, but she looked around the table, realized it was three against one and decided to accept defeat.

After dinner I escaped to the balcony in case Mum and Dad did actual kissing and I vomited. Becky joined me soon after and said, 'What's got into him?'

'Into who?' I asked.

'Into Dad, stupid,' she said, lighting a cigarette and

boom!

dropping the match down on Mrs Rudman's balcony. 'All this cordon bleu business.'

'I bought him a cookery book,' I said.

She gave me a funny look. 'So it's your fault.'

'I think it is,' I said proudly.

'God,' she sighed, 'it's like he's turning into a woman.'

I patted Becky on the back. 'Women going out to work. Men cooking. You've just got to face it, sister. This is the modern world.'

It felt very strange being taught by Mrs Pearce on Monday. I kept wondering if she knew we'd been inside her house, whether she'd found something out of place, whether we were under suspicion. But her behaviour was no different from usual. So I soon relaxed and started to feel rather smug. We'd got away with it. She might have a secret. But we had a bigger one. It was one of the very few times in my life that I knew something a teacher didn't.

Mr Kidd seemed less scary too. We were on to them.

He might have scared the living daylights out of us. But if he knew how close we were getting it would probably scare the living daylights out of him.

We thought we were absolutely brilliant.

And it wasn't until the following Saturday morning that we realized how wrong we were.

I got up early and helped Charlie with his paper round. When it was done we cycled over to the shopping centre for a late breakfast at Captain Chicken. I bought myself a strawberry milkshake and an apple pie. Charlie opted for turkey nuggets and a black coffee, which he thought was more sophisticated.

'Any developments?' I asked.

He took out the orange *Spudvetch!* notebook and opened it at the page where he'd copied out the mystery message.

'I've googled everything,' he said. 'Fardal is a surname. Rifco make bathroom cabinets. Bassoo is the name of a creek in Montana. And Pralio sell sports equipment.' He took a sip of his black coffee. 'On the other hand, you can stick any combination of letters into Google and find something. But here's the interesting thing. Remember Dad saying Coruisk rang a bell?'

'Uh-huh.' I blew bubbles into my milkshake.

'Well—' said Charlie. Then he fell silent.

'What?' I asked.

He was looking over my shoulder. I turned round. A man in a very expensive light-grey suit was walking towards us from the counter carrying a paper cup, a napkin and a burger box. The place was pretty much empty at this time in the morning but he came and sat down on the spare seat at the end of our table.

He was fifty or sixty years old and ridiculously tall. His face was tanned and wrinkly, like he'd spent most of his life outdoors. And despite the suit there was something worryingly military about his cropped grey hair.

He adjusted his suit, opened the burger box, unfolded his napkin, took a sip of hot chocolate, and began eating his chicken burger, carefully keeping his pressed white cuffs away from the onion relish.

'Excuse me,' said Charlie. 'We'd like some privacy. If you don't mind.'

He said nothing. He looked at Charlie. He looked at me. He finished his mouthful. He wiped his mouth with his napkin. 'You think you're pretty clever, don't you?'

It was a posh voice, the sort of voice that introduces classical music on Radio Three. He didn't sound like someone who usually ate his breakfast in Captain Chicken.

I said nothing. Charlie slid the *Spudvetch!* notebook back into his pocket. 'Sometimes we're clever,' he said. 'Sometimes we're stupid. It kind of depends.'

The man smiled and took another bite of burger. Charlie and I began shuffling our bums towards the aisle.

'I don't know exactly how much you know,' the man continued, washing the burger down with another sip of hot chocolate. 'You know a little. That much is quite clear.'

He was clearly not your average weirdo.

'The Watchers brought you to my attention a few days ago. We have had you under surveillance since then. They are of the opinion that you are not dangerous. I'm not so sure.'

The Watchers? Surveillance? Dangerous? I felt the building tilt slightly to one side. Or was it me? I held the sides of my seat for support.

'The Watchers get nervous.' He brushed the bun-crumbs off his silk tie. 'The Watchers do not enjoy people poking into their affairs. And if you carry on as you have been doing, then they may decide that action has to be taken.'

He let the word 'action' hang in the air.

boom!

'Who are you?' asked Charlie.

I kicked him under the table. I wanted this conversation to end. And I wanted it to end now.

But Charlie took no notice. 'What right have you got to come in here and tell us what we can and can't do?'

I kicked Charlie for a second time.

And that's when I saw it again, for a fraction of a second. A fluorescent blue flicker inside the man's eyes. He smiled. 'Who I am is not important. Nor am I going to tell you. Only one thing is important and it is that you stop your little games.'

As he spoke these words he pulled back one of his cuffs and pressed the tip of his forefinger to the surface of the table. I pushed myself further back into my seat. The end of his finger began to glow with an eerie neon-blue light. And the plastic tabletop under his finger started to blister and melt.

'It's very simple,' he explained, beginning to move his hand along the table. 'You have a choice. You can behave. Or you can face the consequences.'

The air began to fill with black smoke and the stink of burning plastic. He was slicing the table in two, the heat from his glowing finger eating through the surface like a soldering iron.

When he'd finished, we could see his polished black

shoes through the gash down the centre of the table.

'Do you understand?'

I nodded.

'Yes,' said Charlie. 'We understand.'

And then the man did what we'd seen both Pearce and Kidd do. He put his right hand over his left wrist. It had always looked as if they were calming themselves down. Now I saw what they were really doing. Around his left wrist was a brass band, just like the ones we'd found in Mrs Pearce's attic. He pressed it briefly with the fingers of his right hand, then let it go.

'Good.' He stood up. 'In that case I shall bid you good day. Charles . . . James . . .'

And with that he was gone.

We sat there, stunned, for several seconds. Then Charlie looked down and said, 'This smells really, really bad,' and a spotty bloke in a Captain Chicken hat started walking towards us, saying, 'What the hell have you done to my table?'

We ran.

Five minutes later we were sitting on a bench in the little park in front of the flats.

'Gordon Bennett!' said Charlie.

'Gordon Reginald Harvey Simpson Bennett Junior!' I replied.

We were silent for a few moments. Then Charlie said, 'You saw that thing he did with the wristband?'

'Yeah,' I said. 'Kidd did the same thing. So did Pearce.'

'I know.' He fished in his pocket, and suddenly there it was in Charlie's hand – a wristband.

'You nicked one?' I asked incredulously. 'From the box in the loft? Charlie, that is seriously not a good idea.'

'Bit late now,' said Charlie. 'She had a whole pile. I was kind of hoping she didn't count them very often.'

'Charlie, you idiot.' Horrible pictures filled my head. The most horrible one involved me being cut in half by a hot neon-blue finger. 'Get rid of it. Get rid of it now. If they find out . . .'

'OK,' said Charlie. 'Point taken. But first . . . a little experiment.'

He pressed the bangle. Nothing. He squeezed it. Nothing.

'That guy was not joking,' I insisted. 'Please, Charlie. Chuck it.'

Then he put it on his left wrist, placed his right hand over it and pressed it.

'Snakes on a plane!' hissed Charlie, pulling his hand away as if he'd just touched an electric cooker ring. 'Try it,' he said, taking it off and handing it to me.

'No way,' I said, holding up my hands. 'Absolutely not.'

'Just put it on,' he insisted, taking my arm. 'This is important.'

I struggled briefly, then gave up. Wincing, I tensed my muscles as Charlie slipped the thing over my wrist.

'Now touch it.'

'Is it painful?'

'No, it's not painful, you big girl's blouse.'

I touched it with the fingers of my right hand and a high-pitched scream roared through my head as if a plane were landing somewhere between my ears. This was followed by a few clicks. Then I heard a voice saying, 'Gretnoid?'

I spun round to see who was talking to me. But there was no one there. We were alone in the park, apart from Bernie, the homeless guy, asleep under the hedge in the corner.

'Adner gretnoid?' said the voice. 'Gretnoid? Parliog mandy? Venter ablong stot. Gretnoid?'

71

boom!

It was coming from inside my own head. It was like having earphones screwed directly into your brain. I took my hand away and tore off the band.

'Heavy, eh?' Charlie nodded.

I decided it was time to go home and lie down.

7

raspberry pavlova

I got into the lift. An elderly lady stepped in behind me with two bags of shopping. Was she a Watcher? Was she going to stop the lift and attack me with a luminous finger? I bent my knees a little, trying to see whether she was wearing a brass wristband. She gave me a worried look and left the lift at high speed when it reached her floor.

Were Pearce and Kidd the Watchers? Were there more of them? And why were they watching?

I got out and sprinted down the corridor, found my key, fumbled it into the lock, ran inside and slammed the door behind me.

'Are you all right, Jimbo?' asked Mum, holding a little orange watering can.

'No,' I said. 'No. I'm not all right.'

'What's the problem?' She put the watering can down on the phone table.

I stared at her. What could I possibly say? I didn't want to end up talking to the police. I didn't want to end up talking to the headmistress. I didn't want to end up talking to a doctor.

Mum gave me a hug. 'Hey. You can tell me. You know that.'

I mumbled a bit.

'Have you done something bad?' she asked. 'Or has someone done something bad to you?' She was very good at this kind of thing.

'A tiny bit of the first thing,' I said. 'But mostly the second.'

'Well, tell me about the second thing. That's the important one.'

I mumbled again.

'Is someone bullying you?'

Yes, I thought, that was a pretty good description. I nodded.

'Do you want me to talk to one of your teachers?' asked Mum.

I shook my head.

She ruffled my hair. 'They do it because they're weak. You know that, don't you? Bullies are cowards at heart. They only feel safe when other people are frightened of them.' She took hold of my shoulders and looked down at me. 'And if you need me or Dad to come into school, just say the word, all right?'

'Thanks,' I replied.

'Hey, Jimbo,' said Dad, sticking his head out of the kitchen door. 'Come and help me decide on the menu for tomorrow night. I need something to follow the salmon mousse and the duck. It's going to be a spectacular, a real spectacular.'

I flicked through *500 Recipes for Beginners,* plumped for the raspberry pavlova, then went and knocked on Becky's bedroom door.

I had to talk to someone. I had to talk to someone immediately. And I had to talk to someone who wasn't going to blab to the headmistress or the police or the nearest mental hospital. Unfortunately the only available person in that category was my sister. She wasn't an ideal choice but I was at the end of my tether. If the only thing she said was, 'That's awful,' or 'Don't worry,' it might make me feel a little better.

'Yeah?' she said.

75

boom!

I pushed the door open and stepped inside.

'Becky?' I said, sitting down on the bed, 'I've got to talk to you.'

'What about?' she asked grumpily, staring into the mirror and applying her black eyeliner.

'This is going to sound really stupid . . .'

'That's pretty much par for the course,' she said, finishing off her eyes and starting to backcomb her hair. 'So why don't you just get it over with?'

'I'm in trouble.'

'Going to chuck you out of school, are they?' she laughed.

'Shut up and listen,' I snapped.

Something in my voice persuaded her that I was serious. She put her comb down and turned to face me.

'I'm all ears, baby brother.'

'You know Mrs Pearce and Mr Kidd?'

'I've been at that school for eight years, Jimbo.'

'OK, OK,' I apologized. 'Well, they're . . .' I took a deep breath. 'They're out to get me and Charlie. They speak this strange language when no one is around. They've got these brass wristbands that send messages into their heads.' I was gabbling, but I couldn't stop myself. 'And they're called the Watchers. At least, I think they're called the Watchers. Although the

Watchers might be someone else. And we were spying on them. And this really weird guy sat down next to us in Captain Chicken. And he told us to stop spying on them. And his finger glowed and he sliced through the table with it . . .'

I ground to a halt. Becky was looking at me as if I had a tap-dancing hamster on the top of my head.

'Becky, Becky,' I stammered, 'I know it sounds unbelievable, but it's true. Really. Cross my heart.'

She stared at me for a few more seconds, then said slowly, 'I don't know what you're up to, Jim. I know I was having you on about getting expelled and all that. It was a joke, OK? And you deserved it. But I am not going to fall for this guff just so you can get your own back. Drop it, right? You're cross with me. Fine. I apologize. End of story.'

She picked up her lipstick and turned back to the mirror.

I didn't even try to sleep. I waited until everyone else had retired to bed. Then I crept out of my room, made myself a Cheddar cheese and strawberry jam sandwich, sat down in front of the TV and discovered that the DVD player was broken.

I watched the highlights of the World Chess Championship. I watched an Open University prog- ramme on diseases in pigs. I watched the first fifteen minutes of a scratchy black and white film called *Son of Dracula*. But I had to switch off the TV when he crawled down a castle wall and turned into a bat. I turned on the radio. I played four games of patience. I played myself at Scrabble. I did the easy crossword in the paper.

At seven-thirty in the morning Dad sauntered into the kitchen in his dressing gown, did a double take and said, 'Goodness me, Jimbo, you're up bright and early for a change. Full of the joys of life, eh? Can't wait to get started on the day?'

And with that he began to rustle up a breakfast of fresh coffee, grapefruit slices, croissants, blueberry conserve and wild mushroom omelette.

Only when Mum and Becky had both emerged from their bedrooms did I finally feel safe enough to sleep. I went through to the living room, lay down on the sofa and passed into a coma.

Mum woke me seven hours later, saying that Charlie was on the phone wanting to speak to me urgently.

I sat up and waited for a few seconds until I could remember who I was and where I was and what day it was. I got to my feet and stumbled out to the hall.

'Jimbo?' he said.

'Nnnn . . .' I grunted. 'Charlie?'

'Yeah, yeah, it's me. Listen . . .'

'Yep.'

'I need you over here, asap.'

'What's the time?' I asked.

'Half five. Get your skates on. Dad solved the puzzle. You remember? Coruisk?'

'So what does it mean?'

'I'll tell you when you get here,' said Charlie.

I looked up. Mum was standing further down the hall, wagging her finger at me. Behind her Dad was slaving over a hot stove.

'Sorry, Charlie,' I said. 'Just remembered. It's Dad's big meal tonight. His spectacular.'

79

'Jimbo,' he insisted, 'this is important.'

'I know, I know,' I apologized. 'But this meal means a lot to him. Can't it wait?'

'Jeez, Jimbo, I thought we were . . .' He trailed off. 'OK. School. Tomorrow. We'll talk then.'

'Course.'

The phone clicked off.

Dinner started with salmon mousse on a bed of green salad with home-made oatcakes. This was followed by duck à l'orange with roast potatoes and honey-glazed carrots. For dessert we had the raspberry pavlova I'd suggested. The food was fantastically good. And because Dad was in such an exceptionally good mood he let me have a glass of wine. For an hour or so I managed to persuade myself that the encounter in Captain Chicken was a figment of my imagination. I didn't think about Mrs Pearce or Mr Kidd. I didn't think about attics or burned plastic. I was with my family. And I loved my family. Except Becky. I hated Becky. But hating your sister was normal.

I felt ordinary and safe. And thanks to all these things I went to bed at ten and slept like a log.

8

goodbye, charlie

Charlie wasn't at school. I'd taken an early bus and waited at the gates. Eight hundred pupils walked past me. But no Charlie. I stayed put till the bell went, then loped up to the main doors.

Perhaps he was ill. Perhaps he was pretending to be ill because he had some cunning plan to work on at home. There was obviously a rational explanation. I just didn't know what it was yet.

Then the headmistress made an announcement during assembly and I knew that things were taking a serious turn for the worse.

After she'd told us about arrangements for the forthcoming sports day, Mrs Gupta tapped her on the shoulder and whispered something into her ear.

'Oh yes,' said the headmistress, 'I nearly forgot to mention. Mrs Pearce and Mr Kidd are both off sick. Their classes will be taken by two very nice supply teachers, Mr

Garrett and Miss Keynes.' She nodded towards the two new faces squeezed in at the end of the line of staff.

Something was badly wrong. It was too much of a coincidence. I tried to persuade myself that Charlie and his dad had solved the puzzle, that they'd gone to the police and that Mr Kidd and Mrs Pearce were already behind bars or heading for the nearest airport. But it didn't seem very likely.

I couldn't concentrate. I got a detention from Mr Kosinsky and another one from Mr Garrett and I simply didn't care.

After lunch I faked a migraine and went to the sick bay. I was given two paracetamol and a mug of tea and groaned dramatically until they rang Dad and told him to come and pick me up.

I carried on groaning dramatically all the way home on the bus. When we reached the doors to the flats, however, I apologized to Dad, told him I'd explain everything later, ran to the bike sheds, undid my lock and broke some kind of land-speed record getting to Charlie's house.

I went through their gate, hit the brakes, turned sideways and sprayed gravel all over Dr Brooks's car. I dropped the bike, ran to the door and pressed the bell.

After a few seconds Mrs Brooks loomed up behind the frosted glass and the door swung open. She lunged towards me, shouting, 'Where the hell have you been, you stupid, selfish, thoughtless little—' Then she stopped. 'Oh, it's you.'

Two hands appeared around Mrs Brooks's shoulders and moved her gently to one side as if she were an unexploded bomb. The hands belonged to Dr Brooks.

'Jim,' he said, his face blank, 'come inside and close the door.'

I stepped onto the mat and squeezed myself round Mrs Brooks, who was starting to cry. Dr Brooks chivvied me down the hall and into the living room.

'Where's Charlie?' I asked.

'Charlie's disappeared,' he said.

'What?' I tried to sound surprised.

'He went to bed last night. Usual time. He seemed, well, like he always does. But this morning . . . he simply wasn't there.' He shook his head slowly. 'We've got no idea where he's gone.'

Out in the hall, I could hear Charlie's mum wailing horribly.

'Look. You know Charlie. He gets into scrapes. He plays silly games. Do you have any idea where he might have gone?'

I took a deep breath. I was going to sound crazy. I was going to be in trouble. But now wasn't the time to be worrying about that. 'Charlie rang me last night,' I said. 'He told me to come over. He had something important to tell me. I couldn't come because Dad was cooking a big meal. It was about that code. Do you remember? Charlie said you'd solved the puzzle.'

'Yes,' said Dr Brooks. 'Yes, we did. Sort of. But I thought that was just a game. Are you saying it has something to do with—?'

'What was the answer to the puzzle?' I asked. 'He said you knew what Coruisk meant.'

He rubbed his face with his hands. 'Coruisk. It's a loch in Scotland. On the Isle of Skye. The numbers after it – the ones in brackets – they're a grid reference. You know, so you can find the place on an Ordnance Survey map.' He paused. 'You're not seriously trying to tell me that he's gone to Scotland?'

'Wait,' I said, holding my head. It was all falling into place. Mrs Pearce went on holiday to Scotland. She owned a book on Scottish castles. The map in the box of wristbands under the water tank – it was a map of Skye.

'Jim?' asked Dr Brooks.

'This is going to sound insane.'

'Go on,' he urged me.

'The code . . .'

'Yes?'

'It was someone's secret. They didn't want anyone to know about it.'

85

boom!

'Who, Jim? Who?'

'Mrs Pearce. Mr Kidd. The history teacher. The art teacher. They were up to something.'

'Jim, what the hell are you talking about?'

'I'm being serious. And they weren't in school today.'

The doorbell rang.

'I'll be back,' said Dr Brooks. 'That will be the police.' He disappeared into the hallway.

They'd taken Charlie, I knew it. He'd used the wristband. The voice on the other end ... They knew. He hadn't behaved. He was facing the consequences.

I had to find him. And to find him I needed clues. I needed the notebook. And I couldn't trust anyone. I skidded into the hallway and ran up the stairs. I reached Charlie's room. I pulled out drawers. I yanked up the loose floorboard. I looked in the wardrobe.

I found them under the mattress. The orange *Spudvetch!* notebook and the brass wristband. I shoved them into my pocket.

I stood up and saw the robot piggy bank on the windowsill. I emptied the contents into my hand. Eight pounds sixty-five. I shoved it into my other pocket.

When I came back downstairs I saw Dr Brooks standing in the middle of the hallway talking to a large ginger-haired policeman.

The policeman looked up at me. 'The doctor tells me you're a friend of Charlie's.'

'Yes,' I said.

'Well, perhaps you can help us,' he said, taking a small flip-top notepad out of his jacket pocket.

'Tell him what you told me,' said Dr Brooks. 'That stuff about Mrs Pearce and whatsisname – the art teacher.'

The policeman's eyebrows lifted. He stared at Dr Brooks. Then he stared at me. 'That sounds interesting,' he said.

'Well,' I began, steeling myself to tell the crazy story all over again.

'I know what' – the policeman smiled – 'why don't I give you a lift home? You can tell me all about it on the way.'

Dr Brooks nodded to me and said, 'It's OK, Jim, you go with Inspector Hepplewhite. We'll be all right here. Just ring and let us know if you remember anything.'

I was about to say that I had my bike in the drive when Inspector Hepplewhite reached out towards the door-knob. A moment sooner, a moment later and I wouldn't have seen it. His cuff lifted slightly and there it was. Round his left wrist. A brass band.

'No,' I said, taking a step back up the stairs. 'Thanks. But I'll be fine.'

'We've got some important things to talk about.' The

inspector began to chuckle in a way that was not very convincing. 'And I'm going to be late for my tea in the canteen. Come on. I can drop you off in a jiffy.'

I looked towards Dr Brooks for help, but he didn't know I needed help.

'I'd rather not,' I stammered.

The inspector walked over to me and I felt his hand around my arm. 'If you know things that are significant, you should tell us. Withholding information is a very serious offence.'

I began to pull away, but his grip was like an anaconda's. And all the time he was smiling a big, friendly policeman smile from the middle of his orange beard. If I didn't think fast, I'd be in that car. Once I was in the car, he'd find the wristband and the notebook and the message. And I'd disappear, like Charlie. There would be no one to look for me. And there would be no clues left except the name of a Scottish loch.

'Fine,' I said. 'I just need to go to the toilet first.'

'I'll wait for you here,' said the inspector.

I walked into the kitchen. There was no back door. I climbed onto the sink and opened the window. I was stepping across the draining board when I kicked over a large casserole dish. I tried to grab it but I was too late. It hit the stone floor with a sound like a gong being struck.

Suddenly the inspector was at the door, yelling, 'Hey! Get back in here!'

'Jim!' shouted Dr Brooks, in close pursuit. 'What are you doing?'

I launched myself through the window to the sound of china shattering behind me. I hit the grass and rolled over, with knives, forks and spoons raining all over me.

I got up, sprinted round the corner of the house, mounted my bike, executed a neat skid round the inspector as he burst out of the front door, rode back over the lawn, then careered through the wooden gate into the park and off through the trees.

I sprinted up the steps of the library, leaving my bike unlocked. I leaped through the doors and aimed myself at the information desk. I was breathing so hard I couldn't speak properly. 'Isle of Skye. Ordnance Survey map. I need the Ordnance Survey map. Isle of Skye. In Scotland.'

'Thank you, I do know where the Isle of Skye is.' With agonizing slowness the librarian extracted a grimy white handkerchief from her pocket and blew her nose.

boom!

Then she repocketed the handkerchief. 'If you'd like to follow me.'

Eventually we found ourselves in the map section. She led me to a shelf of pink spines. 'Typical,' she tutted. 'Everyone's always taking them out and putting them back in the wrong order.'

I pulled a random map out and turned it over. On the rear was a diagram of the entire country divided into little squares. The Isle of Skye was covered by maps 23 and 32. I ran my finger along the pink spines.

The librarian found 32. I found 23.

'Can I take them out?' I asked, extracting map 32 from her hands.

'I'm sorry,' she said, 'maps can't be borrowed. You'll have to read them here.'

It was not a day for worrying about fiddling details like library rules. I said, 'My name is Barry Griffin. I go to St Thomas's,' and sprinted for the exit.

Only when I reached the flats did I realize what a stupid idea it was, going home. Inspector Hepplewhite knew my address. And if he didn't, Charlie's father would tell him.

I overshot the car park, coming to a halt behind the garages. I got off my bike and poked my head round the corner. The car park was empty. The inspector had been and gone. Or hadn't got here yet. Or simply assumed I wasn't stupid enough to come back. My head reeled. If I was going to find Charlie, there was stuff I needed upstairs. I could be in and out in three minutes.

I decided to go for it. I ran across the vacant car park, banged through the swing doors and threw myself into the lift.

I let myself into the flat and shut the door firmly behind me.

I went into my bedroom. I emptied my own savings of nineteen pounds fifty-two from the cigar box and added them to Charlie's money. I pulled the old tent and one of the sleeping bags down from the hall cupboard and stuffed them into my big sports holdall. I grabbed a change of clothes and went into the kitchen and started filling a Sainsbury's bag with food: a loaf, a packet of biscuits, some of Dad's leftovers and a box of

boom!

Quality Street. I opened the wotsit drawer and took out a penknife, the first aid kit, a torch and a roll of string. I went back into my bedroom and found a compass.

As I was doing this, the brass wristband fell out of my pocket. I picked it up and looked at it. Was this how they'd found Charlie? Was it sending out some kind of homing signal? I had to get rid of it. Except that I couldn't get rid of it. It was my one piece of proof, the one object I possessed which showed that I was not a deranged lunatic.

And then I remembered. Dad lost a plane last year. The park people put corrugated iron round the bandstand. The plane flew behind it, the radio contact cut out and it crashed into the boating lake. Radio signals couldn't travel through metal. He proved it by putting the radio in the oven and making it go silent.

I grabbed the roll of cooking foil from under the sink, tore off a large square and wrapped the wristband in several layers before shoving it back in my pocket.

Only when I had finished did I stop and stand still and listen to the ticking of the clock and the buzzing of the refrigerator and realize that the flat was completely empty. No Dad. No Becky. Where were they?

I suddenly felt cold all over.

9

vroom

I took a deep breath. They were late, that was all. Mum was still at work. Becky was still at school. Dad would be . . .

Where would Dad be? I'd done a runner. He'd ring the school. He'd ring Charlie's parents. He might be round there right now. He might be talking to Inspector Hepplewhite. He might be locked up in a cellar some-where.

I rang his mobile. Nothing. I crossed the lounge, opened the glass door, stepped outside and looked over the balcony. Maybe he was on his way back here right now. But the car park was empty.

The glass door slid open behind me. I spun round. 'Dad?'

It was the man from Captain Chicken. The same suit. The same cropped grey hair. The same wristband under the same white cuffs.

boom!

'I'm sorry, James,' he said smoothly. 'You know too much.'

'Where are Becky and Dad?' I said, backing up against the railings, my voice suddenly hoarse. 'What have you done with them?'

'Your father is at the police station. You ran away from Inspector Hepplewhite, remember? But I'm afraid the police won't have any idea where you are.' He shook his head sadly. 'Your sister is with that poorly-washed boyfriend of hers.'

'You . . . you . . . you . . .' I felt very small and very alone and very frightened.

'Goodbye, James. Unfortunately this is the bit where you die.'

I shoved him hard in the chest so that he staggered backwards, then I turned and grabbed the railing. Maybe I could climb over and swing down onto Mrs Rudman's balcony. I threw my leg over.

'James, James, James . . .' he sighed, clutching my arm and dragging me back onto the balcony. 'Don't waste your energy. You see the red Volvo?'

I looked down. A red Volvo was parked by the entrance to the flats. A man in a very expensive light-grey suit was leaning against the bonnet. A second man in a very expensive light-grey suit was standing nearby, idly kicking bits of gravel.

'Even if you got away,' he said, 'you wouldn't make it to the bottom of the stairs.'

My body went limp. There didn't seem to be any point in struggling.

Then I heard a familiar noise. It was still several streets away, but I would have recognized it anywhere. Craterface had taken the silencer off. It sounded like a Chieftain tank being driven at sixty miles an hour. The Moto Guzzi.

'I think we should do this inside,' the man said, tightening his grip and pulling me back towards the door. 'Where no one can see.'

I reached out and grabbed the railing again. If I could hold on for a few minutes until Becky and Craterface got up the stairs. If I could just—

'You're starting to really annoy me now,' he said, prising my fingers off the railing and shoving me through the sliding door into the lounge. The blue light had reappeared in his eyes and it was flickering like crazy.

I grabbed the curtains. They came off the rail. I grabbed an armchair, which turned over. I grabbed the sideboard and we were momentarily covered in a shower of biros and radio-controlled aircraft parts and Mum's decorative plates from Crete and Majorca. As I was manhandled through the hall, I swiped the paper knife from the phone table, twisted round and stuck it into the man's leg.

boom!

He said nothing. He didn't shout. He didn't wince. He merely removed the paper knife, stopped in his tracks, held me against the wall with one hand and twisted the other into a crab-shape several inches from my face. Five hot neon-blue lights appeared on the ends of his fingers and thumb.

And that was when the front door opened. Becky stepped inside, saw me pinned to the wall and screamed like a cat having its tail screwed into a vice.

'What's up?' asked Craterface, coming in behind her.

The four of us stood looking at one another for several seconds, no one knowing quite what was meant to happen next.

Then the man raised his glowing hand towards Craterface. 'You. Back off.'

'Do something!' Becky shouted.

It was all the encouragement Craterface needed. He swept the greasy hair out of his eyes, inflated his chest and said, 'No one tells me to back off, mate.' He flattened his hands, kung-fu style, then leaped forward, roaring, like someone preparing to cut an aeroplane into slices.

The man in the suit let go of me so that he had two hands free to defend himself. Craterface was really very good at the kung-fu thing. He chopped the man in the side of the neck and he tumbled backwards through the kitchen door, fell over and got himself tangled in the ironing board. It was, I think, the first time I had ever seen Craterface looking genuinely happy.

Becky grabbed me by the collar and shouted, 'What the hell is going on, Jimbo?'

'Get me out of here!' I panted. 'Just get me out of here!'

'Wait!' she snapped. 'I need an explanation.'

She didn't get one. What she got were two neon-blue hands on her shoulders. One of the Volvo men had come upstairs to find out what the delay was. There were little blue fireworks in his eyes.

'Oi!' yelled Becky, spinning round.

There were two smoking hand-prints on her jacket and a smell of burned leather in the air.

'My jacket!' she shrieked. 'Look what you've done to my jacket!'

The motorcycle helmet, which had been dangling in her hand, executed a neat curve up over her shoulder and onto the head of the new arrival, who went cross-eyed, tottered a bit, then fell into a heap.

Becky turned to me. 'OK, Jimbo, you win,' she said quickly. 'You can explain later. Let's get out of this place.'

'Thanks,' I said, grabbing the second sleeping bag from the hall cupboard.

boom!

Becky looked at the bag. 'Where are we going? Outer Mongolia?'

'Maybe,' I said.

I looked round and saw the fridge topple over onto the floor with an almighty crash.

'Terry!' shouted Becky. 'Are you all right?'

His ugly face appeared round the door. 'Course I am!' And he dived back into the fray.

Becky picked up Craterface's helmet, threw it to me and said, 'Take this.'

I grabbed his jacket too, for good measure.

All the way down the stairs Becky kept saying, 'This is totally insane. This is totally insane.'

'I know,' I said. 'I know. Please. Just keep moving.'

We ran across the car park and I began stuffing my supplies into the panniers of the Moto Guzzi. Only when I was locking them did I remember the second man in the very expensive light-grey suit, who was now running towards us.

'Becky!' I shouted. 'Watch out!'

She spun round. 'God, Jimbo, you have some really charming friends.'

She hopped onto the bike. I hopped onto the bike. Our pursuer realized he was going to need transport too, and he turned and ran back to the red Volvo. We buckled our helmets on.

'Have you ever driven this bike before?' I shouted.

'Of course not. Terry wouldn't let anyone else near it.'

'Oh my God.'

'There's always a first time!' she shouted.

The Volvo started up, screeched into reverse, then came at us like a fighter jet, with smoke pouring off its back wheels.

'Hang on!' shouted Becky.

I looked up at the flat and saw a kitchen chair fly out of a window. Then my head was yanked backwards, my bum was yanked forwards and we were off.

Considering she was a learner driver, Becky did very well. Considering she was a learner driver being chased by an angry man in a large red Volvo, she was brilliant.

We lurched and roared and skidded. We mounted a pavement and came very close to hitting an ice-cream van. I turned and saw the Volvo lurching, roaring and skidding on our tail. We ski-jumped over a grassy mound and were airborne for a worryingly long time. We hit the ground, banked round a bus shelter and found ourselves on the main road.

So did the Volvo. As we accelerated down the dual carriageway, past the waterworks and the milk depot, I glanced round once more and saw the car only metres from our number plate.

'Faster, Becky!' I shouted. 'He's catching up.'

boom!

I don't know whether she heard me. I don't even know whether she meant to do something quite so dangerous. Either way, without warning, I felt the bike swerve to the right, cut across the path of a large articulated lorry coming up behind us, leave the road and plunge through the shrubbery on the central reservation.

I closed my eyes. Branches clattered across the front of my visor and the bike bucked beneath us like a wild horse. I concentrated on keeping my lunch firmly down. I did not want to be sick inside a motorcycle helmet.

Then, suddenly, there was tarmac under the bike again. I opened my eyes and saw that we were travelling down the dual carriageway in the other direction. Twisting in my seat, I caught one brief and final glimpse of the red Volvo in the middle of the central reservation, its bonnet folded neatly round a tree trunk. Sticking out of the smashed windscreen was a sign reading: NO U-TURNS.

I told Becky she could slow down.

Ten minutes later we pulled up outside Tesco. Becky got off the bike, handed me the keys and said, 'Wait here. I'll be five minutes.'

vroom

'But, Becky . . . ' I complained.

'Listen, mate,' she said, wagging her finger at me. 'If I'm going to Outer Mongolia, I need a toothbrush, I need eyeliner and I need some clean knickers.'

10
the road north

Toothbrush, knickers and eyeliner on board, we roared away into the evening traffic. I directed Becky towards the motorway and after half an hour we pulled into a service station so that we could grab something to eat, fill up with petrol and have a team talk.

We bought ourselves a tray of scrambled eggs and chips and sticky cakes and made our way to a window seat. We squeezed in, Becky speared a chip, I took a sip of my lemonade and she said, 'Explanation. Now.'

I started at the beginning. The expulsion wind-up, bugging the staff room, Pearce and Kidd's mystery language, Charlie saying, 'Spudvetch!' to Mr Kidd, the raid on Mrs Pearce's attic . . .

Becky's chip remained suspended on the prongs of her fork, halfway between her plate and her mouth, throughout my entire story.

'Holy bananas,' she said. 'And this is all true?'

'Of course it is. You saw those men in the flat. They weren't pretending, were they?'

She let out a long, slow, whistly breath, then finally ate the chip.

'Look . . .' I said, reaching deep into a pannier. I took out the wristband and unwrapped the silver foil round it. 'Put this round your wrist.'

'So this is the thing?'

'Yeah, this is the thing,' I said. 'Now touch it with the fingers of your other hand. But be quick.'

She touched the brass bangle and jumped as the plane came in to land between her ears. 'What the flaming . . . ?'

Then the voice started. She whipped round, just like I'd done, thinking someone was standing next to her, talking into her ear.

I snatched the band off her wrist, wrapped it in the silver foil and slipped it back into the pannier.

'OK, OK, OK,' said Becky. 'I believe you. God, that totally freaked me out.'

I took another swig of lemonade. 'And I think it's got a kind of tracer on it, so we can't hang around here too long.'

She started eating her scrambled egg. 'Where are we going?'

'Loch Coruisk,' I said, burrowing in the pannier

103

again and bringing out the Ordnance Survey maps.

'Lock what?' asked Becky.

'Loch Coruisk,' I said. 'It's on the Isle of Skye.' I flattened out map number 32 across the table.

'Why there?'

'There was a message in the biscuit tin in Mrs Pearce's attic. It was in the same language they were using in the staff room. It said "Coruisk". Look . . .' I pointed to a jagged smear of blue in the centre of the map.

'And there was a map reference.' I dug out the *Spudvetch!* notebook and read out the numbers: 'Four-eight-seven-one-nine-six.' I followed the lines down from the top margin and the lines in from the left-hand margin. 'Here.' Where the lines converged there was a tiny square, indicating some kind of building by the mouth of the loch, where it fed into the sea.

'Yes,' said Becky, more insistently this time. 'But why are we going there?'

I looked up. 'I need to find Charlie. And it's the only clue we've got. The only one I can understand, anyway.'

Becky seemed unconvinced.

'This message – it was hidden under the water tank. In the attic. She really didn't want anyone to find it. It has to be important.'

I looked at the map again. It was like something from *The Lord of the Rings*. The loch was surrounded by the

Cuillin Hills. The peak of Druim nan Ramh to the north. The peak of Sgurr Dubh Mor to the south. It was eight miles from the nearest village. It was hard to imagine a more isolated spot.

'Do you realize how far away this place is?' asked Becky.

I crossed my fingers. I needed her. And I needed the Moto Guzzi. 'He's my best friend. And he's been kidnapped.'

'Maybe we should leave this to the police,' said Becky.

'Oh, yes, that's another thing.'

'What?' asked Becky.

'There was a policeman at Charlie's house.'

'And . . . ?'

'He was wearing one of the wristbands. He wanted me to get into his car. I ran away and he went berserk.'

'So the police are after you as well?' said Becky.

'Actually, they're probably after both of us now.'

'Brilliant,' said Becky. 'I'm travelling to the Isle of Skye with my baby brother on a stolen motorbike, without a driving licence, looking for someone who could be in Portugal for all we know. A secret society of mystery maniacs is trying to kill us. The police want to arrest us . . .'

Then I had a stroke of luck. I'd been fiddling with the

studs and tassels on Craterface's jacket when I noticed a large lump in one of the pockets. I stuck my hand inside and extracted a spanner, a packet of cigarettes, a cigarette lighter, a great deal of oily fluff . . . and a wallet.

Becky snatched it out of my hands, saying, 'Oi. You little thief.' But as she took it, the wallet popped open and a wad of ten pound notes spilled across the map.

'What did he do?' I asked. 'Rob a post office?'

Becky was lost for words. Not something I'd seen very often.

'Ugly, but rich,' I said, knowing I was probably pushing my luck a bit too far.

She wasn't listening. She was counting the money. 'Two hundred. Three hundred.' She still had a long way to go. 'The lying pig,' she snapped. 'He told me he was broke. The stinking, two-faced, good-for-nothing, evil, self-centred . . .'

I let her rant for a bit. She needed to get this stuff off her chest. And I quite enjoyed it too. After a couple of minutes she ran out of steam.

I picked up a handful of tenners. 'This lot will get us to the Isle of Skye, won't it?'

Becky looked at me in silence for a few seconds, then hissed, 'Too damn right it will. If that creep thinks I'm hurrying home to see him, he's got another think coming. Let's hit the road, Jimbo.'

On our way out of the service station we remembered that we still had parents, and they were probably not too happy at the moment. So Becky called them on her mobile. Thankfully the answerphone was on.

'Mum. Dad. It's Becky. I've got Jimbo with me. We're both fine. But we can't come home right now. We'll explain everything later. Ciao.'

We filled the tank, bought two pairs of dark glasses and rejoined the motorway.

Night fell and Skye was still three hundred miles away. We turned off the M6 and wove our way down a maze of narrow country lanes until we came to a small wood. We parked the bike out of view of the road, clambered through the bushes and found ourselves a good tent-sized clearing.

There was a message from home on Becky's mobile, but we decided not to listen to it. After all, Mum and Dad weren't going to be wishing us luck.

The food I'd packed was cold and a bit battered,

but the remains of Dad's roast potatoes and raspberry pavlova were still good.

'Know what?' said Becky, brushing the crumbs from her lipstick.

'What?'

'I take back what I said about Dad.' She smiled. 'I don't care if he has got something wrong with his hormones. He produces some quality leftovers.'

We woke at dawn to find torrential rain had hammered its way through the canvas. The bottoms of our sleeping bags were soaked in grimy water. The shoes we'd put outside the mouth of the tent had all but dissolved.

'Why couldn't this have happened in July?' moaned Becky.

I wrung out the sleeping bags while she readjusted her make-up. Once her face was ready we squelched the tent down, squelched our belongings into the motorbike panniers, squelched onto the damp leather seat and made our way back to the M6. Watching the glistening tarmac scoot by beneath my feet, I dreamed of duvets and hot breakfasts, big jumpers and radiators.

We had double beans on toast in Carlisle and spent a long time in the loos drying bits of clothing under the hand dryers. By Glasgow the sun had come out. By Dumbarton I was starting to feel almost human.

The countryside was looking stranger now, older, craggier. We twisted and turned along the banks of Loch Lomond for twenty miles. To our left mist hung between the peaks of high hills. To our right was mile after mile of water, all rippled in the wind and dotted with knobbly little islands with scrubby trees on.

The road climbed. Crianlarich, Tyndrum, Ballachulish. The hills were barer now. In the sun it looked like a picture postcard. In the rain it would have looked like a scene from a horror movie.

My bum was beginning to hurt. We'd been driving for almost six hours now. So I was relieved when the hills started to fall away and we began making our way down towards the sea, to the Kyle of Lochalsh, and the Skye Bridge.

109

boom!

We pulled off the main road and parked in front of a café by the water's edge. It was a popular place. Families were eating picnics on benches. Little kids were playing tag along the quay. Dogs were being taken out of the back of cars so they could pee on the verge.

We clambered off the bike, stretched our aching legs, then went and bought ourselves a couple of ice creams. Gulls wheeled overhead. A fishing boat chugged past.

'Cheers!' said Becky, knocking her cone against mine.

'Cheers!' I said, and for a moment I completely forgot about Charlie. I grinned at Becky. Becky grinned back at me. We were having an adventure. The sun was out, and for the first time in my life I realized that I actually liked my sister.

Then she said, 'I wonder how long we've got.'

'What do you mean?' I said.

She stared at the tarmac and muttered, 'They were nasty people, Jimbo. We don't even know if Charlie's still alive.'

'Shut up,' I replied quietly. 'Please just shut up.'

We finished our ice creams, put our helmets back on, revved the engine and made our way back to the queue for the bridge.

11

the bad step

On Skye we stopped at a Co-op for bread, biscuits, lipstick, strawberry jam and Cheddar cheese. Becky took out her mobile and found that she had no reception. We were now officially off the map.

We headed into the hills. There was a village or two. There was a car or two. But mostly there were mountains, grass, lochs, cattle, sheep, rock and more mountains. It looked like the Land That Time Forgot. If you closed your ears to the roar of the Moto Guzzi, you could imagine a brontosaurus lumbering out of a valley between two cloudy peaks.

I thought about the men in the expensive light-grey suits. I thought about Mr Kidd and Mrs Pearce. And I simply couldn't connect any of them with this place. I began to wonder whether it was all a mistake, whether the map was just a map, a leftover from a holiday spent exploring Scottish castles. I began to wonder whether

Charlie really was in Portugal. Or whether something worse had happened.

The light began to fail. I was tired and I wanted to sleep. But I knew that I wouldn't be able to sleep. Not here. Not without seeing Charlie again.

Eventually the road curved off a hill and made its way into the little fishing village of Elgol. Seeing houses on either side of the road, I felt less nervy. A bedroom light here. A flower garden there. It seemed almost normal.

We turned a last corner and Becky brought the bike to a halt on a tiny stone jetty which cut into the water. An old man was standing on the jetty tidying lobster pots and coiling ropes. Beside him, his cocker spaniel was sitting quietly, panting and scratching its ear with a paw.

Becky lifted her helmet and leaned back to speak to me. 'That's the way,' she said, pointing her gloved hand along the coast. 'Now, let's go and find somewhere to camp.'

The sky was purple and orange in the sunset. The mountains were silhouettes, like jagged strips of torn black paper laid against the sky.

'I want to go now,' I said with determination.

'Jimbo, you're barking mad,' said Becky. 'It's eight miles. It's a rocky path. It's getting dark.'

'You saw them in the flat, Becky,' I said. 'They'll be following us. I know they will. We can't waste any time.

boom!

We've got to help Charlie. I'm going. With you or without you.'

'All right, all right,' she grumped, getting off the bike and helping me to transfer our stuff from the panniers to the holdall. 'I'll come. Not that I've got any choice. Mum would murder me if I went back and said I'd lost you.'

'You're a pal,' I said, shaking her hand.

'I'm a moron,' she replied.

We'd just locked the bike, picked up the bag and started out for the footpath when we were greeted by the old man who'd been tending the lobster pots.

'Evening,' he said in a broad Scots accent.

'Evening,' we replied suspiciously.

'Ah, city folk,' he said, looking at my trainers and Becky's black nail polish. 'You'll no be walking in that get-up, will you? With the night coming down.'

'No. We're going to see a film,' snapped Becky. She was always rather touchy about her 'get-up'.

'Yes. We're walking,' I explained politely. I wanted to get away. I didn't want to stand around chatting to strangers.

'To Camasunary? Or all the way to Coruisk?' he asked.

Then, very slowly, he lifted his pipe to his mouth, so that the sleeve of his oilskin fell away to show a band on his left wrist. I stepped backwards.

'To Coruisk,' said Becky curtly, 'so we haven't got any time to waste chatting.'

I expected the old man to come and grab me by the scruff of the neck. I expected to see his fingers light up. But neither of these things happened. He smiled. Then he chuckled.

'Well, you enjoy yourselves,' he said. 'It's going to be a nice pitch-black night for a walk along the cliff path.' And with that, he turned and walked back up the road, the cocker spaniel trotting at his heels.

'The wristband . . .' I said to Becky.

'I saw it,' she replied.

'They know we're here,' I whispered, looking around to see if there was anyone within earshot, crouching behind a lobster pot or an upturned boat.

'Maybe,' said Becky. 'Maybe it was just a brass wristband, Jimbo. Like people wear. Maybe we're getting paranoid.'

'Maybe,' I said. But I was right. I knew it. He was one of them. The way he showed us the wristband. The chuckle. On the other hand, if he was one of them then we were on the right track. Coruisk was important.

So why didn't he stop us? Perhaps he knew we wouldn't make it along the path in the dark. Perhaps he knew we would find nothing when we got there. Perhaps he knew there were others waiting to greet us at the far end, flexing their neon-blue fingers in the windy dark.

'Well,' said Becky, 'what are we waiting for?'

I fell into step behind her.

We didn't need the torch. The lobster fisherman was wrong. The night was not pitch-black. Ten minutes after we set off, threads of grey cloud dissolved to reveal a perfect full moon suspended above the sea. It felt like walking through a scene from *Son of Dracula*. But at least we could see where to put our feet.

A good job too. The path was narrow and stony and cut into the steep, scrubby cliff rising high above the water. We had to duck under gnarled trunks, clamber over boulders and move fallen branches out of our way. The sea lay to our left like a great sheet of beaten silver.

To our right, rocks, trees and bushes climbed up into the night sky.

Out in the bay an island floated like a great barnacled whale. Beyond it, the ocean, blackness and stars. Everything looked mind-bogglingly big. I was lonely and frightened, even with Becky in front of me. If we tripped and fell, we'd helter-skelter down into the icy water and be swept away. No one would ever know.

To make matters worse, my city-folk trainers were not made for trekking and I was getting a large and painful blister on my right heel. I stuffed the shoe with tissues, gritted my teeth and marched manfully onwards.

After two hours we reached the bay of Camasunary. The path dropped down and the cliff flattened out into a gentle, sloping meadow of spiky grass. We crested a small ridge and the beach lay in front of us. We crossed a tiny stream and stepped into the field.

'Jeez!' I said.

'Now that does my head in,' echoed Becky.

The field was full of rabbits. A hundred. Two hundred. I'd never been frightened of rabbits before. But this lot gave me the creeps, sitting there with their powder-puff tails and their spoony ears like something from a horror film called *Rabbit*.

'Let's keep going,' I said.

We began the second, more difficult section of the path.

Except there wasn't much of a path any more. There were rocks, nettles, thorns, trees and mud, and my blister was getting worse.

After half an hour of slipping, tripping, grumbling and hobbling we came to an unexpected halt. In front of us lay a smooth, steep face of blank rock covered in patches of moss, like a giant granite nose. No mud, no branches, no clumps of grass. Nothing. Starting high above our heads, it swooped down to a ragged edge hanging over the surface of the black water. The map called it 'The Bad Step'. You could see what the map meant.

'You first,' I said. 'You're older.'

'Thanks, Jimbo,' Becky replied. 'You're a real gentleman.'

We couldn't go up and round. And we couldn't go down and under. The slope was just too steep. We had to go over.

Becky shimmied up. I shimmied up behind her. We lay face down on the rock, spread-eagled like sunbathing lizards, and shuffled gingerly sideways.

the bad step

We were doing all right. My trainers were rubbish for walking but the rubber soles stuck to the rock pretty well. Sadly, the moss didn't. I was halfway across when I put my foot on a clump of the stuff, and as I shifted my weight it tore away beneath me.

I shot downwards, braked only by my knees, my fingers and the end of my nose. My heart stopped and my feet slid over the bottom edge into space. I heard Becky scream and closed my eyes, waiting for the inevitable plunge through the air onto the pointy rocks half submerged in the freezing water below.

I came to a sudden halt, my legs dangling in the empty air. My fingers were jammed into a crack that ran across the surface of the stone. It was a narrow crack and my fingers were hurting and I wasn't going to be able to hang on for long. I tried to swing my legs up onto the rock, but I was too far over.

'Jimbo!' shouted Becky. 'Hang on!' I looked up. She was shifting herself slowly down the giant nose towards me with the holdall looped over her shoulder.

'There's a crack,' I said, and at that moment one of my hands slipped free and I screamed.

The toe of Becky's boot found the crack. She took the holdall off her shoulder and lowered it down to me. 'Grab this!' I grabbed it. 'Now pull.'

She pulled. I pulled. The handle stretched horribly. I

swung my right leg. Once. Twice. Three times. Finally, I got it over the lip of the rock. I heaved again and pulled. She heaved again and I got my other foot over the lip and lay flat against the slope, panting.

'Crikey, Jimbo,' she said. 'Don't do that to me again. Ever.'

We waited until we'd got our breath back, then started shuffling sideways, with our toes in the crack. We rounded the curve of the rock and were able to grab a gnarly root and swing ourselves onto the safety of the damp earth.

'Holy hotdogs, Batman,' said Becky. 'That was a close call.'

I put my hand to my face and realized that my nose was bleeding where I'd used it as a brake-pad.

'Well,' she said, 'you don't get this kind of excitement at school, do you?'

Coruisk caught us by surprise. The path led down to sea-level, where we found our way blocked by a little channel leading to the shore. We turned and followed the channel inland. We crossed over a rocky hump and the loch loomed into view, several billion gallons of cold dark water stretching away in front of us.

'Coruisk,' said Becky, standing on the rocky hump like someone who had just climbed Everest. 'We did it, kiddo.'

Around the loch on every side the Cuillin Hills rose into the night. The central strip of water shone blue in the moonlight, but the distant banks vanished in the soot-black shadows of the peaks. High above us plumes of mist were forming on the very tips of the mountains and trailing off into the star-filled sky.

The sea had seemed big, stretching out to the dark horizon. But the size of the silhouetted mountains made the loch seem even bigger. The silence was complete. There were waves on the sea. And the sound of water lapping against rock. The water here was as smooth and motionless as mercury. This was not a place where human beings were meant to be after dark.

'So,' said Becky, 'what do we do for our next trick?'

I thought about Charlie. 'I don't know.' I could feel tears pricking at the corners of my eyes. We'd spent two days getting to this place. We'd risked our lives at least twice. I didn't know what I was expecting to find when we got here. But I expected to find something at least. And this was the emptiest place I'd seen in my entire life.

'Chin up,' said Becky. 'Let's fix ourselves some dinner.'

boom!

We trudged along the edge of the channel, crossed over using a series of stepping stones and looked for a good camping spot. En route we found the ruins of an old cottage that for a few seconds looked as if it might offer some kind of clue as to why Coruisk was so important. But it was just a ruin. Four crumbling walls, a doorway, two window holes, a mud floor. We climbed up to a flat area of grass, neatly protected from prying eyes and the growing wind by a large oval boulder.

Becky erected the tent behind the big stone. I got out some plasters and antiseptic wipes and Savlon and did first aid on my heel and my nose. Once we were snuggled into our sleeping bags we broke out the bread and cheese.

Well fed and footsore, we lay on our backs looking up at the stars through the open tent flap. Becky jammed her iPod earphones in and listened to some Evil Corpse. Or Gangrenous Limb. Or Dead Puppy. Or whatever else she'd downloaded recently.

I tried to remember the names of the constellations. The Bear. The Plough. Orion. Finally, I zipped up the tent, pulled the sleeping bag round my neck and closed my eyes.

'Uh-uh-uh-uh,' moaned Becky tunelessly. Then she stopped. She took one of the earpieces out of her ear, shook it, stuck it back in and tore it out again. I could hear a strange bubbling noise coming out of the tiny white speaker. 'It's broken,' she snapped. 'Again.'

'Your watch,' I gasped. 'Look at your watch.'

She looked at her watch. The face had lit up and the hand was spinning backwards.

'Ouch,' she yelped, ripping it off her wrist. 'It's hot.'

Somewhere inside the holdall, the torch was turning on and off.

Two seconds later the whole tent was bathed in a brilliant blue light.

12
taking the tube

This was why the old man had chuckled. They were out there. He didn't have to get rid of us. His friends would do that. At Coruisk. Miles from anywhere. And there would be no one to save us.

I looked at Becky. She was white. And she was shaking. Or I was. It was hard to tell. It was the middle of the night. But under the canvas it looked like lunch time. In Greece. In summer.

'Becky,' I said, 'I'm going outside.' I had to see what was going on. I had to know who, or what, was out there and what it was planning to do to us. And if there was an opportunity to run, I wanted to run.

'Wait for me.' Becky reached into her pocket, pulled out a large penknife, opened the blade and crouched beside me, next to the zip.

I opened the tent. The unearthly blue light poured through the slit and we had to shield our eyes.

We stuck our heads out and looked up.

'Flipping heck!' muttered Becky.

There was a vast column of blue light, thick as a tube train, going straight upwards into the night sky. I wormed my way out of the tent and crouched in the shadow of the boulder. Becky crouched behind me. Together, we stood up slowly and peered over.

Even from thirty metres away we could feel the heat. The base of the column was rising out of the ruined cottage we'd passed earlier, making the crumbling stones shine so brightly they looked radioactive. Above the ruin, waves of brightness whisked upwards at high speed away from the ground. I took hold of Becky's arm for some small comfort.

Suddenly, there was an ear-splitting *boom!* like no *boom!* I'd ever heard. It made my head wobble. It made my stomach wobble. It made my toes wobble. The light went off. The *boom!* echoed back off the faraway mountains and slowly died away to silence. All we could hear was the blood thumping in our ears.

When my heart slowed down a bit I turned to Becky. 'Well, I guess this has to be the place.'

'Look,' whispered Becky, pinching my arm. 'Down there.'

I followed her eyes to the narrow channel connecting the loch to the sea. A silhouetted man was walking over the rocky ground towards the ruin. Behind him a little boat was moored in the channel, with a second silhouetted man on board.

The first man reached the ruin, turned, waved to the man in the boat and stepped inside. We heard the cough of an outboard motor being started up and the boat pulled away from the shore. There was a short fizzing noise and once again the column of brilliant blue light shot up out of the ruin into the sky.

'Oh my God!' said Becky.

The man had walked into the ruin. He had to be toast now. I was dreaming. I had to be dreaming.

The light shone. The waves of brightness whisked upwards. The *boom!* boomed. My toes wobbled. The light went off. The *boom!* echoed round the valley. And silence returned.

I gagged a bit. 'We just saw someone being killed, right?'

'Eeuw!' said Becky. 'That was not good.'

'We have to go down there,' I said.

'Why?' asked Becky.

'Because . . . because . . .' I said. 'Because that's the thing. That's the reason we're here. We can't sit here just looking at it.'

'No,' said Becky. 'I didn't bring you all this way so you could be cooked alive.'

'So what are we going to do?'

'We're going to sit here and look at it. See if it happens again.'

So we just sat there looking at it. For a long time. A very long time. And it didn't happen again. Becky wandered off to pee and came back again. I fell asleep and woke up when the pins and needles got really bad.

'OK,' said Becky. 'Let's go and take a look. This is driving me nuts.'

We did a commando shuffle through the dark. Down the slope from one shadow to the next. A tree. A rock. A bank of earth.

I thought about Dad, the model planes and the Aubergine Parmesan. I thought about Mum and her natty suits. I thought about my little room with the octopus poster and the cardboard skeleton. I thought about gravity and the Industrial Revolution. It all seemed a very long way away. Like something happening in a model village, tiny and silly and not quite real.

It wasn't fear. It was something way past that. It was

boom!

like walking away from a car accident. I felt shocked and spacey and full of adrenaline.

We reached the back wall of the ruin and crouched down. And that was the weird thing. The stones were cold.

There was no noise from inside, either. I looked at Becky. She looked back at me. The blade of her penknife flashed in the starlight.

She nodded and mouthed the word, 'Go.'

We stood up, tiptoed round to the front of the ruin and leaped through the hole that used to be the front door.

The place was completely empty. Moonlit walls. Dirty flagstones. Some weeds. Some little flowers. Nothing burned. No scorched earth. No crispy little person-remains. Nothing. It was just like it had been when we passed it earlier that night.

Dead or not, the man had vanished. I looked up. Had the blue beam vaporized him? What would happen to us if it came on again? Would we be vaporized too?

'Becky,' I said nervously, 'maybe we shouldn't hang around in here.'

She wasn't listening. 'There has to be a way out. A hidden door. A secret hatch.'

'Becky, please.' I tugged at her sleeve.

She scraped the floor with her boot. She ran her hand

over the stone walls. She ferreted among the scraggy plants growing in the corners.

'I'm leaving,' I said. 'I really don't like this place.'

'Give me the wristband.'

'I'm not sure that's a good idea.'

'Yeah?' said Becky. 'Well, you think of a better one. In the meantime, give me the wristband.'

I gave her the wristband.

It happened as soon as she peeled back the silver foil. The interior of the ruin was illuminated by fifty pinpricks of green light set into the stone walls. Beside the door a panel had appeared.

I snatched the wristband back and wrapped it up in its foil again.

'There's a button,' said Becky.

'Just don't press it.'

'Oh, right,' said Becky. 'So we're just going to stand here and look at it. That's not going to get us very far, is it?'

She pressed the button. The floor beneath my feet dropped away and I found myself being lowered into a round shaft.

'Help!'

'Jimbo!' yelled Becky. She threw herself onto the ground and grabbed my hand, but I was falling too quickly and our fingers were pulled apart.

boom!

She stood up again and jabbed frantically at the button. It was too late. A thick plate was sliding over my head, cutting off the hole and shutting out the light. I banged on the walls and yelled.

Above me, I could hear Becky grunting as she struggled with the covering to absolutely no effect. A striplight came on over my head. I looked around. I was standing in a tall white ceramic tube. The walls were smooth as glass and on one side was a panel of buttons, dials, screens and gauges. Above me, the tube was sealed tightly by the steel plate.

'Jimbo . . . ! Jimbo . . . ! Jimbo . . . !' came the muffled sound of Becky's voice.

I gazed at the panel of buttons. Maybe one of them opened the door. But which one? And what were the others for? Press the wrong one and I might be microwaved, or crushed. The tube might fill with water. Or sulphuric acid. Or cockroaches.

I was finding it difficult to breathe. Was I running out of air, or just hyperventilating? I fumbled in the pocket of Craterface's jacket and took out his spanner. I bashed the wall as hard as I could. It clanged like a church bell and my fingers hurt. I hadn't made a scratch.

I put the spanner back, took out the wristband and unwrapped it. Instantly the panel came alive. Figures and symbols flashed up on a blue screen. Needles shook and quivered. Buttons glowed.

'Jimbo . . . ! Jimbo . . . !' Becky was still shouting faintly.

'I'm still here,' I shouted back. 'I'm trying to get out.'

I wrapped the wristband in its foil and put it back into my pocket. Then I picked up the orange notebook. I opened it at the page where Charlie had written down the code from Pearce's attic: *Trezzit/Pearce/4300785.*

The map reference was Coruisk. This was Coruisk. Perhaps the other numbers meant something too.

'Jimbo . . . !' shouted Becky, her voice dulled almost to silence by the ceiling of the tube.

I crossed my fingers and punched the numbers into the main keypad. 'Four . . . three . . . zero . . . zero . . . seven . . . eight . . . five . . .'

The word 'Pearce' flashed briefly on the screen, followed by a spurt of letters and symbols. I heard a low throb coming from machinery beneath my feet.

I pressed my back against the curved wall. I zipped up Craterface's jacket, braced my feet, took a deep breath and held on tight.

Nothing happened for several seconds. Then I heard the *boom!* Except it was much closer and much louder this time. I thought my ears were going to rupture. Every atom in my body was vibrating. I felt horribly seasick. My clothes were soaked in sweat. I covered my ears with my hands and fell to the floor and curled up into a ball.

The atoms in my body slowly stopped vibrating. My ears still hurt, but the nausea was fading. I got slowly to my feet. The word ZARVOIT flashed across the screen and there was a short *bing-bong* like a doorbell. I heard a little hiss and turned to see that one of the sides of the tube was sliding open.

The tube had gone downwards. I was in a cellar. Or a bunker. Except that there was light pouring through the gap, and it was white and it was bright and it was very much not underground. I gripped the spanner tightly.

It wasn't real. It couldn't be. I was looking out into a vast white hangar. I looked up. No Coruisk. No Becky. No ground. Just a smooth white ceiling twenty metres above my head.

Around the room were huge, high windows. Outside the windows was a black sky thick with stars. This wasn't a dungeon. This wasn't a cellar or a bunker. I must have travelled through some kind of tunnel. I was somewhere else on Skye. Or I was on the mainland. Or I was on that whale-shaped island sitting in the bay.

And that's when I saw them. Seated at a long table nearby. Mrs Pearce. Mr Kidd. The man from Captain Chicken. Inspector Hepplewhite. They were all wearing long violet robes.

This could not be happening. A few more minutes and the alarm would start beeping and I'd head into the kitchen and there would be a big cooked breakfast waiting for me. Sausages, toast, scrambled eggs.

Captain Chicken stood up and started walking towards me.

'Sausages, toast, scrambled eggs,' I said to myself. 'Sausages, toast, scrambled eggs.'

'Welcome, James,' he said, 'and well done. Well done indeed.'

The spanner fell out of my hand and clanged on the floor. There was no cooked breakfast. This was really happening.

'Fantabangle,' said Mr Kidd to Mrs Pearce.

'Mockety,' said Mrs Pearce to Mr Kidd. 'Parlant mockety.'

Captain Chicken grasped my hand and shook it. 'I think we're all agreed. You are precisely the kind of person we need.'

boom!

'A very enterprising young man,' said Inspector Hepplewhite.

'My name is Vantresillion, by the way,' said Captain Chicken. 'Bantid Vantresillion.'

I finally rediscovered my voice. 'Where am I?'

'The Sagittarius Dwarf Elliptical Galaxy.'

'What!?'

'It's about seventy thousand light years from the centre of your Milky Way Galaxy,' said Captain Chicken. 'In the direction of the Large Magellanic Cloud.'

'What!?' He was insane.

'It's often confused with the Sagittarius Dwarf Irregular Galaxy,' he said. 'By you, I mean. Not by us. The Sagittarius Dwarf Irregular Galaxy is, oh . . . much further away. Now . . .' He rubbed his hands together. 'You'll be in need of some sleep, unless I'm very much mistaken.'

He turned and waved his hand over some kind of red sausage sitting on the table. I heard a *pop!* from behind me and turned round.

And this was when I realized I might not be somewhere else on Skye, or on the mainland, or on the whale-shaped island. Because there was a spider walking towards me. A huge spider. About the size of a golden retriever. With the face of a squashed monkey.

I squealed and stepped backwards.

'Don't worry,' said Captain Chicken. 'It's completely harmless.'

The giant monkey-spider walked up to me and held out a hairy leg. 'Shake it, baby!'

I heard myself making a low, moaning noise.

'My name is Ktop-p-páãçôñïî,' said the spider. 'It will make a car crash in your mouth. But you can call me Britney.'

'Go with the spider,' said Vantresillion. 'It'll show you to your room.'

The spider pressed a hairy leg into the small of my back and pushed me gently towards the door. 'Ticket to ride!'

13
short hairy tails

We went out into the corridor, turned left and started walking. I tried very hard not to look at the spider. Everything was white and smooth and hi-tech. There were no lights. The ceiling just glowed a bit. There were no doors. The walls just opened up every so often so that people in purple robes could enter and exit.

'This way,' said Britney.

We turned a corner.

'You come from Earth,' said Britney, trotting beside me. 'I hear it is most delicious. Tell me about bagpipes. Tell me about Buckingham Palace and Elvis Presley. Tell me about cross-Channel ferries and Abba, who are a Swedish pop band that shake my booty.'

'Where's Charlie?'

'Who is Charlie?' said Britney.

We walked in silence for a few more minutes.

'Does my English sparkle?' said Britney. 'Do we groove? Speak it to me from the hip. You are the horse's mouth. You eat the Yorkshire pudding.'

I was very tired. I needed sleep and I wasn't in the mood for an argument. 'Yes, you groove.'

'Disco inferno!' said the giant monkey-spider, waving two legs in the air.

We turned another corner and the white walls gave way to glass. We were walking across some kind of covered bridge between one building and the next. I stopped and looked out. And actually it was even scarier than seeing Britney for the first time. Because all around us, in every direction, stretched a barren, brown desert. No trees, no grass, no water. Just rocks and dust and craters. I turned to look out the other side of the bridge. And what I saw was much, much worse. There were two suns. And they were green. And they were revolving slowly around one another.

I staggered backwards and grabbed the handrail to stop myself falling over. 'So, this is . . .'

'Sagittarius Dwarf Elliptical Galaxy,' said Britney. 'Ten out of ten.'

'But . . . but . . . but . . . How did I get here?'

'No idea.' Britney held up two hairy legs. 'My brain is small.'

'So this place . . . this planet . . . it's . . .'

'Plonk.'

'Sorry?'

boom!

'Plonk.' Britney waved a leg over the barren landscape. 'It is the name.'

'Plonk!?' I said. 'That is the most stupid name for a planet I have ever heard.'

Britney looked decidedly huffy. 'It is a most serious and shiny name in our language.'

'Oh.'

'You have one called Moon,' said Britney. 'That is our word for passing wind out of the bottom. Now follow me.'

'So those people . . .' I said. 'Mrs Pearce and Vantrethingy . . .'

'Not human,' said Britney. 'Short hairy tails and no belly buttons.'

I thought of Mrs Pearce with a short hairy tail and it made me feel a bit ill. So I decided to stop asking questions.

'Whoa there!' said Britney.

We'd stopped by a section of wall with the words ARRIVALS UNIT on it. Britney said, 'Snekkit,' there was a *pop!* and a door appeared in the wall. 'Through here.'

138

We stepped into another corridor. The people here looked almost normal. None of them were wearing purple robes. Most were wearing jeans and T-shirts. There was a DOCTOR WHO T-shirt. There was a XENA WARRIOR PRINCESS T-shirt. One woman with large bosoms was wearing a T-shirt which said SET LASERS TO STUN.

'Your room,' said Britney. 'Snekkit!' The wall opened with a *pop!* 'Go in, human boy.' She was obviously still huffy about the Plonk thing.

I stepped inside. There was a white bed. There was a white chest of drawers. There was a white cubby hole containing a white toilet and a white sink.

Britney said, 'Snore now. Door locking.' There was another *pop!* and the door disappeared. 'Hey!' I banged on the hard white surface. I shouted, 'Snekkit!' thirty times at different volumes in different accents, but all to no avail.

I sat down on the bed, exhausted. On top of the chest of drawers was a kettle and a selection of tea bags and prepacked biscuits, just like in a bed and breakfast.

In the first drawer was a small library of boy books: SAS memoirs, football annuals, superhero comics . . .

In the third drawer there was nothing except some coloured balls the size of large marbles. I picked a few up. As I was doing this, I dropped one. A red one. Except it didn't drop. It just stuck in the air. I reached out and gingerly touched the ball. I could move it easily, but it wouldn't fall. It was like pushing a coin around a table, except in three dimensions. Wherever I shoved it, it simply hung there motionless.

The other balls were the same. I could arrange them in mid-air in any shape I chose. A line. A cube. A smiley face. I put five of them in my pocket. I couldn't wait to show them to Charlie.

Charlie. I'd forgotten about Charlie. I felt a stab of guilt. He was here somewhere. Probably. I hoped. And here I was mucking about with floaty balls and thinking how cool they were.

I had to find him. Except the door was locked and I was shattered. In the morning. Yes, I'd find him in the morning. But right now . . .

I laid my head down on the pillow. It was amazingly soft and comfortable. I was asleep in seconds.

14

little blue suckers

I was sitting in the kitchen with Mum and Dad and Becky. Charlie was there too and we were eating lasagne and it was really, really good lasagne. Except someone was shaking my shoulder, so I rolled over and opened my eyes and screamed.

'Shift your potatoes,' said Britney.

I sat up and rubbed my eyes.

'How is the small one this morning?' asked Britney. 'Are your feelings good?'

'Of course my feelings aren't good. I'm on some stupid planet called Plonk in the . . . in the . . . in the Dancing Hamster Galaxy. And I'm talking to a monkey-faced spider called Britney.'

'Beastly child,' said Britney. 'Get walking. I will take you to breakfast. Put some food in your talk-hole.'

boom!

I made her wait outside while I went to the loo, then she led me through a maze of white corridors to a huge circular hall filled with people. The T-shirt people, not the purple robe people. There was a high domed roof and curving, star-filled windows, and everyone was milling and chatting and eating at long tables. It was like a massive school dining room, with space outside and giant monkey-spiders clearing away the dirty plates.

A middle-aged man with a flowery Hawaiian shirt and a ponytail wandered up to us. 'You must be a new guy.' He held out his hand. 'Bob Smith. Pleased to meet you.'

I didn't shake it.

'Take him,' said Britney. 'He hurts my head.' And with that she turned and scuttled away.

Bob Smith was still holding out his hand.

'Where's Charlie?' I said.

'Who's Charlie?'

'I want to see my friend. And there is no way I am going to shake the hand of some hairy-tailed, kidnapping alien with no belly button.'

Bob laughed. 'I'm human. Like you. Assuming you're human.'

'Oh. Sorry.' I shook his hand. 'Jimbo. My name's Jimbo.'

'You'll be hungry,' he said. 'Coming up the Weff-Beam really takes it out of a guy. Let's get you some tucker.'

I followed him to a round table at the edge of the room. Sitting on the table were a number of little blue suckers. He picked one up. 'Stick it onto your forehead.'

'What?'

'You think of a type of food and it . . . well, it appears. It's totally brilliant. Look.' He pressed a disc to his own forehead and grimaced like he was doing his thirteen times table. There was a *ping!* and a plate of scampi and a pint of lager appeared magically in the centre of the table. He picked them up.

'You have a go,' said Bob. 'You can get anything. Absolutely anything. You can get vomit if you want. Most people try it once. But it annoys everyone. You know, the smell.' He chuckled merrily. 'Oh, and trust me. There is nothing you can do to badger to make it taste good. Baking, boiling, stewing, puff pastry, batter . . . I've tried.'

I put the sucker to my head and tried very hard to clear my mind. If I wasn't careful I was going to get a serving of badger in vomit. 'Brie and marmalade sand-

143

wich,' I said to myself. 'White bread. No crusts. Brie and marmalade sandwich. White bread. No crusts. And some hot chocolate.'

There was another *ping!* and suddenly there it was. Brie and marmalade sandwich. White bread. No crusts. Mug of hot chocolate. Creepiest of all, the hot chocolate was in my battered *Captain Scarlet* mug. Or something that looked very like it.

'Come on,' said Bob. 'Let's find us a seat.'

We sat down and I took a bite of the sandwich. It tasted a bit like Brie and a bit like marmalade and a bit like petrol.

'Yeah,' said Bob. 'It's not perfect, but' – he looked around – 'is this whole place not totally the most incredible thing? I mean, we're on another planet, man.'

'No,' I said. 'Totally the most incredible thing would be finding my best friend and going home.'

'You're not into the whole sci-fi trip, then?'

'Look. No. Wait.' I was holding my head. This was all too much. Seventy thousand light years. The hairy tails.

The disco spiders. 'I mean . . . what the hell is going on?'

'It does kind of throw you a bit, doesn't it?' said Bob, chewing a mouthful of scampi. 'At first, I mean.'

'Yeah. It does. A bit.'

'They can't have children,' said Bob. 'Some kind of genetic malfunction.'

'I don't understand.'

'Fifty years and they'll all be dead.' Bob washed the scampi down with a swig of lager. 'So they decided to repopulate the planet.'

'By stealing people from Earth?'

'We're, like, the closest match. I mean, there's a lot of intelligent alien species out there. But some of them are seven hundred miles long, and some of them look like snot.'

I looked around the room. 'But everyone seems really happy about it. Don't they have, like, families and jobs and friends and stuff?'

'They're sci-fi fans,' said Bob. 'Clever, eh? You know, choosing the kind of people who'd really dig this place.'

'Hang on,' I said. 'They're going to populate a whole planet with sci-fi fans? Is that sensible?'

'I guess you must be an accident,' said Bob.

And that's when I saw him. Hunched over a table on the far side of the room. I'd have recognized him anywhere.

boom!

I leaped to my feet, spilling hot chocolate and sending Brie and marmalade flying and shattering the *Captain Scarlet* mug on the floor.

'Easy, tiger!' said Bob.

'Charlie!' I shouted. 'Charlie!'

I ran across the room, tripping over the legs of a giant monkey-spider carrying a stack of crockery. 'Tighten your pants!' it shouted.

Charlie spun round in his seat. 'Jimbo!' He jumped off his bench and ran towards me and I don't think I've seen anything quite so wonderful in my entire life.

'Charlie!'

'Jimbo!'

We threw our arms round one another and jumped up and down and spun around whooping.

'Charlie!' I said. 'It is so good to see you!'

He grinned. 'I knew you'd make it, Jimbo. I just knew it.'

'You're here!' I said. 'I didn't even know whether you were alive.'

'So,' said Charlie, sitting down again, 'did they capture you or what?'

'No, no, nothing like that. We knew they'd got you. And they tried to get me too. The guy with the suit. And these other men.'

'Uh-huh,' said Charlie.

'But Becky and Craterface, they turned up at the flat and Craterface fought them off and Becky and I borrowed Craterface's motorbike.'

'Uh-huh,' said Charlie.

Something was wrong. He wasn't excited enough. He wasn't interested enough. Maybe it was shock. Maybe it was the petrol-flavoured food. I carried on. 'But the important thing is, we've got to find a way out of here.'

'Actually,' said Charlie, 'I think I'm going to stay.'

'What!?'

'Look at this place. It's brilliant.'

'What!?'

'They've got hover-scooters. I bet you haven't seen the hover-scooters yet.'

'No, listen,' I said. 'Shut up about the stupid hover-scooters. I came all this way to help you escape, so—'

'That's really good of you,' said Charlie. 'But I like it here. I really do.' His voice was calm and he was smiling like he'd become a member of a weird religious cult.

I stood up and leaned across the table. 'Shut up, you idiot. I nearly died looking for you. Your mum and dad are going out of their minds. And now my mum and dad will be going out of their minds.'

boom!

'Give it a few days,' said Charlie in the same creepy, chilled-out way. 'It really grows on you.'

I slumped back down onto my seat. 'They've brain-washed you, haven't they? They've given you drugs. Or put electrodes into your brain. They've turned you into a zombie.'

Charlie laughed. 'Of course they haven't. You're just suffering from jet-lag. Trust me.'

I was too angry to speak. I grabbed him by the collar and shook him hard. 'You're meant to be my friend! You're meant to be my friend!'

'Hey, hey, hey,' said Charlie. It was the same grown-up voice Mum and Dad used when I was getting upset. 'It's going to work out fine.'

'Fine!?' I swung my fist and hit him as hard as I could.

'Ouch!' He put his hand to his face and took it away again. There was actual blood.

I pushed him backwards so that he fell to the ground. Then I turned and ran.

15

orange toilet plungers

I reached the edge of the room. I was about to shout 'Snekkit!' and leap through the door when the lights went out and the entire dining hall went dark. I skidded to a halt. I could see absolutely nothing.

I expected people to start screaming, but all I could hear were excited *Ooohs* and *Aaahs* that died away to a hushed silence. There was a distant whirring noise and a line of soft white light fell across the middle of the room.

I looked up and saw the roof opening like a huge eye to reveal an enormous glass dome. Beyond the dome lay a trillion miles of darkness filled with twinkling stars.

Bob appeared beside me. 'I saw that thing back there. The bust-up with your friend. That was a seriously bad trip, man.'

'What's happening?' I said. 'I mean, the roof and everything.'

'Wait and see,' said Bob. 'It's kinda mind-boggling.'

boom!

The whirring stopped. The roof was now fully open. Way over to my right the two green suns were revolving slowly around one another. Over to my left . . .

'Here comes the ferry,' said Bob.

'The what?'

'The intergalactic ferry,' said Bob. 'Goes round all the neighbouring star systems. Picks up passengers and cargo and stuff.'

A vast object began to slide into view. A spaceship. A real live spaceship. Antennae and gantries and rockets and pods and fins and tubes. Moving as slowly as an oil tanker but a hundred times the size.

'The scorch marks are from jumping in and out of hyperspace,' said Bob. 'It gets pretty hot. And look at the front. You can see the asteroid bumper. That huge panel with all the dents in.'

There was a deep and distant rumble. You could feel the floor vibrating gently.

'Cool or what?' said Bob.

'Cool,' I said. 'Definitely cool.'

'It's not home,' said Bob. 'There's no football on the telly and the scampi's a bit rubbish. But if you're going to spend the rest of your life on another planet, then this one's not a bad choice.'

He was right. Of course he was right. I was lucky. I was alive. I should be grateful.

There was a faint shooshing noise and little tongues of orange flame flickered from twenty rockets down the side of the intergalactic ferry.

'Final adjustments,' said Bob. 'You know, before coming into dock.'

'Wow.'

We stood in silence, watching the ferry fly slowly over the dome until the last tail-fin disappeared and we were left staring up into the night sky.

The lights clicked back on and everyone covered their eyes while they got used to the brightness. The roof began whirring shut and the chatter started up again. Then I heard someone whispering, 'Smelly fart,' in my ear, which was quite odd.

I turned and found myself looking at Charlie. 'Smelly fart,' he said again. 'Gordon Reginald Harvey Simpson Bennett Junior and walkie-talkies and raspberry pavlova. I'm still Charlie. Just . . . come and sit down and talk to me, OK?'

'Shut up.'

'Jimbo, please. Just . . .'

He was still Charlie. Whatever they'd done to him. I couldn't carry on being angry for ever. 'I'll come,' I said. 'But don't give me any more twaddle about how you're staying here, or I swear I'll brain you.'

'Promise,' said Charlie.

boom!

We walked back across the room and he sat me down while he went to get some more food.

Two women at the next table were arguing about whether Daleks were scarier than Cybermen. It puzzled me. The inhabitants of Plonk were meant to be super-intelligent. They had hover-scooters. They had a ferry that went through hyperspace. Why didn't they repopulate their planet with engineers? Or fighter pilots? Or accountants?

Charlie came back carrying a huge bowl containing an industrial volume of tinned spaghetti in tomato sauce. The smell was not good.

He stuck his spoon into the bowl and started fiddling and stirring. Like those kids at school who don't really enjoy eating, but love building snowmen out of mashed potatoes and smiley faces out of peas. I wanted to tell him to grow up and actually talk to me. But it was good sitting here with him, and if he didn't say anything I could just about pretend they hadn't done anything to his brain.

At last he stopped playing with his spaghetti. 'Try some,' he said, pushing the bowl towards me.

'No way,' I said. 'I hate spaghetti.'

'Yes,' said Charlie. 'But this spaghetti is *special* spaghetti.' He had the weird, religious-cult-member face on again.

'Charlie,' I said, trying to control my rising frustration, 'I don't like spaghetti. And you know I don't like spaghetti because the last time I ate a tin of spaghetti I barfed the whole thing up. And you know I barfed the whole thing up because I barfed it up all over you.'

Charlie rubbed his forehead and took a deep breath and looked at me and squeezed his face up like he was having serious trouble on the toilet. 'Jimbo, this is *alphabetti* spaghetti.'

'You're eating alphabetti spaghetti?' I said. 'Well, that's really reassuring. Are you seven years old?'

'Just look at the bowl!' said Charlie.

'No,' I said, folding my arms.

Charlie stood and leaned across the table and shouted, 'How thick are you!? Of course I hate this place. Of course I want to escape. And I had a brilliant plan. But you have totally screwed it up by being a total, total moron. Look at the bloody bowl!'

I looked at the bowl. The letters of the spaghetti were arranged to read:

shut up
they're
listening
to us

'Oh,' I said. 'That's why you were acting weird.'

'Yes,' said Charlie sarcastically. 'That's why I was acting weird.'

'Because you wanted them to think you really liked it here.'

'Yes,' said Charlie sarcastically. 'Because I wanted them to think I really liked it here.'

'So,' I said, 'what happens to you if you don't like it here?'

'They fire you into space?' said Charlie. 'Or feed you into some kind of grinding machine? I have no idea. But it basically starts with a couple of armed spiders dragging you off screaming. Like this.'

He pointed over my shoulder. I turned round. Captain Chicken aka Bantid Vantresillion was standing at the edge of the room in his violet robe, with two giant monkey-spiders at his side. The spiders were wearing crash helmets and carrying orange toilet plungers.

'Seize them!'

The giant monkey-spiders sprinted towards us.

'Run!' said Charlie.

We dodged and dived. We slid along benches and jumped over tables. I covered a woman in mushroom soup. Charlie sat in a bowl of treacle pudding. A spider raised a toilet plunger and a fizzing line of laser-light zapped past my leg, singeing my jeans. Charlie dodged a second one and it set fire to the hair of a sci-fi fan who was eating a knickerbocker glory.

'I love the nightlife!' shouted one of the spiders.

'Bumper cars!' shouted the second.

Somehow we made it to the main entrance. I shouted, 'Snekkit!' the wall opened up and we raced into the corridor.

I have to say we did pretty well. I don't think either of us had run that fast in our entire lives. At one point I shoved a fat guy off a hover-scooter and we both leaped on, but the joystick looked like a tomato and I had no idea how to use it so the scooter just sank to the floor with a squirty hiss. We leaped off and kept on running.

They caught us, of course. They had more legs and the deadly toilet plungers. So I guess we were pretty lucky they didn't fill us full of smoking holes. We ground to a halt and stood with our hands on our knees, puffing and wheezing. A couple of seconds later our arms and legs were wrapped in hairy brown tentacles. The spiders were surprisingly strong. And their breath was appalling.

'Snack them down!' said one of them. 'Alive! For freshness!'

'Foot on the brake!' said the other. 'We do not want the electric prod.'

'No,' said the first. 'We do not want the electric prod.'

Vantresillion appeared behind the spiders. 'Take them to the holding cell.'

'What are you going to do to us?' asked Charlie.

Vantresillion laughed, then turned and walked away.

'Come with us, little bald monkeys,' said the first spider.

We were lifted into the air and they scuttled off at high speed in the opposite direction, jiggling us up and down and not bothering at all about banging our heads on the walls when they went round corners.

Three minutes later they snekkited a door open and threw us into a small room and snekkited the door shut behind us.

This room was different. This room was not white. This room was grey and black and brown. The walls were made of something like concrete and they hadn't been cleaned for a couple of hundred years. There was brown goo running down them and a mess in the corner like something had died there quite recently.

'Lovely,' said Charlie.

We didn't say anything for a while.

I took a deep breath. 'Sorry, this was my fault.'

'It's OK,' said Charlie. 'I forgive you. Sort of.'

Once more we didn't say anything for a while.

'What was the plan?'

'The plan?' asked Charlie.

'Yeah,' I said. 'The brilliant plan. The one I screwed up by being a total, total moron.'

'Oh, that one,' said Charlie. 'Well, if you put those suckers on your forehead and think hard enough, you can make Brussels sprouts that go off like grenades when you throw them.'

'And . . . ?'

'I was collecting them,' said Charlie. 'You know, building up an arsenal, so I could fight my way out.'

'To where?' I said. 'We're seventy thousand light years from planet Earth. Unless you've got some black forest gateau that turns into a spaceship.'

'OK,' said Charlie. 'No need to be sarcastic. At least I was trying.'

There was a sinister grating noise from the other side of the wall.

boom!

'That's probably the grinding machine,' said Charlie. 'Thanks for coming to get me, by the way.'

I nodded. 'No problem. I mean, obviously I didn't have a choice. You being my friend and everything. Plus I missed you.'

'Yeah, me too. I think I'd have gone mad if you hadn't turned up. Everyone talking about *Blade Runner* and speaking Vogon.'

I don't know how long we were in the holding cell. The lights were on all the time and our watches hadn't worked since we arrived on Plonk. We talked about Megan Shotts and the locusts. We talked about Mr Kosinsky's snowman socks. We talked about salmon mousse, and strawberry jam and Cheddar cheese sandwiches.

But thinking about home made us sad. So we played noughts and crosses on the floor by scraping the dirt with the toes of our shoes. Then we tried to name all the countries in the world. Except we kept remembering that we were going to be killed, which was a bit distracting.

Ten hours passed. Or maybe twenty. Or thirty. We got really tired. We tried to lie down and sleep but it was hard to relax lying in brown goo. So we stood up again. And then we got so tired we didn't care about the brown goo any longer so we lay down and slept.

We hadn't been asleep for long when we were woken by two more giant monkey-spiders. Or maybe it was the same ones. It was hard to tell.

'Do the locomotion,' said one.

'Walkies!' said the other.

'Are you going to execute us now?' asked Charlie.

'Hurrah,' said one. 'You are a clever boy.'

'We are the champions!' sang the other. 'But you're not.' Then it snickered gleefully.

We fought for a bit, but it was no use. They grabbed us by the arms and legs and hoisted us over their heads and hauled us off down the corridor.

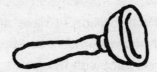

Five minutes later we were taken into a hi-tech white office with blue rubber plants and Bantid Vantresillion sitting behind a desk. The giant monkey-spiders dropped us onto the floor.

'You may go now,' said Vantresillion and the spiders scuttled out.

boom!

'Charles . . .' said Vantresillion. 'James . . .'

'Are you going to kill us?' asked Charlie again, getting to his feet.

'No,' said Vantresillion.

'But the spiders,' I replied, 'they told us . . .'

'They have a strange sense of humour,' said Vantresillion.

'Oh.'

'Normally we'd kill you,' said Vantresillion. 'But I think you may be able to help us.'

I felt a huge wave of relief and everything went a bit wobbly for a few seconds. But Charlie still had his head screwed on properly. 'Great,' he said. 'Just fire away and we'll see what we can do. We like being helpful, don't we, Jimbo?'

'Er, what?' I said. 'Yes, that's right. We like being helpful.'

'Hmmm,' said Vantresillion. 'I have a problem. Every time one of the Watchers travels to Skye to come back to Plonk we lose contact with them.'

'Plonk,' said Charlie, chuckling. 'That makes me laugh every time.'

'Charlie . . . ?' I said.

'What?'

'Don't be rude about their planet, all right?'

'Good idea,' said Charlie. So I reckon he was feeling a bit wobbly as well.

'And every time we beam someone down to find them, we lose contact with them too.'

'That'll be the army,' said Charlie. 'Or the police. Both, probably.'

'But no one knows about the Weff-Beam,' said Vantresillion through gritted teeth.

'Yeah, they do,' said Charlie. 'Jimbo told them, didn't you, Jimbo?'

'Did I?'

'It's OK,' said Charlie. 'You don't have to keep it secret any longer.'

'Right,' I said. I had no idea what Charlie was doing, but I had no other ideas so I decided to go along with it. 'Yeah. We had a notebook. And a map and stuff. From Mrs Pearce's attic. And I gave it to Mum and Dad. So they know all about the Weff-Beam thingy.'

'You're lying,' said Vantresillion.

'Scout's honour,' said Charlie, holding up three fingers. 'Cross my heart and hope to die.'

Come to think of it, he was probably right. Becky had seen the Weff-Beam. She'd go to the police. They'd have the place surrounded by now. Tanks, barbed wire, marksmen.

'I guess they're shooting them as they come up out of the ground,' said Charlie. 'Because they're aliens with tails.'

boom!

'I have lost five Watchers,' said Vantresillion darkly. 'Any more and I swear I will kill everyone on your benighted little planet.'

'You're just kidding, aren't you?' said Charlie, smiling.

Vantresillion leaned over and pulled a black box into the centre of the desk. There were a series of buttons on the box. He placed his finger on the red one. 'I press this,' he said, 'and your planet blows up. No Eiffel Tower. No Great Wall of China. Just a load of smoking rocks in space.'

'What do the other ones do?' asked Charlie. 'Do they make cappuccino?'

I turned to him and scowled. 'Just try and be a bit nicer, OK? He might actually be telling the truth.'

'Look,' said Vantresillion. He spun round and a screen appeared on the wall. In the centre of the screen was a planet. Sort of like Saturn, with rings around it and three moons. 'Zip Seven,' said Vantresillion. 'We've got a Weff-Beam there too.' He pressed the yellow button. There was a loud bang and the planet erupted in a vast ball of fire.

'Holy cow!' said Charlie.

The planet was gone. Just a load of smoking rocks and three little moons drifting sadly off into space.

'My God,' I said. 'Were there, like, people on that planet?'

'Yes,' said Vantresillion. 'But they looked like squirrels and they were stupid and I didn't like them very much.' He took two brass wristbands from his desk and threw them to us. 'Put these on.'

We put them on. He pressed a third button and they snapped tight.

'Ouch!' said Charlie.

I tried to get mine off but it had shrunk and there was no way I could slip it over my hand.

'You go down on the Weff-Beam,' said Vantresillion. 'You talk to whichever moron is in charge down there and you tell them we want the Watchers back.'

'But . . .' said Charlie. I could hear the wheels spinning in his brain. 'They're not going to believe us. "The Earth is going to be blown up." It doesn't sound very convincing, does it?'

'Then you must be persuasive,' said Vantresillion. 'Snogroid!'

A door opened and a spider scuttled in. Vantresillion chucked the spider another wristband. 'Put this on.'

The spider put it on and we heard it snap tight. 'Delightful bangle,' it said. 'And most snug.'

Vantresillion turned back to us. 'You will have five minutes. Then you call me using the wristbands. If you have not solved the problem, then this happens to Charles.' He pressed the green button. There was

163

boom!

another bang and a hideous scream. The spider erupted in flames and the room was filled with brown smoke and the smell of burning hair. When the smoke cleared there was a ring of black ash on the floor and a buckled wristband, still glowing slightly from the heat.

'That should help change their minds,' said Vantresillion. 'Five more minutes and I will do the same to James. After that I will just lose patience and press the red button. Then I will press the last button and get a nice cappuccino.' He thought this was very funny and laughed for a long time. 'Now. Follow me.'

16
the big knobbly stick

Vantresillion strode down the corridor with us jogging behind him. He was carrying the button box and we were wearing the wristbands so there was no point in running away.

'Hey,' said Charlie. 'Look on the bright side. We're going home.'

'Except we'll only be there for five minutes, then we'll be dead.'

'No,' said Charlie. 'Then *I'll* be dead. You get another five minutes.'

'Brilliant. That makes me feel a lot better.'

'You never know,' said Charlie. 'Brigadier-General Doo-Dah might actually believe us.'

'No one ever believes us,' I said. 'About anything.'

'In here,' said Vantresillion. 'Snekkit.'

A door opened in the wall and we found ourselves in the large white hangar where I'd first arrived. The white ceiling twenty metres over our heads. The high windows with the starscape outside. Just as before, Pearce, Kidd and Hepplewhite were sitting at the long table in their violet robes.

'Tidnol,' said Vantresillion. 'Basky dark.'

'Crispen hooter mont,' said Mrs Pearce, standing up. She walked over to us. 'Well, well, well. You turn out to be useful after all. Now that is a surprise.'

'Always willing to help,' said Charlie.

'Get into the Weff-Beam unit,' said Vantresillion. 'And remember. Five minutes. Charles is dead. Ten minutes. James is dead. Then I get bored very, very quickly.'

He shoved us towards the tubular cubby hole. 'Inside. Both of you.'

'It's going to be a bit of a squash,' said Charlie.

'Getting squashed is the least of your problems,' said Vantresillion.

I stepped inside. Charlie stepped in beside me. Vantresillion pushed. Then he pushed a bit harder. Then he said, 'Snekkit,' and the curved door slid shut behind us.

'Fasten seatbelts,' said Charlie, his face pressed against my ear. 'Cabin doors to automatic.'

'So what's the plan?' I asked.

'Absolutely no idea,' said Charlie. 'If we're really lucky,

a paratrooper might kill us with a bazooka as soon as we come out of the ground.'

Then we heard the *boom!* and it was like being hit in the head with a cricket bat. I covered my ears with my hands and every atom in my body started vibrating. My clothes were soaked in sweat and I felt horribly seasick. Charlie must have felt seasick too, because he was actually sick down my back and it smelled really bad.

The atoms in my body stopped vibrating and the nausea started to fade. Charlie said, 'Sorry about that,' and the word ZARVOIT flashed across the little screen beside my head. There was a short *bing-bong* like a doorbell, the roof of the tube slid back and we began to rise upwards.

Sunlight. I could see actual sunlight. We rose a little further and I could see the tops of the mountains. And grass. Real grass.

And then I saw a crazed figure standing above us, with matted hair and mad, staring eyes and a huge knobbly stick in its hands. It yelled like Tarzan of the Apes and

167

swung the stick and whacked Charlie. He screamed and rolled sideways into the grass, holding his shoulder.

Then the crazed figure with the matted hair and the mad, staring eyes and the huge knobbly stick said, 'Jimbo!' and I realized that it was Becky.

'Don't hit me!' I shouted.

'You're back!' shouted Becky. She grabbed me and hugged me, just like I'd done when I found Charlie in the dining hall. And I grabbed her and hugged her back. I don't think I'd ever been more pleased to see her.

'Baby brother!' she said.

'You waited for us,' I said.

'Of course I waited,' said Becky. 'What was I going to do? Go home and get killed by Mum and Dad for losing you? But where in God's name have you been? And why is your back covered in sick?'

Then I remembered. 'I'll explain everything later. We've got to stop the planet being blown up.'

'What!?' said Becky.

I looked around. 'Why aren't the army or the police here?'

'What the hell are you talking about?' said Becky. 'Now just calm down and tell me what happened to you.'

Vantresillion's voice appeared in my head. 'How are we doing, James? Three minutes to go. I'm tapping my fingers. Are you speaking with the person in charge?'

the big knobbly stick

I touched my wristband. 'Er. Yeah. I'm speaking with the person in charge right now. We're going to sort something out. Very soon.' I took my fingers off the wristband.

'Who are you talking to?' asked Becky.

Charlie got to his feet. 'That really hurt.'

'Sorry,' said Becky. 'I thought you were one of them.'

'Becky. Wow. It's you,' said Charlie. 'I didn't recognize you with the cave-woman disguise.'

I turned to Becky. 'What do you mean, *one of them*?'

'That big blue light goes on,' said Becky. 'There's a *boom!* I wander over and whack them over the head. Then I tie them up behind that big rock over there. Where are they all coming from?'

'Ah,' said Charlie. 'You're the reason they've lost contact. Brilliant. Super-intelligent alien civilization foiled by a girl with a stick.'

'Charlie,' I said. 'Shut up. We haven't got much time.'

'Oh yeah,' said Charlie. 'I forgot. I'm still feeling a bit shaken. You know, on account of being assaulted.'

'There's no police,' I said. 'There's no army. What the hell are we going to do?'

Vantresillion's voice was in my head again. 'Two minutes to go. I'm getting twitchy here.'

Charlie was walking round in little circles, squeezing his head. 'OK. Think . . . Think . . . Think . . .'

'You haven't answered my question,' said Becky.

boom!

'Which question?' I said.

'Where in God's name have you been? I've been stuck here for six days living off loch water and Quality Street.'

'Six days?' I said.

'Yes,' said Becky. 'Six days.'

'That's funny,' I said. 'I thought we were only gone for a day. Something must have gone a bit strange with space-time.'

Becky grabbed me by the shoulders and shouted, 'Where in God's name have you been?'

I took a deep breath. 'Plonk. It's in the Sagittarius Dwarf Elliptical Galaxy. It's seventy thousand light years from the centre of the Milky Way. In the direction of the Large Magellanic Cloud.'

Becky shook her head. 'We have to get you to a doctor.'

'One minute to go,' said Vantresillion.

'Becky,' I said. 'Listen. This is important. It is very possible that, in about fifty seconds, Charlie is going to, like, explode.'

Becky stared at me with her mouth hanging open.

'Five minutes after that I'm going to explode too. So I just wanted to say that I love you. And don't stand too close to me. And a few minutes later . . . well, it's probably best not to think about that bit.'

'Thirty seconds . . .' said Vantresillion.

I walked over to Charlie and said, 'You're the best friend ever. You know that, don't you? And I sort of love you too. But not in a girly way.'

'Shut up!' said Charlie.

'Oh, OK, then,' I said huffily.

Charlie touched his wristband. 'Mr Vantresillion . . . ?'

I pressed my own wristband to listen in.

'Yes?' snapped Vantresillion.

There was a pause. 'We have a problem.'

'What?'

'The Watcher are all here,' said Charlie.

'Good,' said Vantresillion.

'But they're tied up.'

'Well, untie them, you brainless idiot,' said Vantresillion.

'I'm standing next to a very large policeman, said Charlie. 'And he's not keen on me doing that.'

'What the hell is going on?' asked Becky.

I calpped a hand over her mouth.

'Fenting Nard!' said Vantresillion. 'Get your friend to stand next to him so I can blow them up together.'

'You can't be serious,' said Charlie.

'Nnnnnnggg,' said Becky, trying to tear my hand away.

'Fenting, fenting, fenting nard!' said Vantresillion. 'Don't move. I'm sending someone down. And when they've

171

dealt with the very large policeman you are going to be *toast*! Do you understand?'

'Absolutely,' said Charlie and took his fingers off the wristband. He turned to Becky. 'Time for you to get your big stick.'

I took my hand off Becky's mouth and she said, 'Would you kindly tell me what is going on? And why is there an imaginary policeman? And who the hell are you talking to?'

But Charlie didn't get a chance to explain because the blinding blue light was pouring out of the sky. Then there was an ear-splitting *boom!* and the light went off and Becky picked up her big knobbly stick and ran over to the ruined cottage and lifted the stick over her head. The cover slid sideways and Mrs Pearce's head emerged from the hole and Becky hit it really hard with the stick and Mrs Pearce squealed and rolled sideways and lay face-down on the earth, completely unconscious.

'Oh my God,' said Becky. 'I've just hit a really old lady over the head.'

'Actually,' said Charlie, 'that's Mrs Pearce.'

'My God,' said Becky. 'I've just hit your history teacher over the head.'

I bent down and started lifting Mrs Pearce's skirt. 'This will make you feel better.'

'What the hell are you doing, Jimbo?' said Becky.

'I need to show you something.'

'You sick and twisted little boy,' said Becky. 'No way am I looking at a teacher's bottom.'

And there it was. Coming out of a neat little hole in the back of Mrs Pearce's knickers. A bit like a long hairy parsnip. The tail.

'Jeez,' said Charlie. 'That is going to be burned into my memory, like, for ever.'

'Becky,' I said. 'Open your eyes.'

'No.'

'Open your eyes.'

'No.'

'Open your eyes.'

Becky opened her eyes and looked down and screamed. Then everything was lit up by a bright blue light and the mountains rang with the deafening *boom!* – except we didn't take much notice because we were all so freaked out by Mrs Pearce's tail. And then we heard someone say, 'Little human scum!' and we spun round to see Vantresillion rising out of the Weff-Beam tube.

Becky ran towards him and lifted the big knobbly stick and swung it, but he was too quick. He grabbed the end and yanked it out of Becky's hands.

'Narking frotter!' he yelled, his eyes sparking with blue light. 'I am toasting you now.' He reached for his wristband.

boom!

'Stop him!' shouted Charlie.

But Becky had already whipped a can of L'Oréal extra-strength hairspray from her back pocket and squirted him in the eyes. He screamed and raised his hands to his face and fell to the ground.

'The wristband,' I said and stamped on Vantresillion's arm while Charlie yanked it off and flung it as hard as he could. We stood and watched it sail through the air until it plopped into the water next to the little boat moored to the rocks.

Vantresillion said, 'Aaeeaaeeaaeeaargh!'

And Charlie said, 'Jimbo, your sister is one feisty chick.'

'I'm assuming that's a compliment,' said Becky.

'Yeah,' said Charlie. 'But when Vantresillion doesn't check in, someone is going to press that button and we're going to explode, so we have to do something spectacular in the next minute.'

Vantresillion got to his feet and staggered around blindly, trying to find us and strangle us.

'Petrol,' I shouted. 'There's petrol in the boat. We set light to the Weff-Beam thing. We blow it up.'

We ran down to the water's edge and tried to lift the outboard motor off the stern but it was too heavy.

'Forget that,' said Becky, holding a red plastic fuel can. 'This is what we need.'

174

We ran back up the grassy slope to the ruined cottage.

'It's closing!' shouted Charlie. 'Quick!'

I grabbed the broken knobbly stick and shoved it into the hole. It splintered and cracked. Charlie and Becky staggered over with a rock and jammed it into the gap. The mechanism squeezed and juddered and gave off a lot of evil brown smoke.

Becky screwed the black top off the red plastic can and poured the contents into the Weff-Beam unit. 'Now,' she said. 'Let's set light to it.'

'How?'

Becky paused for a moment. Then she said a really, really rude word. 'We haven't got a lighter!'

The mechanism juddered and smoked and the rock cracked into two pieces.

'Craterface's lighter!' I searched madly through the pockets. The cigarettes, the wallet, the oily fluff . . . and the lighter.

I threw myself to the ground and shoved my arm down past the lid.

'Stop, you moron!' shouted Charlie. 'You'll blow yourself to pieces!'

He ripped off his shirt and shoved the sleeve into the mouth of the petrol can, then pulled it out and set light to it. The rock finally shattered, Charlie shoved the flaming shirt through the last inch of shrinking gap and shouted, 'Run!'

We ran and hurled ourselves to the ground and waited. And waited. And absolutely nothing happened. Except for Vantresillion wandering into the ruined cottage, moaning, with his arms stretched out in front of him, clawing the air like a lost zombie.

He was standing in the very centre of the cottage when the blue light flashed on. He screamed again, but much, much louder this time. Then he vanished inside the column of light and we couldn't hear him screaming any more. Then the light went off and the *boom!* shook the mountains and we saw that Vantresillion had been turned into a smoking black statue of himself. One arm fell off and smashed on the ground. Then the head did the same thing.

'It didn't work!' said Charlie. 'It didn't—'

And then, suddenly, it *did* work. There was a shuddering *whump!* and the Weff-Beam unit and the cottage and the black statue of Vantresillion erupted in a massive cauliflower of orange flame. We closed our eyes and covered our heads. The heat wave hit us and it was like being run over by a really hot lorry.

We opened our eyes. There was an ominous silence for about two seconds, then a horrible clatter as broken pieces of highly advanced technology rained down around us. I looked up and rolled out of the way just in time to prevent myself being kebabbed by a long spear of ceramic tube-wall.

We got up and picked bits of ash and shrapnel off our clothing and walked back towards the ruin. Except it wasn't there any more. There was a black crater. There was a ring of charred stones. There were some wires. There was a triangle of cracked blue glass.

I heard a little click and felt my wristband loosen and fall to the ground. I heard another little click and saw Charlie's wristband do the same.

He bent down and picked them up. 'You know,' he said. 'Just to be on the safe side.' He drew back his arm and hurled them into the water.

And this was when we saw Mrs Pearce. She'd finally come round and got to her feet. She had her fingers pressed to her own wristband. 'Gretnoid,' she said. 'Nutwall venka berdang.' She pressed it again. 'Gretnoid. Nutwall venka berdang.' Her voice was getting more and more panicky. 'Gretnoid . . . ? Gretnoid . . . ?'

Charlie walked up to her. 'You've lost all contact with Plonk, haven't you?'

She growled at him.

'Brilliant,' said Charlie. 'I'm kind of assuming they can't blow us up now. Or the planet. Is that right?'

'You're going to suffer for this. I am going to make you all suffer so very, very much.'

'How?' said Charlie.

She paused for a few moments, then she slumped to the ground and started to cry. 'Oh God,' she wailed. 'I'm going to be stuck on your stupid, primitive, godforsaken planet for ever.'

'Anyway,' said Becky, 'we're off now. There are five of your friends tied up over there. Behind the big boulder. They're going to need a bit of help.'

We walked back to the tent. The five Watchers were tied up nearby. I recognized two of them from the red Volvo. They were all a bit snarly at first. Then Charlie explained that the Weff-Beam had been destroyed and that they wouldn't be going home. After this they went a bit quiet. A couple of them cried, just like Mrs Pearce.

Becky dug around in the holdall and found a spare shirt for Charlie. We packed up and headed back down to the water. Mrs Pearce was still on her hands and knees, crying, when we walked past her.

'Cheerio!' said Charlie.

She looked up at him and whimpered like a sad dog.

We climbed into the boat and lowered the outboard into the water. Becky yanked the starter cord three times and the engine coughed into life and we puttered down the little channel to the sea.

17
individual broccoli
tartlets

We ran out of petrol halfway, having used the back-up supply to destroy the Weff-Beam. But there were oars and it was a sunny day, and just being on the surface of our own planet was a pleasure.

I tried to explain everything to Becky, but after a while she told me to stop. 'It's doing my head in, Jimbo. I'm tired and hungry and filthy. I've been living in the wilderness for nearly a week, hitting strange people over the head. I need normal. I need ordinary. I need bacon and fried eggs and toast. And I need a long hot shower. I do not need hover-scooters and intergalactic ferries.'

So she went and sat at the bow and Charlie sat facing me while I rowed and we shared our stories about how he'd been captured and how Becky and I had set off in pursuit on a stolen motorbike.

And maybe Bob-with-the-Hawaiian-shirt was right. Maybe it was cool being on a planet on the far side of the known galaxy. And maybe it was even cooler escaping and getting home again. But the coolest thing of all was having my best friend back.

'What about Mrs Pearce?' I said.

'What do you mean?' asked Charlie.

'She said she was going to make us suffer. You don't think she's going to, like, track us down and kill us, do you?'

Charlie put his head on one side and stared at me. 'She's an elderly lady with no job. The police will be looking for her. She has a tail. And no belly button. If I were her I'd be heading for the hills and living off nuts and berries.'

We took turns rowing and after a couple of hours we reached Elgol harbour with two seagulls circling above us and a friendly seal in our wake.

The red Volvo was parked a little way up the road from the slipway.

'So,' said Charlie, rubbing his hands together, 'are we going to break in and hotwire it?'

'Don't be daft,' said Becky. 'I had the driver tied up for three days.' She fished a set of car keys out of the holdall. 'These were in his pocket.'

'You are a true professional,' said Charlie.

'Thank you,' said Becky.

'Can I have a go at driving?' said Charlie.

'Are you out of your mind?' said Becky. 'Get in the back.'

The Volvo was pretty straightforward after the Moto Guzzi. It had four wheels for starters, so it wasn't going to fall over sideways. We scraped a couple of stone walls and bumped in and out of a few ditches over the first couple of miles but Becky soon got the hang of it.

The journey was glorious. All those things I'd never looked at before seemed wonderful now. Cooling towers. Transit vans. Concrete bridges. I looked at electricity pylons and felt a warm glow in my heart.

After three hours we stopped at Gretna Green. Becky ordered her fry-up, I ordered a pizza and

Charlie ordered a black coffee and four apple turnovers.

We had another six hours of driving in which to plan our stories. But we were too tired. After about four minutes Charlie and I fell asleep and didn't wake up till we reached the M25. Luckily, Becky only fell asleep twice, but each time she was woken up by a lorry honking as she veered into the wrong lane of the motorway.

We offered to drop Charlie off first but he reckoned our parents were less likely to kill him.

When we pulled into the car park by the flats I looked up at the tatty, peeling, weather-stained block and I must admit I got a bit tearful. Then I remembered the complications waiting upstairs and my heart sank.

I turned to Becky. 'What are we going to say?'

'We?' said Becky. 'I think that's your job, mate. But if you want my advice, I'd go easy on the aliens-with-hairy-tails-and-space-travel aspect of the whole thing.'

'Gird your loins,' said Charlie. 'Let's get this over with.'

Becky unlocked the door of the flat and we stepped inside. Mum was on the phone. She dropped it and froze for several seconds. Then she screamed. It was actually quite frightening. She threw her arms around me and Becky and squeezed and cried and shouted, 'You're alive! You're alive!'

Then Dad came into the hallway and did the same thing, without the screaming. Then everyone noticed that Charlie was standing to one side looking a bit left out so we grabbed hold of him and had a group hug, by which time all of us were crying, even Charlie, and I'd never seen him cry before, ever.

Things calmed down after a few minutes and we stopped hugging each other. Mum's face went a bit dark and she said, 'Where in God's name have you been?'

And this was the point when I realized we should have worked out a story. 'Well . . .'

There was a horrible silence.

'You disappear for a week,' said Mum, her joy ebbing rapidly away. 'You don't tell us where you're going. We call and you don't ring us back. We've been through hell wondering what happened to you.'

Then Charlie had a brainwave. And I have to say that it was both simple and rather brilliant. 'We were kidnapped.'

'Kidnapped?' said Dad.

'Kidnapped?' said Mum.

'By Mr Kidd,' said Charlie. 'And Mrs Pearce. From school.'

'They took us to Scotland,' I said. 'To Loch Coruisk. On the Isle of Skye.'

'What . . . !?' said Mum. 'What . . . !? What . . . !?' She sounded a bit like a chicken.

'So,' said Dad, shaking his head, 'who wrecked the flat?'

'What?' asked Charlie.

I looked over Dad's shoulder and saw two halves of the snapped coffee table stacked in the corner of the living room and it all came back to me. 'Oh, that,' I said.

'We came back home,' said Dad. 'The fridge was on its side. The sofa was upside down. And we found one of the kitchen chairs in the car park.'

'Obviously we didn't want to be kidnapped,' said Becky, as if this was the most obvious thing in the world. 'So we put up a fight.'

'But . . . but . . . but . . .' said Mum, sounding like a slightly different kind of chicken. 'But why did they kidnap you?'

'I have absolutely no idea,' said Charlie breezily. 'You'll have to ask Mrs Pearce and Mr Kidd. Perhaps they can explain everything.'

'I'm going to ring the police,' said Dad.

'Excellent idea,' said Charlie. 'But I really do think I ought to go home first.'

Becky and I showered rapidly and grabbed some clean clothes and Dad drove us all over to Charlie's house.

We knocked on the door and it was pretty much a repeat of what happened at our house. The hugging, the crying. Except that Mrs Brooks screamed a lot louder than Mum.

Dr Brooks rang the police, and two sergeants arrived ten minutes later. Reassuringly, neither of them were wearing brass wristbands.

We told them the kidnapping story. Like Becky suggested, we missed out the aliens-with-hairy-tails-and-space-travel aspect. And the stealing-a-motorbike-and-a-car-and-driving-without-a-licence aspect. And the saving-the-Earth-from-destruction aspect.

The police asked us whether we wanted counselling. We said we'd prefer a hot supper. They told us they'd be in touch and headed out to their car.

Charlie, Becky and I then wandered into the kitchen to discover that Dad and Mrs Brooks had formed a team. Mrs Brooks was rustling up a Stilton sauce to pour over steamed vegetables, while Dad was putting together some individual broccoli tartlets. Mrs Brooks was really rather impressed.

Indeed, while we were eating supper she said that if he was looking for work, she often needed help with some of her bigger catering jobs. Dad said he was very flattered but he'd have to go away and think about it.

Over a dessert of pears in chocolate custard Mum asked Becky whether she was going to ring Craterface. Except she called him Terry because she was in a good mood because we weren't dead. And Becky said she'd be happy if she never saw the lying skunk again. Which was probably just as well since we'd left the Moto Guzzi in Scotland.

Then there was a loud *pop!* and Dr Brooks appeared carrying champagne and a tray of seven glasses. He filled them, we raised them, Dad said, 'Welcome home,' and Charlie sank his glass in one go and let out one of the loudest burps I have ever heard in my life.

18

a bunker under the brecon beacons

School on Monday morning was particularly excellent. For obvious reasons. When your headmistress stands up in assembly and says you were kidnapped by two of your teachers, but you escaped and they're now on the run from the police, a party atmosphere continues pretty much unabated for the rest of the week.

We were officially cooler than any other pupils in living memory, and I reckoned it was probably a good month before any teacher would feel confident enough to give either of us a detention.

Dad decided to take the job with Charlie's mum. He stuck it for three whole weeks. That was about his limit. She was terrifying, so Dad said. During one particularly stressful wedding reception she did her breadboard-throwing thing. He was inches away from a visit to Accident and Emergency.

Luckily, he was offered a more lucrative and less dangerous job in the Grand Café in town, so he was able to stop working for Mrs Brooks without incurring her everlasting wrath. Even more luckily, the job in the Grand Café was part-time so he was able to come home and cook us beef Wellington and stuffed butternut squash.

The police never came back. I told Charlie something fishy was going on but he told me to chill out and be grateful we weren't taken into custody and injected with truth serum.

So I tried to chill out. And I was doing it really well till we were playing five-a-side football during the lunch break one day a couple of weeks later and I looked across the road and saw a black car with smoked-glass windows parked in front of the laundrette. I didn't tell Charlie. He'd just say I was paranoid.

The following day I saw it when I was standing on the

balcony after supper. It pulled into the car park, idled for a few minutes, then drove away again.

I told Charlie this time. He said I was seeing things. Then we had a class outing to the Science Museum and the black car with the smoked windows was sitting at the side of the street when we got back into the coach. I went a bit crazy at this point. It took Mrs Hennessy a good ten minutes to calm me down and even Charlie said I might have a point.

A few evenings later we met up in the little playground opposite the flats. We sat side by side on the swings. It was getting dark. The orange streetlamps were coming on one by one and the windows in the tower block were lighting up in a chequerboard of different colours.

We were talking about our big secret.

Charlie said, 'Don't you wish you could tell someone? I mean, we could be rich, we could be famous, we could be interviewed by the world's most respected scientists. We could go down in history.' He paused. 'Except of course we wouldn't. Because no one would believe us. We'd probably end up in a psychiatric hospital.'

'Unless we had proof,' I said.

'Yeah,' said Charlie. 'Unless we had proof.'

'Like this, for example,' I said, digging into the back pocket of my jeans and pulling out the floaty balls.

'God,' said Charlie. 'I remember those. Do they still work?'

I placed two of them in the air and let go. They hung there, completely motionless. 'Those are yours,' I said. 'I've got three others. They're, like, a souvenir.'

'Cheers,' said Charlie, sweeping the two balls out of the air and pocketing them.

And that's when I saw the figure emerging from the shadows beneath the trees. My insides froze. 'Charlie . . . ?'

'Oh crap,' he said. 'This is not good, is it?'

I wanted to jump off the swing and run but my legs were no longer taking messages.

The silhouetted figure got closer. 'Hello, James. Hello, Charles.'

It was Mrs Pearce. She was wearing clothes she must have found in a skip. A black plastic raincoat with one sleeve missing. Sandals. Fluorescent-orange workman's trousers. She looked as if she'd washed her hair in engine oil.

'You were probably expecting me, weren't you?'

'No,' said Charlie, in a wobbly voice. 'I mean, actually, Jimbo was. But I wasn't.'

'You destroyed my life. You destroyed everything,' she said. 'And do you know what?'

'What?' asked Charlie.

'I have absolutely nothing left to lose.'

'Really?' said Charlie.

I could see now that Mrs Pearce was holding two objects. In her left hand was a large hammer. In her right was a small pointy gardening fork.

'Now hang on,' said Charlie. 'I think we should talk about this. You know, sensibly. Like grown-ups.'

'Shut up,' said Mrs Pearce. 'I'm going to kill you.'

I looked over her shoulder. The black car with the smoked-glass windows was parked in front of the flats. The driver's door was standing open.

'And I'm going to enjoy it so very, very much,' said Mrs Pearce.

There was movement in the darkness behind her. Two more figures were emerging from the trees. Their clothing was dark and their faces were in shadow. But I could see that they were men. Big men.

Mrs Pearce took a couple more steps and raised the hammer above her head. I screamed and fell off the back of the swing and banged my head on the rubberized tarmac. Mrs Pearce lunged and there was a flash of light and a loud *crack!* and she slumped on top of me, the hammer narrowly missing my head.

I pushed her off and struggled to my feet. There was a feathered dart sticking out of her bottom and she was saying, 'Nnnnrrrrgg . . .'

'Gordon Bennett,' said Charlie.

The two men were walking towards us. They had guns. It seemed like a good idea not to run away. The man on the left bent down, yanked the dart out of Mrs Pearce's bottom, rolled her over and fitted her with a black plastic muzzle. The man on the right walked up to us and said, 'Jimbo . . . Charlie . . .'

He held out his hand and we shook it, robotically, unable to do anything else.

'Who are you?' asked Charlie.

'We're the good guys,' said the man. He was wearing a suit but he had an Action Man scar across his cheek and his head was shaved like he'd just returned from a war.

His colleague hoisted Mrs Pearce easily over his shoulder and carried her towards the park gate.

'What's going on?' asked Charlie.

'We reckoned if we stuck close to you she'd show up sooner or later,' said the man. 'Use you as bait.'

'Bait?' I said.

'There's a couple more still at large in the Peak District

but we'll track them down in the next couple of days. I don't think you've got much to worry about.'

Neither Charlie nor I could think of anything to say.

'Well,' said the man, 'we just wanted to thank the two of you. You got there before us. Job well done. We'd give you medals. But medals mean publicity. And we don't like publicity in the department.'

'What department's that?'

The man looked at Charlie as if he were very, very stupid.

'So, um . . .' said Charlie. 'What are you going to do with her? Mrs Pearce, I mean.'

'She'll be in a disused nuclear bunker several hundred metres under the Brecon Beacons.' The man paused. 'Of course, I may be lying.' He held out his hand towards me. 'Floaty balls, please.'

'What?'

'Floaty balls.'

Reluctantly, I slipped my hand into my trouser pocket, took out my three balls and placed them in his hand. He looked over at Charlie. 'Yours too.'

Across the car park I saw his colleague dump Mrs Pearce's unconscious body into the boot of the car, slam it shut, then climb into the driver's seat.

Charlie handed over the final two balls. The man took his hand away and let all five balls hang motionless for a second. 'God, I love these things.' Then he swept them out of the air and slipped them into his jacket pocket.

'What are you going to do now?' asked Charlie nervously. 'Are you, like, going to wipe our brains or something? You know, so we don't remember anything.'

'You've been watching too many films, Charlie. No. It's much simpler than that. If you say anything, to anyone, we track you down and kill you.'

'Right,' said Charlie.

'It's been good meeting you,' said the man. 'I hope you have a pleasant evening.'

He turned and walked through the gate at the edge of the park. He got into the black car with the smoked-glass windows, slammed the door and drove off into the night.

Mark Haddon is an author,
illustrator and screenwriter who has
written fifteen books for children and won
two BAFTAs. His bestselling novel, *The Curious
Incident of the Dog in the Night-time* was
published simultaneously by Jonathan Cape
and David Fickling in 2003. It won seventeen
literary prizes, including the Whitbread Award.
Mark Haddon lives in Oxford.

Also by Mark Haddon for older readers

THE CURIOUS INCIDENT OF THE DOG IN THE NIGHT-TIME

by
MARK HADDON

Fifteen-year-old Christopher has a
photographic memory. He understands maths.
He understands science. What he can't
understand are other human beings. When he
finds his neighbour's dog lying dead on the
lawn, he decides to track down the killer
and write a murder mystery about it.
But what other mysteries will he
end up uncovering?

'Stunningly good' *Independent*

Winner of the Whitbread Book of the Year and
the Guardian Children's Fiction Prize
Longlisted for the Man Booker Prize
Shortlisted for the Carnegie Medal

978 1 849 92041 4

Also available from David Fickling Books:

Johnny Swanson – Eleanor Updale
Into the Woods – Lyn Gardner
The London Eye Mystery – Siobhan Dowd
The Penderwicks – Jeanne Birdsall

For older readers:
The Boy in the Striped Pyjamas – John Boyne
X Isle – Steve Augarde
Bog Child – Siobhan Dowd
Before I Die – Jenny Downham
Trash – Andy Mulligan

Blackburn
College

Libr

below

THE TERRITORY OF

Language

LINGUISTICS, STYLISTICS, AND
THE TEACHING OF COMPOSITION

Donald A. McQuade

Southern Illinois University Press
Carbondale and Edwardsville

BLACKBURN COLLEGE
LIBRARY

Acc. No. BB52616

Class No. UCL 808·042 MAC

Date 12-11-12

Copyright © 1986 by Donald A. McQuade
All rights reserved
Printed in the United States of America
Edited by Dan Gunter
Designed by David Ford
Production supervised by Kathleen Giencke

This is a revised and enlarged edition of a book formerly entitled *Linguistics, Stylistics, and the Teaching of Composition*, copyright © 1979 by Donald A. McQuade, published by L & S Books.

90   89   88   87   86   5   4   3   2   1

Permission to reprint the following copyright works is gratefully acknowledged:
"The Red Wheelbarrow": William Carlos Williams, *Collected Earlier Poems*.
        Copyright 1938 by New Directions Publishing Corporation. Reprinted by
        permission of New Directions.
"Colloquy in Black Rock": From *Lord Weary's Castle*, copyright 1946, 1974 by
        Robert Lowell. Reprinted by permission of Harcourt Brace Jovanovich, Inc.
From "The Love Song of J. Alfred Prufrock" in *Collected Poems 1909–1962* by T. S.
        Eliot, copyright 1936 by Harcourt Brace Jovanovich, Inc.; copyright © 1963,
        1964 by T. S. Eliot. Reprinted by permission of the publisher.
From "The Love Song of J. Alfred Prufrock": Reprinted by permission of Faber and
        Faber Ltd from *Collected Poems 1909–1962* by T. S. Eliot.

Library of Congress Cataloging in Publication Data
Main entry under title:
The Territory of language.
    Rev. and enl. ed. of: Linguistics, stylistics, and
the teaching of composition. c1979.
    Includes bibliographical references.
    1. English language—Rhetoric—Study and teaching—
Addresses, essays, lectures.   I. Linguistics, stylistics,
and the teaching of composition. II. McQuade, Donald.
PE1404.T47   1986   808′.042′071173   85-2080
ISBN 0-8093-1217-4
ISBN 0-8093-1215-8 (pbk.)

In memory of
Mina P. Shaughnessy

Contents

Preface

The publication of *The Territory of Language* marks the return—in a thoroughly revised and generously expanded form—of a book that became something of an underground classic following its appearance in 1979. *Linguistics, Stylistics, and the Teaching of Composition* offered teachers of writing a broad sampling of the thought-provoking work of some of this nation's most distinguished composition theorists. The volume focused on how composition theory might draw on linguistics and stylistics to elucidate both the nature of the writing process as well as on the pedagogical strategies that could help students establish more practiced authority over the skills needed to write effectively.

Despite the attention it received, the volume disappeared from all but the most resolute of readers' eyes. Printed in a storefront operation in Akron, Ohio, and "distributed" much later from the basement of an academic who has since left the profession for "greener" fields, *Linguistics, Stylistics, and the Teaching of Composition* proved easier to order than to receive. The volume fell out of print within a year. Through the kindness of Edmund Epstein, the editor of *Language and Style, Linguistics, Stylistics, and the Teaching of Composition* was revived briefly as a special edition of that journal. More recently, Kenney Withers, the gracious, intelligent, and dedicated director of Southern Illinois University Press, agreed to publish a revised and expanded version as a service to the community of professionals committed to encouraging scholarship in composition. To reflect the extent of the changes in this new edition and to signal its association with what has become the leading university press in composition studies, the volume bears a new title, *The Territory of Language*.

I have drawn the title of this collection from an especially incisive passage in Mina Shaughnessy's *Errors and Expectations*, a work that remains our profession's most eloquent and humanistic introduction to the challenges and satisfactions of teaching basic writing. From the outset, Mina Shaughnessy writes with great sensitivity about the pressures and confusions students contend with each time they set out to write:

One senses the struggle to fashion out of the fragments of past instruction a system that will relieve the writer of the task of deciding what to do in each instance where alternative forms or conventions stick in the mind. But the task seems too demanding and the rewards too stingy for someone who can step out of a classroom and in a moment be in the thick of conversation with friends.

Confusion, rather than conflict, seems to paralyze the writer at this level. Language learners at any level appear to seek out, either consciously or unconsciously, the underlying patterns that govern the language they are learning. They are pressed by their language-learning faculties to increase the degree of predictability and efficiency in their use of language. This is less a choice they make than an urge they have to move across the territory of language as if they had a map and not as if they were being forced to make their way across a mine field. (P. 10)

There are some striking similarities between what Mina Shaughnessy describes here as the pressures basic writers face and those that teachers of writing encounter each time they work with their students. Until fairly recently, most of us who teach composition approached *our* task with, regrettably enough, little more than "fragments of past instruction." In a similar vein, when we set out to create substance and shape for our writing classes, our pedagogical choices from among what Shaughnessy calls "the alternative forms or conventions [that] stick in the mind" may often have been made with some of roughly the same uncertainty and anxiety that characterize our students' own halting efforts to exercise authority over their compositional skills and the subjects they are expected to write about. We have been reminded by some disgruntled students and dispirited colleagues—although perhaps somewhat less frequently in the past few years—that the effort and responsibility involved in composition courses do indeed at times seem "too demanding and the rewards too stingy." Yet, should we choose to listen more carefully to our students, colleagues, and ourselves, we will understand more clearly that, when it comes to composition classes, what we may well share more specifically with our students is, as Mina Shaughnessy notes, "confusion rather than conflict." Given the possibility that Shaughnessy's observation is reasonably accurate, students and—if I may extend her point—teachers might well benefit if they both could work through "the territory of language as if they had a map and not as if they were being forced to make their way across a mine field." *The Territory of Language* is dedicated to fostering that collaborative spirit.

This volume aims to chart the interconnections of linguistics, stylistics, and the teaching of composition. In doing so, it seeks *not* to fix exactly where the boundaries of these disciplines overlap. Rather, the book is intended to explore a common ground, to clear away some of the intellectual debris accumulated from territorial conflicts of the past few decades, and to encourage a more productive collective effort to cultivate an area which remains for too many teachers of writing a veritable mine field of confusion.

The Territory of Language, like its predecessor, serves as a compendium of reports on significant research and scholarship in composition and offers a medley of practical advice on dealing more effectively with the problems and prospects today's students bring with them to their writing classes. Of the twenty-five essays gathered in *The Territory of Language*, ten are completely new to this edition. Others reflect extensive revision, and, in the case of some research studies and Richard Larson's bibliographical essay, additional attention to recent scholarship. Reorganized into three interrelated clusters of essays, this expanded edition not only reprints, for example, the findings of the first thorough analysis of the composing patterns of basic writers and the results of research on error analysis and sentence combining but also presents the more recent findings of scholarly inquiry into syntactic complexity and the problem of topics in texts. Also included are seminal articles on the linguistic and stylistic evidence for developing a psychology of composing; the importance of acknowledgment in creating a productive community of writers; the tested adaptations of classical rhetorical principles to contemporary writing activities; the use of literary structures to teach writing; the place of traditional and transformational grammar in composition classrooms; a fresh historical overview of the role of grammar in American college composition; and a revised comprehensive bibliographical essay summarizing the interrelations of language studies and composing processes. The section "Teaching the Connections" includes several new essays on such subjects as developing a pragmatic framework for discussing form in writing as well as using abstraction as a speculative instrument in composition. Complementing these important new essays are several essay/reviews of influential composition theorists and a thorough review of the scholarship informing the recent movement toward writing across the curriculum.

A few words about the criteria established for selecting the essays. Significance and readability remain the principal requirements. These essays are presented, then, not only because they make important contributions to composition theory and pedagogy but also because they observe, describe, explain, and speculate about the interconnections of linguistics, stylistics, and teaching composition in terms readily accessible to nonspecialist readers. So too, while several of the essays lead us to the farthest edge of composition theory, none does so at the cost of losing sight of the pressing realities of daily classroom activities. Each, in its unique way, confirms the accuracy of Coleridge's observation in *Biographia Literaria*: "The ultimate end of criticism is much more to establish the principles of writing, than to furnish rules on how to pass judgment on what has been written by others."

The Territory of Language draws together in a single volume significant original essays which would otherwise be scattered throughout any number of professional journals. The book proposes to create a convenient and concentrated forum for enriching the composition theorist's as well as the practitioner's understanding of the assumptions, methods, and results of work in linguistics and stylistics as they apply to strengthening individual and collective efforts to teach writing more efficiently and effectively. The essays gathered here will, I trust, both demonstrate the appreciable progress being made in synthesizing the work of three disciplines as well as set some new, clear directions for collaborating on the considerable challenges that lie ahead.

The Territory of Language appears in print as a result of the encouragement, enthusiasm, hard work, and patience of a number of people. I would like to express my appreciation to the several reviewers of *Linguistics, Stylistics, and the Teaching of Composition* who endorsed the book's being republished in a revised and expanded format. To the twenty-five contributors, who wrote and revised, and revised, and revised, I offer my gratitude and apologize for the delay in putting their work into print. This volume could not have appeared without the kindness, commitment, and patience of Kenney Withers, the director of Southern Illinois University Press, as well as the intelligence, concern, and imaginative attention of Dan Gunter, the editor of this project. They did everything that a first-rate publisher could to support this project. I am also grateful to Ms. Loretta Vincent, who designed the cover. The quality of her work is immediately apparent. I would also like to thank several colleagues and friends who offered invaluable assistance in preparing this volume during what became an especially hectic period in my own work: Ken Bruffee, Fred Buell, John Clifford, Nancy Comley, Jacqueline Costello, Edmund Epstein, Joan Feinberg, William P. Kelly, James Kinneavy, Robert B. Lyons, Elaine Maimon, John J. McDermott, Sandra Schor, Nancy Sommers, Geoffrey Summerfield, Judith Summerfield, Amy Tucker, H. Barbara Weinberg, David Wheeler, Harvey Wiener, and especially Robert Atwan, a superb reader of any text. Nat LaMar generously offered his expert advice on how words work. His elegant intelligence and bountiful goodwill made this a better book. Special thanks to Christine and Marc McQuade for—as always—their gentle cheerfulness, reassurance, and understanding. And as in all such endeavors, my greatest debt is to Susanne Batschelet McQuade, whose intelligence and love contribute immeasurably to all that I do.

Finally, I would also like to say that in dedicating this volume to the memory of Mina Shaughnessy I can only hope that readers will discover in it continued expressions of the strength and spirit of Mina's work.

Mapping the Territory

ROBERT J. CONNORS

Grammar in American College Composition: An Historical Overview

The relationship between the teaching of writing and the various bodies of knowledge and prejudice called "grammar" has always been problematical. In a volume such as this, which investigates, among other issues, the relation of writing to the most modern linguistic phenomena, it might at first seem unwarranted to cover the "bad old days," when pinch-faced champions of "literacy" forced gobs of questionable prescription down adolescent throats. A look, however, into the handbooks and the workbooks that still pour from the presses for use in both remedial and freshman English will show that the old days may be gone theoretically but remain with us on the level of practical pedagogy. We ought, I think, to learn more about them.

English Grammar: Background

In order to understand how grammar has affected the teaching of writing, it will first be necessary to look briefly at the ways in which traditional grammar was taught in America prior to the rise of modern linguistics. The study of formal English grammar became a popular subject in the common schools of America around the time of the American Revolution. Rollo L. Lyman has set 1775 as the date for the beginning of a fifty-year rise of vernacular grammar in elementary and secondary schools.[1] English grammar replaced the study of Latin grammar among the earlier school grades as Latin and Greek ceased to be the absolute core of every curriculum. Soon grammar was so much at the center of elementary study that elementary schools became known as "grammar schools," an appellation that exists even today. Study of English grammar reached its peak influence around 1850, at a time when grammar was the main subject of a pupil's first six grades.

Early grammar instruction—before 1850 or so—had nothing to do with composing essays or even with constructing sentences. It was an absolutely formal discipline that demanded a great deal of rote memorization of terms, complex analyses of given sentences, and suspicious patrols through other sentences searching for "errors." As Charles C. Fries says, the basis of this early formal grammar study was very different from modern linguistic science and had as its end not *"description* for the sake of *prediction"* but *"analysis* for the sake of *classification."*[2] Grammar was not, in any sense, a creative field of study; rather, it was meant as a "mental discipline," training the mind for rigorous thought.

Before 1850, traditional grammar methods were threefold, and none of the three traditional pedagogies was concerned with the development of writing skill. First, pupils were made to memorize the parts of speech, all the "rules" of declension, conjugation, gender, number, case, degree, tense, mood, person, and countless others. Second, they were forced to apply and demonstrate these rules in oral exercises called "parsing," which asked pupils to give definitions and applicable rules for every word in a sentence provided by the teacher. Here is an example of a sentence partially parsed, from what was the paradigmatic grammar text for nineteenth-century America, Lindley Murray's best-selling *English Grammar* of 1795:

> "We should be kind to them, who are unkind to us."
>   *We* is a personal pronoun, of the first person, the plural number, and in the nominative case. (*Decline it.*) *Should be* is an irregular verb neuter, in the potential mood, the imperfect tense, and the first person plural. (*Repeat the present tense, etc.*) *Kind* is an adjective, in the positive state. (*Repeat the degrees of comparison.*) *To* is a preposition. *Them* is a personal pronoun, of the third person, the plural number, and in the objective case. (*Decline it.*) *Who* is a relative pronoun, and in the nominative case. (*Decline it*). . . .[3]

The example goes on, but the point is made. The third sort of grammar exercise was introduced by Robert Lowth in his *Short Introduction* of 1758, and was used by every major grammar textbook through 1850. It consisted of the teacher's providing examples of ungrammatical sentences, either orally or in written form, and asking pupils to correct the ungrammaticality and then state the rules and definitions by which the repair was made. These "false syntax" exercises fostered a spirit of anxiety and suspicion about grammar that was not long in pervading the entire linguistic culture of the new nation.[4]

Around 1850 the methods of teaching grammar began to change as inductive forms of pedagogy were imported from Europe. Creative and compositional elements were gradually added to the memorization and dissection exercises already used. Most important to this movement toward incorporating writing and grammar were the many editions of Samuel S. Greene's *Analysis* of 1847. Greene was the first important grammarian to include the writing of original sentences as part of each of his grammar lessons, usually ending a series of models and parsing exercises with instructions. For instance, "Write fifteen sentences of your own, limiting the subjects of the first five by a compound adjective element, the predicates of the next five by a compound objective element, and the predicates of the last five by a compound adverbial element."[5] In spite of Greene's popularity, however, the field of grammar continued to be overwhelmingly formalistic and abstract, having little to do with communications skills as they really existed. Grammarians contrived to accept Lindley Murray's definition of grammar as "the art of speaking and writing the English language with propriety," and school grammar was still an attempt to instill, through rigid taxonomic practice, this knowledge of correctness.

Teaching of formal grammar in American elementary and high schools reached its high point around 1850 and then began to lose popularity. More and more teachers and school board officials began to see the "mental discipline" claims of grammar instructions as will-o'-the-wisps and the claims that knowledge of grammatical categories fostered literate skills as demonstrably false. William H. Wells, one of the earliest professors of the system of inductive grammar (his textbook appeared in 1846), had lost faith in grammatical study by 1865, when he wrote that a student "may have the whole grammar book by heart, and yet not be able to make a respectable speech. . . . The great object to be attained, is not the mastery of a text-book in grammar, but the acquisition of language."[6] Indeed, some began to question whether English *had* a grammar, so poorly did the language seem to fit into the accepted inflected structure of Latin grammar. In *Words and Their Uses* in 1870 Richard Grant White claimed that English was a "grammarless" language, and many believed the claim.

The traditional teaching of formal grammar was in deep trouble by the 1880s. The state of Connecticut dropped all grammar teaching during this period, claiming it was "hateful" to students and did not help them to speak or write better.[7] On the level of theory, more and more philologists were coming to agree with pioneer linguist George P. Marsh:

> So far as respects English or any other uninflected speech, a knowledge of grammar is rather a matter of convenience as a nomenclature, a medium of thought and discussion *about* language than a guide to the actual use of it, and it is as impossible to acquire the complete command of our own tongue by the study of grammatical precept, as to learn to walk or swim by attending a course of lectures on anatomy.[8]

Marsh believed that in English "grammar has little use except to systematize," and more and more people were questioning why such an abstract system should be at the core of American school education.

Yet grammar, though its early methods were being seriously questioned, was far from defunct. Educators, a conservative group in the nineteenth century, were shoring up fragments against the ruin of their central subject, and between

1850 and 1880 a new pedagogy for grammar was born, one based not on abstract learning of formal grammar but rather on using grammar in sentences. This method, based on Greene's *Analysis*, came to be called "sentence building" or "language lessons," after William Swinton's extremely popular textbook *Language Lessons*, which appeared in 1873.[9] This pedagogy focused on writing and then examining the student's own sentences rather than on rote memorization and parsing. It was given a great boost in 1877, when Alonzo Reed and Brainerd Kellogg first published their *Higher Lessons in English*.

Reed and Kellogg admitted that grammar "is very insecure. Children are not enthusiastic in praise of grammar, most parents recall without pleasure their own trials with it, and many men of culture and of wisdom openly advise its banishment from the school-room."[10] Reed and Kellogg believed that grammar is necessary, but warned that "it must bear on its branches more obvious and more *serviceable* fruit, or the tree will be hewn down and cast out of the way" (p. 3). The answer in *Higher Lessons* was to "make the Science of the Language, of which all the essentials are thoroughly presented, tributary to the Art of Expression" (p. 3). The book was filled with practices, exercises, and drills, but these were not so different from Swinton's drills. What really set Reed and Kellogg apart was their invention of the sentence diagram, the familiar straight-line diagram that was still used in the 1970s to demonstrate sentence structure.

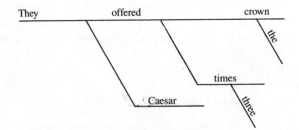

Reed and Kellogg provided a new defense for sentence-based grammar pedagogy, one that soon became extremely popular. It can be said, in fact, that the diagram-based analysis of sentences that *Higher Lessons* originated was *the* essential grammar pedagogy from 1880 through 1970. It was critiqued around the beginning of the century by several theorists, most notably Gertrude Buck,[11] for its mechanical and linear nature; other critics of diagram-based texts called attention to the extremely confusing variation of names and terms in different grammar texts.[12] Despite the criticism leveled at it, however, no system was put forward to supplant the Reed and Kellogg-based "sentence study" method. This became the background method for most of the discussions of "grammar" conducted on the college level prior to 1925 or so, and this traditional grammatical system is the system that came under heavy attack almost as soon as modern descriptive linguistics was established as a discipline. .

Grammar and Rhetoric

When assessing grammar's affect on the teaching of writing, we need to remember that the conflation of grammar and rhetoric is an exclusively modern phenomenon, unknown before 1870 or so. The Greek or Roman rhetorician would have been scandalized by the suggestion that he profess the structure of the language on any level. That job, dirty but necessary, was the responsibility of the *grammaticus*, the lower-grade teacher who made certain that pupils could speak with *correctness*. Only when this knowledge of pure and correct language was assured would the rhetorician take over and teach the pupil to discourse with *eloquence*. This essential split between grammar and rhetoric existed unchanged through the eighteenth century. As the brilliant George Campbell, hardly a purveyor of unexamined tradition, put it in 1776,

> Now, the grammatical art hath its completion in syntax; the oratorical, as far as the body of expression is concerned, in style. Syntax regards only the composition of many words into one sentence; style, at the same time that it attends to this, regards further the composition of many sentences into one discourse. Nor is this the only difference; the grammarian . . . requires only purity. . . . The orator requires also beauty and strength. The highest aim of the former is the lowest aim of the latter; where grammar ends eloquence begins. Thus the grammarian's department bears much the same relation to the orator's which the art of the mason bears to that of the architect.[13]

Campbell is not sneering here at grammar—he discusses grammatical purity at some length when covering good usage—but he does wish to differentiate it clearly from the rhetorical theory that absorbed his interest.

Campbell's attitude toward grammar was not, however, shared by Hugh Blair, whose 1783 *Lectures on Rhetoric and Belles-Lettres* became the most influential of the eighteenth-century rhetorics. Instruction in formal English grammar had begun in both England and America around 1750, and Blair saw, as Campbell did not, that an English rhetoric would have to come to terms with English grammar. Grammar, wrote Blair in one of his two chapters covering it,

> is apt to be slighted by superficial thinkers as belonging to those rudiments of knowledge, which were inculcated upon us in our earliest youth. But what was then inculcated before we could comprehend its principles, would abundantly repay our study in maturer years; and to the ignorance of it, must be attributed many of those fundamental defects which appear in writing.[14]

Blair gave grammar a place in two of his forty-six lectures, covering all the parts of speech and something of the origins of English. This discussion, thought Blair, was necessary, for without a knowledge of grammar as a formal system good writing was impossible. Good style demanded grammatical purity and propriety, and "If any imagine they can catch it merely by the ear, or acquire it by a slight perusal of some of our good authors, they will find themselves much disappointed."[15] This statement became an article of faith for several generations of teachers of vernacular composition, who came to see a complete knowledge of English grammar as a panacea for all ills in writing.

The gradual absorption of grammar by rhetoric began slowly, however. There were early textbooks with titles like *A Grammar of Composition*, but most of the texts of the pre-1850 period are either based upon Blair's *Lectures* and contain much rhetorical theory and a passing mention of grammar, or upon Lindley Murray's *English Grammar* and are overwhelmingly grammatical with perhaps a few pages on "purity, propriety, precision, and perspicuity" in writing. Rhetoricians were generally able to assume preexisting understanding of the "rules" and terms of grammar on the parts of their readers. At the very least, students of rhetoric were supposed to have mastered the necessities of "Correctness," which, as Samuel Newman put it in his *Practical System* of 1827, "is to be learned from the rules and principles of syntax."[16]

Rhetoric, however, was still mostly thought a higher mystery, one concerned with more than the grammarian's correctness. The rhetoric of the period before 1850 was overwhelmingly abstract and theoretical, concerned with systems of rules and principles rather than with creative methods. There was very little actual practice in composition in rhetoric courses before 1875 or so; such courses consisted of lectures on or textbook study of a system. For such a rhetorical tradition, chock full of its own theoretical content, there was little need for the "rules" and definitions of grammar, a separate system.

Beginnings of Composition

But rhetoric in America was changing. As Albert Kitzhaber has shown, the period 1850—1900 was a time when systematic theoretical rhetoric was replaced by an intensely practical course in correct writing, and a large part of this change came about as a result of the mixture of the "practical" sentence-based grammar of Greene and Reed and Kellogg with the newly practical subject of English composition. During the 1850s and 1860s, instruction in actual writing was in its infancy in American colleges, but it became quickly apparent to teachers who demanded writing from students that the older theoretical rhetoric of Blair, like the formal grammar of Murray and his imitators, had no effect on students' abilities to write. Only one early text, G. P. Quackenbos' *Advanced Course of Composition and Rhetoric*, tried mixing the new "sentence-building" grammar with rhetorical lessons.

During the 1860s, however, several phenomena converged to create a new situation for grammar. First, formal grammar, as we have seen, came under attack as sterile and impractical. Second, the teaching of rhetoric came to be more and more concerned with writing, and thus with *correctness* as well as eloquence. Third, the United States culture as a whole began to become more aware of correct speaking and writing as indices of status and professional worth. In 1865 Henry Alford, dean of Westminster, published his *Plea for the Queen's English*, an attack on the poor grammar and bad usage he saw all around him—and noted especially in America. Several American writers answered and debated him, and the prescriptive-usage debate that raged throughout the 1860s and '70s drew the attention of the American intellectual community to linguistic issues as never before.[17] After the Civil War, with the Union saved and the beginnings of the drastic social stratification of the Gilded Age, proper language came to have new importance.

A few theorists saw that rhetoric and grammar would be melded in the developing discipline of composition and strove to create an intellectually defensible systhesis of the two. Some, like grammarian William Wells, saw a new discipline in which practice in writing would be the central pedagogical technique, "where analysis and parsing will find their appropriate place as collateral aids in connection with the daily living exercises in the use of the English tongue."[18] Rhetorician Henry Day, always a theoretical pioneer, published his *Grammatical Synthesis: The Art of English Composition* in 1867. This book, which meant to unite grammar, rhetoric, and logic in one study because all were "grounded in the basis of Thought," never attained great popularity; like most of Day's work it was too original for its own good. *Grammatical Synthesis* showed, however, that by the late 1860s at least some colleges were beginning to mix grammar with composition.

In the 1870s grammatical elements advanced even more rapidly into the teaching of writing, largely because of the influence of Harvard College. Harvard teachers of English had been noticing for some years that their students had trouble with the written language, and as the older academic system of lectures and exams gave way to the newer classroom discussion and essay-writing methods, this problem became even more obvious. In addition, the growing importance of linguistically influenced class structures and Harvard's desire to demonstrate that it had the highest standards and deserved its leadership position led to the introduction in 1874 of a written examination that determined admission to the college.[19] When the Harvard faculty read these first exams they were shocked by the poor writing and the number of egregious grammatical errors produced by the graduates of America's best academies. More than half of the students taking these early tests failed.

This began an "illiteracy" uproar in academia that lasted for more than two decades and resulted in the interment of most of the old traditions of rhetoric and the creation of a new course and subject that soon became *de rigueur* in American colleges: freshman composition courses patterned after "English A," the course Harvard instituted to grapple with its literacy problems. Much anxiety was apparent in the public prints after the mid-seventies bemoaning the "illiteracy of American boys" and suggesting various solutions to the problem. The most popular remedy prescribed for the cure of "illiteracy" was the collection of form-based mechanical lessons that came to be known as "grammar." College students could not write, the reasoning went, because their early grammar lessons had not "taken." Thus the lessons needed to be repeated until the knowledge of parts of speech and rules would transform into the ability to write. We now see this as an *essentially* incorrect idea, and identify students' poor writing in 1874 as a result of their lack of composition practice in the academies and schools. Yet the power of grammar as a panacea for writing ills was still strong in the 1870s and '80s.

Several books appeared in the mid-seventies which reflect the rather sudden introduction of grammar to the composition course. Joseph H. Gilmore's textbook *Outlines of the Art of Expression* set out, quite clearly, to make grammar a college-level subject. Gilmore, a professor at the University of Rochester, stated in his preface:

> This little book has grown, in the author's class-room, out of an attempt to supplement the defective early training of his pupils.
>
> Those pupils had, when they entered college, some practical acquaintance with English composition. . . . *English* Grammar, many of them had never studied at all—few if any, of them, as the author conceives it should be studied.[20]

For Gilmore, grammar was "the art of correctly expressing our thoughts," and his 112-page book mixed formal grammar and prescriptive advice with some low-level stylistic rhetoric. *Outlines* was neither a grammar book nor a true rhetoric, but its combination of sentence-level advice and grammatical rules made it popular until nearly the turn of the century.

Much more popular and important was a book that originated in England, Edwin A. Abbott's *How to Write Clearly* (1875). Abbott had originally written his book to help his students translate Greek and Latin into acceptable English, since "the flat, vague, long-winded Greek-English and Latin-English imposture that is often tolerated in our examinations . . . diminishes instead of increasing the power that our pupils should possess over their native language."[21] Abbott's answer, unlike Gilmore's, was to try to discern the main grammatical principles most commonly violated and to create a new sort of prescriptive rule that would warn against that specific violation. This was often a grammar-based rule but was by no means always a grammatical rule. For instance, where Gilmore covers adverbs according to their traditional definitions and classes, Abbott assumes this knowledge and proffers three specific prescriptions: "Adverbs should be placed next to the words they are intended to affect"; " 'Only' requires careful use"; and "When 'not only' precedes 'but also,' see that each is followed by the same part of speech." In short, *How to Write Clearly* is the first identifiable handbook of composition. Amazingly popular in the U.S., it remained in print from 1875 until 1914 and was required by colleges in all parts of the country.

The Triumph of Grammar in Composition

Gilmore and Abbott together illustrate how pervasively grammar had infiltrated composition by 1880. Curiously, however, we find little evidence of the advance of grammar in most rhetoric texts of the day. Alexander Bain, A. S. Hill, Barrett Wendell, and Fred Newton Scott all wrote extremely popular rhetoric texts that had no important grammatical components at all. Of all the major rhetoricians of the last two decades of the century, only John Genung in his *Practical Elements of Rhetoric* (1886) and *Outlines of Rhetoric* (1893) touched on grammar in any important way.[22] Genung's willingness to deal with grammatical elements (he called them "Fundamental Processes") in his books was part of the reason for his tremendous success: between 1887 and 1894 or so, *Practical Elements* was the most popular composition textbook. Genung realized that rhetoric was going to have to make peace with grammar one way or another and figured that it might as well be done with dignity. "But even in employing grammatical processes as working-tools," Genung wrote, "rhetoric imparts to them a new quality distinctively rhetorical, the quality by which they become methods in an art, means to an end."[23] His *Outlines of Rhetoric* of 1893 was even more open in its acceptance of grammatical theory and syntactic exercises. *Outlines* is a collection of 125 illustrated rules not unlike an expanded version of Abbott's *How to Write Clearly*. Of these, thirty-one were overtly grammatical rules. *Outlines* was the first major text to be so practice-oriented and prescriptively organized.

Genung may have been the only rhetorician of the "Big Four" to include grammatical elements in his rhetoric, but beginning in the late eighties other text authors made the jump from "rhetoric" to "composition." The words "composition" and "by practice" in a book title were often the code terms for books that included lower-level formal sections and sections on grammar. William Williams' *Composition and Rhetoric by Practice* (1888) devoted its first sixty pages to grammar and to sentence practice and remained extremely popular into the 1920s. Williams was immediately copied by Edward Shaw, whose 1892 *English Composition by Practice* was even less concerned with traditional nongrammatical rhetoric than was Williams' book.

The period of the nineties was a time of warfare between the old-fashioned rhetoricians and teachers who believed that grammar and rhetoric should remain separate and the newer teachers and authors who had no such qualms. The old guard, many of whom had been educated in Blair's systematic tradition, looked down on the new field of composition as it burgeoned. They decried the illiteracy of students but insisted that secondary schools take the responsibility for education in grammar and formal correctness. E. L. Godkin, one of the authors of the famous Harvard Report of 1892, pleaded that college teachers be "delivered, in large part at least, from the necessity of teaching the rudiments of the language."[24] It was increasingly clear, however, that they would not soon be so delivered, and younger numbers of the authorial community increasingly produced textbooks that took advantage of the trend toward grammar.

Though more and more traditional grammar was included in college rhetorics after 1895, those who wrote about English pedagogy seemed at that time curiously reticent about admitting that the "practicalization" of the course in rhetoric, so much lauded, really meant the supplanting of abstract lectures by low-level formal exercises. The very word "grammar" seldom appeared in many books except as part of a short discussion about its relation to rhetoric. Hardly mentioned was the fact that basic grammatical correctness was coming to be regarded as the prime desideratum for composition. One must look at some of the student papers of the period and the comments teachers made upon them to realize how essentially formal the criteria for good writing were. At the same time that article-writers in *Educational Review* were discussing "philological training" and "the science of language," however, teachers were making their students buy Abbott's *How to Write Clearly*, A. S. Hill's pamphlet on grammatical correctness, or one of the newer texts that carefully straddled the line between high school and college composition.

Teaching grammatical correctness in college accelerated after 1900, and it soon became obvious that new tools would be needed to make college grammar more effective. In 1907, Edwin Woolley's *Handbook of Composition* reduced the system of English grammar to a series of prescriptive error-based rules. Woolley was much more complete than Abbott, covering 350 rules to Abbott's 56. Woolley's *Handbook* was not a grammar treatise of the old sort; as he said in his preface, "The aim of the book is not scientific, but practical. The purpose is to make clear the rules in regard to which many people make mistakes. No material has been put into the book for the sake of formal completeness."[25] A far cry from the aims of traditional grammarians from Lowth onward, but Woolley defined here the sort of "grammar" that would henceforward be most people's definition: a set of rules about words and sentences that define mistakes as perceived by an English teacher.

The development and use of handbooks after Woolley is another story, one told elsewhere.[26] For the purposes of this essay, it is enough to say that insofar as grammar was part of composition after 1910, it was found in the increasingly popular—eventually almost ubiquitous—handbooks. As the handbook moved closer and closer to centrality in the teaching practices and especially in the paper-grading and marking practices of teachers, the field of grammar became more and more important. For secondary-school students, grammar meant the "sentence-building" book or the "language" book; for college students, grammar meant the handbook.

Rhetoric waned during the period 1910–1930. Frank Scott wrote in 1918 that "for ten years or so there has been a steady diminution of the amount of rhetorical theory offered in [college textbooks]; that which has been retained has been made more and more elementary."[27] Meanwhile, the sort of grammar being taught in college courses reflected the most old-fashioned, rigid, and puristic prejudices of the nineteenth century.

Early Linguistic Theory

If a gap had developed between rhetoric as it perceived itself and the grammar-oriented composition course as it was taught, a gap just as large began to open between the grammar that English teachers taught and the growing insights of the scientific philologists and linguists active in English studies during the late nineteenth and early twentieth centuries. Such important early linguistic scholars as Thomas Lounsbury, Brander Matthews, and George P. Krapp began, in the years after 1900, to suggest that a new way of viewing grammar, one based on a descriptive and flexible objectivity rather than on the prescriptive purism of the older grammar, might be the linguistics of the future.

Support for a universal grammar and a rigid purism in usage declined rapidly among genuine philosophers of language after 1900, but, sadly, little was carried over from the descriptive language studies such as those of Krapp, Otto Jespersen, Henry Sweet, or George Curme. As early as the 1880s a few philologists had criticized teachers' total acceptance of traditional rigid grammar,[28] but before 1900 there was no organized critique of this purblind dependence on an increasingly discredited system.

With the work of Lounsbury, Matthews, and Krapp a new scientific and descriptive spirit appeared in philology. Arguing against a fixed standard of grammatical propriety in *The Standard of Usage in English*, Lounsbury grittily proclaimed that "in order to have a language become fixed, it is first necessary that those who speak it should become dead. . . ."[29] George Krapp, in his *Modern English* of 1909, made an important differentiation between *standard* English as taught by the rigid prescriptive grammarians of the schools and *good*

English, language that treads the boundary between *con*vention and *in*vention. "Language is valuable only as it effects the purposes one wishes to attain," wrote Krapp,[30] unconsciously echoing George Campbell's definition of rhetoric in 1776 as "that art or talent by which the discourse is adapted to its end."

By World War I a whole generation of philologically trained teachers had made themselves conversant with both the history of the English language and with its similarities to and differences from other language systems. This generation of scholars—no more than a few hundred in number, in comparison to the thousands of literary specialists and composition teachers—founded the Linguistic Society of America in 1924. Linguistics thus officially declared itself independent of English, classics, anthropology, and psychology, complaining that "the standing of our science in the academic community leaves much to be desired."[31] In an almost anguished *apologia* for the LSA, published in the first volume of *Language*, Leonard Bloomfield charged that

> Our schools are conducted by persons who, from professors of education down to teachers in the classroom, know nothing of the results of linguistic science, not even the relation of writing to speech or of standard language to dialect. In short, they do not know what language is, and yet must teach it. . . .[32]

Bloomfield's charge was all too sadly true. As I have noted, S. E. Lang, Gertrude Buck, and others had launched various disorganized attacks upon prescriptive grammar before 1910, but no organized group of critics had been forthcoming. By 1925, however, there was already the beginning of a movement to try to set composition on a sounder linguistic basis.

The Antitraditionalists

The National Council of Teachers of English had been formed in 1911, but only slowly did it come to be a prime mover behind attacks on purism and prescriptivism in grammar. Most early NCTE members, it appears, were satisfied with Woolley's prescriptive-handbook approach, but a few of the most active and influential members were aware of the trends in linguistics and began in the late teens to fire off salvoes against prescriptive grammar and usage. Fred N. Scott, as reliably ahead of his time on this issue as on others, attacked inflexible prescriptive standards in the 1917 *English Journal*. In the following year, he was seconded by G. P. Krapp, who was still exploring the question of acceptability of usages, and the youthful Sterling A. Leonard, whose "Old Purist Junk" still remains a classic of witty denigration. It begins, "The purist is surely one of the strangest of God's creatures," and includes the plaint, modern-sounding even in the eighties, that

> in our weary preoccupation with a hundred mere insignificant conventions of wording and idiom we have left almost untouched more fruitful topics. . . . Our

nice conscientiousness has been sadly misled by dictatorial and wise-sounding but often densely ignorant pronouncements, into a teaching, not only of fiddle-faddle niceties, but of positive untruth about present usage. I suggest that for a very considerable part of the actual difficulties and regrettable ill successes of our English teaching—I know at least that it is true of my own—the blind leading of purists is responsible.[33]

Leonard was one of the most important figures in establishing the empirical reality of the doctrine of usage with his posthumously published *Current English Usage* of 1932. (Leonard drowned while boating in Wisconsin with I. A. Richards in 1931; his tragically early death robbed English studies of a natural leader who might have brought about needed reforms much earlier.) But as early as 1917 he had already spoken out strongly in favor of the liberal and reformist ideas he had learned as Scott's student at Michigan.

The decade of the teens also brought forth the first series of attempts to measure empirically the worth of grammar to literacy skills. Most of these early experiments involved elementary and secondary schools and affected college grammar only indirectly. Yet the fact that they were done at all indicates a new professionalism in education, an unwillingness to accept the received wisdom that gramnmar was indispensable. Studies such as those of Hoyt in 1906, Briggs in 1913, Charters in 1915, and Johnson in 1917 cast increasing doubt on the idea that grammar instruction carried over into composition.[34] William Asker in 1923 correlated the grammatical knowledge of high school seniors with their freshman composition grades in college and found that "knowledge of formal grammar influences ability to judge the grammatical correctness of a sentence and ability in English composition only to a negligible degree."[35]

By the 1920s, the antiprescriptivists had begun to assemble an impressive array of theorists and studies unbified by the belief that traditional grammar was not useful. Krapp, Leonard, and Scott insisted that the insights of Bloomfield, Sapir, Jespersen, and other scientific linguists could be ignored only at peril. Around the mid-twenties Charles C. Fries added his voice to this chorus of criticism. Throughout his long and active career in the LSA, the MLA, and NCTE, Fries constantly strove to make English teachers aware of linguistic insights. In Fries's first important book, *The Teaching of the English Language* (1927), he wrote:

Even after more than a hundred years of linguistic study based upon the historical method, the fundamental principles upon which the modern scientific view of language rests and the results of scholarly investigations in the English language have not reached the schools. On the whole the schools still perpetuate with very little change the eighteenth century point of view. . . . This book is an effort to interpret the modern scientific view of language in a practical way for teachers.[36]

Fries discusses at length the folly of rule-worship, the doctrine of the standard of usage, where the concept of acceptable grammar originated, and other elements of informed language teaching. For the next forty years, which included presidencies of the LSA and NCTE, Fries would continue to press the fight against destructive prescription in grammar.

By the mid-twenties the defenders of formal grammar, while ascendant in the classroom, were on the defensive in scholarly journals. Leon Mones was one of the few who made any attempt to defend the teaching of formal grammar against the flood of attacks. Grammar was under such an attack, complained Mones, that "an argument in its favor must ring like either grumpy reaction or hysteric reform. Well, grumpy some of us are, and hysteric too. We have seen the 'No Formal Grammar' army march on to victory and leave chaos behind it."[37] Mones' nostalgia for an ordered past was not the usual position found in journals after 1920, however. The greater number of post-1920 journal articles on grammar either report the findings of ill-designed studies about whether grammar helps students read and write, or attack the idea of prescriptive usage, or report on minor teaching techniques involving grammar without taking sides, or make technical descriptive points within traditional grammar. Meanwhile, in the classrooms, handbooks and their sinister new siblings, "drillbooks" and "workbooks," held almost unchallenged sway.

During this period, the public attitude toward grammar instruction was mixed; most people had hated their school grammar, but large numbers felt it had done them good and many thought traditional grammar needed to be continued.[38] The public had little idea of the formidable forces building a case against grammar instruction within academe until Sterling Leonard's *Current English Usage* in 1932 and Marckwardt and Walcott's *Facts about Current English Usage* in 1938. These books were widely perceived as a surrender on the part of English teachers to an "anything goes" ethic in usage, and various funerals were held in popular magazines for "grammar." When the NCTE in 1935 published its *Experience Curriculum in English*, a document which more or less summed up the pedagogical opinions of the Deweyite wing that composed the group's vocal minority, few were surprised to see a general comdemnation of grammar teaching:

> Because scientific investigators haved failed to show the effectiveness of grammar in the elimination of usage errors, it is not here organized for that purpose. There is no scientific evidence of the value of grammar which warrants its appearance as a prominent or even distinct feature of the course of study.[39]

Linguistics and English: Cross-Purposes

After 1935 a number of factors came together to make the relations between linguistics and composition complex and polemical. Edward Sapir and

Leonard Bloomfield had published their *magni opi*, both entitled *Language*, in 1921 and 1933, and in the thirties their students moved more and more rapidly toward a genuinely scientific linguistics. In practice, this meant that after 1930 linguistics and composition moved further and further apart in terms of their ultimate goals. Linguistics was becoming exclusively interested in comparative and structural description that had nothing at all to do with teaching or specifying good or bad usage. Such labels, dear to English teachers, were becoming genuinely embarrassing to linguists.

Except for a few teachers like Fries, who had deep roots in both English and linguistics, there were not many who could carry the message of this essential disjunction over to English. Since Bloomfield's *Language* in 1933, linguistics had hardly concerned its investigations with writing at all, assuming that writing was secondary to oral speech, but few teachers were even aware of that. Most had never had specific training in linguistics, although the NCTE had been calling for such training for English teachers since 1928.[40] English teachers knew *something* was happening in linguistics, and they had heard it was scientific and impressive; when, they tended to ask, would this new grammar give them something they could use in classrooms to replace the oft-critiqued old grammar?

Such applications were not forthcoming. Linguists after 1940 hardly bothered to criticize the sort of grammar taught in English. They merely rolled their eyes and sighed. The linguistic frontiers were far away from the handbook and the classroom. As many large universities formed departments of linguistics, linguists literally moved away from English and away from the turmoil that continued in English over the use of "grammar" to teach writing.

For the period after 1940 we must carefully distinguish the controversies within the field of linguistics from those in English whose ostensible subject was linguistics. Linguists increasingly disputed analytical techniques, categories, philosophical and psychological perspectives, and purposive paradigms. English teachers disputed two questions: what should "grammar" be and how can it help students read and write better? While this is not the place for a history of linguistics in America (those interested can turn to a number of books on that subject[41]), it must be noted that the knowledge and attitudes of most English teachers were increasingly outdated. Fries' *American English Grammar* of 1940, financed by the NCTE, was meant to inform teachers about contemporary grammatical knowledge and thus reduce the "futile and even harmful practices which have resulted from ignorance."[42] The book seems not to have had much impact, however, despite its practical intentions and readability.

During the forties and early fifties grammar teaching in college was damped down by the growth of two trendy movements: General Semantics and the Communications movement. The General Semantics movement, popularized by S. I. Hayakawa's *Thought and Language* of 1940, concerned itself with words and their representational functions. The "communications" movement in general education wished to concentrate on all four communications skills—reading, writing, speaking, and listening—and thus had a great deal of nongrammatical material to cover. Meanwhile, handbooks of grammar grew from small home-reference manuals into fairly large books that attempted to rule-govern the entire process of composition. It is unfortunate but true that of the dozens of handbooks published between 1930 and 1960 only a handful even attempted to utilize the insights of linguistics, and only one of these had any influence—Porter Perrin's *An Index to English* (1939), which, like all of Perrin's work, was rigorous in its scholarship and not satisfied to mouth the contemporary pieties.

In 1952, the indefatigable Charles Fries published *The Structure of American English*, a textbook which attempted to apply the insights of linguists since Bloomfield to constructing English sentences. Fries's basically descriptive, nonnormative approach would gradually come to be called "structural grammar" and would be one of the key issues in grammatical arguments that would rage a few years later.[43] In 1952, however, *The Structure of English* caused barely a ripple. Many teachers examined it, but few taught it. Most English teachers continued to slumber through a long summer of lethargic acceptance of linguistic ignorance, leading W. Melson Francis to cry in 1953 that

> in no reputable academic discipline is the gap between the pioneers of research and the pedagogical rank and file more shockingly great. . . . Our situation is as anomalous as if our scientific colleagues were to teach geocentric astronomy, pre-Darwinian biology, and chemistry based on the four elements.[44]

The combination of ignorance and willful refusal to abandon traditional grammar and the "standards" that many people thought it represented continued throughout most of the 1950s. Many teachers shared the common public attitude that "standards" had been sliding in English for many years, and especially since Sterling Leonard and Charles Fries and their band of radical hotheads had begun cutting the ground out from under traditional grammar. By the mid-fifties, however, this position was little defended except in *sotto voce* staffroom complaints. Most of the publishing members of the profession were increasingly coming to see a pro-traditional grammar attitude as a hallmark of ignorance and solipsism.

The Great Structuralism Debate

With the mid-fifties we enter a fascinating era, one that really deserves an essay all its own. I cannot do full justice to the complexity of the positions held or the arguments advanced; such huge theoretical shifts rocked both linguistics and composition between 1956 and 1965 that the picture is often less than clear. Before 1956 or so there was relatively little interest in or activity concerning grammar as a intellectual concept or a pedagogical challenge, and after 1965 we emerge into the recognizable modern landscape well described by W. Ross Winterowd.[45] Between those two dates, however, a veritable ferment of interest in linguistics came to English, leaving the discipline shaken and changed forever.

This new era probably began with Fries' 1952 *Structure* as much as with anything else. Though not a popular textbook, it motivated several other authors to write textbooks using "structural grammar" as their essential model. Paul Roberts' *Patterns of English*, Donald Lloyd and Harry Warfel's *American English in Its Cultural Setting* and Harold Whitehall's *Structural Essentials of English* all appeared in 1956. Suddenly, like it or not, English teachers were faced with having to choose between books that tacitly supported the old dispensation and those that trumpeted the new. As happens so often in composition, the knowledge that journal authors had been trying to promote for years was actually delivered by textbooks.

Not, I hasten to add, that the "structural" textbooks took over the field; in fact, they did rather poorly, considering how much had been said about the "new grammar." Some teachers tried the structural approach, hopeful, perhaps that this "new" grammar could rekindle the flame of belief that seemed to be guttering for the old grammar. But Roberts, Fries, and Lloyd-Warfel never became the touchstones they sought to be. Their problems were well diagnosed by Charlton Laird in 1957:

> If we are to attempt teaching English in the near future by extensive use of structural linguistics, we are presented with at least the following staggering facts: (1) structural linguistics is a difficult concept and an exacting practice, when compared, for instance, with an engaging amusement like general semantics; (2) the linguists themselves do not as yet agree entirely, either in the analysis of English or in a method of teaching it; (3) no large-scale test of the approach using unselected teachers has yet been attempted, and (4) there is no immediate prospect of producing a considerable body of teachers versed in structural linguistics.[46]

Laird went on to question the entire structuralist enterprise, but he was aware even as he critiqued descriptivism that the old grammar was no more defensible. His essay provoked several responses.

By 1959, the question of structural linguistics and its relation to English was getting ready to explode. In late 1958 the venerable Wilbur Hatfield had come out in favor of teaching structural grammar in English,[47] and the fuse was lit in 1959 by Harry Warfel's argument in the February *College English*. In his typically winsome and delicate fashion, Warfel began:

> The science of structural linguistics has put new tools into our hands. Just as
> nucleonics has penetrated into the minute operations of the atom, so structural
> linguistics has unlocked the secrets of language. The established conclusions
> and the emerging theories seem likely to force other disciplines to reshape
> current procedures wherever they are dependent upon or impinge upon lan-
> guage. . . . The teaching of composition must undergo a revolutionary
> change.[48]

From this humble beginning, Warfel went on to lecture his audience on the "vast
array of facts" amassed by structural linguists from which come "principles,
rules, and laws that have relevance to general composition." Warfel argued that
the function-based grammar then accepted by most linguists was a better basis
for composition learning than anything else. He inveighed against the "out-
moded gadgetry" of traditional handbooks, workbooks, and grammars, but he
also condemned the (sometimes extreme) "thought" and "general education"
methods of the period. "The study of semantics has been a will-o'-the-
wisp. . . . Most books of reading selections have been productive of little good.
The preoccupation with ideas as opposed to the student's mastery of the
language system has been self-defeating" (p. 212). This hectoring tone continued throughout the article.

Warfel's structuralist boosterism seems vaguely sad and ironic to us
today—"Look upon my works, ye mighty, and despair"—but in 1959 it was
little less than a call to arms. He was replied to quickly, and soon the journals
were filled with essays for and against structural linguistics in English. The
denigration of linguistics in the popular prints was continuing, with Jacques
Barzun leading the charge against the "new grammarians," and from 1960
through 1963, linguistics and its impact on composition were fighting issues.
College English devoted the better parts of four issues to the linguistic controversy between 1960 and 1965, and the battles raged. Structuralists explained
patiently again and again why their discipline better explained the facts of
language than did the traditional grammar,[49] while at the same time numerous
English teachers wrote essays complaining about the nonjudgmental aspects of
descriptive linguistics. Polemicists had a field day; W. Nelson Francis criticized
Barzun and Mario Pei, John Sherwood criticized Charles Fries, A. M. Tibbetts
criticized W. Nelson Francis, platoons criticized Harry Warfel . . . The entire
discipline seemed to feel that a great question impended; as Allain Renoir put it,
"The necessity to make a considered choice between traditional grammar and
structural linguistics is one which teachers of freshman composition can no
longer avoid. . . ."[50]

In the midst of this controversy a number of rational points of view also
appeared. Among those who took this rational middle ground were Renoir, who
admitted that the structuralists' "extreme accuracy in linguistic description is

certainly desirable but by no means necessary to the teaching of composition. The main job of the teacher of composition is *not* to describe language, but rather to teach his students how to *compose.*" And Charles Fries himself, in several magisterial statements in 1960 and 1961, defended linguistics but tried to disassociate himself from its thoughtless popularizers. "Linguistic science, like all science, is concerned with knowing and understanding, not with doing," wrote Fries. If applications were to be made, he was certain that they could not be the result of forcing English teachers to take one or two linguistics courses to master techniques. Nor did Fries believe in the simple-minded adaptations that some of the "linguistic science-fiction" writers like Warfel had proposed. Fries was utterly certain that such adaptations were futile, and his statement is worth noting today:

> In my view, it is not the tools and the techniques of linguistic science that should be brought into the classroom; but in some way, the substance of the knowledge and understanding won by linguistic science must be thoroughly assimilated and then used to shed new light upon the problems that arise wherever language is concerned.[51]

The structuralist controversy seemed to many teachers and English based linguists to be a battle for the very soul of composition teaching itself. Some asked: would the discipline stagnate, a purveyor of outworn and discredited conventions, or would it take the high road of science and accept the future? Others asked: would English surrender to the "anything goes" radical wing or proudly continue its traditional role as safeguarder of standard?

Only a few early saw the futility of the battle, the foredoomed fate of both structuralists and traditionalists. While the usual suspects—Warfel, Fries, Francis, Barzun, Allen, Roberts, and many others—worried the question of structuralism from 1959 through 1963, a young student of Zellig Harris's named Noam Chomsky readied the linguistic revolution that would, at least in America, relegate the entire structuralist enterprise to the history books. As early as 1961 James Sledd saw it coming in a thoughtful article called "A Plea for Pluralism." As usual, Sledd minced no words":

> For American teachers of English, the year's principal developments in language-study have been two. First, Chomsky, Halle, Lees, and their disciples have sustained their attacks on structural linguistics with increasing vigor and success. Second, with increasing success and vigor the evangels of the Anglists have sustained their effort to convert the high schools and colleges to structural linguistics. Yesterday's Left has thus become today's Right, a new Left has emerged which is in some ways closer to yesterday's Right than to today's, and today's Right, internally divided and calling itself the Center, works at ignoring the new Left as it evangelizes the old Right. The result may well be that men who have argued creditably against traditional dogmas will now saddle the country's

schools with the opposite dogmas of American structuralism at the precise moment when many of those dogmas are being discredited.[52]

That is what happened for a little while, but not for long. After 1965, linguistics in America was clearly in the hands of the MIT axis, and the structuralist debate was effectively over. The old Right, handbook traditionalists, remained in English, but even the tenuous bridges between linguistics and handbook grammar that the structuralists had built were impossible to maintain after the ascent of transformational-generative grammar. If Friesian function categories and juncture theory were hard for English teachers to follow, phrase-structure rules and obligatory transformations were completely impossible for most of them. After 1965, linguistics as an ongoing exploration had less and less to do with teaching English. As genuine linguistics became less accessible, "grammar" in English became the strange amalgam of buzzwords, legends, handbook nostrums, half-understood transformational concepts, and decayed eighteenth-century prescription that most of us know today.[53] Traditional grammar did not flourish openly, especially after the famous and seemingly final verdict of *Research in Written Composition* in 1963 that "the teaching of formal grammar has a negligible or, because it usually displaces some instruction and practice in actual composition, even a harmful effect on the improvement of writing,"[54] but it continued its malevolent half-life in its accustomed lair: handbooks and workbooks.

In 1963, the concerted leap forward in rhetorical theory that we now think of as the "rhetorical revolution" was just beginning, and some nonmainstream linguistic theories such as tagmemics were instrumental parts of it. A few enthusiasts believed that transformational-generative theory could be made the keystone of the new rhetoric, but results were inconclusive, and the full story of TG applications takes me beyond 1965, where I arbitrarily mean to end this history.

The tale of grammar is by no means over; even today sentence diagramming has voluble champions, and traditional grammar, against all odds, is attempting a comeback. A great deal of the history of composition in America seems to be a clumsy shuffle-dance of grammar with rhetoric, with first one and then another leading. It will not end soon, for the wish for certainty and algorithmic closure represented by the one struggles always with the desire for originality and creativity represented by the other. So long as language is part science, part art, and part magic, the grammarians and the rhetoricians will be struggling with each other to lead the dance.

EDWARD P. J. CORBETT

Teaching Style

If your educational experience in any way resembled mine, you have been uncertain about what style is. *Style* was a familiar enough word for you, but your concept of style was probably vague. You sensed that certain authors had a distinctive style, but you were not quite sure what it meant to say that an author "has style" and even less sure about what made a style distinctive. In reading a piece of prose, you experienced an undeniable effect, but you could not designate just what it was in that collection of sentences that caused that effect. Consequently, you still may not know how to analyze style or how to talk about it in any meaningful way.

Style may be a vague concept to us because our own teachers spent little or no time talking about style. They may have used such general terms as "lucid," "elegant," "labored," "Latinate," "turgid," or "flowing" in commenting on an author's syle, but they never bothered to analyze the features or the constituents of the styles that bore those epithets. Those were largely impressionistic labels, and if we too regarded a certain author's style as, say, "turgid"—whatever *that* was—then we agreed with our teacher's classification of the style. But if we felt that this same author had a "lilting style," we knew no way of describing a "lilting style" or no way of refuting our teacher's judgment. So we dutifully copied down in our notebooks the appropriate epithets for each author we read and discussed in class, and we delighted in moving on to talk about more determinable matters, like the content or the structure of the piece of literature. If we listed ourselves as members of that post–World War II generation of students who regularly practiced the Brooks-and-Warren method of close analysis, we could talk about the linguistic features of a poem with great specificity. Yet we may well have been stymied when we wanted to talk about the linguistic features of a prose text.

If you could put these questions concerning style (what is it? what effects does it produce in a reader? what does one look for in studying it?) to a Renaissance schoolboy, he could give you satisfactory answers. His education was predominatly language-oriented. From the beginning to the end of the school day, he was steeped in words—English words, Latin words, sometimes even Greek words. He had to recite the grammatical rules that he had memorized the night before; he had to parse sentences; he had to translate Latin sentences into English sentences or English sentences into Latin sentences; he had to be able to write original sentences according to a prescribed pattern; he had to paraphrase sentences in a variety of ways; he had to be able to recognize, classify, and define the schemes and tropes in a passage being studied (and there were more than a hundred of those listed in the Renaissance rhetoric texts). T. W. Baldwin's *William Shakspere's Small Latine & Lesse Greeke,* or Sister Miriam Joseph's *Shakespeare's Use of the Arts of Language,* or Donald L. Clark's *John Milton at St. Paul's School* will give you a generous sense of the language-arts regimen that the Tudor school boy was subjected to in the grammar schools.[1] If we required of our students what Renaissance school-masters demanded of theirs, we would no doubt face a general revolt.

This rigorous regimen, however, produced students who really learned grammar and rhetoric and who knew not only the meaning of style but also the procedures for analyzing someone else's style and improving their own. They could tell you that style represented the choices that an author made from the lexical and syntactical resources of the language. Style represented a curious blend of the idiosyncratic and the conventional. The more idiosyncratic a style, the more distinctive it became; the more conventional, the more bland it likely became—although not necessarily less serviceable for being bland. In one sense, then, "Style was the man," because it represented the characteristic way in which a person expressed his or her thoughts and feelings.

For that reason, everyone can be said to "have a style." But some styles are more pleasing, more distinctive, more effective than others. Some writers can command several styles—a range of styles into which they can readily shift as the subject-matter, the occasion, or the audience necessitates. There are high styles and low styles and middle styles. In his book *The Five Clocks*, Martin Joos compares these various styles to what he calls the five registers—the frozen, the formal, the consultative, the casual, and the intimate.[2] Joos also notes that sophisticated language-users can shift into and out of these registers as the occasion demands. Some people do not command the full range of styles or registers, simply because they have not yet acquired the full repertory of diction and syntax needed for stylistic versatility. As the philosophers would say, they have the command *potentially* but not *actually*. Our task as teachers is to turn the *potency* into *act*.

If we as teachers want to engage our students in the study of style, the first point that needs to be made is that the circumstances in which we teach may not allow us to deal with style at all. Many of us teach in a curriculum so crowded that there simply is not enough time to deal adequately with style. And the study of style does take time. The Renaissance schoolmaster had the same group of pupils for the full academic year, often had them six days a week for six to eight hours a day. That generous allotment of time allowed for relentless recitation, rigorous drill, and reinforcing repetition. And the curriculum then was not as cluttered as it is now. If you cannot devote at least two weeks to the study of style, either in a concentrated period or in scattered sessions throughout the semester, you had better not deal with style at all.

The relative sophistication of your students in language matters may also determine whether you can deal with style in the classroom. I can imagine some teachers saying, "Good heavens, I have all I can do just to get my students to the point where they can consistently write sentences that parse. My students have to learn how to walk before I can teach them how to run." There is no question that a minimal grammatical competence is a *sine qua non* for stylistic studies. If style represents the choices one makes from the available grammatical options, then students must have at least a basic awareness of what the grammatical options are if they are to profit from stylistic studies. But a deficiency in conscious knowledge of grammar is not an insuperable disqualification for studying style. Many students can learn their grammar while studying style. I have found that students are invariably fascinated by style—not only because it offers something new and different but also because it provides an element of fun in changing words and shifting parts. And in such a positive and creative atmosphere, students may well be more inclined to develop an interest in grammar or at least to absorb grammar subconsciously.

Studying style in English courses can have two focuses or objectives: to learn either how to analyze someone else's style or how to improve our own. These two objectives are ancillary rather than countervailing. As teachers, we can pursue either or both, but we should determine our main objective for the course at the outset. Learning how to analyze someone else's style belongs primarily to the literature class; learning how to improve one's own style belongs primarily to the composition class. But there is no reason why both kinds of learning cannot take place in both classes. In fact, learning how to analyze someone else's style in the composition class is almost a necessary prelude for learning how to improve one's own style. By analyzing an accomplished writer's style, we can recognize the marks of effective style, and then we can begin, either consciously or unconsciously, to incorporate some of those features into our own style. The process works in reverse too. By deliberately working on our own style to refine it, we learn what to look for in analyzing someone else's style.

Studying style begins with some awareness of what we should look at or look for. In the chapter on style in my *Classical Rhetoric for the Modern Student* and in my "A Method of Analyzing Prose Style, with a Demonstration Analysis of Swift's 'A Modest Proposal,' " I outline the features that can be observed and analyzed.[3] I divide these features into four main categories: diction, sentence patterns, figures of speech, and paragraphing. But my designating those main cagetories may not be very helpful to you. What about diction? What about sentence patterns? Just what aspects of diction and sentence patterns are significant?

Let me be a little more specific here. A writer's choice of words contributes to the effects that style has on readers. If we think about it for a moment, we must acknowledge that choosing a big word or a little word, a general word or a specific word, an abstract word or a concrete word does make a difference in what the text conveys to us either explicitly or implicitly. And when we observe that certain kinds of words are recurrent, when we observe that sets of words exemplify certain motifs, these words become even more significant because of what they tell us about an author's characteristic way of saying things. A writer's working vocabulary—the stock of words that a writer actually uses in a piece of writing rather than the words that he or she can recognize in someone else's writing—reflects the range of a writer's knowledge and interests. The larger one's working vocabulary, the more likely it is that one can choose precise diction. Shakespeare's working vocabulary of over 21,000 words was an extraordinary lexicon—and not only for his time.

The study of the lexical element of style involves fewer objectively observable items than the study of any other stylistic element. By the term "objectively observable item," I mean an item which can be definitely classified by observation rather than by judgment. For instance, one can decide whether a particular word is monosyllabic or polysyllablic by simply looking at the word. The decision, however, about whether a word is abstract or concrete, general or specific, often involves a judgment, because those dichotomies are more relative than absolute. Consider, for example, a sentence like "The wealthy Texan owned huge herds of cattle." Is the word *cattle* general or specific? It is more specific than *livestock* but less specific than *steers*. Because of the relativity of the general-specific dichotomy, the classifier has to make an arbitrary judgment about the word *cattle* in this particular context. In this respect, it is worth remembering that any tabulating of percentages of words in a text according to whether the words are abstract or concrete, general or specific, formal or informal, denotative or connotative is likely to be somewhat less than precise, simply because in many instances the yes-no decision represents someone's arbitrary judgement.

When we move on to study collocations of words in sentences, we find not only more objectively observable items but more significant features of writing habits. Most of the stylistic features of sentences are objectively observable items: length of sentences (in number of words); grammatical types of sentences (simple, compound, complex, compound-complex); rhetorical types of sentences (loose, periodic, balanced, antithetical); functional types of sentences (statement, question, command, exclamation); types and frequency of sentence-openers; methods and location of expansions in sentences; amount of embedding. Analysis and classification of features like those tell us a great deal about the level of a writer's "syntactic fluency."

Syntactic patterns also tell us something about the way a writer structures his or her thoughts, about a writer's "epistemic orientation," to use Richard Ohmann's term.[4] The frequent occurrence, for instance, of balanced or antithetical patterns in Dr. Johnson's sentences suggests that he tended to structure his thinking in terms of parrallel or opposing dichotomies. The many levels of subordination in John Henry Newman's prose suggests that he tended to see things in terms of hierarchies. The stringing together of independent clauses in Hemingway's prose, often with redundant use of coordinating conjunctions, indicates that Hemingway tended to view the phenomenal world as a flux of discrete, coordinate elements. Henry James's heavy use of parenthetical elements reflects a mind disposed to meticulous qualifications. And so on.

The gathering of data about syntactic patterns involves a lot of tedious counting and tabulating. Data of that sort were not previously available because the counting and measuring had to be done by hand and took hours and weeks. When Edwin Lewis and L. A. Sherwin did their studies in the 1890s of sentence and paragraph length in the works of several British writers, they did all their counting by hand.[5] Today, the computer facilitates such tedious data-gathering, and as a result, stylistic studies of large corpuses of prose and poetry have proliferated.

Collecting data—once tedious and time-consuming—still must be done. We are much more impressed when someone pronounces that a certain writer strings together unusually long sentences and supports that claim with the empirically derived evidence that the writer's average sentence length is 37.8 words. And we are further impressed by the disclosure that 18 percent of that writer's sentences are ten or more words longer than that average.

How much of a corpus has to be studied before valid generalizations can be made about someone's style? I have told undergraduate students studying style—either their own or some professional writer's—that they must analyze somewhere between 1000 and 1500 words of a piece of prose. That is not very much really—at most four double-spaced typescript pages, maybe two pages of printed text. But it is substantial enough to allow for some valid inferences to be drawn. Students writing a dissertation or a scholarly article on someone's prose style should be reminded not only that they would have to study a much larger corpus but also that they would have to study several specimens of a writer's prose, pieces written at different periods and on different subject matters for different audiences. As in any inductive study, the larger and the more representative the sampling, the safer the conclusions will be.

The gathering of data is a necessary stage but should not be the stopping point. Necessary as the gathering of the data is, what one does with the data matters more. Data—even raw statistical data—can convey some illuminating information. But often the full or the most salient significance of the data depends upon interpretation. The act of interpretation calls upon all of one's intellectual and imaginative powers; it requires that one shift from the role of a mere counter to the role of a critic.

Critical interpretation demands that one be able to detect the relevance or the relationship of the data to the exigencies of the rhetorical situation—to the occasion, purpose, subject matter, audience, or author of the discourse. We may find, for instance, that in a particular discourse, the author used an unusually high percentage of interrogative sentences—let us say 18 percent, almost one out of every five sentences. Why? A question like that poses a real challenge for the critic. The critic may find the answer by relating the statistical fact to the nature of the subject matter that the author addressed. The writer may have been writing on a subject about which he was uncertain. He was exploring the subject, probing for answers. So he frequently resorted to questions, knowing that sometimes asking the right questions can be as illuminating as proposing hesitant answers. Or the critic might relate the statistical fact to the disposition of the audience for this piece of discourse. The author, let us say, knew that his audience harbored a certain hostility to the position he was espousing. He knew that he could exacerbate that hostility if he were dogmatic in his pronouncements. So he decided that it would be a prudent strategy to soften his assertiveness by frequently resorting to the tentativeness of questions. But looking closely at his questions might reveal, for example, that many of them are framed as rhetorical questions in which the writer has subtly implied the answers he wants to elicit from his audience.

That kind of interpretation, that kind of relating of fact to function, may be beyond the capacity of some students in basic writing courses. After all, that kind of interpretation requires a great deal of linguistic and rhetorical sophistication. Some students may not be mature enough to make such connections and to come forth with anything more than the most superficial interpretation. But the present incapacity of some students for such critical insights is not the issue. They have learned something valuable about the text simply from gathering the data. They have learned something too from the mere *attempt* to interpret the data. Inadequate as their interpretation may be, they have grown a few inches in the attempt.

In addition to diction and syntax, there are other aspects of style that we might have our students look at: the incidence of figures of speech, the rhythms of sentences, the manner of paragraphing.

A figure of speech may be defined as any artful deviation from the ordinary way of speaking or writing. The classical rhetoricians commonly divided the *figura* into two main groups: schemes and tropes. A scheme involves a deliberate deviation from the ordinary pattern or arrangement of words. In addition to common patterns like parallelism and antithesis, schemes include such artistic patterns as the inversion of the natural or normal word order (*anastrophe*), deliberate omission of the normally expected conjunctions in a series of related words, phrases, or clauses (*asyndeton*), repetition of the same word or group of words at the beginning of successive clauses (*anaphora*), repetition of initial consonants in two or more adjacent words (*alliteration*), and reversal of the grammatical structures in successive clauses (*chiasmus* or *crisscross*). Tropes, the second main kind of figurative language, are deliberate deviations from the ordinary *meaning* of words and include such familiar figures as metaphor, simile, hyperbole, synecdoche, metonymy, oxymoron, and irony.

In the schools of rhetoric, pupils were expected to be able to identify, define, and illustrate the figures they encountered in the texts they read and to be able to invent similar figures. Their task was complicated by the fact that the number of schemes and tropes had proliferated enormously. *Rhetorica ad Herennium*, an influential Roman rhetoric text, listed 65 figures; the 1577 edition of Henry Peacham's *The Garden of Eloquence* identified 184. Undoubtedly, the proliferation of the figures resulted from overly subtle anatomizing, but amazingly, once students were made aware of the many kinds of artful deviations from the normal meanings or arrangements or words, they readily found the figures in the prose and poetry they read. In the second edition of my *Classical Rhetoric for the Modern Student*, more than half of the schemes and tropes illustrated there were supplied to me by two classes of freshman students who, over a six-week period, searched for examples in their reading. They found a surprising number of examples in magazine advertisements and television commercials. Once students become familiar with a wide range of schemes and tropes, they find them everywhere, even where authors were not conscious that they were creating figures.

What should teachers encourage students to look for when studying the figures, and what does the occurrence of figures tell them about an author's style? First of all, we ought to ask them simply to look for the schemes and tropes. When they find them, they ought to identify and tabulate them and perhaps draw up some statistical information about them. If there are many schemes and tropes, they can begin to classify them into groups or clusters. A particular author, let us say, uses mainly schemes of repetition. Most of this author's metaphors are based on agricultural analogies. Certain patterns or motifs begin to emerge that tell students something about a particular author's mind-set. The presence—or the absence—of figures tells students something about the texture and flavor of an author's prose.

In the modern classroom, teachers rarely, if ever, consider prose rhythms, but our forebears in Greek and Latin schools regularly engaged their pupils in analyzing and composing various prose rhythms. The Greeks and the Romans, of course, had developed elaborate prosodies for their synthetic languages, and since a good deal of their formal communication took place in the oral medium, they were much more conscious than we of the sounds and rhythms of words when they composed their orations. We have only to read sections of Cicero's rhetoric texts or his orations to find out the careful attention this rhetorician gave to the composition of euphonious prose.

English-speaking people probably lost their ear for verbal rhythms when written or printed documents superseded oral discourse as the primary mode of communication. In the late eighteenth century, the elocutionary movement in England, fostered by former actors like Thomas Sheridan, tried to revive interest in the sounds of prose.[6] Although English teachers continued to teach students how to scan lines of poetry, they began to lose all interest in the aural dimensions of prose early in the twentieth century, along about 1915, when teachers of speech formally divorced themselves from the National Council of Teachers of English and formed their own speech association.

But at a time when the aural element has become dominant again and music is the favorite medium of young people, perhaps we should revive the study of prose rhythms in the classroom. Litterateurs like George Saintsbury have shown us that there is an elaborate prosody for scanning prose rhythms,[7] but I would not recommend that we spend valuable time in the classroom exploring the technicalities of that system. If we would revive the practice of reading prose aloud, we might be able to cultivate our students' ears for the harmonies of prose. In the February 1977 issue of *College Composition and Communication*, Thomas Kane published an engaging article about what teachers might do in the classroom to cultivate a sense for the ring and rhythm of well-constructed sentences.[8] Prose, of course, is most often read silently, but curiously enough, euphonious sentences somehow disclose their meanings more easily than awkwardly constructed sentences do, even when read silently. Rhythm is a neglected area of stylistic study, but the classical rhetoricians were right when they preached that the harmonies of prose did make a positive contribution to the conveyance of a message.

For the classical rhetoricians, stylistic study rarely extended beyond the limits of the sentence. Maybe the reason for that neglect was that the concept of paragraphing had not yet developed, even in their writing system. The typographical device of paragraphing was largely the invention of printers, and it was not until the late nineteenth century that a systematic rhetoric of the paragraph was developed by Alexander Bain.[9] Recently, however, such rhetoricians as Francis Christensen, Alton Becker, Paul C. Rodgers, and Frank

D'Angelo have convinced us that there is such a thing as a "style" of paragraphing.[10]

What should teachers and students look for in studying the "style" of paragraphing? They can, for example, examine the length of paragraphs, measured in number of words or sentences per paragraph. Information about the average length of paragraphs reveals whether an author tends to break up the discourse into small units or into large units and whether an author tends to develop topics elaborately or minimally. Teachers and students can also note whether an author uses explicit topic sentences and where those topic sentences are placed in the paragraph. Moreover, they can observe the coherence devices that an author uses to articulate sequences of sentences within and between paragraphs. Using Francis Christensen's system, they can diagram the levels of coordination and subordination in paragraphs. They can also catalogue the methods of development that an author uses. Indeed, the kinds of choices that an author makes in composing a paragraph are comparable to, if not identical with, the kinds of choices an author makes in composing a sentence. There is, then, a style of paragraphing.

Each aspect that teachers and students can look at when studying someone else's style can be applied to studying specimens of their own prose. And I would strongly urge teachers to analyze their own style. They can take a paper of 1000 to 15000 words that they wrote for one of their college classes or a paper that they have published and subject it to some of the kinds of counting and measuring that I outlined. They will find the investigation fascinating, and they will discover some surprising features about their style—some felicitous characteristics and some regrettable mannerisms.

Improving our students' analytical skills is a proper concern of English teachers, but improving our students' synthetical skills should be our main concern as teachers of composition. And let me suggest, although in the broadest terms, the kinds of exercises that can help our students refine their style and enhance their stylistic virtuosity.

In my own rhetoric texts, I have suggested a number of imitative exercises that have proven fruitful for me and for my students. Let me just mention those exercises, without elaborating on them. (1) Simply copying verbatim admired passages of prose. (2) Copying a passage but changing one element in it—for instance, changing all the past-tense verbs to present-tense verbs. (3) Composing a sentence on the pattern of a sentence written by some admired author. (4) Taking a sentence that someone else has written and seeing in how many different way one can say essentially what the model sentence says. (5) Taking a group of isolated kernel sentences and combining them into a single sentence.

You can get more details about these exercises by consulting the chapters on style in my two rhetoric texts, in Francis Christensen's article "A Generative Rhetoric of the Sentence," in the two NCTE monographs on sentence-combining by John Mellon and Frank O'Hare, in Walker Gibson's *Tough, Sweet, and Stuffy*, in Winston Weathers and Otis Winchester's *Copy and Compose*, in Joseph Williams' *Style: Ten Lessons in Clarity and Grace*, or in Thomas Whissen's *A Way with Words*.[11]

Perhaps the classroom practices I have suggested here are wholly impracticable for your situation. With all the requirements—and time constraints—of a composition course, the study of style may be more than you can handle. Or some of your students may be so minimally literate that engaging them in any of the analyses or exercises I have proposed would prove futile. But even if your students are not ready to engage in stylistic studies, you can do so yourself. Such a regimen promises to help you grow immeasurably in your awareness of the remarkable richness and variety of our language and in your resourcefulness as a teacher of language, literature, and composition.

Additional Readings

Those interested in pursuing the study of style may consult the following selected readings, as well as the books and articles cited in the notes.

Bennett, James R., et al. "The Paragraph: An Annotated Bibliography." *Style*, 11 (Spring 1972), 107–18.

Corbett, Edward P. J. "Approaches to the Study of Style." *Teaching Composition: 10 Bibliographical Essays*. Ed. Gary Tate. Fort Worth: Texas Christian University Press, 1976, pp. 73–109.

Corbett, Edward P. J. "Ventures in Style." *Reinventing the Rhetorical Tradition*. Ed. Aviva Freedman and Ian Pringle. Ottawa, Ontario: Canadian Council of Teachers of English, 1980, pp. 79–87.

Davidson, Donald. "Grammar and Rhetoric: The Teacher's Problem." *Quarterly Journal of Speech*, 39 (December 1953), 425–36.

Fleishauer, John. "Teaching Prose Style Analysis: One Method." *Style*, 9 (Winter 1975), 92–102.

Graves, Richard. "A Primer for Teaching Style." *College Composition and Communication* 25 (May 1974), 186–90.

Love, Glen A., and Michael Payne, eds. *Contemporary Essays on Style: Rhetoric, Linguistics, and Criticism*. Glenview, IL: Scott, Foresman, 1969.

Milic, Louis T. "Theories of Style and Their Implications for the Teaching of Composition." *College Composition and Communication*, 16 (May 1965), 66–69, 126.

Milic, Louis T. *Style and Stylistics: An Analytical Bibliography*. New York: Free Press, 1967. Since 1967, the journal *Style* has been publishing the annual bibliographies on style and also several special bibliographies on style.

Price, Marian. "Recent Work in Paragraph Analysis: A Bibliography." *Rhetoric Society Quarterly*, 12 (Spring 1982), 127–31.

Secor, Marie J. "The Legacy of Nineteenth-Century Style Theory." *Rhetoric Society Quarterly*, 12 (Spring 1982), 76–94.

Vitanza, Victor J. "A Comprehensive Survey of Course Offerings in the Study of Literary Style in American Colleges and Universities." *Style*, 12 (Fall 1978), 342–82.

Weathers, Winston. "Teaching Style: A Possible Anatomy." *College Composition and Communication*, 21 (May 1970), 144–149.

Weaver, Richard M. "Some Rhetorical Aspects of Grammatical Categories." In his *The Ethics of Rhetoric*. Chicago: Henry Regnery, 1953, pp. 115–127.

W. ROSS WINTEROWD

Brain, Rhetoric, and Style

It may be well to start our speculations with the obvious before we begin to probe the not-so-obvious and even the esoteric. Obviously, then, the skilled writer of exposition must be able to generalize (state or adumbrate a thesis) and then to organize the exposition of that thesis in some meaningful way. This idea can be stated in a variety of terms: the writer of exposition must be able to think deductively, must be coherent in the development of ideas, must be "logical." And just as obviously, the skilled writer must be able to supply appropriate local detail, to texture the exposition so that it is something more than an elegant structure in which all of the major segments fit.

In this essay, I will argue that the writer needs those skills which are characteristic of both the left and the right hemispheres of the brain; I will further suggest that some unsuccessful writers are extremely left-hemispheric while some are extremely right-hemispheric; finally, I will suggest that the skills of both hemispheres can be taught (though a great deal of empirical work must be done before we will be on solid ground in this regard).

So this essay will concern composition, but our interest does (and must) spill over from that homely subject into the headier realms of poetry. In fact, I believe that there can be no sharp division between composition theory and literary theory without the impoverishment of each. I intend *not* to keep a sharp focus in these pages, but to maintain a lambency of interest.

As composition is the construction of texts, so reading is their reconstruction, and composition theory must take account of reading theory. In fact, it is virtually impossible to consider the construction of texts without also dealing with their reconstruction.

All of which is to say, really, that the following essay will deal with reading and writing in the light of brain theory—the reading of *anything* and the writing of *anything*.

This discussion calls upon the most reliable theories of brain function and uses the consensus of brain researchers for its conclusions and speculations. The reader must determine for him- or herself where conclusiveness ends and speculation begins, for I do not hesitate to use brain theory and research metaphorically, heuristically. The facts about the brain are accurate; in this paper, I often use them as speculative instruments.

And yet I think that alert readers will know perfectly well when the paper becomes highly speculative, for I have made every attempt to keep not only my audience but myself oriented. No small task, when one considers the drama and glamour of brain theory, the seductive possibilities of using one finding about cognition or brain mechanism for much more than it is worth.

All in all, however, I have approached my materials with caution. I hope that my readers agree on two points: where I am relatively assured in my conclusions, I have good warrant for my certainty; when I am less assured, I have nonetheless pointed the way for future inquiry and research.

By "rhetoric" in the following discussion, I mean the generation, reception, and pragmatics of natural language and even more narrowly, reading and writing.

The story of brain and language began in the mid-nineteenth century when, performing an autopsy on an aphasic, the French neurologist Paul Broca found massive damage to an area of the left cerebral cortex and concluded that this area—now identified with his name—was the speech center. It is indeed known to be *one* of the areas controlling speech.

Since Broca's discovery—and especially since the end of World War II—brain research has been pursued with increasingly dramatic results.[1] An ecumenical endeavor involving neurologists, neurosurgeons, biochemists, linguists, and psychologists (among others), brain science has, as the following pages will demonstrate, much to contribute to rhetoric and stylistics, and, conversely, both of these fields have much to contribute to brain science. For example, in discussing the brain as mechanism of language, A. R. Luria tells us that expression begins with a *motive* or general idea, while perception (decoding, understanding) ends with the interpretation of the motive lying behind the utterance.[2] That is to say, rhetoric is the alpha and omega of the brain's handling of speech, for rhetoric is, in large part, the study of motives.

However, I do not want to give the impression that brain research is meaningful to rhetoric and stylistics only in the large philosophical sense; its details help clarify many of the premises of these fields and suggest pedagogical strategies.

Left-Brain, Right-Brain

Our interest in the brain centers on hemisphericity, the different ways in which the left hemisphere (LH) and the right hemisphere (RH) function.

The LH controls the right hand, and the RH controls the left hand. By and large, in right-handed people language is a function of the LH, often called the "dominant hemisphere." Localization studies by such researchers as Wilder Penfield have resulted in "maps" detailing the areas of speech mechanisms.

The two hemispheres of the brain are joined by the *corpus callosum*, a white sheet of axons or nerve fibers that provides the communicative link between the two halves of the brain. If the corpus callosum is severed (through a surgical procedure known as *commissurotomy*), the left hand quite literally does not know what the right hand is doing if there are no visual or verbal clues. Obviously, commissurotomized patients are a major source of knowledge about the functioning of the hemispheres.

Information from the left side of the visual field is transmitted to the RH, and information from the right side of the visual field is transmitted to the LH. Since language is, by and large, a function of the LH, if the right portion of the visual field is covered in a split-brain (commissurotomized) patient, only the RH receives information, and as a result, the patient cannot name items shown to him or her even though there is evidence that this patient knows what the items are. For instance, in the situation just described, a patient will be able to use a spoon properly, but will not be able to name it.

While it is generally agreed that the LH is the side of the brain with language, the role of the RH in regard to language is disputed. One study suggests that the RH does have language, which is released when the control of the LH is weakened or removed as in the case of massive injury to or removal of the LH.[3]

An even more dramatic view of the RH and language is provided by the study of three subjects, nine and ten years old, who had either the RH or the LH removed before five months of age. The study concludes the following: (1) both the LH and the RH are efficient in phonemic discrimination; (2) both the LH and the RH provide "an adequate substrate for semantic skills"; (3) the LH is far better at syntax than is the RH. "What is the characteristic of the left hemispheric defect? It appears to be an organizational, analytical, syntactic, and hierarchic problem rather than a difficulty with the conceptual or semantic aspects of language."[4] In regard to the LH, those adjectives have resonance: organizational, analytical, syntactic, hierarchic.

Perhaps the best-known terms for characterizing the hemispheres are J. E. Bogen's *propositional* (LH) and *appositional* (RH), in regard to which he hazards the generalization that "simultaneous patterns rather than sequential order distinguish appositionality from propositionality."[5] As we shall see, the terms "propositional" and "appositional" have great meaning for the present discussion, implying as they do that the LH is sequential, logical and that the RH, on the other hand, works with an all-at-onceness, atemporaly and nonsequentially.

In this discussion, I will suggest that language use can be rated on a scale according to its degree of propositionality or appositionality. On the one hand, some language use approaches the pure propositionality of mathematics or symbolic logic; that is, it is structure almost without specific content. Other language use is almost purely appositional in the sense that idea after idea or image after image occurs in a string of appositions, with no apparent propositional connection. At these extremes, language is, I think, pathological, and indeed the best illustrations of what I mean come from the language of schizophrenics.

In a later section of this paper, we will return to my notions of propositional and appositional language, particularly in relation to the teaching of written composition.

To characterize the RH, then. It is often called the "dark," "intuitive" side of the brain. In the normal right-handed person, either it has very little language or its language function is suppressed by the "dominant" LH. The RH is superior at establishing part-whole relationships, that is, at gestalt formation or closure.[6] (As will be seen, this idea is extremely important.) For instance, with the left hand (controlled by the RH), the split-brain patient is proficient at determining what a whole object will be on the basis of feeling one part of that object; from the part, the patient can infer or construct a gestalt. With the right hand, this is impossible.

As Bogen points out, perhaps the RH's lack of the linear concept of time in ordering thought is the most important distinction between the two modes. (This will be important to us when we consider reading.)

The RH emotes, learns, remembers, and initiates responses. It is superior in "managing spatial tasks."[7]

Robert D. Nebes provides a succinct description of the activity of the RH:

> It is evident that the right cerebral hemisphere makes an important contribution to human performance having functions complementary to those of the left hemisphere. The right side of the brain probably processes information differently from the left, relying more on imagery than on language, and being more synthetic and holistic than analytic and sequential in handling data. It is certainly important in perceiving spatial relationships. It is also probably the neural basis for our ability to take the fragmentary sensory information we receive, and construct from it a coherent concept of the spatial organization of the outside world—a sort of cognitive spatial map within which we plan our actions.[8]

If we think about the process of speech—which characterizes the LH— we begin to get a notion of how the LH must operate: "what is essentially involved in language production is the programming of an idea, itself containing no intrinsic temporal order, into a sequence of linguistic units, which are also intrinsically unordered."[9] As Luria characterizes the process, first "the motive or general idea of the expression . . . is coded into a speech scheme and put into operation with the aid of internal speech; finally, these schemes are converted into narrative speech, based on a 'generative' grammar."[10] The temporal nature of these operations is illustrated by the fact that, in some cases at least, the speaker must choose or project a structure before selecting a lexical item, as in the following: "That she didn't recognize Jim surprised Mary."

In sum,

> The left (dominant) hemisphere (in right-handers) begins to play an essential role not only in the cerebral organization of speech, but also in the cerebral organization of all higher forms of cognitive activity connected with speech—perception organized into logical schemes, active verbal memory, logical thought—whereas the right (non-dominant) hemisphere either begins to play a subordinate role in cerebral organization of these processes or plays no part whatsoever in their course.[11]

I cannot resist ending this characterization of the hemispheres with a paradox—which will seem a good deal less paradoxical as our discussion progresses. I have implied that the LH is the logical half of the brain and that the RH works in images, alogically. Now ponder Einstein's description of his own cognition:

> The words of the language, as they are written or spoken, do not seem to play any role in my mechanism of thought. The psychical entities which seem to serve as elements in thought are certain signs and more or less clear images which can be "voluntarily" reproduced and combined.[12]

As Nebes hints, perhaps the apparent inverse relationship between creativity and verbal skills could be due to the overtraining of verbal skills at the expense of nonverbal abilities.[13]

Brain, Creativity, and the Comp Class

It is a common experience in composition classes to find two diametrically opposed styles, the one which is highly general, the student writer never seeming able to get down to cases, and the other which is extremely specific and concrete, but chaotic, as if the writer is unable to order ideas and impressions, unable to establish the logical connections and hierarchies among them. In the one style, we have the skeleton of coherence without the substance of tangible content; in the other, there is substance without form.

We can characterize the highly abstract but "coherent" style as propositional and the concrete style as appositional. We will further discuss the characteristics of propositionality and appositionality, but for the moment, we must relate these styles to brain function.

As we have seen, the LH is the propositional side of the brain; it works well with deductive structures, handling the ghostliness of symbolic logic and the bare-bonedness of the syllogism and the sorites with a proficiency of which the RH is incapable. The RH is the appositional side of the brain, "seeing" with an all-at-onceness, taking a gestaltist view of sensory input, perceiving patterns in the gouache which the LH would process as merely a jumble of disconnected fragments. (It is the RH that enables us to recognize faces.)

That much said, we can look at some specific examples of propositional and appositional styles.

Some years ago, quite by chance, I found an article on schizophrenic language.[14] When I read the piece it occurred to me that the author, Brendan Maher, could well have been speaking of the more extreme cases of propositionality and appositionality that I had discovered in my composition classes. Here are two examples of schizophrenic language:

PROPOSITIONAL
The subterfuge and the mistaken planned substitutions for that demanded American action can produce nothing but the general results of negative contention and the impractical results of misplacement, of mistaken purpose and unrighteous position, the impractical serviceabilities of unnecessary contradictions. For answers to this dilemma, consult Webster.

APPOSITIONAL
I hope to be home soon, very soon. I fancy chocolate eclairs, Doenuts. I want some doenuts, I do want some golden syrup, a tin of golden syrup or treacle, jam. . . . See the Committee about me coming home for Easter my twenty-fourth birthday. I hope all is well at home, how is Father getting on. Never mind there is hope, heaven will come, time heals all wounds, Rise again Glorious Greece and come to Hindoo Heavens, the Indian Heavens. The Dear old times will come back. We shall see Heaven and Glory yet, come everlasting life. I want a new writing pad of note paper.

"Normal" students write themes that are only a shade less schizoid than the passages quoted above. The following two themes are reproduced exactly as I received them, with all errors intact.

PROPOSITIONAL
Before a person can say whether the best things in life are free, he must first deturmine what in his opinion the best things are. Naturally every person has his own ideas concerning the objects or things that are important.

I believe that friendship, health, and beauty are three of the most important things a person can enjoy. When I say "beauty" I mean having things around you that you like or being places that make you feel good.

When I say that friendship is not fun, I don't mean that you can go out and buy five dollars worth of it when you need a friend. Instead of using money you use yourself. Your ideals and attitudes to buy friends. To fit into a group you must drop some and maybe most of your attitudes before you will be considered normal in the group. If you don't, you will be considered rebellious or off-beat and become an outcast from that group. Therefore, to have friends is to pay by changing yourself for their benefit.

Good health is very important to me because without it I can not enjoy myself. To maintain a healthy physical condition one must get the proper amounts of exercise, food, and sleep. Exercise and sleep are free but food is by no means free. Every time one turns around he is paying for food by working at some type of job to get money for food.

Beauty is the only thing that comes close to being free. Aside from having to buy most of the articles that a person likes to have—such as a car, skiis or any other material object—beauty is mostly free. I love to go into the forest and enjoy nature's beauty. The trees, forest creatures, brooks and streams all mean a lot to me. I enjoy hunting and camping in the forest and just walking there alone, thinking to myself. But to keep these forests we must pay to see that some careless hunter or camper doesn't burn them down. We have to set aside parks and wilderness areas so they aren't cut into lumber by the mills. These parks all cost money. Everywhere you go, you have to pay some way or another.

APPOSITIONAL

                              Are Motion Pictures Too Real?
"Film" Scene Is 'Too Real' "

Sao Paulo, Brazil (Reuters)—An assistant movie director shooting a Brazilian style western, fell dying with a rifle bullet in his back during a gunfight scene, Meridional News Agency reported here Wednesday.

Police halted film-making while they tried to find out who fired the fatal shot at Martino Martini as film extras blazed off blank ammunition.
So far there has been no explanation of how there came to be a live bullet among the blanks.

Martini was a talented young member of the "new wave" of Brazil's film industry. The film, "Obliged to Kill," was to be completed in 10 days' time."

Senta of Vienna

"Brunette Senta Berger of Vienna has long been a glowing face in nondescript German movies. Last year fame took a leap across Europe and the world after she played the lusciously blonde German girl friend of a Russian soldier in the American-produced "The Victors." "I (Senta) was the aggressive girl in the film scenes. I stood out because when you're aggressive, audiences watch you." Senta also stood out, as mail from men everywhere proclaimed, because she is full-faced, full-bosomed, full-hipped—a frankly full female."

"The 'Love Goddess' who never found love."—Marilyn Monroe

"Here (Miss Monroe) fans saw her pictures as reflections of her beauty, fame, fortune, and sex. They show the evolution of the Love Goddess in all her sexuality—the role that Marilyn knew and enjoyed and most feared to lose. First—and most famous—was the 1949 nude calendar pose, which brought her a worldwide flood of welcome publicity while she was just a long-haired model who had a few walk-on parts in the movies."

Elizabeth Taylor and Sophia Loren among the few, are too explicit in their acting on and off the scene. Producers seem to put realism in front of morals and dignity.

The public wants more sex from female actresses, more realistic looking and sounding killings, etc.

The Walt Disney type program is fast becoming absolute. Programs on the educational line seem to have died. I want to go to a movie to be intertained by good acting, but moral conduct.

Now days, I walk away from a movie with a sick feeling in my stomach.

My feelings are caused by simpley vulgar intertainment. Of course, there are a few good movies, such as Lorance of Arabia and others, but to the handfull that are acceptable in my terms, there are hundredes that are poor. The producers' ought to put this realistic tought into good and moral acting.

Not this garbage that is turned out in mass production.

"Of Human Bondage"

"Some women can't help what they are . . ."

"There would always be men in her life . . . all kinds of men . . . and always Phillip to come back to . . . to degrade and despise."

As the billboard, a half naked woman!

The propositional and the appositional styles can be contrasted on the basis of these factors, among others:

PROPOSITIONAL	APPOSITIONAL
Stated topic (enthymeme)	Implied topic
Organizational rigidity	Organizational flexibility
General examples, if any	Specific examples
Backgrounded style[15]	Foregrounded style
Little presence[16]	Great presence

In the propositional essay, the topic is clearly stated; at the end of the second paragraph, we know that the writer considers health, friendship, and beauty to be three of the best things in life, and we can predict with virtual certainty that the essay will explore these three values to determine whether or not they are free. The progression will be, in Kenneth Burke's term, syllogistic.

It follows then, that organization is predictable. The first two paragraphs enunciate the topic (which might, indeed, have been stated in one complex sentence), and the following three paragraphs each explore one aspect of the topic. Our expectations concerning organization are thwarted only by the writer's failure to supply cloture in the form of a summative paragraph.

There are no real examples in the piece, no narrative concerning a friendly relation, no anecdote concerning ebullient good health, no specific image of a beautiful place. The prose floats at least thirteen feet above the rich earth of specificty.

This lack of examples creates the backgrounded style and deprives the writing of presence, which is the sort of palpability that evokes attention from the reader.

Comments on the appositional essay would be the obverse of those on the propositional: the topic is unstated, there is no real organization, and the examples (which are the substance of the essay) create foregrounding and presence.

Although the ability to carry on propositional thinking is undoubtedly a sign of maturity, maturity in writing involves the ability to unite the appositional with the propositional in appropriate contexts. Such is the implication of Aristotle's mention of inductive thinking and of the whole concept of presence. (Such also, of course, is the implication of the poetic theory that this discussion will elaborate.) Of course, writing teachers have intuitively understood this point all along. The master comment on the propositional theme above would be, I suppose, "Get down to cases. Give me some concrete examples. Help me to see what you're talking about, to experience." The "master" comment on the appositional theme would be, "Get a thesis, state it or imply it clearly, and then organize and explore your ideas."

When we give such advice, we are quite literally asking students to change the ratios between their cerebral hemispheres. In this regard, Luria tells us that

> it must be remembered that the absolute dominance of one (the left) hemisphere is not by any means always found, and the law of lateralization is only relative in character. According to recent investigations (Zangwill, 1960; Subirana, 1969), one-quarter of all persons are completely right-handed, and slightly more than one-third show marked dominance of the left hemisphere, whereas the rest are distinguished by relatively slight dominance of the left hemisphere, and in one-tenth of all cases the dominance of the left hemisphere is totally absent.[17]

Clearly, in the classroom we must take account of the fact that we will encounter instances of extreme LH or RH dominance, and I would postulate that in the example themes above, we have seen probable instances of such dominance. The situation becomes even more complicated when we realize that literacy may create or facilitate lateralization.[18] Learning to read and write may well increase the dominance of the LH.

Can we conclude, then, that the appositional writer may increase proportional skills through intensive practice in reading and writing? Such would seem to be the case. Are appositional writers in general less literate than propositional writers are? At present, there is no answer to that question. In the absence of such evidence, I would suggest that carefully structured reading and writing exercises may well increase the versatility of the appositionalist.

Drawing on work that I have done in the past[19] and on my experience with secondary students in the Huntington Beach Union High School District, I am at present constructing materials intended to give the appositionalist propositional skills. The materials are yet to be tested, but, in general, they are based on a progression from algorithmic to heuristic to aleatory exercises. In the materials, this progression will be applied to instruction in all of the "stadia" of discourse: sentence, paragraph, essay.

The paragraph is the handiest example of what I am getting at. Drawing on both tagmemic theories and the theories of Francis Christensen,[20] I ask students to construct paragraphs according to algorithms—for instance:

(1)	Make a general statement about your English class.	My English class is boring.
(2)	Qualify, restrict, or explain that statement.	We never do interesting things in the class.
(3)	Illustrate the restricted statement three times.	We spend a lot of time diagramming sentences.
		The teacher makes us read a lot of old-fashioned poetry.
		Every day we do grammar drills in our workbooks.

The result is a recognizable paragraph, with levels of generality and local details.

The next step is heuristic: to recombine the "tagmemes" in the algorithmic paragraph in as many ways as possible:

(1) In my English class, we spend a lot of time diagramming sentences. The teacher makes us read a lot of old-fashioned poetry, and every day we do grammar drills in our workbooks. My English class is boring. We never do interesting things in the class.

(2) Because we never do interesting things in my English class, it is boring. We spend a lot of time diagramming sentences, and the teacher makes us read a lot of old-fashioned poetry. Not only that, we do grammar drills in our workbooks every day.

(3) We spend our time doing uninteresting things in my English class: diagramming sentences, reading old-fashioned poetry, and doing grammar drills in our workbooks. My English class is boring.

The aleatory phase of instruction relies on creative devices such as metaphor and analogy to suggest relationships that can be expressed in paragraphs, the forms for which students have presumably "internalized" through their algorithmic and heuristic work. For example,

> Compare a recent journey—to another country, another city, another part of your own city—with each of the following:
>> threading a needle
>> a nightmare
>> attending a play or a film
>> eating a tart apple
>> smelling a freshly painted room
>> touching suede
>> solving a math problem
>
> Use the ideas that your comparisons generated to write a paragraph—or several paragraphs—about the journey.

One other possibility concerning the appositionalist is intriguing and deserves careful investigation. If the general skills of propositional thought are both learnable and transferable, then it might well be possible to increase the appositionalist's versatility by providing him or her with extensive exercises in propositional reasoning, e.g., syllogisms, enthymemes, sorites, and problems in symbolic logic.

As to the propositionalist, I can only suggest that intensive exposure to the most appositional of all written discourse may well bring about greater versatility. I am speaking, of course, of the reading the writing of lyric poetry. However, the common method of "explaining" the lyric poem by propositionalizing all of its images (a subject which is explored fully in a later section of this paper) should, according to my logic, tend to increase the propositional nature of the writing. It would seem, then, that "reader response" criticism and free writing would be in order.

Finally, of course, the ultimate goal is to increase the creativity of all writers—the ability to generate writings (whether poetic or nonpoetic, temporal or atemporal) that satisfy the writer's need for expression, the reader's need for understanding and empathy, and the world's need for meaningful communication. This creativity consists of the ability to use both propositional and appositional modes appropriately, and it comes about only in the proper environment.

Insofar as the composition classroom is an environment, it must be characterized by an atmosphere of freedom and writing tasks that are liberating. (Drills and exercises can be liberating at certain times for certain purposes with certain students.)

Carl Rogers defines creativity as "the emergence in action of a novel relational product, growing out of the uniqueness of the individual on the one hand, and the materials, events, people, or circumstances of his life on the other."[21] The conditions that foster creativity are psychological safety ("Accepting the individual as of unconditional worth. . . . Providing a climate in which external evaluation is absent. . . . Understanding empathically") and psychological freedom.[22]

In his magnificent book *The Act of Creation*[23] Arthur Koestler has developed a model of the creative act. The creative person has been able to bisociate by leaping from one matrix to another. An excellent example of both matrix and leap is provided by James L. Adams in *Conceptual Blockbusting*.[24]

At sunrise on the first morning, a monk laboriously climbs to the summit of a mountain, where he spends the rest of the day and all of the night meditating. At sunrise on the second day, he comes down the mountain on the same trail by which he ascended. Is there any time in his journey downward at which he would be in exactly the same spot as he was on the journey upward?

If one stays in the verbal matrix, this is a difficult problem to solve, but if one leaps to the visual matrix, the solution becomes obvious. Picture the monk going upward and downward simultaneously. Obviously he would meet himself at some point on the trail.

Koestler sets up three categories of creativity: comedy, in which there is a collision of matrices; science, in which there is an integration of matrices; and art, in which matrices are juxtaposed. The comic effect comes about, for example, through the juxtaposition of the ridiculous with the sublime; Kepler analogized the role of the Father in the Trinity with that of the sun in the solar system, thus integrating two matrices; in tragedy the matrix of the play is juxtaposed with the audience's knowledge that the play is just a play.

As there is matrix-hopping, so there is hemisphere-hopping: in fact, the two are apparently the same at times. Fluency in thought, like fluency in writing, is the ability to use both the appositional and the propositional, an ability that is very much like John Crowe Ransom's description of metaphysical poetry (as opposed to physical and Platonic poetry):

> Platonic poetry is too idealistic, but physical poetry is too realistic, and realism is tedious and does not maintain interest. The poets therefore introduce the psychological device of the miracle. The predication which it permits is clean and quick but it is not a scientific predication. For scientific predication concludes an act of attention but miraculism [in the form of the metaphysical conceit] initiates one. It leaves us looking, marveling, and reveling in the thick *dinglich* substance that has just received its strange representation.[25]

The RH is the master of the appositional, *dinglich*, all-at-onceness of images; the LH is the master of metaphor, analogy, and proposition.

The fluent writer is a hemisphere-hopper.

Right-Handed Metaphor and Left-Handed Synedoche

In a paper that I coauthered with Timothy Crusius, one of my students,[26] we analyzed the nature of metaphor. As Christine Brooke-Rose[27] and Laurence Perrine,[28] among others, have pointed out, metaphor can have any of a great variety of grammatical forms. For example:

> *predicate nominal sentence*
>   All the world's a stage. . . .
> *genitive construction*
>   the bird of time
> *appositive*
>   the black bat, night
> *vocative*
>   O wild West Wind, thou breath of Autumn's being. . . .
> *deixis*
>   Be watchful of your beauty, Lady dear!
>   How much hangs on *that* lamp, you cannot tell.

Indeed, metaphor may depend on context alone:

> Eat, drink, and be merry, for tomorrow you die.

This would not be metaphorical if uttered by a guard delivering the last meal to a condemned prisoner.

The metaphor, then, with its variety of grammatical forms, emerges through our knowledge of the world (and in this discussion, I ignore the difference between metaphor and simile). If I say "From Los Angeles, I sailed to New York in a great silver ship," your metaphorical interpretation of that statement will depend upon your knowledge of United States geography and modern transportation systems, though, of course, it is quite possible that I took a sailing ship through the Panama Canal or around the Horn.

Whatever its form, the metaphor is meaningless as metaphor unless, to use Richards' terms, we can identify its tenor and vehicle, which is to say, in fact, that all metaphors are somehow a vehicle predicated of a tenor, or, if you will, that all metaphors can be expressed as a predicate nominal sentence.

	Tenor	(is/are)	*Vehicle*
All the world's a stage	world		stage
the bird of Time	Time		bird
the black bat, night	night		black bat
O wild West Wind, thou breath of Autumn's being	wild West Wind		breath of Autumn's being
Be watchful of your beauty . . . that			

lamp. . . .	beauty	lamp
Eat, drink, and be		
merry. . . .	life	a day
Sheathe thy		
impatience	impatience	sword
the tawny-hided		
desert crouches	desert	lion

I am not arguing, of course, that when we process language we go through the kind of transformation that I have illustrated, and specifically I am avoiding the argument over the nature of deep structure or whether it has any psychological reality. Quite obviously, however, metaphors are, to use Bogen's term, propositional in nature.

Not only are they propositional—they are verbal in a specific way. Suppose I say to you, "Eat, drink, and be merry, for tomorrow you die." And suppose you ask me what I mean. I can propositionalize: "Well, I was only trying to tell you that 'life is but a day.'" Suppose further that you are still unsatisfied and ask me to clarify my meaning; I will tell you bluntly that I mean "life is short." With "short" I will have arrived at an intermediate term, beyond which I can still go to make my meaning more explicit: Life is only a few hours in the sum of eternity; birth is like waking in the morn, and death is like going to sleep at night; in one day, there is time for few pleasures. . . .

Another example. A particularly obstreperous child says to me, "Oink, oink!"

"What do you mean by that?"

"I mean that *you are a pig.*" (propositionalization)

"Why am I a pig?"

"Because you're *unpleasant.*" (intermediate term)

"Why am I unpleasant?"

"Because you're greedy, rude, fat, smelly. . . ."

In both of these examples, we have seen that there are intermediate levels beyond which we can go in explanation of the metaphors and also that there are rockbottom levels beyond which we cannot go. The rockbottom level is the most specific level of explanation.

It is now perhaps apparent why I say that metaphor is a particularly verbal kind of figure. We explain metaphor by resorting to sets of terms, not to counter-images. (Shortly, we will be considering imagery, and we will see that explanations of images take place through the construction of counter-images; this difference in explanatory strategies clarifies the difference in function and effect between metaphor and image.) I believe that we always explain metaphor with rockbottom terms or with further metaphors, which in turn can be explained with rockbottom terms:

> Eat, drink and be merry, for tomorrow you die.
>> Birth is (like) waking in the morn, and death is
>> (like) going to sleep at night.
>>> Life is a day.
>>> Life is short.
>>> Enjoy yourself while you can.

The particularly verbal nature of metaphor becomes clearer when we compare metaphor with image. One of the most famous of all imagist poems is this, by William Carlos Williams:

> The Red Wheelbarrow
>
>> so much depends
>> upon
>>
>> a red wheel
>> barrow
>>
>> glazed with rain
>> water
>>
>> beside the white
>> chickens.[29]

How do we begin to "explain" this image? To be sure, we can metaphorize it: red wheelbarrow (tenor) is purity, childhood, life, machine, etc. (vehicle). However, such a reading of the poem is simply unwarranted, as our complete uncertainty about vehicle indicates. In the case of imagery, it seems that the poem should not mean, but be. And yet the poem does mean, but not in any metaphorical sense. Whereas metaphor in poetry is relatively easy to explain or "explicate," the image is elusive and difficult.

Take the first few lines of "The Love Song of J. Alfred Prufrock," for example. Ignoring certain "embedded" metaphors, we can see that these lines present an alternation of metaphors and images:

> Let us go then, you and I,
>
> When the evening is spread out against the sky
> Like a patient etherized upon a table;   *metaphor*
>
> Let us go, through certain half-deserted streets,
> The muttering retreats
> Of restless nights in one-night cheap hotels   *image*
> And sawdust restaurants with oyster-shells:
>
> Streets that follow like a tedious argument
> of insidious intent   *metaphor*
> To lead you to an overwhelming question . . .
>
> Oh, do not ask, 'What is it?'
> Let us go and make our visit

> In the room the women come and go   *image*
> Talking of Michelangelo.[30]

Note how relatively easy it is to explain the meaning of the metaphors. Since the evening is spread out against the sky like a patient etherized upon a table, the evening is passive, inert, in someone else's hands, sick, hovering between life and death, stifling. But note also how difficult it is to explain the "meaning" of the images. "In the room the women come and go/Talking of Michelangelo"— but what does that *mean*?

In fact, I think, the only way for me to explain what that image means is to present counter-images and thus to construct a set of images, of which the original would be a part. The original image, then would be a synecdoche, a part standing for the whole category that constituted the meaning of the one image for me.

My purpose here is to discuss the nature of poetry, not literary criticism, and yet I cannot resist an instructive and essentially relevant digression to illustrate my point about metaphorical versus synecdochic explication. Years ago, I read Yeats' account of the composition of "Leda and the Swan." As I recall, Yeats talked about getting so caught up in the image of the poem that nothing else mattered, and I think that the experience of the poem gives the reader something of the inexpressible—or at least inchoate—intensity of a painting of the same subject. Insofar as the poem "works," it does so as an image, not as a statement. But what can one say about an image? As we have seen, it is relatively easy to talk about metaphor, to explicate the metaphor in essentially metalinguistic terms. No metalanguage serves to clarify the image as image, however. (How would one give a metalinguistic explication of "The Red Wheelbarrow"?)

It turns out, I think, that the need to explicate—whatever the source of that need—forces us to metaphorize the image, a result that in itself is neither good nor bad. For instance, here is Richard Ellmann on "Leda and the Swan":

> Could power and knowledge ever exist together in this world, or were they, as he (Yeats) had reason to suspect, contraries ever at war? Was wisdom the ripe fruit obtainable only when the sense of taste was gone?[31]

In this ingenious (and to me, at least, particularly rich) interpretation of the poem, Ellmann uses the gambit of metaphorization:

> Zeus is power.
> Leda is knowledge.
> Rape is war.

I am hinting strongly, of course, that metaphor relates closely to what we know about the LH, that it is easier to explain "meanings" in LH than in RH terms, and, finally, that explications which we might characterize as RH will sound naive, typically beginning with that sure clue to the affective "fallacy," "This reminds me of . . ."

Let's think about images in poetry. One of the powers of metaphor, certainly, is that it propositionalizes imagistically (or usually does so): "night is a black bat," "the stars are the candles of the night," "life is but a walking shadow," "we devour our time like am'rous birds of prey," and so on. "Eat, drink, and be merry" is more powerful than its reduced propositionalized version ("life is a day") precisely because it is more imagistic in quality. But as we have seen, one of the important characteristics of metaphor is its amenability to metalinguistic explanation.

The image has a "purity" which is quite arbitrary and depends wholly on the reader in that any reader can metaphorize any image, as we have seen to be the case with both "The Red Wheelbarrow" and "Leda and the Swan." When the image is "pure," explication becomes difficult, if not impossible, for, as we shall see, it is difficult to talk about the meanings of images.

I want to use "Prufrock" as my example, for it is the first modern poem that I took seriously. In 1948 on the banks of the Truckee River in Reno, Nevada, I decided to make the first step toward overcoming my all-too-obvious philistinism: I would get to know Eliot. (Joyce was second on my agenda. Twenty-nine years later, I realize that I have not reached my cultural goal and never will. Nonetheless.)

I began to read "Prufrock," resolving that I would understand its every word and then memorize the whole. The details of this experience—even the setting—still live vividly for me. With the first few lines, I gained a trememdous sense of power, for I could well understand the evening's being an etherized patient stretched out against the sky. I had words to express my understanding and sensed that I could argue cogently in favor of my interpretation.

Immediately, though, I was frustrated. How could I explain the full sense that I got from the images? (I did not yet have that term.) What did sawdust restaurants with oyster-shells "mean"? Even more puzzling: women in a room talking of Michelangelo? Of course, I resorted to a strategy that embarrassed me even then: "These passages remind me . . ." The only way I could begin to express what had happened to me in my reading was to give examples of similar scenes and events from my own experience. Even at the age of eighteen, I realized that such naive understanding was unacceptable—though I was not awfully precocious, and though I was a student at one of the most humble and practical state universities. I was stymied—in just the same way that most readers of poetry are stymied when they want to or are forced to discuss their experience of imagistic poetry.

We have not, I assure you, wandered from our purposes: to discuss LH and RH in the experience of reading poetry. We have seen that there is good reason to characterize metaphoric interpretation as LH, and there is equally good reason to characterize the interpretation of images as RH.

You will recall our characterization of RH thought as appositional, holistic, imagistic. There is good reason to believe that the RH power of imaging is necessary even for some kinds of propositional thought. For example, in solving problems involving certain kinds of disjunction, the RH seems to be essential. In answering the following, the LH seems adequate: "Jim is taller than Bill. Who is taller?" But in the following, experiments have shown that imaging seems necessary: "Jim is taller than Bill. Who is shorter?"[32] And, of course, if our logic follows, the metaphor (which propositionalizes images) must be bihemispheric while the image can be associated largely with the functions of the RH. (Does bihemisphericity explain the power of metaphor, which, Longinus tells us, simply sweeps us away and thus is the most rhetorically cogent of the figures?)

Particularly skilled at establishing part-whole relationships, the RH is quite literally synecdochic in operation, synecdoche being the figure in which part stands for the whole: *All hands on deck! A fleet of twenty sails. I give my heart to you.* (Metonymy is the figure in which something closely associated with the object term is substituted for the term: *The crown commands. The pen is mightier than the sword.* For our purposes, the distinction between synecdoche and metonymy, like that between metaphor and simile, is ignored.)

To understand the argument regarding images in poetry, one must understand the psychological concept of the *cognitive category*,[33] itself a metaphor that explains a perfectly obvious property of thought: the tendency of the mind to categorize, the necessity to do so. When a child first learns to recognize four-footed creatures, all quadrupeds are quite likely to be "doggies." Experience enables the child to make differentiations and thus establish new, refined categories: "moo-cows," "kitties," "horsies." The child—or adult— makes differentiations very rapidly, on the basis of one or two examples. When the child sees one "horsie" and differentiates it from "doggie," the new category is established, the one horse being a synecdoche, a part representing the whole category. For many freshmen in college, a poem is a poem is a poem, but after a brief time in a literature class, the "poetry" becomes lyrics, narratives, sonnets, odes, etc. Thus, cognitive categories are hierarchical in arrangement and are created by and large through the observer's purpose.

In the experience of reading, an image is a synecdoche in just this sense: it is meaningful to the reader insofar as he or she can relate it to a set of like images, i.e., place it in a cognitive category. For this reason, in its effect the image is likely to be highly personal, even idiosyncratic. An eminent brain researcher, Sir John Eccles, states the idea this way:

> Our speculation has been extended to cover in principle the simplest aspects of imagination, imagery or the re-experiencing of images. In passing beyond this stage we may firstly consider a peculiar tendency to association of imagery, so that the experience of one image is evocative of other images, and these of still more and so on. When these images are of beauty and subtlety, blending in harmony and capable of being expressed in some language, verbal, musical or pictorial, so that transcendent experiences can be evoked in others, we have artistic creation of a simple or lyrical kind.[34]

While we might argue with the adjective "simple" in the above, certainly Eccles describes the lyrical experience.

All of this means, then, that a perfectly forthright explanation of the "meaning" of a poetic image is likely to be unacceptable in the academy, where the tradition demands "logical," impersonal explications.

In a brief essay, Roman Jokobson makes suggestions that relate to my argument here.[35] He points out that aphasia suppresses either the ability to express similarity (metaphor) or the ability to express contiguity (metonym). It would seem, then, that metaphor and metonym (or synecdoche) are polar functions of language, even if they cannot be associated directly with LH and RH.

Another intriguing hint comes from a theory about the genesis of language. Harry J. Jerison postulates that language evolved as a marking system, not as a system of communication.[36] Wolves and other predators mark their territory with urine, their highly developed olfactory sense making this possible, whereas man, who has never had a highly developed olfactory system, signaled with sounds. In other words, language was first used to produce (evoke) images, and it still is so used. Whether or not Jerison is right—and we will never know—certainly the power of the image is mysterious and basic, felt in our right-handed, logical culture, but largely inexpressible because of our hemispheric bias.

According to the logic of this argument so far, the bilateral symmetry of the organ within our skulls—anatomical symmetry with complementarity of function—destines us for the poetic experience, both productive and receptive. If it turns out in fact that most people take no joy in poetry, find no real meaningfulness in it, we must look for a social influence of enormous power—enough to overcome "basic human nature," and we realize that even jails have not been successful at that.

I would suggest that we look at our right-handed schools, which both reflect and influence the development of our culture. In most literature classes—from the public schools through graduate seminars—it is impossible to respond to the synecdochic quality of poetry in the way that I have argued is necessary, using the LH-RH distinction at least as the analogical basis for my argument.

The emphasis on *explication de texte* and the critical essay warps the total poetic experience and serves, I think, to alienate people from poetry.[37]

LH, RH, and Reading

What we know about brain function helps us understand the process of reading. In the following, I will not cover territory already explored in standard sources, but will attempt to suggest new directions for inquiry and explain some of my own recent insights.[38]

First, I would like to point out some obvious, but generally unnoticed, characteristics of texts and the reading process.

Texts can be roughly categorized on the basis of their temporal organization and their poetic or nonpoetic character. (For "temporal organization" we could substitute "appositional or propositional organization" or "lyric or nonlyric form.") Most novels and dramas, narrative poems, and other works take chronological sequence as their principle of organization. Lyric poems and some modern works of prose fiction and drama do not take chronological sequence as their organizing principle. Nonpoetic works such as sets of instructions, journals, logs, and so on are chronologically organized. Nonpoetic works such as collections of sayings, the larger structure of the present discussion, and other writings do not take chronological sequence as their organizing principle.

Recently, I encountered a perfect description of an atemporal, nonpoetic text: specifically, a study of William Faulkner, written by John T. Irwin. Irwin's description is well worth repeating:

> As I look back on the writing [of the book], I suppose that, stylistically, I was trying to weave a kind of seamless garment, and that that was necessary because the structure of what I was trying to reveal exists only as a whole, exists not as the sum of its elements, not by the simple addition of those elements, but rather through the simultaneous multiplication of every element by every other element. What I tried to evoke was a kind of synergism in which the structure in its irreducible wholeness is infinitely more than simply the sum of its parts, for, strictly speaking, *considered as structure, a continuous system of differences*, it has no parts, no independently meaningful, logically separable units. . . .
>
> At one point I simply had to ask myself if I thought that it was possible to present a holistic, simultaneous structure in the temporal, successive medium of written discourse. My answer was, "Of course not"—not if by "present" one meant "explain." But it seemed to me that I could come as close as possible to presenting that structure by trying to embody it in the structure of my own text. The model I used as a starting point for that attempt was the musical, motival structure of Lévi-Strauss's *The Raw and the Cooked*. In order to achieve the multiple counterpointing effect that is the great strength of that method, I had to try to create within my text a kind of multidimensional imaginative space in

which there existed the possibility of simultaneously placing every element side by side with every other element.[30]

In this connection one might also—with great trepidation—evoke Marshall McLuhan.

Diagrammatically, what I am saying works out like this:

	TEMPORAL		ATEMPORAL
	novels	.	lyric poems
POETIC	dramas	.	some novels
	etc.	.	some dramas
		.	etc.
		.	
		.	
	sets of	.	collections of
	instructions	.	sayings
NONPOETIC	journals	.	essays
	logs, etc.	.	etc.

The distinction between poetic and non-poetic writings is determined by the reader, a bald statement that could well be (and indeed has been) the subject of a long essay in itself. What I mean is simply that the poetic/nonpoetic distinction is determined by the purpose of the reader. I can read *Heart of Darkness* as a fiction (poetic), as a treatise on colonialism (nonpoetic), as a document in the autobiography of Conrad (poetic or nonpoetic).

Related to, but distinct from, the contrast between poetic and nonpoetic writings is the nature of the reading experience itself. In *informational reading*, the purpose is to learn something, to gain information, the reader always aware of context, the text relating to or having the potential of relating to something "out there" in the real world of concepts and ideas. It is the kind of reading that most reading theorists talk about: the efficient processing of a text for meaning, which is commonly defined as "the reduction of uncertainty."[40] I am suggesting that most reading theorists deal with the multiple experiences of reading as if they were intended solely for the purpose of gaining information about the world "out there."

But there is another world, the world of the possible, which is the root of the distinction that Northrop Frye makes between poetic and nonpoetic texts. The poetic text delineates a possible world. The text that delineates an actual world is not poetic.[41]

I am not suggesting, of course, that the distinctions I outline are clearcut. Is a work such as *In Cold Blood* or even *The Grapes of Wrath* a delineation or an actual world? The answer, as I have said, lies in the purpose of the reader, but it is obvious that some texts, like *The Grapes of Wrath*, have more potential for being taken as nonpoetic than do others, such as *Vathek*.

When the work is (taken as) poetic, the delineating of a possible world, the reading experience is quite different from that of the nonpoetic work in that the reading becomes solipsistic, the purpose being to immerse oneself, not to test the text against reality or to gain information. If there is such a phenomenon as informational reading on the one hand, there is also such an experience as *esthetic immersion*.

At the moment, I am reflecting on my own writing problem here. It seems to me that I need some way to "verify" the distinction I am making between informational reading and esthetic immersion. I need support—preferably in the form of unimpeachable authority—but I think there is no such "outside support" to be found in the scholarship of reading or of literary theory. The best authority is oneself, one's own experience of reading. In the experience of esthetic immersion, the ties with reality (with the "context," in Roman Jakobson's term) are either cut or suppressed. One lives more or less exclusively in the world of the work, and there are no "practical" consequences to the reading. Everyone who passionately reads poetry or fiction has had this experience.

But there is a paradox. Since we read with our minds, not our eyes, the text is meaningful only insofar as we can relate it to our own experience, and as we make this relation, we change the nature of our experience by expanding it, so that, through reading, we gain knowledge. Consider (with Kenneth Burke) *Madame Bovary*, a prime example from the naturalistic school. Flaubert has "displaced" the mythic underpinning of his tale to give it its lifelike quality. But, as Frye says,

> The realistic writer soon finds that the requirements of literary form and plausible content always fight against each other. Just as the poetic metaphor is always a logical absurdity, so every inherited convention of plot in literature is more or less mad.[42]

As Burke points out, the novel is nothing more than a definition of the god-term of its title, Madame Bovary. Just as the poet displaces myth to give it credibility, verisimilitude, life-likeness, so the reader who is esthetically immersed displaces. The esthetic purpose of reading *Madame Bovary*, is to define "*Madame Bovary*." Once that definition is made, the reader has a powerful tool for understanding reality; he or she is in command of the complex concept "*Madame Bovary*," which can be used to illuminate and deal with experience. In the reading, the naturalistic content is "displaced" to make way for the experience of the novel. For this reason, the most improbably possible world can be as real in the act of reading as the most probable. In esthetic immersion, *Madame Bovary* is no more real than one of Philip José Farmer's outrageous fictions. The more "real" the novel is to the reader, the less of a poem it becomes. The poem has a reality of its own. This reality is, of course, in the mind of the reader, a mythic reality.

Frye's outline of the process whereby we grasp the mythic reality of the fiction—the plotted poetic work—squares nicely with brain theory. When we read a fictional work,

> continuity is the center of our attention; our later memory, or what I call the possession of it, tends to become discontinuous [appositional]. Our attention shifts from the sequence of incidents to another focus: a sense of what the work of fiction was all *about*, or what criticism usually calls its theme. And we notice that as we go on to study and reread the work of fiction, we tend not to reconstruct the plot, but to become conscious of the theme, and to see all incidents as manifestations of it. Thus the incidents themselves tend to remain, in our critical study of the work, discontinuous [a-temporal], detached from one another and regrouped in a new way.[43]

The fiction becomes mythos and thus takes on the character of lyric.

Put into "brain" terms, Frye is describing the reading of fictions in this way. The images (RH) are perceived in their temporal sequence (LH). In retrospect, the sequentiality of the images disappears, and the work becomes a gestalt (RH). Any one of the images becomes a synecdoche (RH) for the whole. In discussing *Moby Dick*, for instance, any one of its synecdochic images, frequently the substance of one chapter, can become "the point of entry"— "The Candles," "The Try-Works," "The Doubloon." In this sense, the mythos of the fiction is analogous to the cognitive category.

The experience of reading should convince us that the most closely reasoned essays have the same organizational principle as fiction: the temporal, in that A must come before B in order for B to make sense, and B must come before C—though it is the case that few essays in my experience have this kind of tight logic, most not being of the nature of St. Thomas Aquinas. Once we have finished reading, we have the "meaning" or the equivalent of mythos, but seldom can we put the details of the argument together in a satisfactory fashion.

Other dynamics are working here, however. In writings based on temporal sequence, it should be the case that readers would attempt to "reduce" them to mythos or "meaning." One of my students has suggested, though, that there may well be—and probably are—readers who tend always to be reductive and others who tend always to be constructive. In her experiment, Judith Walcutt presented a variety of kinds of prose to readers: poems, recipes, sets of instructions, and so on. She revealed these texts to her subject readers in small increments, in effect uncovering them virtually line by line. What she found is that some readers always tend to "reduce," to seek out the central mythos or meaning, while others construct their own possible worlds—poems, fictions, fantasies, speculations—on the basis of the individual segments of the text as they are revealed.

Reductive readers seem determined to make *the* sense out of the text; constructive readers seem to be triggered into their own creative processes by the synecdochic nature of the individual segments of the text. In our terms, reductive readers seem to be LH, while constructive readers seem to be RH.

So far we have been dealing primarily with those texts which are organized on the basis of what Kenneth Burke terms syllogistic progression.[44] Lyrics and other writings do not have such a structure. The sections of "The Waste Land," for example, could well be rearranged without affecting the integrity of the work as a whole.[45] Or compare *Moby-Dick* with *The Moonstone*. To be sure, *Moby-Dick* has a chronological organization based on the sequence of the voyage, but its organization is primarily lyric, the individual chapters being synecdochic for the whole.

We will return to the atemporal (lyric, appositional) mode hereafter, but for the moment, I would like to relate our key terms—esthetic immersion and informational reading, temporal and atemporal organization—more clearly to what we know about brain function.

Ordinary consciousness, Robert E. Ornstein says, "involves analysis, a separation of oneself from other objects and organisms."[46] The experience of esthetic immersion in reading is, then, not ordinary consciousness, but extraordinary. One does not analyze, does not "stand back" and achieve separation from the text. The informational reader must maintain contact with context, with the world "out there" which the text deals with; the text at every moment relates to context and, conversely, gives one access to context. Esthetic immersion, resulting from a willing suspension of disbelief, breaks that contact.

Esthetic immersion is a matter of attention. If I am reading a set of instructions for operating a new electric razor, the razor itself—"out there"—will be literally or figuratively before me; there will be an attention ration between the set of instructions and their referent. But, as Frye points out, in poetic discourse there is not such ration, poetic discourse constructing, by definition, only possible worlds, worlds, that is, of the imagination.

Attention is, to be sure, neurologically determined. "It is well known to psychologists that those features of the most elementary, involuntary attention of the type which is attracted by the most powerful or biologically significant stimuli can be observed very early on, during the first few months of the child's development."[47] Voluntary attention, however, "is not biological in its origins, but a social act. . . . It can be interpreted as the introduction of factors which are the product, not of the biological maturing of the organism, but of forms of activity created in the child during his relations with adults, into the organization of this complex regulation of selective mental activity.[48]

In Piaget's characterization of cognitive growth, one finds two parameters. First, the child discovers "otherness," that he or she is separated from the world "out there," a process that begins almost at birth and is completed at about eight years. Second, the child develops the ability for operational and abstract thinking, "the possibility of utilizing formal operations, which are completely abstract, conceptual tools."[49] The child begins to understand reality, gains the ability to use abstract thinking to deal with that reality, growing from the world of story to the world of science, developing the possibility of using reading as a tool for manipulating the world, i.e., the possibility of informational reading.

For the child, "Little Red Riding Hood" is an experience; for the adult, this myth can be regarded as an allegory concerning puberty and the onset of menstruation.[50] When the tale is used in an attempt to understand some facet of reality (of context), the reading is informational, not esthetic immersion.

Now, it is obvious that the development of cognition creates the possibility for using stories, particularly in Western societies, which are characterized as LH.[51] Crimes based upon fictions—cinematic, video, or prose—are only the most blatant examples. Nonetheless, the ability to experience stories—with wonder, intense curiosity about "what happens next," with terror, with absorption—remains always a possibility, though Western cognitive styles and, in particular, Western pedagogy tend to suppress and devalue this ability. *After* the experiences of reading, the adult also has the possibility of using the story as a cognitive instrument, a definition of a situation, the title or the name of a character becoming a tool of communication or a pivot for rational thought. During the experience of esthetic immersion, the story is *never* an instrument; I would like, almost, to say that it is prerational.

Note well: I am not dichotomizing; I take account of *both-and* as well as *either-or*. Almost simultaneously, the story can be *both* myth *and* instrument for the reader, so infinitely complex is the experience of reading.

The story is temporal (LH), *in medias res* being the most apparent example. "Processing" a story must be very much like processing a sentence or other verbal sequence, which in surface form must be a spatial-temporal sequence, the events in the story, like the phonemes or graphemes in the sentence, coming one after another, both conveying meanings, which by definition are atemporal. An analogy is the "deep structure" of a sentence, which has no linear or temporal dimension, so that both *I smoke cigars* and *Cigars are smoked by me* convey the same meaning in the sense that (a) predication and reference are the same and (b) roles are the same, i.e., in both versions we know that the same person is performing the same action with regard to the same thing. Any sensory array can be dealt with in two ways: serially (one at a time) or holistically. In reading, it appears that the RH processes data visuospatially, while the LH processes it verbally. "Thus, while the left hemisphere goes through and sequentially transforms each letter into an internal acoustic code (i.e., names them), the right hemisphere examines all the letters simultaneously looking for a variation in shape."[52] If the terms "event" or "scene" are substituted for "letter," this must pretty well describe the process of reading temporally organized works.

However, we must distinguish between process and experience, since reading *anything* must involve somewhat the same process at one level. Even though reading a mystery by Dorothy Sayers (syllogistic progression) and a collection of poems by Adrienne Rich is based on the same "decoding" procedures, these procedures can be and usually are radically different in the larger sense—that is, we read the Sayers mystery from first page to last sequentially to get the meaning, but we can and probably do read the collection of poems in an almost random way. The experience of reading each may be immersion in the world of the possible, but there are differences, of course, for reading a murder mystery is not reading a series of poems. The similarity of the two experiences is in the connections that one does or does not make between the texts and the world "out there"—the immediate *uses* that one makes or does not make of the reading.

The best example of the atemporal text is the lyric. (Not all lyrics are appositional in form since the completely appositional lyric can be rearranged significantly with no loss of "coherence.") Many lyrics—perhaps the best ones—simply evaporate when one attempts to explicate them, for they are experience, transmitted from poet to reader, near the subjective pole of the subjective-objective dichotomy. Eccles gives a spectrum of experience that illuminates the nature of the "pure" lyric:

(a) The vision of an object. (The object can be touched, photographed, etc.)

(b) A pin prick. (Can be seen by an observer; can be duplicated in an observer; observer can see the wince of pain and hear the cry.)

(c) Ache or pain in a visceral organ. (Cannot be seen or duplicated, but can be generally described, even in a clinical sense.)

(d) Mental pain or anguish. (Not a consequence of physical stimulation, but can achieve public status through descriptions and clinical reports.)

(e) Dreams, memories (fantasies, etc.). Gain public status through "the wealth of communication that there is between observers."[53]

The subject matter of the lyric—dreams, memories, reveries, fantasies—is RH. The imagistic quality of lyrics is RH.

We can perform an experiment that will demonstrate the reading experience offered by the lyric—and again, I differentiate experience and process, for in process, the reading of a lyric might well be as sequential as reading a set of instructions (or, might be "attacked" as if the steps in their sequence were arranged appositionally, the holistic processing of serial displays being always a possibility). The inner process of reading a lyric, regardless of attack strategies, is quite different from the inner process of reading instructions.

Reprinted below is Lowell's "Colloquy in Black Rock." Read this poem in the following way: jump about from stanza to stanza, image to image, even word to word in a quite random way, until you feel you "know" the poem. Then ask yourself the sense in which you know it. As yourself, further, how you might go about transmitting that knowledge to another; ask yourself, indeed, whether you have knowledge of the poem in any traditional sense, i.e., in any sense that would allow you to provide a conventional, logical *explication de texte*.

Colloquy in Black Rock
Here the jack hammer jabs into the ocean:
My heart, you race and stagger and demand
More blood-gangs for your nigger-brass percussions,
Till I, the stunned machine of your devotion,
Clanging upon this symbol of a hand,
Am rattled screw and footloose. All discussions

End in the mud-flat detritus of death.
My heart, beat faster, faster. In Black Mud
Hungarian workmen give their blood
For the martyr Stephen, who was stoned to death.

Black Mud, a name to conjure with: O mud
For watermelons gutted to the crust,
Mud for the mole-tide harbor, mud for mouse,
Mud for the armored Diesel fishing tubs that thud
A year and a day to wind and tide; the dust
Is on this skipping heart that shakes my house,

House of our Savior who was hanged till death.
My heart, beat faster, faster. In Black Mud
Stephen the martyr was broken down to blood:
Our ransom is the rubble of his death.

Christ walks on the black water. In Black Mud
Darts the kingfisher. On Corpus Christi, heart,
Over the drum-beat of St. Stephen's choir
I hear him, *Stupor Mundi*, and the mud
Flies from his hunching wings and beak—my heart
The blue kingfisher dives on you in fire.[54]

I posit that your experience of the poem can now be characterized something as follows: your "knowledge" consists of a series of images in apposition and a mood or emotion. I think, indeed, that the following equation is valid: *images in apposition + mood or emotion that they engender = knowl-*

edge of the lyric. Our knowledge of the lyric is RH and thus difficult to express, unless we propositionalize, so that perhaps the only true "explication" of a lyric is another lyric.

A more superficial point can be made about "Colloquy in Black Rock": it offers many possibilities for rearrangement—but that, of course, is precisely the nature of apposition.

The power of the lyric is the experience that our right-handed civilization is organized to deprive us of. Which leads me to conclude with this from Eccles:

> Entrancing displays of imagery that are reputed to be of great beauty and clarity can be experienced by ordinary people under the influence of hallucinogenic drugs such as mescaline or LSD. In parenthesis it should be noted that there are very few transmutations into literature or art of the transcendent esthetic experiences alleged to be enjoyed by drug addicts. One would suspect that in these conditions there would be an especial tendency for the formation of ever more complex and effectively interlocked patterns of neuronal activity involving large fractions of the cortical population of neurones. This would account for the withdrawal of the subject from ordinary activities during these absorbing experiences. Not unrelated to these states are the various psychoses where the inner experiences of the patients also cause them to be withdrawn.[55]

LH, RH, and Presence

One of the most important documents in "the new rhetoric" is *The New Rhetoric: A Treatise on Argument*, by Chaim Perelman and L. Olbrechts-Tyteca.[56] Among several key notions in the work is that of *presence*, the means whereby style gives arguments status, vividness, and extralogical power.

Presence seems to have these characteristics. First, that object or concept to which one directs attention assumes thereby more presence than other objects or concepts. In other words, the act of attention endows presence. Second, the image creates presence. Third, presence is conferred by holism. Perelman says,

> *Presence* acts directly on our sensibility. As Piaget shows, it is a psychological datum operative already at the level of perception: when two things are set side by side, say a fixed standard and things of variable dimensions with which it is compared, the things on which the eye dwells, that which is best or most often seen, is, by that very circumstance, overestimated. . . . Certain masters of rhetoric, with a liking for quick results, advocate the use of concrete objects in order to move an audience. . . . It should also be observed that the effort to make something present to the consciousness can relate not only to real objects, but also to a judgment or an entire argumentative development. As far as possible, such an effort is directed to filling the whole field of consciousness

with this presence so as to isolate it, as it were, from the hearer's overall mentality.[57]

And Perelman quotes Bacon:

> The affection beholdeth merely the present: reason beholdeth the future and sum of time. And therefore the present filling the imagination more, reason is commonly vanquished; but after that force of eloquence and persuasion hath made things future and remote appear as present, then upon the revolt of the imagination reason prevaileth.

After reading Perelman, we have a fairly good sense of what presence consists in, and yet an exact specification eludes us.

Aristotle, of course, had the same intuitions about presence that Bacon, Perelman, and many others have had. Logical proofs, he tells us in the *Rhetoric*, are developed through deduction on the basis of the enthymeme or through induction on the basis of example. In rhetoric, of course, the example does not have the power of statistical validity—and yet, Aristotle and our experience tell us, it does have great power: the power of creating presence.

As you can well forsee, I am about to argue that presence in argument comes about largely through RH functions. I am referring to the synecdochic power of the example-image, with its ability to evoke a cognitive category and to change that category by becoming a part of it. In this sense, the image not only creates presence by "triggering" the imaging power of the RH, but is also strictly dialectic, in that it adds to the available cognitive data of the perceiver.

We can postulate that the image affects cognition in at least two ways: first, by adding to and thus changing the category through enlargement, and, second, by triggering the creation of a new category. Paradoxically, the enlargement of a category always involves the creation of a new category due to hierarchical structure.

We can further postulate that some examples are *confirmative*, or *disconfirmative*, evoking in the reader (or hearer) that set of images, memories, and associations that represent an already existing category and thus creating presence, which results in adherence to or rejection of an idea through tacit demonstration that the subject under consideration is familiar. In this sense, they serve as the grounds for argument, and, as Perelman explains, argument can begin only on the basis of shared assumptions.[58]

Some examples are *constructive*, creating presence by triggering the construction of whole new cognitive categories in the reader or hearer and thus making whole new avenues of thought possible.

Some examples, of course, are *misfires*, neither confirming nor constructing either because they have not received attention or because they are so far outside the audience's experience that they cannot evoke or trigger the formation of a new set.

One function of style, assuredly, is to serve as an attention-getting device: inflection and emphasis in spoken discourse and figures of grammar in written.

I would argue that, to a large extent, presence is the lyric component of argument. The purest deduction is an abstract set of statements which are relationally valid; the purest induction is a set of examples in apposition. Deduction is typically LH; induction is typically RH. Rhetoric—as Aristotle posited—must use both deduction and induction, for rhetorical situations and subject matter are both right-handed and left-handed.

This discussion of presence leaves me dissatisfied, uneasy, realizing as I do that it consists largely of hints and generalities when the topic assuredly deserves a more thorough handling. Yet I have decided not to omit this section, for I would hope my stumbles, misfires, and occasional insights will generate interest and further thought and research.

Conclusion

Earl Miner has addressed himself to brain theory as it relates to the old speculation about literature as knowledge. Miner tells us that

> the poet has not the Eureka discovery but the constant assistance of the right-hemispheric Muse. The artist must draw continually on typical right hemi-spheric activity. When that proves infeasible, "inspiration" is gone, "invention" is dried up. And while sustaining creativity with the right, the artist must also continually draw on left-hemispheric activity for elaboration and consistency of detail. Much more must the poet among artists rely on the linguistic performance of the left, as well as transformations of other things on the left, to give his sustained creativity an intelligibility and word-brightness. It is such distinctions that give aesthetic knowledge its appositional character, its virtual or provisional status.[59]

From the standpoint of the aesthetic reader, bihemispheric activity seems equally crucial. For example, I have assembled some evidence (tentative though it may be) that extremely LH readers have no sense of the kind of episodic knowledge that poetry conveys. A typical comment, from one of my friends, is that poems and stories are "meaningless" to him: he is unable to imagine or visualize the synecdochic content.

If my speculations are correct, poetry is the paradoxical attempt to convey episodic knowledge verbally, which, of course, can never be totally successful.

My friend Jay Martin has posited that Henry Miller confronted himself with a dual problem, to speak the unspeakable and to say the unsayable. As both Miller and D. H. Lawrence demonstrated, the unspeakable can be spoken, though often at enormous personal risk and sacrifice; however, each also demonstrated the ultimate futility of attempting to say the unsayable, and both artists, late in their careers, turned to painting.

In an inspired, fascinating, and outrageous book, *The Origin of Consciousness in the Breakdown of the Bicameral Mind*, Julian Jaynes has posited that consciousness as we know it developed very late in the evolution of humanity.[60] Lawrence and Miller struggled in their work to reunite consciousness, to bring about a harmonious balance between the propositional knowledge of the LH and the appositional knowledge of the RH, and in this, I think they were typical of all poets.

But, of course, our concern is not with brain physiology and most assuredly not with cell structure and function. In fact, the rhetorician is not so much interested in brain as in mind.

Modern brain studies—as this discussion has tried to show—give us a new and unique understanding of mind, which must result in productive new directions for theorizing, scholarship, and experimentation in rhetoric and stylistics. If the paper stimulates that activity, it will have served its purpose.

DAVID BARTHOLOMAE

Released into Language: Errors, Expectations, and the Legacy of Mina Shaughnessy

At the bedrock level of my thinking about this is the sense that language is power, and that, as Simone Weil says, those who suffer from injustice most are the least able to articulate their suffering; and that the silent majority, if released into language, would not be content with a perpetuation of the conditions which have betrayed them. But this notion hangs on a special conception of what it means to be released into language: not simply learning the jargon of an elite, fitting unexceptionably into the status quo, but learning that language can be used as a means of changing reality.—
Adrienne Rich, "Teaching Language in Open Admissions (1972)" in *On Lies, Secrets and Silence*

I

When Adrienne Rich reprinted her essay "Teaching Language in Open Admissions" in 1979,[1] she added in a headnote that the "profound" experiment of open admissions was, perhaps, "naively optimistic," citing a history of broken promises, disappointments and betrayals. Basic writing teachers found themselves overworked, underpaid and often excluded from the protection of tenure-track positions. Working-class and minority students were left to compete for resources which, she said, should have been open to all. And, in a final image, Rich added that "on the corner of Broadway near where I live, I see young people whose like I knew ten years ago as college students 'hanging out,' brown-bagging, standing in short skirts and high-heeled boots in doorways waiting for a trick, or being dragged into the car of a plumed and sequined pimp."

I imagine that all of us who began teaching, or who began teaching seriously, in the late '60s and early '70s have stories to document our various disappointments, including our disappointing realization that the best teachers we knew could not or did not transform American society, the university system, or the cities we lived in. As Mina Shaughnessy convincingly and eloquently argued, however, it is teachers' expectations that justify a curriculum and enable students to imagine the radical transformation that can make learning more than a gesture of obedience to those in power or an accommodation to the status quo.

In reprinting her essay, Rich acknowledged her debt to Mina Shaughnessy, from whom, she says, "I learned—in a time and place where pedagogic romanticism and histrionics were not uncommon—a great deal about the ethics and integrity of teaching." Shaugnessy remains a figure who can teach us much about the ethics and integrity of teaching. Her work was cautious and meticulous. It made no promises about a new society, but showed us, I think, how to pay careful, sympathetic attention to the experience of students who were being released into language and, in particular, into a language that belonged to others, not to them—that belonged to us and to our universities, to our projects and agendas and our peculiar notions of power and freedom. The question remains whether entering that language, entering the privileged discourse of an academic community, can be more than either learning the jargon of an elite or fitting unexceptionably into the status quo.

Shaughnessy taught us to understand the problems and achievements of basic writers at a time when both were hidden to the profession, and in doing so she made possible a new kind of college English class—a class for academically unprepared students that could provide both access to college reading and writing tasks and an orientation to the goals and values of academic life. This was her charge to the profession—to teach not only skills but also an understanding of context and purpose, so that the act of writing could enable students, as she said, to begin their lives anew. I would like to review her contribution to the teaching of English and return, at the end of my essay, to the way she speaks to us still in the current debates over the literacy crisis.[2]

II

I have a vivid memory of attending the 1975 MLA Convention in San Francisco and hearing Mina Shaughnessy give a talk at the plenary session of the newly formed Division on Writing. It was a time when I was struggling to come to terms with the new direction in my professional life imposed by my first full-time appointment as a basic writing teacher and an administrator in charge of a basic writing curriculum. I had committed my career to the students she called Basic Writers and to the task of easing their precarious entry into the world of the university. At the same time, however, I was painfully aware that my ability to understand or alter their actual performance as writers was severely limited. It was a time of crisis, a crisis I found I shared with most everyone I met who was doing this kind of teaching and taking it seriously. The crisis had partly to do with the enormity of the task presented to us, having to make writers out of young adults who, many of them, had done almost no writing at all. But the crisis was due as well to the fact that we were so profoundly unprepared and that the existing models of instruction, what there were, so often ran against both our common sense and our sense of justice.

Professor Shaughnessy's talk, entitled "Diving In: An Introduction to Basic Writing,"[3] outlined a kind of pilgrim's progress, where the pilgrim was the basic writing teacher struggling to evolve a pedagogy consistent with the needs of students and the requirements of conscience. Shaughnessy saw teachers' development in a series of stages, each stage punctuated by a crisis when the existing metaphors—metaphors for teaching and for writing—became inadequate and had to be replaced by new ones. Her talk was given a resounding reception, and the reason for this reception, I think, was that she had given labels and order to the discouraging confusion of our professional lives, and she had done so in a way that made us believe that growth was possible (and occurring). Through her own tremendous warmth and dignity, she gave the work we were doing a dignity, humanity, and complexity that made it seem the proper focus of a professional life.

In the talk, after describing the stages in which the teachers are preoccupied with their students' perceived incompetence (these stages are called, drawing upon familiar metaphors, "Guarding the Tower" and "Converting the Natives"), Shaughnessy went on to describe a point where, faced with the continual evidence that the existing notions of who these students are and how they must be taught are inadequate, teachers reconceive the problem. Rather than ask, "How is it that these students cannot learn simple lessons?" they learn to recognize the way in which these lessons are not simple at all, that, in fact, they only appear simple to those who have already learned them. And, as Shaughnessy observes,

> This insight leads our teacher to the third stage of his development, which I will name SOUNDING THE DEPTHS, for he turns now to the careful observation not only of his students and their writing, but of himself as a writer and teacher, seeking a deeper understanding of the behavior called writing and of the special difficulties his students have in mastering that skill. ("Diving In," 236)

This stage in the growth of a teacher can lead to the fourth stage, "Diving In," the point at which a teacher turns to other disciplines, such as linguistics and developmental psychology, in order to gather new data and new research methods to develop the kind of systematic inquiry that can transform the study of basic writing into a discipline.

For many teachers, the starting point for such a study is Shaugnessy's book, *Errors and Expectations*.[4] The book provides, literally, the record of her reading of four thousand student essays written by incoming freshmen at City College of the City University of New York between 1970 and 1974. The purpose of the study was to "be precise about the types of difficulties to be found in basic writing (BW) papers at the outset and, beyond that, to demonstrate how the sources of those difficulties can be explained without recourse to such pedagogically empty terms as 'handicapped' or 'disadvantaged.' " The book contains many examples of student writing, each included to "deepen one's sense of pattern and thereby [develop] the ability to make swift assessments and classifications of writing difficulties." Her study provides both a lesson in how to read this peculiar genre of student prose and a model of what it means to know one's students and, through such knowledge, become a teacher.

Shaughnessy's work, then, is an exercise in classification and interpretation, and the method is basically inductive. Rather than beginning with a set of rules—rules meant to describe "correct" writing—and letting those rules generate a pedagogy for the unruly, she begins at a more appropriate beginning, with the writing of basic writers, in order to discover categories of error, characteristic patterns of variance from the standard written idiom. Through a close reading of this staggering number of essays, she catalogues and describes errors of the following broad types (and these labels provide the chapter headings): Punctuation and Handwriting, Syntax, Common (errors of tense, inflection and agreement), Spelling, Vocabulary, and errors in performance Beyond the Sentence. By studying errors in the context of students' actual performance, Shaughnessy allows us to see basic writers as writers rather than as a group lacking skills that are somehow acquired prior to writing. This perspective acknowledges the place of error in all writing (including our own), and it provides a way of seeing error in the context of attempts at communication and understanding, where writing is an attempt to approximate a discourse and not just another way of taking a test.

Shaughnessy's study insists, then, that teachers and students see error relative to an actual writing situation, where some errors are serious and some not so serious depending on a student's project and a reader's responses. Shaughnessy goes one step further, however. The significance of various errors, she argues, must also be perceived in the context of an instructional sequence and in the context of research on language development. (I'll talk more about this research later.) If we ask students to take on a way of "talking" that is not immediately their own (and we do this when we ask any student to write), we are inviting them to make mistakes, to become confused and awkward, to err in reaching beyond their immediate skill. Some error, in other words, can be seen as a sign of growth, as a sign of students' implicit faith in writing and their willingness to take risks and experiment with a language that is not "naturally" or immediately their own. If errors—errors of syntax, errors in word choice, errors of judgment—can be seen as evidence of students' attempts to approximate the language of a more privileged group (of those who speak and write freely at the university, for example), then it may not be at all appropriate to point to an error and say, "Don't do that." To say that is to say "Don't do more than you can do," a directive that will most likely be taken for exactly what it represents by students who are excluded from the mainstream of university life. "Don't make mistakes," "Don't use jargon," "Be simple and direct"—all of these phrases quickly translate into "Don't try to be what you are not" or, more succinctly, "Go away."

The value of Shaughnessy's work extends in several directions. The method of analysis and system of classification provide the basic grammar and vocabulary for all further studies of error in writing.[5] And an understanding of the method of analysis, more than the specific exercises, enables teachers to carry the genius of the book to their own classrooms. As teachers and students learn to perceive patterns in the apparent confusion of student writing, that writing comes to represent something other than confusion. Such a process puts students in a position to objectify the strategies, rules, and ad hoc heuristics buried in their use of the language of written discourse (a language which they too easily assume uses them). Rather than sitting down to a workbook to learn the English sentence, students can begin with the study of their own sentences. And such a pedagogy frees the teacher from the faulty logic that connects a sign with a cause, the logic that has allowed teachers to conclude that a student misspells because he can't spell or writes a sentence fragment because he can't write a sentence. In place of this Shaughnessy offers both a theory of error that allows us to see error as other than random and a method for analyzing error as part of the process of articulation—where an error can be seen in relation to a student's attempt to cope simultaneously with the demands of a language, a rhetoric, and a task.

Because of this theory of error, the book can be seen as a central document in the general scholarly attempt to develop a philosophy of composition, one that can inform composition teaching and research at the broadest levels. If error can be seen, as Shaughnessy demonstrates, as something other than an a accident of composing or a failure to learn—if, that is, we can discover regular, predictable patterns of error in student writing—then it will be those patterns rather than the correct features that will provide the key to learning about the development of writing ability, since those errors provide insight into the most profound contact between the learner and that which is being learned.

There are, of course, errors that are accidents, slips of the pen, but there are many errors that are not, and some of these errors are the logical products of idiosyncratic rule systems. If language learning is a process of forming and testing hypotheses about language in order to bring idosyncratic systems into alignment with conventional ones, then the regular but unconventional features in student writing will reveal the rules and hypotheses that govern students' idiosyncratic or approximate versions of the standard idiom.

A basic writing class is the place where this conflict between idiosyncracy and convention is acted out most dramatically. A student doesn't know how to spell a word, but he invents a spelling and he invents it not out of nothing but out of his understanding of the rules that govern the way words are spelled in English. A student uses commas and periods in a manner that seems to have little to do with the structure of the sentence, but, perhaps, she is applying her version of some advice she once heard about long pauses and short pauses or about marking off "complete thoughts." The syntax of a sentence in a student paper becomes "derailed" (to use Shaughnessy's metaphor) when a student presses forward, following the various (but perhaps competing) available sentence patterns for an imagined utterance. A verb is incorrectly inflected but this can be seen to be the result of interference of spoken with written language. In each of these cases one can see a student acting systematically from within a system that challenges or misapproximates the standard system governing conventional, written English. When a student enters into the language of others, when that language is not a language of the student's own invention, he or she approximates—but only approximates—the sentence that is sanctioned or expected by the closed world the student seeks to enter.

This method of analysis can be extended, however. The moment teachers move their attention beyond the sentence, where errors are errors in taste, judgment, or understanding, this procedure for interpreting student error becomes more challenging and, in a way, more revealing. When a student fails to complete an argument or to develop a discussion or to put two sentences together, and when a student fails to do this as basic writers often fail to do it, then the hidden rules and conventions of academic discourse become suddenly visible. The errors represent the fault lines when two systems—an idiosyncratic system and a conventional system—press against each other. Shaughnessy's work suggests this as an area of research, but error beyond the sentence, particularly in the work of the basic writer, has received little direct scholarly attention.

It is here, I think, at the intersection of idiosyncracy and convention, where the skilled and unskilled adult writer have the same writing problem, where the sign of failure for one is the sign of achievement for the other. Both stand (if not for the same reason) outside the predictable range of set, prepackaged discourse. It's the average writer—the "C" student who appears with telling regularity in every class, year after year—who writes the predictable five-paragraph theme in support of a commonplace ("Sports are valuable because they teach us sportsmanship.") Both the skilled and unskilled writer are characterized by the fact that their writing locates them outside of, in opposition to, that conventional discourse with its preset contours, phrases, examples, and outcomes.

Contemporary literary criticism celebrates an image of the writer as one who no longer resides comfortably within a field of conventional learning and conventional discourse, who must, in fact, push against the force and dominance of conventional systems in order to preserve an identity (or the fiction of an identity) as an "I," a speaking subject. Here, for example, is Edward Said's account of the position of the contemporary critic. It could, in its outlines, stand as a representation of the situation and the dilemma of the basic writer:

> The problem we face today when we study Joyce, or when, untrained in classics or religion, we read Hooker, or when we deploy psychology in the study of a literary text, is a problem of irregularity, of discontinuity. That is, less background, less formal training, less prescribed and systematic information, is assumed before one begins to read, write, or work. Thus when one begins to write today one is necessarily more of an autodidact, gathering or making up the knowledge one needs in the course of creating.

Deprived of a set, "knowable" cultural tradition, and working within an ethos that is set against the commonplace, Said's modern writer is a "wanderer, going from place to place for his material, but remaining a man essentially *between* homes."[6] For an expert writer, this is a willed condition, something one achieves by writing, and not a function of one's high school education or socioeconomic status. Said's metaphor, however, also describes the basic writer, wandering between the old neighborhood and the university, belonging to neither, and left to invent academic expertise every time he sits down to write. To the degree to which the basic writer is aware of this dilemma, of the problem of convention and one's relation to convention (and I believe this is one of the first lessons a basic writer learns), he has a more mature, more complex understanding of writing than does the average student, the student who is comfortable with the five-paragraph theme. The basic writer, and I'm speaking now from my own experience in the classroom, is closer to that orientation toward language we call "critical thinking" than the mainstream freshman who decided early on that correct, orderly prose was good enough, and that the conventional five-paragraph theme was an adequate representation of a person's experience and intellect.

The image of the writer as one who stands outside a closed discourse (wandering between homes) underlies the current literature on Writing across the Curriculum, where a student on the outside works to write his way inside an academic discipline, like anthropology, by learning to write as an anthropologist, by learning to approximate the discourse that constitutes that discipline and represents its specialized, privileged way of seeing and reporting on the world.[7] The experience of the basic writer, as Shaughnessy demonstrated, allows us to resee our own experience, showing us the hidden rules, agendas, and projects that underlie a way of talking and writing that we take for granted. The study of error beyond the sentence, particularly those errors produced by students most dramatically excluded from the privileged world of academic discourse, even the generalized discourse of the freshman English class, can reveal rules that govern our "normal" ways of establishing authority, marshalling evidence, extending a discussion, and completing an argument. When we come to better understand what is involved as a student moves into a discourse, we can be better teachers of writing. We can teach more, that is, than the "jargon of an elite."

This, I think, is an honorable goal. It is a way of allowing students to enter into and participate in our academic projects, to learn them from the inside, as writers, rather than from the outside, through textbooks and tests and papers that ask students to repeat names and dates and canonical interpretations. It is honorable, I think, even if we teach students to see the world as we see it or to read primary texts as we read them, even if we do not teach students to use language to "change reality" and undo or deconstruct the systems we, as professionals, labor to preserve and extend.

III

The theory of error in *Errors and Expectations* is represented not so much by abstract discussion as by the way Shaughnessy selects and analyzes her examples from student essays. While much of the energy in the book is spent looking at student writing in order to classify types of errors, Shaughnessy offers more than just a list, since an equal amount of time is spent inferring the emotional, linguistic, rhetorical, and intellectual context within which a particular student was writing. These inferences provide the foundation for conclusions about the causes of the errors themselves. Let me try to piece together just a short example of this process of interpretation.

Shaughnessy's discussion of syntax is based upon the assumption that a reader can move inside the head of a basic writer and reconstruct both the conditions that led to the "derailment" of syntax and the meaning that was scrambled by the lack of syntactic options available to the writer while in the throes of composing. What we're offered is a narrative that fills in what would be a pause in a transcript of a writer composing orally:

> In the following sentence . . . the writer has modified the noun *job* by simple expedient of placing his adjectival elements after the noun, a "logical" strategy

but not unfortunately a conventional one unless he makes use of certain forms that attach such elements to the sentence:

> Now mostly every job you go to get *worthwhile* or *making a decent salary something to live off* is asking for a college degree.

A similar problem arises in this sentence, where the writer's thought calls for some kind of appositional structure that will further define "intellectual period." For want of such a structure, he relies on juxtaposition alone:

> I think the author tried to show, that due to the intellectual period in which we live *the need to categorize things in every respect of life* we tend to lose the natural beauty of what is happening around us. (*Errors and Expectations*, p. 66)

In the section on punctuation, and in particular after some examples of writing where commas and periods have been omitted, transposed, or interchanged, Shaughnessy draws the following conclusions:

> What one senses through such punctuation is a caution about losing control of the sentence by allowing it to become too long—too full, that is, of embedded structures, which to the unpracticed writer may well echo their deeper origins as sentences. Yet combined with this effort to simplify individual sentences grammatically by breaking them up into smaller segments is another effort to link sentences rhetorically by pressing commas into service as conjunctions, by over using words like *and, but, that* or *because*, or by ignoring terminal punctuation altogether. (*Errors and Expectations*, p. 28)

What is remarkable here, aside from the sophistication of the analysis, is the tremendous sympathy that enables her to enter into the minds of student writers, and writers whose writing and thinking are so unlike her own.

With some notable exceptions, much of the research done on composition before the publication of *Errors and Expectations* was represented by frequency counts and computer tabulations of objective features of prose (as, for example, in the studies of syntax). It was not uncommon, in fact, to hear statistical research being praised at the expense of the anecdotal accounts that had characterized another tradition of scholarship in composition. Much of that criticism, and much of the heavy praise for "objective" research, came from people who didn't teach writing and who lacked the day-by-day contact with writers and their problems that makes the impressions and speculations of writing teachers, at least the best of them, like Shaughnessy, so valuable. Shaughnessy, like Ann Berthoff, has demonstrated how teaching and research can together be part of a professional life.[8]

Shaughnessy also helped to return a sensitivity to context to composition research. Her analysis of the work of basic writers is grounded in her reading of a writer's situation, a situation richly imagined, acknowledging the social and psychological context for an act of writing. She brings impression, speculation, and interpretation together with theory and systematic analysis to give us a more complete picture of a writer at work than any we previously had. In *Errors and Expectations,* she reconstructs the way writers work, the way they think and feel, and this provides crucial information about the composing process. Much of the most valuable research of the last few years, drawing on case study analysis and protocol analysis, has extended this view of the composing process of basic writers.[9]

IV

One could imagine Shaughnessy's study ending with the categories of errors she finds, but such a taxonomy, as she says, would misrepresent the complexity of the problems and possible responses. Any list of "Basic Writer's Errors" would only become another version of the "25 Common Errors Writers Must Avoid." The value of the taxonomy in the book is the method it defines, where one looks long and closely at a student's writing to determine what patterns emerge. Through the perception of such patterns, one can discover that errors are not random, but products of systematic decision-making—that is, evidence that there is a grammar to students' ungrammaticality—and one can begin to speculate on the causes of the specific errors, rather than begin with the buckshot approach of teaching to all possible error. What makes this book so valuable, then, is the model of interpretation it provides. As Shaughnessy says (speaking, again, of punctuation errors):

> It becomes important, then, to do more than list, prescriptively, the ways in which the student breaks with the conventional code of punctuation. Rather, the teacher must try to decipher the individual student's code, examining samples of his writing as a scientist might, searching for patterns or explanations, listening to what the student says about punctuation, and creating situations in the classroom that encourage students to talk openly about what they don't understand. (*Errors and Expectations*, p. 40)

It is important to add that the power derived from this kind of inquiry is not limited to the teacher alone: when students learn to see their writing in this way, to shift their perspective and view their writing as a reader, to see the decisions made and the options lost, they learn the key to controlling and experimenting with their language.

To say, then, that we must enable students to achieve a distance from what they do is not the same as saying that we must teach them skills they don't possess or that we must teach them something they are incapable of doing, although these are the prejudices that continue to characterize most basic writing courses. In the face of a seeming chaos of error, teachers often make the wholesale judgment that such writing is evidence that students "can't write a sentence" or "don't know how to think" and proceed to begin at what is taken as the beginning by teaching the sentence, or the grammar of the sentence, and thought or paragraph patterns. Writing and thinking are conceived, then, in terms of constituent skills, skills which could be defined, outlined on the board, and taught one by one.

Such a pedagogy meets the immediate needs of teachers frustrated by their failure to understand what could be happening in the heads of students whose writing is so radically different from their own. And it is the convenience of this pedagogy, which frees all parties, teachers and students, from ever having to talk about writing, that leads teachers to hang on to it in the face of evidence that it produces limited returns—in the face, too, of evidence not only that these students can, of course, think, but also that in their conversations and in their essays they can produce many coherent and controlled utterances. The skills curriculum is founded neither on any investigation of the language students produce nor on any systematic investigation into how writing skills are acquired.

Such negative judgments about these writers are not based on a notion of fluency but of competence, and talk about competence puts everyone on shaky ground. A teacher I once worked with came to me with a student paper that began with the following: "A decision that I had to make that didn't came easy. The time was when I had to diside if I what to play basketball in my last year of junior high school (eight grade)." This instructor said in despair that not only did this student not know how to spell or how to write a sentence, but he didn't even know the difference between "what" and "want." The words on the paper were allowed to stand for the student, and the only meaning to be found there was derived from the single perception that the language went counter to the reader's expectations. As a consequence, the teacher concluded that the student must have suffered from some species of conceptual deficit, not even knowing the difference between "what" and "want." But this is simply not adequate to explain why, for instance, although "diside" is misspelled, "decision" is not, or why the paper contained more correctly than incorrectly formed sentences. With a closer look, it is not difficult to see the syntax behind the passage above. The student began by stating his subject, "a decision that I had to make that didn't came easy," but either got lost or felt it would be appropriate to stop after the long restrictive clause and restated the subject, "the time was," and began again to complete the sentence. And, finally, assumptions about this student's incompetence don't account for the fact that, when asked to read the passage aloud, the student automatically corrected "if I what to play" and "eight grade."

This teacher was unable to read a paper like his student's, to pay the kind of attenton to the text that would allow him to see the deviations from the conventions of the standard dialect, and to determine their meaning through the context of perceived intention. This failure is a peculiar one given the fact that this reader spent most of his adult life perfecting his skills as a reader of texts and could, if confronted with an e. e. cummings poem, for instance, account for the ways it deviates from conventional expectations in elaborate and sympathetic ways. He would see as much meaning, in fact, in the deviations themselves as he would in the ostensible, paraphraseable message presented in the words. Our literary training prepares us to see literature as a record of struggles with words and meaning, but to shift this habit of attention from supposedly "elevated" modes of expression to the verbal wrestlings of our students does not come easily: the nature of and the reasons for the violation of literary conventions are so much more evident to us than the nature of and the reasons for the violations of the conventions of what is taken to be a standard idiom. In our students' writing the variation is not seen as an expression of deliberate or learned behavior, but only as evidence of the absence of learning or the lack of deliberation. The individual errors are allowed to stand for Error, the proof that the poor kids can't write.

One basic principle emerges from the study of error in *Errors and Expectations*. To an inexperienced teacher, the writing of basic writers may appear to contain nothing but a chaos of error, but a close, careful analysis will reveal very little that is random or "illogical" in what they have written. The errors are not evidence that basic writers are slow or incapable of learning but, as Shaughnessy argues, that these writers are beginners and must, like all beginners, learn by making mistakes. And, in fact, the keys to their development as writers "often lie in the very features in their writing that English teachers have been trained to brush aside with a marginal code letter or a scribbled injunction to 'Proofread!' "

Shaughnessy's idea that errors may hold the "key" to basic writers' development as writers is important and needs further discussion. One aspect of this truth should be obvious by now. If we make a careful inventory of the nature and cause of the errors unique to a particular writer, our instruction can be not only efficient but more humane. Rather than conclude that a student can't write a sentence, we can conclude that he often comes unglued with embeddings signalled by "wh" words. Or rather than conclude that a student can't spell, we may find that she confuses homonyms (like "their" and "there") or has trouble because he neither speaks nor hears certain final consonants. Each case would call for a specific pedagogy. And, of course, it is comforting to both teacher and student alike to discover that in a paper containing perhaps thirteen errors, the errors fall into three basic patterns. This kind of close and systematic analysis of error provides, then, both a pedagogical and diagnostic tool.

Shaughnessy also argues that error is a key to understanding language development. This can best be explained by referring to two concepts drawn from the study of error in second language learning.[10] The first says that where a student is working with a new language and is not yet fluent, any statement deliberately intended to communicate will be meaningful. It will be systematic, rule-defined, and coherent. It will, that is, possess a grammar. And, secondly, the rules of that grammar will be derived from:

1.) the rules of the first language (which, in this case, would be the mother tongue or spoken dialect—the analogy between learning to write and learning a second language is complicated by the fact that writing calls upon skills—like punctuating—that are in addition to oral skills and not learned the same way or defined by the same rules),

2.) the rules of the target language (which here would be the dialect of formal, written discourse),

3.) some truly idiosyncratic dialect that belongs only to this writer at this point in his development.[11]

The best evidence, then, that a speaker possesses the construction rules necessary to acquire language is the occurrence of systematic errors, or rule-governed behavior.

In the case of a writer learning to use the formal, written dialect, what we see during the learning process is either the transfer of one "language" to a situation where it is inappropriate or the creation of an "interlanguage," an "approximate system" which is evidence of the writer's transitional competence.[12] As the writer tries to approximate the vocabulary and movement of academic prose, her approximations are often only partially conceived and, at some points, she reverts to the spoken idiom, relying on its rules and strategies. Or, in the case of an approximate system, an interlangage, she relies on her knowledge that language can be made predictable and either overgeneralizes or creates a hypothesis that is "false." The interlanguage is not necessarily appropriate to an audience expecting either the first or second language, but it is coherent in itself and certainly not a sign of random behavior. In fact, it could be said to represent a particular stage of learning.

The concept of an approximate system is important for the way it modifies the notion of a spoken dialect interfering with the written dialect. The concept of interference makes the learner passive, caught between social or class roles, one of which must be overcome. Seeing those errors which reveal an interlanguage or approximate system allows us to see the ways in which basic writers are actively generating rules and strategies, and it allows us to chart and draw upon their particular learning styles.

Such an analysis allows us to distinguish three "types" of error, types that correspond to the categories in each area of Shaughnessy's study. First there are errors that are truly accidental. These may be slips of the pen, the kind that are common to all writers, where we leave out a word, or write "an" for "and," or write a word we never had in mind at all or jumble syntax as our hand rushes to keep up with our brain. Teaching to this kind of error requires that we teach students to see it in proofreading, often a surprisingly difficult task for writers unused to seeing writing as black marks on a page. Secondly, there are also errors caused when one dialect interferes with another, and this is not only a matter of idiom but also, given the unique contours of the formal written dialect and the difficulties of producing words on a page rather than sounds into the air, a whole range of other errors as well, from errors of syntax to errors caused by habits of pronunciation, as when "given" is substituted for "giving" because the two sound the same in speech. The third kind of error comes from the application of rules that belong only to the writer's approximate system, where the writer uses his own powers of analogical thinking to make an unfamiliar and irregular language predictable. There is evidence of this, for example, when a student adds inflectional endings to infinitives, as in this sentence: "There was plenty the boy had *to learned* about birds."

The conclusion that Shaughnessy draws from this third type of error is that "The student who learned to make these errors reveals through them all the linguistic sophistication he needs to correct them." The issue, then, is not a student's capacity to master formal English but "the priority this kind of problem ought to have in the larger scheme of learning to write," the formulation of a pedagogy that will enable us to assist the natural learning process, and the willingness of the student to spend the time it takes to learn. A theory of error does not carry with it any magic solutions. For both student and teacher this kind of learning means hard work with few immediate rewards. A theory of error will, however, suggest a place to begin.

The theory of error that runs through *Errors and Expectations* suggests its own pedagogy, one that is radically different from most existing strategies. The pedagogy that breaks writing up into constituent skills, as "skills" are defined by the traditional study of sentences and paragraphs, makes no sense if the source of error is the conflict caused by the interference of two existing grammars or the result of incomplete or inappropriate generalizations about language. Such courses, which rely heavily on workbook drill, deny both the student's individual competence and her own sequence for learning. And the "skills" assumed to be basic or constituent have little to do with the way writing proceeds or language is learned. The pedagogy suggested by contrastive analysis, where a teacher uses grammatical analysis to describe the points of variance between the first language and the target language in order to predict problem areas, can be criticized from the evidence that the existing interlanguage is, in fact, idiosyncratic, unique in many respects to each writer and unique to a specific stage in that writer's development. It also seems as though errors due to an idiosyncratic rule system are much more frequent than errors linked to language transfer.[13]

What we are left to conclude is that one important skill basic writers need to learn is how to read their own papers, the same skill needed by their teachers. Students need to learn how to distance themselves from and analyze the writing on the page in order to determine what information that writing holds about their performance as a writer. This is probably the most difficult skill a teacher has to teach, since a student's failure to "see" errors or to "see" the marks on the page or to "see" the information carried in his sentence—and to see what possibilities each of these reveals—is not usually due to laziness or a failure to read "carefully" but to the very real perceptual and conceptual difficulty of objectifying language and one's performance as a writer.[14] When asked to read their own writing aloud, students typically hear a voice but don't see black and white marks on the page and, in many cases, automatically read the correct form. They read in terms of their own grammatical competence.

Much of the research on error that immediately followed *Errors and Expectations* searched for the cause of error (see, for example, the essays by Ken Bruffee and Donald Freeman in this volume). The belief was that the more we knew about the causes of error, the better we could tailor instruction to head off those errors in the first place. This direction for error analysis has been complemented by recent research, much of it at the University of Pittsburgh, directed at the procedures students use to correct errors. Rather than asking what the source of an error might be, this research turns to protocols of students trying to correct errors they've identified in their own writing to see what they do next. If students have incorrectly marked sentence boundaries, this research is interested in both where, on a second pass, students put commas and periods and how they describe what they are doing when they change the punctuation in a paragraph or an essay. Students can adjust the rules they use to mark sentences, and their next approximation, which will be driven by a revision of the rule that produced the error in the first place, will give us access to the range and variation of their understanding of (in this case) the rules governing the identification of sentence boundaries. In addition students' own reports on the changes they make allow us insight into what might be called the "editing process." Glynda Hull has shown, for example, that students will follow one of three correction strategies: comprehending, intuiting, and consulting. In order to see and correct some errors students must percieve that something is wrong with the meaning of a text. Correction, here, begins with an act of comprehension. This is often the case with syntax errors. To see and correct other errors, students must consult an existing verbal representation of a rule ("Let's see, you use commas when . . ."). Or, as is often the case, students turn to their sense that something is wrong, even if the "wrongness" cannot be described, and intuit that a certain change is appropriate. While this taxonomy can be used to catalog types of errors, it has immediate pedagogical value since it provides insight into the procedures novice and expert writers use to solve the types of linguistic problems that are part of the act of editing. Students need to learn to read their own writing, then, but they also need to learn to edit.[15]

There is, of course, another problem in learning to edit, perhaps one almost as difficult, and that is motivation. How does one convince a student that it's worth the time and effort to see that a piece of writing is correct? The only answer, I suspect, is to enable students to see that correctness is in service of something other than producing a correct paper, something the student can believe in. Since it is no longer enough to appeal to correctness as a sign of godliness or gentility, this is a perplexing problem. Shaughnessy suggests that we appeal to the needs of a reader and what happens to that reader when the static of error gets in the way of the information on the page.

These are the problems teachers should be devoting themselves to, and the pedagogies that emerge must offer strategies for editing, since insisting on correctness at the moment of articulation enforces a rigor we seldom demand of ourselves. We rely on our freedom to go back and hold our writing at arm's length. And, while students need to learn how and when to worry about correctness, they also need to learn how and when to tap into the generative power of language, which requires that the editor be shut off and we be free to experiment and take risks.

If a student can learn to read his own writing as an editor, then it would appear that the most useful strategy would be something like the following. Those errors, particularly accidental errors, that are slips of the pen or result from distractions caused by the demands of making letters on a page, will disappear as a writer becomes more coordinated and more fluent. The same is true of many interference errors, since practice with the formal dialect will make this peculiar vocabulary, idiom, and syntax more readily available, and less likely to be blurred or confused. If these errors will disappear in reasonable time anyway, and research should give us fairly reliable information on what they are, then it makes no sense to waste time teaching to them. Not only is such teaching inefficient, but it is also likely to produce the kind of nervousness about making mistakes that will keep a student from experimenting with a new language in the first place.

Beyond this "level" of error would be the errors that students, with encouragement and guidance, have the resources to correct on their own as they become more proficient as readers. In a conference, a teacher can enable a student to "see" errors he has missed in his own editing. This is often best achieved by reading the paper aloud, or having the student read the paper aloud, stopping to correct mistakes and to explain what he is doing and why. When dealing with whole classes of students, teachers can assign students the task of regularly circling their own and each other's errors, and teachers can highlight an area of text, drawing a line next to three lines of prose on a student's paper and telling her that somewhere in there, there is an error. And, after students have found errors in their own writing, it should be up to them to find patterns among those errors, to give them names and find their own resources for correction. This exercise begins slowly and needs prodding, but it can become the most effective strategy in a teacher's repertoire, since it draws upon the student's own language competence. It encourages students to practice authority over their writing and responsibility for it.

Where error is the result of some idiosyncratic set of rules, this kind of self-consciousness about one's language is most important. We need to develop methods of bookkeeping to distinguish between those patterns of error that mark a stage of lerning and those that indicate that learning has stopped, where the learner is no longer testing rules but relying on set patterns. Where, then, a learner has overgeneralized a rule, drill is not an appropriate strategy at all, since, if learning is going to take place, the writer must turn his attention from the percepton of rules to the activity of testing rules and seeing their limits.[16]

What would remain untouched after all this is a core of error that the student cannot find or does not have the resources to correct, and this would require some formal instruction. The difficulty here is finding a way to talk about the writing, since such talk will inevitably revert to grammatical terms and concepts. Shaughnessy isolates four key grammatical concepts teachers and students will need to share for such conversations to be possible: the concept of the sentence, of inflection, of tense, and of agreement. With each key concept, Shaughnessy offers examples of how each might best be taught. The great responsibility that faces the teacher and the profession, however, is developing the ability to determine the occasion when a student's problems require this kind of instruction. Diagnosis may be more an art than a science. The problem is partly knowing *how* to make such a diagnosis, but it is also a problem of knowing when. When in the course of working with a student can we determine with authority that such instruction is necessary? And when, given the internal sequence of the student's language development, will such instruction complement rather than hinder the learning process?

Finally, it is interesting to note that in locating the resources needed to draw the sorts of inferences she does about the composing process of her students, Shaughnessy does not refer to the formal study of linguistics or rhetoric but to the information she gets, both directly and indirectly, from her students and her colleagues when they talk about specific papers or problems. And she refers to her own experience "as someone who writes and therefore understands the pressures and peculiarities of that behavior." Shaughnessy is clearly also drawing upon a thorough understanding of developments in linguistics, rhetoric, second language learning, and the range of disciplines brought together in the formal study of the composing process. For the classroom teacher without a familiarity with these disciplines, however, the point is that a key resource is our shared experience as writers. This is where a basic writing teacher's education can begin.

We are bound together by the difficulties and triumphs of expression. This is important for us to know, since it is a corrective to the notion that our students' behavior is alien or incomprehensible, and it is important for our students to know, since it can free them from the damaging belief that through some perverse fate they have been deprived of a gift granted to others. In fact, because writing is such a lonely activity, and writers are bound by the assumptions they carry with them to their desks, it is crucial for students to hear about our struggles with writing and the strategies we've evolved to overcome them. They tend to enter into writing with the belief that good writers sit down, start with an introduction and write through to a conclusion without making any mistakes along the way. Such a vision makes it rather easy to believe one can't write, and it is likely to leave the writer stuck, making his first sentence also his last.

V

Shaughnessy has convincingly demonstrated that "There are 'styles' to being wrong," and that learning to read closely to see the style of error is a crucial skill for a teacher of composition. This is one of the reasons, as I have suggested, that perhaps the best preparation for a composition teacher, including a teacher of basic writing, is a literary education.

A style, as a literary education teaches us, is more than a sign of an individual linguistic performance; a style is allusive, derivative; it refers out to a language that is a cultural legacy and that an individual writer can finally neither invent nor control. Or, as Geoffrey Hartman has recently said, "Style is not cognitive only; it is also recognitive, a signal betraying the writer's relation, or sometimes the relation of a type of discourse, to a historical and social world."[17] "Betraying" is a loaded word here, of course. Shaughnessy charts one form of betrayal when she observes the following about the work of a basic writer:

> Often, but not always, the content that is carried in such writing is short and bare, reinforcing the impression of the reader that this writer is "slow" or intellectually immature. Yet the same student might be a spirited, cogent talker in class. His problem is that he has no access to his thoughts or personal style through the medium of writing and must appear, whenever he writes, as a child. (*Errors and Expectations*, p. 192)

The writer is "betrayed" here because his writing makes him appear slow or stupid, and he is not. He has an adult mind, but he has "no access to his thoughts or his personal style" because of a problem he has with writing.

While it is undoubtedly true that this writer is neither slow nor stupid, Shaughnessy's account of the nature of his problem is sentimental and, as a consequence, not very useful as a description of the relationship between language and thought for a teacher or a researcher considering the tenuous and problematic relations between basic writers and the world of "adult thought." Clearly the student cited above has an adult mind, but it is not the "mind" represented by written, adult, academic discourse. *That* mind does not exist outside of language; it does not stand before language waiting for a language that is fluent enough to express it. That mind is, itself, a discourse.

Shaughnessy acknowledges this at other points in *Errors and Expectations*, although the contradiction is persistent. At times writing is in service of "personal thoughts and styles," and at times it is in service of the institution, an institutional way of thinking and being present in the world.[18] She is, at best, ambivalent in her role as a mediator between the world of the student (which is outside the conventional language of academic discourse) and the world of the university (which is inside).

When, for example, she talks about more advanced student writers, she talks about writers who have moved into a language they do not yet fully control:

> for all the gains in vocabulary that the writer at this stage can claim . . . the pre-packaging feature of language, the possibility of taking over phrases and whole sentences without much thought about them, threatens the writer now as before. The writer, as we have said, inherits the language out of which he must fabricate his own messages. He is therefore in a constant tangle with language, obliged to recognize its public, communal nature and yet driven to invent out of this language his own statements. But invention is difficult at these early stages when the cliches and conventions of the formal style are fresh to the writer and before he is confident or knowledgeable enough to translate more freely into language that is closer to his thoughts. (*Errors and Expectations*, p. 208)

Clearly, knowledge and confidence are necessary goals of a basic writing course, but the key question is whether at the end of a course of instruction students are translating into a language that is closer to their thoughts or closer to ours. The question, I suppose, is whether there is a point at which students are no longer betrayed by the language that represents them on the page. This is, let me add, a pressing pedagogical issue, not just the stuff of debates at meetings of the poststructuralists, since it has to do with the final stages in a basic writing curriculum and the degree to which the work set for students should be overtly and insistently parodic and imitative. Should students, in the end, write *for* the university, or should they write against it or in spite of it?

While Shaughnessy is often ambivalent about this in *Errors and Expectations,* her tendency, I think, is to say that students should write against or in spite of the formal conventions of academic discourse. The adult writing she holds up as a model is by Orwell, Baldwin, and Hoggart, work that she says shows an "easy" merging of experience with idea. She wants to believe that the right use of language can bring together personal experience and the world of ideas while retaining the integrity of each. The movement between experience and idea in the work of Orwell, Baldwin, and Hoggart may show a stylistic ease and grace, but it is dangerous to ignore the difficult personal histories that underlie this artistic achievement. Hoggart, for example, chronicles the pain, loss, and humiliation that was a necessary part of his education away from the working-class home of his family. The ideas that came to represent his experience served also to separate him from that experience, from the past, and from his family; the transition was difficult, at times provisional. The separation was measured by the way he had learned to think and feel as well as by the neighborhood he moved into and the things he did with his time.[19]

Late in her book, where she talks about what students can gain by a course of instruction in basic writing, Shaughnessy speaks of the way that the acquisition of the "language of academia" comes only at the sacrifice of those qualities that give "life," "power," and "authenticity" to her students' writing:

> Many teachers would view any such transposition as an intolerable kind of academic colonizing, discouraging the student from developing his "native" talent with language and imposing upon him a model of competence that is by comparison barren. Yet the differences we note grow out of real situations that will not dissolve simply because of our preferences for expressive over discursive, for personal over public, or spoken over written styles. (*Errors and Expectations,* p. 239)

As I understand professional writing, and by that I mean the writing that does the work of institutions, there is no easy merging of experience with idea, and yet I'll confess that I do not find the model of competence represented by academic writing (including the academic writing done by undergraduates) to be "barren," at least not if the assignments are carefully written and if students are given real work to do.[20] In fact, I think that the styles and projects of academic discourse can be exciting, creative, and liberating, even at the point at which they confine students to work that is, at least for undergraduates, ours and not theirs, and even to the degree to which that writing does not "change reality" or reshape the university and its disciplines. There are reasons, I believe, for students to learn to work within our community that are more important and more powerful than the dream of preserving their freedom.

My purpose here, however, is not to take issue with Shaughnessy's notion of "native" intelligence, but to turn again to the question of literacy and the process by which one acquires the skills of the higher literacy demanded by a university education. This process begins, I believe, when students are released into language, and not when students develop fluency with a neutral, transparent language that allows them access to their personal thoughts. It requires, that is, that students be given access to the culture, the closed culture, of the world they would enter. They must enter another's thoughts by using another's language. The question is whether they can do this and still remain themselves; it is a question of whether they can, as Shaughnessy says, use someone else's language and yet create out of this language their own statements. This is a very complicated and subtle act of appropriation. Teaching it requires a very different understanding of central concepts—"basic skills," "self-expression," "rhetorical patterns"—than that represented by most basic writing courses and most colleges and universities.

Let me turn to two recent proposals for curricula to teach general, cultural literacy. Richard Lanham in *Literacy and the Survival of Humanism* proposes a single conceptual framework—and interpretive scheme—that can unify the university curriculum by organizing and interpreting all texts, artifacts, and varieties of human performance according to a single theory of human behavior.[21] It is this scheme that allows students access to the competing voices and projects of the university community: "One thus avoids with a single step all the protracted and sterile debates about which texts are canonical and which are not, which periods and subjects and which derivative."

At the risk of turning this radical proposal into parody, let me try to summarize Lanham's argument. Human behavior, Lanham says, is governed by three motives: purpose, game, and play. Composition instruction, as Lanham argued earlier in *Style: An Anti-Text*, has tried to banish play and competition by teaching a single-minded rhetoric of purpose (where good writing is clear, brief, and sincere—known as the CBS theory of writing—and never opaque, elaborate, and self-consciously artificial). The university curriculum, in a sense, has followed suit, leaving nonpurposive behavior for literature, creative writing, and other humanities courses, and assuming that the rest of the curriculum is busy training students for a trade or a profession. This split misrepresents the work that goes on in the disciplines, including English, and, according to Lanham, it threatens our well-being.

Students can learn to observe and appreciate the range of our behavior by learning to analyze and imitate the styles of texts. They can learn, that is, to look both "at" and "through" the texts we assign them to read. A text here can be literally a text—a textbook, a literary text, a piece of scholarly writing (it makes no difference which, since any of these can be seen as either working, playing, or competing)—or it can be any variety of human performance. Lanham argues that the university curriculum must "orchestrate" these three motives and that the humanists must "harmonize" them. The starting point for such an education is the composition course:

> The writing course, when it actually works, mixes all three motives just as the curricular purposes mix in good teaching. The study of prose thus provides, once we understand it aright, a model for motive. It can, then, act as a do-it-yourself curriculum guide, can do something for students besides sharpen their verbal pencils.

The writing course is also, however, a training course. In it, students imitate and parody "all kinds of prose," not just the transparent essays (clear, brief, and sincere essays) that model purposive behavior. A composition course like this will, Lanham argues, give students a "conceptual framework that will allow them to find, and to create, some order among the humanistic disciplines," and it will make students "self-conscious about their own complex motives, their layered purposiveness."

This is, clearly, a program of instruction that celebrates the various languages of academic and public life. The chapter of the book that describes the UCLA writing program is a humbler account of what the first steps look like. The basic writing program there, as described elsewhere by Mike Rose, is currently a collection of courses, all of them, however, governed by the powerful principle that the work the students do should situate them in the context of some subject matter and some adult, academic object. Or, as Rose says, "a remedial writing curriculum must fit into the intellectual context of the university. Topics should have academic substance and, when possible, should require the student to work from text."[22] To this degree they follow Lanham's stipulation that composition courses be imitative or parodic and that they provide set interpretive schemes to analyze and connect diverse textual materials.

E. D. Hirsch, speaking in the name of Mina Shaughnessy, has offered a very different proposal, one that places a core curriculum not only at the center of a university education but as a solution to declining writing skills. Hirsch's argument is bold, compelling, and, as he acknowledged, somewhat dangerous. Hirsch argues that while it is possible to talk about generic writing "skills," skills that are independent of any given subject and any approach to and understanding of that subject, those skills alone do not produce writing. What we have ignored, he says, is the cultural aspect of writing. "No amount of training in the skills of composition, in the writing process, and in the basics will by themselves convey the additional cultural information that underlies advancement in general literacy."[23] By "cultural information" he means a general knowledge of names, book titles, key terms, famous ideas and the like. But he means more than this as well:

I said that the craft-approach neglects the cultural dimension of writing. Alternatively, one could say that we have stressed the process and product of writing at the expense of the huge domain of tacit knowledge which is never written down at all, but which, though quite invisible, is just as operative as the visible written words. A writing task could be compared to an iceberg whose visible tip is arrangement, syntax, rhetoric, spelling, coherence and so on, but whose much bigger invisible base is tacit cultural knowledge—not just linguistic knowledge, and knowledge about the topic, but also, and most important, knowledge of what others also know and expect about the topic, about the form, about the writer, and about the world. In short, the cultural dimension is that whole system of unspoken tacit knowledge that is shared between writer and reader.

To give students the cultural literacy they will need in order to be able to write, Hirsch argues, there must be a commonly agreed upon curriculum; educators need to agree about "the *kinds* of materials we shall teach, and also about some of the particular facts and texts we shall teach." And this, he acknowledges, raises difficult and far-reaching political questions.

I think it is possible to agree that certain texts and ideas are important, even central, to a university education. In fact, it is hard to imagine the college or English department that doesn't operate under a tacit agreement to this effect. And, as I've argued, I think that to learn to write students must learn to work their way into the culture of a privileged community. We can speed this process up by providing students access to the canon. I'm not sure, however, that the sum total of the books will be equivalent to the "tacit knowledge" that is shared between similarly educated readers and writers. A student can read the *Phaedrus* and, in a sense, "have" some Plato to use in the classroom or in an essay, but I'm not sure whether that same student would have the *Phaedrus* as we have it (and I think I can generalize here), since we have learned not only the *Phaedrus* but a way of reading the *Phaedrus*; we have learned to notice some things and ignore others, to remember certain stories and forget the rest, and our students, if they have not learned this way of reading, may ignore and forget the wrong things.

For many teachers, the key response to Hirsch's proposal will be "Who gets to choose the reading list?" And Hirsch wisely recognizes that this will have to be a matter of public policy. It should not be left up to university faculty alone. The point is, however, that whether we develop and publish such a reading list, students enter into universities, departments, and classrooms where unspoken reading lists are already in operation. The lectures they hear, the texts they read are all situated within a culture that has set boundaries and predictable terrain. For me, the unanswered system in Hirsch's proposal is what students are going to be led to *do* with those books and ideas. How will the act of writing be brought to bear on the texts that make up the new canon? I see no reason to imagine that students' writing could not be critical as well as synthetic, that students could not be taught to extend or challenge or question ideas as well as report on them.[24] But developing such curricula is no simple task. I see few basic writing courses across the country that allow students any active involvement with the real work of the university, whether that work be located within the projects of individual disciplines (like a history department) or whether that work be the general intellectual project of inquiry, interpretation, and report. It is in this area that we have yet to complete what Mina Shaughnessy began.

In her essay for Gary Tate's *Teaching Composition,* she wrote:

> Still, the special conditions of the remedial situation, that is, the need to develop within a short time a style of writing and thinking and a background of cultural information that prepare the student to cope with academic work, create a distinctive tension that almost defines the profession—a constant, uneasy hovering between the imperatives of format and freedom, convention and individuality, the practical and the ideal. Just where the boundaries bertween these claims are to be drawn in basic writing is by no means clear. Some would argue for a gradual exposure to academic subjects and skills through the extension of the remedial concern . . . others would press for a concentrated, direct apporach to the distinctive tasks of academia, arguing that for students to lay claim to their critical and analytical powers and to cultivate the formal discursive style associated with academic work is no less 'creative' or 'personal' than the activities (poetry, stories, etc.) usually associated with those words.[25]

And, she concluded, "The debate has not yet surfaced among basic writing teachers in formal or scholarly ways. It is more an undercurrent that unsettles staff meetings and most probably confuses students who must often move between semesters from one pedagogy to another."

The distinctive tension, I think, remains. We have courses in basic writing, and yet they are courses that most often lack a subject, a context and, in a sense, a home. We have students who wander, not as Said's writer wanders, resolute in his refusal to be appropriated by outworn systems, but wander without purpose or direction, doing what they can, and using what we have taught them, only to survive. The project that can both honor and complete Shaughnessy's work is the project that will turn again to the requirements of academic writing, or any writing that moves a writer into a privileged and closed discourse, to find a subject and a context for basic writing students and to develop a course of instruction that will extend what she has taught us about the ethics and integrity of teaching.

ELAINE P. MAIMON

Knowledge, Acknowledgment, and Writing across the Curriculum: Toward an Educated Community[1]

I

The word *knowledge* in its earliest uses in written English in the fourteenth century meant acknowledgment, confession, recognition of another's claims. The *Oxford English Dictionary* records such uses beginning in the fourteenth century ("c 1375 Fairf. Bid him opin knawlage make & lette for na shame to shew his sake"). Knowledge in this early sense is defined in the context of public space, one person making open acknowledgment to others in the community. Public utterance can become knowledge when speakers or writers understand how to acknowledge their debts to the words of others. Such acknowledgment does more than create context; it creates a shared world.

When scholars acknowledge the work of others, they connect their own statements to a continuum, an ongoing conversation, oral and written, which along with graphic and numerical representations, defines civilization and civility, both words deriving from *civilitas* (community). Participants in this ongoing conversation produce texts, patterns of symbols understood within the communities that create them. "Interpretive communities," says Stanley Fish, "are made up of those who share interpretive strategies not for reading but for writing texts, for constituting their properties."[2] Those who create the constituent parts of a text determine what is regarded as conventional or characteristic in that symbolic pattern. We understand the shape and significance of what we interpret because we have written and spoken enough to acknowledge the similarities and dissimilarities between utterances. Those who themselves actively formulate symbolic representations—those who write or paint or create mathematical formulae—determine the context for what various communities interpret. When we read the acknowledgments at the end of an author's preface, we see an explicit account of communities in the making.

When I conduct workshops in writing across the curriculum, I suggest that faculty members in all disciplines ask students to read the acknowledgments in every assigned textbook. From this assignment students learn that historians, sociologists, nurses, and computer scientists are also writers who sought advice on numerous drafts. Moreover, instructors who make this assignment will focus their own attention on the acknowledgments they have read and written. As readers, they may remember the communities invoked by the authors' thanks. As writers, they may recall their own experience of sharing work-in-progress with students and colleagues who praised and argued, advised, and cajoled. Such memories may finally help instructors to see themselves as writers as well as specialists within a field.

Scholars who remember their own dependence on acknowledgment will be more likely to create writing communities within their classrooms. The creation of such communities defines writing across the curriculum, not the number or length of required papers. Instructors create writing communities by teaching students that those who write determine what becomes characteristic within a discipline and that writing is essential to the ongoing formulation of what constitutes a field of study. Instructors welcome new members into specialized communities by providing opportunities for writing and rewriting, reading and rereading, questioning and responding. After frequent exchanges with classmates and with the instructor, students' acknowledgments, written as a preface to completed papers, become intellectual histories of the processes of choosing public voices.

To illustrate acknowledgment as it has worked in a specific interpretive community, I propose as an example the readers of *The Territory of Language: Linguistics, Stylistics, and the Teaching of Composition.* This interpretive community is one of the many smaller communities subsumed in the larger concept of the educated world, which scholars in all disciplines, teachers and students, can construct through participation. The key is dialectic: scientists and literary critics, teachers and students, exchanging ideas to create a context for understanding. I will then suggest a pedagogy of collaborative learning and writing across the curriculum as a way to participate with newcomers in expanding the boundaries of an educated world.

II

In the preface to the first edition of this volume, when Donald McQuade acknowledges Mina Shaughnessy, he recognizes the tangible help she gave him, in person and in writing, toward formulating connections among linguistics, stylistics, and the teaching of composition. McQuade also identifies an interpretive community of scholars who take composition seriously and who believe it is connected to other academically respectable subjects like linguistics and stylistics.

After Shaughnessy wrote *Errors and Expectations,* more scholars in English departments could understand the intellectual connections among composition, linguistics, and stylistics. Even though Shaughnessy built on a substantial body of work accomplished by Edward Corbett, James Kinneavy, Francis Christensen, Kellogg Hunt, and others, most members of English departments—particularly those in the East—were so focused on literary study that they gave scant attention to the connections between stylistics and composition. Most linguists, studying speech not writing, showed little concern for theories of composition. Certainly, the English department in which I did my graduate work in the late sixties would have thought that the connections were bizarre or trivial because, fundamentally, they believed that composition was unteachable, that the ability to write was part of essential undergraduate equipment, like cashmere sweaters or button-down shirts. Students who arrived unprepared did not belong.

Mina Shaughnessy helped many English teachers to see that writing ability is not a possession that someone does or does not own but a process that can be learned. She viewed the basic writers at the City University of New York not as beggars, bereft of collegiate accoutrements, but as newcomers, inexperienced with the language of the academy. Because Shaughnessy saw the problem as remediable, a matter of language, she read and acknowledged the appropriate scholarship: William Labov, Charles Fries, Otto Jespersen, Edward Sapir, Stephen Ullman, Karl Reisman, I. A. Richards, R. C. Gardner, and W. E. Lambert.[3] Shaughnessy's distinctive footnotes summoned scholars who had rarely before cohabited between the covers of the same book: sociolinguists, structuralists, traditionalists, semanticists, anthropologists, literary critics, second language specialists, and anyone else from any field who could help teachers of basic writing to map the frontiers of literacy.

One reason for the profound effect of *Errors and Expectations* is the participatory nature of the volume. The reader finds references in every chapter to conversations with colleagues who were also struggling to understand and to teach fundamental linguistic interactions that they themselves probably had learned effortlessly. The preface to *Errors and Expectations* opens with a scene in a "worn urban classroom" at CCNY, where Shaughnessy is sitting alone, confronting her students' "disturbing essays with their tangles of errors and puzzling incompetencies."[4] Their sentence fragments reflect their initial isolation and her own. She writes this book, she says, to share methods and insights, and sharing, not solitude, is the prevailing mood for the rest of the volume.

The latter part of the preface announces Shaughnessy's formal acknowledgments, including one to Marilyn Rosenthal, a linguist, who "read the chapters on syntax and common errors from a linguist's perspective" (p. viii), a stance different, Shaughnessy notes, from that of an English teacher. Rosenthal, we are told, suggested changes in terminology to clarify Shaughnessy's vocabulary of linguistic analysis. That acknowledgment represents the many acts of translation across disciplinary boundaries that make *Errors and Expectations* distinctive.

Besides the traditional placement of thank-you's at the beginning of the volume, Shaughnessy's acknowledgments spill out beyond the preface to the notes at the bottom of many pages. There, she does more than document scholarly quotations. She thanks teachers who have shared with her a lesson or provided a significant example: "I am indebted to Sarah d'Eloia for this and the preceding example"; "I am indebted to Kenneth Bruffee of Brooklyn College for this example," etc. (pp. 75, 238). Besides this evocation of her own colleagues in the City University, Shaughnessy invites all readers into the ongoing conversation. She immerses us in examples, making us colleagues who are free to disagree with the inferences she draws, In these ways, Shaughnessy helps to create an interpretive community: she takes seriously a subject which some previously thought trivial; she connects that subject with the world of traditional scholarship; she joins with others who are seeking new ways to address seemingly insoluble problems; and she involves the reader actively in making interpretations.

In the years following the publication of *Errors and Expectations*, composition teachers have formed a new interpretive community. Insights that were astonishing in 1977—errors are windows to the student's mind; the editorial capacity may impede language's generative power; writing is a human activity, not a set of chronologically attained skills—have become assumptions today, at least among most readers of *The Territory of Lanugage*. Some English professors still carry membership cards in a different interpretive community and are therefore not reading this book at all. The major interest is in interpretation, theory, or the history of literature, and their teaching of composition— when they deign to do it—reflects what Richard Young calls "the current traditional paradigm,"[5] one that assumes that the texts which students produce accurately represent what they know. If students write three fragments, they must need a lesson on subject and predicate, even if a majority of sentences in the draft are grammatically complete. This other interpretive community is also identified by disjunction: the instructor's meticulous, sophisticated analyses of the unconventional in literary texts existing side by side with a determinedly literal interpretation of students' errors.

A reader of *The Territory Language* could undoubtedly identify members of this other interpretive community by reading the acknowledgments in the books they publish and by observing the sessions they attend at their annual meetings. But I do not wish to convey the impression that interpretive communities are monolithic, with clearly identifiable boundaries. Nor do I believe that the profession of English studies today offers us only two warring camps (although the mundane experience in many English departments may belie that disclaimer). Membership in an English department in itself implies certain shared assumptions: e.g., writing and reading are essential activities; life is enhanced through aesthetic appreciation; linguistic form in and of itself is a significant area of study. It is within this shared context that members of English departments—literary critics and composition specialists—are able to dispute their differences. Likewise, English professors as a group share certain assumptions with the larger academic community and with the educated world as a whole.

Interpretive communities can be imagined as circles within the larger circle of the academic community which is itself encompassed by the educated world. Some of the inner circles are concentric—e.g., literature specialists are included within the larger community of English specialists. Some of the inner circles are overlapping, like Venn diagrams, with shadings and crosshatchings to show the shared territories and boundaries.

An interpretive community, in the larger sense of the educated world or in its smaller concentric and overlapping subdivisions, provides a context for understanding the language of that community. As Stanley Fish says, "understanding is always possible, but not from the outside." People always communicate, he says, "*from within* a set of interests and concerns."[6] Mina Shaughnessy in *Errors and Expectations,* Donald McQuade, and all of us writing here in *The Territory of Language* communicate with each other and with readers within the shared context of a body of scholarship that makes it possible to understand that the teaching of composition is a serious endeavor and that the subject is integrally connected with linguistics and stylistics. In fact, this volume creates a larger section of shaded area in the overlapping circles of linguistics, stylistics, and composition.

III

No matter what the context of our subcommunities, all scholars— composition specialists, linguists, critical theorists, criminologists, botanists, anthropologists—share membership in the academic world. We know the moves of the academic game. We know how to be polite—or pointedly impolite. We are in control. Most of our students (not just basic writers) feel like outsiders in the collegiate world.[7] They bring with them other contexts, other concerns. Shaughnessy proposes that teachers must understand something of the students' world (or various worlds) if we wish to find a shared context between them and us. Without that shared context we simply cannot communicate. She encourages us to read works outside the canon of English studies—especially sociology, psychology, and anthropology—to understand and appreciate the cultural context that students bring to college.

We still know too little of that context, and the subdivisions are as diverse as our students. But let me venture a few generalizations. Students value sincerity and confuse belief with reasoned argument. As a consequence, they find academic assignments difficult to accomplish because the academy demands evidence, ground for belief. But to the students, the grounds seem to change from classroom to classroom. Biology professors expect evidence based on systematic observations of phenomena, while literature professors want testimony from authoritative sources. The word "evidence" itself, deriving from a Latin root based on *videre* (to see), changes in meaning according to the perspective of the instructor. Students, who do not understand the special expectations of academic subcommunities, often interpret this variability as caprice.

As Shaughnessy notes in *Errors and Expectations,* for many students "academic writing is a trap, not a way of saying something to someone" (p. 7). Even after twelve years of schooling, most students bring scant experience in explaining or arguing an idea to strangers who will refuse to be convinced simply by the writer's good will. They lack fluency in all genres of written expression, but they have particularly narrow experience in the discourse conventions of exposition and argument. As David Bartholomae has shown, they will frequently draw on more familiar discourse conventions, the soap opera or grammar-school history lesson on "great men."[8]

If we as teachers can see students' cultural contexts as different rather than in error, we can serve as the native informants to introduce newcomers to the academic community which is a smaller circle within the educated community. The educated community, as Mina Shaughnessy notes, is the creation of the language of books, "a language that has been developed over several centuries by writers who were discovering and exploiting the analytic powers of written English . . . the common language not only of the university but of the public and professional world outside" (p. 187). When students read their academic assignments, they encounter this written language, which, unlike the ebb and flow of talk, is linear, demanding, highly allusive, referring to the words and ideas of others, living and dead. Students feel like outsiders to a conversation within which others already know the important names and key phrases. When students are asked to write in response to their reading, they cannot discover a way to get in, let alone find anything to say that follows the rules of this elaborated discourse.

Feeling estranged from the academic community, students too often regard the print in their books as reading and the scrawls of their own pens as writing. That disjunction makes them passive readers and blocked writers. Teachers can help students to see that authors of printed material are not magicians who waved a wand to produce difficult reading assignments but writers who procrastinated, worried, and revised. Even though beginners can hardly be expected to model their own prose style on the example of professionally finished documents, they can become more confident if they understand their kinship as readers and writers with all those who have struggled to go public with ideas.

Too many students believe that writers are the people who were anthologized in their high school short story collections. Since few students aspire to be anthologized, they do not think of themselves as writers. The club of writers, they think, is an exclusive one, which will never let them in. They soon discount the importance of a club that they believe will not accept them. Students will lose interest in writing unless they perceive that writers and readers are potentially the same people and that they themselves are members of that club.

The educated community understands that writers are not necessarily people who publish; writers are people who write and then read, read and then write. Some writers write stories and poems; others write reports, case studies, and proposals. But most experienced writers share certain practices. They write much more than they keep. They read their own manuscripts critically and make choices about what to develop and what to throw away. They reformulate their own material so that later drafts are connected to earlier ones in ways that only the writer may fully understand. They resist the temptation to finish prematurely and sometimes tinker too long. They frequently ask colleagues and editors to comment on work-in-progress, but they also know how to reject advice as well as how to accept it. In fact, experienced writers know that no matter how much help they seek, they alone are responsible for final decisions about their own work.

Experienced writers can tolerate the solitude of the silent library because they have learned not to be alone there. Writers hear the voices of colleagues asking questions about the formulation of ideas, reminding them about absent readers, pointing to potential dissonances. Inexperienced writers hear voices, too, but these sounds are too often mocking and disdainful: "You can't write," they chide. Or they ask the student's preoccupying question: "Do you belong here?" When writers hear the voices of colleagues, they can talk back to them on paper, and that dialogue can drown out the voices of self-doubt and discouragement.

Writers publicly recognize and record such collegial assistance through the convention of the acknowledgments page. Not only do the acknowledgments invite writers—including student writers—openly to give witness to the help they receive, liberating them from solitude, allowing them to connect their thinking to the idea of others, but the acknowledgments also identify the interpretive community to which writers belong or to which they seek membership. Acknowledgments define the intellectual context, the cultural and critical traditions.

Requiring students to write acknowledgments makes sense, however, only if we teach them how to talk about their work with one another and with the instructor. Students, like most of us, tend to be possessive and defensive about their ideas, afraid to give thoughts away, as if conversation will deplete their intellectual supply. When students read published acknowledgments, they encounter models of intellectual sharing without the individual author's losing autonomy or shirking final responsibility. In class discussion or in small group work, we can help students to interpret these brief intellectual histories of the nurturing of ideas through exchange.

Another way to help students to learn collaboratively is to teach them to ask each other for advice and to acknowledge that advice.[9] In my classes, writers must prepare a cover sheet for any draft which is to be reviewed by a peer reader or by me. The cover sheet poses three questions: How close to being finished are you? What steps do you plan to take to complete the project? How might readers help you at this stage? The process of asking for advice is much more important than giving it. Learning to ask means learning to gain some distance, to formulate the questions writers need to hear at 3:00 A.M. when there is nobody around to ask. In fact, I remind my students again and again that I do not ask them to read each other's drafts so that someone else will fix their papers for them. Writers are responsible for their own work. I ask students to work collaboratively for two major reasons: to gain enough distance from their own prose to ask the right questions, and to learn to work tactfully and constructively with other people. Nonetheless, they must keep notes on the specific help offered by classmates and on the ways that conversations with others might have inspired their own thinking. Before students submit a paper for a grade, they use these notes to write their acknowledgments.

When students work collaboratively, they learn independence, not dependence. They learn the fine but crucial line that divides requests for assistance from exploitation. They know that some professional writers have been sued by people whom they gracefully acknowledged because the borrowed material should have appeared within quotation marks. They learn the reasons, not just the forms, for documentation. They also understand that if they seek help with the actual phrasing of sentences, they have acquired a co-author whose name belongs with theirs on the title page of the paper. Therefore, they learn the difference between acknowledgment and co-authorship. They learn to avoid plagiarism by first understanding intellectual responsibility. Furthermore, they begin to see that writing is one instance of the many social situations that present the perils of exploitation. Students must work with other people because conversation is essential to growth, but social interaction always necessitates responsibility and honesty. A university campus is a place to practice the art of conversing freely without taking advantage of anyone.

Perhaps a typical acknowledgments page written by one of my freshman composition students will clarify these points. The writer of the paper, Merry Wolfson, thanks a number of people who helped her to write a critical analysis of James Joyce's "Araby":

> I would like to thank Amy Miller for finding some more symbolism in the story, as well as for reading my paper and helping me with it. Also my thanks go to A. J. Mayer, Sahar Al-Amri, and Lori Shields, who also read and commented on this paper. To Dr. Maimon I owe thanks for getting me started on the right track and asking some very interesting and important questions. Many thanks to all.

By thanking Amy Miller for helping her to find "more symbolism," Merry Wolfson not only admits that she had help and expresses appropriate gratitude but also demonstrates her tacit assumption that in the context of my class, the English department of Beaver College, and the academic community in general, a student does not read "Araby" in the same way she might read a Harlequin romance. She looks beyond literal significance to piece meaning together through nonlinear acts of interpretation. Merry also thanks me for asking her questions, not for giving her answers, and for getting her started, not for calling time.

Merry, like my other students, has achieved public statement by first engaging in private exploration. My students write journals, letters, discovery drafts, and other private and semiprivate documents to discover what they want to say. Writing is a powerful act of self-exploration, and many writers will choose to stop with self-clarifying entries in a private journal, in response, for example, to the following: "Write in your private journal about your own first crush. How old were you? How were your actions and reactions similar or dissimilar to those of the narrator of 'Araby'?"[10] If Merry had chosen to stop there with an expressive response to "Araby," she could have gone public with another set of ideas. In my class students write approximately 1000 words per week for fifteen weeks but must go public with only four 1000-word papers, which are graded for the effectiveness of their public statement.

Because the composition course which I teach is the introductory level of a full-scale writing-across-the-curriculum program, Merry's assignment to write literary analysis represents only one genre from among the required papers. For their three other 1000-word essays, students must write a scientific case study, a paper of philosophical argument, and a brief exploration of a question requiring library research, with the questions defining the genre more precisely. In this way, students are introduced to the interpretive communities of literature, philosophy, and science, not to become technicians of the special conventions of writing in these disciplines, but to learn that various contexts exist and matter. As a result of their sojourns in a number of interpretive communities, students learn to avoid a monolithic view of discourse and to pose questions about aim, audience, and situation. After such initial analysis, they will communicate more effectively within understandable contexts.

When a composition course introduces students to the concept of thinking in contexts, then instructors in other courses can build on students' sophistication. Instructors in various disciplines can give assistance with their own specialized dialects when necessary, while reminding students that the university is multidialectal. Students can learn to regard the voice of the specialist as appropriate on some occasions but not on others. Biology instructors can help students to understand that a group of scientists, like a group of close friends, will typically (in the journal *Science,* for example) communicate in telegraphic phrases, since more elaborated communication would waste time and, in fact, sound unfriendly to members of the group. When an acquaintance from another subcommunity joins the conversation, the group switches to a less condensed, more explanatory mode of communication. To do otherwise would be exclusionary and rude. Biologists can encourage apprentices to write laboratory reports when necessary and to write widely intelligible explanations of their laboratory work when appropriate. When students write such explanations in a biology class, their instructors notice enhanced understanding of the concepts in biology. If students talk these concepts over with peers, read drafts of laboratory reports, and record emotional responses in journals, they will employ writing as a way to become better biologists.

But if students write in journals without ever going public with their work, they will not achieve knowledge in the etymological sense of recognizing others' claims, understanding the connective tissue that joins all intellectual explorers. Certainly, all successful writing across the curriculum programs that I know of teach writing as a powerful tool for learning by integrating journals and other ungraded writing assignments into all classroom activities. But an exclusive concern with self-discovery denies the writer's urge to share ideas with a larger community. Students can, of course, read each other's journal entries, but such activity teaches communication only with those who have agreed in advance to be kind.

I am suggesting that the acknowledgments page, not the journal as others have proposed,[11] is emblematic of writing across the curriculum. Acknowledgment links the private with the public, self-knowledge with the context of community. Writing across the curriculum will come of age when we can connect the private and the public, the energy of creativity with the control necessary for public statement, the assignment of journals with the assignment of acknowledgments.

If the acknowledgments page is the emblem of writing across the curriculum, then the faculty writing workshop is the key. The maturity of writing across the curriculum depends on a continuing opportunity for faculty members from different departments to meet together to speak the same academic language. The workshop reminds instructors that they all belong to the same widely defined interpretive community, even though their special interests bond them into smaller circles within the educated world. All share the challenging task of helping students to enter the educated world and of assisting them in finding some special allegiance to a subcommunity.

Faculty workshops help to transform the fragments of the multiversity into a university by promoting conversation across the disciplines. This conversation is carried on in what James Kinneavy calls the "dialect of the educated reader." "The college," he remarked about faculty workshops at Beaver College, "was a collegium, a unified body of academics, speaking the same language about the problems of various disciplines."[12] One reason that writing across the curriculum has evoked so much enthusiasm in diverse institutions is that its preparatory workshops have created a context for faculty exchange, which is the fundamental prerequisite for curriculum change. The conversation among faculty members becomes a widening circle that eventually includes the students in a shared world.

IV

Throughout this essay, I have been working on the assumption that a shared world is possible. I do not believe it can be found, like some lost Atlantis, but I do think it can be made. I have also been assuming that education is not only possible but essential. I have used the phrase "the educated world" not as something elitist and exclusionary but as the inclusive and expanding artifact that we build against chaos. Some may see this artifact as a Tower of Babel, characterized by a confusion of tongues. The builders of the biblical tower, however, had no intention of living inside it. They wanted to use it as a way to get to heaven. My building, not so much tower as shelter, is itself the locus of meaning, a place to live in together, learning to reach tentative, temporary agreements about the work of building, of making meaning.

Education invites newcomers into the house without striking from their hands the means of making something new. Hannah Arendt writes that "education is the point at which we decide whether we love the world enough to assume responsibility for it." That is, we teach when we decide that we have responsibility for maintaining and extending a civilized community by keeping the conversation going. Arendt continues:

And education, too, is where we decide whether we love our children enough not to expel them from our world and leave them to their own devices, nor to strike from their hands their chance of undertaking something new, something unforeseen by us, but to prepare them in advance for the task of renewing a common world. [13]

We as teachers must bring our students into the conversation of civilization, while at the same time learning not to wince when they say or do something unforeseen by us. Sometimes the unforeseen will be an error. Then we must learn to understand it as a risk taken by a newcomer who is still learning the conventions of the educated world. Sometimes the unforeseen will shock us in a form that looks like mockery and caricature of ourselves at our worst—pedantic, heavy, speaking in unnecessary and overelaborated jargon. These errors are hardest for us to forgive, but we must learn to see them as developmental. Would we punish a child who raids her mother's closets and stumbles into our sight in high heels and out-of-date dresses?

Sometimes the unforseen will be a startling expression of originality and individual talent, which is after all, as T. S. Eliot says, nurtured by a tradition. We will experience these delightful surprises if we encourage our students to choose. When students realize that the verb "to choose" comes from the Anglo-Saxon root meaning to relish, to enjoy by tasting, to exercise preference among available possibilities, they will understand that freedom is not flight from responsibilities but an active participation in our shared world. They will also choose knowledge as a way first to recognize the claims of others, and then to cause knowledge to grow, through their own ability to make something new, something unforeseen by others. Then together we can build *civilitas*, a civilized community that constantly makes and remakes its symbols.

Exploring the Language

KENNETH BRUFFEE

Getting Started

For years, I have noticed that for many students one of the hardest things about writing is getting started. I don't mean sitting down to write, although eventually that may come into it also. I'm talking about actually beginning to generate sentences. That this aspect of writing is painful we all know. I had the devil of a time getting started writing this paper. I suppose most writers have had that experience. And most people who come into the Brooklyn College Writing Center—which is not a service for basic writing students alone but for all Brooklyn College students, and for faculty as well—most people who go there ask for help in getting started, or in organizing their ideas, which often turns out to be the same thing. The worst paragraph in nine out of ten student papers, papers written by relatively competent writers as well as basic writing students, is the first paragraph. We all seem to have trouble getting started.

For as long as I have known this, I have had an uneasy feeling that the trouble writers have getting started was somehow telling me something more about writing, about verbal utterance, perhaps about language itself, than I had yet grasped. I don't think I have quite tracked that uneasy feeling to its lair. But I think I may have been able to follow it into the countryside where it is at home. The conclusion I think I have been led to is this: that a writer's difficulty getting started has to do with his difficulty knowing and understanding the structure of the utterance he is setting out to make—not what he wants to say (although naturally that may create some problems too) but how he wants to say it. Once we know, however vaguely, the order or form of our discourse, we can begin that discourse, but not before. And this principle applies as well to a single sentence as it does to any large rhetorical form such as, for example, an essay or even a whole book.

This hypothesis came to mind during a recent rereading of Noam Chomsky's *Syntactic Structures*. *Syntactic Structures* was published in 1957— over twenty years ago. During those twenty years a great deal of work has been done attempting to understand, develop, apply, prove, and in some cases refute the immense contribution made to linguistic theory by that book and by Chomsky's subsequent work growing out of it. In reflecting on that contribution and our effort to digest it, it occurred to me that while many of us may have been taking Chomsky's highly general notion of a "transformational grammar" too generally, I began to wonder, at this distance, if it isn't possible that we ought to be seeing transformational grammar as only one special case of a still more general theory of language which has yet to be formulated.

I will not attempt to formulate that possible theory here. I intend only to try to point out what it seems to me might be something of the nature of that theory as it seems implied in Chomsky's work, and to suggest what some of its possible practical implications might be. In doing this, I am sure to be like one of the blind men trying to describe the elephant by touching only one of its members. Nevertheless I feel that the effort is worth making, however partial and distorted the resulting view, first because it seems to me that a new, more general "field theory" is long overdue in linguistics; and second, because even the partial description of a fragment of what such a "field theory" might be like may be of some immediate use to those of us who teach writing.

I am going to be talking here about the *generation*, that is, the production or "performance" of sentences—language on the hoof, so to speak. I am well aware that this is very dangerous ground. And I am aware also that Chomsky—and he is not alone among linguists in this regard—resists the notion that a grammar can explain how we spontaneously generate sentences or how we are to analyze all the sentences we spontaneously generate. In *Syntactic Structures* Chomsky insists, indeed, that a grammar can only explain how to analyze an utterance that the grammar itself generates.[2] Our grammars can cope with our "performance" of a language only from the point of view of a more highly generalized idea of our "competence" in it.

I respect this self-imposed limitation on the grammatical technology which Chomsky offers, and I am aware also that there are functional limitations to transformational technology itself. At the same time, I would agree with John Lyons that Chomsky's most important contribution to our understanding of language is not technological but conceptual. My own view would be that Chomsky's greatest contribution in the long run may be, however, somewhat more general than John Lyons would have it: "the mathematical rigor and precision with which [Chomsky] formalized the properties of alternative systems of grammatical description."[3] At the same time, I think Chomsky's contribution may be somewhat less general than his view that "the structure of language is determined by the structure of the human mind" (Lyons, p.15), at least insofar as that is genetically transmitted structure. Instead, I suspect that Chomsky's lasting contribution may be an implication inherent in his transformational grammar, the implication that language is nonlinear and discontinuous.

Chomsky begins *Syntactic Structures* by rejecting two earlier conceptions of language, both of which assume that language is linear and continuous. One of these conceptions, leading to what he calls finite-state grammars, holds that the characteristics of any language unit (however defined or described) are determined—and by extension generated—in a continuous temporal sequence, or, so to speak, from left to right. According to this view, each event in a sequence of utterances would be derived from the immediately preceding event (Chomsky, p.24), or, to put it another way, each action in speech would be accounted for by the immediate history of the action. The second conception of language as linear and continuous leads to phrase-structure grammars. These differ from finite-state grammars in that each element's form does not depend necessarily on what immediately precedes it. However, phrase-structure grammars are similar to finite-state grammars in the sense that each element's form is defined by its immediate "constituents" and by a surface structure determined by a sequential set of "rules." This conception of language is basically a storage-retrieval notion. It is a step beyond simple left-to-right grammars. Yet although here the sentence string, we might say, curves—and in some cases curves deeply—the continuity of the line as a coherent generative nexus does not break.

What Chomsky suggests in place of these rejected conceptions of language is a radically different one, according to which elements "look back" beyond the last unit generated to earlier ones in order to determine their form (Chomsky, p.38). This dynamic process depends neither on contiguity nor, as subsequent experimentation has shown,[4] on the storage capacity of "short-term memory." According to this view of language, elements (however defined or described) which have their own internal structure may be related to earlier elements or units in a way which is independent of the surface structure of the unit itself (Chomsky, p.41). What determines the form of any given element in an utterance is not necessarily what immediately precedes it, or what precedes *that* element, now set aside for the moment and "stored." What determines an element's form is a set of underlying "transformational" options and obligations. These transformations are not just formal and relational rules as in phrase structure grammar, but potential and anticipated *changes* in forms, in relations, and above all in further relational rules. It is this view of language which I would call generatively—that is to say temporally—*non*linear, and *dis*continuous.

This conception of language has a great many larger implications, I think, only a few of which have yet been developed. One of the implications of the view that language may be generatively nonlinear and discontinuous, for example, is that if language units may "look back" not only to immediately preceding units but also beyond those to still earlier ones, they must also be capable of "looking ahead" to language units yet to be uttered. That is, the general principle of which transformational grammar is a special case would seem to be that what we say and the way we say it may be based in some way not only on what we have just said and what we said a few moments ago, but also on what we anticipate saying sometime later.

This conception, that utterance may be affected in some way by future eventualities, rings true to me, because it is consistent with other things I know about language. For one thing, forethought is certainly part of the larger rhetorical use of language. I say what I am saying now in part because I am leading up to what I have in mind saying next. This analogy with rhetoric is not, however, one I would want to stress here, because it is inexact. What I am concerned with is something less conscious than rhetorical forethought. It is more a matter of an understanding at the threshhold of awareness, a sense of the structure of the whole thing we intend to say. Partly, indeed, because it is not wholly conscious, the sense of the whole structure of an utterance that I am getting at here would be so powerful that it would affect the way we *begin* a unit of utterance, such as a sentence, as well as the way we proceed and the way we end it.

A more exact analogy is what seems to happen when we read. In fact it is more than an analogy, since we seem to experience reading almost as a sort of vicarious speech, utterance produced in our imagination by proxy. Some of the work of Kenneth Goodman, as I understand it, seems to suggest this. When we read, Goodman seems to show, we "read ahead" in a very practical way. How I now read the first part of this sentence (both what I understand it to mean and the way I deliver it aloud) depends to some extent on what I anticipate reading in this later part. This principle surely applies when we have read a passage before. But it also seems to apply when we read a passage for the first time. The way I construe the beginning of a sentence is based in part on a guess I make about what is going to happen in the rest of the sentence. If I guess incorrectly, I make a mistake at least in the tone with which I read the passage (if I am reading aloud) and perhaps even in the way I perceive what is written on the page. As a result, I may read the whole sentence incorrectly; eventually, if the disparity between what I expect to be there and what is actually written becomes great enough I will stop, go back to the beginning, and start again, this time with a better-informed anticipation of the structure of the sentence. That is, I would have misread something at the beginning of the sentence because what I anticipated would happen later doesn't happen; or, conversely, if I read the beginning of the sentence correctly, I did so in part because my anticipation was correct.

This principle of anticipation in reading is further verified, I think, in E. D. Hirsch's *Validity in Interpretation.*[6] Hirsch says there that when we begin reading a work of literature—a story, say—we make a "genre guess" about what we are going to be reading later, about how the story is going to turn out. This "genre guess" about what will follow affects not only how we understand the beginning of the story, but also how we perceive it. My experience teaching fiction to students who had read very little fiction seems to suggest that Hirsch is right. When students who are familiar with a very small repertoire of fictional genres read a story which seems at first to fit one of the genres they know, but which turns out in fact not to fit it, they become very uncomfortable and, as they put it, "bored." A "cowboy story" like Crane's "The Bride Comes to Yellow Sky" which doesn't end in a shootout, or a "love story" like Elizabeth Parsons's "The Nightingales Sing" which doesn't end in a clinch, leaves these students at first totally bewildered. It turns out that they in effect "lock themselves out" of such stories by their conventional anticipation, the conventional "genre guess" they make when they begin reading the story. The way they perceive details at the beginning of the story furthermore is itself determined by what they anticipate will happen later on.

It is something like this, I am suggesting, which happens when we speak and when we write. When we begin generating a new sentence we make a structural prognostication analogous to Hirsch's "genre guess" about how we will be saying what we have to say in the rest of the sentence. This structural anticipation of what we might call a "sentence genre guess" about what will happen in the future, along with of course our knowledge of past utterance, affects what we say in the present. I have applied the term "discontinuous" to this conception of language, because what we misleadingly call the sentence "string" does not merely spin out of us like the web from a spider. It is in part drawn out by as yet nonexistent entities, units of language which are as yet unarticulated and have as yet no real verbal form. They exist only in some sense we have of language structure, of language potentiality.

One value of this conception of language is that it seems to help explain, with reference to large formal written utterances—such as this paper—why "getting started" writing is so hard. And it also helps explain why teaching students how to organize their work and helping them to "get started" writing turns out so often to be about the same thing. Until we have some sense of what we are going to say—of the overall structure of the whole utterance—we cannot get started. We may not have to know all that we are going to say, but before we can introduce whatever we are going to say we have to have some idea of how we are likely to say it. This principle would seem to apply to short utterances—single sentences—especially those made in a formal context, as much as it applies to longer ones. If this is true, and if we consider an "introduction"—that is, the beginning of any utterance however long or short—as an integral part of the whole utterance, which of course it is, then what we seem to be saying is that what we anticipate saying affects how we start.

I would like now to offer a few examples of single-sentence utterances which may show that this discontinuous conception of language is not simply a matter of semantical-rhetorical-cogitative forethought, but that it is really some deeper sort of structural matter. I hope these examples will also show how this view of language generation might affect our practical understanding and explanation of how we write. I shall draw my examples from Mina Shaughnessy's excellent *Errors and Expectations*,[6] because that book is the richest source of real-life, student-generated sentences—language on the hoof—that I know of, and also because it is the only book I know which systematically analyzes sentences such as these by applying the normal linguistic tools available to most writing teachers. Shaughnessy does not ask why the sentences her students generated are "wrong." She assumes instead that every one of them has been generated by an intelligent human being as the best solution which that person could offer at that moment to a difficult problem of expression. And she examines these sentences with an exactitude, intelligence, and respect which has heretofore been reserved almost exclusively to works of literature. She asks what these sentences say about what her students were thinking, and classifies their styles of thought in order not merely to change the students' writing "behavior," but in order to educate them. In this respect, and in many others, Shaughnessy's book represents to my mind the highest sort of educational endeavor. In the next few paragraphs I shall attempt to build modestly on that firm foundation.

I should point out first that the basic, explicit conception of language in Shaughnessy's book, especially in the chapter on syntax from which my examples are drawn, is linear and, in most respects, continuous. Shaughnessy tends to talk in metaphors of railroading (sentences get "derailed" at certain "junctions" and so on). This figure clearly suggests a concatenary, continuously sequential view of language. Shaughnessy takes this view for several good reasons, as I see it. First of all, she is, as I have said, addressing writing teachers in familiar linguistic terms. Using these terms, she is able to illuminate brilliantly the student writing she discusses. Secondly, a linear view of language is entirely appropriate in many respects to explaining the process of writing, which does depend a good deal on a well-trained memory. Shaughnessy describes, for example, the inexperienced writer who "does not easily recall what he has written once his hand has moved on to another part of the sentence."

At the same time that she assumes as a practical base for analysis of writing a linear conception of language, however, Shaughnessy is also aware implicitly of the discontinuous nature of utterance, which the work of inexperienced writers makes sometimes all too painfully evident. She refers to the nonlinear "dimensions" given to sentences by parenthetical phrases (Shaughnessy, p. 32). She tells us that the inexperienced writer who must learn to recall what he has written is limited not merely by "the constraints he has set for himself" in what he has just written, but also by what he wrote "a few words back" (p.59). And she contends that "the perception of the sentence as a structure rather than a string of words is probably the most important insight a student can gain from the study of grammar" (p.133).

What Shaughnessy of course does not assume is the extension of this principle of discontinuity which I have been suggesting here: the notion that the forms of utterance are determined not only by "looking back" but also by structurally "looking ahead." Shaughnessy explains most syntactic errors by suggesting that the writer did not know how to continue the form with which he began his sentence. What I would like to do here is examine how in some cases the sentences generated by inexperienced writers may be explained in the converse way. That is, I will try to show that part of the difficulty these students are having may be caused by their not knowing how the ending which they intend to give a sentence implies the way that sentence must begin. I am suggesting that some of these writers' troubles are caused not by being unable to finish what they start, but by being incapable yet of getting started saying what they already know how to finish.

This principle sheds some light especially, I think, on Shaughnessy's sample sentences in which the end of the sentence is conspicuously more clearly expressed than the beginning. The following is a rather obvious example of the type of sentence I have in mind.

> (1)   In my opinion I believe that you there is no field that cannot be effected some sort of advancement that one maybe need a college education to make it.
>
> (Shaughnessy, p. 62)

Here it seems to me that the predicate is unexceptionable. What the student seems to intend saying is, "No matter what field people choose, they need a college education to make it." or perhaps even simply, "*I* need a college education to make it." The difficulty the student seems to have had in this example is not in writing a predicate to fit a clearly conceived subject, but in writing an adequately modified subject to "introduce" a preconceived, and well-conceived, predicate. The writer knew where he wanted to go; the trouble he had was in getting started.

This principle seems to be at work also in the case of a student's three separate attempts to compare the life he expects to lead after college and the life his parents have led.

> (2)   *First try*
> The life that my parents led and the life that I am going to lead will reflect the opposite of them trying to maintain an image on the block.

Second try
The life that my parents led and the life I am going to lead is the opposite of their struggle.

Third try
The life of my parents and the life I am going to lead will be the opposite of their life styles.

(Shaughnessy, p. 57)

Common sense seems to tell us that since the first half of the sentence in these three attempts remains more or less intact, the problem must lie with the changing second half. But as Shaughnessy points out, if in making a comparison a writer "names the two elements in his comparison first. . . . [then] he cannot pursue the comparison easily in that sentence because the verb then serves both members of the comparison." Add to this that in each of these tries the predicate is correctly expressed—that is, each try involves a different but adequate way of predicating the comparison—then it seems reasonable to suggest once again that what the student does not know how to do is write the beginning of a sentence which is mandated by the "structural sentence genre" he anticipates using, a "genre" he otherwise knows so well that he can even write three quite adequate variations of it.

Another example. Shaughnessy explains the following sentence with the acute observation that the introductory adverbial element (*even if . . .*) causes "the writer to lose his subject, or to think that he has already provided one," that is, that the error is in the predicate, and it is caused by poorly understanding or forgetting what precedes it.

(3) Even if a person graduated from high school who is going to college to obtain a specific position in his career should first know how much in demand his possible future job really is.

(Shaughnessy, p. 59)

This sentence looked at from the point of view of structural anticipation seems to suggest, in contrast to Shaughnessy's explantion, that the writer knew when he began what he wanted to say in the sentence ("X should first know how much in demand his possible future really is"), but he did not know how to express a complicated "X" in such a way that he could say what he anticipated saying about it.

Some of Shaughnessy's examples of redundant coordinate conjunctions also seem to confirm this view, although the argument here becomes more complex. If, as she says earlier, inexperienced writers tend to know and depend excessively on *and* and *but* for articulation, then in the following sentence it would seem that it is not the familiar *but* which causes the writer trouble, but rather the unfamiliar articulator *even though*.

(4)   Even though colleges do not train people for some jobs that are in demand but they train people for other important jobs without which a society would find it difficult to exist.

(Shaughnessy, p. 60)

The student's error here might be, as Shaughnessy says, adding an inappropriate *but* between the clauses. It seems equally possible, however, that the problem is instead that the writer's repertoire of sentence "genres" does not yet include the whole structure of an *even though* or *although* sentence. This is not an easy structure for an inexperienced writer to learn, because it links two clauses not where the linkage reasonably belongs, between the clauses, but at a distance, from a position at the beginning of the sentence. In order to put that articulating element properly at the beginning, the writer has to know in advance that the two clauses will not be linked in the way he is used to. Here, the *even though* can as easily be seen, I think, as an inappropriate way to begin a sentence in which the writer assumes two clauses must naturally be linked with *but* or *and*.

(4a)   Colleges do not train people for some jobs that are in demand, but they train people for other important jobs without which a society would find it difficult to exist.

One last example. The sentence reads:

(5)   It is important for young people attend college.

(Shaughnessy, p. 67)

Shaughnessy's suggestion for interpreting the thinking which lies behind a sentence like this is a good one: that the student did not recall, when he got to *attend*, that he began with a prepositional structure which requires an infinitive verb. That is, the writer is not yet equipped to complete what he set out to say. According to this interpretation, the correct version of the sentence the student intended is:

(5a)   It is important for young people to attend college.

I would suggest, however, that another perhaps equally valid explanation might be that the student *did* know what he wanted to say, and said it. He anticipated a sentence structure which includes an inflected form of the verb, "young people attend college." What seems to me possible is that he did not know how to "introduce" that structure.

(5b)   It is important *that* young people attend college.

Having shown in more detail some of the possible practical implications of a discontinuous theory of language generation, I am now going to take the liberty in conclusion of supposing that the reader agrees with me that the interpretations I have offered of the nature and cause of these sentence errors are plausible. If that is the case, then we have two alternatives to consider. These alternatives may be expressed, if I may borrow Shaughnessy's metaphor, in this way: Do these sentences start off on the right track and become derailed, or do they plan to catch a perfectly reliable train, but jump desperately on only at the last moment just as it leaves, having got lost on the way to the station? Are these writers having trouble finishing up, or in getting started?

Supposing that these are at least debatable alternatives, I would like to conclude with a larger proposition. I would suggest that linguistic theory as it exists today is not yet generalized enough either to explain why these alternatives are not mutually contradictory, or to offer a basis for choosing between them. I would suggest that linguistics still lacks a unified "field theory" of sufficient generality to encompass and explain both the readily apparent continuity and linearity of language, *and* its evident nonlinear and discontinuous nature. Such a unified linguistic theory would provide a basis which we do not yet have for resolving many aggravating problems, such as those which Shaughnessy raises. Why is it, for example, that inexperienced writers of the sort she is concerned with tend to break parallel constructions "at the point where the verb enters (or ought to enter) the construction?" And "how much of the syntactic difficulty at this and other levels of student writing is rooted *not* in a writer's unfamiliarity with basic syntactic structures but in his attempt to use these structures in the formal register of textbooks and teachers?"

Answers to questions such as these require more than the fragmented approach to the study of language represented by communications theory, grammatical technology developed under laboratory-pure conditions, and such sub-fields as psycho- and sociolinguistics which are derived in turn from disciplines—in this case experimental psychology and sociology—which, it seems increasingly clear, are themselves almost hopelessly fragmented.

We require, I think, more than a new mix of what we already know, and we require courageous speculation that reaches beyond the parochial limits of both behaviorism and neo-Cartesian rationalism. For linguistics to develop further as a field of knowledge, for it to be able to help us understand language at the level we refer to broadly by the term "style," and certainly for it to begin helping writing teachers on anywhere near the scale that help is needed, we require a new paradigm by which we perceive language as a single matrix of processes in which utterances evolve.

Of course, to create such a general theory will be no easy task. How do we go about it? We need not follow Chomsky all the way to a mentalist theory of language, in which innate "ideas" or ideal preconceptions are seen as the ultimate source of the underlying structures of utterance. I would suggest that we examine instead the possibility that spontaneously generated sentences are subject to the unalienable fact of the continual *de*generation of experience into memory, conscious and unconscious, and the subsequent and continual spontaneous *re*generation of experience through memory and fantasy into projections upon the present and upon the as yet *un*generated future.

If I were forced to put the whole matter in the simplest possible way, I might have to recommend that the whole linguistic enterprise go back and reread its Proust, its Whitehead, and its Freud. This may seem like a weak suggestion: thoroughly unscientific. But I believe that one of the questions most ignored by linguistics today is the nature and role which the imaginative faculties of mind play in generating language. In order to help people write better, I think, we have to find out more about how the mind spontaneously generates sentences in the first place. To accomplish this, examining the role of the projective power of the imagination might not be a bad way of getting started.

FRANK J. D'ANGELO

Topoi and Form in Composition[1]

When rhetoric was incorporated into English departments in the late nineteenth century, the function of the rhetoric instructor changed from that of lecturing on rhetorical matters to that of assigning and correcting written themes. Thus rhetoric's association with oratory was cut off. The term *rhetoric* itself was gradually replaced by the term *composition,* which came to be associated exclusively with written discourse.[2]

Although American composition textbooks continued to deal with rhetoric in the form of argumentation (argumentation was one of four forms of discourse—description, narration, exposition, and argumentation), the theory of the formal topics, as it relates to classical invention, disappeared from composition textbooks in the late nineteenth and early twentieth century. The practice of the formal topics, however, did not disappear. It simply took a different form. It is there, buried in composition textbooks, under the guise of "methods of developing paragraphs."[3] These modes of developing ideas (such as comparison, contrast, definition, cause and effect) closely resemble the classical *topoi.* They are, in fact, structural counterparts of the formal topics which appear as "relationships" in paragraphs and which are used to organize those paragraphs. At a later date, they reappear in textbooks as methods of developing complete essays.

There are traces of the classic *topoi* not only in the names of the categories used to label the methods of development but also in the concept of the topic sentence. In developing paragraphs, the writer is advised to embody the main idea in a "topic" sentence. (The word *topic* comes from the same root word, *topos,* meaning "place," as does the classical *topoi.* Then he or she is instructed to search for the "means" of developing that subject (comparison, contrast, definition, exemplification, and so forth). In other words, the methods of development are presented as inventional strategies for the logical development of ideas, although the term "invention" is seldom, if ever, used.

I would like to suggest that this shift from thinking of invention as the search for ideas before one begins to write to thinking of it as an ongoing process that continues throughout the arrangement of those ideas makes good historical sense. In classical antiquity and perhaps up to the invention of printing, the art of invention had to be concerned as much with the retrieval of information as with developing lines of reasoning, since there were few available books or manuscripts. Thus the art of invention was closely allied with the art of memory. But in an age when knowledge is more easily accessible in books or through computer retrieval, the emphasis in rhetorical invention might more properly be on developing lines of reasoning about a subject and upon the representation of meaning in writing.

In brief, what I am suggesting is that implicit in the nineteenth century concept of methods of development and the twentieth century concept of patterns of organization is a view of invention that considers the *topoi* (i.e., the methods of development) as methods of reasoning which a writer can employ in constructing paragraphs and longer stretches of discourse, rather than a view that sees the *topoi* as sources to which writers can turn for subject matter. In this view, composition is a sequence of connected activities that results in a unified piece of writing. Invention, arrangement, and style are part of an organic whole. Patterns of organization based on the *topoi* appear in writing because a mental process puts them there, because a conceptual structure supports them. Underlying these larger organizational patterns are schemata or paradigms which are the structural counterparts of the *topoi*. These paradigms guide thought in the act of composing. The assumption is that the modern writer has access to a wealth of ideas, but that he or she needs a heuristic procedure for developing these ideas.

To illustrate the foregoing ideas more concretely, I would like to examine the structure of an essay which exemplifies this view of the composing process and then discuss its pedagogical implications. But before I begin this examination, I would like to make a few comments about paradigms.

A paradigm is a pattern of organization based on the topics of invention. It is a model or design that is abstract and general. It is an undetailed, general plan. It is not to be confused with a traditional outline that is detailed and specific. Unlike a traditional outline, a paradigm is an idealization, a conception of a pattern in its absolute perfection. It represents the writer's competence, that is, the writer's ability to use language. But competence is always spilling over into performance, so that it is possible to use these formal patterns in the act of writing. Because a traditional outline is so detailed, with its divisions and subdivisions, it can be used only for the specific piece of writing for which it is intended. A paradigm, however, represents a global pattern that can recur from one essay to another. In other words, a writer can use the same general plan and write completely different essays with it. This should not be surprising since a paradigm is the organizational form that a specific topic of invention or mode of development takes. Thus, it is possible to view a particular topic or mode (for example, comparison and contrast) as the principle method for organizing that discourse. A traditional outline is static; it represents a finished product. But a paradigm is dynamic; it represents stages in thinking.

A paradigm is a form of reasoning that leads the mind from one thing to another. But because thinking in composition is directed toward the whole person, a paradigm engages not only the intellect, but also the emotions and the innate moral sense which serves as the basis of ethical decisions. In other words, a paradigm is a structural form which integrates logical, emotional, and ethical appeals by incorporating emotional and ethical terms into the sentences that comprise the paradigm.

The following essay, taken from Bertrand Russell's *Autobiography*,[4] is a good example of an essay that uses the formal topics as a strategy of invention and the resulting paradigm as a principle of organization. As you read this essay, notice that although the paradigmatic form is logical, the logical form organizes the emotional and ethical elements necessary to secure the reader's belief and conviction. Russell achieves this integration of form and meaning by including ethical and emotional terms in the sentences that make up the paradigm, words and phrases such as "passions," "the longing for love," "the search for knowledge," "the unbearable pity for the suffering of mankind," and so forth.

The essay is reprinted below for ease of reference. I have indented the sentence levels so that the logical divisions stand out clearly:

WHAT I HAVE LIVED FOR
Bertrand Russell

1

1   Three passions, simple but overwhelmingly strong, have governed my life: the longing for love, the search for knowledge, and unbearable pity for the suffering of mankind.

2   These passions, like great winds, have blown me hither and thither, in a wayward course, over a deep ocean of anguish, reaching to the very verge of despair.

2

3   I have sought love, first, because it brings ecstasy—ecstasy so great that I would often have sacrificed all the rest of life for a few hours of this joy.

3   I have sought it, next, because it relieves loneliness—that terrible loneliness in which one shivering consciousness looks over the rim of the world into the cold unfathomable lifeless abyss.

3   I have sought it, finally, because in the union of love I have seen, in a mystic miniature, the prefiguring vision of the heaven that saints and poets have imagined.

4   This is what I sought, and though it might seem too good for human life, this is what—at last—I have found.

3

3   With equal passion I have sought knowledge.

4   I have wished to understand the hearts of men.

    4   I have wished to know why the stars shine.
    4   And I have tried to apprehend the Pythagorean power by which number holds sway above the flux.
       5   A little of this, but not much, I have achieved.

4

  3   Love and knowledge, so far as they were possible, led upward toward the heavens.
  3   But always pity brought me back to earth.
    4   Echoes of cries of pain reverberate in my heart.
       5   Children in famine, victims tortured by oppressors, helpless old people a hated burden to their sons, and the whole world of loneliness, poverty, and pain make a mockery of what human life should be.
         6   I long to alleviate the evil, but I cannot, and I too suffer.

1   This has been my life.
  2   I have found it worth living, and would gladly live it again if the chance were offered me.

Because a paradigm is based on the principle of repetition, in getting at the underlying paradigm, we must look for patterns of repetition, both semantic and syntactic, within each sentence and between sentences. In this essay, Bertrand Russell uses several methods of repetition. Sometimes he repeats words ("three *passions* . . . these *passions* . . . with equal *passion*"). Sometimes he uses synonyms ("three *passions* . . . *love* . . . *knowledge* . . . *pity*"). And sometimes he repeats entire grammatical patterns ("I have sought love . . . because it brings ecstasy. . . . I have sought it . . . because it relieves loneliness. . . . I have sought it . . . because . . . ").

Since there are other ways of looking at form in composition, in trying to get at the "topical" pattern, we would want to abstract only those sentences that relate to the specific formal topic of invention under consideration: division into parts, definition, comparison, contrast, and so forth. We could abstract the appropriate sentences exactly as they appear in the text and put them into a paradigm that represents the text's meaning. However, if it appears necessary, we could regularize the text to reveal the underlying pattern more clearly. We can do this by using a sentence paraphrase, recasting the sentences in simpler form. The resultant paradigm will represent the topical structure of the essay.

The thesis sentence of the paradigm marks the origination of a pattern that is transmitted through space and time. The supporting sentences represent stages in thinking, and the clincher sentence exemplifies closure. When we isolate the abstract paradigm, the organic unit seems to fade into the background. The pattern seems static. Yet the enduring pattern is wholly derived from aspects of the various temporal sections of the essay. The pattern endures in isolation, but it also exhibits itself in the whole.

In beginning our analysis of the Bertrand Russell essay, notice that the opening sentence is not only the thesis sentence, but also the sentence that indicates the plan of development. The word "three" suggests that a pattern of enumeration will follow. The word "passions" indicates a complementary pattern of classification. The sentence, in outline form, looks something like this:

> Three passions . . . have governed my life:
>   the longing for love,
>   the search for knowledge, and
>   unbearable pity for the suffering of mankind.

This thesis gives us a clue, a hint for what is to follow.

The second sentence in this paragraph qualifies and expands the idea of passions in the first sentence. The explicit tie-in is the repetition of the word "passions":

> These passions, like great winds, have blown me hither and thither, in a wayward course, over a deep ocean of anguish, reaching to the very verge of despair.

In paragraph 2, no one sentence advances the pattern. There is, for example, no topic sentence. Instead, the first three sentences advance the pattern by giving the reasons why the author sought love. So we provide a sentence that can serve as the organizing sentence of the paradigm and add to it those sentences or phrases that constitute its support. The result is the following pattern:

> [I have sought love . . .]
>   I have sought love, first, because it brings ecstasy . . .
>   I have sought it, next, because it relieves loneliness . . .
>   I have sought it, finally, because . . . I have seen . . . the prefiguring vision of the heaven that saints and
>   poets have imagined.

The first sentence of the next paragraph enumerates the second of Bertrand Russell's passions, knowledge:

> With equal passion I have sought knowledge.

And the subsequent sentences in that paragraph form the support structure:

> With equal passion I have sought knowledge . . .
>   I have wished to understand the hearts of men . . .
>   I have wished to know why the stars shine . . . And
>   I have tried to apprehend the Pythagorean power by
>   which number holds sway above the flux . . .

The first sentence of the fourth paragraph repeats the words "love" and "knowledge" of the two previous paragraphs and continues the main idea. It is a transitional sentence. The second sentence of that paragraph advances the overall pattern by enumerating the third passion that has governed Bertrand Russell's life. So we use this sentence and add to it the supporting details, but this time regularize the support pattern to make it parallel the structure of the support patterns of the previous paragraphs:

> But always pity brought me back to earth . . .
>   [I have pitied] children in famine . . .
>   [I have pitied] victims tortured by oppressors . . .
>   [I have pitied] helpless old people a hated burden to their sons . . .
>   [I have pitied] the whole world of loneliness, poverty and pain . . .

Finally, the first sentence of the last paragraph completes the pattern, and coupled with the first sentence of the essay it acts as a frame device for the entire essay:

> This has been my life.

If we put the various stages of the process together, we get this overall pattern:

1

Three passions, simple but overwhelmingly strong, have governed my life: the longing for love, the search for knowledge, and unbearable pity for the suffering of mankind.

These passions, like great winds, have blown me hither and thither, in a wayward course, over a deep ocean of anguish, reaching to the very verge of despair.

2

[I have sought love . . .]

I have sought love, first, because it brings ecstasy . . .

I have sought it, next, because it relieves loneliness . . .

I have sought it, finally, because . . . I have seen the prefiguring vision of the heaven that saints and poets have imagined . . .

3

With equal passion I have sought knowledge . . .

I have wished to understand the hearts of men . . .

I have wished to know why the stars shine . . .

I have tried to apprehend the Pythagorean power by which number holds sway above the flux . . .

4

Love and knowledge . . . led upward toward the heavens.

But always pity brought me back to earth.

[I have pitied] children in famine . . .

[I have pitied] victims tortured by oppressors . . .
[I have pitied] helpless old people a hated burden to their sons . . .
[I have pitied] the whole world of loneliness, poverty and pain . . .

5

This has been my life.
I have found it worth living, and would gladly live it again if the chance were
offered me.

If we "normalize" the pattern, taking a few more liberties with the
phrasing, we get the following paradigm:

1   Three passions . . . have governed my life: the longing for love, the search
    for knowledge, and unbearable pity for the suffering of mankind.

2   [I have sought love.]
    I have sought love because it brings ecstasy.
    I have sought it because it relieves loneliness.
    I have sought it because it contains a vision of
    the heavens that saints and poets have imagined.

3   I have sought knowledge.
    I have wished to understand the hearts of men.
    I have wished to know why the stars shine.
    I have tried to apprehend the Pythagorean power
    by which number holds sway above the flux.

4   [I have sought pity.]
    [I have pitied] children in famine.
    [I have pitied] victims tortured by oppressors.
    [I have pitied] the whole world of loneliness,
    poverty and pain.

5   This has been my life.

This pattern represents the paradigmatic structure of the entire essay. It is
the master technique for adapting the writer's thought to the reader. In this essay,
Russell wants to convince the reader that life is worth living. He does this by
reflecting on his past and by appealing to the reader's emotions, by evoking
feelings of love, justice, and pity for the sufferings of mankind. But words such
as "love," "knowledge,"—"justice," and "pity for the sufferings of mankind"
take on an ethical sense when they are presented as values by someone whose
life reflects their meaning.

The overall logical pattern is that of informal classification reinforcd by
enumeration. There is a genus-species relationship between the word "passions" in the opening sentence and the specific passions that follow—the
longing for love, the search for knowledge, and unbearable pity for the suffering

of mankind. The logical structure of the classification pattern is informed by the formal topics of genus and species which help to organize the ethical and emotional appeals.

Paradigms can be depicted in a number of ways. They can be instantiated as complete sentences:

> Three passions have governed my life.
> The first passion is the longing for love.
> The second is the search for knowledge.
> The third is pity for the suffering of mankind.
> These are the passions that have governed my life.

Or they can be depicted by a more abstract scheme that emphasizes their relationship to the formal topics:

> *Classification Paradigm*
> Introduction (states the *genus*)
> Type 1 (*species* 1)
> Type 2 (*species* 2)
> Type 3 (*species* 3)
> Types 4, 5, 6 . . . (species 4, 5, 6 . . .)
> Conclusion (restates, summarizes, etc.)

The parts of a paradigm do not necessarily bear a one-to-one relationship to corresponding paragraphs. The divisions represent chunks or sections of the essay. These sections can be paragraph divisions, or they can be larger thought units, as the following scheme indicates:

> Paragraph 1 (introduction)
> Paragraph 2 (statement of the *thesis*)
> Paragraph 3 (type 1)
> Paragraph 4 (qualification of paragraph 3)
> Paragraph 5 (type 2)
> Paragraph 6 (digression)
> Paragraph 7 (transitional paragraph)
> Paragraph 8 (type 3)
> Paragraph 9 (conclusion)

The point to remember about paradigms is that they are a kind of verbal schemata. They are one of the ways by which writers represent meaning to themselves. They are also acts of rhetorical choice. The sentence form of the paradigm is the means that writers use to represent meaning to others.

If we accept this view of paradigms as structural counterparts of the formal topics, what are the implications for the teaching of composition?

The first implication is that in teaching rhetorical invention we might point out to students the close relationship that exists between the formal topics and form in composition and ask them to use the categories of invention to discover form and meaning in their own writing.

The second implication is that in teaching rhetorical invention we might more profitably begin with paradigms of various kinds, in their abstract form as well as in their actual shape in a discourse, and then go back and relate them to the topics of invention. Since one of the biggest failings of students is an inability to follow a logical plan of development in their writing, it makes sense to start with form and structure first. But because these paradigms can also serve as explicit methods of invention, students will be learning discovery procedures at the same time that they are learning something about form.

The third implication is that in teaching form and arrangement we might ask students to construct the sentence form of paradigms before they write their essays. By putting their ideas into the form of a paradigm, students will get an opportunity to analyze the underlying reasoning process of the entire essay, the appropriate supporting evidence, the emotional and ethical appeals, the values embedded in those appeals, and the means of adapting their ideas to their readers.

The final implication is that a paradigmatic view of the composing process is developmental. This means that no longer should teachers of composition conceive of themselves too narrowly as purveyors of superficial skills. Rather, they should think of their roles more properly as that of facilitators in the important task of helping students to develop mental abilities that will govern much of what they do in later life. Acquiring, understanding, and using paradigms can help them to ascend to higher levels of linguistic and conceptual development.

LESTER FAIGLEY

The Problem of Topic in Texts

My daily trip to the mail box often yields one or more real-estate ads, one of the side effects of the great Sun Belt land rush. These ads come in two genres. Some are disguised as regular first-class mail, sometimes using a law firm's stationery. Other ads arrive in odd-sized, multicolored envelopes that brazenly announce themselves as junk mail. Both genres use the same selling tactic, promising free gifts for visiting a real-estate development. An example of the red, white, and blue genre begins:

> ONE OF THESE FABULOUS AWARDS IS
> YOURS ABSOLUTELY FREE!

> 1. Lincoln-Mercury Cougar
> 2. RCA Color Console TV
> 3. Carphone RC22 Telephone

The AWARD you receive will be determined by matching the AWARD NUMBER above to the AWARD NUMBER SHEET at PEDERNALES RIVER RANCH. You have been computer selected and WILL RECEIVE one of these awards just for visiting!

The opening of this ad illustrates some of the problems of defining topic in a written text. In terms of text features, the most likely candidate for the topic of this segment is "award." "Award" is repeated in each sentence and serves as the antecedent for the list of prizes following the first sentence. From my experience with this genre, however, I know that the topic will shift from "award" to what is being offered for sale, in this case "Pedernales River Ranch." Furthermore, I know that the intent of this document is to get me to buy land, not to give me an award.

This short example illustrates a crucial problem for those who study the structure of texts because any adequate notion of text structure depends on being able to identify what a reader will consider as the topic in a stretch of text. Yet, as the real-estate ad shows, identification of topic is not simply a matter of recognizing features in a text. I will argue in this essay that topic in written texts arises from a complex relationship of text features, the reader's knowledge of the subject of the text, and the reader's recognition of the intent of the text in a particular context. Before I set out my argument, I would like to consider further why an understanding of the phenomenon of topic is critical to the study of written texts. To begin I will review the debate over paragraph structure that appeared in composition journals in the mid-1960s. This debate is instructive because the inability to define topic proved to be the bane of theories of paragraph structure.

The Problem of Defining Topic in Paragraphs

In the mid-sixties the paragraph was one of the most prominent subjects of discussion among composition teachers. That interest led to a series of articles appearing in successive issues of *College Composition and Communication*. The October 1965 issue contained Francis Christensen's "Generative Rhetoric of the Paragraph," which advanced the cumulative sentence as the structural paradigm of the paragraph.[1] In the December issue, Alton Becker proposed a model of paragraph structure based on arrangements of semantic "slots"—such as "topic-restriction-illustration" and "problem-solution"—in "A Tagmemic Approach to Paragraph Analysis."[2] Paul Rodgers then offered a third view in the February 1966 issue with "A Discourse-Centered Rhetoric of the Paragraph," arguing that paragraphs are orthographic conventions not controlled by rules governing their structure.[3] In the May 1966 issue, Christensen, Becker, and Rodgers agreed to comment on each other's work. Their reflections, along with those of Josephine Miles and David Karrfalt, brought several issues underlying the paragraph debate into focus.[4]

Christensen and Becker recognized the similarities of their positions. Both assumed that texts are processed hierarchically, that a reader moves from understanding words to understanding phrases to understanding sentences and paragraphs. Both thought of paragraphs as "macrosentences" or "metasentences." In spite of their differences, both Christensen and Becker worked squarely in the tradition of structural linguistics, starting at the bottom and working through linguistic units at successively higher levels of structure. Rodgers pointed out, however, that this notion of structure depends on recognizing the topic of the paragraph. Becker defined his "T slot" as where "the topic is stated," and Christensen was similarly vague. Rodgers maintained "The 'statement of topic' has never, to my knowledge, been defined thoroughly. Until we define it, we shall not be able to describe it to everyone's satisfaction or even to agree upon its location."[5] Rodgers proposed that we should look not at paragraphs but at semantic units that he called "*stadia* of discourse." A stadium of discourse, according to Rodgers, may or may not conform to paragraph boundaries. Rodgers admitted that he had no way of defining a "stadium of discourse."[6]

Work following the "Symposium on the Paragraph" tended to show that the issues raised by Rodgers, Christensen, and Becker were complex and that their models of paragraph structure lacked explicitness.[7] The key issue remained how to determine the "topic" of a paragraph, a concept that Alexander Bain had introduced a century before in 1866.[8] Even during Bain's lifetime, his principle that well-formed paragraphs have topic sentences was challenged. In 1900, John F. Genung agreed with Bain that " in all cases the topic should so control every part of the structure [of the paragraph] as to be clearly apprehended," but he noted that "Different kinds of subject-matter, however, may cause [the topic] to be apprehended in different ways: it may be definitely pointed out, in so many words; or it may be left for the reader to gather and mentally realize as the total effect."[9] Genung's observation that all paragraphs do not have overt topic sentences was emphatically made again in 1971. In a corpus of twenty-five essays from *The Atlantic, Harper's,* and other journals, Richard Braddock estimated that only 13 percent of contemporary nonfiction paragraphs begin with a topic sentence and only 3 percent end with one.[10] Braddock's figures, often quoted by critics of the paragraph theorists, contributed to the dwindling interest in paragraph structure among many composition researchers.

Failure to define "topic" in paragraphs proved to be one of the more conspicuous weaknesses in the theories of Christensen, Becker, and Rodgers and remains a troublesome problem not only for attempts to describe the structure of a particular text but also to explain the rhetorical effectiveness of that text. Before we can build a theory of how texts are rhetorically effective, we must first know what a reader is going to find important in a text. The problem of topic leads to another critical question: Is the structure of a text similar to the structures found in smaller linguistic units, such as sentences, or is structure in a text a fundamentally different phenomenon?

I take the position that describing structure in a text requires approaches that are fundamentally different from those used to describe smaller linguistic units. In this essay I examine discourse topic from three viewpoints: one focusing on the relationship between topic and text features, one focusing on the relationship between topic and the reader's knowledge, and one focusing on the relationship between topic and the situational context. I conclude by arguing that topic can be best understood as a combination of these three relationships.

Topic and the Text

The Prague School

Efforts to identify topic in terms of text features directly or indirectly evolve from work of "Prague school" linguists. The tradition of looking at topic within sentences dates at least to work by Vilém Mathesius in the 1930s.[11]

Mathesius and his coworkers studied the syntax of Slavic languages, which have extensive systems of inflectional endings more closely resembling Latin than English. The Slavic inflectional system permits wider potential variation in word order than is possible in English, but in fact, few of the possibilities are realized. Mathesius found that to a great extent word order is governed by the surrounding discourse. He divided sentences into two parts—the *theme* (what the sentence is about) and the *enunciation* (what is said about the theme). He made the general observation that in Slavic sentences, the theme comes before the enunciation. Other linguists continued Mathesius' division of sentences into two parts, using the terms *theme-rheme* or *topic-comment*. Although what is meant by these terms varies from linguist to linguist, the essential notion is that the theme expresses the topic of a sentence and the rheme is what is said about the theme. In English the theme is most often the grammatical subject and the rheme is usually the predicate.

A later generation of Prague school linguists extended the theme/rheme notion to entire texts. The most influential of these linguists is František Daneš, who theorizes that each utterance can be analyzed at three levels: a semantic level, a grammatical level, and an utterance level. [12] The semantic level includes case relationships such as actor, action, and goal. The grammatical level describes categories such as subject, verb, and object. The utterance level is divided into two subcategories—topical structure (theme-rheme) and information structure (known vs. unknown information—also referred to as "old-new" or "given-new"). [13] Daneš insists that while theme and given information are usually the same, in some cases they are different. He points out that the theme is not necessarily given information. For example, theme and given information do not co-occur in certain emphatic constructions, such as "Disco music I can't listen to."

More important to the present discussion is how Daneš applies the theme-rheme notion to units of discourse longer than sentences. He describes three kinds of topical progression. The first is simple linear progression. Consider the following set of sentences:

(1) The recorded history of Vietnam began in 207 B.C., when the renegade Chinese warlord Trieu Da established the Kingdom of Nam Viet.
(2) Trieu Da's non-Chinese kindgom was overthrown by the Chinese in 111 B.C.
(3) The Chinese held the North for more than one thousand years. [14]

In the simple linear progression, the rheme of sentence 1 becomes the theme of sentence 2, the rheme of sentence 2 becomes the theme of sentence 3, and so on:

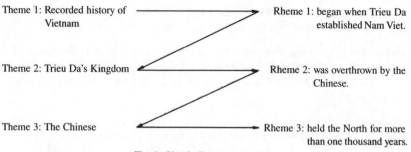

Fig. 1. Simple linear progression

The second type of progression is continuous theme progression. In this instance, the same theme is used in a succession of sentences, as in:

(1) Ho Chi Minh was at various times known at Nguyen That Thanh, Le Thuy, Song Man Tcho, Nguyen O Phap, and Nguyen Sinh Chin.
(2) He had almost as many political stances as aliases, presenting himself as a Nationalist, pro- and anti-French, Chinese, or Japanese, as the situation demanded.
(3) He organized the Indochinese Communist Party in Hong Kong in 1930.

It can be represented as:

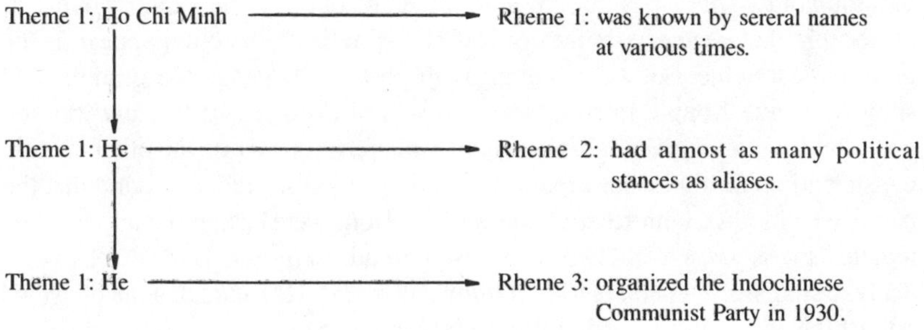

Theme 1: Ho Chi Minh ——————————▶ Rheme 1: was known by sereral names
                                              at various times.

Theme 1: He ———————————————▶ Rheme 2: had almost as many political
                                              stances as aliases.

Theme 1: He ———————————————▶ Rheme 3: organized the Indochinese
                                              Communist Party in 1930.

Fig. 2. Continuous theme progression

The third type is thematic pregression with derived themes. Daneš claims that in texts like the one below, the theme is implicit:

(1) The narrow coastal plains of South Vietnam are characterized by sandy beaches, wide, flat river valleys, extensive marshland, and rice fields.
(2) The central highlands are a mountainous region, extensively forested and very rugged.

(3) The Mekong Delta comprises a very flat, low-lying area of extensive rice paddies and swamps, cut by rivers, streams, and canals.

Daneš would maintain that the topic of the text above is something like "the terrain of South Vietnam." Such an implied discourse topic, which he calls the *hypertheme,* comes from the aggregate of sentences. He represents the hypertheme as [T]:

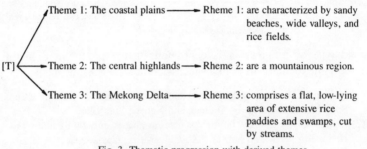

Fig. 3. Thematic progression with derived themes

He calls the themes of the individual sentences *derived themes.*

Daneš' extension of Prague school theory has inspired several recent applications to the study of writing. Vande Kopple tested how maintenance or violation of two of Daneš' progressions affect readability and memory of a text. Observing that sentence themes or topics in English most often appear as the grammatical subject or as an initial noun phrase other than the grammatical subject, Vande Kopple manipulated two sets of passages so that one version consistently placed given information in topic positions while the other version consistently placed new information in topic positions. Students found that the passages with given information in topic positions were easier to read, and they recalled these passages better. Witte used an adaptation of Daneš' scheme to analyze students' revision of a short informative text. He found that the revisions rated high in quality provided more elaboration on fewer subtopics than did revisions rated low in quality.[15] Witte demonstrated that Daneš' system can provide a simple measure of idea development.

Another notion implicit in Daneš' topical progressions is that sentence topics are directly related to the topic of discourse. Witte and I designed an experiment to test the relationship among sentence topics and perceptions of the discourse topic. We wanted to know if consistent assignment of a particular subtopic to grammatical subject positions would affect what readers take as the topic of the passage. We manipulated a test passage about the conversion of World War II transport aircraft to civilian airliners in much the same way as did Vande Kopple. In one text we consistently placed the names of the airliners in subject positions. In another we placed the names of the manufacturers in subject positions. In a third passage we alternated airlines and manufacturers in subject positions. Fifty-one college students participated in our experiment, with seventeen reading each passage. After students had finished reading, they performed an interruptive task and then wrote a phrase that would serve as a title for the passage that they had just read. Of the seventeen students who read the passage with airliners in subject positions, eleven gave a title exclusively naming the planes, such as "Commercial Aircraft after World War II." But most students who read the passage with manufacturers in subject positions or the passage that mixed airliners and manufacturers in subject positions supplied titles that stressed the conversion of the planes from military to civilian use, titles such as "Converting Wartime Planes to Peacetime Use." These results indicate that consistent assignment of a particular topic to grammatical subject positions does affect readers' perception of the discourse topic.[16]

In spite of these successes, the Prague school approach to topic in texts has serious limitations. To begin with, many stretches of discourse cannot be analyzed using Daneš' three kinds of topical progression. Consider the following pair of sentences:

(1) The porter carried my bags down the steep hill to a pension.
(2) The lounge was filled with elderly English women drinking tea.

Intuitively we might call this a simple linear progression. But if we assign *lounge* as the theme of the second sentence, it has no direct antecedent in the first sentence. To connect these two sentences, we must know that *pensions* are small European hotels that usually have lounges. Thus to handle even routine discourse, Daneš' progressions must be augmented with some way of accounting for semantic association, such as Halliday and Hasan's notion of lexical collocation.[17]

A second limitation is that Daneš' progressions do not explain adequately the role of *anaphora* in signalling the topic of a stretch of discourse. Anaphors can be pronouns, general lexical items (e.g., "car" referring to "Chevrolet"), or other expressions that refer back to a previously mentioned element in a text. Anaphoric expressions maintain focus on a particular topic. Notice in the following example how the pronouns in the last sentence connect the paragraph, even though they are separated from the referent by several sentences:

Although he knew it had turned cold in the high country, Harry decided to take the chance that the pass was still open. The road started up into the trees, and the rain started falling harder. The incline grew steeper, and the rain changed to sleet. The road was beginning to get slippery. At 8,000 feet, wet snow began clinging to the windshield, building up faster than the wipers could push it to the side. The headlights penetrated only a few feet in front of the car. There was no place to turn around on the narrow road. He realized he'd made a bad mistake.

Daneš' topic progressions do not explain the connecting function of anaphora nor why this passage maintains a consistent focus on Harry's attempt to drive over the pass. The pronouns in the last sentence signal to the reader what is centrally important.

Third, there are numerous other textual markers of topic besides topics in sentences. Rhetorical questions direct readers' attention to a topic. Parallelism, demonstrative adjectives ("this", "that"), cleft sentences ("It is ice cream that kids like"), and pseudo-cleft sentences ("What kids like is ice cream") often perform the same function. Of course, written texts give other options for marking topics, such as headings and boldfacing.

A more serious limitation is that Daneš's progressions offer no way of accommodating knowledge that is not prompted by the previous text. As I was writing the present section, my five-year-old son, prompted by hearing the name "Beatles" mentioned, uttered the following:

(1) John Lennon was the most talented Beatle.
(2) Someone shot him.
(3) They caught him.

Notice that in sentences 2 and 3 the information referring to previous text, in each case "him," appears at the end. My son assumed that the referent of "they" is understood, and he uttered sentence 3 with the same lowered pitch and stress on "they" as if the referent had been present in his previous sentence.[18] The point here is that extralinguistic factors have as much to do with determining what is given and new information as what is present in the text itself. Ellen Prince points out that there are at least three distinct notions of "given" or "old" information among linguists who have used these terms and that no two of them mean exactly the same thing by "given."[19]

The short example from my son points to the major theoretical weakness in Daneš' approach to topic in discourse. This weakness is best illustrated by the third type of topical progression he outlines—the progression that postulates a hypertheme. What Daneš is saying, in effect, is that some texts have a topic that cannot be inferred from any particular sentence but to which all sentences are connected. This progression allows for the reader's active role in determining a topic from some texts. Daneš, however, offers no explanation of how a reader might come to understand the topic of a stretch of discourse apart from sentence topics. I will return to this point later, but now I would like to move on to another text-centered effort to understand topic in discourse.

The Propositional Approach

During the 1970s, other European linguists and some psychologists and reasearchers in artificial intelligence in America began looking at the problem of how readers infer a topic in a stretch of discourse. The linguists' interest grew from efforts to formulate text grammars that would describe the structure of texts as well as the structure of sentences. The psychologists and researchers in artificial intelligence were interested in how texts are processed and stored in memory.

One of the questions psychologists had to address is how readers arrive at a general notion of what a text is about. But before psychologists could attempt empirical investigations of meaning, they had to find some way of describing meaning. Psychologists have generally elected to represent meaning in a text as a *text base* consisting of a series of *propositions*.[20] Propositions are composed of one predicate term and one or more arguments. Verbs, adverbs, adjectives, or relations between propositions function as predicates. The remaining key words are argument terms. Arguments fulfill case relations such as agent, object, and instrument. In most models the predicate term is placed first in the representation of a proposition, and all terms are capitalized to distinguish them as concepts. For example, "Mary read the book" would be represented as (READ, BOOK, MARY). Propositions can be embedded within other propositions to account for more complicated sentences.

The method for analyzing propositions developed by Walter Kintsch has been used often in research on comprehension. In Kintsch's method, repetition of argument is a necessary condition for coherence; that is, propositions in a coherent text are connected because they share at least one concept. Kintsch's model is also hierarchical. In a short text, a proposition near the beginning of the text is at the top of the hierarchy, and propositions which repeat arguments are at successively lower levels. Several insights into how people comprehend texts have come from experiments using Kintsch's methodology. Reading times have been linked to the number of propositions a text contains as distinguished from its word length, giving one indication why conventional readability formulas are inadequate as measures of ease of comprehension.[21] More important to the present discussion are experiments examining which propositions in a text subjects are likely to remember.[22] Researchers have consistently found that propositions higher in the hierarchy are remembered better than propositions lower in the hierarchy. This finding has come to be known as the *levels effect*.

To analyze longer texts Kintsch incorporated the theory of text structure offered by the Dutch linguist Teun van Dijk. Van Dijk distinguishes between a text base or *microstructure,* which contains all propositions in a text, and a *macrostructure,* which represents the "gist" of that text.[23] Macrostructures are said to consist of *macropropositions* derived in ways similar to Kintsch's method for ranking propositions in a hierarchy. Thus the macropropositions function as labels for segments of the text, and Van Dijk claims that the macrostructure represents the overall topic of discourse.

Kintsch and Van Dijk have worked together for several years in theorizing and testing models of how texts are processed. Their first model, proposed in 1978, is based on the assumption that as we read we understand meaning proposition by proposition (the microstructure) and at the same time abstract the "gist" of that text (the macrostructure).[24] They analyzed the micro- and macropropositons from a test paragraph and calculated the probability that people would recall each individual proposition. Their predicitions turned out to be reasonably accurate when compared to data from experiments with actual readers. Additional experiments supported the hypothesis that two kinds of processing go on during reading—processing at the microlevel and processing at the macrolevel.[25]

In spite of the fact that Kintsch and van Dijk's 1978 model has been tested empirically and most of its assumptions have been supported by data, it has serious limitations for explaining how readers recognize topic in a stretch of text. Let's look at another example:

> The New York Yankees defeated the Boston Red Sox, 1-0, yesterday afternoon in the final game of the 1961 regular season. The Yankees have already clinched the American League pennant. They will open the World Series on Wednesday at Yankee Stadium against Cincinnati. Three Yankee pitchers, Bill Stafford, Hal Reniff, and Luis Arroyo, allowed the Red Sox only three hits.

Without going into a detailed analysis, the proposition contained in the first clause (DEFEAT, NEW YORK YANKEES, BOSTON RED SOX) would be at the top of the propositional hierarchy with all other propositions subordinate to it. If we asked readers to give the topic of the passage, they probably would respond with something like the top proposition. Likewise, if readers were asked to recall the entire passage, we could predict with some confidence that the proposition at the top of the hierarchy would be the one most frequently remembered. These hypothetical findings support Kintsch and van Dijk's processing mode.

I decided to test this hypothesis, but I added two more sentences at the end of the same passage:

> The New York Yankees defeated the Boston Red Sox, 1-0, yesterday afternoon in the final game of the 1961 regular season. The Yankees have already clinched the American League pennant. They will open the World Series on Wednesday at Yankee Stadium against Cincinnati. Three Yankee pitchers, Bill Stafford, Hal Reniff, and Luis Arroyo, allowed the Red Sox only three hits. A home run by

Roger Maris in the fourth provided the only run in the game. Maris' 61st home run of the year came off losing pitcher Tracy Stallard.

The propositions in the last sentence would be represented at the very bottom of the proposition hierarchy because they are subordinate to propositions in the previous sentence, which in turn are subordinate to propositions earlier in the text.

Forty undergraduate students participated in this experiment. Students first completed a ten-item quiz to test their knowledge of baseball. Next they read the passage. They worked for two minutes on a word puzzle that served as an interruptive task. Then they were asked to supply a phrase that could serve as a headline if the passage they had just read had appeared in a newspaper on the day after the game. Finally, students were asked to write down everything that they remembered about the passage.

For a title, twenty-two students gave something like "Yankees Defeat Red Sox"—the proposition at the top of the hierarchy. However, seven students wrote titles like "Yankees Begin World Series," and nine other students wrote titles like "Maris Breaks Record with 61st Home Run"—a proposition near the bottom of the hierarchy. The assignment of titles was not as arbitrary as the data suggest. On the basis of the quiz on baseball, I divided students into high-knowledge and low-knowledge groups. Of the twenty-four students in the low-knowledge group, nineteen supplied "Yankees Beat Red Sox" titles," three gave "Yankees Begin Series" titles, and two gave no title. On the other hand, high-knowledge individuals exclusively supplied the "Maris Tops Ruth" titles. Those familiar with baseball knew that from a baseball fan's point of view Maris' home run, breaking Babe Ruth's season record of sixty home runs set in 1927, far overshadowed the importance of the particular game in which it occurred.

The results of my modest experiment do not necessarily disprove Kintsch and van Dijk's 1978 model of text processing. What they do show is that readers make connections on the basis of prior knowledge as well as what is in a text, an aspect to which Kintsch and van Dijk devote much more attention in their 1983 book on discourse comprehension.[26] Prior knowledge influences what a reader considers to be the topic of a text and what a reader remembers about that text. Thus, to account for what is perceived as the topic, we must in some way take into account a reader's knowledge. In the next section I will look at how some researchers have attempted to incorporate the reader's knowledge into a model of comprehension.

Topic and Readers' Knowledge

The approaches to topic that I have discussed to this point all focus on the text. The Prague school places topic in nominals at or near the beginning of sentences. Kintsch and van Dijk's 1978 model locates topic at the top of a propositional hierarchy. But the different interpretations of topic for the baseball example suggest that any approach to topic that considers only text elements will be inadequate to explain what a reader perceives as most important. One line of research has used ambiguous passages to examine the relationship between knowledge of the world and comprehension. A group of researchers read the following passage to selected college students:[27]

> Rocky slowly got up from the mat, planning his escape. He hesitated a moment
> and thought. Things were not going well. What bothered him the most was being
> held, especially since the charge against him had been weak. He considered his
> present situation. The lock that held him was strong but he thought he could
> break it. He knew, however, that his timing would have to be perfect. Rocky was
> aware that it was because of his early roughness that he had been penalized so
> severely—much too severely from his point of view. The situation was becoming
> frustrating; the pressure had been grinding on him for too long. He was being
> ridden unmercifully. Rocky was getting angry now. He felt he was ready to make
> his move. He knew that his success or failure would depend on what he did in the
> next few seconds.

Physical education majors thought the passage was about wrestling, while other students thought it was about a prisoner. Additional passages were tested at the same time, including a passage that could be interpreted as about either playing music or playing cards. Again background knowledge influenced how students interpreted the passages. Music majors interpreted the the passage as about music. Only one student in five was aware that another interpretation was possible.

Prior knowledge also influences how much people remember about texts. Several experiments have established that people with knowledge of the subject matter of a text will remember more about that text than people with little or no knowledge of that subject.[28] I obtained similar results in the experiment with the baseball passage. I examined what the students remembered about the passage, looking for six facts that no individual probably would have known before reading the passage—the score of the game, the names of the three Yankee pitchers, the number of hits the Yankee pitchers allowed, and the inning in which Maris hit the home run. High-knowledge individuals on the average remembered over two of these facts while low-knowledge individuals remembered almost none.

A week later I asked students to again remember everything that they could about the passage. High-knowledge individuals, as I expected, remembered more about the passage than did low-knowledge individuals, who had virtually forgotten the contents altogether. Even more interesting was the way that the high-knowledge individuals remembered the passage. Although Babe

Ruth was not mentioned in the original passage, seven of sixteen high-knowledge people mentioned Ruth in the delayed-recall test. Furthermore, high-knowledge individuals tended to reverse the order of the original paragraph, placing Maris' sixty-first home run at the beginning. These distortions suggest that the readers' knowledge not only influences how they find the topic, but also how they later reconstruct the topic.

One of the first theorists who argued that memory is reconstructive was Frederick Bartlett. In a book published in 1932 titled *Remembering*, [29] Bartlett reported experiments using Eskimo folktales which showed that people consistently distort what is culturally unfamiliar in recalling a passage. Bartlett used the term *schemata* to describe structures of knowledge, a term that Kant had used two centuries earlier to describe categories of knowledge. Although Bartlett's work is now viewed as a pioneering effort, it was dismissed at the time because of the exotic nature of the passages he used and the behaviorists' general prejudice against verbal data of any kind.

It was not until the mid-1970s that researchers again became interested in schemata. [30] The ability of schema theory to explain how inferences are made is especially important to understanding how people derive topic from discourse. People use schemata to make predictions about the world, extrapolating from part to whole. In many cases these predictions are incorrect, just as in J.G. Saxe's poem, "The Blind Men and the Elephant," adapted from a Middle Eastern folktale. Six blind men sought to observe an elephant. The first touched the elephant's side and concluded that the elephant was like a wall. The second felt a tusk and compared the elephant to a spear. The third grabbed the trunk, claiming that the elephant was like a snake. The fourth touched its leg and thought the elephant was like a tree. The fifth held an ear and judged the elephant to resemble a fan. The sixth held the tail and found the elephant to be like a rope. Readers approach a text much like the blind men in Saxe's poem. They make predictions, starting with the title and its projection of what the text is going to be about. These predictions frequently have to be rejected or modified. If a reader cannot discover any topic, the text will seem fragmented and unorganized.

When students read the baseball passage, they use their knowledge of written texts and the world to construct a topic. The first sentence was characteristic of a sports news story. Readers used schemata associated with baseball. Nowhere is baseball explicitly mentioned, yet no reader mistakenly identified the sport. Most readers found the remainder of the text consistent with their initial prediction. Some readers, however, found the configuration of the text inconsistent with their knowledge of baseball and sports reporting. These readers activated schemata associated with baseball records. They rejected their initial schema of a game report and replaced it with a schema of a major baseball record.

When readers do not arrive at the topic that the writer intends, schema theory offers three explanations of what goes wrong.[31] First, a reader might lack the appropriate schemata. Second, a reader might have the appropriate schemata but may not find the clues in the text that suggest those schemata. Third, a reader may derive a topic different from the one intended by the author. Schema theory provides us with a way of accounting for why different readers might arrive at different topics for the same text. But, at the same time, schema theory leads us into the very troublesome problem of being sure we can correctly determine a writer's intentions—a problem that any theory that looks at ways of identifying topic eventually confronts. Whether we can know a writer's intentions has prompted intense—and continuing—debate among literary critics. In the next section, I will look at how a few philosophers and linguists have considered intention in texts.

Topic and Context

In the two previous sections, I have considered topic as a textual and as a cognitive phenomenon. Texts, however, are not simply analyzable objects or mental stimuli. People write texts in specific situations for specific readers, to serve specific purposes. Written texts, therefore, are social acts that convey the writer's intent or point. A writer's intent is not the same thing as the topic, but perceptions of topic are often dependent upon perceptions of intent. A famous example of a text whose intent was misunderstood occurred during the American Civil War. On the morning of July 1, 1863, the first day of the Battle of Gettysburg, Robert E. Lee's Confederate army overran two Union army corps blocking the western and northern approaches to Gettysburg. Lee's divisions sent the federal troops fleeing to high ground on the east side of Gettysburg, the only good defensive position left for the Union army to make a stand. Lee recognized the opportunity for a decisive victory. He wrote an order to Lieutenant General Richard S. Ewell to take Cemetery Hill, a height dominating the right flank of the Union line. Ewell had just replaced Thomas J. J. ("Stonewall") Jackson, whose own troops had killed him by mistake at the Battle of Chancellorsville two months earlier. Lee's order to Ewell was worded as a request ("press those people in order to secure possession of the heights . . . if practicable"), the way his orders to Jackson had always been worded.[32] Ewell apparently missed the point. He sent out patrols, but he did not send his divisions forward. The Confederates missed the chance to seize the dominant position on the battlefield.

George G. Meade, the commander of the Union Army facing Lee, realized the precariousness of his situation and rushed fresh troops to Cemetery Hill that night. Lee's attack on Cemetery Hill the next day was turned back, as was the desperate effort against the Union center on the third day known as

"Pickett's Charge." Lee's beaten army marched south to Virginia, never to return to Northern soil again.

In some sense Ewell probably understood what the message was about, but he failed to interpret the communicative intent of Lee's order. The study of communicative intent in language has come to be known as *pragmatics,* following from the division set out by Charles Morris.[33] Morris proposed that language could be analyzed three ways: "syntactics" (the study of form), "semantics" (the study of meaning exclusive of context), and "pragmatics" (the study of meaning in context). For many years pragmatics was a realm explored only by a few semiotic theorists. One of the first linguists to advance a theory of how context determines the effects of individual sentences was J. L. Austin.[34] Austin's "speech-act" theory proposed that sentences can be classified according to the speaker's or writer's intent as well as according to their form, the usual method of linguistic classification. Other theorists have elaborated Austin's proposals. For example, John Searle analyzes at four levels: as *utterance acts* possessing linguistic meaning (that is, a text that is grammatical), as *locutionary acts* possessing propositional content (that is, a coherent text), as *illocutionary acts* possessing intentions that a writer wishes the reader to recognize (such as a request), and as *perlocutionary acts* bringing desired effects upon readers (such as changing the reader's beliefs).[35] A writer successfully communicates if a reader recognizes the writer's illocutionary intentions, but writers are successful as persuaders only if the reader acts according to the writer's perlocutionary intention. In other words, the intent of a writer's request may be clear, but the reader may not want to do what the speaker requests. Thus according to speech-act theory, Ewell either understood the illocutionary intent of Lee's order to be a "request" instead of a "command," or he chose not to fulfill the illocutionary intent.

One problem in speech-act theory has been that very few statements announce their illocutionary intent. We don't say things like "I assert that I teach at the University of Texas," nor do generals write orders that begin "I command you to do this," unless they anticipate possible insubordination. People must infer what the speaker or writer intends in nearly all cases, a fact that would seem to encourage misunderstanding.[36] But we accurately interpret the intentions of most texts because of our previous reading experiences, our experiences with human behavior, and our experiences with the world in general. We know, for example, that form letters in odd-sized, multicolored envelopes announcing that we have won a contest are in reality gimmicks to get us to buy something. We make such inferences by what we have learned to be normal in certain contexts.[37] Defenders of Lee have argued that Lee had no such trouble giving similarly worded orders to Jackson in earlier battles. Ewell's failure to understand Lee—if we can rule out deliberate misconstrual—was probably caused by his lack of familiarity with Lee's politely worded orders. He had not learned what, for Lee, was normal discourse in a combat situation.

Another problem is that many speech acts are nonliteral. These acts range from remarks such as "It's a swell day for a picnic" uttered during a blizzard to extended satirical essays such as Swift's "A Modest Proposal." In a paper published in 1975 titled "Logic and Conversation," H. P. Grice extended speech-act theory to instances of nonliteral texts, acts which he called *implicature* and which others have called *indirect speech acts*.[38] Grice claimed that people make several assumptions about a text. He called these assumptions, taken together, the *Cooperative Principle*. He expressed these assumptions as maxims and grouped them under four categories:

1. QUANTITY. Make your text no more or less informative than is required.
2. QUALITY. Say only what you believe to be true and have adequate evidence to support.
3. RELATION. Be relevant.
4. MANNER. Be brief and orderly. Avoid obscurity and ambiguity.

According to Grice, such rules underlie not just texts but all rational behavior. The rules themselves are simple but powerful in potential applications, both to literal and nonliteral texts. For example, Lee's order violates the fourth category, Manner, which specifies that no statement should be left open to interpretation in a particular context.

A primary contribution of speech-act theory has been to show how much written communication depends upon the goals, expectations, and mutual knowledge of both readers and writers. "Topic" in discourse is closely linked to what a writer hopes to accomplish in that text and the reader's ability to recognize those intentions. Searle calls the reader's recognition of the writer's intentions the *illocutionary effect*. If a writer is to achieve an illocutionary effect, he or she must know not only a great deal about language and discourse but also a great deal about an intended reader's knowledge, attitudes, and capabilities.[39] Furthermore, a writer often must anticipate how a reader will interpret a text in a particular situation, such as in the midst of a major battle.

Toward An Understanding Of Topic In Texts

The various approaches to topic in texts present a paradox. Those who attempt to define topic in terms of text elements would argue that topic is necessarily signalled by elements in the texts. Furthermore, as I noted in my criticism of Daneš' topical progressions, topics in texts are marked by anaphora and several syntactic devices such as cleft sentences. Those who take the opposing position claim that perceptions of topic in a particular text can differ because of differences in readers' knowledge and the contexts in which it is read.

Perhaps the problem is not so much in which approach to topic is correct but whether the term *topic* is a useful one for describing the phenomenon. Two major notions of topic need to be sorted out. One notion is what I will call *index topic*. Index topics are what allow a reader to identify what a writer is talking about and to connect groups of sentences. Let's look at how index topics function in the real-estate ad. I have numbered the sentences for purposes of discussion:

> (1) ONE OF THESE FABULOUS AWARDS IS
>   YOURS ABSOLUTELY FREE!
>
>   1. Lincoln-Mercury Cougar
>   2. RCA Color Console TV
>   3. Carphone RC22 Telephone

(2) The AWARD you receive will be determined by matching the AWARD NUMBER above to the AWARD NUMBER SHEET at PEDERNALES RIVER RANCH. (3) You have been computer selected and WILL RECEIVE one of these awards just for visiting!

(4) This in NOT a vacation timeshare or a land development sale but a unique and fascinating NEW CONCEPT designed to provide wholesome alternatives to existing leisure and travel oportunities. (5) YOU'VE PROBABLY NEVER SEEN ANYTHING LIKE IT BEFORE! (6) PEDERNALES RIVER RANCH is open from 9:00 a.m. to 6:00 p.m. Friday, Saturday, Sunday, and Monday

A reader begins processing this text by choosing an index topic in the first sentence. The reader is alerted to "awards" by the demonstrative "these." If "award" is repeated or referred to in the second sentence, the reader will maintain "award" as the index topic. "Award" is repeated, and its role as the index topic is confirmed. The third sentence appears to shift "you" to the index topic, but readers accommodate the presence of narrators ("I") and addressees ("you") in texts as secondary topics. Narrators or addressees can assume topic prominence, but in general the focus is on the object under discussion.

The fourth sentence presents another problem, beginning with an un-specified "this." The reader must rule out "award" for a referent and must search for another index topic. The most likely candidate is "Pedernales River Ranch." The "it" in the fifth sentence also refers to Pedernales River Ranch, confirming that the index topic has shifted.

The process of finding and tracking index topics is also known as *focusing*. Candance Sidner describes focusing as a three-step process. First, the hearer or reader chooses a focus. Second, the hearer uses this focus to interpret anaphoric elements. Third, if the hearer decides an anaphoric expression refers to something other than the focus, she determines the focus has changed.[40] While readers rely on prior knowledge and contextual information to track index topics, these topics are marked syntactically and follow the constraints of particular languages.

The second notion of topic is what I will call *discourse topic*. Discourse topic is a more elusive notion than index topic because it is not always marked by overt elements in a text. It is more like what is called the "upshot" or the "gist" of a text. I discussed earlier van Dijk's attempt to represent the gist of a text as a macrostructure consisting of a series of macropropositions obtained by applying reduction rules to a propositional representation of a text. The goal is to show how a summary can be systematically derived from a text. Without going through the machinery of van Dijk's analytical scheme, the macroproposition of the first three sentences of the real estate ad would be something like "You will receive an award" or "You will receive an award for visiting Pedernales River Ranch."

But when I receive ads like the one for Pedernales River Ranch, I rarely read past the first paragraph. If someone were to ask me what the text is about, I would say, "It's another something-for-nothing real-estate scam." If I were asked to elaborate, I would say, "The ad promises you a gift for subjecting yourself to hard sales pitch, but what they don't tell you is that the cars they're giving away may be three inches long." For me, the gist of this ad is not the same as a summary of its contents. My knowledge that the prizes may be bogus obviously does not come from the text but from conversations with people who have "bit" on such ads. This is not to say that the text has a minimal role in determining the discourse topic. Under normal circumstances I could not validly interpret the gist of these sentences to mean the sky is going to fall tomorrow. The point is that cultural constraints—in this case the practices of land speculation in America—have as much to do with determining discourse topic as textual constraints.

To be fair, van Dijk makes provisions for "pragmatic macrostructures" to allow for such interpretations, and van Dijk and Kintsch discuss at length the influences of contextual cues, genre expectations, and differences in readers' knowledge, beliefs, attitudes, and goals on text comprehension in their 1983 book. Nevertheless, I maintain that the way in which I "read" junk mail is more typical than exceptional. When I read a scholarly article that follows the *APA Style Sheet* (e.g., an article in *Research in the Teaching of English*), I generally read the abstract first, then turn to the "discussion" section to find out what claims the author makes, then turn back to the "methods" and "results" sections to see if the experiment supports the claims. When I read literary criticism, on the other hand, I usually try to find out what question the author wishes to address before I start reading the essay.[41] These strategies do not simply reflect personal idiosyncracies but my familiarity with certain assumptions particular to academic disciplines.

The problem of topic in texts illustrates the limitations of studying texts as objects containing quantifiable units. The problem of topic takes us beyond the text as object, forcing us to recognize that the reader is an active participant in forming structure in a text. A more fruitful approach to topic and to questions of text structure in general is an interactionist approach, an approach that takes into account that the knowledge we use to interpret texts is socially transmitted and is an important aspect of culture.

ANDREW KEREK, DONALD A. DAIKER, AND MAX MORENBERG

The Effects of Intensive Sentence Combining on the Writing Ability of College Freshmen

In reviewing the state of research on writing less than a decade ago, Sherwin was able to cite only three studies concerned with transformational sentence combining (henceforth SC), concluding cautiously that the approach was "a promising way to help students toward greater skill in writing."[1] Research since then has strengthened—and perhaps begun to make good—that promise. A number of recent experiments involving primarily elementary and secondary school children have produced impressive evidence that SC practice, whether oral or written, indeed enhances students' syntactic maturity.[2] The results of these studies not only verify the normative data that Hunt[3] and O'Donnell et al.[4] have established for syntactic maturity at various grade levels in English, but also strongly support Hunt's insight that by stimulating elaboration and expansion *within* sentences, SC exercises can actually accelerate the students' syntactic growth and thus enable them to write on developmentally higher levels of syntactic fluency. Nevertheless, in spite of its repeatedly confirmed effectiveness in building certain types of syntactic skills, SC was bound to remain largely irrelevant to the ultimate concerns of the composition class as long as it failed to produce corresponding gains in overall writing quality.[5] It was therefore a crucial step forward when O'Hare was able to demonstrate for the first time, even if on a limited scale, that growth in syntactic maturity correlates significantly with subjectively judged gains in writing effectiveness.[6] O'Hare's findings were later confirmed for the same grade level by Combs[7] and Pedersen.[8] Because of its far-reaching implications for the teaching of composition in general, the evidence that has emerged from all these studies invites further extensive corroboration.

The substantial experimental study[9] on which the present paper is based fits into and expands this context of inquiry. It was intended to test the effectiveness of SC further as an approach to the teaching of writing, especially by seeking answers to a number of curricular and pedagogical questions left open by previous investigations. Above all, we were interested in how well SC worked on the college level, specifically in the freshman English class, which has so far been entirely bypassed by significant SC research. The normative figures that Hunt reported in his two pioneering monographs show a syntactic abyss separating twelfth graders from skilled adult writers, a gap about as wide as that dividing twelfth graders from fourth graders.[10] Since Hunt's data suggest that normal syntactic development continues beyond high school into adulthood, we hypothesized that even for college freshmen intensive SC practice should effectively stimulate and accelerate growth. In the process, as a side benefit, we would obtain normative data for this age group not currently available in the published literature. More important from our point of view, if increased syntactic fluency has proved to correlate with a significant improvement of writing quality in, say, seventh grade, we intended to test whether such a correlation could also be demonstrated for college freshmen. These, in essence, amounted to the two major hypotheses of the experiment.

Perhaps our most substantial departure from past experimental procedures involved the status of SC itself within the total composition course. In previous experiments, and apparently in some nonexperimental writing programs that incorporate SC, such practice has been treated as an adjunct or supplement to more conventional components of the course syllabus and as such used only for limited portions of the writing class.[11] But no one seems to know for sure how much SC per day or per week is sufficient or optimally effective, and indeed every recent experiment appears to have followed a different arbitrary formula.[12] In the present study, SC was *the* course. The experimental group consisted of genuine SC classes where students approached all questions of writing—rhetorical as well as syntactic and stylistic—exclusively through exercises calling for the judicious manipulation and synthesis of sentences. We emphasize "rhetorical" because most of these exercises invited the students to consider the contextual demands of the total discourse. (We found, in fact, that you can effectively and pleasantly put across just about any aspect of writing by discussing SC options—thesis, organization, coherence, emphasis, tone, rhythm, problems of grammar and punctuation as they arise, even diction.) A typical SC exercise would ask the student to combine into an effective whole—generally a paragraph or a short essay—a series of basic kernel sentences taken from William Strong's *Sentence Combining*[13] or supplied by the researchers. Such "open" exercises, in which no specific instructions for the combining were given other than that the final product ought to be "effective," alternated with semi-open, patterned types, which lent themselves to the use of certain free modifiers such as absolutes, appositives, and participial phrases. The emphasis throughout the course was on the students' *active* involvement in the writing process, on the one hand by producing from day to day the "best" possible version that they could come up with for particular combining sets, and on the other by participating in an intensive discussion and revision in class of their own and their peers' responses to the same task, learning in the process to weigh the syntactic, stylistic, and rhetorical consequences of given options. "Signaled" exercises calling for specific grammatical transformations, though widely used in previous experiments and common in SC texts, were altogether avoided in this course, and—in contrast to Christensen's Rhetoric Program, for example[14]—the use of grammatical terminology was minimized; one of our implicit goals was, in fact, to test the well-motivated claim that SC can be effective without requiring students to be trained in formal grammar.[15]

Furthermore, unlike the control classes, which followed the traditional local syllabus and used *The Harbrace Reader* and McCrimmon's *Writing with a Purpose,* the experimental sections did not engage in the reading and rhetorical analysis of essays by accomplished writers. It is a prevalent but as yet untested traditional asumption that the analytic-interpretive skills students may develop through the reading and discussion of model essays somehow directly and significantly transfer into active expressive skills, that is, into control of formal linguistic devices required by the writing process. Even if such transfer did occur, we argued, it was likely to be significantly less productive and of less direct practical benefit to the students of composition than controlled experience in syntactic and rhetorical decision-making in their own writing. But would not the experimental group, then, doing no reading at all as part of the course, fall behind in reading comprehension, as one might charge—even though it might register gains in some parameters of writing, possibly at the expense of that decline? In fact, we made a much stronger claim: that, as Stotsky and others[16] have speculated, intensive practice in putting sentences together would actually enhance the student's ability to take them apart and thus to interpret passages. Accordingly, we hypothesized that SC practice would have a positive effect on reading comprehension.[17] In short, since the respective syllabi followed by the experimental and control groups were unambiguously different, we expected that the results of this study, if significant, would suggest a clear choice between the two approaches to composition.

In other than the dependent variables just outlined, the two groups were entirely comparable, with all major independent variables carefully controlled. The total experimental population consisted of 290 freshmen controlled at Miami University in the fall of 1976, randomly assigned by computer to twelve sections of the required freshman writing course;[18] these were evenly divided into "experimentals" and "controls." Neither in SAT/ACT scores nor in the reading and writing pretests did the two groups show any statistically significant difference. The instructional staff for the project was selected with special care. Rather than adopting O'Hare's procedure, for example, who had the same two teachers (including himself) teach both the experimental and control classes, we chose for each group volunteer instructors who were commited to and enthusiastic about their respective approaches, and would have been more than gratified to see their own approach proven best. To see whether the relative experience and maturity of the teacher made any difference—whether, in fact, instructors with little or no teaching experience could cope with SC in the classroom—we had half of the experimental classes taught by faculty members and the other half by graduate assistants. These were meticulously matched on the control side, with the cooperation of the department chair and the director of freshman English, in terms of rank, years of teaching experience, and degrees of demonstrated teaching effectiveness. Furthermore, both groups wrote the same number of compositions during the term (both in and out of class), including a two-hour pretest and a two-hour posttest, each taken under identical conditions for all classes. Each test yielded approximately 600 to 700 words, generally considered adequate for syntactic analysis.[19] Two similar topics were used for the tests, with one-half of each group writing on one topic on the pretest and the reverse topic on the posttest, each subject thus producing an essay on both topics. Since the mode of discourse elicited by a question could affect the syntactic characteristics of the resulting paper,[20] each topic was carefully constructed to prompt an expositiory paper—the type of writing most emphasized in both the experimental and control sections of this program, and in freshman English classes in general. Both topics, however, lent themselves to narative and descriptive detail, which tend to make writing more concrete and more substantial.

The assessment of the experimental treatment involved both quantitive and qualitative procedures. The former consisted of a detailed analysis of pre- and posttests for words per clause, words per T-unit, and clauses per T-unit, according to by now well-known procedures,[21] by a team of graduate students fully trained for the purpose. On the other hand, the procedures for the subjective rating of writing quality used in this experiment substantially exceed the scope of those employed in previous SC research, and—we believe—surpass them in validity, accuracy, and reliability. These qualities are to a large extent a function of having available a sufficient number of qualified raters to evaluate a sufficient number of writing samples a sufficient number of times in a sufficient numer of different ways—although one would be hard pressed to define sufficiency itself other than by assuming that better raters and more ratings will produce more accurate results. In research of this sort three modes of rating have been common: (1) the holistic or impressionistic method (used by Mellon, for example); (2) the forced-choice technique (adopted by O'Hare and by Combs); and (3) the analytic approach (employed by Pedersen), each of which in and by itself has certain limitations.[22] But all used together, applied to the same corpus of writing, as in this experiment, could be expected to yield optimally accurate and reliable results.

The ratings were performed by a team of twenty-eight judges—some local, some from neighboring universities, all with advanced degrees in English, and with an average of thirteen years of experience in teaching composition. The team stayed on the Miami campus for an entire week, working full time in a single large room each day, with appropriately spaced breaks to counter fatigue. Pre- and posttests from the control and experimental sections, all written on the same type of theme tablet, had been Xeroxed (on the same machine), assigned random numbers and secret codes, and then ordered by random number, so that it was impossible for a rater to discover the identity of a paper. The critieria for the holisitc and analytic ratings were explained in a detailed rubric given to each rater, and reviewed periodically during the tightly supervised rating sessions; they included six categories—ideas, supporting details, organization and coherence, voice, sentence structure, and diction and usage. Each paper was read four times holistically and four times analytically, each time by a different rater, and assigned scores on a scale of 1 through 6. In the forced-choice rating, ten different judges, were to choose the "better" paper within each of 134 pairs, where each pair consisted of one experimental and one control posttest from students with identical or near-identical holistic scores on the pretest.

The results of this experiment strongly confirm the claims advanced for SC in recent years: SC clearly helps accelerate syntactic growth even among young adults, and it is significantly more effective than the conventional essay-analysis approach in increasing the overall writing skills of college freshmen. Among quantitative measures of syntactic maturity, in the subordination ratio (clauses per T-unit), posttest differences between the two groups remained not significant,[23] as they were on the pretest. But in mean clause length (words per clause), which Hunt claims is the syntactic factor that best differentiates adolescents from professional writers,[24] the experimental group gained .89, nearly one whole word (up from 8.75 to 9.64), whereas the control group dropped .13 (down from 8.80 to 8.67). This difference is statistically significant at and beyond the .001 level of confidence. Note that in fifteen weeks the treatment group increased its clause size by almost half of the growth experienced, according to Hunt, in the previous *eight* years of normal development.[25] The same group showed a nearly as impressive .74 word gain in T-unit size (words per T-unit), up from 15.31 to 16.05, in contrast to the .05 word drop (from 15.00 to 14.95) by the control group. The posttest difference between the groups, 1.1 word, is again significant at better than .001. The growth, then, is precisely in the direction that Hunt leads us to expect—a relatively stable subordination ratio (the index in which at about this age a young writer's development has just about reached the ceiling set by the language), and a vastly exploding clause size, which also jacks up T-unit size, as students learn to add details and hence substance to their sentences.

But, undoubtedly, the major thrust of this study is in the evidence it has yielded for a significant correlation of these syntactic maturity gains with improved writing in free compositions, no matter how writing quality is measured. In the holistic rating, which best reflects the overall quality of a paper, the experimental group registered a posttest gain of .53 on a scale of 6 (up from 3.20 to 3.73), in contrast to the gain of .21 by the control group (up from 3.16 to 3.37); again this posttest difference is significant at .001. The experimental gain of .53 is perhaps comparable to a veteran baseball player boosting his batting average 53 percentage points in half a season—no trivial accomplishment. The forced-choice rating gave similar results: experimental papers were picked as better at a ratio of almost 2 to 1 (79 to 42, with 13 ties), again statistically a staggering difference.

With the superiority of the experimental group clearly established, it was instructive to see which components of writing were responsible for the qualitative gains. The posttest scores showed no significant difference in only one factor: organization/coherence. It is noteworthy that even in this one category SC practice did not have a negative effect, nor did the control group register significant gains. On the other hand, the experimental papers came out on top in posttest scores in the rest of the analytic categories: diction and usage (at .05), ideas (at .01), sentence structure (at .01), supporting details (at .001), and the category of voice (at .001), which we had defined as the individuality of a paper—the qualities that make it different, unique, memorable, and to that extent interesting. It appears, then, that these five of the six analytic qualities were responsible for the favorable overall judgments that gave experimental papers the significant edge in holistic and forced-choice ratings. It is interesting that not only did those qualities stressed in the SC class—sentence structure, supporting materials, and voice—appreciably raise the general effectiveness of writing; sentence combiners significantly outgained control students even in the one quality most cultivated in the conventional class—ideas. Recall Christensen's claim that "solving the problem of *how to say* helps solve the problem of *what to say*."[26] O'Hare came to the same conclusion—that perhaps indeed "knowing *how* does help to create *what*."[27]

Incidentally, the class-by-class breakdown of the results shows that while, as expected, classes taught by those with more teaching experience generally scored higher on both sides, relative lack of experience did not prevent an instructor from using SC procedures with success. In fact, the effectiveness of the method generally *overrode* the lack of experience. On the holistic rating, for example, one experimental graduate assistant registered higher gains than any instructor on the control side, and all graduate assistants in the experimental group gained more than any but two instructors of the control group (one of them a graduate assistant). Or in the forced-choice rating, all experimental instructors had a higher percentage of winning papers than any but one control instructor. Thus, in general, not only did the two sets of expermental instructors consistently outscore their control counterparts, but in many rated categories experimental graduate assistants, though with little teaching experience, out-gained experienced faculty in the control group.

While the results of this experiment convincingly demonstrate and emphatically support previous claims for the beneficial effects of SC practice on writing skills, it is somewhat difficult to try to isolate those ingredients of the experimental treatment that really did the job and to link them directly to these results. We can—and do—say to our colleagues: "Here is good evidence that SC works in the freshman English class. Why not try it yourself?" But it is not at all clear why SC *should* work. For example, among others voicing reservations about the SC method,[28] Marzano has questioned O'Hare's claim for a signifi-cant correlation between syntactic maturity growth and writing quality gains on the ground that a correlation does not necessarily *prove* causation.[29] Our study unequivocally supports O'Hare's findings, but again it can establish only a reasonably high probability for the cause, not invincible proof. Indeed, no one seems to be absolutely sure why students who practice intensive SC generally become more skillful and effective writers. Does SC tap some deep cognitive skills, enhancing their growth? Or are the benefits primarily psychological—perhaps increased control over the available linguistic choices simply makes writers feel more confident, giving them the incentive and the courage to use their growing repertoire of options in novel and interesting ways? Perhaps the increased control over form does encourage invention and help generate ideas; the strong showing of our sentence combiners in the latter category seems to support this assumption.

In attempting to interpret the impressive cumulative results of recent SC research, bear in mind that since its "modern" inception—indeed revival—a little over a decade ago, SC has noticeably eased away from its initial linguistic orientation. When in 1965 Hunt first suggested the use of "sentence-combining transformations" (thus, in quotation marks) to help build structural depth and complexity into student writing, he explicitly linked them to "recursive" proc-esses "operating on the strings underlying 'kernel sentences.' "[30] But more recently, as SC has gained ground in educational research and its underlying principles have become attractive to nonlinguists, it has shed much of its linguistic jargon and formalism in favor of emphasis on the general principles themselves and on their most effective classroom applications. Viewed in this light, SC may be a refinement of exercises "long in use in grammar textbooks"[31] and referred to by Sherwin as "plain," as opposd to "transformational," sentence combining.[32] If, as it appears, this distinction corresponds to the one between "open" and "signalled" SC exercises, i.e., those without and those with explicit transformational instructions, then our experimental classes may indeed have utilized a rather traditional "device for structuring the process of composing a sentence."[33] Of course, they went far beyond that, using the device for structuring the *total* process of composing. The point is that, while allowing for and encouraging almost unlimited creativity in syntactic form, SC is basically a device—perhaps one of several devices—providing *controlled* experience with writing. As such, it may be as old as it is significant.

Indeed, upon learning about our work, colleagues occasionally exclaim: "But I've been doing that for years—without knowing what it was called!" At the same time, we have found that the *idea* of SC as a way of teaching writing frightens some people in the profession—the term seems almost stigmatized, still suggesting to some dull and mechanical transformational exercises calling for a fancy linguistic terminology or for odd signalling symbols, to others something too empty to be suitable as the methodological principle of a composition course. The favorable results of the Miami project flatly refute these fears. Perhaps what scares some people is that SC seems so simple, say, in comparison to a secure, bulky handbook on rhetoric—which, of course, in a way, it is. In some sense it takes you "back to the basics"—and yet, as Strong points out,[34] it takes you far beyond them. Day in and day out, we observed how SC leads students to discover and use in novel and creative ways the complex linguistic knowledge that most are unaware of holding in their heads. And they seem to enjoy this discovery. At the end of the course we asked all experimental students to tell us about their experience in and atitude toward SC. Did they like it as an approach to writing? Did they feel that such practice for a semester helped them become better writers? On a scale ranging for a low of 1 to a high of 7, the responses averaged about 5 points. Would they recommend such a course to a friend? Exactly two-thirds of them responded favorably (5 to 7). Perhaps one respondent's terse complimentary comment about the SC class best summed up the feelings of many: "For a frosh comp course," he said, "it ain't bad."

STEPHEN P. WITTE, JOHN A. DALY, AND ROGER D. CHERRY

Syntactic Complexity and Writing Quality

Introduction

Background of the Present Study

For almost two decades, some of the most visible and influential research in written composition has followed Kellogg W. Hunt in examining student writing from the standpoint of syntax.[1] Most of this research relies at least to some extent on one or more of the quantitative indices posited by Hunt as gross measures of syntactic sophistication—mean number of words per clause, mean number of words per sentence, mean number of words per T-unit, mean number of T-units per sentence, and mean number of clauses per T-unit.[2] Although ill-defined conceptually, the phenomenon these indices purportedly measure is variously referred to as syntactic complexity, syntactic maturity, or syntactic fluency.

Researchers using Hunt's syntactic indices generally pursue one of two lines of inquiry. Hunt's own research—together with the researches of, for example, Roy C. O'Donnell, W. J. Griffin, and R. C. Norris, and Murray F. Stewart—is primarily concerned with identifying normative levels of syntactic complexity for different age groups.[3] Other researchers pursue a second line of inquiry, seeking to measure the degree to which the syntactic skills of different experimental groups are enhanced through sentence-combining exercises. Among the studies using Hunt's indices to measure syntactic growth as a result of such treatment are those by John L. Mellon; Frank O'Hare; J. E. M. Mulder, C. Braun, and W. G. Holliday; Stewart; Max Morenberg, Donald A. Daiker, and Andrew Kerek; and Lester Faigley.[4]

Most of these studies seem to be motivated by the assumption that a more sophisticated command of syntax in writing is positively associated with writing quality. Although Hunt himself does not argue explicitly for a direct relationship between syntactic complexity and writing quality, the nature of his samples and the higher levels of syntactic complexity found for his older, and presumably better, writers at least imply a positive relationship between syntactic complexity—as measured by his indices—and writing quality. So too with the normative research of O'Donnell, Griffin, and Norris, and Stewart.[5] For each successively older, and presumably more skilled, group of writers, these researchers report longer T-units, longer clauses, and more clauses per T-unit. In fact, each of these normative studies *suggests* that as writers grow older their writing becomes better as it becomes syntactically more sophisticated or complex.

The findings of these normative studies have influenced the direction of pedagogical research. In fact, Hunt's earlier studies (e.g., the 1964 and 1965 reports) prompted instructional researchers such as Mellon and O'Hare to look for ways of teaching students to write sentences that were syntactically more complex or sophisticated than would be typical for their age group. We believe it no exaggeration to say that the sentence-combining research cited above is predicated on the assumption of a positive and linear relationship between writing quality and syntactic complexity. If increasing syntactic complexity were not assumed to increase writing quality, then there would have been no reason to investigate the use of sentence-combining instruction in writing classes. Indeed, it is no accident that most experiments designed to enhance syntactic complexity through sentence-combining exercises also looked for, and found, parallel gains in writing quality. All of this, of course, suggests that the underlying assumption of a positive linear relationship between writing quality and syntactic complexity is valid. However, in the few studies that regress data for Hunt's indices against ratings of writing quality, Hunt's indices predict very little of the variance (usually less than 7 percent) in the quality ratings.[6] Moreover, in these same studies the indices proposed by Francis Christensen fared no better.[7]

Limitations of Previous Research

While previous research in the area either assumes or suggests a positive linear relationship between syntactic complexity and writing quality, as defined by Hunt's indices, to our knowledge no one study has directly addressed the question of whether this relationship is in fact linear. And even when researchers conducting experimental studies in sentence-combining methods have indirectly explored the relationship between syntactic complexity and writing quality, they have not been able to do so unambiguously.

Two related problems in experimental studies of sentence-combining instruction have precluded a clear and unconfounded test of the linearity assumption. The first problem stems from the limited range of syntactic complexity displayed in essays rated for quality in experimental studies. In virtually all sentence-combining studies, the range of syntactic complexity is relatively narrow. For example, in the Miami University sentence-combining experiment, essays by the control and experimental groups displayed a posttest mean difference in clause length of less than one word and a posttest mean difference in T-unit length of only 1.1 words.[8] Nevertheless, the Miami investigators report that the experimental group—the group exposed to sentence-combining practice—wrote essays at the end of the experiment that were significantly better (p $\langle$ .001) than those written by the control group. Similarly narrow ranges in syntactic complexity are found in many normative studies, which tend to associate chronological age and syntactic complexity. For example, the investigation by O'Donnell, Griffin, and Norris of syntactic growth revealed a mean difference in clause length of only 1.2 words between grades three and seven; and Hunt found mean differences of only two words per clause between grades four and twelve.[9] In both experimental and normative studies that have employed Hunt's indices, similar restricted ranges of syntactic complexity often appear.

It is possible, however, that a limited range of syntactic complexity in essays used to elicit quality ratings might significantly attenuate any effects of syntactic complexity on judgments of writing quality. Thus, until something approaching the full range of possible values for syntactic complexity is used in a rating situation, the relationship between complexity and quality must remain ambiguous. A clear test of the relationship between syntactic complexity and writing quality would require ratings of essays along an extended range of complexity values.

The second problem, which is in some ways the obverse of the first one, appears exclusively in the experimental studies. These studies usually investigate the relationship between syntactic complexity and writing quality to one degree or another. Most of these studies employ an essay-rating procedure that requires raters to judge the quality of particular essays in relation to other essays read during the rating session. Standards are thus inferred and rating criteria established in terms of differences that exist among essays within the pool of essays rated. Consequently, evaluations of essays are, in fact, relative judgments of writing quality. Because discourse mode, purpose, and topic are often controlled in such studies, and because raters are often instructed to ignore handwriting and mechanical problems such as spelling, small differences among the essays in terms of syntactic complexity may exaggerate differences in quality. Such rating procedures may bias results by cuing distinctions along dimensions—such as syntactic complexity—which under other circumstances may not have a pronounced effect on judgments of quality. Undue attention to syntactic features may produce results that suggest a positive relationship between writing quality and syntactic complexity but that may in reality be an artifact of the rating procedure. Before differences in quality can be attributed to levels of syntactic complexity, the potential bias that may result from rating essays in relation to one another must be assessed. This can be done by contrasting ratings given to the same essay under two conditions: one where the essay is read alone and another where the essay is read as one essay in a series of essays. To demonstrate an unambiguous relationship between writing quality and syntactic complexity, it is necessary for essays differing in syntactic complexity, but read by themselves without any contrasting essays, to vary systematically in quality ratings.

Purpose of the Present Study

In this study we attempt to clarify the relationship between syntactic complexity and writing quality by addressing directly (1) the issue of extremes in syntactic complexity and (2) the issue of dependence among ratings of texts. We examine quality ratings for texts that differ in syntactic complexity and assess whether there is a significant linear relationship between perceived writing quality and syntactic complexity. In this respect, the present study resembles certain aspects of sentence-combining studies. However, the present study differs from those studies in two ways. First, we extend the range of syntactic complexity values in stimulus passages. In previous research, differences in levels of complexity among the texts rated have been small; in contrast, the texts in our study represent a wide range of complexity values. Second, we contrast conditions under which raters form judgments of writing quality. In one condition, raters are exposed to a series of passages that vary widely in syntactic complexity. In the second condition, raters evaluate only a single passage. The latter condition eliminates the influence of previously rated passages on judgments of writing quality.

Investigation I

Purpose

The purpose of our first investigation was to examine the relationship between syntactic complexity and writing quality by having teachers rate a series of texts that varied widely in syntactic complexity. This investigation required teachers to read and evaluate five short passages that were written on the same topic but that differed in syntactic complexity. The entering expectation was for a positive linear relationship between syntactic complexity and writing quality.

Subjects

Sixty-two high school teachers served as evaluators in this investigation. All participated in the investigation as part of a graduate course in communication. Passages on two different topics were used so that an internal replication would be possible and to preclude a confounding between any effect and discourse topic. Thirty-five teachers read and evaluated short passages on the topic of making aluminum; the remaining twenty-seven read papers on the use of alcohol and marijuana. In this investigation, the ratings of the passages on the "alcohol and marijuana" topic were used as part of the replication study. Because the procedures for creating the experimental stimuli and for collecting data were identical for each group of five passages, those procedures will be described only once.

Materials and Procedures

The investigators composed five short texts for each topic. The five passages in each set represented five different levels of syntactic complexity, ranging from very simple to very complex. However, the passages were, as much as possible, similar in all other respects. Discourse mode, discourse purpose, and content were held constant across all five passages in each set.

The first set of five passages was based on the "aluminum" task used in Hunt's 1970 study of syntactic complexity.[10] The original "aluminum" passage, which served within the first set of passages as the passage with the lowest level of syntactic complexity, reads as follows:

Aluminum

Aluminum is a metal. It is abundant. It has many uses. It comes from bauxite. Bauxite is an ore. Bauxite looks like clay. Bauxite contains aluminum. It contains several other substances. Workmen extract these other substances from the bauxite. They grind the bauxite. They put it in tanks. Pressure is in the tanks. The other substances form a mass. They remove the mass. They use filters. A liquid remains. They put it through several other processes. It finally yields a chemical. The chemical is powdery. It is white. The chemical is alumina. It is a mixture. It contains aluminum. It contains oxygen. Workmen separate the aluminum from the oxygen. They use electricity. They finally produce a metal. The metal is light. It has a luster. The luster is bright. The luster is silvery. The metal comes in many forms.

This passage consists entirely of single-clause sentences, each of which is a single T-unit. It is a passage notable for its syntactic *simplicity* rather than its complexity. For the other end of the spectrum of five passages on the first topic, we constructed a passage delivering the same content, but in a much more syntactically complex way. Two sentences from the passage at the other end of the spectrum will illustrate the differences in syntactic complexity:

Aluminum, an abundant and useful metal, comes from bauxite, a clay-like ore. Although bauxite contains several other substances, workmen remove them by grinding the ore and placing it in pressurized tanks where the other substances form a mass which is removed by filters.

This latter version differs in important ways from the simpler passage. Some sentences from the original version, for example, appear as appositives in the first sentence of the more syntactically complex version. Other sentences from the original version are reduced to subordinate or relative clauses in the second version, while still others become participial constructions, adjectives, and prepositional phrases. Such reductions to dependent-clause status or to less-than-clause status have the effect of (1) increasing the average length of resultant clauses and T-units and (2) increasing the ratio of dependent clauses to independent clauses (i.e., the mean number of clauses per T-unit). Complementing the increase in syntactic complexity is a corresponding decrease in the total number of words needed to deliver essentially the same content.

Similar differences exist between the least and most syntactically complex passages devised for the second topic. Those five passags were all based on a sentence-combining exercise entitled "Alcohol and Marijuana" from William Strong's *Sentence Combining: A Composing Book* (New York: Random House, 1973). Because this passage is considerably longer than the least complex "aluminum" passage, only the first part of the original is reproduced below:

Alcohol and Marijuana
There is much talk. The talking occurs today. The talking is about evils. The evils are from marijuana. But few people talk about alcohol. Alcohol represents a hazard. The hazard is to health. The hazard is greater than marijuana. Consider an example. Consider our consumption. The consumption is of alcohol. The nations [sic] drinks 650 million gallons. The gallons are distilled spirits. The drinking is done each year. Americans guzzle 100 million barrels. The barrels contain beer. The guzzling is done each year. We also drink wine. The volume is 200 million gallons.

These first 19 sentences from the simplest version of "Alcohol and Marijuana" indicate that the passage is comparable with respect to syntactic complexity to the least complex version of the "aluminum" passage. The following two sentences are from the most syntactically complex of the five versions of "Alcohol and Marijuana."

Although much is said today about the evils of marijuana, few people talk about alcohol, which may represent as great a health hazard and social threat as marijuana. Consider, for example, Americans, who each year drink 650 million gallons of distilled spirits, consume 200 million gallons of wine, and guzzle 100 million barrels of beer.

Using the procedures set down in the Miami University sentence-combining study for segmenting extended texts into clauses and T-units and for counting words,[11] we calculated the mean T-unit length, mean clause length, and mean number of clauses per T-unit for each of the five passages in the two sets used in the present investigation. These descriptive data appear in table 1 below.

Table 1. Syntactic Descriptions of the Two Sets of Passages Used in Investigation I

	Aluminum			Alcohol and Marijuana		
Pass	Words/ T-unit	Words/ Clause	Clauses/ T-unit	Words/ T-unit	Words/ Clause	Clauses/ T-unit
1	23.00	11.50	2.00	21.50	10.75	2.00
2	16.00	10.67	1.50	16.15	10.50	1.54
3	12.67	6.71	1.89	10.65	8.19	1.30
4	7.22	5.91	1.22	8.44	8.44	1.00
5	4.34	4.34	1.00	5.46	5.46	1.00

Although questions may be raised about the artificial nature of these stimuli, we decided to compose the passages rather than use student essays in order to gain better control over not only the levels of syntactic complexity but also the content. Such controls were mandatory for a direct and unambiguous test of the relationship between writing quality and syntactic complexity. It is impossible to find actual student essays that deliver exactly the same content and exhibit the range of syntactic complexity necessary to test the linear hypothesis. By using these stimuli, we avoided several problems that we identified in the earlier literature on syntactic complexity and writing quality.

Having constructed these brief texts, we presented each of the sixty-two teachers with a packet of materials that included the five passages on one of the two topics. Each of the passages was followed by a rating form that asked the teacher to rate the passage on five evaluative scales: high quality/low quality; effective/ineffective; good/bad; interesting/uninteresting; clear/unclear. The polarities of the scales were randomly set, and the five passages were randomly sequenced within each packet.

The teachers' responses to the scales were averaged across the scales after analyses revealed that the five scales formed highly reliable composites. For the "aluminum" passage, the average internal consistency estimate (alpha) of the five-item measure was .90; for "Alcohol and Marijuana" it was .91.

Results: "Aluminum"

The one-way, repeated-measures analysis of variance revealed a significant main effect for syntactic complexity: $F(4,174) = 34.99$, $p < .0001$. Means and standard deviations for the evaluations appear in table 2.

Table 2. Means and Standard Deviations for Evaluations of Passages on the Two Topics*

	Aluminum		Alcohol and Marijuana	
Syntactic Complexity Level	Mean Qual. Score	S.D.	Mean Qual. Score	S.D.
1	24.34 a	7.42	28.48 b	7.21
2	28.23	5.99	26.74 b	4.11
3	22.31 a	6.06	24.63 a,b	7.65
4	20.80 a	7.41	21.00 a	7.14
5	11.54	5.10	9.15	5.57

* Means sharing a common letter are not significantly different from one another. Comparisons are made only within essay topic.

The Newman-Kuels procedure recommended by B. Winer for multiple comparisons was used to perform follow-up analyses.[12] These analyses indicated that (1) the simplest passage syntactically (passage 5) was rated significantly lower in quality than all other texts in the set; (2) the fourth most complex passage (passage 22) was evaluated significantly higher than all others; and (3) no significant differences in quality existed among the passages that were next to the lowest (passage 4), third highest (passage 3), and highest (passage 1) in syntactic complexity.

Results: "Alcohol and Marijuana"

The one-way, repeated-measures analysis of variance indicated a significant effect for syntactic complexity: $F(4,134) = 48.89$, $p < .0001$. Means and standard deviations for the evaluations are summarized in table 2. The Newman-Kuels procedure revealed that (1) the least syntactically complex passage (passage 5) was evaluated significantly lower in quality than the other passages; (2) the passage highest in syntactic complexity (passage 1) was rated as better than the two passages lowest in syntactic complexity (passages 4 and 5) but not better than the third most (passage 3) or the fourth most (passage 4) syntactically complex passages; (3) the passage next to the highest in syntactic complexity (passage 2) was rated better than the lowest (passage 5) and the next-to-the-lowest (passage 4) passages but not better than the third from the lowest (passage 3); and (4) the third most syntactically complex passage (passage 3) was evaluated as better than the lowest (passage 5) but no better than any of the other passages.

Discussion of Results of Investigation I

The results of our first investigation suggest that syntactic complexity affects teachers' judgments of writing quality. Our analyses reveal that for both sets of texts the least syntactically complex passage (passage 5 in both cases) was rated significantly lower in quality than the other four in each set. Our analyses also indicate a consistent attenuation of differences in writing quality beyond the least complex passage in both sets: the magnitude of the differences in quality among the four most complex passages in each set was consistently smaller than the differences between the least complex passage and the four others. The patterns of these differences in quality, however, are not entirely consistent across the two topic sets. One inconsistency appears in the quality ratings assigned to the most complex passages. The most complex passage (passage 1) on the use of alcohol and marijuana was rated more positively, although not significantly more so, than the two passages (passages 2 and 3) nearest to it in terms of syntactic complexity. In contrast, the "aluminum" passage given the highest quality rating was not the most syntactically complex one. Rather, it was the fourth most complex passage (passage 2). The most syntactically complex "aluminum" passage (passage 1) was not seen as significantly better than either the second lowest (passage 4) or third lowest (passage 3) passages in syntactic complexity.

In short, we did not find a linear pattern where significant differences in quality between passages appear at each point along the continuum of syntactic complexity. Rather, it seems that the predominant effect is due to passages that are extremely noncomplex syntactically. The magnitude of differences between passages diminishes markedly after the least syntactically complex passage is considered. This is especially so for the "aluminum" passages, where a plot of the effect of syntactic complexity on writing quality suggests a nonlinear pattern. Nonetheless, for both topic sets, syntactic complexity seems to have had large and significant effects on the teachers' judgments of writing quality.

Investigation II

Purpose

For our second investigation of the effects of syntactic complexity on writing quality, we had teachers read and evaluate a single text. The entering hypothesis was for a positive relationship between writing quality and syntactic complexity, although a relationship of smaller magnitude than that found in our first investigation. We expected a smaller effect because the teachers participating in the second investigation would rate a single passage without comparing it to any others. Syntactic complexity would thus be less salient as a differentiating variable. The second investigation provided (1) an additional test of the linearity hypothesis and (2) a test of whether the findings of previous research have been biased by raters having made judgments of essays in the context of rating a number of essays.

Subjects

Two hundred and fifteen high school teachers participated in this phase of the investigation. One hundred and eleven teachers evaluated one of the five "aluminum" essays, while the remaining 104 evaluated one of the five texts on the use of alcohol and marijuana.

Procedures

As in the first investigation, the use of passages on two different topics allowed us to conduct two independent studies at the same time. Because the two studies were conducted simultaneously, only one description of the procedures is presented here. The texts used in the two studies in the second investigation were the same ones used in our first investigation. The essays were randomly assigned to the teachers, and the teachers used the same evaluation scales that were used during the first investigation. Estimates of the internal consistency (alpha) of the ratings were again high, .88 for the "aluminum" passages and .89 for the "alcohol and marijuana" passages.

Results: "Aluminum"

A one-way analysis of variance performed on the ratings of the passages indicated that syntactic complexity significantly affected the quality ratings assigned to the "aluminum" passages: $F(4,99) = 3.85$, $p < .006$. Table 3 summarizes the important numerical information.

160   WITTE, DALY, CHERRY

Table 3. Means and Standard Deviations for Evaluations of Brief Passages Read Independently of Other Brief Passages*

Syntactic Complexity Level	Aluminum			Alcohol and Marijuana		
	Mean Qual. Score	S.D.	N	Mean Qual. Score	S.D.	N
1	23.05 b	8.31	22	24.28 a	6.51	18
2	23.44 b	5.23	18	27.17 a	4.49	23
3	21.09 a,b	6.56	22	26.90 a	4.47	21
4	19.32 a,b	7.22	22	26.11 a	4.40	27
5	16.20 a	5.74	20	18.23	7.24	22

* Means sharing a common letter are not significantly different from one another. Comparisons are made only within essay topic.

A follow-up analysis using the Newman-Kuels procedure revealed that the least syntactically complex passage (passage 5) was evaluated as significantly lower in quality than either the most complex passage (passage 1) or the next-to-the-most complex passage (passage 2) but not significantly lower in quality than either passage 3 or passage 4, the two passages closest to passage 5 in terms of syntactic complexity.

Results: "Alcohol & Marijuana"

A one-way analysis of variance revealed a significant effect for syntactic complexity: $F(4,106 = 10.21, p < .0001$. Table 3 again summarizes the relevant numerical data. Results obtained by the Newman-Kuels procedure for multiple comparisons indicated that the only significant effect for syntactic complexity was between the least syntactically complex passage (passage 5) and the remaining four.

Discussion of the Results of Investigation II

The results of the two studies conducted during our second investigation suggest that syntactic complexity has some effect on judgments of quality. The patterns of means for both topic sets indicate that the predominant effect is again for the least syntactically complex passage in either set (passage 5 in both cases) to be rated significantly lower in quality than any of the other texts in a given set. Beyond this effect for syntactic complexity, no significant differences among ratings emerged when ratings were assigned independently of one another.

Discussions of Investigations I and II

It is important to contrast our two investigations in terms of the limitations in previous research on syntactic complexity and writing quality described in the introduction. Recall that our first concern was with the restricted range in syntactic complexity found in previous studies, studies that seem to assume a positive linear relationship between syntactic complexity and writing quality. In both of our investigations, we used as stimulus passages brief texts that spanned a greater range in syntactic complexity than the writing examined in most previous research, especially pedagogical research on sentence-combining instruction. It was fortuitous that we did. In every case, the least syntactically complex passage had a significant impact on the results. Differences consistently emerged between the quality ratings assigned the least complex passage and the other, more syntactically complex passages on the same topic. Usually, the differences in the ratings assigned the passages within the mid-range of syntactic complexity were not significant. It is important to note that these mid-range passages were comparable in syntactic complexity to the essays studied in, for example, Faigley's generative rhetoric experiment and the Miami University sentence-combining experiment.[13] Had we chosen to use only passages within the mid-range of complexity, no significant effect on writing quality would have emerged. In that case, our findings would have paralleled more closely those of studies that have regressed data for one or more of Hunt's indices against quality scores.[14] In short, in order to obtain large and significant effects for syntactic complexity, it is necessary to use stimulus essays that span a wide range of levels of syntactic complexity. It is essential that relatively extreme values, especially at the lower end of the spectrum of syntactic complexity, be used if an effect is to be obtained.

Previous research, whether normative or experimental, has consistently implied a positive and linear relationship between syntactic complexity and writing quality. The results of the present study on this issue are mixed. In three of the four analyses we performed, the most complex passage received a lower mean quality rating than the next-to-the-most complex passage. In only one of the four analyses presented here was the difference in quality between the most complex and the next most complex passage statistically significant. In the other three analyses we performed, the differences in quality among the three most syntactically complex passages were not statistically significant. In short, the only time a significant difference in quality emerged among the three most complex passages was when the next most complex passage was judged to be of significantly higher quality than the most complex passage. Thus, at the upper end of the syntactic complexity range, a positive and linear relationship between complexity and writing quality does not appear to exist. However, all four analyses performed in the present study indicate that the least syntactically complex passage is inferior in quality to all other brief texts with which it was compared. Thus our analyses suggest that a positive and linear relationship between writing quality and syntactic complexity obtains only when ratings of texts at the lower end of the syntactic complexity range are contrasted with texts in the middle or higher ranges of syntactic complexity. Plots of the mean values suggest a tendency towards a positive linear relationship only when ratings of extremely noncomplex passages are included. And beyond the extremely non-complex passages, there is little evidence of a systematic relationship.

We were also concerned in the present study with the potential effects that multiple essays have on the quality ratings assigned to individual essays in a set. Our first investigation used a rating procedure similar to that used in much composition research, whether experimental or evaluative. In that investigation, teachers read five passages, all on the same topic but differing with respect to level of syntactic complexity. In our second investigation, teachers read only one brief text. Differences in the quality ratings assigned the same brief essays during the two investigations indicate the impact of multiple essays on judgments of writing quality. These differences can be examined in two ways.

First, the magnitude of the relationship between syntactic complexity and writing quality can be compared for the two investigations. For both the "aluminum" and "alcohol and marijuana" passages, the magnitude of the effect due to syntactic complexity was greater in the first investigation than in the second. When raters had the opportunity to read and, in essence, compare five brief passages, syntactic complexity—which was manipulated within topic sets—had a larger effect on judgments of quality than when raters could not compare one passage to another. It is possible that when the raters were unable to make comparisons among passages, syntactic complexity did not figure as a salient cue in their judgment-forming processes. Without having to evaluate other essays that vary in syntactic complexity, raters may not rely as much on syntactic complexity to form judgments of quality.

Second, the differences between the quality ratings assigned each brief passage in both investigations can be examined. One tendency was for the more extreme quality ratings to occur with the multiple-text procedure. For the "alcohol and marijuana" passages, teachers who made judgments of writing quality relative to other passages rated the least complex passage (passage 5) significantly lower than did the teachers who read passage 5 in isolation: $t(47) = 4.83, p < .05$. The teachers who rated five passages in a set also rated the most complex passage (passage 1) significantly higher than did the teachers who read only that text: $t(43) = 3.03, p < .05$. A similar pattern emerged in the ratings of the "aluminum" texts. The teachers who read all five "aluminum" passages rated the least syntactically complex passage (passage 5) as significantly lower in quality than did the teachers who read and rated only that passage: $t(53) = p <$

.05. In addition, the teachers who rated five "aluminum" texts gave significantly higher quality ratings to the most syntactically complex passage (passage 1) than did the teachers who read only that one text: t(53) = 3.00, p ⟨ .05. These results strongly suggest that the potential for extreme quality ratings is greater when papers are rated relative to one another in a group than when single papers are read and evaluated in isolation.

The research we have reported here suggests that studies using procedures that call for raters to evaluate a series of essays may be biased by those procedures. Such procedures can exaggerate the magnitude of effects due to characteristics of the essays rated. The investigations we have reported here also suggest why, in spite of their expectations to the contrary, composition researchers have not been able to demonstrate that syntactic complexity is strongly related to writing quality. Our research suggests that syntactic complexity may, after all, be an important pheomenon to investigate in experimental and normative research in composition. But it also suggests that unless there is a wide range of levels of complexity in the writing samples examined, researchers are likely to be disappointed in their attempts to show a relationship between syntactic complexity and writing quality.

References

Christensen, Francis. "A Generative Rhetoric of the Sentence." *Notes Toward a New Rhetoric: Six Essays for Teachers*. New York: Harper and Row, 1968.

Daiker, Donald A., Andrew Kerek, and Max Morenberg. "Sentence-Combining and Syntactic Maturity in Freshman English." *College Composition and Communication,* 29 (1978), 36–41.

Fagan, W., C. R. Cooper, and J. Jensen, eds. *Measures for Research and Evaluation in the English Language Arts*. Urbana, IL: National Council of Teachers of English, 1975.

Faigley, Lester. "Generative Rhetoric as a Way of Increasing Syntactic Fluency." *College Composition and Communication,* 30 (1978), 176–81.

_____ "The Influence of Generative Rhetoric on the Syntactic Maturity and Writing Effectiveness of College Freshmen." *Research in the Teaching of English,* 13 (1979), 197–206.

Hunt, Kellog W. *Differences in Grammatical Structures Written at Three Grade Levels, the Structures to be Analyzed by Transformational Methods*. Technical Report, Cooperative Research Project No. 1998. Tallahassee: Florida State University, 1964. ERIC Document 003 322.

_____ *Grammatical Structures Written at Three Grade Levels*. NCTE Research Report No. 3. Urbana, IL: National Council of Teachers of English, 1965.

_____ *Syntactic Maturity in School Children and Adults.* Monographs of the Society for Research in Child Development, 35 (1970), (1, serial no. 134).

_____ "Early Blooming and Late Blooming Syntactic Structures." In *Evaluating Writing: Describing, Measuring, Judging.* Ed. C. R. Cooper and Lee Odell. Urbana, IL: National Council of Teachers of English, 1977.

Kerek, Andrew, Donald A. Daiker, and Max Morenberg. "Sentence Combining and College Composition." *Perceptual and Motor Skills,* 51 (1980), Monograph Supplement No. 1.

Mellon, John. C. *Transformational Sentence-Combining: A Method for Enhancing the Development of Syntactic Complexity in English Composition.* NCTE Research Report No. 10. Urbana, IL: National Council of Teachers of English, 1969.

Morenberg, Max, Donald A. Daiker, and Andrew Kerek. "Sentence Combining at the College Level: An Experimental Study." *Research in the Teaching of English,* 12 (1978), 245–56.

Mulder, J. E. M., C. Braun, and W. G. Holliday. "Effects of Sentence-Combining Practice on Linguistic Maturity Levels of Adult Students." *Adult Education,* 28 (1978), 111–20.

Nold, Ellen, and Sarah W. Freedman, "An Analysis of Readers' Responses to Student Writing." *Research in the Teaching of English,* 11 (1977), 164–74.

O'Donnell, Roy C., W. J. Griffin, and R. C. Norris. *Syntax of Kindergarten and Elementary School Children: A Transformational Analysis.* NCTE Research Report No. 8. Urbana, IL: National Council of Teachers of English, 1967,

O'Hare, Frank. *Sentence Combining: Improving Student Writing Without Formal Grammar Instruction.* NCTE Research Report No. 15. Urbana, IL: National Council of Teachers of English, 1973.

Stewart, Murray F. "Syntactic Maturity from High School to University: A First Look." *Research in the Teaching of English,* 12 (1978), 37–46.

_____ "Freshman Sentence Combining: A Canadian Project." *Research in the Teaching of English,* 12 (1978), 257–68.

Strong, William. *Sentence Combining: A Composing Book.* New York: Random House, 1973.

Winer, B. J. *Statistical Principles in Experimental Design.* New York: McGraw-Hill, 1971.

Witte, Stephen P., and Lester Faigley. *A Comparative Evaluation of Analytic and Synthetic Approaches to the Teaching of Writing.* Texas Writing Research Group Technical Report No. 1. Austin: University of Texas, 1981. ERIC Document 209 677.

DONALD C. FREEMAN

Linguistics and Error Analysis: On Agency

When you come to remedial composition as late in life as I did, you realize very quickly that the world is a much less orderly place than you had thought. Yet the problems in the prose of students in the remedial situation are a never-ending source of fascination to me; equally, I confess, attempts at their solution often are a source of the most exquisite kind of frustration. As a linguist, I realize that my discipline has been greatly oversold as a panacea for the ills of written expression; at the same time, I persist in the illusion that linguistics can make a contribution to the teaching of composition. What follows is an attempt at beginning such a contribution.

There are many areas of teaching composition in which linguistics can be of little or no assistance. I doubt that linguistics can do much to help us with such questions as logic, organization, connotation, or diction. I think it *can* help on the question of simply getting students to *write grammatical sentences*. Partly for this reason, the following discussion is based solely on sentence-level analysis. This position may seem to be a restriction of the potential contributions of linguistics, but this skill—simply writing grammatical sentences—is, in the experience of every composition teacher I know, the hardest single thing to teach the student in a remedial composition course.

The way linguistics can help get students to write grammatical sentences is in the construction of a new system of error analysis, and, through that analysis, construction of a pedagogical grammar: a handbook organized in structure and sequence for the classroom sitation, and based as far as possible on modern linguistic insights. [1] Developing a system of error analysis can be done, in my view, only by extensive analysis of problem essays from the real world. I recognize that error analysis is only half, and perhaps not even that much, of the task which faces us. But I believe that remedial strategies for improving student writing can arise only from an empirically grounded system or error analysis; they cannot be constructed a priori. In this respect, I favor the inductive method of Mina Shaughnessy over the deductive method of E. D. Hirsch, Jr. [2] I am going to sketch out briefly here one little corner of what such a system might look like using the sentence as the basic unit; plainly, the insights of recent work in text grammars, speech acts, and related areas will play an important role in any elaboration of a system of this kind. The theoretical basis of this discussion is a deliberately simplified version of the so-called standard theory of trans-formational-generative grammar.[3]

How can this version of modern linguistics help us to construct a system of error analysis? I believe that the set of analytical pigeonholes that we now use to classify the range of problems in composition is constructed wrongly. Much of current error analysis, as that analysis is reflected in the organization of most existing handbooks, consists of putting square pegs in round holes. Subject-verb agreement, for example, is a host of errors, not one: in Temple University's internship course for teachers of composition, a graduate student analyzed a large sample of real-world sentences and concluded that there are at least eight different kinds, most of which have very little to do with one another. Other studies arising from this course have yielded comparable results for such categories as faulty parallelism and diction. Similarly, as will be suggested in what follows, a group of what have been thought to be heterogeneous and unrelated errors can, under this kind of analysis, be considered under a single rubric.

Modern linguistics has changed the size, shape, and number of many analytical pigeonholes in the theory of language. For example, generative phonologists have shown that the change from hard *g* to soft *g* in the pair *regal* and *regicide,* and from hard *c* to soft *c* in *medical* and *medicine* are the product of one linguistic rule,[4] not two; transformational syntacticians have shown that the sentences *colorless green ideas sleep furiously* and *lazy over the jumped fox quick dog brown* are ungrammatical in two ways, not just one.

Modern linguistics has also fostered a view of the overall structure of human language strongly compatible with what we do in the remedial situation: that language has not only a surface structure, the organization of the sentence as we hear it or see it on the page, but an underlying structure roughly correspond-ing (and how roughly is by no means agreed upon) to its propositional content. To use classical examples, again, the sentence *Invisible God created the visible world* contains, in its underlying structure, three propositions: *God created the world, God is invisible,* and *the world is visible.*[5]

Propositional analysis of this kind is analogous in important ways to what we do when we analyze tangled syntax in problem essays: we conduct a rough-and-ready analysis of the underlying structure of offending sentences, and then try to figure out how and where they went off the rails. I am proposing as a basis for a new system of error analysis, a slightly, but only slightly, formalized version of this procedure, and I am going to develop it from a real student essay.

Can I Take You to the Movies?

I prefer movies to plays for a number of reasons. First, movies have a wide variety of technical advantages that plays just can't compete against. Casting of movies is varied, whereas in a play the actors have to be limited to a certain number due to the size of the stage. Advantages in terms of make-up and costume design also make a movie more enjoyable as well as a worthwhile visual experience in comparison to a play.

Editing, cutting, and being able to alter the finished product are only a few examples of the technical superiority that a movie has over a play. The finished movie with all its corrections and adjustments help to make the movie as perfect as possible. A play, however, since they are performed live leave mistakes, even in the case of professional actors, to present a real problem that a movie has already been able to take care of. Since a movie has no restrictions in terms of scenery the advantages and different places a movie can be shot at also make for a major advantage. A movie can take place all over the world, and special effects such as earthquakes cause for more excitement and in turn a superior product.

Casting, which in theory is unlimited in movies is severly [sic] limited in plays which, once again, proves to be an advantage for movies. The availability of famous actors for even a cameo role can make a movie worthwhile; plays on the other hand can't afford to pay a stars salary for only a moments work. The number of actors, itself is a factor in this comparison to [sic]. A play being restricted to a limited number of scenes and major roles doesn't have the accass to the amount of stars that a movie does.

Costumes and make-up play a more visual role in movies than they do in most plays. With the natural limitations that plays carry with them, they don't have the advantages of camera angles and other filming techniques that a director can use in a movie. The camera can fool the human eye, and in conjunction with make-up and costuming makes for a much more enjoyable performance.

In closing, I hope I have accurately shown that movies have many advantages over plays, and, overall, presents a more diverse and entertaining medium than that of a play. For the reasons stated above, I hope to have explained why movies appeal to me more than plays do.

This essay is a typical product of a middle-level remedial composition course. It has many of the subjective, impressionistic features we attribute to what we call the "remedial" essay: its syntax is clotted; it is wordy and vague; it has a kind of lameness to it. There is here, typically for the remedial essay, no sense of someone *acting* in the world, an intuition to which I should like to return.

We can also observe a number of objective features in this prose which correspond at many points to the subjective ones: excessive use of the passive voice, faulty number agreement in pronoun reference, subject-verb agreement errors, vague pronoun reference, faulty parallelism, periphrastic constructions like "in terms of," "in comparison to," and "make for," and faulty personifications: "plays can't afford to pay a stars salary . . ." The essay certainly provides us with ample justification for the requisite number of red marks, and enough *topoi* for the divinely ordained twenty-minute conference.

But somehow these features fail to capture the essence of the problem in this essay; moreover, I believe it is wrong to treat them as unconnected to one another, as existing grammar books do. There is a thread connecting the seemingly diverse problems in five sentences which to me typify this essay's difficulties. That thread is what I would like to call *agency,* and whatever remedial exercises one designs on the basis of analysis should direct the student toward increasing the sense of agency—of someone acting on someone or something in a world. In what follows I do propose some revisions, but I am more concerned at this point with constructing the system of error analysis that must precede these proposals for revision than with the revisions or the remedial exercises themselves. Here is the first of these sentences:

> Editing, cutting, and being able to alter the finished product are only a few examples of the technical superiority that a movie has over a play.

This sentence seems to me to fall apart because of the gerunds. The standard transformational analysis of gerunds is that underlying them are predications with subjects: X edits. X cuts. X is able to alter, etc. But, in the context of this essay, *Who* edits, cuts, etc? A film director. And there is a cause-effect relationship between these actions (which have an agent) and the technical superiority that this student is claiming for movies over plays. If the student revises toward greater overt agency, the vagueness of this sentence can be greatly reduced:

> Because a film director can edit, cut, and alter the finished product, a movie is technically superior to a play.[6]

Sentence 2 seems to me to run afoul of a second class of verb-related nouns: *-ion* and *-ment* nominals.[7]

> The finish movie with all its corrections and adjustments help to make the movie as perfect as possible.

Who corrects and adjusts? Again, our old and hard-working friend, the film director. In using these verb-related nouns the student has created what has been aptly termed a "wall-eyed sentence." The nouns are grammatically subordinate to "the finished movie," but are also, by virtue of proximity, candidates for the subject of "held," which magically becomes plural as the finished movie helps make the movie perfect. When the student revises toward greater agency, this redundancy, along with the opportunity these nouns create for subject-verb agreement error, disappears:

> As the director corrects and adjusts in finishing the movie, he can make the final product as perfect as possible.

Sentence 3 presents somewhat more complex problems:

> A play, however, since they are performed live leave mistakes, even in the case of professional actors, to present a real problem that a movie has already been able to take care of.

Here the agents, the professional actors, are grammatically subordinated into some kind of sentence adverb, and further effaced by the periphrastic "even in the case of." *Who* makes mistakes? Plays don't; they don't even leave mistakes (rather, mistakes remain in them—another agency problem). Professional actors make mistakes. And if the student is encouraged to elevate this agent-action nexus to the main subject-verb nexus of the sentence, much of the muddy verbosty disappears. And, because this revision necessarily simplifies the sentence's clausal structure, the opportunities for subject-verb agreement errors[8] diminish:

> Even professional actors make mistakes, which in movies can be edited out, but in live plays cannot.

The same problem—too deep a subordination of the only possible agent-action nexus in the sentence—afflicts sentence 4:

> With the natural limitations that plays carry with them, they don't have the advantages of camera angles and other filming techniques that a director can use in a movie.

The only possible agent, the director, is subordinated in a *that*-clause which modifies a compound noun phrase which is in turn subordinated to the direct object of the sentence. If, in revising, the student can be persuaded to contruct the sentence around this crucial agent-action nexus, the result is much less vague:

> The director of a movie can use the advantages of camera angles and other filming techniques that the director of a play, with its natural limitations, cannot.

Finally, sentence 5:

> The camera can fool the human eye, and in conjunction with make-up and costuming makes for a much more enjoyable performance.

Here the subject of "makes" is grammatically "the camera," but conceptually it is three things: the fact that the camera can fool the eye, makeup, and costuming. I think, however, that the real culprit here is not so much faulty parallelism, but yet another word derived from a verb—here, the adjective *enjoyable*. *Who* enjoys? The audience enjoys, or we enjoy. *What* do we enjoy? We enjoy movies more than we do plays. Again, a revision by the student in the direction of greater agency clarifies an otherwise loose and unwieldy sentence:

> We enjoy movies more than we do plays because of the greater visual effects of makeup, costuming, and camera techniques, which can fool the human eye.

I have some observations to make about this exercise as a whole. If I have selected the right sentences as illustrations, their problems suggest that nouns and adjectives derived from verbs create difficulty. Verbs and words derived from verbs have more obligations than other words do; they require subjects, expressed or implied, or at least an awareness of the part of the writer that the subject of a verb-derived word is empty. Transformational analysis of these words and the difficulties they entail makes this property of verb-derived words more explicit, and should guide the design of remedial strategies and exercises.

A second observation is that agency problems often are signalled by high incidence of abstractions, often complex ones, in subject position. Of the eighteen sentences in this essay, seven have abstractions as subjects: "casting of movies," "advantages in terms of makeup," "editing, cutting, and being able to alter the finished product," "the advantages and different places a movie can be shot at," "casting," "availability," and "number." Abstractions have far fewer, if any, opportunities to be agents. Only three human subjects appear—all of them first person singular, in the obligatory and familiar opening and closing formula—and human beings are the best agents of all.

These proposed revisions are far from perfect: on the one hand, they probably are better than we could reasonably expect from remedial students; on the other, they certainly can be improved upon (one difficulty in proposing revisions is keeping intended meaning more or less constant). The revisions are in any case in isolation from their contexts, and it is precisely in this area of supra-sentence revision that text linguistics and discourse analysis may have more to tell us. The remedial procedures—a set of suggestions for revision—are very much subsequent to the construction of a system of error analysis of which this paper is a very small and highly tentative part.

What I am suggesting, basically, is that linguistics can be of the greatest help to the teaching of composition not in presenting a bundle of rules to be taught directly to students—that approach, in the sixties, was an unqualified disaster—but as a tool that can provide a set of heuristic devices for the construction of a pedagogical grammar in which it might be better, instead of sections on, say, subject-verb agreement, pronoun reference, and parallelism, to have a section on agency, where the particular kinds of these errors illustrated here would be discussed in one place, and other kinds lumped together in other sections as yet unlabeled and unknown (for example, morphology, or word-formation, is a reasonably unified topic, but no pedagogical grammar book I know of treats it in a unified way). A forthcoming study[9] of linguistics and the teaching of grammar shows that linguistic theory of a rather sophisticated sort can provide arguments for ordering, in a pedagogical grammar, topics like subject-verb agreement, for which there is a mechanical procedure for determining whether the rule is applied correctly, before topics like pronoun reference, where there isn't always such a procedure. Analytical insights of modern linguistics, in short, even the very crude versions of them I have shown here, can help construct a new system of error analysis with differently shaped clusters of persistent student problems related to one another in ways not hitherto—or even yet—perceived. And these insights also can provide a well-motivated and non-ad-hoc basis for sequence in the composition curriculum.

Three general objections frequently are made to proposals of this sort. Linguists argue, on the one hand, that this particular kind of language in use is much too complex and unsystematizable for the analytical procedures of formal linquistics, and, on the other, that the linguistic system used is much too simple-minded. These objections seem to me to be opposite sides of the same coin: the goodness of fit—or lack thereof—between the formal elegance of modern linguistics and the manifest inelegance of the remedial situation. It appears, for example, that I would adjure students always to place agents in subject position with as little subordination as possible, and to avoid verb-derived adjectives and nominals, when in fact both the passive voice and the gerund, to name but two of the troublesome constructions discussed here, have their uses. Throughout this essay I have used the term "agency" in an extremely loose sense, without the formal rigor of the case grammarians, and I have based discussion on a model of tranformational-generative grammar now very considerably altered from its original version in significant details.

To these objections I rejoin that there is a very considerable distinction between a scholarly grammar and a pedagogical grammar. In the present state of our knowledge we cannot hope to systematize all of the problems in the teaching of remedial composition. In this programmatic statement I have sought to use what I believe to be one of the greatest strengths of modern linguistics—its analytical powers—to describe one small part of those problems: a part not hitherto thought to be a coherent entity. From this description should follow a set of remedial strategies such as exercises and revision procedures, which would have as their aim not essays composed of monotonous sequences of agent-action-goal sentences, but an awareness in the student of (in the present case) agency as an important and identifiable component of writing, just as, say, parallelism and punctuation are important and identifiable components of writing. Future work along these lines should seek to isolate and describe other parts, and fit these parts into a structure, a pedagogical grammar, which will look quite different from existing pedagogical grammars and from scholarly grammars.[10]

For this effort to have any reasonable chance of success, questions internal to linguistic theory will have to be disentangled, to the extent that they can be, from questions internal to remedial composition. I have therefore, based this discussion on a model of grammatical theory which at least has the advantage of a reasonable degree of currency. Like any field of serious inquiry, linguistics is in a state of constant ferment and change. But I think linguists cannot—must not—delay making significant contributions to the analysis and remedy of writing problems until the structue of English is fully described and agreed upon. The entire history of modern linguistics strongly suggests that this consensus will never be attained. Like the teaching of English composition itself, the contributions of linguistics to that enterprise will be messy and piecemeal for the foreseeable future.

A third and more serious objection to what is proposed here is raised by composition teachers: that analysis of this sort is within the reach of any good, experienced composition teacher's intuitions. Composition teachers have always known, for example, that there is an implied subject for the verb-derived noun *adjustment*; it is a common remedy to suggest that students revise muddy sentences so that the agent is in subject position instead of in some subordinate clause. In response to this objection, I would argue that linguists have made few if any discoveries about the structure of English (as opposed to the structure of linguistic theory) that composition teachers have not already known as independent facts. But there is a difference between a fact and a systematized fact. It is a fact that if you sit under an apple tree in late September, an apple is likely to fall nearby, and it is a fact that the sun rises and sets at predictable times. But these facts look very different when embedded in a theory of gravity, inertia, mass, and acceleration.

Similarly, it is a fact that the so-called "misrelated modifier" occurs when a participial clause does not modify the subject of the sentence in which it occurs; it is a fact that vagueness occurs when a student uses gerund subjects, verb-derived nouns, in such a way that the subjects of the verbs from which the gerunds are derived cannot be clearly identified. But these facts look very different when they are seen as part of a theory in which both clauses and derived nouns are related to full predications whose structure can provide a principled basis for analysis and remediation.

Pedagogical grammar has been apple-dropping, in my judgment, for quite a long time. Much of it always will be, probably; but after a quarter-century of intensive research in the structure of English, linguistics should be able to systematize some aspects of pedagogical grammar for the teaching of composition. The most promising locus for this sort of enterprise, I contend, is in the development of an empirically based system of error analysis. This essay is a small step in that direction.[11]

JOSEPH M. WILLIAMS

Non-Linguistic Linguistics and the Teaching of Style

Not too many years ago, a seminar at the MLA set as its topic why linguistics in the service of literary criticism had been such a failure. That seminar could have asked why it had also failed in composition, for at that time, those attempting to exploit linguistics in teaching writing could have pointed to little that was promising and to less that had been delivered, particularly on any of those occasionally extravagant predictions made in the '50s and '60s. It's certainly not too late for such a seminar, because in the few years since then, not many of even the more modest promises have been realized.

William Labov, Ralph Fasold, Walt Wolfram, Shuy, and Stewart[1] have provided us with sophisticated descriptions of social dialects. And others, Kenneth Pike and Frank D'Angelo,[2] have associated contemporary grammatical theory to the traditional arts of discovery and arrangement. And then there is sentence combining, perhaps the most promising development in the last several years.

Ironically, of course, systematic sentence combining, intellectually legitimized by transformational grammar, might never even have been conceived had Noam Chomsky not made a theoretical error in *Syntactic Structures*,[3] had he realized then, as he did later in *Aspects*,[4] that a grammar generating sentences recursively would not need sentence-embedding transformation. And had there been no sentence-embedding transformations in 1957, then Donald Bateman and Frank Zidonis in the early 1960s and later John Mellon and Frank O'Hare[5] might never have recognized how transformational grammars could be used in teaching composition.

Regardless of its legitimacy, of course, if sentence combining fulfills its most modest promise, students will develop a maturity of style earlier than they otherwise might have. And if it even partly fulfills it more dazzling promises, it will help students think, organize, and argue beyond their grade level.

Now certainly, our least task in teaching composition is to develop in our students a level of minimal syntactic competence, however we define that competence. But minimal competence is surely not our only task, nor even our most important one. We don't judge carpenters by how accurately they cut their wood; accuracy is a prerequisite for becoming a carpenter. In the same way, minimal linguistic competence, defined as control over the grammar of standard written English and the ability to write sentences at an appropriate level of syntactic maturity, is only a prerequisite for learning how to become a writer able to meet the demands of a literate adult life.

And it is this question that I want to address here: why contemporary linguistics has offered so little that takes us beyond describing the grammar of standard written English and beyond providing some of the theory for setting a level of syntactic maturity at 1.74 clauses per T-unit and 11.5 words per clause.[6]

Some of the reasons for this failure are easy enough to propose. H. L. Mencken, not half in jest, I think, offered one:

> With previous few exceptions, all the books on style in English are by writers quite unable to write. The subject, indeed, seems to exercise a special and dreadful fascination over schoolma'ams, bucolic college professors, and other such pseudo-literates. One never hears of treatises on it by George Moore or James Branch Cabell, but the pedagogues, male and female, are at it all the time. In a thousand texts they set forth their depressing ideas about it and millions of suffering high-school pupils have to study what they say. Their central aim, of course, is to reduce the whole thing to a series of simple rules—the overmastering passion of their melancholy order, at all times and everywhere.[7]

I can't recall which of my graduate-school teachers it was, but what he said about discovering the structure of the language we were working on, Kikuyu I think, seems relevant to this problem of discovering and describing the structure of not just minimally competent but rhetorically appropriate language. He said that if we wanted a really sound analysis of Kikuyu, it would probably be easier to teach linguistics to a Kikuyu than for a linguist to learn Kikuyu. It would be a little unfair, I think, to claim that in the same way it is probably easier to teach linguistics to a native speaker of clear and graceful prose than to teach clear and graceful prose to a linguist, for of course there are many able writers among linguists—Jim Sledd, Raven McDavid, Dwight Bolinger, and, certainly, many others.

But I think the general force of the analogy holds. English-speaking linguists are competent to deal with the grammar of English. But I am less certain that those who have tried to use linguistics in teaching writing have demonstrated any special sensitivity in describing what invests prose with more than mere grammatical or quantitative acceptability. In fact, I think a case could be made that even those concerned with developmental quantitative syntactic maturity may be so basically mistaken about what constitutes it that, if they are not teaching the wrong thing, then they may not be teaching at least one very important right thing. But more of that later.

However mistaken many editors and writers may be about the folklore of grammatical usage, they usually write well, or at least they recognize good writing when they see it. They may not be able to explain in the most fashionable grammatical terminology why a piece of writing is good or bad, but their sensitivity to clear writing parallels that sense of grammaticality which we attribute to native speakers of a language and by which we test our grammatical descriptions.

Now these are, admittedly, comments ad hominem. But I think we have to distinguish between defining syntactic maturity on the one hand by quantifying grammatical features of writing and, on the other, by making informed judgments about a passage, and then manipulating the passage in search of grammatical features relevant to our sense of stylistic acceptability, much the same way as we manipulate the grammatical structure of sentences in search of grammatical acceptability. It is a distinction that goes to the heart of the way in which linguistic stylistics has been practiced for the last half century, particularly, but not exclusively, in regard to the teaching of writing.

When we teach writing, what we teach about style depends on what we think we can verify and publicly demonstrate. And what we are able to verify and demonstrate usually depends on the categories and processes and relationships in our theory. If our theory includes the category "word," and we can agree on how to apply the definition, then we count words. If the system includes the category "clause," we count clauses. If it includes "transformation," we count transformations.

When a theory becomes so intrinsic a part of our intellectual baggage that, as with the dialects we speak, we eventually become unaware that we are speaking through the vocabulary of a particular theory, then we may also become unaware that we are not likely to look for anything except those features toward which our theory directs us, much less what other features there might be, not defined by our theory.

This problem is particularly acute when the theory we use in an investigation of one area was originally devised to answer not the questions we have posed about that area, but rather some other set of questions. This is the case with all current theories of syntax pressed into the service of style and composition.

Before 1957 (the date is symbolic) descriptivists were most concerned with gathering reliable data from observed linguistic behavior and with formulating empirically vertifiable discovery procedures that would systematically process the data into a constituent-structure grammar, a grammar usually organized from the bottom up, from phoneme through morpheme and syntagmeme.

After 1957, public behavior as a source of data gave way to introspection; formalizable discovery procedures gave way to informal heuristic methods based on paraphrase, ambiguity, anomaly, and so on; and a concern with constituent structure alone gave way to a concern with relating surface and increasingly remote structures. Generative grammars are rhetorically organized not from the bottom up but from the top down, with sentence in the initial statement and statements subsequent to it moving through semantics and syntax to statements about acoustic features.

At first glance, one would think that generative grammars would have revolutionized the study of style, emphasizing as they do the intuitive sense of linguistic appropriateness, and explanatory rather than descriptive statements. But descriptive and generative grammars share two features that for our purposes are, I think, fatal to their uncritical use in stylistic analysis. First, neither directly addresses how the structure of a sentence is experienced, from the point of view either of the speaker/writer or of the reader/listener. Both are, to this degree, text-centered. And yet if style is a component of rhetoric, as it must be in the teaching of composition, and rhetoric is the art of moving audiences, such text-centered theories must in some critical respects miss the point.

This preoccupation with text-defined structures has been particularly reinforced for those of us trained in graduate schools of English where for so many years the New (now old) Criticism dominated critical thinking. Like linguistics, the New Criticism is an enterprise that centers on the text, excluding on principle any critical consideration of the intention of the writer or the experience of the reader. But even if we set aside the question of whether the affective and intentional fallacies are indeed fallacies in literary criticism, I cannot conceive that they should determine how we think about style and composition.

The second flaw is that both descriptive and generative grammars either initially or eventually make the sentence the highest hierarchical structure in the system. Although there has been a good deal of work recently put into the functional analysis of sentences and into text grammars,[8] just about all of those investigations begin with terms drawn from a theory of sentences in isolation. Our ignorance about the structure of discourse has prevented us from formulating a theory of sentences whose categories and relationships would intersect with, or at least impinge on, the categories and relationships constituting that theory of discourse. One principle in constructing theories of systems composed of hierarchically interlocking sub-systems is that boundary conditions are set from without rather than from within, and that to some degree parts take their character from the whole they constitute. In the case of sentences, they are constituent parts of, and therefore shaped by, a larger whole, the discourse they occur in.

It is the difference between A. A. Hill struggling, in his *Introduction to Linguistic Structures*,[9] to move from phoneme to morpheme, from lower to higher, and Chomsky and Morris Haile, in *The Sound Pattern of English*,[10] demonstrating that a syntactic description, the higher hierarchical system, is a prerequisite to a phonological description, the lower hierarchical system. If sentences are shaped by the discourses they appear in, quantitative analyses cannot capture that shape, particularly when only those features relevant to the structure of sentences constitute the terms of the theory.

A particularly relevant example of the problems raised by these points is the research into sentence maturity, based largely on the T-unit, and its ratio to words and clauses. Let me say at the outset that I think the work of Kellogg Hunt, Roy C. O'Donnell, and others[11] on syntactic structures at various levels is an invaluable resource. Without it, we would be much the poorer. But it is an entirely text-centered study that does not make clear whether 1.74 clauses per T-unit and 11.5 words per clause have any affective reality. We have no idea at what point a text composed of T-units increasingly below those figures would be perceived as "immature." Or what happens when the clause ratio goes down and the word ratio goes up. Or vice versa. Or whether there is such a thing as too much maturity. And if there were, how we would know.

Hunt and O'Donnell left a gap in their counts, I think. They provide data on several grade levels through the 12th, and for superior adults, presumably those writing for publication. What we do not find are data gathered from the prose of nonsuperior adults, those who write for the everyday purposes of commerce and industry, who write hasty and unedited but surely, in some sense, mature prose. In order to fill this gap, Rosemary Hake and I collected samples of prose written for internal use at a large manufacturing concern in the Chicago area. We asked the supervisors providing the samples to judge them as well or badly written by whatever intuitive judgment they wanted. The documents judged badly written had a clause-to-T-unit ratio of about 1.5, roughly equivalent to the prose of a ninth grader. The documents judged as well written, on the other hand, had a clause-to-T-unit ratio of about 1.3, equivalent to the prose of a seventh grader.

Now clearly something is wrong here. None of these documents could be mistaken for the work of a seventh grader, or even a ninth grader. Whatever syntactic maturity infuses these texts, clause-to-T-unit ratios seem not to be affectively salient, at least in the way we might predict, and certainly not independently of other features.

I would like to discuss one syntactic feature which I will simply claim is more affectively salient than almost any other syntactic feature that invests a passage with the *appearance* of maturity. And that is the abstract nominalization, the noun formed from the cognate verb. I have elsewhere reported on some of the work that Professor Hake and I have been doing in this area, so I will summarize it here only briefly.[12] We have found that an essay written in a nominal style not only tends to be graded higher than precisely the same essay written in a verbal style, but also tends to be perceived as better organized, better supported, and better argued than the corresponding verbal paper. Here is an example:

> My *preference* is for *life* in a large city because there I would have a *freedom* to do things that can't be done in a small town. In a small town, a person's *life* has to be like his neighbor's. There is a *need* for his *conformity* to their *beliefs* in regard to proper *behavior.*

> I *prefer* to *live* in a large city because there I would be *free* to do things that can't be done in a small town. In a small town, a person has to *live* the way his neighbors do. H *needs* to *conform* to what they *believe* is the proper way to *behave.*

Although the frequent use of these abstract and deadly nouns rather than those concrete and lively verbs contradicts everything we tell our students about good writing, a great many teachers of English, perhaps most, apparently take a nominal style as evidence of thoughtful, mature writing. Nominalizations reduce the proportion of clauses to T-units because clauses become noun phrases, thereby increasing, of course, the words-per-clause ratio:

> When we *discussed*   why he *failed*   it *influenced*   what we *decided.*
> Our *discussion*   of his *failure*   *influenced*   our *decision.*

In our experimental verbal papers, for example, the clause-per-T-unit ratio was about 2.4, considerably above the superior adult's 1.74. Our nominal papers had a clause-to-T-unit ratio of about 1.6, about on a par with an eleventh grader. Yet it was these latter papers, the nominal papers, that usually received the higher grade. This supports the observation that longer clauses characaterize more mature writing, but contradicts the corollary observation that, as writing matures, the ratio of clauses to T-units increases.

So among a text-centered T-unit analysis, a reader-centered affective analysis, and a textbook-centered rhetorical analysis, we have a contradiction. Insofar as nominalizations are concerned, if we urge our students to write in that concise and verbal style we all say we support, then they will write like high school students in the length of their clauses, and like superior adults in the number of their clauses, but in the process perhaps elicit from their teachers the unfavorable judgments that seem to be associated with a verbal style. On the other hand, if we train them to increase the number of words per clause, they must correspondingly decrease the number of clauses, and if they associate nominalizations with more complex writing, as almost all writers do, they will write in a style that we all say we condemn for its lack of grace and vigor, but which seems to get better grades. That ghostly chortle belongs to H. L. Mencken.

We might be able to resolve part of this contradiction if we simply modified what we say to match how we actually respond, or at least how most of our evaluators responded, much as we have been asked to modify our attitudes about standard English. But that won't do because, unlike dialects, a heavily nominal style is not only rhetorically mendacious but cognitively difficult. Several experiments done in the early '60s by E. B. Coleman[13] provde some evidence that in comparison to a verbal style, a nominal style is more difficult to process. Professor Hake and I recently developed some additional evidence. We gave two passages differing only in their nominal and verbal syle to more than seventy typists at different levels of ability and education. On a words-per-minute basis, they typed the verbal style about 15 percent faster than the nominal, and made about 20 percent fewer errors. So we can choose between these styles not simply on the basis of taste but, if pushed to the wall, on a cost-accounting basis as well.

Now if a nominal style is so affectively and cognitively salient, why is it that studies of syntactic maturity have devoted so little attention to it? In the first place, despite some references to transformational grammar, these analyses use a syntactic theory derived for the most part from traditional and descriptive grammars. The theory simply has no well-defined and prominent category that accommodates nominalizations, that demands that nominalizations be one of the first categories attended to. In the rhetoric of traditional grammar, the most prominently displayed categories are called *noun, verb, adjective,* and *adverb*; *declarative, interrogative,* and *imperative*; *simple, compound, complex,* and *compound-complex*; *active* and *passive*. But we have no reason to believe that those categories are the most salient to the experience of a sentence.

Hunt devoted a few words to the subject of verbal nouns and, under a different heading, a few more to gerunds.[14] But he did not discuss them together, because gerunds with their empirically observable-*ings* are objectively different from abstract nominalizations of the *discover/discovery, translate/translation, report/report* types. So his theory distinguished that which, from the point of view of the *text grammar,* was structurally different, but which from the point of view of the *text experience* may be identical. But even if his theory had provided a clearly defined category of verbal nouns in general, it would not have singled out nominalizations as any more or less affectively salient than any other category. No statistic based on text-centered analytical categories has any prima facie relevance to what is rhetorically salient, or by extension, to what we should be teaching.

I think the problem is even more complicated than I have just described, because affective salience is not a simple function of particular syntactic features but of features foregrounded in a context that is both linguistic and nonlinguistic. I overgeneralized a bit when I said that our evaluators generally seemed to prefer a nominal style. Some of the pairs of papers they read were intrinsically well organized, well supported, well argued; others were disorganized, weakly supported, illogically argued, and so on. The high school teachers in the group generally preferred the nominal papers regardless of their intrinsic quality. But the college teachers were more selective. They generally preferred the nominal version of the good papers, but among the bad papers they either failed to prefer one over the other, or preferred the verbal.

In other words, in different nonlinguistic contexts, the same linguistic features were perceived in different ways. We think that a reader reading a nominal style in an intrinsically good paper sensed a match between an abstract, i.e., educated or mature, style and clear thinking; a competent reader reading a nominal style in an intrinsically bad paper responded to the abstract style as an attempt to cover up with turgid language an absence of careful thought.

If this is so, then it leads to an important though certainly not new principle of stylistic analysis. Any conception of a whole must come from a sequential perception of its parts; but it is equally true that the sequential perception of the parts depends on a developing conception of a whole. How we understand the general stylistic demands of the genre is an obvious example. Our understanding of the specific relationship between speaker/writer, reader/audience, subject matter, and situation in light of the informing intention of a passage is a much more complex event. The beginning of Lincoln's Second Inaugural Address is in a relatively nominal and passive style:

> At this second *appearing* to take the oath of the presidential office, there is less occasion for an extended *address* than there was at the first. Then a *statement*, somewhat in detail, of a course to be pursued, seemed fitting and proper. Now, at the *expiration* of four years, during which public *declarations* have been constantly called forth on every point and phase of the great *contest* which still absorbs the *attention*, and engrosses the energies of the nation, little that is new could be presented.

He could have written more directly:

> As I appear here for the second time to take the oath of presidential office, I have less occasion to address you at length than I did at the first. Then it seemed fitting and proper for me to state in detail the course I would pursue. Now after four years have expired, during which I have been constantly called on to declare publicly on every point and phase of the great contest which still absorbs the *attention*, and engrosses the energies of the nation, I could present little that is new.

Because we know Lincoln was a serious man speaking on a serious occasion, we respond to the indirect style of the original version by directing our attention away from Lincoln and toward the serious occasion.

None of this should surprise us since that idea has for a long time been the staple of gestalt psychology. But it does have some important consequences in the analysis and teaching of style, not the least of which is, first, the importance of perceived intention as an informing principle that shapes the developing perception of a whole and, second, the potential meaninglessness of statistics. It certainly suggests that a reader who senses a specific and clear-cut intention reads and integrates all the details of the text to that intention. And that is the mirror image of what many teachers of composition have observed, that if a writer has a sense of his intention and direction, he will make fewer errors of all kinds, from organization to grammar to spelling.

If this is the case, then there are some special questions we should ask about sentence combining and other teaching methods that concentrate on sentence style.

Professor Hake and I have been conducting another research project, this one comparing the effects of sentence combining with sentence imitation. One group of high school students, over a hundred, are combining sentences; the others are imitating the same sentence structures that are the goal of the combiners. One difference between what we are doing and what most other sentence-combining projects that I have heard about are doing is that in every case, the students are working with sequences of three sentences constituting a short discourse. Another difference is that we have avoided narrative and descriptive sentences and are working almost entirely with expository forms. For example, this is what the combiners end up with, and the imitators begin with:

> This country should ratify the ERA because women must have rights equal to their responsibilities. Our society needs a law which would guarantee that everyone is equally protected from discrimination. Such protection will come, though, only when we all recognize what we lose in an unjust world.

We have no comparative results yet; however, the teachers teaching the units have reported that when students combining sentences are not familiar with the content of the kernel sentences (which was often the case because I had no idea how little most tenth graders know about anything—what the CIA is, what interest on a bank account is, what the Viet Nam war was), they have a difficult time doing the combining exercises. But the sentence imitators, who are given familiar topics to use in their imitations, seem to have little trouble. We believe this happens for the following reason: when a student has a clear conception of the content he is working with and is, in effect, provided with an intention that infuses that content, he can manipulate the grammatical structures and their logical relationships with relatively little difficulty. But when the content makes little or no sense to him, then the logical relationships are very unclear, and when the logical relationships are unclear, then the syntactic relations will also be unclear. The imitators, on the other hand, are provided with subjects that they know something about, and so are able to formulate a reasonably clear intention that lets them match their own ideas and intentions to our syntactic patterns.

Now what does this imply? It may be that sentence-combining exercises allow students to make readier use of their store of ideas and information because more complex sentences let them integrate more ideas more easily. If the experiments conducted so far have emphasized narrative and descriptive writing, as do most of the exercises I have seen, then we might explain the success of sentence combining, as others have, as the students' increased ability to express what they already know in larger structures—structures that, if they are narratives, are in effect preshaped by the recollection of the event—by what must be virtually an inherent sense of storyhood.

But expository writing sets different demands. The subject matter is usually not as immediately available as the matter of a recollected narrative. The shape of the discursive essay does not present itself as readily as the shape of a story or the description of a scene. Successful expository writing depends on a control of syntactic structures, but more so than narrative writing on seeking out an informing intention and on generating ideas other than those that are merely ready to be released by complex syntactic structures.

So it may be that practice in the traditional arts of invention and of formulating a clear intention, in shaping a discourse on the one hand, and practice in sentence structure on the other will have mutually beneficial effects. As one is strengthened, so is the other. Whether combining or imitation is the more effective in developing more effective sentence structures remains to be seen.

I have one final reservation about the research into syntactic maturity based on contemporary syntactic theory, about defining maturity on the basis of feature counts and creating exercises designed to raise those counts to appropriate levels. I suggested it when I wondered whether it were possible to be too mature. The major problems of contemporary prose written by adults, both in our edited public discourse and in our unedited private memos and reports, are not the problems of immature, undeveloped sentences, but of sentences that are too indirect, too long, too verbose, too complex, too abstract, to be easily understood. If anything, it is this postremedial problem of tangled and turgid writing that a theory of style should address, the kind of writing we find in sentences such as:

> There is now no effect mechanism for introducing into the initiation and development stages of reporting requirements information on existing reporting and guidance on how to minimize burden associations with new requirements.

The clause-to-T-unit complexity of that passage is 2.0, and the words per clause average is 16, very mature indeed. In this light, the premium placed on quantitative linguistic complexity without the qualification of a linguistic definition of clarity should make us pause.

We need a theory of sentences in which clarity would be a concept that we could not escape addressing, and that would ineluctably lead to exercises that would concentrate on clarity along with complexity. The fact that we are a long way from such a theory does not mean that we do not know what we must know in order to formulate one.

For one thing, we require a much fuller and more careful analysis than we have of topicalization, both how it occurs in a sentence and the rhetorical functions it can serve. We need, as odd as it sounds, a good description of the way sentences end. The categories of rheme or comment that match theme and topic are too crude to account for the problems of stress and emphasis. Incidentally, in addition to their familiar topicalizing function, nominalizations have another rhetorical use, to end sentences with an emphatic thump.

We shall certainly need a category in the analysis that we might call *metadiscourse:* all the elements in a sentence that refer to the process of discoursing, as opposed to the specific reference of the discourse. I have in mind what goes on in a sentence such as:

> I believe that in regard to the American pharmaceutical industry, we can say that there seems to be excessive federal government regulation.

On its most ordinary interpretation, the sentence is not about me as a believer or about us as sayers, but about the American pharmaceutical industry. That is the topic of the sentence, that for which the rest of the sentence exists. The comment, the statement about the topic, is *excessive regulation by the federal government.* Everything else—*I believe that in regard to* and *we can say that there seems to be*—is metadiscourse, discourse about discourse, elements referring not to the referents external to the discourse but to the act of discoursing, to how we should take the truth value or probability of the propositions about those external referents.

We also have to distinguish very clearly how semantic concepts such as agency, action, and patient intersect with these rhetorical functions. For example, *American pharmaceutical industry* is the topic but is also the patient of the action underlying the climax of the comment: *regulation/regulate.* The agency is at the end of the comment: *federal government.* The order is not agent-action-patient but patient-action-agent. Were there a perfect intersection between topic and comment and agent and action/patient, the sentence would have read:

> I believe that in regard to the federal government, we can say that there seems to be excessive regulation of the American pharmaceutical industry.

But that would have changed the perspective of the sentence, requiring a different perspective in any discourse in which such a sentence appeared, and that would in turn require a different intention infusing the perspective of the discourse infusing the perspective of the sentence.

Note that to describe these aspects of rhetorical structure we have not yet needed any grammatical terminology. Eventually, of course, we would. The topic is not expressed in the subject of the main clause but as the object of a compound preposition *in regard to*; the comment is the complement of the metadiscourse verb *be*. The agency is the object of the preposition *by* in a noun phrase; the action is the noun in the predicate noun phrase; and the patient is the object of the compound preposition. Had there been a perfect correlation among these three levels of discourse, among the rhetorical, grammatical, and semantic structures, the sentence might have read:

> The federal government is *excessively* regulating the American pharmaceutical industry.

semantic structure	agent	action	patient
grammatical structure	subject	verb	object
rhetorical structure	topic	comment	
	The federal government	is excessively regulating	the American pharmaceutical industry.

There is a fourth level of analysis that intersects with the semantic structure expressed by the particular words: the structure of real-world events. Contrast these three sentences:

(1) The forest   provided me with   everything I needed.
(2) I   found   everything I needed in the forest.
(3) Everything I needed lay waiting for me in the forest.

In the real world, forests and things cannot act; I can. But the *forest* is a seeming agent in (1), a literal locative in (2) and (3). *Everything* is a seeming agent in (3), an object in (1) and (2). *I* am the agent in (2), a dative object in (1) and (3). We can see the difficulties raised by introducing this level of analysis in these two sentences:

> A great idea suddenly came to me.
> I suddenly got a great idea.

What is most important in all of this, I think, is that the grammar of the sentence need not be the *first* level of analysis. When we begin with grammar, with subjects, verbs, and objects, those categories become the presiding terms of our analysis and all other terms and levels of analyses flow from them. But if we begin where the experience of the sentence is, with the rhetorical and semantic structure and then integrate a necessary gramatical description with those levels, we have the beginnings of a theory which would allow us to deal with the experience of a discourse rather than the solipistic terms of a theory of sentences. [15]

Several years ago, when as a graduate student I first became interested in stylistics, I asked a visiting fireman from MIT about the rules (that overwhelming passion of our melancholy order) that might explain good and bad writing. He shriveled me with a glance and announced that that was not linguistics. I was too chagrined to ask him what it was (fearing he would answer "remedial composition," perhaps), and I labored along on and off for several years, doing that thing that had no name. In fact, I think now I was doing linguistics all along. I—like most of us interested in style and both composition and literature—had simply been asking questions that required theories different from those we were using on Kikuyu.

Now I prefer to think of it all as non-linguistic linguistics. The secret to using the term is to pronounce the initial *linguistic* in a slightly condescending tone. I would like to think that the second linguistics, the kind I have been discussing here, would at some point include a good deal of what the first linguistics is all about. But it doesn't start there.

An Afterword

Professor Hake and I have completed the first stages of the combining/imitation research. The preliminary results appear in *Sentence Combining and the Teaching of Writing,* edited by Donald A. Daiker, Andrew Kerek, and Max Morenberg (Conway, AR: L&S Books, 1979). I can summarize the results here, though.

On the basis of pre- and posttest essays, we classified the students into three groups: (1) Those whose papers were judged incompetent both before and after their course of study; (2) those whose pretest essays were judged incompetent but whose posttest essays were judged competent; and (3) those whose pre- and posttest essays were both judged competent. An analysis of their T-units revealed the following:

	Pretest Incompetent ⟶	Posttest Incompetent	Difference (37 students)
words/T-unit	15.51	16.45	+ .94
clauses/T-unit	1.83	1.87	+ .04
words/clause	8.47	8.79	+ .32
	Incompetent ⟶	Competent	(76 students)
words/T-unit	15.69	13.01	− 2.68
clauses/T-unit	1.99	1.59	− .4
words/cause	7.88	8.27	+ .39
	Competent ⟶	Competent	(99 students)
words/T-unit	11.86	15.56	+ 3.70
clauses/T-unit	1.68	1.82	+ .14
words/clause	7.05	8.54	+ 1.49

These results agree in some respects with what other researchers have reported: Students increase the length of their T-units if they are given encouragement and practice in doing so. But the curious exception is the group that began incompetent and became competent, and the astonishing difference between the T-unit counts of the incompetent and competent before the instruction began.

It is not difficult to find a logical explanation for this: incompetent students write long and uncontrolled sentences; competent sudents control their sentences. As incompetent students become competent, they control their sentences better by shortening them; competent students control their sentences and so can increase them under control. The difference between the imitators and the combiners was not statistically significant.

In the matter of more holistic and trait judgments, we found that among the students who began and remained competent, the imitators did significantly better than combiners. The evaluation instrument asked graders to find flaws in four different dimensions: overall sense of wholeness, logic and organization, style, and usage/mechanics. (The instrument was developed by Professor Hake at Chicago State University.)

An analysis of the flaw counts among this most competent group provided the following data:

Imitation (38 students)

	Pretest	Posttest	Difference
D_1	3	1	-2
D_2	9	5	-4
D_3	9	4	-5
D_4	6	8	$+2$
Total of 2–4	24	17	7

Combining (41 students)

	Pretest	Posttest	Difference
D_1	3	1	-2
D_2	9	8	-1
D_3	9	8	-1
D_4	4	4	0
Total of 2–4	22	20	-2

Control (20 students)

	Pretest	Posttest	Diffeence
D_1	3	1	-2
D_2	9	9	0
D_3	8	7	-1
D_4	6	5	-1
Total of 2–4	23	21	-2

Evaluators found significantly fewer flaws in logic/organization and style among the imitators. This result supports our original thesis: When students are provided with model structures to impose on experience of their own devising, they will be better able to impose similar structures on self-generated content during real writing tasks; students who are provided with content in the form of kernel sentences and are expected to generate their own structures for that content will be less able to impose structures on their own content later.

We have not yet completed the analysis of the papers from those students who began incompetent and remained so or from those who became competent. But on the basis of the T-unit differences among these groups, we expect to find that students at different levels of ability—resolutely incompetent, incompetent but able to improve, and already competent—will respond to different kinds of exercises in different ways.

The paper in the sentence combining collection mentioned before elaborates this possibility that different rhetorical models call for different kinds of exercises at different stages in that growth.

As for the formal model suggested at the end of the paper, I think I would like to expand it just a bit. There are, I think, not three but four levels of analysis relevant to the central structure of each sentence, and those four levels divide into parallel sets of two vs. two.

The grammatical and semantic levels are still clearly enough defined:

SUBJECT	VERB	OBJECT
AGENT	ACTION	GOAL

As for practical analysis of this canonical intersection, it is sufficient to ask only two questions:

1. If the subject is not an agent, what case is the subject?
2. If the agent is not the subject, where is the agent?

The fine categories generated by most case-grammarians are too detailed for the practical analysis of style, much less for its teaching. As I. M. Schlesinger has pointed out *(The Production and Comprehension of Utterances* [New York: John Wiley and Sons, 1977], pp. 31ff.), we probably metaphorize most instrumental (and I suspect locative) subjects into agents, anyway. If agency is indeed the stylisically most salient case (as it certainly is in teaching "good" writing), then we need only look for a canonical coincidence (or lack thereof) between subject and agency, and then if the subject is not an agent, for the location of agency. These two levels, we might note, constitute an intersection between a relatively fixed functional position and a variably placeable meaning.

We can find the same relationship when we move from this grammatical-semantic level of sentences to a discoursal-rhetorical level of texts.

Let me simply sketch out the following: The topic of a sentence typically begins with one of the first noun phrases and continues through a transition (I think *pivot* would be a better word) to a comment. The topic is that from which the rest of the sentence logically follows; it is that about which the sentence is saying something. It is usually the subject:

Style   is difficult to define.

But it may be in an introductory prepositional phrase:

About style   we can say little with certainty.

Or a front-shifted object:

What style is   no one can say precisely.

The function of topic is usually expressed positionally, but it regularly coincides with the discourse (not metadiscourse) subject.

The rhetorical meaning of topic, on the other hand, is as flexible as the semantic meaning of subject. It usually announces information most psychologically accessible, that information which is oldest, least surprising, most familiar, most predictable, most easily recoverable from the preceding discourse. This rhetorical meaning we might call *theme*. We can then use *rheme* to identify information that is least psychologically accessible, information that is the newest, least familiar, least predictable, most surprising.

Now, just as semantic cases can be permuted through relatively fixed grammatical functional positions with attendant stylistic consequences, so can rhetorical meaning be permuted through relatively fixed discoursal functional positions. But the coincidence between topic and theme is as canonical as the coincidence between subject and agency:

My second point   is   your stupid terminology.

Though we may want to invest *second point* with some special rhetorical significance, in any unmarked context *second point* is obviously less rhematic than *your stupid terminology*. If so, *second point* should coincide with the topic position. (And to complicate matters, we have here a metadiscourse topic followed by a discourse comment. It is a matter I won't pursue here.)

But it does not have to:

Your stupid terminology   is   my second point.

If we grant that *your stupid terminology* is not predictable from the previous discourse and that *my second point* is at least not surprising, then we have permuted a rhetorical rhematic meaning into a topic function/position, pecisely parallel to permuting a semantic goal meaning into a subject function/position. And if we manipulate the articles in this following set of sentences, we can represent four permutations among subject/agent/topic/theme and object/goal/comment/rheme:

Those animals must have fled from a fire.
That fire must have driven away some animals.
A fire must have driven away those animals.
Some animals must have fled from that fire.

We thus have this canonical paradigm:

internal: {	grammar:	SUBJECT	AGENT	OBJECT	position/function
	semantics:	AGENT	ACTION	GOAL	meaning
external: {	discourse:	TOPIC	COMMENT		position/function
	rhetoric:	THEME	RHEME		meaning

To oversimplify not too much: Style is defined at least partly by how we can manipulate the categories of meaning through the categories of function and position.

LOUIS T. MILIC

Composition via Stylistics

From the beginning of my career as a teacher of composition (over twenty-five years ago), I have held certain beliefs, for which I have had no substantial evidence, about the proper conduct of the task. For example, I have always been persuaded that a course in freshman English should be so suffused with information about language and about English (its history, structure, features, resources) that in some ways it might be indistinguishable from a course in English linguistics. The faith underlying this belief (quite commonly held at one time) might be described in the following terms: if the student becomes aware of the role of linguistics in his environment, if his consciousness of what principles come into play when he is speaking, reading, writing is heightened, inevitably his skill in these activities will increase. This is a tenable proposition and it may well be true. I have, however, lost faith in it but not because the results I have achieved as a teacher of composition have convinced me of its defects. I do not think I have been (or am) a better teacher of composition than any of my colleagues. I can claim to have maintained, despite regular and severe discouragement, an intense interest in the process and a curiosity about the possibility of a solution.

The problems that face the teacher of composition in college are certainly greater than those facing the teacher of any other elementary subject (e.g., mathematics). They are so extensive as to throw into doubt anything that the teacher may try to do and range from the difficulty of defining achievement or progress to the near impossibility of stating what the subject matter itself consists of.

The most obvious problem is the prodigious yet increasing illiteracy of each successive generation of students. It is probably correct to associate this tendency with the abandonment by the young and the population at large of printed materials as sources of entertainment in favor of television and auditory stimuli. The most important consequence of the freshmen writers' unlettered background is that they arrive in college without the repertory of Standard Written English structures that earlier generations (entertained by reading *Gulliver, Robinson Crusoe,* Zane Grey, *Zorro*, or even *True Romances*) had stored in their nervous systems. They do not know what writing should look like and are therefore at a hopeless disadvantage when they address the task of writing a composition.[1]

Essentially, then, one task of the college composition teacher today is to find a substitute for the background of literacy that the student lacks. A major problem is still that we have not yet adjusted to the special difficulty of teaching those who are non-literate in the sense I have described. We continue to use the methods that may have been appropriae at a time when social circumstances were widely different, when leisure activities, high school preparation, means of communication, attitudes toward knowledge and the make-up of the college population itself diverged sharply from today. If we could act on Paul Roberts' facetious dictum—"Anyone who has written a million words has no writing problem"—we might not have the teaching problems that we do. But, at the rate of five thousand words per semester, it would take the student fifty years to arrive at the condition described (summers included), and who would read all those papers? Evidently what is needed is an efficient method of teaching composition, and the "natural" method (writing a million words) is not efficient.

A neglected but central question is how to determine whether progress is taking place.[2] This question finds its answer in the nature of the task itself: what are we trying to teach? Most composition courses proceed under extremely vague notions of the task being attempted and the criteria for estimating improvement. Indeed, it appears probable that many instructors "go through the motions," assign papers, correct them, discuss some readings, lecture on principles, and at last conclude with a grade whose significance is uncertain.

Much composition teaching is to great extent the study of errors.[3] In the average classroom, the student gets his paper back from the teacher marked with correction symbols (e.g., *agr* for agreement error, *ref* for reference error) which he is expected to act on. To correct his errors, he must look up the diagnostic symbol in a handbook, read the relevant discussion of the error, try to understand its relevance to his mistake, apply the principle and make the required change in the original wording. The student is usually incapable of doing any of this except for the simplest errors (spelling, vocabulary, agreement). Teachers resort to such markings as *awkward, incoherent* and *vague* more often than necessary because they are unable to make a sufficient analysis of the type of error they have noted. The complexity of student miswriting is puzzling to the instructor without a deep interest in syntax and rhetoric. To illustrate, here are four genuine sentences extracted from some recent freshman essays:

1. To speak properly, not just pronunciation but also grammar and syntactically, a person should have the right techniques.
2. This action alarms the driver of the oncoming car of his negligence of keeping on the correct side of the road.
3. These usually add strength to what is being communicated, for instance, if one wishes to show hatred, squinting and frowning will usually succeed.
4. This information we can improve on with a wider perspective of information.

The sentences just cited were taken from impromptu papers written for the purpose of placement on the second day of the second quarter of a required freshman English course, the topic being nonverbal communication. Though it is true that the sentences are shorn of context, it is nonetheless possible to draw some conclusions from them, specifically: which of the four writers could benefit from college-level instruction in composition and which should be returned to a lower level for more basic instruction or perhaps even discouragement.

The most serious defect is in sentence 3, which contains a comma fault, rightly judged by most teachers to be the sign of a very low degree of writing sophistication. Similarly, sentence 1 contains an alarmingly unparallel arrangement in the parenthetical structure separating the front adverbial from the subject, with a pleonasm thrown in. Sentences 2 and 4, on the other hand, are syntactically adequate and contain no major grammatical defect. Unfortunately, they appear to be almost meaningless. No one can decode sentence 4 without more data, which could not be found in the contiguous sentences of the original essay. Sentence 2 contains perceptible meaning but vacillates between a given sense and its opposite. If I had to place the writers on the basis of these single sentences, I would express the least hope for the writer of sentence 4, whom I would suspect of having no idea what he was about, and only a bit more for the writer of sentence 2, whose difficulties are lexical, idiomatic, and semantic. Both sentences are in different ways literally incoherent.

I would be more optimistic about the writers of the odd-numbered sentences, despite the flaws they exhibit, because a purpose exceeding the available techniques appears to animate them, the reverse of the case of the even-numbered writers. If the grammar or the rhetoric of sentences 1 and 3 is adjusted, they not only make sense but show some ambition. The effort to build a parallelism, to illustrate a generalization, is risky if one doesn't have the technique, but such risks should be encouraged.

Of course, the common difficulty in correcting wayward writing is that it is impossible to tell what the student intended to say if he did not write it. This is a difficult proposition to refute. Those teachers who take refuge in it simply transfer to the student the necessity of correcting the paper, limiting their comments to question marks, symbols of obscurity and doubt, and expressions of puzzlement and skepticism. With mature students, such a procedure can be challenging and eventually productive. For the beginning writer it is nothing of the sort. If a class of students has been assigned a composition on a stated topic, the instructor has undoubtedly developed some expectations about the range of responses he is likely to receive. He is aware of the likely approaches to the task and can even predict the form of a number of the sentences that will be submitted. Any set of sentences placed before him can be interpreted in the light of all these contextual clues. In addition, the teacher may know the individual students and their propensity to certain typical errors. In other words, despite the theoretical integrity of the view that meaning cannot be inferred from a meaningless sentence, teachers can usually do so and ought to, since they are not a typical but a special audience.

Given all these problems and others large and small too numerous to mention, how is composition to be taught, assuming that it can be done at all. There is no question that it can be done. In fact it could be done in rather interesting ways, if cost were no factor: isolating the students from distracting and corrupting influences (creating a new New Atlantis, a good place or "Eutopia"), allowing them to steep themselves in the classics of prose, urging them to write six hours per day and discuss the results with a variety of interested, learned, tactful, and encouraging teachers in an environment beautiful to the eye and restful to the ear . . . But cost is a factor and any course today must be taught efficiently, i.e., in classes of twenty-five to thirty-five, each one making up no more than half the teachers' workload and about one-fourth of the student's. Under such circumstances indirect methods and wasted motion must be abandoned.

For that reason (the need for efficiency) I have come away from the belief that teaching the student about language and assigning papers on language-related topics will result in improvement in writing. It might eventually, especially if begun not later than the ninth grade. But the available time is so short that there is really no leisure for any topic that does not bear directly and immediately on the writing problem. There is therefore insufficient opportunity for a survey of modern grammar, a history of the language, a historical survey of dictionaries, an excursion into rhyme, meter, and poetry.[4] There is room for only one aspect of classroom instruction: whatever will fill the gap produced by the systematic avoidance of the forms and structures of Standard Written English.

In a normal course of study in primary and secondary school, before the age of television, a student might be expected to have read a certain range of well-known ("classic") authors in his native language (from Bacon and Shakespeare to Edith Wharton). In addition he would likely have been spending his leisure time reading trashy adventure stories, westerns, romances, sports writing, and the like, thus getting the necessary exposure to the resources of style that the English language contains. In the course of his schooling these resources would gradually percolate into his writing until he had achieved an instrument for communication with undeveloped possibilities: immature, to be sure, probably awkward and uncertain, but a basis. Note that such a result did not come about because of a stress on "basics" in high school nor because of spelling bees or word-study, though these may all have helped in some ways. The major influence was exerted by the same natural method which teaches us to *speak* our mother tongue. This is what is in great part missing today and what stylistics can attempt to provide a substitute for.

But to apply stylistics in composition, it is necessary to have a terminology. The several topics that must be touched on include vocabulary, rhetorical devices, punctuation, morphology, and syntax. A language has long existed in school classes in English among which such terms as *synonym, noun, metaphor,* and *parallelism* may be found and with which some students have at least an auditory familiarity. To deal with these and less familiar items by definition ad hoc may be satisfactory for everything but grammar. Grammar, however, remains an exception because it is not a set of terms but a system, whatever manner of grammatical description is adhered to. Whatever else may be true about a freshman class today, one thing is sure: no single member of it has an explicit knowledge of any usable grammar of his native language. And if any two students in a class should have some knowledge of grammar, there would certainly be little correspondence between them. If grammar is essential to stylistics, a prior component of any style-based composition course must therefore be a brief exposition of grammar. Whether it is the case that an explicit grammar is essential has been debated. The workshop method involves an inductive even intuitive process of substituting one formulation for another. Apart from the difficulty of referring to things without names which this method has, without a grammatical underpinning it lacks the means of generating a wide range of possible alternatives.

Unfortunately, any suggestion that grammar be included in a composition course is likely to fill the teacher with despair, for he believes that if grammar enters his syllabus there will be no room for anything else, given the complexity of modern grammatical description. Moreover, teachers often feel inadequate to the task of giving a competent account of modern grammar even to a class of freshmen. Certainly the task can be difficult if a high level of fidelity to the most recent developments is maintained. But an important distinction exists between linguistics and stylistics. Stylistics requires some knowledge of linguistics but includes other topics as well. Linguistics for stylistics is not the same as linguistics for itself. Stylistics is a practical field and does not demand a theoretical grasp of the processes under scrutiny. Specifically the grammar that I advocate is a simplified version of the tagmemic system called Sector Analysis, which was devised by Professor Robert L. Allen of Teachers College.[5] Pedagogically it is suitable for easy learning, as has been demonstrated numerous times by its inventor, using classes of fifth-graders. It may be supposed that college freshmen would not find it beyond their powers. Practically, it is more suitable for this purpose than other grammars, not only because it does not break with traditional description, but because its design accords very closely with the needs of the apprentice writer. In two weeks of instruction, the student can be introduced to a linear description of the English sentence, which will permit him not only to analyze illustrative sentences but to discover the nature of his own practice. Other grammars deal much less directly—perforce, since this is their intention—with the surface structures of the language. Sector Analysis describes the ideal and the existing sentence as a string of positions (same of which may be vacant in any given case), which can be filled by a variety of structures. The basic form of the sentence is the following:

L F] S X M V O C B [E

L: conjunctions like *and, but*

F: front adverbial, including adverbs, phrases or clauses

S: the subject sector, capable of accepting a wide variety of structures, primarily nominals

X: the first auxiliary of a verb group, sometimes zero, as well as any form of *be* when it is not an auxiliary

M: middle modifiers like *often*

V: the verb group minus its first auxiliary, the verb itself when there are no auxiliaries.

O: the object sector (like S above)

C: the complement sector, which accepts the widest variety of structures, such as indirect objects, predicate nouns and adjectives, adjectivals, adverbials.

B: verb particles (*up* in "make up the test")

E: end adverbial (like F).

When sectors L, F, and E are removed from a sentence, what remains is the "trunk," which constitutes the basic S-V-O unit. The following sentence will illustrate the application of the formula:

As we observed in the chapter on punctuation,] students
F
who speak in sentences / do/n't necessarily / know / ana-
S   X   M   V
lytically / what they are.
C̃   O

The auxiliary *(don't)* overlaps the X sector *(do)* and the M sector *(n't)*, the actual locution being the unit *not necessarily,* which belongs in the latter. The tilde over the C indicates that the sector has been shifted from its normal place. The three included clauses may be broken down as follows. (It should be noted that included clauses have the I sector in place of L):

As / we / observed / in the chapter on punctuation
I   S   V   C

who / speak / in sentences
I   V   C
what / they /are
I   S   X

Two of the includers fulfill roles which in trunks would be represented by such sectors as S and O.

Although the above sketch is far from being an adequate description of the grammar of the English sentence, it provides a usable outline which permits the student under supervision to perform certain operations which can improve or change his original attempt on some basis other than the correction of errors.

The major advantage of this simple grammar is that it can be mastered quickly. Its main disadvantage is that it masks some of the complexities of English syntax, but that is more of a disadvantage to the student of linguistics than to the freshman writer. A further advantage is the provision it makes for word order—actually the order of sector or constructions—the alteration of which is an important means of achieving emphasis in English. The sentence matrix can easily be applied to the student's own writing to yield such easily tallied data as his own habitual patterns, whether he is given to front adverbial clauses, parentheticals, appositions, shifted particles. Whatever is learned in this way is self-knowledge, facts about a process always previously considered mysterious. The realization by a student that he has a singlular manner of writing—a style—may be very encouraging to him.

The basis of progress in composition is the realization that there is more than one way to say anything. This principle of synonymity, the crucial theorem of stylistics, must be developed in a rational and gradual manner if the course in composition is to be efficient. It should be recalled that the best usual course in composition consists of two components (if we disregard the readings which are insufficient to have any effect). The instructor lectures on various topics concerned with the process of composition, such as organization, paragraph structure, vocabulary. The students write a number of themes in the light of the injunctions offered by the instructor. The lectures unfortunately do not accomplish anything and do not influence the work of any student who is actually in need of the information they contain. Their presence in the course is the result of a lack of alternatives. I overlook here the workshop or tutorial method which appears to differ from this procedure in that the student's writing is the basis of all discussion. In practice, however, it serves as the text for brief lectures on vocabulary, organization, and the like, more pragmatic perhaps but not really different from the standard model. If they do not lecture, the instructors discuss readings, usually in spite of themselves, from the thematic rather than rhetorical viewpoint. The theme-writing component is based on the supposition that in half-a-dozen themes the student will produced a valid sampling of his linguistic resources and allow the teacher to make an estimate of his writing ability and potential. Naturally, the statistical basis of this latter is shaky when it is considered how many structures the language contains and how few a sample of three thousand words can include. The procedure might be sounder if the student's compositions were treated as an inventory of the different structures in his idiolect and a ratio were devised to serve as a measure of his ability. The post-mortem treatment of papers in the standard course shows the same misplaced emphasis on the correction of errors rather than on synonymous alternatives. This time-honored system has never worked except with students so well prepared that they were not in need of it.

To return to the original point (given the illiterate condition of our present students), an *efficient* means is needed to make up for the lack of a background of reading twelve years in extent. To remedy such a deficiency is impossible, so it is well to aim lower. One alternative might be to expend the course time in a study of a systematic treatise of the stylistic resources of English, such as exist for French and Latin, for example.[6] No such work exists for English, of course, though works for the use of Japanese or other foreign speakers have been compiled. Despite this lack of source material, the sentence matrix can serve as the basis for a set of exercises designed to expose the student to a wider range of structures than he possesses.

In presenting the outline of such a course as I now favor built on the materials I have mentioned I am faced with the nagging quandary facing anyone who pretends to teach writing to native speakers—where to begin? Because the end product (writing) must be produced from the beginning, there is no obvious place to start. If one starts with organization, what of sentences or words? If one begins with words, how is the student to produce good paragraphs before the end of the term? There is no solution except to teach everything at once, which is plainly impractical.

What I am describing here is such a course as my experience suggests would make the best use of the materials I have developed to solve the problem as I have diagnosed it. I would begin with an introduction to the sentence matrix, followed by an application of it to selected examples drawn from readings. Such a procedure involves the close examination of texts, a new and valuable experience for such students as I have described. Next, I would move quickly to paragraph design, using an analytic scheme consisting of the seven relation-ships which can exist between successive propositions,[7] by examining sample paragraphs from both standard sources and from student papers. A study of the former would reveal appropriate models which students could follow to remedy the deficiencies in the latter. Patterns for generating good paragraphs also result from this procedure, as well as a new awareness of connectives, their use and variety. This order of presentation is a compromise designed to produce im-provement in student writing as early as possible. In a leisurely course, paragraphs would enter perhaps halfway. Paragraphs, incidentally, are the largest units systematically studied in this course. If paragraphs and sentences are inadequate, the organization of the whole will hardly be perceived; if success in sentences and paragraphs is achieved, larger organizational problems will be easier to solve. The remainder of the course is devoted to the sentence matrix and its implications. This work is both theoretical and practical and it proceeds extensively by means of exercises to explore the expressive resources of the language in the stylistic equivalents which it affords.

A stylistic equivalent is a synonymous alternative for a word or structure. No systematic treatment of these exists in English. Dictionaries and grammars index the language according to the words and the structures in use. No work makes available to the reader the means of expressing a given meaning. If we wish to state the temporal aspect of an event, for example, we are provided in English with a considerable range of options. The day after today can be referred to by a single word *(tomorrow)* placed in the F, M, or E sectors. As a phrase or clause ("in twenty-four hours," "after the sun rises," etc.), it is limited to the F and E sectors, though there are circumstances when it might occupy the C sector. It may also be expressed in a separate sentence: "This will occur tomorrow."

Stylistic equivalents are classified on the basis of their degree of departure from the initial sentence. The range is from zero-order, which makes no alteration in the sectors of the initial sentence, to third-order, in which the initial arrangement of sectors is scrapped and another substituted. To illustrate, let us consider a fairly common sentence structure (analyzed into sectors):

1.   Though few people are aware of it, / the aurora / is
            F   S   X
      regularly / seen / in northern latitudes.
            M   V   C

In the lowest (or zero) order of stylistic equivalence, changes are made only within sectors, thus producing such sentences as these:

2a.   Though few people *realize* it, the aurora . . .
2b.   . . . the aurora is regularly seen in northern *regions*
2c.   . . . in *polar* latitudes.

The systematic application of this process will generate many sentences and call into play a consideration of vocabulary, in particular the discrimination of synonyms. In my view, it is only in this practical and immediate way that vocabulary should be studied in a composition course. Formal treatment tends to be digressive and theoretical and places the emphasis on the nature of the word rather than its use.

The first-order equivalent involves the substitution of the contents of an entire sector. Some versions of our original sentence:

3a.   . . . the phenomenon known as "aurora borealis" is
       regularly seen . . .
3b.   . . . the aurora is *often* seen . . .
3c.   . . . the aurora is regularly *observed* . . .
3d.   . . . the aurora is regularly seen *near the North Pole.*
3e.   *Surprisingly,* the aurora . . .
3f.   *Although it is not generally known,* the aurora . . .

These substitutions involve a yet more elaborate range of possibilities without, however, affecting the basic structure of the sentence. Discussion surrounding these manipulations inevitably includes consideration of modifier types and semantic paraphrase as well as synonymy.

Second-order equivalence occurs when the word-order is shifted primarily by the movement of entire sectors:

4a.   The aurora / is / regularly / seen / in northern latitudes, /
          S   X   M   V   C
       though few people are aware of it.
          E
4b.   *Regularly,* / though few . . ., / the aurora / is / seen . . .
          M   F   S   X   V
4c.   *Regularly* / *is* / the aurora / seen / . . . , *though few* . . .
          M   X   S   V   E

This mode of alteration of sentences relates to some of the more important aesthetic effects available in English prose and calls into play a large number of rhetorical devices. The manipulation of word-order will doubtless appear most unfamiliar to the "unread" student. It should therefore be stressed in order not to permit this valuable range of effects to remain hidden and unused. The most extensive departure from the initial sentence is found in third-order equivalents. In these the original number of sectors and their arrangement may be wholly modified or even abandoned:

5a.   Though . . . , / the aurora / is / a regular sight /
          F   S   X   C
       in northern latitudes.
                 C_2
5b.   It / is / not / generally / known / that the aurora is
       S X M_1 M_2 V   O
       regularly seen . . .
5c.   Do / you / know / that the colorful display of the northern
       X   S   V   O
       skies is a regular event?

Third-order stylistic equivalents are really semantic-syntactic paraphrases of the original base and may take the most distant forms. Although some of them can be produced by the native speaker searching for a means of achieving clarity, being able to manipulate them effectively implies some knowledge of English style and the resources of the language.

It would be folly to claim for the suggestions that I have made that they constitute a complete (or new)[8] course in composition. They leave out of account such considerable topics as invention and organization of the whole and treat vocabulary and mechanics as incidental. It is scarcely worth mentioning that the research paper, library research, and methods of documentation are totally ignored. The emphasis is on the close and actual manipulation of language in the context of an understanding of the main structure of English, the sentence. It may be objected that this process is too demanding for the type of student I have visualized and that, even if successful, it is insufficient. I shall deal with these objections in order.

Although the "aurora" sentence is far from sophisticated, it could be argued that is is unlikely to appear in a student's paper. The following sentence, however, is a genuine student sentence:[9]

> 6. People / are / judged / by what they produce on the job.
>   S   X   V   C
>   what / they / produce / on the job.
>   I S   V   C

Assuming for simplicity's sake that the context involves the writer's own anxiety about employment, we may proceed to ring the changes on this illustration:

7. (zero and first-order)

People	are	judged		by what they	produce	on the job
Workers		valued			perform	at work
The young		evaluated			do	in the office
Minorities		estimated			accomplish	at their post

> 8a. (third-order)
>   Their production on the job / is / what judges people.
>   S   X   C
> 8b. Work / is / the basis of evaluation.
>   S   X   C
> 8c. Production / causes / favorable judgment.
>   S   V   O
> 8d. In the long run, / it / is / work that counts.
>   F   S   X   C

Anyone familiar with the language and its resources could continue the third-order list to much greater length. How to enable the student with an impoverished vocabulary and no adequate access to the forms of Standard Written English to do so is evidently a problem whose solution must be found in the pages of a workbook or a set of exercises yet to be devised. But I reject the contention that this student is incapable of some part of 7 and 8 above. If that student can even produce a single synonym, he is on the way to an understanding of stylistic equivalence and can eventually produce complex forms.

As for the objection that proficiency in this technique would not insure a student's ability to write an entire composition, although this claim has some apparent plausibility and the evidence does not exist to refute it, I am persuaded that it is untenable. Any teacher knows from experience that the student who can manipulate alternative formulations can write and that incapacity on the whole is associated with the inability to produce alternative formulations.

Writing papers, learning to paragraph, becoming acquainted with the English sentence and its system of alterations—that is basically what I see today as the proper content of a freshman English course. I cannot speak from successful experience but I believe that great emphasis must be placed on the students' own productions and on their extensive revision. Once produced, the students' writing begets their loyalty and they become eager to improve it. That this can be accomplished by means of systematic drill with only incidental lectures seems at least possible. We know very little about success in writing but we do know that a student who is not writing cannot improve. Revising for the correction of errors is insufficient because it concentrates on the incidental rather than the fundamental. Students err and continue to err because they have no background of literacy. Correcting errors only stops the bleeding; it does not make the body healthy. The complex and rich resources of English prose, which stylistics can open to the student, must somehow be deployed as the corollary of health. By using systematic shortcuts, as consumer testing agencies open and close car doors 20,000 times to simulate a decade of use, we may be able to simulate a dozen years of reading.

SANDRA SCHOR

Style through Control: The Pleasures of the Beginning Writer

As a teacher of writing and an occasional writer of fiction and poetry, I would like to propose today that "style" is a term wholly out of place in a class of beginning writers. In its place I want to suggest the word "control," and I want to talk about why "control" may be a more suitable byword during the first semester or year of a writing class.

E. D. Hirsch, Jr., in *The Philosophy of Composition*,[1] supports Louis Milic's assumption that "learning the craft of prose is learning to write the *same* meaning in a different and more effective way," an assumption about the conscious aspects of style which Hirsch and others agree justifies the teaching of writing. While Milic's insight may be practical for advanced students of writing, one has inevitably to wonder how it can be applied, without frustration, to beginning writers. Clearly it is a call for control, yet a control too refined, one that does not take into account the beginning writer's fundamental failure to bring to his or her writing ordeal a meaning hospitable to the struggle for greater effectiveness. At the very earliest levels of learning to write, levels at which we find the majority of college freshmen today, a writer is often so intimidated by previous failures and so grossly limited in writing experience—in diction, syntax, and especially in his capacity to endure as a writer—as to obscure meaning, particularly from himself. Although he may be willing to articulate his meaning at some length verbally, more often he hastens to agree with a teacher's asessment of what his sentences are getting at. A change of form in his writing often yields a major revelation of content. It brings an idea into focus, or, more spectacularly, locates an idea scarcely hinted at in the original. If beginners say something in a way that is not "effective" it is not because they have no style, but because they have not yet had the experience of producing content of a "writable" or controllable dimension. In other words, they have not yet developed, through the practice Milic himself recognizes as necessary if anyone is to learn to write,[2] the skill and the patience to push their thinking to those more interesting boundaries available only to writers and the most remarkable of Peripatetic thinkers. Nowhere do beginners have a body of writing in which a drift of style can legitimately be detected, nor do they know the bittersweet pleasure of a writer forced to reveal himself by what Milic has called "the constant linguistic necessity."[3]

Milic draws a distinction between stylistic options "made unconsciously while the language-generating mechanism is proceeding" (i.e., during the act of putting words on paper) and conscious rhetorical choices "made while the mechanism is at rest" (during the revision stage).[4] I am suggesting that writing experience in both stages—and nonpunitive experience at that—provides the writer with the gross control of language necessary to the discovery, expression, and adjustment of meaning. Eventually, further writing experience provides data in which all the options of an experienced writer can legitimately be identified as "style."

Perhaps I can make this position plainer by testing some popular definitions of style on the writing of a student—let us call her Karen—in one of our basic writing courses.

We may take *style* to mean those recurrent features of a text that an author habitually uses, in the sense that a writer cannot help writing the way he or she does. Or we may take style in its ornamental view to mean deviations from a "neutral"—even a "naked"—norm. According to this definition, the writer dresses the same meaning in a different suit of clothes for different occasions. Or we may take style to mean those features that suggest what is implicit and unstated about a writer's attitude toward his subject, for example, whether a writer's concerns about freedom, injustice, and patriotism are expressed in abstract nouns or, as Camus' are, pronominally in the first person. Now I would ask that you substitute for the word *writer*, the name of our student Karen, a placidly inexperienced nineteen-year-old on whose earliest essay, submitted in your class of beginners, I ask you to focus your memories.

Is Karen's style of writing recognizable in those recurrent features which she can't avoid expressing? (Aren't these recurrent errors or, at best, features of monotony?)

Is Karen's style the manner in which she deviates from a neutral norm? And do her deviations suggest that she is adroit enough to change the dress of her message at will? (Aren't they really circumlocutions and syntactic traps into which she helplessly falls, hobbled as she is by a limited and insecure syntactic repertory?)

Measured by the third definiton, is Karen's style the details by which her writing gives her away, implies her attitudes, and suggests her personality? After reading Karen's first essay would you risk delivering a verdict on her, call her aggressive, playful, daring, understated? More often her writing is precisely the evidence that misleads us into thinking she is a zero, a shallow, depersonalized individual known to her readers through her use of the passive voice, her frequent nominalizations, and a tendency to abstractions and unsupported generalizations. Is there a real Karen detectable under these bland features that every writing teacher knows have no life signs? Those of us who have been teaching for a while know better; the truth is we are no longer surprised when a dignified, interesting, if vulnerable and unsure, young woman named Karen shows up in our office for her first conference. This student, with considerable personal grace and enough presence to get through a conference with a professor, is still a long way from exhibiting style in her writing. Handicapped, she hasn't had enough experience to try out the structures that will hold her ideas and generate more of them. She not only has little to say but few structures to say it in and less confidence that she can succeed.

We don't know exactly when Karen started writing. For us Karen's life as a writer begins with her placement essay, a document singularly out of touch with the personality of its writer. Here are excerpts from two placement essays, let us say Karen's and another student's, not the best we've seen, but clearly not the worst. (I should point out that at Queens College the writers of these essays were not admitted into the freshman course but were placed in the writing course that precedes freshman composition).

(1) Anybody who doesn't read once in a while is missing an awful lot. Most people who read get a lot of knowledge of what is happening all around them. Reading can be very enjoyable if you know what you are reading. When you read a book that is interesting and a book that you like, you just think about that book, you get so absorbed in the story, that sometimes you don't want to put it down.

Some people read for a hobby or they have to read a book for class. If you like the book it will take no time to read. I know when I read a book that I enjoy, it could be mystery, drama, or comedy, I get so wrapped up in what I am reading, that I just can't put it down or think of anything else.

Occasionally, there are people who read books that are boring to some people. There are people who have no knowledge of reading. Either they don't care or are just plain lazy. People are just lucky to have eyes to see and to read because it is a wonderful thing to do in your pastime. If people knew just how fortunate they were if they knew how to read, there would be a better world.

(2) The word laughter can be one of the best things to do these days. If not for laughter in the country everything would be one big mess. We don't have too much peace around the world today so laughter or laughing can make things around you and people much more pleasant. Laughter is when people tell jokes and laugh. Laughing is the knack to tell whether the joke was good or not. If not then you'll just have to try again. There is also a sarcastic laughter when people commit a stupid thing and laugh, it wasn't funny but just plain stupid. Telling jokes is also the best way a person gets out of a bad mood, so maybe instead of getting down or feeling sorry for yourself, laughter can be the best thing to get you out of that bad mood. It is stupid to laugh at immature things, so

when somebody cracks a joke think about whether it was funny or not. Laughing at everything can be a sign of not being grown up. Sometimes laughing at everything isn't the best thing to do. Laughter is what brings some people into show business for the comedians. If not for the audience, comedians wouldn't be around too much longer. There are many high paying salaries for comedians because his job is to make the audience laugh, by telling jokes or doing some funny stunts. Making people laugh can be very entertaining and the comedian telling the jokes can be very self-satisfying for him and the audience. These are some of my thoughts on what laughter does and some of its meanings.

What kind of writing is this? I'd like to share with you some quite unexpected insights I gained into this kind of writing from the work of investigators into an analogous kind. I refer to the work on the style of suicide notes in articles, both popular and scholarly, that range in title from "Suicide Notes Are Dull"[5] to "Some Effects of Motivation on Style of Encoding."[6] After reading these articles, it struck me that the stress on the inexperienced writer of a placement essay and the stress on an imminent suicide may be so similar as to produce similar stylistic patterns in their writing. Edwin S. Schneidman, a specialist on the sociopsychological causes of suicide, remarks that suicide notes are "like the postcards sent home from the Grand Canyon, the catacombs or the pyramids—essentially unimaginative . . . and not at all reflecting the grandeur of the scene being described or the grandeur of the human emotions that one might expect to be engendered by the situation." He goes on to say "some notes are like last minute shopping lists . . . 'fix the spark plugs on the car,' while others get in one last lick, 'you drove me to this.' " Certainly the notes are "belabored" and yield very little drama.

But why do we expect grandeur of a suicide? The suicide feels like a zero and, pitifully, has no sense of the grandeur of this exquisite and horrifying human ordeal. The writer of the placement essay is put into a remarkably similar do-or-die mentality. While he is not literally suicidal, his life as a student, his self-image as a student, is on the line. Is there an observable stylistic connection between the two? Charles E. Osgood, who comes to his study on the effects of stress on encoding as a psycholinguist, hypothesizes about the relationship of stress to style as shown in suicide notes. He says that the increased stress of the moment causes greater stereotyping of choices. These limitations show up in less diversity of vocabulary, greater repetitiousness, and more terms which permit of no exception (such as *always, everybody, no one*, and *forever*).

Those of us who read placement essays will certainly recognize these stylistic constraints as the very same signals we look for in tagging a writer for a remedial course: limitations of vocabulary, broad generalizations that begin, "Everybody in the world today" and "People who read books always . . ." as well as unintegrated lists of ideas and a pervasive repetitiousness. Osgood goes

on to talk about the high instance of evaluative terms and ambivalent constructions, although some of the aberrations he expected never materialized,
such as the total disorganization of language skills, a general structural distur-
bance, and decreased length of sentences—none of which seemed characteristic
of the suicide notes studied. Grammatical problems, which appear to transcend
moments of stress, can be counted on to show up routinely in the writing of
anyone afflicted with poor grammar.

My question is, does it make sense to talk about improving the style of
writers of suicide notes? Well, we hardly need to say that the potential suicide
can write about his anxieties and terror only when that anxiety has been
alleviated and and he is again in control. It may well be oxymoronic to talk about
the "style" of suicide notes. In the same way, it seems to me outrageous to talk
about the "style" of beginning writers. Beginning writers need to experience
writing for a long period of time under conditions without stress, without
penalty of a grade closing down on them whenever they exhibit a completed
sentence. Just how reliable the placement essay can be is a subject of some
dispute. Certainly it would be a contribution if we could alleviate the stress of a
test situation. But, imperfect and stressful as placement essays are, they still
appear to be the best instrument for testing writing that we have.

But why subject our students to the tyranny of the suicidal placement
essay all semester long? I know from the number of excellent and humane books
that have recently come across my desk that the wind traveling through the
country's writing classrooms has been changing. But I also hope we understand
that by changing the climate in which writers write, we are not talking only
about the survival of good writing. Keeping the stress of the placement exam out
of the classroom may mean the survival of many of our students *as* students
because under stress they do not learn to deal with the complexities of college-
level thinking.

Another way we increase the pressure on writers who possess little
self-confidence is to charge them to write in their own "voice." It is as though we
were addressing clients in Overeaters Anonymous who are publicly shamed
when they are told, "You are what you eat." "Write in your own voice" means
exactly that. "Aha! Now we see what you are. You are what you write."
Although later on I shall question Richard Lanham's thesis in *Style: An Anti-
textbook,* here I must agree with his attack on the dogma of sincerity.[7] How
many beginning writers have one "voice"? A nineteen-year-old who cannot
decide on a major, who cannot see a job out there in his or her future, whose
handwriting slants in a different direction in every paragraph, sometimes in
every line? The voice of that formative personality can begin to produce writing,
and thinking, in quantity. Perhaps what we mean by "voice" applies only to a

given piece of writing: "Write this essay in a consistent voice, one that shows control and purpose."

It may be only through prolific writing that writers can recognize the cycle of acts[8] they perform every time they sit down to write. Only prolific writing will create the multitude of options in subject as well as in syntax, and, in the case of basic writers, in grammatical forms. Who but teachers can resupply the students' exhausted energy and good will as they continue daily to face those baffling options? They find out that daily writing and daily response to writing is the way they learn to choose one option over another. The expanse of work a writer produces is a great flood of evidence, as we discover when we lug home student journals and free writing—the evidence that tells us the beginner has moved past the "I have nothing to write about" stage and into experience. As he or she writes, and thinks, and writes some more, these experiences become, willy nilly, more and more complex, more and more tangled in other experiences. One piece of writing nudges another. The more complexity beginning writers face, the sooner they are themselves struck by their inability to cope. Too many decisions now demand their attention. As Karen writes, she finds out for herself that survival depends not on mastering a style, but on controlling all the ideas and impulses and words that wobble just beyond her control, competing to be organized and contained.

It is probably not necessary to go into all the routines and nightclubby stunts that entertain classrooms of beginning writers. But if it is *control* we are after, then let us consider Milic's assumption and start by getting control of meaning. Writing frequent essays and reading the writing of one's peers allow the entire class to become its own showcase for looking at the process of getting and holding on to a subject. And if frequent writing ultimately leads to control, then a writer's control of subject will imprint his style no less than will the arrangements of his ideas, the syntactic shapes of his sentences, or his chosen lexicon. Whatever a writer chooses to write about—God, home, injustice, or Louis Armstrong—mirrors the writer's personality no less than do sentences computed for the number of appositives or embedded restrictive clauses. It is therefore sensible to offer our students as much chance as we can for invention, for development, for bringing the subjects they are writing about closer to their own experience. As Norman Holland pointed out, identity refers to the way individuals *relate* to things "out there." In this connection, I seriously question Lanham's thesis of enabling students to "find a central style by playing at and with a great many styles."[9] This is far too advanced a game for beginning writers.

Lanham also says, "What to say should be supplied. A range of opinions ought to be furnished and surveyed along with a range of styles," and "if a student hasn't any opinions, let him be given some."[10] Opinions and topics are not what students need. They have plenty of their own. What they need is the training to recognize as topics the ideas that burden them, so as to begin projecting a style through subjects that concern them. Assign a structure? Covertly, by concealing a structure within an assignment that is virtually guaranteed to elicit a certain shape (for example, a narrative or a comparison).[11] When we assign a topic, do we not assume a certain professionalism of beginning writers? Do we not assume, in fact, that they know how to manipulate their experience so cleverly as to have it explicate a topic unrelated and uncongenial to their lives? Commercial writers feign a passion in order to improve their chances of selling their work. Why impose that subterfuge on beginners and expect the results to bear a style? Adolescent writers, as Lanham correctly understands, have many selves. Then why give them additional ones? A beginning writing class could do little that is more profitable than spend a part of every meeting exploring the implications of ideas students already have for papers. Ideas and topics, although agreeably left to the students, need not be relegated to the weekend when the paper is privately wrestled into print. That is the everyday business of a writing class. Subjects need to be X-rayed in class. For inexperienced writers, the sifting through of subjects for ideas and attitudes may generate the kind of conscious control over material that eventually permits the unconscious elements of style to emerge. Performing such normally private work in public shows inexperienced writers how to expand the parameters of a subject. It avoids shutting off the subject prematurely. When a student hears the discussion of a subject by twenty or so other personalities in a class, he effectively avoids confining his subject in the pre-cooked shape of his own "style." At the same time, hearing a multitude of voices shows the magnitude of a subject, freeing the implications locked in a subject and extending the range of the writer whose subject it is. In this connection, I refer you to John Gardner's excellent essay "Moral Fiction" in the Winter/Spring 1976 issue of *Hudson Review* (later expanded in *On Moral Fiction* [New York: Basic Books, 1978]).

An important responsibility of the beginning writer is to gain control of sentences, because it is a progression of sentences that forms the whole essay. We've learned a lot about sentence-combining and I want to encourage applying sentence-combining techniques to the creation and criticism of students' own writing. Sentence patterns and the conventions of grammar create expectations which beginning writers either fulfill or, in their awkwardness and inexperience, disappoint. Milic quotes Hemingway as follows:

> In stating as fully as I could how things really were, it was often very difficult and I wrote awkwardly and the awkwardness is what they called my style.[12]

It is probably fair to say that Hemingway is talking not about sentence patterns alone nor subject alone but the marriage of the two. Even for those of us who have grammar in our pockets, the excitement of writing is the marriage of heaven and hell, the unspeakably suspenseful connection between subject and syntax. How much more so for the beginning writer who, until he achieves some sense of control, is likely to feel only the baffling pain and in no way the pleasure. He is, as Milic describes the constraints of every writer, "imprisoned by his idiolect,"[13] though the impoverished idiolect of the beginner constitutes heavy chains indeed and the torment of a one-foot prison cell. I suspect that Hemingway may be showing us the kind of groping through awkwardness that in the end is the residue of our struggle we call *style*. A student of mine first became conscious of syntactic "style" by mastering the kind of noun clause that exists in "That my mother is an amateur psychiatrist will surprise no one who knows her." Every paper for the rest of that semester contained at least four such constructions, awkwardness notwithstanding. Teachers of writing understand that students escaping the clutches of a limited syntactic repertory for the first time become a captive audience for options out of which emerges a style.

Another activity we should avoid overemphasizing if we are to attend to control first and shelve style temporarily is an undue attention to audience. We want freshman writers to be able to deepen ideas and not merely tint their surfaces different colors. Implications for varied audiences can be delayed until *after* a writer learns control, after he permits himself the nagging discomfort of an inadequate word, or after he finds satisfaction in the tiniest revision. Perhaps writing for an audience has been granted undue attention to beginners as a way of substituting thrills for process where interest in freshman composition lags. But this kind of exercise encourages writers to see writing as ornamental. In rewriting, students should not be out for the thrills of ornamentation, but for the process of unfolding a complex idea and for the more lasting pleasure of holding the interest of their readers as they do so. Why ask beginners to write differently adorned versions of an identical text for a shifting audience, when they cannot spare time away from finding out what they mean and saying it? Shifting audiences merely increases the variables they must contend with.

A more traditional classroom procedure whose usefulness may also be strained is handing in the "final" draft. The cycle of recursive acts that writing requires—getting started, refining a thesis, unifying paragraphs, writing forward-moving sentences, getting reactions from readers—always invites rewriting and adjustment. This is not to suggest that every revision guarantees improvement, nor that every paper should be revised; however, the recursive elements in the writing process should be isolated and understood by students as constituent acts in every episode of writing. Tuning up a deficiency, such as stating a thesis, may after all be left for the next paper instead of pursued to the death in the tired one just abandoned. At one of our staff meetings at Queens College, we heard one of our graduate fellows[14] say that he pursues a thesis privately, in a conference, with each student whose essay shows the lack of one. This is, I think, critical recognition of the work required to gain control of one's subject. The thesis is the writer's personal handle on his or her subject. The thesis asserts something about the scope of a writer's material, but is also defines the writer's attitude. Once the writer's attitude is stated, phrasing, ironic diction, and other stylistic indications unconsciously fall into place. In the experience of composing, the *subject* takes the writer all the way from invention, through control of material, to style.

My personal task, when I write, is to permit the material to show me its implications. This blooming from the inside requires control, and control means shaping, the fighting back of excesses, the directing and restraining of material as it is burgeoning. Control means I find out what I have to do with my subject to support my assertion. The sentences I write and the rhetorical choices I make will also, consciously and unconsciously, show my attitude. When I think of my style I think of all my shortcomings as a writer. I think of my tendency to modify, to get ornate, my weakness for a tempting phrase even for its own sake, and a certain relentless drive toward making things more complicated than they have a right to be, probably in the struggle to pin down exact relationships between the parts. When I think of my style I think of working hard to overcome it, of fighting against the odds of a strong and sinister drift, for some of which I ask my readers to pardon me at this very moment.

Of course, what I have at my disposal is a tremendous motivation to do the bloody thing over, strip away and come back up with something dead center. But however hard I work against the drift of my style, there is bound to be some drifting. I suppose that my willingness and my capacity to tolerate drudgery do finally land on a sentence here and there which comes close to what I discover I want to say and can control saying. Still, an irresistible analogy or other temptation gives me away.

What I feel about the potential style of my students is close to what I feel about my own, except that, as *they* begin, they must work to overcome limited resources of many kinds—unreliable inflections, merged constructions, shallowness of subject, the constraint of stress, impatience. Serious academic or business writing now requires that they write accurately, explicitly, and often; and that they practice the repertory of their language as it is available to them in published texts and through each other's and their teacher's writing. Style will emerge gradually as they acquire the control necessary to formulate an idea in writing.

RICHARD L. LARSON

Language Studies and Composing Processes

Linguistics, as I understand it, studies how a language works: what it consists of, how its elements interact and collaborate, and what characteristic patterns govern the operations of that language as it is spoken or written by people who have used it from birth. The linguist seeks to define the options available, and those not usually available, to a native speaker or fluent writer of a language. The linguist may also chronicle the changes that take place in a language, in successive periods of time, or as one moves from region to region, country to country. In other words, a linguist is a describer of language; he or she does not make "rules" or enforce them, but does suggest what rules appear to operate among fluent users of a language—rules that any user should observe, and break only for special reasons, if he or she wants to communicate effectively in the language.

The teacher of composing, on the other hand, guides students in carrying out one or more processes. These processes—which we now know are cyclical (the jargon term is "recursive") and hierarchical (small, brief steps are parts of larger ones) and not linear—begin with the first germination of an idea or perception of a need to communicate and end when the finished communication is transmitted to its destination. Although these steps result in the production of units of language in speech or on paper, they involve, even before that act, inward reflections on a subject and on data—inward reflections formulated, to be sure, in language but not necessarily carried on in accordance with the rules a linguist might have identified. Even during those portions of the processes where the composer utters or writes down units of language for listeners or readers—a step that Linda Flower, our most persistent and informative researcher on composing processes, has called "translating"[1]—it is by no means clear that he or she bears deliberately in mind, or draws consciously upon, any processes that linguists can describe; of course, if the composer is a fluent user of the language what he or she produces will probably conform in many respects to the linguist's descriptions of language. Nonattention to the insights offered by linguists is particularly likely if the composer is engaged in "free writing"[2]— the deliberate effort to compose without in any way limiting or controlling the flow of language.

Of course, when the composer revises or edits his or her work, he or she is often guided by what the linguist has learned about acceptable or nonacceptable ways of handling language (within a dialect or within the more standard form of language), and by what linguists have identified as ways of managing the resources of the language. But editing is nearly the last stage in the processes of written composition (some might say that proofreading follows it), and composing processes include so much more than editing that they might seem to profit only in a small way from knowledge of or insights gained from the formal study of language. In students' writing, certainly what precedes the final editing relies on guidance from sources other than linguists: though students are urged, or required, to edit advanced drafts of their work, they are earlier and more often guided by rhetoricians' advice about form (say, the form of a complex text) or about content (say, ways of exemplifying and confirming a generalization) than by advice about features of language that a linguist studies. Well-edited papers that conform precisely to linguists' descriptions of what is acceptable to native speakers of the language can be, as we all know, pretty empty and boring.

I offer these generalized observations in order to introduce, and partly to explain, the extended professional controversy that has gone forward these past twenty or so years over the role of language studies and linguistics in the teaching of composition. The controversy first came clearly into focus in 1963, with the publication of Richard Braddock, Lowell Schoer, and Richard Lloyd-Jones' *Research in Written Composition*.[3] These authors found no evidence whatever, even in the few well-planned research studies they located, that the teaching of formal traditional grammar—the only form of linguistic study whose value in teaching composition had at the time been seriously investigated—had any beneficial effect on students' learning to compose. In fact, they cited studies to show that extended attention to grammar was connected with a lessening of students' ability to compose effectively. I do not believe that Braddock, Schoer, and Lloyd-Jones suggested any one single explanation for these findings, but one may speculate that instruction focused on formal grammar fails to illuminate—and may even ignore altogether—those processes by which writers produce their writing. Braddock and his colleagues indeed imply that teaching which focuses on grammar deflects students' attention from the acts and processes of composing, even though it is on the performance of these acts that the students' writing is ultimately judged.[4] In 1969, J. Stephen Sherwin reviewed the work of Braddock and his colleagues, and also many of the studies not summarized by them, and came to similar conclusions along with inferences similar to those just cited.[5]

The findings of *Research in Written Composition*, buttressed by the studies of Sherwin and others, became after 1963 the received wisdom about any possible connection between the formal study of language and the act of composing. Though curriculum consultants in the schools largely neglected those findings, and though school board members and administrators, in calling teachers "back to the basics" in the 1970s, implied their disbelief in the findings, scholarly writings on the teaching of composition tended to take them as fact.

There were, to be sure, a few dissenting voices. In 1974, Elaine Chaika argued that "learning to write is a language-learning problem," and described her techniques for helping students deal with that problem by engaging them in the examination of "basic sentence relations." Asserting the fundamental linguistic premise that "language is rule-governed behavior," and implying that students should learn the rules and their applications, Professor Chaika reviewed various teaching emphases based on "the latest psycholinguistic and syntactic theory" and concluded not only that "the number of deviant sentences drops sharply over the semester," but that students found her course "interesting," saying that "grammar lessons helped teach them to write."[6] What Professor Chaika was doing, I think, was to record the successes of an informed and maybe even gifted teacher; whether she was reporting activities and results that could be exported into other classrooms was less clear.

But until 1981 not many scholars echoed Chaika's views, even though many classroom teachers were acting, or were forced to act, as if knowing about the language (its grammar) facilitated "correct" composing. In 1981, Martha Kolln of Pennsylvania State University, in an essay provocatively titled "Closing the Books on Alchemy," took Braddock and his colleagues to task for overstating their conclusions. Reexamining the studies cited by Braddock's team, Kolln found that the studies did not indeed support those conclusions, and labeled as "alchemists" those who had banished language study from classrooms in deference to Braddock's conclusions. She ended with a dedicated assertion of the values to students of studying grammar: "Our goal should be to help them [students] understand consciously the system they know subconsciously as native speakers, to teach them the necessary categories and labels that will enable them to think about and talk about their language, so that when they use it consciously, as they do in writing, they will do so with control and grace and enthusiasm."[7] Knowing grammar, Kolln implied, would indeed help students compose the language effectively.

Kolln's convictions, as one might well expect, were not allowed to stand unchallenged. One respondent, writing in a later issue of *College Composition and Communication*, reminded readers of the number of studies that found no connection between learning grammar and learning to compose, faulted Kolln's reasoning (because the evidence calling into question the value to student writers of studying grammar is "flawed," he found her saying, there must be value in studying it), and declared himself an alchemist.[8] Another respondent, who withdrew his response from publication evidently because *College Composition and Communication* had not printed it instantly, also would have arrayed before readers the studies allegedly demonstrating the error of Kolln's view. But Kolln stood her ground, arguing that "the rhetoric of grammar has its place in the study of rhetoric."[9] And she has received theoretical support recently from a colleague who contends that being able to conceptualize a process and to verbalize the concept, such as grammatical relationships, helps students to make secure their understanding of that process.[10] The issue of whether studying grammar facilitates the processes of composing, clearly, is not dead.

Until the early 1960s, the chief language system considered in research or commentary on the uses of language study in the teaching of composition was what we call, for want of better terminology, "traditional grammar." But in the mid-1960s a grammar called "transformational-generative," derived initially from the work of Noam Chomsky, began to attract widespread attention, with many scholars (such as Richard Ohmann and Kellogg Hunt) championing it warmly as a way of looking at language and styles.[11] Despite the fervor with which they embraced transformational-generative grammar, not a few of these linguists denied in so many words that it offered much help to the teacher of composing. A representative example of such reasoning, published in 1967 by Mark Lester (a scholar committed to transformational-generative grammar as a theory of language), argued that while transformational grammar held great promise for advancing stylistic analysis, it held little promise for the teaching of composing because the study of composition is a study of single performances, conducted after the fact, while the ability of a writer to compose is a part of his "competence," which is a result of inate capacity and cannot be learned. Lester said that we are, and are likely to continue to be, ingnorant in our conscious minds "of how or by what steps or processes we perform any complex process of skill." (Lester, of course, wrote before the first observational studies of composing processes—those by Janet Emig and Linda Flower—appeared.) Lester added that he had taught a section of freshman English using transformational grammar; the students had liked the subject, but he had spent so much time teaching the grammar that he had had little time to teach writing.[12]

Nor was Lester a lone voice. Even experimental researchers, using earlier versions of transformational theory, have voiced reservations about its value in teaching writing. An example is a study conducted a few years ago in New Zealand that used transformational grammar (in the form presented in the well-known University of Oregon Curriculum Study Center materials) as one approach in an experimental evaluation of three methods of teaching writing. The researchers in New Zealand found that transformational grammar did not benefit the overall quality of students' writing, as judged by carefully trained readers, and that students' attitudes toward this grammatical system were sharply negative.[13] This is, indeed, one of the studies cited by critics of Kolln in rejecting her contention that the study of grammar benefits the composing writer.

Still, transformational-generative grammar—for all its differentiation of people's "competence" in executing a process from their "performance" of that process at any given moment—nonetheless claimed to set forth a model by which the forms of language that we observe are created. That is to say, far from simply describing relationships among units of language and offering rules governing the occurrence of certain forms, transformational grammar proposed a model of language that suggested a system of steps by which shorter stretches of language are changed into longer stretches of language. In short, transformational grammar offered a view of processes for composing language. In the late 1960s, the insights derived from this study of how longer units of language are created began to be put to use. At that time, the major names associated with this research were those of Kellogg Hunt and Roy O'Donnell. Hunt's *Grammatical Structures Written at Three Grade Levels* (1967), mentioned earlier, was essentially a study of children's language development. That study hypothesized that language development, or maturation, could be studied through the uses made by children of some operations of language (making shorter stretches of language into longer ones) easily described in terms of transformational grammar. The study was continued, and major findings confirmed, by Roy O'Donnell in *The Syntax of Kindergarten and Elementary School Children* (1967).[14] And the move from that hypothesis to a central question of whether students' acquisition of mature habits of using language could be facilitiated by direct teaching of transformational processes proved not to be a long step, or one slow in coming. The first scholar to take the step was John Mellon, whose *Transformational Sentence-Combining* (1969)[15] argued that the study of transformational grammar can and does favorably affect students' ability to produce "mature" sentences (i.e., sentences characteristic of adolescents' and adults' writing). However, Mellon's study failed to find that the effectiveness of students' written scripts, judged holistically, improved after they had studied transformational grammar. It was left to Frank O'Hare, whose *Sentence Combining: Improving Students' Writing Without Formal Grammar Instruction* appeared in 1973,[16] to show that by using the insights of transformational grammar without teaching the terminology of the conceptual system, a teacher could not only enhance students' ability to produce more "complex," "mature," discourse, but could also enhance their ability to produce writings that were considered effective when judged holistically.

One result of this research was that this derivative of transformational-generative grammar, which had come to be called "sentence combining," very swiftly acquired an influence on the teaching of composing that most scholars were working to deny to "traditional" grammar and that had never been won by other grammatical conceptions that surfaced in the 1950s and 1960s (such as "structural" grammar and "sectoral" grammar). Other research studies followed O'Hare's, among the more notable being a study conducted at Miami University of Ohio by Donald Daiker, Andrew Kerek, and Max Morenberg, who found that an experimental group of freshman taught sentence combining in the basic composition course "clearly progressed toward levels of syntactic maturity characteristic of professional writers."[17] Driven by such findings, sentence combining soon became in the practice of many teachers a central emphasis in the teaching of writing. Texts such as William Strong's *Sentence Combining*[18] rapidly grew popular, as did *The Writer's Options*, a text by Daiker, Kerek, and Morenberg themselves.[19] Professional conferences could be counted upon to feature panels and workshops on sentence combining at almost every time slot on the program, and elements of sentence combining began to appear in rhetorics and handbooks.

No matter that other writers were posing some unsettling questions: that Lester Faigley was asking whether the profession had a clear notion of what "growth" and "maturity" in writing were;[20] that Susan Peck McDonald was wondering what to make of statistics showing that the average students in a small state college were achieving gains of several years on numerical indices on "maturity" in writing after a few weeks' drill in sentence combining;[21] that the linguist Joseph Williams was asking how long, after all, were the sentences in "mature" professional prose and whether the effective use of shorter sentences was not also a sign of stylistic "maturity";[22] or that Michael Holzman was finding in sentence combining only the most conspicuous application of a crude "Scientism" to the humanities.[23] Sentence combining seemed to "work"—after all, it was perhaps the only teaching technique that could be shown, quantitatively, to do so—and teachers in a field not conspicuous for its ability to demonstrate successes wanted a winner.

What, besides its statistical credentials, has made sentence combining so influential? One probable reason is that sentence combining is an operation that can be applied—indeed often is applied—at a recognizably important point in almost everyone's composing processes: the point of revision. In other words, sentence combining is a procedure that can easily become part of a recognized step in composing. As the importance of revision (which we know can occur throughout the process of composing) is highlighted, and as teachers increasingly attend to the "stance" or "voice" created by a writer's language, the availability of a neatly teachable procedure for revising language invites teachers to instruct students in that procedure. Some steps in revising—e.g., checking whether one has one's "focus" right, testing the plan of organization—are hazy, difficult to discuss. In contrast, combining and recombining (even decombining) sentences are precise operations not open to the charge of looking toward superficial "correctness," and consistent with long-standing admonitions of the handbooks that writers should seek "sentence variety." Why indeed should sentence combining *not* have been influential?

Two quite recent developments in linguistic theory also offer some promise of influencing writers (and teachers of writing) at the point of revision. Both deal with units of language beyond the sentence—an interest that is itself of rather recent origin. One is scholarly attention to "cohesion" (often taken to mean the kinds of linkages that can be made in English between individual sentences in a text) and "coherence" (often taken to mean the available patterns of connection among parts of a text that give readers a sense that the text is a whole rather than an assemblage of parts). This scholarly study began with M. A. K. Halliday's and Ruqaiya Hasan's famous study, *Cohesion in English*,[24] and has continued in essays such as Jeanne Fahnestock's "Semantic and Lexical Coherence,"[25] Betty Bamberg's "What Makes a Text Coherent?"[26] and Sandra Stotsky's "Types of Lexical Cohesion in Expository Writing"[27]—to name only a few of the many recent essays and monographs on this subject. All of these studies look at connections and patterns of language across sentences, and in several of them (notably Stotsky's) the authors suggest improvements on the system offered by Halliday and Hasan for classifying linkages between sentences.

If these studies of cohesion and coherence influence the practice of composing today (and there is yet no hard evidence that they do), that influence too comes at the point of revision. What our scholars are offering, it may be suggested, is an enumeration of the options available for maintaining cohesion and coherence, as well as a suggested array of tests by which a writer can check the cohesion and coherence of his or her text. No one is yet suggesting that the options for assuring cohesion and coherence are generative, in the sense that they can influence the locating and evaluating of ideas for writing, or that they can influence the actual drafting of prose text. Having been made more sensitive to the presence or absence of coherence and cohesion than older textbooks could make them, and knowing more of the elements of language that establish these qualities, writers can, at least in theory, revise more productively and effectively, and teachers can teach revision more usefully. But none of our studies on cohesion or coherence have yet led teachers (or writers) to the point where they can usefully teach, or test, the overall planning of a text: the succession of steps by which a writer moves from the beginning to the end of what he or she has to say in such a way as to make that progression clear and suitable to the writer's purpose. Language studies have yet to illuminate for use the cognitive operation of planning.

The second development in linguistics that may influence writers is the appearance of a body of theory called "text linguistics." Extended discussion of this complex theory, as set forth (for example) in William Vande Kopple's "Functional Sentence Perspective, Composition, and Reading"[28] and "Some Exploratoroy Discourse about Metadiscourse,"[29] is not possible here. But in its first applications, the theory suggests that readers can understand sentences more readily if they are constructed so that items or ideas previously referred to are mentioned first in the sentence (as "topic") and ideas not previously mentioned come later (as "comment"). Readers, that is, prefer to meet "old" or "given" information before they receive "new" information. In "Functional Sentence Perspective," Vande Kopple reports some research that tends to confirm the theory. A highly sophisticated extension of text linguistics is offered by Stephen Witte in "Topical Structure and Revision: An Exploratory Study,"[30] which advances a plan for identifying the "topical structure" of a paragraph (the number of different "topics" discussed in sentences in that paragraph, and how they are deployed in relation to each other). Identifying the "topical structure," Witte argues, can assist readers in understanding and writers in revising the text. One reason revision sometimes fails, Witte suggests, is that writers do not understand what they have done in the paragraphs they are revising. Knowing how to understand those relationships, Witte implies, might help writers to revise more effectively.

Work on text linguistics and functional sentence perspective has emerged in American scholarship essentially since 1981; the work is too new to permit us to determine whether it can, or will, affect composing and teaching. If it does affect composing, it will most likely do so at the point of revision— helping writers to see more clearly where readers may have problems with their texts and how to recast their texts (if they are so moved) to minimize those problems. If functional sentence perspective survives the close scrutiny of professional debate, however, it might come to function as a set of principles that guide drafting, the actual generating of language in the first instance. It might influence the deliberations through which writers pass in constructing sentences. But none of this work holds promise *at the moment* for influencing the invention of ideas or the planning of extended stretches of text.

I have written about theories of language from the perspective of their effect on the work of the writer during the process of composing, for I believe that only those theories of language that can have such an effect will benefit the teaching of composing: only those that help the composing writer choose new structures, that can become part of the writer's equipment for getting down ideas, can claim the teacher's attention. Most of the theories I have discussed can affect composers only at the point of revision, though it remains possible that sentence combining and functional sentence perspective may come to affect the initial drafting and even the planning of sentences, thus claiming a larger sphere of influence that they have claimed to date. This proposition—that in order to claim the attention of teachers a thoery of language must assist writers in generating text—obviously applies to and is supported by one major recent rhetorical system: that known as "tagmemic rhetoric," which grew directly from the work of linguists. "Tagmemic rhetoric," set forth most eloquently by Richard Young, is best known and most easily studied through *Rhetoric: Discovery and Change,* a textbook written by Young, Alton Becker, and Kenneth Pike.[31] Another good source is Young's published, but not widely circulated, report of his experiments at the University of Michigan in the teaching of tagmemic rhetoric.[32] But these documents do not reveal the roots of the system or the sources of its value for those who write.

The earliest introduction of tagmemic rhetoric into the professional literature on composition that I know, and one of the seminal expositions of the theory, is an article by Kenneth Pike in 1964 entitled "A Linguistic Contribution to Composition."[33] In that article Pike describes the experience of training students to analyze and write descriptions of some 260 languages by breaking the descriptive problems into very small pieces, and then asks the question: "Would it be possible to explore a number of the axioms of such a language theory, in order to develop exercises based on these axioms about language structure but specifically designed to develop writing competence?"[34] It is from the study of language, particularly of phonetics but also of the occurrence of words in specific utterances, that Pike draws some of the major assertions of tagmemic theory, namely:

> *A unit to be well defined must be treated in reference to its contrast with other units, its range of variation, and its distribution in class, sequence, and system.* . . .
> Only if a unit has been contrasted with other units is it well defined.
> Similarly, a unit is well defined only if its range of variation is made explicit. . . .
> A unit is, in addition, well defined only if its distribution is specified, with the unit seen as occurring as a member of a *class of alternatives.* . . .
> A unit is well defined only if its distribution is specified in reference to the particular *sequence of specific items with which it can occur, or with which it characteristically occurs.* . . .
> A unit is well defined only if its distribution is specified in reference to its occurring in a system. . . .[35]

To define a unit of language or (by extension) of any kind of item or experience, one needs to take three steps: (1) contrast that unit with others that are like it but not identical to it; (2) see how far the unit can change and still be identified as what it originally was; and (3) observe in what patterns of experience it occurs or can be placed. In Pike's theory, a method of description that started as a way of enlarging our understanding of language acquires the ability to enlarge a person's understanding of any subject. A procedure for analyzing language becomes a procedure for analyzing any matter about whose identity and features a person wishes to learn more.

It is from his studies of grammar and phonetics also that Pike draws the fundamentals of what has come to be called his "tri-modal perspective":

> Lanaguage units can be viewed as particles, or as waves, or as points in a linguistic field. . . .
>
> For some analytical purposes the observer must view behavior as a sequence of particles (or segments). . . .
>
> For some other purposes, however, the observer must study the same units as waves in which the borders may fuse into one another in a physical continuum.
>
> For still other purposes the observer must treat language as some kind of field. In this view the units become intersecting points of contrasting features . . . of form and meaning. . . . in the network of a background system.[36]

That is to say, one can look at a unit of language—or any other unit of experience—as it exists in isolation from other units, or as the unit becomes or blends into other units, or as the unit participates in an ordered system in which it has relationships to other units. Once again a procedure for analyzing language has become a generalized procedure for inquiring and learning about objects or experiences.

Pike's essay even contains, in its conclusion, some seeds of the application of what we now call "Rogerian theory" to the study of human communication: "Change passes over a bridge of shared components. Tagmemic theory suggests that change never occurs in terms of action at a distance, but only over a bridge made up of some shared component."[37] For someone to effect change in another by communicating with that other person, Pike seems to imply, the person communicating must find and use points of agreement between the two, or shared assumptions, or shared values, rather than viewing the person being addressed as an adversary, separate, at a distance. Such a perception can direct one's efforts at locating ideas and emphases in composing; it can help in the creating of what one will compose.[38]

Pike elaborates his views in reference to the analysis of longer units of discourse, including works of literature, in an essay called "Beyond the Sentence" (1964).[39] In the same year, Hubert M. English, Jr., a colleague of Pike, restated and illustrated the possible applications of tagmemic theory to the study of composing in an article entitled "Linguistic Theory as an Aid to Invention."[40] English recapitulates the main points in Pike's system for analyzing elements of language and shows by examples how the system applies both to bits of sound in language and to subjects for extended discourse.

I am not asserting here, of course, that the system devised by Pike for describing the operations of language matches or facilitates a creative process which the human mind can readily and easily employ. We do not have the evidence necessary before we can make such an assertion. What I am suggesting is that Pike, Alton Becker, and most especially Richard Young have taken a procedure for describing language and converted it into a process which, if followed systematically by writers, can yield ideas for writing—ideas that might not otherwise have come to the mind of the writer. It is not that Young, Becker, and Pike have a facile way of applying language study directly to the teaching of writing. Rather, they see the need for the writer, before he or she writes (or while he or she is in the act of writing), to gain control over a subject and try out ways of looking at the same subject, not to mention ways of presenting that subject to audiences who hold particular views about that subject. Discovery is a part of the process of composing. It occurs in different ways, at difficult times, in different writers. Pike's and Young's work applies to an "earlier" step in the processes of composing than do the insights furnished by transformational-generative grammar. (We should recognize that writers may make discoveries and incorporate them into their text at any time before they complete their final drafts.) However, both can guide the writer, if the writer so wishes, as the writer carries on the act of composing.

Despite recent advances in our understanding of composing processes that have come from the work of Janet Emig, Donald Graves, Linda Flower, Carol Berkenkotter, and Sondra Perl—to name only five—we are in only the early stages of learning how writers write.[41] In particular we know little about how they come to find occasions and subjects for writing, or come to experience the need and desire for writing. Very possibly it will take extended work by psychologists and psycholinguists to illuminate the processes of perceiving and forming ideas that lead to the desire to communicate and set in motion the processes of inquiry. But if most ideas must be formed somehow into langauge before—or at the moment when—we begin to write, the possibility remains that those who study ways of describing and managing language may be able to furnish additional insights into the ways in which writers (and speakers) compose. In order to furnish these insights, scholars will need not only to analyze in detail the ways in which units of language already uttered seem to work, but also to observe the ways in which people arrive at their written and spoken utterances. It may now remain for those (like Emig, Graves, Flower, Berkenkotter, and Perl) who observe composers at work to ascertain whether findings from language studies do indeed illuminate the composing processes of human beings or in any way facilitate those processes.

Teaching the Connections

ANN E. BERTHOFF

Abstraction as a Speculative Instrument

All studies are language studies, concerned with the speculative instruments they employ.—I.A. Richards[1]

Like imagination, meaning, representation, interpretation, intention, and form, abstraction is an idea we can't do without when it comes to thinking about the teaching of composition—which is to say, when we undertake to think about thinking. The fact that the first six do not commonly appear as terms in discussions of rhetorical theory and composition pedagogy is one measure of a significant failure in our profession, but the fact that *abstraction* appears continually is, unfortunately, not a sign of health. Abstraction is rarely well defined as a term and the complex concept it names is not generally well formed. For some, abstraction is a power of mind to be encouraged and trained; for others; it is a stylistic fault to be avoided. The fact that abstraction has a wide range of meanings is not in itself a danger; ambiguities, as Richards was fond of pointing out, are "the very hinges of thought." The trouble arises when the ambiguities are not recognized. In what follows, I will suggest reasons why abstraction is poorly understood and will try to show the effects of fundamental misconceptions of its linguistic and psychological character. I will also be concerned to define how abstraction might serve as a speculative instrument in our study of composition.

For those who make the mind out of the senses—as Coleridge said of Locke—abstraction is the opposite of reality. Language, in this view, is unreal in itself, and the more abstract it is, the more unreal: as we move towards abstractions in our language, away from the particularities of space and time and the nameable details of sensory knowing, the farther we move from reality. When reality is posited as "out there," language is seen, logically enough, as a veil or barrier separating us from what is real, that is to say, the deliverances of our senses. In this perspective, abstraction is troublesome, considered the source of dangers to which we must be alert. The strong implication is that although we cannot get rid of abstraction, we should at least try to control its hazards by being "specific" and "clear." We may remember that Swift ridiculed the early proponents of the plain style in the figure of those academicians whose servants carried around sacks of objects which were deployed instead of words in their exchanges. Some modern theories of style entertain comparable suspicion of the abstractions that language makes possible, but distrust of abstraction in current rhetorical theory is more fundamentally an epistemological matter. It derives not from a rationalist rhetoric but from Bertrand Russell's logical atomism and the correspondence theory of truth. We meet it continually in the slogans and models of General Semantics, as popularized by Stuart Chase, S. I. Hayakawa, and James Moffett—the primacy of what is happening, the idea of language as a map for the territory of reality, the Ladder of Abstraction.

So regarded, in the linguistic perspective as it were, abstraction is, generally speaking, held to be hazardous. It is this conception teachers have in mind when they issue warnings *not* to "generalize." On the other hand, when abstraction is considered a "cognitive skill," it is equated with the capacity to generalize and is regarded as an important behavioral objective and a reliable index of intellectual achievement. It is this conception teachers have in mind when they ask "Where are your generalizations?" When *abstracting* is reduced to *generalizing*, there is a strong need for other terms to name what has been left out: thus *poetic, expressive, personal, creative, affective, right-brain, nonlinear,* and *holistic* activities, behaviors, and operations are identified. There is no end to the attempt to address by lexical means the problem created by a logical and epistemological misconception.

Positivists conflate abstraction and generalization both as acts of mind—or, as they say, "behaviors"—and as rhetorical strategies, because they do not recognize that abstraction proceeds in two modes; more accurately, they do not accept the idea of perception, artistic creation, and mythopoesis as being kinds of thinking which entail abstraction. The fact is—and it has long been established by studies of perception, by the analysis of dreams, and by the interpretive review of artistic creation—that we abstract not only by means of generalizing but also by means of what Susanne K. Langer calls "direct, intensive insight." Two formulations of hers can provide us with a working concept of abstraction:

> The perception of form . . . arises from the process of symbolization and the perception of form is abstraction.

> Abstraction is the recognition of a relational structure, or *form*, apart from the specific thing (or event, fact, image, etc.) in which it is exemplified.[2]

Symbolization, form, recognition, structure: all these concepts are needed for an understanding of abstraction as the fundamental act of mind. Symbolization keeps us from stretching abstraction to cover all responses to all stimuli, in which case its usefulness as a speculative instrument for the study of meaning is minimal. (Just so, if *communication* is stretched so that it includes the wiggles of sea anemones, it can't be of much use when we want to characterize the human use of signs.) The relation of abstraction to forming is also crucial, since it gives us the genus for a definition of abstraction. By identifying abstraction as the perception of form and the recognition of structure, we can thus proceed to differentiate "the ways recognition is achieved."[3]

Abstracting by means of generalizing goes by many names, of which "reasoning" and "concept formation" are the commonest. Abstracting by means of apprehending gestalts—nondiscursively—is characteristic of what Cassirer calls "mythic ideation," in which parts stand for wholes, images bear conceptual significance, and spatial or temporal contiguity represents causality. Silvano Arieti's term for this mode of abstracting is "paleologic," in contradistinction to earlier practices of speaking of "pre-logical thought." Freud's "primary process," in which condensation and displacement remain undifferentiated, is another well-known name for the abstracting which shapes our dreams and the delusions of the insane.[4] The two kinds of abstracting are active and interactive in the mind, a reflection of the fact that whatever happens in one hemisphere of the brain is very complexly related to what happens in the other half. But the essential point is this: generalization requires abstraction, but we can have abstraction without generalization.[5] Abstraction seen as the recognition of form; as the symbolic representation of our recognitions; as enabling, but not requiring generalization—this is the conception of abstraction which can help us think about the composing process and composition dialectically.

Now, if we consider the Ladder of Abstraction in this light—one of the chief models of the positivist understanding of the relationship of language and thought—it will be evident that it is incapable of representing abstraction in the nondiscursive mode. It is, in fact, a ladder of the degrees of generality, but that is not to say that it correctly or adequately represents the process of generalizing. (As I have noted elsewhere, only Buster Keaton could manage the Ladder of Abstraction dialectically.) Let us look carefully at these inadequacies.

Some of those who deploy the Ladder of Abstraction speak of moving *down* it as well as *up*, but the usual explanation is that students—everybody— should properly begin with particulars and move on up the rungs, always remembering that they are dangerously out of touch with reality, which is constituted by particular things. Consider the Ladder of Abstraction in the Light of Lev Vygotsky's summary of his theory of concept formation: "When the process of concept formation is seen in all complexity, it appears as a *movement* of thought within the pyramid of concepts, constantly alternating between two directions, from the particular to the general, and from the general to the particular"[6] The principle that simple particulars come first; that sensory knowing is a datum; that it is natural to move from particulars to specifics to "abstractions"—that principle is false. Perception is dependent on a primordial abstraction, as all cognition is on *re*cognition. Consider the Ladder of Abstraction in the light of Rudolf Arnheim's recapitulation of his brilliant account of how the child apprehends visual forms:

> The touch image of a surface, a shape, or an angle must be composed by the brain, just as it must create the visual image from a multitude of retinal stimulations. . . . The artificial distinction between perception and conception has been superseded by evidence that perception does not start from particulars, secondarily processed into abstractions by the intellect, but from generalities. 'Triangularity' is a primary percept not a secondary concept. The distinction between individual triangles comes later, not earlier. Doggishness is perceived earlier than the particular character of any one dog.[7]

The Ladder of Abstraction, by encouraging the identificaiton of particularity with an unmediated sensory experience, misrepresents the dialectic of thought and feeling. Consider the Ladder of Abstraction in the light of Ernst Cassirer's critique of the Realist epistemology it models:

> Intellectual expression could not have developed through and out of sensuous expression if it had not originally been contained in it; if, as Herder said, sensuous designation did not already embrace a basic act of 'reflection.' The characteristic meaning of language is not contained in the opposition between the two extremes of the sensuous and the intellectual, because in all its achievements and in every particular phase of its progress, language shows itself to be at once a sensuous and an intellectual form of expression.[8]

The Ladder of Abstraction falsely models concept formation and it ignores abstraction in the nondiscursive mode, viz., imagination, mythic ideation, primary process. It confuses abstraction with generality. It is entirely consonant with the idea that words name things without the mediation of an interpretant; it provides no way of representing context or perspective or purpose. The Ladder of Abstraction, insofar as it represents a philosophy of language and a theory of knowledge which can neither account for the process of making meaning nor give an account of meanings, should be abandoned in the interest of our learning to think with the concept of abstraction, to employ abstraction in all its complexity as a speculative instrument for the study of composition. Before turning to what it could help us explore, I want to consider the effect on research methodology and pedagogy of an unenlightened conception of abstraction as, simply, generalization and as the unproblematic antithesis of the concrete.

In a praiseworthy attempt to analyze the development of writing ability from high school into the later years of the university, Aviva Freedman and Ian Pringle aimed to measure intellectual growth, not just "rhetorical ability."[9] They wished to measure abstraction because it is "cognitive" and not just "rhetorical," explaining that they chose as "a potential index . . . the levels of abstracting, or rather the students' capacity for abstracting as revealed in the writing" (p. 316). They carefully distinguish what they did from other attempts to measure abstracting capacity by focusing on T-units or by identifying as especially significant " 'statements at a high level of abstraction'," defined by some researchers as those which " 'propose principles or generalizations concerning life at large' " (p. 317). They note their decision not to base their ratings on "abstractness of the diciton or the abstractness of individual propositions" (p. 317). Here, then, is the summary of their purpose:

> What we were interested in getting at in our analysis of these students' writing was not only the level of abstracting from experience that the essay was operating on, but also the degree to which the students had themselves formulated these abstractions. In other words, we wanted some mesure of the number of rungs up the ladder of abstracting that the students themselves had climbed, as evidenced in their writing. (p. 318)

If formulating abstractions is what these researchers want to look at, how, one wonders, is that to be studied otherwise than in rhetorical terms? How is abstracting "evidenced" by writing, if not in the language of the discourse—and isn't that what rhetoric is concerned with?

There are laudable statements throughout the article about the dangers of judging rhetorical skills as necessarily significant (unless, interestingly, they have *not* improved), but the only clue as to how one would go about judging the ascent up what they call the ladder of *abstracting* is said to be a "second-level classification"; in cases where a writer goes on to compare, say, authors and periods, that is, when he or she forms more general classes, that is said to be an even higher level of abstraction. "The student's capacity to abstract" is to be determined by how "the primary data" has been "classified, ordered, and integrated by the writer within some superordinate hierarchic conceptual pattern" (p. 317). Apparently, they see classification, ordering, integration as matters not of "rhetoric" but of "cognitive process."

Freedman and Pringle display an ambivalent attitude towards rhetoric. They take as their own the conception of rhetoric which has been called, in an execrable instance of scientistic jargon, "the current-tradition paradigm." This ahistorical and wrong-headed identification of rhetoric with *bad* rhetoric accounts for their dismissal of "rhetoric" as helpful to them in their study of students' "capacities for abstracting"; nevertheless, they employ a "rhetorical instrument" to describe "the features of successful expository prose" (p. 316). Rhetoric is identified with judging in terms of vividness, stylistic effectiveness, tone and other such "mentalistic" criteria (where is "flavor"?); by contrast, intellectual processes, conceptualizing, creativity, generalizing, and, of course, "abstracting" are important to the measurement of cognition. By failing to articulate any relationship between "the cognitive aspects of the process" of writing and "the rhetorical features of the completed product," though they declare its existence (p. 322), Freedman and Pringle do not recognize that they are dichotomizing what should be kept in dialectical relationship: they have given us another version of the positivist view of language as the garment of thought.

The dichotomy of rhetoric, which is considered suitable only for evaluating style, and abstracting, which serves as a measure of intellectual power, is analogous to the perennial dichotomy of the product and process. In both cases, failure to recognize and represent the dialectical character of the relationship is symptomatic of the failure to begin, as Vygotsky urged, with "the unit of meaning." Freedman and Pringle are committed to process; they understand its pedagogical importance and have taken as a point of departure in their research the sound principle that composition is properly evaluated only in the context of its creation and shaping. But apparently they think that by speaking of *abstracting* instead of *abstraction* they have made their allegiance clear and that nothing more is required. When they convert the Ladder of Abstraction to "the ladder of abstracting," the superficiality of this tactic is revealed, since the ladder in no way represents what Freedman and Pringle call "the heuristic power of the process" (p. 314); in no way does it model that dynamic alternation which Vygotsky identifies as the essence of concept formation. In my view, unexamined assumptions and ill-formed concepts cannot be improved by tinkering with the models which represent them.

As an example of what I mean, let me note what happens in the discussion of "second-level classification": it is seen as less of an achievement than the formulation of those generalities reached at higher rungs of the Freedman and Pringle ladder of abstracting. But as we surely know—it is a self-evident fact and requires no research to be established—our students can name general classes very much more easily than they can specify. To rename a parsnip as a *vegetable* or an *ingredient* is a far surer sign of conceptualization in progress than renaming it *food* or *something you can buy at the grocery store*. Freedman and Pringle recognize this fact when it is considered as a matter of "rhetoric": they would not be taken in by big words or "generalizations about life at large," which they have wisely dismissed as unsound indices of intellectual power and command. But they apparently do not recognize that the same holds true when we are considering thought as a matter of "abstracting." It is their ladder of abstracting which traps them into considering that higher is better.

I believe that experimenting with ways of developing the rhetorical counterpart of concept formation is the research composition pedagogy most needs. I also believe that abstraction can serve us as a powerful speculative instrument when we come to consider the pragmatics of that relationship of language and thought. The questions I want to raise are these:

Josephine Miles has said that logic, rhetoric and grammar provide ways of analyzing a writer's language, the means he uses to take him where he wants to go: What would happen if we analyzed and evaluated compositions, not in that split-level way which results from dichotomizing language and thought, product and process, rhetoric and cognition, but as a matter of interpreting symbolic expressions and representations of intentions?

I. A. Richards saw rhetoric as a study of "how words work":[10] Could we approach student writing, looking for ways of relating how words work in relation to how concepts are being formed?

If we think with the concept of abstraction as the recognition of form, can we devise questions which would help us to determine if students are indeed forming concepts? Would they be like these?
—Has the student analyzed the question? Are the terms of the question/topic renamed, critically deployed? Is the question questioned?
—Is there any sign of a recognition of presuppositions? Are assumptions identified or examined? Are alternate perspectives or contexts considered?
—Do the transitions signal actual shifts or are they merely additive?
—If texts are cited, are they properly adduced? adequately explained? Is there evidence that the student can paraphrase in the interest of critical explanation?
—What about analogies: are there any? are they cogent? If there is an extended metaphor, is it logically developed?
—Are the specifics appropriate to the class names? Do the class names have the appropriate degree of generality?
—Are there any formal definitions? Are they logically sound, i.e., with both classification and differentiation? Are the examples characterized and evaluated? When conceptual terms are used, are they developed by means of *specific* names, i.e., intermediary between a high degree of generality and a low?
—Is there any attempt to develop an argument by means of the opposite case? borderline and model cases?
—What is the logic of error: are sentences faulty because of pleonasm and idiomatic snarls or because semantic requirements have not been met?
—Does the writer have a working lexicon for the definition of relationships, or are *enhance* and *contain* the all-purpose verbs, once *is* has been exhausted?
—Does the writer demonstrate an understanding of how to draw out the implications of an assertion or a description? Are concepts transformed to activities? titles to situations? events to a characterization of a state of affairs?
—Is there any sign that the writer has an understanding of the uses of style for the sake of articulation and emphasis? Are there any judicious repetitions? phrases in apposition? parallel structures?
—Has the semicolon been "dialectically" deployed?

The real challange to pedagogy is to teach our students how to make such questions their own. Our students, using abstraction as a specuative instrument, can learn to draw on the resources of language itself in order to discover their intentions and articulate the relationships which thinking identifies. Thinking with the concept of abstraction as the recognition of form is a way to make thinking about thinking integral to the composing process; it is more likely, then, that our students will learn to see revision as a dimension, not a stage, of the composing process. The current rage for revision, like the earlier "prewriting" fad, will have little salutary effect on composing practices, if the underlying conception of language as muffin tins does not change. Abstraction can help everybody think clearly about how words work.

But for the time being, I want to concentrate on how abstraction can guide *our* practice, both in the evaluation of writing and in designing the assignments which elicit what we get. The idea that abstraction is the recognition of form can help us speculate about how our students are forming concepts and sentences alike. Keeping abstraction-as-forming in mind can help us judge cogency of argument, as well as appropriateness of diciton; soundness of definition, as well as control of syntax; the balance of particularization and generalization, as well as pacing of exposition. And because it can help us evaluate, abstraction as a speculative instrument can guide us in designing courses and assignments. In composing our courses in composition, what we most urgently need, I think, is an improved understanding of "development": abstraction, understood as the recognition of form, could help us speculate about what we are up to when we try to teach development. What would happen, for instance, to the notion of "supporting detail"? Consider the following; it comes from a text for teachers of writing:

> As an entity convenient to the creative effort for beginners, the topic sentence needs limiting right away from the start. Students need to state the topic of their paragraphs—and they need to state their opinions, reaction, attitude towards, or judgment about the topic there too. Thus a topic sentence that reads in a descriptive essay like 1 below is merely a statement of fact in which the writer proposes no generalization to support. Hence he runs into trouble in developing a point. In 2, however, there is a limitation and control right from the outset: 1. The room has black walls. 2. The room is dreary.

The doctrinaire assumption expressed here about the need for limits derives from the idea that generalizations are simply proposed—not formed, arrived at, but simply posited. If generalizations are not regarded as the results of forming concepts, then it follows that limits will not be seen as having any heuristic value; they will be seen simply as constraints. Instructing students to compose paragraphs by beginning with topic sentences and then "adding specificity and detail" (as this writer goes on to say) is certainly consonant with the idea that rhetoric is one thing and abstracting quite another. The speculative instrument of abstraction as forming trained on this misconception could help us reclaim what we surely know about the composing process, to let it help us realize that the way to substantiate generalization is not to limit (constrain) from the start but to amass particular observations and nascent classifications from tentative or hypothetical points of view generated by a purpose, and to discover limits in the very process of ordering and balancing, specifying and classifying, describing and defining. The composing process *is* the process of forming concepts. Thinking with the concept of forming could help us assure that purpose had a chance to come to life—which is to say, we would never have assigned A Descriptive Essay in the first place.

What is the relationship of fact to generalization implied in the passage quoted? A statement of fact is not the same thing as a proposition, nor does a statement of fact *propose* a generalization; statements of fact are one kind of support for generalization. Perhaps that is the point being made, but the implication seems to be, rather, that *in this case*, the statement of fact (sentence 1) proposes no generalization, whereas in sentence 2, *because* it is not a statement of fact, there *is* a generalization which can then be supported. But of course without context there is no way of knowing whether sentence 2 provides a very particular detail, a rather specific observation of a fact or feeling, or a tentative judgment, a generalization. The implcit dichotomies in this analysis of two topic sentences are fact/impression, objective/subjective, limitless/generalizable; they are illogical and unsupportable.

In an effort to forestall having students turn in an unstructured, pointless list, this textbook writer claims that only the expression of attitude has the power to elicit supporting details, since it is a generalization. The instruction guarantees, I would say, a paratactic line-up of impressionistic, adjective-ridden sentences. There is no reason whatever for expecting that the The-cat-is-on-the-mat predication of sentence 2 will necessarily encourage development any more certainly than would the recording in sentence 1 of a surely extraordinary fact, that the room has black walls! There is plenty implicit in that image: think of it as nondiscursive abstraction and see what you can find. Encourage students to think with that image, and generalizations will be drawn out, developed. Generating a "chaos" of names in response to *walls* and *black* will yield not just synonyms (though they can be useful) but meanings—and meanings become the means of making further meaning. Inviting students to compose sentences, then, from and with these words is to assure that the dialectic will get started, that concepts will be formed, because it is the nature of syntax to bring thought along. Making the heuristic powers of language accessible to students is the surest way to teach them how to move from abstraction in the non-discursive mode to abstraction in the discursive mode. The best way to get the dialectic going is to get the sentence going; the easiest way to do that is to convert assertions, statements of fact, expressionss of opinion to "iffy" questions—the strategy C. S. Peirce called *abduction* and Paulo Freire calls *problematizing: If the walls are black* . . .

Abstraction in service as a speculative instrument could help protect us against the "gangster theories" (I. A. Richards' phrase) represented in the disquisition on topic sentences I have cited and in other such wrongheaded instruction. Thinking with the concept of abstraction as forming could certainly reveal the inadequacy of seeing development as a matter of getting the right topic sentence and adding on the allegedly "supportive details." But I want to make the further claim that abstraction-as-forming can help us keep meaning in focus by defining the commonalities of language and thought. And this is surely what we must do if we are to make the case that writing is a mode of learning and a way of knowing.

In my view, the real usefulness of abstraction as a speculative instrument will become dramatically apparent as we undertake the definition of the role of writing in the arts and sciences. That is because it can show us how to think of forming concepts as a matter of composing. I am convinced that our colleagues will not be attracted by the maundering banalities of reading specialists, the abstruse treatises of psycholinguists, the question-begging models of cognitive psychologists (whose understanding of language is generally no less primitive than that of the behaviorists), or the intellectual shallowness of most rhetoricians; and if they are contented at first with the quick answers some composition specialists give them to their naive questions ("How can I teach writing and cover all the material in my course?"), they will soon be back, sometimes merely irritated, but often with a new consciousness of the complexities of thinking about thinking. It is at this point that abstraction can clarify Richard's claim that "all studies are language studies, concerned with the speculative instruments they employ."

Collegiality is fostered in those concerted efforts which typically follow in the second and third phases of instituting programs in "writing across the curriculum." We might be surprised to find that we have something to learn, especially from scientists. In discussions of writing in the disciplines, it is generally assumed that it is the job of the invading rhetoricians to teach the historians and the biologists and the anthropologists. And so it is: we must certainly work hard to demonstrate that wrting is not editing and we will of course want to show how writing can function as a mode of learning. But once we have engaged our colleagues in this enterprise of teaching writing as a composing process, we should open our minds to the fact that we have something to learn from teachers in other disciplines when it comes to thinking about thinkng. For one thing, we could quickly discover that the aim of a context-free description of something happening in the immediate environment based on observation whose purpose it is to gather "data" is recognized by working scientists as an illusion. They write up their experiments in a way that suggests a controlled single-mindedness, but the actual process is quite different. Like writing, scientific research is a composing process—full of accident, confusion, contradiction, befuddlement, as well as the temptation to smooth out what is fundamentally complex and to ignore the genuinely problematic. It will be easier for us to persuade our colleagues that writing is both a creative and a critical activity of forming if we undertake to discover that this is, precisely, how best to define the search for evidence, the presentation of cases, the preparation and execution of experimentation, the articulation of interpretation.

We will discover in thinking with our colleagues about writing and the teaching of writing that we are engaged in a philosophical enterprise. J. Robert Oppenheimer, a scientist and a great teacher for whom thinking about thinking was a pleasure as well as a professional duty, had this to say:

> Science is a search for regularity and order in those domains of experience which have proved accessible to it. I am not sure that the effect of the impressive victory of man's mind in this enterprise has not been to make us a little obtuse about the role of the contingent and particular in life. It is true that many particulars can be understood and subsumed by a general order. But it is probably no less a great truth that elements of abstractly irreconcilable general orders can be subsumed by a particular. And this notion might be more useful to our friends who study man and his life than an insistence on following the lines which in natural science have been so overwhelmingly successful. [11]

It has been my aim here to suggest that abstraction employed as a speculative instrument can help us re-think the nature of the relationship of "the contingent and the particular" to "the general orders."

GEOFFREY SUMMERFIELD AND JUDITH FISHMAN
SUMMERFIELD

States of Mind, Acts of Mind, Forms of Discourse: Toward A Provisional Pragmatic Framework

The psychological heft of a role has more existential presence than daily life. —
Norman Mailer, Marilyn

*As for the rhetorical exercises in which we were successively Xerxes and Themistocles,
Octavius and Mark Antony, they intoxicated me; I felt like Proteus.—Marguerite
Yourcenar,* Memoirs of Hadrian

An unremarked but striking feature of *The Development of Writing
Abilities*[1] and of *Writing and Learning across the Curriculum*[2] is this: that the
most impressive student texts quoted in the two books were written by students
not in *propria persona* (as "themselves"),[3] but in role.[4] Part of our case is not
only that this may well be more than a coincidence, but also that it may be
debilitating and counter-productive to confine students in composition to the
role of student-as-writer-for-a-reader-who-is-a-teacher-as-examiner/grader.
Such a confinement denies the rich possiblities for the production of controlled
and venturous discourse that writing-in-role offers.

James Britton, Nancy Martin, and their colleagues make various scattered and pregnant observations on role, and we are grateful for those. But our
purpose is to induce students to take the possibilities and promises of role
further. In effect, we believe it's both possible and desirable to construct a role-
based framework for composition. If *propria persona* student texts, in the
transactional mode, are on the whole rather neutered and derivative, with no
clear sense of energetic intent or of audience; and if, conversely, texts written
from within role are strong, vivacious, and compelling; then such a consistent
difference needs to be acknowledged, and its implications for the teaching of
composition must be teased out, clarified, and applied, so that our students may
be brought to explore and exploit the distinctive possibilities for strong discourse that writing-in-role offers.

Our title speaks of a "pragmatic framework"; what we mean by this is
simply that, as teachers of composition, we cannot rest content with a theoretical

framework that is, in itself, so elegant and intellectually rewarding that it gives us something of the same kind of pleasure as a "theory of history," say, or a theorem, or a game of chess. The salient question is rather, pragmatic: does such a framework actually *enable*—as our students' pens begin to approach, then move across, their pages? So, we search for a framework which offers not only theoretical coherence, tolerably free of contradiction, and economical in its hypotheses—closely shaved by Occam's razor—but also a genuinely fruitful occasion for our students, a dependable handle, a clearer way of focusing, an enabling constraint. Our aim is to elicit forms of discourse that enjoy a clear sense of audience and a coherent sense of functions. When we offer our work as "provisional" we are simply acknowledging that, as always, there is room for improvement.

Our practice is to nudge, provoke, lead, or push our students into a vicarious situation, or context. When they enter it, the very act of entering generates "states of mind"—what Suzanne Langer calls "virtual experiences" and Erving Goffman "realms of being".[5] It is appropriate to speak both of entering a state of mind and of a state of mind entering us, of our being "engrossed." Depending on the situations, there is no limit to the variety of possible "states of mind": their crucial feature is that they are "reactive," so that when students are "put" into a situation, a context, they willy-nilly find, as soon as they begin to internalize, to *realize* their situation, that they are engrossed in/ by various states of mind—surprise or rage, horror or delight, fear or loneliness, and so on. Following a hint from William James—"No reception without reaction, no impression without correlative expression"—we provide the initial action: students simply have to react; they don't have "to make anything up."

States of mind tend, invariably, to generate "acts of mind": speculation, surmise, problem-solving, anticipating, remembering, seeking out causes, and so on. And it is these "acts of mind" that, in turn, generate discourse.

The two fundamental relationships that we all have with our worlds are those of spectator and participant. (We borrow these terms from Denys Harding, acknowledging our debt with pleasure, but both Britton and Erving Goffman have explored these relationships thoroughly and to good effect. The uses, however, that *we* make of them are not to be blamed on either Harding, Britton, or Goffman.)[6]

Consider now this situation: a prisoner-of-conscience in solitary confinement. In what ways is the prisoner to be construed both as a spectator and as a participant? It is a deplorable fact of our century that it has produced a rich literature of solitary confinement. For us, two of the great texts are Edith Bone's *Seven Years Solitary* and Jacobo Timerman's *Prisoner Without a Cell, Cell Without a Number*.[7] But even if you have not met any such texts, it will not take you much time and effort to recognize that the individual in the cell at this very moment, as you read these words, probably depends for sanity and moral survival on his spectatorship of his previous life—of virtually anything that comprises part of his preconfinement life. When we examine, say, the case of Edith Bone, this spectatorship—vicarious, internal, and retroactive—is precisely what we find. Each day she "visited"—inside her head—one of her friends; she travelled, step by step, bus by train, to their home, paid a call, and engaged in conversation. Conversely, Edith, the prisoner, is "spectator of her own future"; she regards, and explores, the unknown years that lie ahead.

In such ways the individual both sustains and re-appraises her values. As Harding and Britton have argued, the spectator-relationship allows for evaluation and revaluation, for an exploration, modification, and refinement of values. Conversely, when Edith Bone, for example, taunts her guards, demands to see the prison governor, or goes on a hunger strike, she is acting on, living out, her values, as a participant.

Our practice, then, is to involve our students in such a variety of constraining situations that they will perforce generate texts in the roles of both spectator and participant, not to mention the richness in between those two poles where one is a participant-spectator. For the sake of clarity, we tend initially to push them to one end of the spectrum or the other—as a participant within the hurly-burly, the unpredictability of act, or as a detached observer, Wordsworth's *spectator ab extra*.

In all of this, the distinctive virtue of "role" is this: that the individual student can summon up and draw on the rich resources of her own "funding"— what she knows and has known, what she feels and has felt—without acknowledging or confessing it *in propria persona*; the very fiction, the sheer vicariousness, of role is an enabling feature of the act. "This, my text," the student can say, "represents someone other than me, my self," but, paradoxically, it will be "informed" by the resources of the self, the "hidden" self. Students can represent and present their "truths"—delicate, difficult, sensitive truths, perchance—and offer them confidently as belonging to an other, the other of the role. An example may serve here: in the "prisoner-of-conscience solitary-confinement" sequence, we start with a ten-minute introduction to Edith Bone's story. Then students are allowed a pencil and only two sheets of paper. They are offered the chance to write a letter from prison to parents or closest friend/lover/husband/wife/children and are warned that this may be the last letter they will *ever* be allowed to write. (In the threatened withdrawal of writing, they gratifyingly discover some sense of the peculiar privilege of being able to write.) We suggest that they may wish to explore both their hopes and their fears, and to offer these as some consolation or warning to their nearest and dearest. One of the features of such texts that strikes us vividly is the immediacy, the intensity, of their realization of the sheer solitariness of "solitary confinement" (something they have never *actually* experienced). The clue is offered when, subsequently, students write retroactive explanatory commentaries on their texts; and the consensus is that we *all* know loneliness, what it feels like, how we cope with it. Retrieved *actualities* are used in the task of realizing a vicarious, virtual, experience.

Here, now, is Stacey Silverman's first letter from prison; like most of the students represented here, she is a student in English 110, the first of two required freshman composition courses at Queens College.

February 4, 1984

Dearest Mother and Father,

Why was I given a voice, so only I could hear the screams of my torment? And why when I am silent does the serenity pierce my eardrums like gun fire? I long to hear the voice of another animal. I have taken to shouting kind words to the far end of the room, so the echo brought back to me is the voice of another being who shares this bleakness with me. I pray to God every time I close my eyes, that when I open them, I will be in a crowded room, but it never happens.

There is a wooden chair standing by the huge bolted door towards the corner of the room. It is covered with layers of dust. I think it must have occupied that same spot for years. I fear what has happened to that chair will happen to me.

When the jailer led me to this room, he looked annoyed at having to walk the extra flights down to this hell that I must now call home. Just before he shut me into my aloneness, he maliciously grunted, "I guess I won't be seeing you around anymore." With that he slammed me in. I quickly rushed to put my ear to the door, and strained to hear his footsteps, which grew fainter and fainter. Then there was silence.

I fear the worst for myself now. I will undoubtedly go insane. No one could possible save their mind in this position. The constant pressure of solitude is unbearable. I will, however, make it to tomorrow. It takes more than just one day to die of loneliness.

With love,
Your daughter

This letter is, however, intercepted by the prison authorities and passed by the governor to the resident psychiatrist (or, as one student felicitously wrote, "spychiatrist"). The clinical task, then, is to read the letter very closely, observe all its various expressions of "states of mind," and to offer both a diagnosis and a prognosis. The constraints are effectively felt as *pragmatic*: the governor is a "busy man"; he hates jargon; his duty is to "take action" and he needs clear guidelines; above all, he doesn't want a suicide on his hands, especially of a prisoner who is potentially very "valuable from an intelligence point-of-view." The student, in role as psychiatrist, must function as a participant-observer; and the resulting text must constitute what we choose to call "an authentic forgery."

The felicity of this term is that it acknowledges a familiar paradox—that in our various roles in life, we construct precisely such "forgeries," which must read as plausibly authentic. Anyone in training as a lawyer, a doctor, or whatever will be familiar with the tightrope of authenticity/role/"forgery". We wear the "clothes" of our profession, and they feel, for some time, like "new" clothes; they fit perfectly well, but they don't feel altogether comfortable, and yet one day we wake to discover that they have become part of our "selves."[8]

As prisoners, our students discover that every prison has rules of order. In our case, the prisoners also devised rules—Rules for Staying Sane—an exercise in paring text down to its essentials, since they had to be written on a small scrap of paper to be attached to the cell-wall. After three weeks, without warning, they were told they could go free; as a way back into the world which is the world of all of us, they wrote one last letter. Here is Peter Mazzola's:

Dear Anthony,

It has been 20 years since I have seen the light of day. I have spent the better part of my life in solitary confinement. I cannot believe that I was freed from my prison cell just last week. Like a child, I must now re-learn how to communicate with others. You are the first.

Being in solitary confinement did irreparable damage to my psyche. All that I have witnessed or learned in the past is, in effect, wasted. When I first entered prison, I entered an unwilling subject, railing at the guards who slid my meals under the door. I was determined to find a way out of this mad-house at all costs. After countless efforts, and many beatings, as a consequence, my morale became somewhat "bent." Although I realized that I was not going to escape immediately, I always had the notion in the back of my mind that my time to escape would eventually come. It was just a matter of buying time, waiting for the right opportunity to come.

I think it was 10 years before I totally gave up all hope of resuming a normal life. I had become like an animal, driven by hunger. I no longer thought about the guards and what they were doing outside my cell. I did not think along the lines of my past or future. I simply existed. My words were reduced to simple utterances, and while I often talked to myself about many things regarding the prison, I found myself forgetting the significance of what I was saying. I do not recall what exactly, on a day-to-day basis, I did. I just remember the times that I had been hurt badly, and the duration of my suffering.

I never did have a chance to develop many friendships in the past, present company excluded. Certainly, my prison sentence destroyed the future of any "social life" that I might have had. As I have mentioned earlier, I do not think that I will ever lead a normal life in the future, although I will try my best to live constructively. Maybe I'll get a job stationed at an ocean oil-rig. I hear the pay is good, or at least it had been prior to my confinement. Besides, I won't have to come in contact with too many people outside of my co-workers. (I fear people now.) I will try to catch up on my reading, in the meantime, on how the world has been for the past 20 years.

Many things have changed since I left the "civilized" world. For one thing, I hear that man is now able to fly to the moon in spaceships! Imagine that! What will they think of next? The cities seem a lot more crowded. My stay in New York this past week has been quite an experience. I can't remember the last time that I had to pay so much to do so little. I almost didn't want to ask about my room. I spent an hour rehearsing my lines. I looked in a history book the other day and read that we are in a Cold War with Russia. When was Kennedy shot? It must have occurred a month after I left. Anyway, Johnson seemed to have carried a good administration afterwards.

But enough talk. I have long forgotten the beauty in idle nature. The grass, the trees, the birds in the sky. I forgot what the color blue looked like! I am free to walk the streets, buy food, even watch a movie or two. I am not kept under surveillance, and I can take a bath as often as I like, any time I want to.

Fashions have changed too! Why, just the other day I saw a girl walking down the street with PURPLE HAIR! I have resumed my long-lost hobby of coin collecting. Do you know that they stopped minting silver coins the year after I left? I didn't know that silver had become so valuable.

At any rate, I will try my best to keep up-to-date on the situation of the nation, although I will always remain a silent person in the crowd, somewhat hesitant in receiving hospitality and friendship. I forgot most of the manners I had so been accustomed to using. Just the other day I was leaving my apartment, and I slammed the door in the landlady's face. Without even looking back to apologize, I continued walking just as if nothing had happened. Things will never be the same, and yet I still have "blind hope" in my possession. Every day now since I left prison, I have kept praying and praying. . . .

Peter

Two examples of "prison writings" from our freshmen at a crowded, noisy college in New York City, where the confinement is hardly solitary. But, you may well ask by now how exactly are purely participant texts created? What do they look like? Surely, when we are embroiled in *act*, we cannot simultaneously create a text representing the inner utterance that accompanies that act? The answer, quite simply, is *fiction*. Every participant text is, inevitably, a fiction. Let us look at a characteristic participant text, and then explore its discourse.

So warm and dark. I feel so comfortable. No need for anything. Just dark warmthness. There are walls. What is this sound in the walls and up above as if something moves through the wall and pounds overhead. What could it be? Are there others like me through the walls? I try to break the wall, but it yields to my force, then rebounds back in place. What is out there? I'll stay dark and warm, forever? What? Moving now? Turning and turning. Pressure all around. Am I to be crushed? Greater and greater, the pressure builds. The floor is now the ceiling or is it the walls? What is happening? Pressure building. New sounds. Sounds of fear and pain. Pressure building now, four fold building, crushing, building, crushing, then gone, as my atmosphere drains away from me through a hole in the ceiling or floor or is it one of the walls? I feel I shall never know. The walls moving now, getting closer, pressing against me, crushing, squeezing. The hole now opens and begins to engulf me, the walls crushing me, pushing into this hole, into the throat of some great beast. Being swallowed whole. What will I find at the end of this throat? Moving, crushing, why? Then I break free. The light, painful and blinding—am I to be burned by this light? No, too cold, so very cold—am I to freeze? But then comes the pain and I gasp for air and I AM ALIVE!

Eric Capponi's text is clearly a fiction, setting up a teasing relationship with its reader, somewhat like a riddle. The "narrator" is generating a moment-by-moment narrative, a text whose emergence, segment by segment, is simultaneous with the events it records, a text that is, in effect, a transcript of utterances: unvoiced utterances that move, so to speak, through darkness, asking a lot of questions. The effect is that the text, from moment to moment, does not know what it is going to be next. It is as if Eric replies with his fiction to John Donne's argument: "In the wombe wee have eyes and see not, eares and heare not" (*Death's Duell*, sermon preached at White-Hall, Lent, 1630).

Eric's text represents what we have chosen to call "an extreme situation." We are currently developing a useful typology of situations—useful in the sense that we are working to isolate those situations that seem to offer students specially fruitful matter for texts, in both participant and spectator roles; one subtype comprises "extreme" situations—e.g., birth, death, hallucination, fever, nightmare.[9] The task of representing such situations from both participant and spectator positions, respectively, offers students the opportunity to discover, among other things, the primal structuralist principle that "the meanings are to be found in the differences." Comparison is one of the most enlightening parts of their enterprise.

Look again at Eric's text, and you will see that it is almost consistently *paratactic*.[10] James Notopoulos, in his paper on Homer,[11] has observed that "parataxis is first of all a state of mind." We wish immediately to add that, complementarily, *hypotaxis*, also, is a state of mind. And, furthermore—and this is for us both rather provisional and very useful indeed—we suggest that participant texts seem predisposed, because of the nature of the "state of mind," to take a paratactic form; conversely, that spectator-texts seem inevitably to move toward the relative complexity of hypotaxis.

The implications of this for our work in composition seem very rich indeed. Sentence-combining exercises, however ingenious, constitute operations on language that work from the outside in. If, however, the texts are, contrastively, generated by paratactic states of mind and hypotactic states of mind, then the relative coordinate simplicity and the relative interwoven complexity are generated as virtually inescapable representations of their respective states of mind.

That the correlation—

> participant: parataxis
> spectator: hypotaxis

should be found to be recurrent, is hardly surprising, even though it has gone as yet unremarked, for parataxis is precisely the appropriate—even inevitable— form for the unrolling of an event, recorded even as it happens, i.e., a simultaneous participant text. Conversely, *hypotaxis* is an ineluctable feature of the structures of our very perceiving/thinking/representing: it draws on the semantic fundings and syntactic orders of long-term memory. And it is an inherent neurological datum that long-term memory functions in part through generalization (i.e., typification); just as it is inherently a part of the spectator's representation that it should see the thing *whole*, from a position of relative detachment, "placing" or construing the particular event within the context (explicit or implicit) of the spectator's value system. It is for such reasons that all narratives proffered by spectators incorporate evaluation as an essential element of their discourse.

Further support for these findings comes out of intensive work we are doing with narrative, and here represented by those compelling human interest stories that newspapers print to fill up space: what newspaper people call "fillers." We know of colleagues in creative writing classes who use such "data" to spur students to try fiction; for the fillers, as texts, represent a point of view— the news reporter or editor who has already selected the bare bones out of what we can readily imagine to be a richer, more resonant, more extended version of the story. We see, after all, only a slice, or what Goffman calls a "strip," that has been cut from a "stream of ongoing activity." The "creative" writing student might be asked to recast the story from a particular character's point of view, or to begin farther back in time than the events represented, or to extend the action beyond the "end."

We, too, invite writers to enter the story—as participants and as spectators, both as involved spectators and detached spectators—and we observe that the story enters them in a variety of ways—as story, with its tensions and resolutions, with its suggestions of human character and voice, with its intricacies of plot, and nuances of setting, and with its insistence on evaluation.[12] For stories, no matter whether they are long or short, our own or others', whether they are heard or read or told, are conveyors of values, of our own and of the cultures within which we live. We cannot/do not tell (or write) a story without either an explicit or implicit statement of *why* we are telling the story in the first place, and conversely, we do not hear (or read) a story without our habitual insistence and reliance upon the same conventions. How many of us know the storyteller who goes on and on and on and on—and we wait, perhaps with increasing impatience, for the punch line—the "point."

Here, now, is a filler:

SIX-YEAR-OLD BOY
QUITE A DRIVER

Six-year-old Charles Boyd wanted to visit his father at work Monday morning in Kings Mountain, N.C., so he hopped into his mother's car and started driving.

One-half hour and five miles later, just as he was getting ready to turn onto Interstate 85, the car rolled off a road and bumped to a stop.

Charles opened the door and climbed out, startling the man who had been driving behind him.

"He thought he was following a drunk, but he never saw the driver," Kings Mountain police dispatcher Roy Dyer said.

A little lost, Charles rode with the man to Garlock Industries in Gastonia, where his father works. That's about 20 miles from his home.

Dyer said an officer asked Charles how he worked the brakes and the accelerator, "and he said he looked through the windshield until it was clear, and then he'd get down and push the gas. Then he'd jump back up and steer until the car slowed down."[13]

First, as "participants," students write as one of those involved in the event as it is happening; they select a role as Charles; the driver behind ("Mr. X"); Roy Dyer, the police officer; Charles's father; or his mother. In one class we debated whether or not to include Charles's mother in our list of participants; she, after all, is not explicitly named as a participant in the newspaper version. Lisa Portnoy's portrayal of Charles's mother, however, convinces us that she was indeed a participant:

"Charlie, Charlie, where are you?"
Damn kid, I hate playing hide and seek.
"Charlie, you get in here right now or you're gonna get it."
He wants another one. The hell with that. I can't even handle this one. No more babies for me.
"Charlie, Charlie!"
I'll bet he's hiding outside. Damn kid.
"Charlie! Charlie!"
Oh my god, where is my car?
"CHARLIE!"

"Oh no, oh no, oh no. Help, my baby's been stolen, my car's been kidnapped. Help."

Calm. Be calm. Breathe. O.K. Breathe some more. Go back inside. Call police. Be calm. Breathe. Pick up phone. Dial. Very good. Calm. Take deep breath. Oh, why the hell aren't they answering?

"Oh, help, someone has stolen my baby and my car. Yes, he's six. Blonde hair, blue eyes. Yes, about 40 lbs. Omigod. Have you found him? Is he dead? Is my baby o.k.? Where is my baby?"

"What, no. No. He . . . what? No. My husband is driving him home? Could you explain this to me again? Yeah. O.K. Thank you."

I'm gonna kill him.

Lisa's text—as participant—typifies over fifty students' responses in two freshman composition classes: they represent the event as if it is happening by "filling in" the "once," by seeing it for what it is—an event that is happening as it does and will never occur again in the same way. Lisa breathes the life of particularity into the event by allowing Charles's mother to speak; she takes on flesh, comes to life. We feel her "states of mind": irritated, annoyed, puzzled, persistent, bewildered, exasperated, breathless, anxious, incredulous, resolute ("I'm gonna kill him"). The text captures the immediacy of the moment, its verbs cast in the present; the voice is both monologic (talking to herself) and dialogic (calling to the absent Charles, speaking to the nameless police officer). Her text represents utterances, is paratactic. The participant, uncertain, inconclusive, speculative, is so deeply involved in the event that she cannot see the forest for the trees; she sees the part but not the whole; she does not evaluate. Interestingly, once Lisa's "mother" knows that Charles has not been kidnapped or harmed—she's "gonna kill him." The first sign of relief to the participant who, now, instantaneously, has become spectator, is to prepare for the future—the "present" gives way to the past as she anticipates the future.

When students represent the same event as erstwhile participants-who-have-become-spectators, they remove themselves in time from the event as it is happening and look back upon the event as it happened; they are no longer in but out, no longer there, but here, and the forms of discourse reflect the difference. The move parallels what we do in our daily lives when we tell of something that has happened to us: we remove ourselves in the telling; we become—even if we are still emotionally involved in an event—spectators of our own lives. And often we tell precisely because we are trying for distance. We look back, remember, reflect upon—and evaluate.

Mr. X, for example, as participant, raised numbers of questions as he tried to make sense of the "driverless" car in front of him:

I can't believe it—am I seeing things?
Is the guy crazy, drunk, asleep, short?

Is it a remote controlled car?
Is it a drunk midget?
Is there a driver?
Am "I" having a nervous breakdown?
Is it some old lady who can't see over the wheel?

Now, "looking back" as spectator, Mr. X puts many of the pieces together to construct a representation of the event, he orders it anew, and orders it within the particular evaluative frame he has "chosen." We might say that the choosing chooses him, unwilled, for it emerges out of his own conceptual, evaluative frame—what psychologist George Kelly would call a "template," a "transparent pattern,"[14] through which he sees the world—so that depending upon what the spectator foregrounds and backgrounds (hypotaxis), we see how he sees the world, how he informs the event through his own values. Here again are several different Mr. Xs—after the event:

What an amazing little boy.
I'm sure I wasn't that smart at that age.
I really felt sorry for that little kid. He must
    have been desperate to see his father.
If he were my kid, I'd give him the beating of
    his life.
Thank God, no one got hurt.
Somebody could have been killed.
Now, at least I know I'm not crazy.

We push further—asking writers to write as spectators who were not involved in any way in the event: they can be teacher, another parent, child psychologist, journalist—whatever spectator-role they choose. Here is Neil Frederickson, a "journalist," taking a strong stand on the issues he *sees* within the text. (Neil is a student in English 120, a second required composition course at Queens College.)

Unwatched children are becoming more and more frequent in today's modern society. Witness the case of Charles Boyd, a six year old, who, while left unattended, decided to drive to his father's place of employment 20 miles away, on his own. Finding the car keys, which had carelessly been left lying around, young Charles started the car and managed to drive five miles before running off the road.

Charles showed great imagination in driving the car, but this does not deny the fact that he is only six years old and could have caused an accident on the highway. It was sheer luck that no one was hurt and Charles was stopped before an accident occurred. Even so, when he stopped, he was far from home and could have fallen victim to any number of road hazards, not the least of which was possible kidnapping. Luck was again with Charles, that a kind man was in the car behind him and was able to help him.

Not all children would be so lucky. There are many more cases where such situations end in disaster. But what can be done about the problem? Certainly, the first thing is to try not to leave such young children unattended. Have a neighbor look in on the child once in a while. But if it is necessary to leave the child alone, make sure he knows what he can and can't do. Also, don't leave any hazardous or tempting things (like car keys) lying around. Educate the child well and try not to leave him unattended for too long a period. Remember, the safety of your child is your responsibility, whether you are there all the time or not.

When we contrast participants' texts and closely-tied spectators' texts with Neil's distanced-spectator's text, we find that the "once" has been transformed: where the participant-spectator has been eager to realize the event, to capture the intensity of the moment, the remoter spectator sees the once as a "case," a type, representative of what can happen to "unwatched children." Charles, who had been "Charlie" to Lisa, becomes "the child" to Neil. The particularities of the "case" are selected to fit the narrator's evaluative framework: the keys had been "carelessly" left "lying around": Charles had been left "unattended": the man in the car behind had been "kind". It had all worked out all right in this case—but "not all children would be so lucky." The event, now represented in past tense, is subsumed in the general "truth," in the present continuous: "Unwatched children are becoming more and more frequent. . . ." The event becomes subordinate to the message, the informative to the conative, as the present and past give way to the future; and the indicative and interrogative give way to the imperative:

Have a neighbor look in . . .
Don't leave the child alone . . .
Educate the child well . . .
Remember . . .

Our correlation now becomes richer:

Participant: parataxis/particularization
Spectator: hypotaxis/generalization

But again, not surprising. We know that we simply cannot store, neurologically, event upon event, instance upon instance, without typifying. The event becomes a type; the once, representative; the particular gives way to the general. And while we may remember and savor the particularities of daily events and of those that have made a difference in our lives, the "instances" give way to sorting, classifying, contrasting, generalizing, evaluating. And we find that we do not need to teach these fundamental acts of mind: we merely make them explicit.

The movement from participant to spectator and an understanding of what such a shift entails in terms of textual options and constraints are the fundamental moves that we aim for. We offer this theoretical framework to our students incrementally, trying to sense the moment, the occasion, when such framing will provide them with a handle—a grasp of the issues involved in their making of texts. They accept the frames as a means whereby they can reflect on the texts they have already made. In this sense, most of our "teaching" involves a retroactive pedagogy, a set of aids to reflection.

As teachers of composition, we must envisage and frame our own autonomous *terminus ad quem*: for us, this is a mind within each student which has come to appropriate more fully the entailments involved in the production of a text, a clearer and more confident sense of the available options, and a more sophisticated sense of textuality and of utterance. By the end of a fourteen-week semester, our students will have produced about twenty-five texts, including some abandoned false starts and proto-texts to be continued in their own time. And lodged somewhere inside their heads they will have a reasonably well-ordered sense of this:

PARTICIPANT	SPECTATOR
parataxis	hypotaxis
particularity	generalization
private	public/social
present tense	past/future
ellipsis[15]	redundancy
uncontextualized and	contextualized and
unevaluated	evaluated

The heightened sense of textuality that they evince is an essential part of their writerly/readerly awareness of what is involved when they themselves write, in fuller possession of their powers. They will have begun to guide their doings, to make their own more canny choices, and will have experienced something of the exhilaration, the potential, the sheer reach of role.

SONDRA PERL AND ARTHUR EGENDORF

The Process of Creative Discovery: Theory, Research, and Implications for Teaching

Like a potter who molds a shape from a lump of clay, so any person engaged in the act of creating begins with what is at first unformed. Our interest in this essay is to explore the process through which explicit form comes into being. Traditionally this process has been considered too vague or inaccessible for systematic scrutiny: however, a new line of philosophical inquiry—the philosophy of experiencing—now provides us with a grasp on some of its elusive aspects. We hope to show here the value of experiential formulations for unraveling the complexitites of the creative act.

We will begin by locating our concern through examples drawn from writing, Plato's *Meno,* and psychotherapy. We will then introduce some notions from the philosophy of experiencing, followed by a review of the findings from a study of the composing process. In the final section we will discuss some implications for the teaching of writing.[1] Throughout, our concern will be to show how creative discovery results from a reflective act in which symbols arise out of inchoate experience.

Knowing But Not Knowing: The Quandary of Self-Expression

"I know what I want to say but I don't know how to say it." It is hard to imagine that anyone who writes is spared this experience. Somehow people manage to overcome it. Yet does anyone know clearly how this happens?

Students who complain that they "know but don't know" commonly receive the suggestions cherished by traditional pedagogy: begin by making an outline; write topic sentences; then fill in the gaps. Teachers recommend this practice because it "makes sense" and is believed to work. But can any advocate of outlines and topic sentences explain how one proceeds from "knowing but not knowing" to being able to write anything at all? Many teachers use other skillful means to "get students to write": having them jot down random ideas or encouraging spirited classroom discussion. But called upon to give a plausible account of how it is that these means work, most teachers, in our experience, are at a loss to do much more than assent, "I try to stimulate thinking" or "You can often get students started by having them bounce their ideas off one another."

Even more problematic is the request by a student for advice on how to proceed when the teacher's skill is not available: what should a student do in a state of "knowing but not knowing" when no teacher is there to help? Some teachers make themselves available to listen so that students may "talk out" their ideas. They thereby provide an example of the kinds of help that students may seek from people other than their teachers. But what should this help actually do? Apart from the trivial point that the end result should be that the student now knows how to say what was formerly obscure, how is one to gauge the helpfulness of whatever assistance *is* available *while* it is going on? What *precisely* should the help address? In other words, how can a teacher help a student create form from something that is at present formless, without clear shape?

We expect to provide responses to the questions we have raised here in the discussion that follows. For the present, we hope simply to have pointed clearly to the experience we have named "knowing but now knowing: the quandary of self-expression," and to have stated two central problems: (1) how to account in cogent, formal terms for what takes place through creative self-expression; and (2) what to offer people in the way of clearly operational and experientially relevant tools so that creative self-expression can be brought more directly within their grasp.

Meno's Dilemma and Psychotherapy

"Knowing but not knowing" is by no means a new phenomenon. Nor are the dilemmas that students in such a state pose to their teachers. In Plato's account, Meno asks Socrates, "But how will you look for something when you don't in the least know what it is? How on earth are you going to set up something you don't know as the object of your search?"[2] Socrates responds with a demonstration. He "teaches" one of Meno's slaves how to construct a square that has twice the area of a given square without ever giving the boy the answer. One point of the exercise is to show that thoughtful inquiry can quite feasibly begin with "knowing that you don't know"; in fact, Socrates shows that this state of perplexity lies closer to finding the correct answer than the blithe ignorance in which one assumes one knows when in fact one does not. Later in the dialogue, Socrates elaborates on this point by celebrating the virtues of true *knowledge*, which only comes after one has managed to think and work through the answers for oneself, over the less secure and less stable *opinions*, which come from unreasoned hunches or from mouthing another's beliefs.

While many educators have been inspired by Socrates' example, teachers in schools and universities rarely follow it. How often is a professor heard to say, as Socrates did to Meno, "It isn't that, knowing the answers myself, I perplex other people. The truth is rather that I infect them also with the perplexity I feel myself"?[3] As in ancient times, Socrates' way of teaching is more likely to be found *outside* formal institutions of learning. But we *have* progressed. Those who follow closely in the Socratic tradition are no longer condemned by the state as "corruptors of youth." We simply banish them to the mental health fields and call them psychotherapists.

Psychotherapy patients are people who may be likened to the baffled student of writing in one important respect: they "know but they don't know." They know they want to be or to act otherwise, but they are at a loss to achieve their ends. If they are in a state that therapists call "motivated for treatment," they behave like Meno: thoroughly perplexed, skeptical about the possibility of setting up something they don't know as the object of a search, yet nevertheless capable of mustering a certain willingness to look and inquire. For example, a patient-therapist dialogue might proceed as follows:

> Patient: I feel terrible. I have a pain in my back. I can't do any work. I know all the reasons intellectually for why I'm feeling this way—problems on the job, a home—but knowing that stuff doesn't do any good. There's something I'm missing."
>
> Therapist: What *are* you missing?
>
> Patient: If I knew that, I wouldn't be telling you about it.
>
> Therapist: Fair enough. So let's go to work with this feeling you have that something's missing. Even if you can't *say* what this missing thing is, try and let that sense you *do* have of it come clearer. Pay attention to the way it feels inside . . . that whole business of the reasons you already know not being enough and you needing to find something else.

In this way therapy begins to engage the specific sense this patient has of "something missing," a knowing-that-something-crucial-remains-unknown. The patient brings this feeling to therapy as a complaint. Therapeutic inquiry transforms the complaint into the central subject to be reflected upon. Although the therapist might offer interpretations of the patient's experience, these would only be valuable to the extent that they bring this experience more explicitly within the patient's grasp.

Habermas' reading of Freud's papers on technique lead him to conclusions that run parallel to ours. He locates the central psychotherapeutic process in the tradition of critical thought:

> Initially psychoanalysis appears only as a special form of interpretation. [But] psychoanalytic hermeneutics, unlike the cultural sciences, aims not at the understanding of symbolic structures in general. Rather, *the act of understanding* to which it leads is self-reflection.
>
> [This] includes two movements equally: the cognitive, and the affective and motivational. It is critique in the sense that the analytic power to dissolve dogmatic attitudes inheres in analytic insight.[4]

Troubled therapy patients adhere to some particular approach to their experience despite mounting evidence (their own suffering) that situations in their lives demand something more of them. Therapy offers a context in which that adherence can be relaxed sufficiently to allow patients to engage their experience in fresh reflection. Through creative self-discovery, they are able to provide themselves with more adequate self-conceptions as heuristics for easing the next bit of further living.

Empirical support for this view of psychotherapeutic process comes from a ten-year series of studies of psychotherapy.[5] In this research success in psychotherapy did not correlate with the nature of therapists' interpretations. Rather, what mattered was the extent to which patients (1) engaged aspects of their experience that they at first could only sense, and (2) "stayed with" these aspects until they were able to find some means to express them. Thus, both teachers and therapists work with people's sense of knowing-but-not-knowing. Psychotherapy provides an example of how this quandary may be resolved through a reflective process: turning toward and engaging the sense of what lies beyond one's current capacity to express.

The Relation between Symbolizing and What Lies Beyond: The Philosophy of Experiencing

It seems to be a contradiction to speak of what lies beyond our expressive capacities when, in order to refer to this beyond, we must make use of those capacities by employing words, formulations or symbols. Logically, one cannot symbolize the "cannot-be-symbolized." Yet, in fact, we have already gone beyond the merely logical possibilities of language in the previous sections. There we used words to refer to the common experience of having something to say without yet having the words to say it. Even single words like "ineffable," "inchoate," "implicit," can point to the presence of "something" we experience that extends *beyond* words.

Many philosophers have referred to the "beyond" in experience. For example, Wittgenstein warns us not to look for the meaning of a given word *in* the word itself or in other words, but rather in the word's *use*, which extends beyond what any words themselves express.[6] This "realm beyond," which encompasses more than what lies within our capacity to express, also presents itself as "what lies beyond our current thinking." To take another example, in his treatise on thinking, Heidegger, enjoins us to think what has not yet been thought.[7]

Many thinkers since Kant have claimed that all valid thought and expression are rooted in the wider realm of prerepresentational experience. But the presence of a "realm beyond" is often invoked in obscure terms that mystify and leave us with the sense that the "beyond" does no more than impose embarrassing limitations on our capacity to think and to symbolize our experience. Until very recently, no one has provided clear guidelines to show how such experience may be employed in or used as a reliable criterion for what we say or think. For all their concern with the realm beyond, even such powerful thinkers as Wittgenstein and Heidegger have not made clear *how* we "have" this realm available to us.

In an effort to resolve these difficulties, Eugene Gendlin has opened a new line of inquiry in philosophy through elaborating ways in which the functioning of what remains implicit—the "beyond"—can be studied in explicit terms.[8] We will not attempt to do justice to the range and depth of Gendlin's work here. Our goal is simply to present several of the basic observations and formulations in his philosophy.

Experiencing has been excluded by the standard models and theories of human functioning. Its absence accounts for the failure of traditional sciences to grapple adequately with such crucial phenomena as love, death, and creativity. Such corners are commonly assumed to be solely the province of the arts and literature. In contrast to this assumption, Gendlin has shown that systematic inquiry *is* possible in the domain of experiencing when methods of observing and conceiving the subject of the inquiry are brought into line with the nature of what is to be studied.

What is this experiencing? It is, first of all, "empirically" observable, although in an expanded sense of what "empirical" is usually taken to mean. For you, the reader, it is the *phenomenal* sense or feel of how you are right now as you read this. If you are pleased or dissatisfied about something, these sentiments may be part of it. But your phenomenal sense need not be limited to sentiments or emotions alone. You might also, for example, be in contact with some sense of why you are reading this, or with the way some event that happened yesterday still reverberates in you, or with how some important challenge that will be facing you colors the way you have been going about your life lately. Of course this short list will not come close to exhausting all that you might sense at this moment. In fact, words could never exhaust experiencing, for with each new formulation, experiencing is extended. You may have already recognized this: each new phrase on the page may bring out some aspect of your experiencing that may not have been clearly in mind before.[9] If you "drop" your attention from the particular words or images that are occurring to you right now, you may note a global, perhaps ineffable, yet nonetheless unmistakable sense or mood—just "under" the words or images—that encompasses *all* of how you are at this instant. *This global sense or mood, which is more encom-*

passing than any formulation of it, is what we refer to when we use the terms
"preconceptual," " felt sense," and experiencing.

What people can experience directly and bodily as the concrete data of existence is the flow of experiencing. According to Gendlin, "it is the felt apperceptive mass to which we can inwardly point" (p. 27). Any aspect of this flow that receives our attention soon yields to other aspects so that we observe that experiencing consists of continuously unfolding orders rather than finished products. What a given aspect eventually comes to *mean*—the explicit significations that come to mind with reference to what may have initially only been dimly felt—may be said to have "existed" in a sense *before* they became explicit. But this sense is

> not the sense of marbles in a bag. These "implicit" meanings are not complete and formed (under cover, as it were). When they become "explicit," they become different from what they were, when they were "implicit." They were "preconceptual" aspects of this protean type of order, and only as they interact with symbols do they become completely formed. (Pp. 28–29)

In attending to an aspect of our experiencing we may find that it "breaks open" or "subdivides" or "differentiates" into "parts" and then more parts and on and on. In so observing we may further conclude that experiencing is precisely that realm which has "no given discrete units . . . except as units are further specified and created. By the application of some scheme there will be units. With respect to another scheme, different units arise" (p. 29). And thus we come to recognize the ever-increasing complexity of experiencing. Although by no means merely random or arbitrary (one does not, in a flash, become the King of Siam or the Empire State Building), this complexity is observably greater than any one logical scheme:

> A logical scheme can be applied to this or that aspect or relation, thereby symbolizing it, but the "preconceptual" order cannot be logically represented. It is *supralogical*, or, if you wish, *prelogical,* capable of functioning in the creation and application of very many different logical schemes. (P. 29)

In stipulating observable qualities of experiencing, Gendlin moves beyond merely decrying the limitations of symbolic form or invoking "nebulous feeling" as the basis of thought and expression. He has introduced a method for studying systematically the interactions between symbols and what lies beyond them, which makes it possible to show how "feeling" and "cognition" function together. For example, one class of relations between symbols and experiencing is exemplified in the common use of demonstrative pronouns such as "this" or "that funny feeling I get." In these examples, terms serve mainly to refer to or point to some sensed datum. This is a class of relations Gendlin calls "direct reference." In another class of relations, words or images may give a reader or viewer a "new experience." In such cases symbols create or "lift out" a new aspect of experiencing. Gendlin calls such instances "metaphor." In a third class of relations, some already available aspect of experiencing responds to a "known" symbolic formulation. Thus, when someone says "tree," we *recognize* what they mean. Our experiencing of that object responds to a name for it. Gendlin calls this "recognition."[10]

Gendlin has constructed an "open" system that does not violate the humanist injunction against reducing experience to some trivializing scheme. His philosophy of experiencing is also responsive to science, which values theories capable of generating empirically testable propositions. However, studies of experiencing differ from more standard research on human phenomena. First, the philosophy of experiencing fosters an *empirical holism* which, unlike strict behaviorism, does not limit its concern only to what is observable. But also unlike mentalist strategies, it does not weave schemes to account for observations and then elevate those schemes to the status of a priori structural antecedents of the phenomena studied. Instead, empirical holism is capable of focusing on the finest behavioral sequences while retaining the sense that what is observed may only be selected manifestations of vast, inricate processes. To the extent that these processes remain largely *implicit*, they may not *yet* be amenable to explication.

A further difference is that studies of experiencing are concerned with the movements and flow that experiencing presents to us. This means a shift in research strategy away from studying "traits" or other "contents" of personality or mental structure to considering process. It also means abandoning conceptual tools that cast human phenomena in static or fixed terms in favor of ones that can apprehend on-going change. In the following section we will describe a study of students' writing that exemplifies the approach of empirical holism and its concern with process.

A Study of the Composing Process

What happens when writers sit down and begin to write? How does the process of creating and elaborating meaning unfold, and what conclusions can be drawn from observing this process directly? These were the questions that guided one of the authors in an investigation of the composing process of college writers.[11] One of our purposes in this section is to present some of the relevant findings that emerged from this inquiry. We believe that these findings have implications for teaching that extend beyond what is defensible on statistical grounds alone. Our second purpose, therefore, is to show how these findings take on more general significance in the light of Gendlin's philosophy of experiencing.

The Study

In order to understand how college students write, the author worked with five students who were judged to have writing problems. Each of the students met for five 1½-hour sessions with the author. On four occasions they were directed to compose aloud, that is, to articulate as much of the flow of their thinking as they could. They wrote on four different assignments, two in the extensive mode (impersonal, expository style) and two in the reflexive (personal style, touching on writer's own experience). One additional session consisted of an interview on perceptions and memories of writing and writing instruction. Since the writing sessions were taped, the author had before her a record of each student's composing operations and the order of their unfolding. By coding each of the operations, she was able to view the separate features of the composing process and the manner in which each related to the whole. What follows are some of the principal observations that arose from this method of inquiry and three of the conclusions to which they point:

A. *Writing as Creative Discovery.* Except when students appear to be writing some pat version of what they have read or written before, they are surprisingly consistent in articulating an attitude of "I'm making this up as I go along." This is readily understandable at times when students begin by saying, "I don't know what to write, so I'll just write anything." At these times, writing anything that would "get them going"—that would lead to getting a partial text down on the page—has a clarifying effect. Once having managed to write, they are then more likely to say, "Oh, now I see what I want." In this way "making it up" often leads to a sense of discovery.

"Making it up as I go along" also characterizes the attitude of students who begin writing with a clearly articulated sense of direction. Through the act of writing they continue to change and elaborate on what they have to say. It was as if they do not know all there is to write until they have written it. Yet even the act of writing does not then insure that they "have" it. Writing further frequently has the effect of leading them to consider whether they want to keep what they have just written.

Based on this observation, it is tempting to conclude that writers *discover* what they have to say as they write. If that were the only conclusion, however, we would miss the point that this discovery process unfolds by virtue of the writer's own activity. If writing is made possible by the discovery of what one wants to say, it is just as true that the discoveries come about through the writing itself. Thus *writing* is what makes discovery possible by creating the possibilities for discovery. For this reason we conclude that writing involves *creative discovery*.

When inclined to appreciate words poetically, we would not blink at the term *creative discovery*. But once we leave a poetic frame of mind and demand precise definitions we are likely to ask, "Which is it? Either something clearly exists and the first time one happens upon it should be called discovery, or the thing does *not* exist and its coming into existence is a *creation*." Note the words "something clearly exists . . . or the thing does *not* exist." This objection is not simply a plea for clarity. It is an articulation of a theory, now enshrined as common sense, that is a heritage of Aristotle's brillance 2,500 years ago. Heidegger calls it the "thing model"—one tenet of which is that something either does or does not exist.[12] Due to its basis in dualism, we find the "thing model" inadequate for grasping the creative process of becoming. In the philosophy of experiencing, Gendlin has provided alternative formulations.

We may state Genlin's model abstractly in the following way: living is an interacting between bodily processes and all else that is constitutive of our environing world. Experiencing is the preconceptual manifesting of the way in which our bodies—which are biological organisms further structured linguistically, socially, culturally and historically—have already begun to organize the situations in which we live. Most of the flow of experiencing remains implicit—preconceptual—until we focus our attention on what we can at first only sense, in such a way as to find some relevant aspect. *Discovery* is involved in that we have some hint of what we are seeking and are impelled to look for it. This discovery process, to be understood, must also be granted its creative features. What we discover forms out of the flow of experiencing, a further differentiation of, or elaboration from the sense with which we began. What comes to light cannot, therefore, be said to have existed before in quite the form it takes when finally explicit. Through providing our own context for the further symbolizing of our experience, we *create* the meanings we *discover*.

B. *"Going Back as the Way to Go Forward"*: *The Logic of Creative Discovery*. Students appear to write by shuttling back and forth from their sense of what they wanted to say to the words on the page and back to address what is available to them "inwardly." Thus the process of creative discovery appears recursive in two ways. (1) When given a topic, students ask themselves about it and begin to articulate the two or three aspects of the topic that come most readily to mind. They break the topic down into manageable pieces or focus on a key word and develop associations to that word. In both cases, they frequently turn back to themselves to call upon what they "know." By using only demonstrative pronouns or vague epithets to refer to this knowing as "that" or "this answer I got," they give the strong impression to an observer that what they "knew" first came to them as only a vague sense that they could not yet articulate clearly. (2) Once words are down on paper, students consistently return to read and reflect on what has already been written before developing their ideas further. Thus the planning of what they will write is impelled forward once students translate some of their ideas into written form. It is through seeing those ideas on paper and reflecting on them that the students develop them further. In this way, the writing of symbols that refer to an aspect of experience provides grounds for developing that aspect so as to engender further symbolizing.

On the basis of these observations, the author originally proposed a model that takes the movements that occur during composing into account. One feature is called *retrospective structuring*. This refers to the way in which the writer turns back to lay hold of and take forward the sense, however inchoate, of what is already there to say. Writing is the carrying forward of an inchoate sense into explicit form. This proceeds further when what has been written can be read, sensed anew, and used to provide a further differentiation of the sense one now has of what one wants to say.

Retrospective structuring is writer-based.[13] It is the feature of the composing process that builds on the writer's sense of what needs to be said in order for the text to make sense to the writer. Composing also involves another feature that is reader-based. This refers to the need for the text to make sense to people other than the writer. For that to happen, the writer must "project" whether readers, who do not have access to the sense evoked in the writer by the writer's own words on the page, will nonetheless grasp what the writer intends to say. Crafting one's sense of what one wants to say so that it will be intelligible to others is the feature of composing called *projective structuring*.

Projective structuring presupposes some capacity to edit—to judge discourse objectively and to apply formal rules. It also relies on the cultivation of aesthetic distance, or the ability to view one's writing as an artifact and to assess its formal characteristics. But most essentially, it depends on the writer's capacity to distinguish between a felt sense of what is being intended and the formulations devised to say it. Only through this distinction can projective structuring proceed. One must be able (1) to lay hold of the sense of one's intention and (2) to compare it with one's sense of what readers will need to be told before they can grasp it, so as (3) to assess whether a given set of formulations provides an adequate vehicle for translating a private datum into publicly accessible form.

Retrospective and projective structuring, then, refer to the alternating postures writers assume in composing, and from which they creatively discover what they want to say, externalize what they mean or intend by placing words on the page, and recreate that externalized meaning to ready it for the eyes of others.

Stated generally, both retrospective and projective structuring are features of creative discovery, which moves forward by "going back." It does this going-back in two senses: (1) one must "go back" behind the initial formulation to the concretely felt experiential datum, for that is the source of new or improved differentiations of it; and (2) one must also "go back" on or loosen the hold that some already constituted formulation—even a direct referent such as "that vague sense I can't talk about"—has on the relevant experiential aspect. Going back in this way is tantamount to providing oneself the degree of freedom needed to formulate the experiential aspect further. New steps or differentiations arise through the particular way in which symbolizing and experiencing interact. This way of interacting is what we call *the logic of creative discovery*.[14]

C. *Distinguishing Rules for Products from the Process of Creating: An Evocation of the IOFI Principle*. The written products of unskilled writers are often criticized, with good reason, for lack of organization, illogical relationships, and an abundance of outright errors. As a consequence, teachers often assume that the students' approaches to writing must be disorganized, illogical, and full of errors as well. Observations of unskilled writers during the act of writing indicate, on the contrary, that they are capable of engaging in consistent, well-ordered composing processes. In fact, it seems to us that these students perform some of the crucial functions of creative discovery quite skillfully. They write by continually referring back to the sense of what they want to say. In doing so they also seem to acknowledge that as yet unformed ideas may eventually point to the need to change already formulated statements.

Here we see evidence that even unskilled writers may, to some degree, understand implicitly what has only recently been stated explicitly in the philosophy of experiencing: (1) Meaning does not exist in some place, ready to be encoded, decoded, or printed out, as a machine or "thing" model might lead one to predict. Rather, it is to be found through creatively engaging one's own as yet unformulated sense of what one wants to say. (2) Any formulation of an aspect of experiencing is only one of many possible versions, and may need to be reshaped in the light of a clearer sense, yet to come, of what that version is intended to mean.

The reader will note, however, that a grasp of the meaning of these principles alone is only sufficient for one of the two delineated features of the composing process: retrospective structuring. Careful observations do reveal difficulties in unskilled writers' composing processes. What seems particularly unskilled about the way these students write is that they apply prematurely a set of rigid, critical rules for editing to their written products. As a consequence they frequently lose track of what they mean by becoming caught up in correcting details on grammatical or logical grounds before they have clearly sensed and expressed in some form what they mean to say. To state the problem differently, these writers act as if they believed that the form of what arises through creative discovery must immediately conform to a priori specifications for acceptable products. The premature application of such rigid rules thwarts the very process through which these students might eventually produce more refined products. The result is a fragmented, disjointed text.

In contrast to the belief imputed to these students, we categorically insist that rules for judging products must not be confused with guidelines for producing such products. The failure to make this distinction keeps these writers from recognizing that one does not "polish" a text by a more or less mechanical application of rules so much as by carrying forward, clarifying, and differentiating what one means to say through the operations of projective structuring. The knowledge of what the rules require is undeniably an important element for projective structuring. But the rules must not be mistaken for the process of further crafting and molding that brings a piece of writing into conformity with them.

Once again we are struck by an analogy with psychotherapy. Unskilled writers who are prematurely critical of work that remains largely unwritten have a counterpart in psychotherapy patients whose "block" to creative self-reflection is their propensity to condemn what is not yet realized in themselves. In both cases the difficulty is not in lacking personal experience to draw upon nor in having no access to that experience. Rather, the central difficulty arises from "literalizing" a set of rules.

Unskilled writers read a partially written product they have just generated and sense an inadequacy. They unfortunately proceed from this sense as if it were a directive to "correct" their product. We believe that their writing would be significantly enhanced if, instead, they would respond to any sense of inadequacy that arises in them as an indicator of needing to refer to their sense of what they mean to say and to develop that sense further. (We will expand on this point in the following section.) Similarly, troubled therapy patients tend to construe the disproportion between private fantasies of greater personal well-being and their less satisfying, living reality as grounds for castigating themselves for not meeting their own standards. The therapist's job is to help them unravel the strains of their troubled state so as (1) to sense more clearly what standards they have been applying, (2) to determine whether these standards are appropriate, and when and if they are, (3) to use them as guides for further growth rather than as cause for self-punishment.

The "literalizing of rules" that we attribute to unskilled writers and troubled therapy patients has its ground in a more fundamental misunderstanding. It is one that assumes that the meaning of symbols resides solely in the symbols themselves. This fallacy is commonly termed "reifying" or "taking the word as the thing." The value of Gendlin's work is that is provides us with a formulation that takes us beyond the negative proscription, "Don't reify."

In Gendlin's theory of meaning the sense of any symbol, conceptualization, or formulation resides in its particular relation with the aspect of experiencing it refers to, "lifts out," meets in "recognition," etc. Experiencing is what gives sense to symbols. The symbols themselves "instance" experiencing. Sense may therefore be said to come from the way that a symbol is an instance of the experiencing that gives rise to it. Gendlin thus concludes that meaning arises when experiencing "instances" itself through symbols. He calls this the "instance of itself" principle, or IOFI.[15]

One concrete implicaton of the IOFI principle is that to "get at," clarify, or create meaning we must achieve access in some way to the experiencing that is its source. The IOFI principle therefore provides a theoretical rationale for employing experiential methods—ones that bring us in contact with direct experiencing—as a way to foster creative discovery. We now turn to a presentation of how such methods may be used in the teaching of writing.

Implications for Teaching

In the preceding sections we have continually referred to the process through which inchoate musings develop into articulated products. We call this creative discovery. In this section we will offer ways to help bring this process more firmly within the grasp of teachers and students. Our suggestions are designed to direct attention to the vague sense that comes to us before we have a clear grip on what we want to say. We wish to cultivate this sense of what is not yet known, since, as we have tried to show, it is out of this wider preconceptual realm that our first tentative formulations emerge.

The instructions we offer are modeled after those that have been proven successful for facilitating self-reflection in therapeutic settings.[16] Before we begin, a note of caution: by pointing students to the "sense" or "feel" of their experiencing, we do not mean to imply that their classes be transformed into encounter groups or therapy sessions. Calling on the capacity to sense or feel must not be confused with evoking specific feelings or emotions such as anger or joy. The capacity to sense or feel is wider and provides for much more richness and variety than any set of emotional states that can be named and categorized. It is precisely just such an understanding that offers the basis for a crucial distinction: referring students to their felt sense of something is not to be confused either with sanctioning mindless emoting or with violating the sanctity of private sentiments.

Given the widespread confusion in our culture on precisely this point, we believe that any public use of experiential techniques be introduced with a statement like: "I'm going to ask you to pay attention to all that you can sense or feel about this (topic) (question) (etc.) You're likely to find that it might be vague at first. But in a few moments, more things may come to you about it. Maybe even more things than you can say here. In deciding what to say, it might be useful to ask yourself two questions: 'What is really important to say about all this?' and 'What feels OK to say about it here?' "[17]

Where to Begin

Frequently the most difficult aspect of writing is getting started. Nothing is clear; nothing is determined. There is the sense that one wants to or must do it along with, perhaps, a few vague ideas but not much else. What to do? Our suggestion is to turn attention to the concrete feel of how the writer is experiencing the initial difficulty. Therein lie, implicitly, the resolutions of the quandary. Teachers can show students specifically how to engage in this productive reflection by giving instructions like the following:

"I'm going to ask some questions that may not have easy answers. Don't be discouraged if answers don't come to you right away. I would like you to ask yourself these questions, privately. Then see what comes to you. It may take awhile. Thirty seconds or even a minute might go by. And even when something does come, it may only be a hazy feeling at first and you may not have any words for it right away."

A teacher might then say: "Ask yourself, 'Where am I with this (topic) (question) (issue) (etc.)?' and don't even try to answer. Just wait and see what comes to you. (Pause.) Try paying attention to what might only be the hazy feelings you have about it. (Pause.) See if, in addition to noticing all you know about this, you can also acknowledge within yourself all you don't yet know."

Through adding such instructions to whatever other pedagogical skills they find useful, teachers may become more effective at converting a stifling sense of perplexity into a datum to be scrutinized. The sense of knowing-but-not-knowing then becomes the source one looks to for the greater clarity that is yet to emerge.

Encouraging and Refining Minimal Symbolizations

Teachers who understand that finished products do not first emerge full blown, like Athena from the head of Zeus, do their students a service by tempering any naive expectations accordingly: "What first comes to mind may be fuzzy or vague. Even the first clear ideas or words you get may not be the ones you eventually decide to stick with." But whatever first comes may nonetheless provide a "handle" to grasp over the course of working toward greater clarity. Thus teachers can encourage students to say or jot down whatever words or thoughts first come.

Showing student that they can actually begin with the very "jumble in their heads" and that their first unclear references may nonetheless help chart their future course, is the practice we call encouraging minimal symbolization. One of its principal corollaries is that the order of a set of ideas may be allowed to emerge from the clarifying of them, rather than being rigidly imposed at the outset. To point this out, teachers might say, "Don't worry if the thoughts you have don't seem logical right now. You'll be able to make them logical later on. Right now it's more important to work with whatever comes to you the way it comes."

Encouraging minimal symbolization as a first step departs from the traditional pedagogical instruction to "plan what you're going to write and then write it." It is a departure in that it acknowledges explicitly that "planning" and "writing" overlap and interact: what was planned may need to change in the writing of it, just as what is written may have to be altered in the light of future planning.

Teachers can assist students in carrying their minimal symbolizations forward by providing other instructions as well. After students have produced a partial text, teachers might say, "Check back with the sense of what you're trying to say and then ask yourself, 'Are these words right? What would I need to add or change to capture even more fully what I'm trying to say"

These instructions provide concrete directives to aid in carrying out the writer-based or retrospective structuring feature of the composing process. Students are encouraged first to shape the discourse for themselves and in this way achieve as close a fit as possible between the words on the page and the aspect of their experiencing they wish to convey.

Allowing for "Leap Steps"

Encouraging minimal symbolization means, as a corollary, recognizing that the relation may not at first be clear between the next incipient formulation and those that preceded it. Of course, to expect otherwise is to fail to acknowledge that a creative sequence is precisely one in which an emergent element leaps ahead and is not strictly predictable from what came before. One may, from hindsight, creatively discover some "logic" in the creative leap and impute this logic to the sequence that unfolded seemingly without order. But if such logic was operating, it was implicit. Explicating such implicit logic always involves a further clarifying. To put this differently, the reasoning that connects an idea that first dawned with another idea that came to mind afterwards, is the product of a third step of creative discovery.

Putting this understanding of leap steps to practical use requires further departures from traditional pedagogy. One departure applies to "tangents," which teachers commonly treat as ipso facto irrelevant or incidental. Teachers would do well, instead, to make use of an operational criterion: rather than assume that whatever they cannot follow must be irrelevant, teachers might say, "What you just came up with is hard for me to follow because I don't see its connection with the rest. But you wouldn't have said it unless it made some sort of sense. See if you can find your way back to whatever you were feeling that led you to those words. It might clarify things if you then try to talk more about it or use some other words to say it."

Often further reflecton reveals that a seeming "tangent" does make sense but in relation to another part of the discourse. Such "illogical" ordering often stymies students. It doesn't follow their outlines and certainly no one has informed them that thinking could be so disorderly! To help them capitalize on the creative potential of tangential thoughts and to minimize their frustration with the "illogical" ordering, teachers can prepare students by reassuring them that useful ideas will not necessarily come to them in the order that they will finally appear on the page.

Leap steps can also be cultivated as a particularly constructive means to escape from the inertia of "being stuck." When stuck, students often reread what they have already written, using the words on the page to bring them closer to their next formulation. Another strategy worth learning is to project ahead to what will be, but has not yet been, constituted by words. To make this forward movement possible, students can ask themselves, "Where is all this leading?" "What else do I know about this topic that I haven't written yet?" "What is not in here that needs to be?" Leaping ahead in this way gets writers going by bringing them more clearly into contact with the sense of what they have yet to say.

Constructing Presentable Form

Students, and others, need to learn that the first formulations they give to their private thoughts are best not judged by the same criteria that are applied to polished prose. Relaxing these criteria, however, does not mean abandoning them. Clarity, reason, logic, structure, precision, and any other attribute that makes for incisive discourse all have their place. But concern for these qualities should be postponed until retrospective structuring, the feature of composing that is writer-based, has generated an initial text.

Refining requires a greater emphasis on projective structuring or the reader-based posture. It is through viewing a text from the perspective of what would make sense to others that one can discover the further revisions that are necessary. This is one of the most difficult aspects of writing to master.

Projective structuring can be facilitated if the strands of the process are laid out clearly. It is most important to emphasize that while a knowledge of rules for editing is indispensable, the process of revising cannot be reduced to mere correcting or editing. *Revising is further writing.* To make this concrete for students, we suggest a two-phase sequence.

In the first phase students may be encouraged to view their first drafts for logic and coherence. They are, so to speak, asked to construct an "outline" from the ideas on the page. To help them do so, teachers can instruct students to jot down answers to questions like the following: "What am I trying to say here?" "What are the main points I have so far?" "Is each of these points explained and does each one lead smoothly to the next?" "Are there any gaps in what I've written so far?" "Do I jump around too much?"

These questions serve as an initial means for enabling students to "move away" from the text and to review it in an ordered fashion. Reversing the traditional sequence, so that "outlining" follows rather than precedes initial writing, has several advantages: it frees students from the expectation that their initial writing must conform to some logical, a priori scheme; it helps "pry" them loose from the words on the page by asking them to clarify further the sense that those formulations are intended to capture, and it enables them to see more clearly where something is lacking.

In the second phase students may review their written products from the point of view of their readers. Thus they are instructed to ask themselves, "What do I have to write here so that someone who doesn't know what I know about this topic will be able to understand what I'm trying to say?" The very asking of such a question is the first step in cultivating the reader-based posture of projective structuring.

These instructions cannot insure that students will know how to revise adequately or how to apply the rules for evaluating finished discourse to their written products. They nonetheless can help students create for themselves an appropriate frame of mind in which to make use of whatever formal knowledge they do have.

Conclusion: The Teacher's Posture

Teaching, as we understand it, is quite different from merely holding forth before a captive audience. It is, in our sense of it, providing a context in which others can engage in creative discovery. Seen in this way, teaching is more than the imparting of any body of knowledge. We have tried to illustrate what this more fundamental aspect of teaching entails by drawing parallels between such otherwise divergent activities as psychotherapy and the teaching of writing. In both we have seen that "setting up what we don't know as the object of our search" constitutes the essential beginning. This process is a venerable one. Those who practice it may justly claim as mentor Socrates, who said,

> One thing I am ready to fight for as long as I can, in word and act: that we shall be better, braver and more active . . . if we believe it right to look for what we don't know.[18]

Adhering to this credo, however, is no easy task. As Heidegger writes:

> Teaching is even more difficult than learning . . . because what teaching calls for is this: to let learn. The real teacher in fact, lets nothing else be learned than— learning.[19]

As in the ideal of the supremely skillful therapist—encountered, perhaps, far more often in myth than in fact—the "real" teacher does not interpose his or her own formulations, as if ready-made answers or "useful information" could substitute for the search others must undertake for themselves. Thus, Heidegger also observes that the "conduct" of a "real" teacher

> often produces the impression that we properly learn nothing from him, if by "learning" we now suddenly understand merely the procurement of useful information.[20]

What then is the proper role and function of a "real" teacher? How does such a teacher behave in relation to students? Heidegger concludes:

> The teacher is ahead of his apprentices in this alone, that he has still far more to learn than they—he has to learn to let them learn. The teacher must be capable of being more teachable than the apprentices.[21]

To be more "teachable" than one's students recalls Socrates' claim that all he did was infect others with the perplexity he felt himself. In our scheme we take both to mean that to teach creative discovery one must be well along the way toward it oneself.

ELLEN W. NOLD

Alternatives to Mad-Hatterism

"Why is a raven like a writing desk?"

"Come, we shall have some fun now!" thought Alice. "I'm glad they've begun asking riddles—I believe I can guess that," she added aloud.

"Do you mean that you think you can find out the answer to it?" said the March Hare.

"Exactly so," said Alice.

"Then you should say what you mean," the March Hare went on.

"I do," Alice hastily replied; "at least—at least I mean what I say—that's the same thing, you know."

"Not the same thing a bit!" said the Hatter. "Why, you might just as well say that 'I see what I eat' is the same thing as 'I eat what I see'!"

. . . and the party sat silent for a minute, while Alice thought over all she could remember about ravens and writing-desks, which wasn't much.

In this episode in *Alice's Adventures in Wonderland*,[1] the Mad Hatter acts as a writing teacher: he reflects to Alice a more concise surface representation of what she meant by her own "I can guess that" after the March Hare reminds her that saying what she means is not the same thing as meaning what she says. This reminder is the crux of the teaching of writing to children above the age of about ten or twelve. For maturing writers, writing is not merely the representation of speech, as the linguist Bloomfield asserted in 1930.[2] Writing requires a detachment, an imaginative attention to audience and genre, a control of a special dialect called a "grapholect"—all of which make the process of writing far more complex than informal speech to an audience.

Unfortunatley, teaching composition is not accomplished by merely reminding students that they must say what they mean or correcting their habits until they miraculously stop making annoying mistakes. The Mad Hatter and the March Hare represent the stance decried by Francis Christensen when he spoke of teachers who only expected students to write better, but did not teach them to do so.[3] In their struggle to eschew Mad-Hatterism, however, teachers are often at a loss. How does one *teach* composition?

The first part of the answer must be that one must understand, even if only provisionally, the process of writing in order to conceive of a basis from which to intervene in the process. The "teaching" methods (one might better call them "expecting" methods) current in many places are mainly noninterventionist. An instructor might intervene in the process in order to give an assignment—if just to write about some topic—and then to "correct," willy-nilly, the written product. Since the student usually does not act upon the corrections, often does not even read them, no teaching is accomplished. The gains in compositional skills after this kind of "teaching" may be attributed only to the inevitable effects of maturation and practice. Teachers who conceive of their noninterventionist methods as the only ones rightfully and logically conclude that they have not "taught" writing. Only they state the truth in a false maxim: that writing cannot be taught by any method. But many courageous, insightful, and interventionist teachers have proven this maxim false.

A Model of the Writing Process

In order to teach composition, one must have a conception of the process in which he is intervening. Figure 1 shows a schematic representation of the process as I conceive it and teach it to the teachers and tutors who work for me.

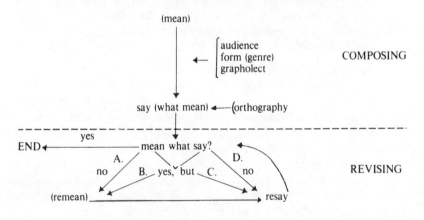

Fig. 1. The writing process

The figure represents an idealized version of the writing process of a skilled writer. It is a kind of theory, and as such, it has not been tested. The only points it has to recommend it are: (1) it is the product of years of introspection about my own writing processes and (2) it looks like many of the models of the writing process that colleagues of mine have recently advanced.[4] We may provisionally accept it as a convenience, a jumping-off point for a discussion about teaching composition.

In figure 1, I have divided the process into two parts: *composing* and *revising*. Composing is the first-time production of discourse, more or less subject to prior planning. In the writing of even a first draft by a skilled writer, both composing and revising take place. In fact, in a dysfunction commonly referred to as "writer's block," the revising process wholly or partially cripples the composing process. The writing process of beginning writers, which normally includes composing but not much revising, is not much different from the production of informal speech, except that in speech, an audience gives the speaker verbal and nonverbal feedback. As is well documented by psycholinguists,[5] corrections of speech occur usually at predictable junctures. Compared, however, to the extent of revising that occurs in the writing process of skilled writers, revising in informal speech is almost negligible.

In composing, the writer begins with a mysterious process indicated by (mean) in Figure 1: the job of finding and formulating meaning. Researchers in the composing process like Linda Flower and Richard Hayes of Carnegie-Mellon University[6] are trying to define what happens when someone (mean)s. According to psycholinguist Walter Kintsch, the meaning most probably takes the form of hierarchical propositional form.[7] But as we writers know, what we (mean) is not always clear to us in our first draft of a discourse; hazy intentions of meaning may clear up as we begin to compose. The word "mean" is in parenthesis because I postulate that meaning is essentially nonlinguistic and, hence, it is only approximated by ordinary language. Specialized languages can, for all practical purposes, express meaning exactly, but only in limited fields of inquiry.

Also impinging on the writing of a first draft—at least by mature writers—are considerations of the audience, the form (mostly couched in terms of "what kind" of piece it should be and "how long" it should run), and, rarely, the modifications of the grapholect or orthography that might be required to achieve an effect on an audience. The grapholect includes all the normalizations of regional dialects and personal ideolects that occur when one writes for a fairly wide audience. In addition, there are requisite orthographic conventions to be followed in writing the grapholect. Because young children must spend so much attention on the orthographic demands of writing and because they have not developed concern for the reader's differing point of view, considerations of audience, form, and grapholect do not figure strongly in their composing processes. But as the physical and orthographic process become more automatic, as less memory is required for forming letters and spelling words, more attention may be given to the demands of audience and form, of graceful, first-time production of prose. Fostering the ability to produce written prose easily— in short, fluency—should be a major goal in the teaching of composition to beginning writers—whether they be six, eighteen, or fifty-three years old.

But, as I see it, fluency in composing is not the end-goal of the teaching of writing in the schools, especially in the curriculum of the secondary schools and in the institutions of higher education. At these levels, the schools should take advantage of the developing memory, experience, and detachment of the older student to focus on the second stage of the writing process: revising. In speech, revisions are usually limited to changes in the syntax or semantics of single sentences, often in response to a real audience's misunderstandings, but for mature writers the revising process is largely introspective. Mature writers take into account not only the syntactic or semantic infelicities of single sentences but of larger elements of the discourse. Revising, then, is not just correcting the lexicographic and syntactic infelicities of written prose—though at the lower grade-levels these aspects are stressed. It also includes (1) changing the meaning of the text in response to a realization that the original intended meaning is somehow faulty or false or weak (represented by arrow A in figure 1); (2) adding or substituting meaning to clarify the originally intended meaning or to follow more closely the intended form or genre of the text (represented by arrow B in figure 1); (3) making grammatical sentences more readable by deleting, reordering, and restating (arrow C in figure 1); and (4), correcting errors of diction, transcription, and syntax that nearly obscure intended meaning or that are otherwise unacceptable in the grapholect.

Revising, then, requires an ability to read well one's prose and to test it with a double set of standards: (1) does this prose reflect clearly what I want to say? and (2) is it accessible to my audience's understanding, given their predispositions, knowledge, and other constraints on understanding? Because the standards often conflict, a mature writer must learn to make compromises and concessions that demand flexibility and creativity. It is no wonder that the whole, complex revising process is mastered late in development, if it is mastered at all.

Teaching for Perceptible Change

Twenty years ago, freshman composition courses were abolished in many colleges and universities because there was no clear evidence that composition was taught. Although some of the problems of proof lay with the research methodology, many of the problems arose because, indeed, composition was nglected. The composition curriculum lacked a sequence of instruction based on any approximate notion of the process in which the instructors were intervening or on any consistent diagnosis of individual students' needs. In addition, confusion reigned about what particular and definable changes in a composition might arouse an outside judge to say that X composition was indeed better than Y. Although these questions are far from being definitively answered now, more attention than ever before is being given to them.

Based on research into the evaluation process,[8] I recommend the se-

	Student's ability in:		Teaching focuses on:	
	Writing	**Reading**	**COMPOSING**	**REVISING**
STAGE 1	More than 15% mechanical errors	Less than 5th grade	Lexicography Grapholect	Arrow D
STAGE 2	Between 5-15% mechanical errors Steady control of the grapholect	Between 5th and 9th grade	(mean) Form	Arrow A Arrow B
STAGE 3	Fewer than 5% mechanical errors Ability to form a thesis and marshall evidence Ability to organize an essay, if only in stock ways	Above 9th grade	Form	Arrow C

Fig. 2. The teaching sequence

quence of instruction represented in figure 2. At Stage 1, the major focus is on fluency because when there are more than 15 to 20 percent orthographic and lexicographic errors in a composition, processing the written text is so difficult that it seriously impedes the smooth interpretation of meaning. In psychologists' terms, the load on short-term memory becomes so great and the time to closure on each particular proposition so long that a representation of the shape of the meaning, the sense of the passage, is seriously disrupted.[9] Of course, Stage 1 students have problems reading their *own* writing. Revising at this stage should focus on arrow D type of activity in figure 1: changing the orthographic representation of sentences until they can be read in the conventional manner. In addition, efforts should be made to teach the Stage 1 student the specialized dialect. In calling for the main foci on orthography and the grapholect, I do not mean to imply that no attention should be given other concerns: for instance, the creation of a recognizable beginning, middle, and end of a personal narrative or an understanding of paragraphing. But attention given these concerns should be minimized in favor of actual, repeated practice in the physical act of writing until the student becomes reasonably fluent in both writing and reading.

At Stage 2, the focus shifts to getting, examining, ordering, and elaborating upon ideas of a specific audience. The reason for this shift is clear: once a text may be read with a minimal effort, the reader then pays by far the most attention to the soundness, elaboration, and order of the ideas. This precedence of "content" over "form" in the evaluation of papers written by people at Stage 2 is the bane of those researchers who view evaluation as a mechanical process of counting "errors." At least with papers written by most college students (except for Open Admissions and other special admits), the mechanical approach is simply useless.

To say that English teachers are more confident in their abilities to teach Stage 1 skills than those delineated for Stage 2 is an understatement. Rhetoric after rhetoric ignores or brushes over the problem of "finding something to write about," a real difficulty in the necessarily artificial atmosphere of a composition course. The subsequent problem of coherently explaining what one thinks to a given audience is reduced to the formulaic five-paragraph theme (one to state the thesis, three to explain three examples, and one to conclude with a restatement of the thesis) or its modern counterpart, "functional writing" as taught by A. D. Van Nostrand.[10] This reductionism, however, is quite useful to the Stage 2 student, who is often unaware of the existence of perceptible structure in others' writing and, hence, of the need for perceptible structure in his own.[1] For many students in Stage 2, drilling in simplified forms is a necessity.

Composition instructors are far more likely to be aware of teaching materials that stress the simplified forms than those which may be used to aid the teacher in aiding the student in the production of ideas. Most present-day instructors are only dimly, if at all, aware that the "topics" or "themes" they assign arise from the traditional Aristotelian/Ciceronian notion of *topoi*. In the history of rhetoric, the meaning of *topoi* has moved from the place associated with already conceived and ordered ideas to a more open-ended, abstract "place" where one could search for arguments—comparison, degree, cause/effect, definition. At present, the topic is not in the student's arsenal, but the teacher's. Like the Mad Hatter's riddle, it is supposed to inspire a clever answer because it is such a clever question. Unfortunately, the student usually has nothing on his side to help him; like Alice, he tries, but doesn't remember much.

Unbeknownst to many instructors, the ancient notion of topoi for the student has been revived and given another Greek name: heuristic. Heuristics are open-ended questions that stimulate ideas and thereby increase the probability that a solution to a question will be discovered. A simple set of topics is Kenneth Burke's "Who? What? When? Where? Why?"[12] Another is suggested by W. Ross Winterowd's article called "The Grammar of Coherence."[13] Couched in questions, this set might read:

(1) With what other items is my subject coordinate?
(2) What are the opposites of my subject?
(3) What causes my subject; what does it cause?
(4) What conclusions are drawn regarding my subject?

(5) What are the alternatives to my subject?
(6) What includes my subject; what does my subject include?
(7) What chronological sequences are associated with my subject?

The most elegant and most rigorously validated heuristic is one based on the linguistic theory called tagmemics, first articulated by Kenneth Pike in *Language in Relation to a Unified Theory of Human Behavior*.[14] The pedagogical applications of tagmemics are contained in *Rhetoric: Discovery and Change*, by Richard Young, Alton Becker, and Kenneth Pike. Based on a notion of seeing a subject as first a particle, then a wave, and then as part of a field, tagmemic heuristics have shown themselves useful in teaching students to discover ideas about which to write.[15] Unfortunately, the textbook by Young, Becker, and Pike is not appropriate for most Stage 2 students, and other, more popular materials have been slow in coming.

At Stage 2, students should be encouraged to begin examining their own processes of writing, particularly the crucial shift from (mean)ing for oneself to explaining (mean)ing to an audience. Stress should be placed on the difference between "getting ideas down on paper" in one's own process of invention, of (mean)ing and, after closure, shaping those ideas for an audience. In (mean)ing, great fertility ought to be the goal; in the other aspects of composing and revising, pruning, ordering, and shaping are the goals. Students should learn that even good ideas that do not fit the form or the purpose of a piece must be deleted. After struggling with producing ideas and then again after struggling with pruning them, students should talk to each other about the struggle. In addition to passing around finished pieces of writing for admiration and evaluation (a practice, unfortunately, not much followed), selected students should give presentations (complete with illustrations, drafts, wadded pieces of paper) of the process of their conception and ordering of ideas. The poorer students will gain from hearing how hard the better ones strived, and it will occur to them that effort, not magic, was a large determinant of the better students' success. Similarly, the instructor should also illustrate his or her methods of composition so that the class sees that even the teacher goes through messy and often frustrating gyrations to come up with a finished draft. I well remember the sighs of relief that issue from my composition students the first time I haul out the drafts for a published paper: they learn that attention and hard work and a sensitivity to audience determine more the success of a writer than does that mysterious force called "talent."

Stage 3 is marked by two changes. First, the student is encouraged to drop fixed forms in favor of forms that better suit the structure of his material and/or the structure of his audience's preconception of the material. Longer, more complex structures in reading are introduced and perhaps imitated.

Second, the student learns about complex sentence structures and all the stylistic niceties of really well-written prose: parallelism, absence of extra words, ellipsis, sophisticated indication of the relationships between abstraction levels of contiguous sentences, such as semicolons and colons. Most helpful in this stage is the notion of sentence-combining, first introduced by John Mellon and later developed by Frank O'Hare.[16] Solidly based on transformational-generative grammar, sentence-combining increases the syntactic repertoire of students by giving them practice in combining short sentences into longer ones, usually with cues about how the combining is to be accomplished. Researchers claim that facility in composing already-provided sentences in the exercises carries over into facility in composing the students' own sentences in free writing.[17]

Stylistics comes last in the teaching sequence because research shows that sentence structure and other variables related to style are significant in the evaluation process only after the given topic has been addressed, organized, logically presented, and elaborated upon.[18] In terms of producing perceptible change in composition skills, a syntactically sophisticated, short, redundant, illogical essay will be rated lower than a slightly awkward, long, elaborate, logical one.

Examples of Productive Methods of Teaching Composition

As long as we spend our time foolishly as composition teachers, our efforts will proceed glacially, if at all. The biggest time-waster in all of composition teaching is red-penciling all the errors and infelicities on a paper and sending the paper back to the student to glance at and shove into a desk drawer. How do we stop wasting time? Answers:

(1) Instead of red-penciling, keep track of the *kinds* of each student's errors on a separate page. Keep your pen off the student's paper (except perhaps to make check marks) until after you have read the paper once.

(2) Work on at most three of a student's problems in one paper; if the problem is major, like a mangled organization, work on only that problem.

(3) After a paper is revised, check for a solution to the few problems you mentioned before. If they are solved, move on to a couple of new problems.

(4) After solving a specific problem, try to state a more general solution. For instance, after rewriting a muddy thesis in the first paragraph of essay #1, generalize: "If you try to make your thesis as specific as you can, while still adumbrating the major points you make later, you'll be in good shape. Remember: a thesis often has to be rewritten as the paper takes form."

(5) Set up methods by which the students can communicate to you about the processes of their writing. Ask them what they think needs to be reworked, where they got stuck, which parts were most interesting to write. In this way,

you can judge the development of their skills in revising as well as in composing. Pay attention to making the process of composing more efficient for each student, taking into account his or her preferred modes of operation.

Let's suppose that the essays reproduced below were written by your freshmen English students in class on the first day. Each student took forty-five minutes to write on the following question: "Marijuana is now an illegal drug in California, although the penalties for its possession have been reduced recently. Do you agree or disagree with this decision? Give reasons for taking your position." (In the research project in which these essays were actually written, they were all retyped and recoded to control for the effects of handwriting and the rater's biases about sex and background. Unfortunately, teachers cannot control for these real biases, except to be aware of them and to ask for typed copies when possible.)

STUDENT 1

There are many questions that I and other people have about marijuana. The affects of marijuana on the body and the brain are not quite understood. One thing that is known is that it distorts space and time. Because Marijuana does distort space and time I am against the use of it in any way except for the use of it as a medacine.

I feel that people are using marijuana to excape reality. They are tired of putting up with them selves and others, so they try to escape what is real and go into the limbo of marijuana. The only problem with useing marijuana to escape your own personal hange ups is that no matter how far you go you will eventually end up right back where you started from. People have to learn to deal with the problems that they have, not escape them. If people go on trying to excape the problems of the world and them selves they will create many more problems than they had before.

I am against legalizing marijuana and I think that stricter laws should be drawn up and put before the people. I also think that people should be more informed to what marijuana does to your mind and your body.

STUDENT 2

I do not agree with the penalities they have on marijuana because in the first place I think marijuana should be legalized. I don't think anyone can be a judge on a given subject unless they have experienced the act. I am willing to bet that most of the people who voted against legalizing marijuana has never tried it. Yet they feel alcohol is O.K to have legalized. I have seen the effects of both alcohol and marijuana. Most people who drink too much alcohol start acting loud and violent. They can never remember what they did the day before. And they have a terrible hangover the next day. Smoking marijuana is a different kind of high. You don't feel sick inside. It puts you in a peaceful state. Usually one wants to be alone and just think. This is good because then you don't bother anyone. But if you smoke marijuana make sure you have lots of food around because you will definitely get the munchies. I don't know the medical effects of marijuana but I know it can't be any worse than sclerosis of the liver.

Therefore reducing the penalties for possession of marijuana does not do any good because this is just telling the public you can smoke marijuana but just don't get caught with a large amount.

STUDENT 3

The lowering of penalties for possession of marijuana in California resulted in benefits for both the state and the individual.

The state profited from reduced court loads which allowed more efficient handling of serious crimes. The police, being freed from searching for marijuana offenders, could devote more time to protecting individuals from violent crimes.

Removing marijuana offenders from jails gives another advantage in that the offender is no longer associating with hardened criminals. Allowing private use without fear of being arrested for a felony lessens the guilt and fear of what is usually a social event with neither offender nor victim.

STUDENT 4

While recent reductions in the penalties for marijuana possession and use do not necessarily portend decriminalization, these revisions are a justifiable step toward adjusting the penalty to fit the crime. For many years, the severity of the penalty did not befit the nature of the crime, resulting in numerous inequities. Finally, marijuana use has been "legislated" a fair position in the criminal spectrum.

The basic nature of classifying the offense has been purely subjective, being a wholly personal view. If an individual regarded marijuana usage as bad or detrimental, physically or morally, then this person could reasonably label its use as a crime. Logically, the reverse is true. Provided its use is a purely enjoyable experience, which generally affects only the individual, there would be absolutely no crime involved. The foundation of past laws has been the supposition of gradual and inexorable succession to more dangerous physically and socially, narcotic drugs, some of which are virtually hopelessly addicting. For years these views, generally held by a minority, dominated marijuana legislation. This is another instance of people, doubtless with good intentions, of attempting to govern the actions of others. Gradually, more and more such laws governing private conduct or so-called victimless crimes are being repealed, perhaps revealing a changing social atmosphere.

While decriminalization could initiate an undesirable and substantial increase in marijuana use, it is unlikely that such a penalty reduction will do so. Various offenses, such as selling or possessing large quantities, are still subject to rather severe penalties, and this is likely to remain so. Obviously, this creates a somewhat ironical situation, since those who choose to use it must get the marijuana from somewhere. Still, those who formerly used marijuana will most likely continue to use it, and probably with somewhat less anxiety. Because it is still penalized, there will probably not be any significant increase in the numbers of users. Hopefully, apprehension will lead to unfortunate record or background consequences, as it may have in the past.

Because of personal nature of the "offense," partial decriminalization was the correct move. Considering that there was no violence involved, a stiff classification was totally unnecessary. While decriminalization is undesirable, this legislation was both desirable and appropriate.

What conclusions, what plans of action, do these essays suggest? Before we begin drawing conclusions, we must first adopt a healthy skepticism about the reliability and validity of the exercise we have just given our students. First, as researchers and teachers, we know that a student's performance varies widely, depending on the topic he is assigned. In a research project I conducted two years ago, twenty-two students wrote four essays each on a different topic; each essay was rated by six different raters on a four-point scale. A little more than half the students produced on unrepresentative essay—that is, one of the four essays averaged either a full grade or more above or below the average for the other three essays. Other researchers have noted similar instabilities in an individual student's performance.[19] Our diagnostic in-class exercise, then, is fairly unreliable: to make a cut-and-dried decision about "what kind of writer Johnny is" from performance on one topic is unfair and unwise.

In addition, the validity of the exercise is in question if we contend that our in-class exercise tested the writing skills of these college freshmen. As we have seen, the writing process of skilled writers involves both composing and revising. In forty-five minutes, there is little time for REVISING; for students who have a hard time thinking of anything at all to say, revising probably occurs less than for students who are already facile with a specific topic, who write fluently and who have time to go back over their work. We have strong evidence that in-class themes indeed do not test the important revising skills that are the focus of most freshman English classes.[20]

Our tendency to jump too quickly to conclusions now tempered by these warnings about the reliability and validity of our practices, we determine that one of our main goals in this freshman English course is to teach short essay writing in test situations, since this art is highly rewarded in college. (We have decided further to test again to determine more fully our students' abilities in take-home essays a little later in the course.) The present sample, then, is a valid (though still not highly reliable) sample of these students' abilities in test situations.

These students' papers are arranged in order of the grades given them by four readers in a research project. On a four-point scale, Student 1's essay was given three 1s and one 2, while Student 2's essay was given two 2s and two 1s. Student 1's paper is more logically argued than Student 2's: Student 1 gives a justification for her opinion that marijuana should not be legalized (it distorts time and space, allows people to escape rather than confront problems), but Student 2's argument begs the question ("I do not agree with the penalties they have on marijuana because in the first place I think marijuana should be legalized"). Student 1's paper is better organized: the first paragraph sets out the presupposition for the argument; the second paragraph expands the argument; the third tries to conclude. It's pretty obvious that Student 2 didn't stop a moment before he began to write to consider a structure: he just begins with a fat, overblown paragraph that sets out every argument he can think of in the time allotted and then concludes in a short last paragraph that contains nothing of relevance to the first, but which presents probably his strongest argument, the inconsistency of the penalties for large and small amounts.

Why was Student 1's essay rated lower? Because of her lack of control of lexicography and the grapholect. In my first dealings with her, I would treat her as a Stage 1 student, working with her on her spelling and her relationship with the reader. To help with the first, I would make check marks in the margins to the left of each line in which there was a misspelled word and ask her to pick out the word. In this way, I would see how aware she was of her problem and what strategies she used to determine whether a word was misspelled. There are patterns in her misspellings: they appear to arise from mispronunciations: med*a*cine, pro*u*blem, e*x*cape. I would have her begin a spelling book, chronicling the correct spelling of every word she misspelled; this book she will consult in the final revising stage of her writing. In a class session on the academic's relationship to his audience soon to follow this exercise, I would use her and her classmate's sentences addressing the reader as "you" to illustrate the improper tone. Depending on her motivation, Student 1's work could quite quickly outstrip Student 2's, and she could soon be a solidly Stage 2 student.

It may be surprising that Student 3's essay received exactly the same rating as Student 2's; two 2s and two 1s. After all, Student 2 commits egregious errors. In addition to the infelicities already discussed, there are: (1) rash generalizations ("I don't think anyone can be a judge on a given subject unless they have experienced the act"); (2) meanderings from the subject ("But if you smoke marijuana make sure you have lots of food around because you will definitely get the munchies"); (3) disagreements in pronoun reference required by the grapholect. Student 3, on the other hand, writes much more complex sentences, exhibits none of the grapholectical problems of the first two essays, and organizes his argument transparently.

Why was Student 3's essay graded so low? Because of its clipped and unelaborated nature. The strange shift from past to present tense in the last paragraph may afford us a clue to some of the problems this student faced. In the first two paragraphs the student argues from past experience: reducing penalties on marijuana benefits society by clearing the courts to process more "serious" crime and by freeing policemen to work on violent crime. But the student, sitting in the test room, does not have the work data to support his contentions. Uncomfortable with this position, he shifts to the present tense, indicative of a hypothetical argument: the marijuana offender does not hobnob with the hardened criminal and gains psychological security. But by failing to elaborate on his answer, either by supporting his claims or spinning out his story, the student has not "played the game" of essay writing. An effort at support or elaboration, even when the elaboration is off the point (as in Student 2's efforts), is better than no elaboration at all.

All three of the students discussed previously probably need two exercises: (1) to discuss and then to practice the process of writing essays in short periods, and in particular (2) the ways of getting, rejecting, and formulating arguments on a topic. Students 1 and 3, in discussing their methods of writing, could probably teach Student 2 a thing or two. An exercise in in-class writing that forced the students to wait a significant portion of the time allotted for writing in just thinking and making notes before writing connected discourse would probably improve the products significantly. The teacher might demonstrate, in response to a question selected by the class, his own invention and ordering process, explaining why he rejected ideas, chose others to predominate. In these ways, alternatives to unproductive behavior are illustrated and practiced.

Productive methods of teaching composition are based not only on an awareness of the implications of theory and research for the teaching process and on a disciplined, orderly attempt to produce discernable change. They are also based on asking the student important questions about his work to determine where to begin. Student 4's essay shows a near perfect control of the grapholect, a sophisticated sentence structure, an ability to form a complex answer to a question and to attempt to support that answer with relevant arguments. Raters gave this essay three 3s and one 2. But there are curious confusions and inconsistencies, particularly about his arguments concerning the validity of the bases on which to assign a "seriousness" rating to the crime of smoking marijuana. In a highly confusing second paragraph, he seems to equate the "personal" view of marijuana with the moral basis of making the decision, but then argues that its use is purely personal in order to justify its reduction in penalties. If he can catch this inconsistency and clear it up, he is a Stage 3 student. If not, he is a Stage 2 student.

Determining how introspective he is, how far along in his development of the revising prcess he is, requires that we ask him about his paper, most preferably in tutorial. After he reads the paper out loud to familiarize himself with the content (and for you to see if he catches and corrects the very awkward constructions in the second paragraph), suppose the following dialogue occurs:

Teacher: Glad to see you caught that phrase in the second paragraph: "to more dangerous, physically and socially, narcotic drugs."

Student: Yeah. That was terrible. But I was really rushed.

T: That is the problem with essay tests. Your hurriedness may have led you into some larger difficulties, too. What would you rewrite in this essay if you could? Or is everything all right?

S: Well, I felt that the sentence at the end of the third paragraph was weak.

T: How?

S: Seems I got off the subject of whether there'd be more users into the whole thing about whether there'd be records of penalties.

T: I thought that was irrelevant, too. What would you do?

S: Uh. I think I'd just take it out, 'cause if there're reduced penalties, records wouldn't matter much.

T: All right. Anything else?

S: Not really.

T: O.K. One paragraph that really bothered me was the second one. What's that one about?

S: Well. (Pause) It compares the old method of assigning how serious a crime is to what the new method is, or the most logical method is.

T: And what's the old method?

S: Well, that's the method in which an individual merely regards something as physically or morally wrong. And . . .

T: Yeah. But later on in the paragraph you talk about people, which is plural, who attempt to govern the actions of others because, as you imply above, they see that marijuana smoking leads to harder drugs.

S: Oh.

T: Let me draw a map here to show you where the inconsistencies are.

In this dialogue, the teacher discovers that, though the student can pick out some obvious irrelevancies, he cannot see how mangled the argument in the second paragraph is. By beginning to draw him a map, to show him his classifications overlapped and became confused, the teacher does two things: she sharpens his perceptions about how a good reader reads and reasons and she sharpens his formulation of his meaning. The subsequent assignment will be to rewrite the second paragraph, perhaps expanding it to two, in order to build his argument upon a more solid base. This revision will not clear up all the problems in the essay, but it will efficently use both the teacher's and the student's time. In the next interview, she can check whether he really did understand her objections, and she can probe into the problems of the third paragraph. The solutions to these problems ought to be arrived at much earlier than for the second.

The necessity to ask instead of to guess, to teach good writing rather than to expect good writing, implies the need to provide students with more high-quality time with the instructor and with each other. It implies more time spent in workshop sessions and tutorials and less time spent in lecture settings, more time spent interacting with students and less time interacting with red pencils, more effort spent in teaching students to help each other and less effort preparing talks on the semicolon. Finally, more attention should be given to understanding our own and others' writing processes and to reading about research and theory in composition. In this way, the composition instructor acts the role of the professional rather than the role of the Mad Hatter.

D. G. KEHL

Composition in the Mimetic Mode:
Imitatio and *Exercitatio*

In *Zen and the Art of Motorcycle Maintenance*, Robert M. Pirsig describes the experience of teaching freshman composition: "What you're supposed to do in most freshman-rhetoric courses is to read a little essay or short story, discuss how the writer has done certain little things to achieve certain little effects, and then have the students write an imitative little essay or short story to see if they can do the same little things. He tried this over and over again but it never jelled. The students seldom achieved anything, as a result of this calculated mimicry, that was remotely close to the models he'd given them."[1] The reasons why imitation as a method of teaching writing did not seem to work for Phaedrus at Bozeman are perhaps as many and varied as the reasons a multiplicity of other methods may not work—whether at Missoula, at Iowa City, or at Princeton.

Generally, the rationale for use of readers, anthologies of essays, stories, and sometimes poetry, in teaching writing seems to be two-fold: (1) examples of "inspiring," "stimulating," "provocative" writing will stir young minds to discuss and write about the ideas presented, and (2) reading and discussing well-written pieces will produce effective writers—somewhat in the manner of osmosis. All too often both the composition teacher and his students resemble the frustrated Romantic in C. S. Lewis' *Pilgrim's Regress*, at a loss over what to *do* with the grass and trees: there are George Orwell and Francis Bacon and Sam Clemens and E. B. White and Huxley and Hazlitt and Thurber and Thoreau—but what do I *do* with them?

No attention is given to imitation in most rhetoric texts and only scant attention in just a few. As for readers, the essays most often seem to have been selected for their thematic, rather than their stylistic, import. The titles of a few readers suggest the intent of conscious imitation of exemplary models: *Models for Writing* by Hogins and Yarber (SRA), *Models for Thinking and Writing* by Taylor (World), *Prose Models* by Levin (Harcourt), *Models for Composition* and *Models for Composition 2* both by Glatthorn and Fleming (Harcourt). In their preface to *Models for Composition*, the editors write: "One effective way to teach a student to write is to present him with models of good writing and invite him to emulate them. In choosing this approach the authors affirm their belief that techniques of the craft of writing can be observed and, with proper guidance and analysis, mastered."[2] The same editors write that their sequel anthology is "dedicated to the principle that a student can learn to write through careful analysis and emulation of models of widely acknowledged excellence."[3]

The idea of learning to write by imitation of admirable authors is not new. Quintilian, the first-century Roman rhetorician, wrote: "There can be no doubt that in art no small portion of our task lies in imitation, since, although invention came first and is all-important, it is expedient to imitate whatever has been invented with success. And it is a universal rule of life that we should wish to copy what we approve in others."[4] Similarly, Goethe wrote in 1827, "If you see a great master you will always find that he has used what was good in his predecessors, and that it was this which made him great."[5] But perhaps no one has offered more clearly than Ben Jonson the formula for writers: given *Ingenium* (natural wit), what remains is *Lectio* (reading), *Imitatio* (imitation), and *Exercitatio* (hard work, practice). The writer, according to Jonson, must "be able to convert the substance, or Riches of another Poet, to his own use. To make choice of one excellent man above the rest, and so to follow him, till he grow very *He*: or, so like him, as the Copy may be mistaken for the Principal. Not as a Creature that swallows but what it takes in, crude, raw, or undigested; but that feeds with an Appetite, and hath a stomach to concoct, divide, and turn all into nourishment. Not to imitate servilely, as Horace saith, and catch at Vices for Virtue; but to draw forth out of the best and choicest flowers with the Bee, and turn all into Honey, work it into one relish, and savour: make our Imitation sweet: observe how the best writers have imitated, and follow them."[6]

The teaching of composition has long stressed two parts of Jonson's formula: *Lectio*—wide reading of a variety of materials and styles—and *Exercitatio*—practice in writing. But omission or neglect of the middle process—*Imitatio*—often leaves the student, and sometimes the teacher, confused about the relation between what is read for Monday and Wednesday and what is written for Friday's theme. All too often in the teaching of composition there is this missing connection. Many composition teachers seem to think that if students read effective writing and perhaps spend fifty minutes discussing its content, they should be able to write better on the next theme. But somewhere between the act of reading the anthology and the act of writing the theme there must come not only the observance of effective use of rhetorical strategies in achieving particular effects but also the practical application to one's own writing. This application can be aided by *Imitatio*, the process by which the student-writer seeks to emulate effective strategies of style to achieve his own purposes.

Accomplished writers have credited *Imitatio* as a means of their learning to write. Robert Louis Stevenson, one of the master stylists in English literature, wrote: "Whenever I read a book or a passage that particularly pleased me, in which a thing was said or an effect rendered with propriety, in which there was either some conspicuous force or some happy distinction in the style, I must sit down at once and set myself to ape that quality. . . . I got some practice in rhythm, in harmony, in construction, and the coordination of parts. . . . I have thus played the sedulous ape to Hazlitt, to Lamb, to Wordsworth, to Sir Thomas Browne, to Defoe, to Hawthorne, to Montaigne, to Baudelaire, and to Ober-mann." "Like it or not," he concluded, "that is the way to learn to write. . . . It was so, if we could trace it out, that all men have learned. . . . Perhaps I hear some one cry out: But this is not the way to be original! It is not, nor is there any way but to be born so. Nor yet, if you are born original, is there anything in this training that shall clip the wings of your originality. . . . Before he can tell what cadences he truly prefers, the student should have tried all that are possible; before he can choose and preserve a fitting key of words, he should long have practiced the literary scales."[7]

Ben Franklin remarked in his *Autobiography* how he admired and imitated *The Spectator* of Addison and Steele: "I . . . read it over and over, and was much delighted with it. I thought the writing excellent and wished if possible to imitate it. With that view, I took some of the papers, and making short hints of the sentiment in each sentence, laid them by a few days, and then without looking at the book, tried to complete the papers again by expressing each sentiment at length and as fully as it had been expressed before, in any suitable words that should occur to me. Then I compared my *Spectator* with the original, discovered some of my faults, and corrected them."[8] Addison, the imitated, was also imitator, as he wrote in *The Guardian* (September 4, 1713): "In imitating great authors, I have always excelled myself."

To what extent does one learn to write as one learns to speak—by imitation—and how practicable is the method in teaching freshmen? Opinions vary among contemporary writers. Stuart Chase has called the method "danger-ous," saying, "It never did me any good."[9] Similarly, Herbert Gold considers it a "poor method" but "a good way to learn typing."[10] The consensus, nonethe-less, seems to be a guarded approval. Poet and teacher Howard Nemerov has said, "So far as I learned to write at all, it was first by becoming enchanted with literature, by hero-worship, by imitation, by inventing my own five-finger exercises, later by the criticisms offered by my teachers—and perhaps even more—the criticism offered (on a reciprocal basis, to be sure) by friends of my own age who were also engaged in the project of learning to write."[11] Especially significant in Nemerov's statement are the implicit references to Jonson's quaternia: natural intelligence, interested reading and sensitivity to rhetorical strategies, imitation and disciplined practice. Lacking any of the four, the method will fail, as it did for Phaedrus in Pirsig's work.

Perceptive analysis is essential in *Imitatio*. The late Joseph Wood Krutch noted, for example, that although imitation is "perhaps the most important method" of learning to write, "the teacher should analyze the specific faults committed by the student. He should also help him to realize that he must have something to say. Muddled thinking is as important as anything else as a cause of muddled writing."[12] It is necessary, as Jonson said, to "digest," to "concoct, divide, and turn all into nourishment," that is, to analyze the particular strengths of the model as well as the weaknesses of one's own writing, to observe the effects achieved by the model and be certain the adopted strategies fit the intended purpose. The interrelatedness of Johnson's four concepts is further suggested by Eudora Welty's view of *Imitatio* as "an extended form of reading,"[13] *Lectio*.

Imitatio as a method is admittedly fraught with dangers. A Burmese proverb says that "sparrows who emulate peacocks are likely to break a thigh," and a Japanese proverb says, "The crow that imitates a cormorant gets drowned." The lesson is clear: "models" should be congenial to the students; perhaps, at least initially, the sparrow might emulate an effective sparrow, the crow a proficient crow. The poet and teacher X. J. Kennedy has said that *Imitatio* is "the method by which most pros learn. But it is essential that the would-be writer do his own choosing of those admirable authors who meaningfully speak to him. That is: as teachers, we do the would-be writer little good to impose models upon him. But we can, of course, acquaint him with all the good writers we can, that he may choose among them for himself."[14] Similarly, the late Lionel Trilling said, "I am all for it [*Imitatio* as a method of teaching writing] if it is done out of natural impulse, because the young writer admires the established author he is imitating."[15]

The reference to "natural impulse" suggests another controversial question related to *Imitatio*: assuming that it has value for the young writer, should it be conscious and deliberate or unconscious and inadvertent? Allen Tate has said, "We all begin by imitating an older writer; but this is of little value if, like Stevenson, we go about it deliberately."[16] "Imitation often happens inadvertently," Wallace Stegner says; "I have never myself tried to use it as a conscious method."[17] Similarly, Richard Wilbur says, "Unconscious imitation of a great number of writers at once is the best way to grow, I should think."[18] Lewis Mumford essentially agrees: "Conscious parodies are useful, because they exaggerate the vices of a style; but *conscious* imitation should be avoided."[19] On the other hand, Leslie Fiedler says, "All young writers imitate somebody. The point is to be conscious of what you are doing."[20] Perhaps it is valid to say that all beginning writers inadvertently imitate, in varying degrees, other writers they admire. But even inadvertent imitation requires that the writer be cognizant of his purpose and the effects to be achieved by particular stylistic strategies.

It is important to recognize that conscious, deliberate imitation will work for some students, but not for all. Poet and teacher Donald Hall has said: "Imitation works for some students. I would always assign it in a course, not because it will benefit every student, but because it will benefit some of them."[21] For that matter, it is highly unlikely that any single method of teaching writing will be equally beneficial for every student.

Another danger of *Imitatio* as a pedagogical method lies in staying too long with a single author. Lewis Mumford has said, "No young writer can avoid imitating the authors he likes; the only thing to be guarded against is staying too long with a single author or choosing an inferior one" (letter). Similarly, Richard Wilbur has said, "I think it bad to imitate *one* writer only, because nothing should be purely an exercise, and one should be developing one's own voice" (letter). Staying too long with a single author, choosing an inferior author, engaging in servile, slavish imitation—these can be detrimental to one's own style, causing one to pick up stylistic mannerisms unsuited to one's particular temperament or purpose—as Stevenson perhaps did.

Imitatio should not—and need not—become onerous, cumbrous, con-straining. It is true, as Eudora Welty has said, that although imitation is "a good exercise," it "can't put original thought onto paper, which is what real writing is" (letter). At the same time, it is true, as Voltaire is reported to have said, that "imitation, when good, is the most perfect originality." There is considerable difference between imitating and *counterfeiting*, copying to deceive; between imitating and merely *stimulating*, feigning a surface similarity; between imitat-ing and *aping*, slavishly and mechanically duplicating; between creatively imitating and merely *parroting*.

Sometimes imitation takes the form of inversion. "To do exactly the opposite," Lichtenberg wrote, "is also a form of imitation."[22] In any event, true *Imitatio* need not squelch originality. Coleridge wrote that "to admire on principle [perhaps *rhetorical* principle also?] is the only way to imitate without loss of originality."[23]

For *Imitatio* to succeed, the would-be writer must make full use of the other three Jonsonian concepts: *Ingenium, Lectio,* and especially *Exercitatio.* "For a man to write well," Jonson says elsewhere in *Timber: or Discoveries,* "there are required three necessaries: to read the best authors, observe the best speakers, and much exercise of his own style."[24] Writers (and/or the teacher) must invent their own five-finger exercises. One approach is to ask students to select a work (or author) which they especially admire, attempt to decide specifically why they admire it, and then seek to emulate some of its strategies to achieve suitable purposes of their own.

Perhaps the most logical and successful movement is from general to specific, beginning with imitation of a whole piece—for example, its tone, its voice, its point of view. As a preliminary assignment in *Imitatio* and *Exercitatio,* parody works well (for example, an essay parodying the tone, point of view, and voice of Swift's "A Modest Proposal" or "An Argument Against Abolishing Christianity" or Philip Wylie's "Science Has Spoiled My Supper"). Subsequent exercises might include an essay imitating the structural patterns or mode of discourse of the model. (A process-analysis essay which works well for this purpose is "How to Iron a Telephone Book," by Fred Dickenson, *The New Yorker*, January 17, 1959, pp. 247 ff.)

After some reading, analysis, and discussion—for example using the late Francis Christensen's generative rhetoric of the paragraph and the sentence,[25] students might imitate the texture, the levels of generality, of particular paragraphs. One beneficial exercise is to analyze several different paragraphs on the same subject (such as a description of waking up "the morning after the night before"; for example, paragraph one of chapter 6, Kingsley Amis' *Lucky Jim* [N.Y.: Viking, 1953], and Peter DeVries' descripion of the same experience in chapter 18 of *Let Me Count the Ways* [N.Y.: Bantam, 1965]—and then write a paragraph imitative but uniquely suited to its own purpose.

Perhaps the rhetoric of the sentence lends itself even more readily to beneficial imitation. As Donald Davidson pointed out, "Imitation of sentence patterns is a useful means of getting experience in writing sentences that have an effective design. It has exactly the same purpose that the copying of a master's work may have for an art student. From doing, or trying to do, what the master does, the student learns what good work is. Imitation is a means of acquiring skill; it is the way in which we naturally learn a great many things, from infancy on into later life."[26] Again, after wide reading, analysis, and discussion of effective use of rhetorical strategies, such as the periodic sentence, the cumulative sentence, parallel construction, structural-strategic patterns in a variety of selections (for example, Bacon's "Of Studies," stories by Hemingway, etc.), the would-be writer might beneficially imitate effective sentence types and patterns. For example, in Walter Van Tilburg Clark's story "Hook," a periodic sentence effectively describing two hawks battling in mid-air— "Talons locked, beaks raking, they dived earthward"—elicited this student imitation: "Engines roaring, gears shifting, they raced down the dragway." A richly textured cumulative sentence used in Clark's story to describe the mating of hawks can be analyzed according to the generative rhetoric of the sentence:

    2 On a hilltop projection of stone two miles inland,
1 he struck her down,
    2 gripping her rustling body with his talons,
    2 beating her wings down with his wings,
    2 belting her head when she whimpered or thrashed,
    2 and at last clutching her neck with his hook/
1 /and/ succeeded.
    2 /when her coy struggles had given way to stillness/

Such analysis then produced the following student imitation:

    2 At the forty yard line
  1 Grabowski snared the pass,
    2 jumping high in the air between two defenders,
    2 stiff-arming another,
    2 cutting sharply outside,
    2 breaking two tackles at the thirty-five yard line/
  1 and/scored.
    2 /after outdistancing the last pursuer by ten yards/

Another possibility is imitation of sentence models—whether examples by professional writers or for-the-nonce examples or even numbered patterns—by adding subordinate and coordinate levels of generality. Such an exercise produced the following student sentences:

  1 The rattlesnake slithered from beneath the leaves,
    2 moving forward,
      3 its vertebrae gliding gently over rough stones,
        4 its tail vibrating,
          5 only the tip held high.
  1 They drove wrecklessly [sic]
    2 Cotton at the wheel with a profound mission,
      3 his red hair flying wildly,
      3 his hands clutching the wheel,
    2 his passengers in the back,
      3 braced and frightened,
      3 wondering where it all would end and hoping it
        would be soon.
  1 They laughed at her mercilessly,
    2 Tony with gleaming eyes that sparkled through
      tears,
      3 his face reddening,
      3 amusing himself at her distress,
    2 his brother dry-eyed,
      3 chuckling more and more maliciously at her every
        attempt to rectify the blunder.
  1 My parents interrogated me,
    2 Dad with his nasty temper,
      3 his face red,
      3 his eyes piercing,
    2 Mom with her accusing stare,
      3 obviously hurt to find me so immoral.
  1 She's lying on the bed,
    2 paws flopped carelessly,

2 tail slowly twitching,
3 beating an imatient rhythm,
3 reminder that a cat has no master.

Another beneficial exercise asks students to imitate the succinctness, the rhthym, the sensory imagery, the syntax of a short poem, such as Ezra Pound's "In a Station of the Metro," William Carlos Williams's "The Red Wheelbarrow" (or "This Is Just to Say"), Robert Herrick's "Upon Julia's Clothes," Theodore Roethke's "My Papa's Waltz," or Carl Sandburg's "Fog." Initially, students can be asked to make just a slight change in the poem—a word, a phrase, an image, a line—then to make others, and finally to write a similar but different poem. They might be asked to write an imitation of Whitman's "The Dalliance of the Eagles," substituting "lions," D. H. Lawrence's "The White Horse," substituting "white Porsche," X. J. Kennedy's "Nude Descending a Staircase," substituting "nerd" or "jock," Marianne Moore's "The Wood-Weasel," substituting "gerbil," Sandburg's "Jazz Fantasia," substituting "Rock Fantasia." Or, as Nancy R. Comley and Robert Scholes have suggested in their essay "Literature, Composition, and the Structure of English,"[27] students would profit from imitating E. A. Robinson's "Richard Cory," assuming a townsperson's point of view and voice, or Gwendolyn Brooks's "We Real Cool," assuming the role of one of the pool players at the Golden Shovel twenty years later. Such emulation exercises are almost limitless; each teacher and student must design his or her own.

Whether or not a student-writer can imitate successfully is perhaps to some extent an individual matter. But most assuredly, a famliarity with diversified styles, an awareness of varied effects which can be achieved, and an appreciation of stylistic artistry can enhance one's own writing. The key to effective writing is to understand which words, which rhetorical strategies, work, and when, and for what. Given a measure of *Ingenium,* the process of *Lectio, Imitatio,* and *Exercitatio* will help in achieving this end. But why then did *Imitatio* never seem to "jell" for Phaedrus and his freshmen at Bozeman? Perhaps it was because of any one or more of the dangers discussed above, or perhaps because one or more of Jonson's concepts were deficient or lacking. But perhaps Jonson himself, in his discussion of *Exercitatio,* provides the most suitable response to Phaedrus and his freshmen: "If his wit will not arrive suddenly at the dignity of the Ancients, let him not fall out with it, quarrel, or be overhastily angry, offer to turn it away from Study, in a humour; but come to it again upon better Cogitation; try another time, with labour. If then it succeed not, cast not away the Quills yet, nor scratch the Wainscot, beat not the poor Desk; but bring all to the forge, and file again; turn it anew."[28]

JAMES L. KINNEAVY

The Relation of the Whole to the Part in Interpretation Theory and in the Composing Process

If I were a committee, this study would be labeled a "progress report." Indeed, it is an example, if not a model, of "exploratory discourse." For it presents an important problem and an ongoing attempt to arrive at a solution. There is a hypothesis, but not yet a thesis.

The hypothesis has a very practical origin. It is concerned with the failure of our attempts to integrate several "parts" of the composition to the whole. There are seventy years of research which demonstrate overwhelmingly that the isolated teaching of grammatical skills has little or no transfer to use in actual composition.[1] There are parellel studies in library science which demonstrate that library skills taught in isolation also fail to transfer to real situations.[2] There are similar studies in mathematics education which demonstrate that a curriculum which is too oriented to the teaching of mere computational skills produces fewer problem-solvers than a curriculum which forces students to use computational skills in verbal and more abstract settings.[3] I suspect that the same can be said of the insulated teaching of logical skills.

My question about all of these skill operations is the same: "What catalytic agent enables the student to see the relevance of skill exercises to actual writing situations?" I can sympathize with those who, in the present literacy crisis, fault us with neglecting these skills. Students do need vocabulary development, sentence maturity, paragraph instruction, introduction to library techniques, etc. Yet I know that isolating the skills and teaching the skills to the neglect of the act of writing is almost certainly a waste of time—as much of this research tells us.

On the other hand, there is much evidence that beginning with the whole and moving only incidentally to the parts (mechanical skills of punctuation, spelling, sentence skills, paragraph skills) does not seem to be entirely successful either. At the University of Texas, where I teach, there has been a rhetorically based program for years, with emphasis on writing eight or nine fairly long themes a semester. For quite some time there was not even a handbook for grammar and usage employed. Yet several tests recently have convinced us that these skills were being ignored, that the whole does not necessarily take care of these kinds of parts. Our experience is not at all unqiue.

We need the parts and we need the whole. Beginning with the skills, the parts, and moving to the whole does not seem to work. Beginning with the whole and moving only incidentally to the parts seems to be not entirely successful either. Is there a way out of the dilemma?

I had, in earlier work, been concerned with the relationships of part to whole, but had not found a satisfactory model for explanation of the composing process. However, I now believe that the treatment of whole and part in interpretation theory seems more promising than the model of Piaget which I had used in handling the nature of description, or the model of mereology of Lesniewski, which I had tried and rejected in the same circumstances, but for different reasons.[4]

The treatment of the whole-part relationship in interpretation theory is embodied in the notion of what is usually called the hermeneutic circle. One writer succinctly explains the circle as follows:

> We understand the meaning of an individual word by seeing it in response to the whole of the sentence; and reciprocally, the sentence's meaning as a whole is dependent on the meaning of individual words. By extension, an individual concept derives its meaning from a context or horizon within which it stands; yet the horizon is made up of the very elements to which it gives meaning. By dialectical interaction between the whole and the part, each gives the other meaning; understanding is circular, then. Because within this "circle" the meaning comes to stand, we call this the "hermeneutical circle."[5]

By rhetorical, if not poetic, justice, the hermeneutic circle had its origins in rhetorical theory, particularly in the organic metaphor of the head and limbs of Plato's *Phaedrus*. Gadamer tells us that Luther and his successors

> applied this image, familiar from classical rhetoric, to the process of understanding and developed the universal principle of textual interpretation that all of the details of a text are to be understood from that contextus (context) and from the scopus, the unified sense at which the whole aims.[6]

Others go even further back in their search for the origins of the hermeneutic circle and find it in Heraclitus, Parmenides, Socrates, Plato, Aristotle, Cicero, Quintilian, Celsus (the jurist), and later in Hegel, Fichte, and Schelling. It crystallized in Frederick Ast, was developed by Schleiermacher and Dilthey, and was expanded to include all understanding by Heidegger.[7]

This notion of interpretation or understanding is obviously the inverse of rhetoric, as Schleiermacher remarked.[8] In fact, the processes of producing or composing a text and of interpreting it are very similar, a similarity to which some have called attention.[9]

Both involve the act of interpretation. The writer interprets the world to the reader by means of a text; the reader interprets the text of the writer in order to interpret the world. The world, the text, and the act of interpretation are all involved in both activities, though in the reverse order.

It is not therefore surprising that, as Gadamer has pointed out, Melanchthon set out to write a rhetorical treatise on the *commonplaces* (a rhetorical term) of Christian doctrine but ended up writing a treatise on how to interpret the Scriptures.[10] It seems only proper, then, that the hermeneutic circle, having originated in rhetoric and having subsequently been enriched in interpretation theory, now returns, like Joseph from Egypt, back to the promised land to help the homefolk.

One of the most important tenets of the circle creed seems particularly promising for composition theory. There is a strong concern for the continually changing relation between whole and part,[11] the relative notion of what is whole and what is part,[12] the dialectic that continually functions between whole and part,[13] and the reciprocal interdependence of each on the other.[14]

Now I believe that this model of the composing process is consistent with what we know about the habits of professional writers as well as students. Indeed, while reading about the dialectic of the hermeneutic circle, I was continually reminded of passage after passage in the *Writers at Work* series of interviews of professional writers by the *Paris Review*. The interviews focused specifically on the working habits of composition. The changing notions of part and whole, the taking over of a plot by a character who was initially a minor personality, the additions and deletions of small and large segments, the provisional writing and rewriting in order to achieve an elusive whole, etc., all seemed to me to be accurate instances of the hermeneutic dialectic.[15]

One way of looking at the part-whole relationship is to distinguish among levels. Linguists, rhetoricians, structuralists, and interpretation theorists are among those who have successfully used this technique. Thus, linguists often view the sentence as the whole and the lower-level components as parts. On the other hand, the sentence, as such, is not a major concern with many literary critics. Thus, what is a whole at one level of analysis or production may be viewed as a part at another level, and the relationship of a part to a whole at one level may be completely different from the relationship of the same part to a whole at another level.

As has already been pointed out, level differences are not new to language theory, either in rhetoric or in interpretation. Much existing work has been done at different levels by modern scholars. Part of this success has been brought about by applying the same model to different layers and analyzing for similar component relationships. In rhetoric I think immediately of the success of the tagmemic particle-wave-field model, which Pike and others apply very successfully at the phonemic level, at the morphemic level, at the paragraph level, at the utterance level, and at the full conversational and behavioral levels.[16] I have tried to do the same with the semiotic structure of "component-reference-use" at different levels of interpretation and composition.

In some respects, both models work effectively at different levels. But we are also learning, that, in important respects, the levels are not symmetrical. E. D. Hirsch, Jr., quoting Bazell, has insisted on this and has suggested that the more we move into the larger rhetorical patterns of composition, the more asymmetrical the levels become.[17]

Although there is some evidence to support this position, more investigation must still be made at many of the levels and comparisons among the levels have also to be made. In an attempt to compare (and contrast) some emphases at quite different levels, I have assembled the following chart. Emphases in composing theory are represented on the left-hand side of the page and emphases in interpretation theory are given on the right-hand side of the page. These names or movements are only intended to be suggestive, not at all to be exhaustive.

It is, however, a curious fact (for which I have no adequate explanation), that theories of producing and theories of interpreting emphasize quite different aspects of the two processes. For this reason, it will be necessary to switch back and forth between the productive and the interpretive processes, given the scholarly emphases.

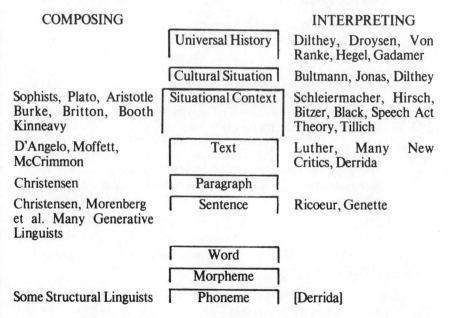

Fig. 1. Persons and movements emphasizing different levels

At the lowest level of the chart, it is possible to find some who have viewed the structure of the phoneme as the microstructure which can be used as the model of all higher level analyses. The success of de Saussure at the phonological level has indeed left a distinct impression on much subsequent study, particularly with structuralists and poststructuralists in France. Thus Derrida, in *Of Grammatology*, says:

> Linguistics thus wishes to be the science of language. . . . Let us first simply consider that the scientificity of that science is often acknowledged because of its *phonological* foundations. Phonology, it is often said today, communicates its scientificity to linguistics, which in turn serves as the epistemological model for all of the sciences of man. [18]

Lévi-Strauss has, on the other hand, warned of the dangers of a simplistic analysis of all levels of culture in terms of phonemic and distinctive features. [19] As will be pointed out later, he categorically rejects the notion that the myth is made up only of linguistic structures. However, he cannot resist comparisons. Having suggested that the myth is the sum of all of the individual variants of a myth (a criterion beyond the individual text, therefore), he concludes, "To put it in even more linguistic terms, it is as though a phoneme were always made up of all its variants." [20]

Sentence Emphases

However, it is the work of Lévi-Strauss himself using the sentence as a basis for analyzing myths that has attracted much of the attention of the structural and poststructural French thought in this connection. Paul Ricoeur, a contemporary hermeneutic theorist, is impressed with the centrality of the sentence. Writing in 1969, he states:

> The question is to know if all the levels are homologous. All of my investigations will rest on the idea that the passage to a new unity of discourse, constituted by the sentence or the utterance, represents a cut, a mutation, in the hierarchy of levels. I will not, moreover, exhaust the question of levels. I will even glimpse at possibly other strategic levels such as the text, the internal coherence of which calls for a different sort of intelligibility than the sentence or than the word in its position in the sentence. [21]

It is at the level of the text that the hermeneut usually operates, he maintains. [22]

However, writing a year later, he returns to the centrality of the sentence. Despite the fact that the written text is not *langue* but *parole,* he says, using the terminology of de Saussure,

> the specificity of writing with regard to effective *parole* rests on traits susceptible of being treated as analogous to *langue* in discourse. This hypothesis of work is perfectly legitimate; it consists in saying that under certain conditions the

large unities of *langue*, that is to say the unities of a degree superior to the
sentence, offer organizations comparable to those of small unities of language,
that is to say those of a degree inferior to the sentence, those precisely which are
the *result* of linguistics.[23]

He cites the analysis of the Oedipus myth by Lévi-Strauss as an example of such
a procedure and adds that Roland Barthes and A. J. Greimas follow the same
technique. He summarizes:

> One finds in these authors the same postulates as in Lévi-Strauss. The unities
> above the sentence have the same composition as the unities below the sentence.
>   For the cluster of relations of which Lévi-Strauss carries back the
> mytheme is again of the order of the sentence and the play of oppositions which
> are located at the very abstract level of the mytheme is still of the order of the
> sentence and of meaning.[24]

The reason he gives for this is that the relations between the components of the
myth (and other sociological relations, such as those of blood relationships) can
be expressed in "the form of the sentence." [25] This is a strange argument, the
validity of which I shall return to later after looking at the other analyst who is
often credited with finding in the sentence the structural model for higher level
analyses.

Beginning his analysis of narration in "Discours du récit," Gérard
Genette poses the foundation of his analysis as follows:

> Since every narrative . . . is a linguistic production assuming the relation of one
> or of several events, it is perhaps legitimate to treat it, as monstrous as this may
> seem, as the development given to a *verbal* form, in the grammatical sense of the
> term, the expansion of a verb. *I walk, Peter has come* are for me the minimal
> forms of the narrative, and inversely the *Odyssey* and the *Remembrance [of
> Things Past]* do nothing more than amplify (in a rhetorical sense) statements
> such as *Ulysses returns to Ithaca* or *Marcel becomes a writer*. This authorizes
> us, perhaps, to organize, or at least to formulate, the problems of analysis of
> narrative discourse according to categories borrowed from the grammar of the
> verb, and which here can be reduced to three fundamental classes.[26]

He then calls his three classes those of time (tense), mood, and voice, terms
borrowed, he says, from grammar. He concludes the long paragraph by repeating: "Once again it must be said that there is here only a borrowing of terms, but
that there is no pretense to a rigorous homology."[27]

His *time* has to do with the order of events, the duration of events, and
the frequency of events. His *moods* concern, he says, problems of distance
which American critics of the Jamesian tradition generally treat in terms of the
opposition between showing and telling. The third category of *voice* treats
problems of first and third person narration and their interrelationships.[28]

There is, therefore, something of a grammatical framework of analysis erected by Genette for his lengthy investigation of narrative structures. None-theless in his analysis of the order of events there is no recourse to technical issues of tense at all. Nor is there any attempt to reduce structures to the order of the sentence. His typical microanalyses of short passages from the *Odyssey* and *Jean Santeuil* use, for example, five sentences which are not equivalent to the five events being analyzed, then three sentences embodying nine events but with only two temporal units involved, and then a passage of fourteen sentences embodying fifteen events but only seven temporal units. The macroanalysis of the *Remembrance* uses ten segments for the entire novel, a few comprising only a page or so of text and several comprising hundreds of pages.[29]

In fact the structures he finds within these micro- and macrostructures are not patterned like sentences at all, nor do they reflect any tense design either. The same may be said of his mood and voice analyses. Consequently, though Genette begins with a framework that seems analogous to one drawn from grammar, the superstructures he discovers are not grammatically homologous at all.

The same must be said of the myth structures of Lévi-Strauss. It is true that he plasters his walls with single sentences drawn from the many versions of a myth. He then arranges, deranges, and rearranges these sentences in clusters to arrive at the structure of the myth, the clusters being certain repeated thematic patterns. Relating this work to linguistic structures, he says,

> To sum up the discussion at this point, we have so far made the following claims:
> (1) If there is a meaning to be found in mythology, it cannot reside in the isolated elements which enter into the composition of a myth, but only in the way in which these elements are combined. (2) Although myth belongs to the same category as language, being, as a matter of fact, only a part of it, language in myth exhibits specific properties. (3) Those properties are only to be found *above* the ordinary linguistic level, that it, they exhibit more complex features than those which are to be found in any other kind of linguistic expression.[30]

The basic constituent units of myths he calls mythemes, and he uses sentences to serve as the mythemes with which he builds his mythic structures. However, these isolated units do not constitute the myth.

> From this springs a new hypothesis, which constitutes the very core of our argument: The true constituent units of a myth are not the isolated relations but bundles of such relations, and it is only as bundles that these relations can be put to use and combined so as to produce a meaning.[31]

Indeed the final formula for myth which he gives in "The Structural Study of Myth" has no grammatical or sentence parallel at all. Therefore it is difficult to see that either Genette or Lévi-Strauss has postulated a sentence structure for the study of discourse. In fact, Ricoeur's argument that myths and blood relations have sentence structures because they can be written about in sentences would make all structures in all disciplines sentential. And the argument that because Lévi-Strauss starts with sentences as mythemes, the large structure is sentential is also fallacious. One could also argue that the cathedral at Rheims has the architectural structure of a molecule of stone because it is made of stone.

In one sense the most unabashed sentence emphasis in the analysis of language has been that of many of the speech-art theorists. The work of Austin and Searle exemplifies this emphasis. Searle is very aware of this stress. He is also aware of the objection that might be made to such a technique. He says,

> It still might seem that my approach is simply, in Saussurian terms, a study of "parole" rather than "langue." I am arguing, however, that an adequate study of speech acts is a study of *langue*.
>
> There are, therefore, not two irreducibly distinct semantic studies, one a study of the meanings of sentences and one a study of the performances of speech acts. For just as it is a part of our notion of the meaning of a sentence that a literal utterance of that sentence with that meaning in a certain context would be performance of a particular speech act, so it is a part of our notion of a speech act that there is a possible sentence (or sentences) the utterance of which in a certain context would in virtue of its (or their) meaning constitute a performance of that speech act.
>
> Therefore, it is in principle possible for every speech act one performs or could perform to be uniquely determined by a given sentence (or set of sentences), given the assumption that the speaker is speaking literally and that the context is appropriate.[32]

Searle is attempting to justify his study of discourse (*parole*) to linguists interested in the kind of language analysis which linguists usually make (*langue*). However, his technique is open to objection from the opposite position, that of scholars interested in the full text. From this point of view he might just as well be accused of reducing *parole* to *langue*. And this is what he actually does—analyze a speech act by analyzing an equivalent sentence. For example, Searle's analysis of a *promise* speech act is made by analyzing sentences like "X made a promise."

I really don't know of any evidence that enables an analyst to reduce a whole discourse to a single equivalent sentence, or even a few of them; Searle doesn't even give an example. Actually, Searle ordinarily limits himself to the single sentence. Most discourse analysts would respond that a good deal has been lost when one tries to abstract a discourse in that way. As Paul Valéry has said, "Résumer une thèse, c'est en retenir l'essentiel. Résumer une oeuvre d'art, c'est en perdre l'essentiel."[33]

In literary criticism, such a reductionism was called by one famous critic the heresy of paraphrase. But Searle exempts literary discourse from his analysis—though for different reasons than those which promoted Cleanth Brooks' condemnation of such summarizing.

However, many scientists would not even concede the first half of Valéry's statement. The summary of an elaborate proof is not equivalent at all to the proof. And no logician would grant the position that a given particular proof can be analyzed by analyzing the nature of proof itself. Yet that is what Searle is doing. Such a position ignores the individuality of any given speech act. On this account all proofs are the same, all promises are the same, etc. No one would deny that they have something in common, but they also have something individual.

Searle, however, in the process of analyzing his isolated sentences, finds it necessary to posit "appropriate conditions" in the speech-act situation in order that a promise, a request, a command, etc., be meaningful. A promise, for example, predicates a future act of the speaker, the listener must prefer that future act over its opposite, the act must be one that the speaker would not normally do anyway, the speaker must sincerely intend to do what he promises, and the promise "counts as the undertaking of an obligation to do the act."[34]

In other words, although Searle bypasses text in his analysis, he does not bypass situational context. Indeed, he continually refers to something like a "suitable context," or an appropriate context.[35] Promises, in fact, extend beyond the situational context into the cultural context.[36] This analysis, it might be added, has proven extremely useful. A possible source for this emphasis on the context of situation in the ordinary language philosophers may well have been Malinowski, especially as he was transmitted through Firth. Langendoen remarks in this connection,

> It is interesting to observe that the Oxford philosophers have maintained an outlook on semantics that bears great resemblance to that of Malinowski, Firth, and their linguistic followers, although there does not seem to have been much exchange between these two groups.[37]

Mary Louise Pratt, writing eight years after Searle, recognizes the danger of reducing texts to single sentences. She writes,

> Searle claims that "the characteristic grammatical form of an illocutionary act is the complete sentence" (it can be a one-word sentence) (1969:25), and indeed, speech acts have been discussed mostly in terms of single-sentence utterances. Nevertheless, it is clear that the appropriate conditions for explaining, thanking, or persuading, for example, must at some level of analysis be seen as applying to explanations, thankings, or persuadings that are many sentences long. This is an issue to which few speech act philosophers (and few linguists) have addressed themselves, and to which I shall return in the next chapter.[38]

In the next chapter she continues,

> More broadly, the question is whether and to what extent the terms and catego-
> ries designed to describe language at sentence level can be applied at the level of
> discourse, that is, to utterances of more than a single sentence. (In some cases,
> the real question seems to be whether terms originally developed by sentence
> theory actually belong to discourse theory). These are questions that no one has
> so far answered, and that most linguists and language philosophers lamentably
> tend to avoid by choosing one-sentence examples.[39]

She rejects Ohmann's attempt to get around this difficulty.[40] She herself
uses several full texts and a good number of multi-sentence parts of texts in
attempting to establish more clearly the appropriate conditions of "The Literary
Speech Situation," as the largest and most important chapter of her book is
called. She recognizes that both Searle and Grice were, in effect, working out
the components of the situational contexts for different kinds of utterances.

Speech-act theory, then, early emphasized sentence, bypassed text, and
moved into situational context. In Pratt, at least, there is a respect for sentence,
partial text, full text, and situational context. And occasionally Searle but
especially Grice and Pratt insist on the operation of cultural or institutional
norms in order to understand some kinds of utterances. Thus they range in
emphases from sentence to cultural context.

On the production side of the chart, Bazell has shown convincingly that
the phoneme level is a very different structure from the morpheme level; and
both of these are quite different from the sememe level (roughly the word
level).[41] He does not discuss higher levels in any detail at all except to remark
that each situation is so different that the structure would have to be distinct.[42]
Generative grammar, though not ordinarily considered a part of composition
theory, yet does imply a production technique.

Still on the production side of the chart, I have placed the names of
Christensen, and then those of Morenberg, Daiker, and Kerek. These represent
the scholars who believe that the sentence is the basic structure of the composition as a whole and that to teach the sentence is to teach the theme. I will return
to Christensen later. In the meantime let us turn to the experiment in Miami,
Ohio, by Max Morenberg, Donald Daiker, and Andrew Kerek.

The analogue in classical rhetoric, incidentally, for such a position
would have to be that of the Sophists ridiculed by Plato in the *Phaedrus*. Some
Sophists presumably reduced all persuasion to matters of style, such as figures
of speech and of thought, and structures of prose rhythm. For this reason, some
historians have practically equated the sophistic concept of rhetoric to the
stylistic. Yet this analogue, I shall attempt to show later, is not even fair to the
Sophist more frequently accused of such a position—Gorgias.

Morenberg and his colleagues, however, have proposed a version of the centrality of the structure of the sentence to the structure of the composition as a whole that claims more than the wildest Sophist or stylist ever did in the history of classical rhetoric. Working with twelve classes of about twenty-five students each, Morenberg and his colleagues taught *only sentence-combining* to the six experimental freshman composition classes for a semester. By sentence-combining I mean the joining of several simple sentences together into more involved sentences using phrase or clause embeddings. The control classes read and discussed anthologized essays on current topics, engaged in some grammar work, and studied rhetorical principles. Both groups wrote eight compositions as the term assignments, the first serving as the pretest and the eighth as the posttest.[43]

Variable controls were very rigid, possibly more so than in any other major study in composition research of which I am aware. The pre- and posttests were graded by three different groups operating with different norms. The first grading was by English teachers who simply gave a holistic grade (on a scale of 1 through 6) to the essays. The second grading was by another set of English teachers who gave a final score based on a consideration of six component factors: ideas, supporting details, organization, voice, sentence structure, and diction. This second scoring was called the analytic grade. The third set of graders scored the themes on syntactic maturity only. Syntactic maturity scores are based on the number of words per clause, the number of clauses per thought unit, and the number of words per thought unit; a thought unit is defined as a main clause with all of its modifiers, clausal and nonclausal.

The results obtained after one semester's work were spectacular. The experimental group's scores on all three ratings were significantly greater than the control group's (in some instances in the .001 degree of significance). Despite the fact that the experimental group had read no anthologized essays and had engaged in no reflective discussions on current topics as had the control group, the experimental group scored significantly higher in "ideas," "supporting details," "voice," and "syntactic maturity" than did the control group. Let me quote the authors in their announcement of the most interesting finding:

> The results of the multiple regression indicate that the single best predictor of the holistic score is the quality of a paper's structure. More specifically, the single analytic factor of sentence structure predicts 64.6% of the variance of the holistic rating.[44]

What this means is that the ordinary English teacher, whatever he says he grades for, really seems to grade a theme by the quality of its sentence structure. The other eight factors, it might be remarked, accounted for only 6.7 percent of the variance. All of these findings would seem to support the centrality of the sentence in the composing process.

Now there are some interesting speculations that might be made about these findings. One of them is the ominous suggestion in rhetorical production that the structure of the sentence is central to the essence of the theme itself. This would seem to parallel the structuralist statements of Ricoeur and others.

There are some serious reservations that must be made about this study before such a claim could be made, however. It must be pointed out that the control group did not do nearly so much writing as the experimental group (counting daily sentence-combining as writing). Secondly, maybe English teachers are not the great judges of a theme's values that they are usually assumed to be. Conceivably by quite specific norms, such as, for example, factual and organizational criteria such as are used to judge the usual newsstory in journalism, or the rigid evidence that a scientist might require, or the careful definitions that a logician might demand in a classification paper, these papers might rate as vacuous, illogical, and undefined. Thirdly, another parallel structured writing program with equivalent writing practice might account for comparable results.

One final reservation that must be made about the Miami study, however, is probably the most serious one. Unlike all the other sentence-combining research studies, Morenberg and his colleagues insisted on putting the sentence into a context, often a paragraph or an entire theme. The sentence, therefore, was incorporated into the whole. O'Hare had recommended such a rhetorical incorporation, although he had not carried it out in his work;[45] but Mellon had designedly avoided such an incorporation as had Hunt before him.[46] Consequently, the Miami study represents a combined text and sentence emphasis.

An interesting phenomenon common to all four of the sentence theories of discourse which have just been reviewed is that in each case there was an initial commitment to the sentence and then the gradual working up toward a partial-text, whole-text, or situational-context level in order to make sense of either the production or the interpretation. The sentence combiners began with only isolated sentence combinations in Hunt and Mellon, suggested the desirability of a rhetorical context in O'Hara, and supplied the paragraph or text in the exercises of Strong and the research work of Morenberg and his colleagues. Although Lévi-Strauss begins with sentences, he works through the level of motifs (partial texts) to whole texts and many-text versions of the same myth, all for the purpose, of course, of analyzing the culture of the group under consideration. Genette, beginning below the level of the sentence with the verb, occasionally considers single sentences, but usually works at the level of the part text (the large segments of Proust, for example). Speech-act theory has followed a similar progression. Searle and Grice, attempting to account for individual sentence meanings, have ended up positing appropriate conditions in the situational context. And Pratt, the most recent theorist in the speech-act tradition, is really much more concerned to delineate the conditions of the literary speech-act situation than she is to analyze individual sentences. In addition, she also investigates full and partial texts.

Some sentence patterns, in particular those of Francis Christensen, have been imposed on the paragraph with some success. However, Alton Becker, taking a tagmemic approach, criticizes Christensen for this imposition.

> I think Rodgers is right when he criticizes Christensen (and, indirectly, Josephine Miles, and, I might add, a number of "generative" linguists) for seeing the paragraph as a "macro-sentence or meta-sentence."[47]

Rodgers, in fact, accuses Becker of precisely the same illicit procedure.[48] It certainly does seem true that not all paragraphs can be analyzed by the structures of the Christensen sentence (indeed, he never claimed that they could). It is also obvious that other than presently known sentence norms are necessary to account for certain literary paragraphs (i.e., stanzas) or expressive paragraphs. In fact Christensen's basic structure seems to be a classificatory one, ill suited to other than classification kinds of paragraphs.[49]

It is interesting to note that the Christensen formula was not applied to the entire theme in the Nebraska Curriculum Demonstration Center materials, although I have heard that the attempt was made. However, there are those who maintain that a theme is just an expanded paragraph, although there is no evidence of which I am aware that supports this notion. Given the limitations of the Christensen paragraph, it might be said that a theme would be like blowing up a tire and expecting an automobile to result.

There are no interpretation theories coordinate to the composition theories at the middle levels of the hierarchy—as far as I am aware—although some reading theories (especially Goodman) reach up into those levels, but without specifying the paragraph as such, for example.

Text Emphases

At the level of the full text, from the standpoint of interpretation theory, there are certainly those who have insisted on the autonomy of the text. In one sense that is what the Luther revolution in interpreting the Bible was about. For him, outside norms were irrelevant—the Bible was the "whole" and the parts were to make sense within it as a unity.[50] All scripture was for him *"sui ipsius interpres,"* its own interpreter.[51]

A good many practitioners of the new criticism were, in a sense, literary protestants. Their creed might well have been summarized in "the text, the whole text, and nothing but the text." They are equally afraid of being contaminated by the intentional or the affective fallacy. Their position, it might be defended, was justified at the time because of the inordinate importance given during the preceding period of literary criticism to the historical context and the life (situational context) of each author. This is a movement in the opposite direction from some of those which we have analyzed above. Their counterparts in composition theory, I have suggested, are theorists like D'Angelo, McCrimmon, and (with reservations) Moffett. Indeed, most freshman English texts with their deification of "theme" present almost a solid front for the autonomy of text. The freshman English theme as it is usually taught is most frequently written without an explicit aim, takes no particular view of its subject matter, is oriented to no particular medium, and is preferably done with no serious thought preparation. In other words, it is aimless, modeless, mediumless, and unprepared. No serious professional writer would dream of producing a text under any of these conditions.

There are a few exceptions to this view, both in English and speech communiation, as we shall see later. But the typical English teacher in composition, like the typical English teacher in interpretation of literature, is a true-blue believer in the autonomy of text.

Situational Context Emphases: Antiquity

Nevertheless the dominance of the autonomy of text has not always been the rule in the history of rhetoric. In antiquity, at least, three (or four) important doctrines militated against it. The most important of these was the notion of *kairos*. If I hesitate to translate the word, I have the authority of S. H. Butcher, who says that *kairos* is a word which has no "single or precise equivalent in any language."[52] Liddell and Scott give four basic meanings to the word, three of which are relevant here: (1) fitness, proportion, due measure; (2) the critical time or occurrence, the right time; (3) the state of affairs. Actually in the Presocratics, in Socrates and Plato, in Aristotle, and as late as Dionysius of Halicarnassus, the word usually meant a combination of these three meanings. Funaioli defines *kairos* as follows:

> The καιρός, when resolved into the rhetorical skill . . . can be defined as 'that which is fitting in time, place, and circumstances', which means the adaptation of the speech to the manifold variety of life, to the psychology of the speaker and hearer: 'variegated, not absolute unity of tone.'[53]

This notion runs through Hesiod, Pindar, Philolaus, the Pythagoreans, nearly all of the Sophists, Socrates, Plato, Aristotle, and later Greek writers.

English and American classical scholarship has not given as much attention to this notion as has German and Italian scholarship. Guthrie, an English historian of Greek culture, remarks on this: "Some have made a great deal of this καιρός-*Lehre*, in which among other things they see medical influence."[54] In strictly rhetorical scholarship it has, to my knowledge, been almost completely overlooked.

Protagoras represents one interesting variation in the theory. He saw in the "situation" or the "experiences" the elements of a strife which had to be mastered. By mastering these elements of experience, man becomes the master or measure of experience or all things *(Panton chrematon metron estin anthropos)*—I am here following Untersteiner's translation.[55]

The element of strife in experience represented a concern of nearly all of the Sophists. They were well aware that what was just in one situation was not just in another, that justice had an element of the probable in it that could go either way in a given set of circumstances. Consequently Protagoras maintained that it was man who mastered this indeterminancy. By looking at things indifferently man could put different values on them and could *by persuasion* make it possible for something of a lesser grade of knowledge to take on a higher level of knowledge.[56]

To adapt to these different situations, Protagoras seems to have been the first to devise the notion of the topics and to have extended the ambivalence of the opposites to all spheres of practical activity (there are two sides to everything).[57] Scott Consigny, in his article "Rhetoric and Its Situations," rightly recognizes that the topics were an attempt to get at the diversity of situations.[58] But it should be pointed out that the topics in classical rhetoric only took care of the subject matter issue in the situation—the *kairos* involved much more than subject matter.

Gorgias, however, was the Sophist who centered his entire system of thought around the *kairos*. Zeller lists among the major rhetorical works of the Sophist a questionable *Peri Kairou* by Gorgias.[59] In contrast to Protagoras, Gorgias felt that the *kairos* was the irrational power that broke up the oppostion of the antitheses in the situation and made possible *by persuasion* of self and of others the perception of something as objectively knowable, the ability to decide between right and wrong, and the capacity to discern the ugly from the beautiful.[60] This irrational power of the situation in effect made the decisions. There is thus an important distinction from the position of Protagoras. Whereas in Protagoras man mastered experience, in Gorgias experience was the master— the situation determined whether something was ugly or beautiful, whether the act was just or unjust.[61]

This is true of all fields which Gorgias investigates. Untersteiner examines the application of this doctrine in several areas. He then concludes. "The ethic, esthetic, and rhetoric of Gorgias are all based on καιρός."[62] This statement comes after he had devoted some seventy-six pages to examining the epistemology of Gorgias, also based on *kairos*. In other words, Gorgias had a situational epistemology, rhetoric, ethic, and esthetic—all founded on the persuasive power of the logos. In each area the situation (*kairos*) could make one element in the antithesis appear more probable (and therefore more persuasive) than the other element by forcing the decision—remember that the word *pithanon* in Greek meant both probable and persuasive.

The contingent nature of such a morality, epistemology, and ethics struck Socrates as particularly harmful, says Guthrie.[63] To place the basis of virtues in conventions, varying from place to place, was dangerous. As Guthrie says, outlining Socrates' position:

> Serious thought about the laws of human behavior had begun with a radical skepticism, which taught that it rested on no fixed principles but each decision must be made empirically and *ad hoc*, based on the expediency of the immediate situation (*kairos*). From this theoretical soil grew the pride of youthful rhetoric in its ability to sway men to or from any course of action by mastery of the persuasive use of words.[64]

Socrates and Plato repudiated such an epistemology, such an ethic, and such an esthetic. Indeed, Plato's world of ideas where justice, beauty, goodness, and courage were immutable and true and not subject to the vagaries of situational probabilities can be considered the response of Plato to the Sophistic, especially Gorgian, relativism.

But Plato did not, interestingly enough, reject a situational rhetoric. Near the end of the *Phaedrus,* when Socrates has outlined what the study of an ideal course in rhetoric should entail, he concludes:

> But it is only when he [the student of rhetoric] can state adequately what sort of man is persuaded by what sort of speech; when he has the capacity to declare to himself with complete perception, in the presence of another, *that here is the man and here the nature that was discussed theoretically at school—here, now— present to him in actuality*—to which he must apply *this* sort of speech in *this* sort of manner in order to obtain persuasion for *this* kind of activity—it is only when he can do all this and when he has, in addition, grasped the concept of *propriety of time* . . . it is only then, and not until then that the finishing and perfecting touches will have been given to his science."[65]

The climactic words in this translation, *propriety of time,* are the English rendition of *kairous* in Greek. And the whole passage is a fair summary of one important facet of *kairos* doctrine.

Aristotle uses the notion of *kairos* in many of his works,[66] and sees medicine particularly as a typical illustration.[67] The concept, if not the word, pervades the *Rhetoric*. Aristotle, while agreeing with Plato on the importance of *kairos*, nonetheless disagrees with Plato on the dangers of the mere probabilities in such situations. Aristotle feels that the existence of a probability at

least precludes the determinism of a certainty. The probable allowed the inter-
vention of man and permitted man to achieve some mastery over the situation.
Thus the sciences and the areas of the probable are the sciences of the free.[68] In a
sense, Aristotle reverts to something like the position of Protagoras: man is the
master of the situation.

Dionysius of Halicarnassus, teaching in Rome twenty years after the
death of Cicero, states that nobody until his time, not even Gorgias, had defined
the notion of *kairos* adequately.[69] Nevertheless, the word passed into the *koine*,
the Greek common language used throughout the Mediterranean world from
Syria to Gaul in the Hellneistic and Roman period. It is an important word in the
koine of the New Testament, used eighty-six times (a significant number),[70] and
in some very notable passages. For our purposes maybe one of the most
revealing uses is in Mark I, 15, where Jesus, having just come out of the desert
after his forty-day fast and temptation, inaugurates his public ministry. Jesus'
first quoted words are: "The time [*kairos*] is fulfilled, and the kingdom of God is
at hand; repent ye, and believe the Gospel." This is a very rhetorical statement,
both practically and theoretically. The words for believe and belief are derived
from the noun *pistis,* the word used throughout Greek rhetoric for the rhetorical
appeals or proofs (ethical, pathetic, and logical, in Aristotle). Mark's choice of
two words with long rhetorical traditions in Jesus' first recorded statement to the
Mediterranean world is significant. And, of course, the emphasis on situational
context is obvious. Throughout the New Testament, persuasion to belief is made
to depend on the rightness of the time: *pistis* depends on *kairos*. This idea is so
pervasive in the New Testament that the theologian Tillich maintains that the
word *kairos* reached its deeper meaning of a fullness of time, or a decisive time,
only in the early Christian period.[71] In Tillich, the *kairos* is so important for the
fundamendal receptivity of both individual and whole cultures to the kingdom
of God that he makes the notion the cornerstone of his entire theology, as
another eminent theologian, Erich Przywara, has remarked.[72] In any case, the
Greek New Testament certainly continued the relationship between persuasion
and *kairos*.

Among the Romans the notion seems to have been almost dissolved into
that of fitness or propriety (*prepon*). Even among the Greeks the two notions
were very closely allied. Consequently, when we are looking for a version of the
importance of the situation in Cicero or Quintilian, we should ordinarily look at
the associations made with the concept of fitness, which Cicero usually trans-
lated as *decorum*. Since this notion has received much more attention in
rhetorical and ethical circles than has the notion of *kairos,*[73] I won't delay long
on this second important depository of the situational context. It might be
pointed out, however, how much Quintilian expanded the areas to which fitness
applied compared even to Cicero, where the concept is almost unbiquitous. The

difference is in the explicit specification of areas. Pohlenz remarks that Cicero, like Isocrates and Gorgias before him, had joined the *kairos* and the *prepon* in such passages as *De Oratore*, III, 210: "id quidem perspicuum est, non omni causae nec auditori neque personae neque tempori congruere orationis unam genus," and he also refers to *Orator*, 21 and 74. In addition he cites from Quintilian, in what he calls a summary statement combining *kairos* and *prepon*. It concerns:

> . . . quid dicta (31), cur (39), apud quem (43), quando (46), locus et tempus (48), causae (57), apud judicem (75), whereby one can also bring in other things.[74]

The third notion in Hermagoras, Cicero, and Quintilian in which the notion of situational context is embodied in the distinction between the hypothesis and the thesis in the stasis-doctrine. The hypothesis was an actual issue embodied in a real situation; the thesis was an abstract and general discussion of an issue. Cicero rejected the thesis as being irrelevant to rhetoric. Here, as in the notion of decorum, Cicero insisted on a real situation.[75]

Thus, if we separate the notion of the topics from that of the general *kairos*, there are four major concerns in antiquity attempting to cover the problem of the situational context: *kairos, topoi, prepon,* and *hypothesis*.

Situational Context: Modern Emphases

The full history of the disappearance of the concept of *kairos* from the subsequent rhetorics has yet to be written. And the ascendency of the notion of the autonomy of text is a historical trend that has yet to be documented. Religious authority, the rise of print, and other influences probably have something to do with these two competitive tendencies.

At any rate, at the present time the autonomy of text is challenged by many who argue beyond the text to some norm for understanding. In law, of course, legislative intent and legal precedent are norms beyond the text. In rhetoric, there are those who, like Black and Bitzer, argue for the preeminence of the rhetorical situation and tend to minimize the text in favor of history.[76] In Biblical criticism the Catholic Church has always asserted the norms of tradition and authority in interpreting the Bible. Today in Biblical criticism and in general hermeneutics there are the demythologizers who maintain that the message of the Bible must be separated from the local and temporal cultural myths in which it was necessary to embody the message. All of these movements challenge the autonomy of the text. Their parallels in composition theory are the people who assert the importance of the dramatistic situation (Burke), the importance of a specific audience and purpose (Booth, Britton, and Kinneavy).

One important voice who repeatedly called for consideration of the situational context and whose voice is often ignored even by some of his closest followers is that of Freud. (Incidentally I prefer the term *situational context* because it is more general than *rhetorical context*. Besides a *rhetorical context* there could be distinguished a *literary context* [as Pratt has done], a *religious context* [as Tillich has done in *The Religious Situation*],[77] a political situation [Nazis used the term *kairos* for the idea that the *political* situation was right for the adoption of their ideas],[78] a scientific context, etc. Consequently, it seems better to revert to the general term of Malinowski, accepted generally by anthropologists today.) A typical warning can be seen from this quotation from *The Intrpretation of Dreams:*

> At the same time I must expressly warn the investigator against overestimating the importance of symbols in the interpretation of dream-translation to the translation of symbols, and neglecting the technique of utilizing the associations of the dreamer. The two techniques of dream-interpretation must supplement one another; practically, however, as well as theoretically, precedence is retained by the latter process, which assigns the final significance to the utterance of the speaker, while the symbol translation which we undertake plays an auxiliary part.[79]

The message of this admonition is seen again and again in Freud.[80]

Beyond text are levels like the entire corpus of a particular writer, or his complete life, or the complete culture within which the work was produced, or even universal history.[81]

Given all these levels and the possibilities of asymmetrical systems within them with different whole-part relations, the important question for the teacher of discourse composition is: At what point(s) does transfer of grammatical, library, usage, and even logical skills take place so that they are effectively used in composing? In other words, how are parts woven into the whole?

The long discussion of levels and varying emphases, both in rhetoric and interpretation, may enable us to return to the first tenet of the hermeneutic circle creed in order to see the operation of the whole part-relationships of a discourse and its components posited in a situational and a cultural context.

This paper, in fact, can serve as a vivid illustration of the four relationships between whole and part: their continual changes, the relative notion of what is whole and what is part, the dialectical relation of each to the other, and the reciprocal interdependence of each on the other. First let me consider some of the higher levels in the chart and then I will turn to some of the lower levels.

The first version of this paper was given at the 1974 Conference of College Composition and Communication. Against the background of the "Back to Basics" movement in the situational context, I was protesting a tendency to equate "Basics" with mechanics; my emphasis was on the entire text of a theme, not just on its mechanics, as I delivered a talk on "Holism and Merism in Composition Theory." In 1977 at the same conference, my talk was part of a panel on hermeneutic theory and the composing process (situational context). As a result I added the hermeneutical circle as a rationale and method for integrating the relationships of whole and part. I also added the long section on levels, and talked briefly about the intermediate levels, to which I had paid little attention in the 1974 talk.

In November, 1977, at the Western Speech Communication Conference in Phoenix, I gave the third version. I felt that a speech audience would understand an emphasis on situational context (in view of the stand on rhetorical situation by people like Bitzer and Black). Therefore I emphasized situation more and pointed out to that audience the extreme importance of *kairos* in early classical rhetoric (an importance speechwriters have ignored). In addition, I enlarged the speech (I was allowed an hour in that situational context) and consequently I added some emphases at various levels which I had not hitherto included, particularly the three theories of Morenberg et al., of Genette, and of poststructuralists interpreting Lévi-Strauss as supportive of this position. In front of a speech audience I felt that I could also make some derogatory remarks about the text emphasis on the part of both the English composition teacher and the English literature teacher. Consequently the operative *parts* within the speech changed radically and the notion of *whole* moved solidly into situational context. In brief, the notion of parts had moved from a grammatical and mechanics concern to the sentence and the notion of whole had moved from text to context.

Just before Christmas, 1977, I was asked by Don McQuade if I had anything that might be publishable in a forthcoming special issue of *Language and Style*. I sent him a copy of the Phoenix talk, offering to spruce it up for final publication if he was interested. He asked me to make several minor adjustments for the larger audience of *Language and Style*. I felt that the more linguistic audience of *Language and Style* might seriously criticize the paper if it ignored speech-act theory, especially since Pratt's application of speech-act theory to literary discourse had just appeared. Notice that both of these considerations derive from situational context. Consequently I added the section on speech-act theory and attempted to make the paper more intelligible to a larger audience than the typical CCCC crowd.

Although the entire manuscript had now almost doubled from even its 1977 size, I excerpted the sections on sentence theories of discourse (Miami, Genette, Lévi-Strauss) and juxtaposed them to the historical notion of *kairos* at a talk in Denver this year. Nearly all of that was new material for the CCCC audience.

This printed version, therefore, represents a fifth whole with different parts of a developing, continually changing, reciprocally dependent dialectic between various notions of whole and part, limiting the notion of part to a larger segment of discourse—something between paragraph and text.

The lower levels have also been strongly influenced by the various situational contexts. The terms "holism" and "merism" have given way to "whole" and "part." In the 1977 CCCC talk, E. D. Hirsch—rightly, I believe— felt that "hermeneutic" would be a more frightening word than "interpretation" theory. I used "rhetorical situation" for the speech audience in Phoenix (because that is the term used by speech scholars), but reverted to "situational context," Malinowski's earlier and more general term.

All of this seems to suggest that the proponents of situational context are right—situational context seems to be the critical level. Only in the dialect with the situational context do the word, then the sentence, the section, and even the text encounter the real tentativeness, changing relationships, relativity, and reciprocal interdependence which are determinative. This corresponds to what we know about the learning of a foreign language: we learn it rapidly and efficiently when we have to use it in Mexico City, or Bordeaux, or Freiburg in order to buy plane tickets, or order food, or find a lodging, etc.

In the classroom then, when we can pose real communication situations there is the highest likelihood of transfer of skills. Otherwise the situational context has to be simulated. And the further away the level is from the situational context, the less likely is there to be the motivation to transfer. This is my hierarchy hypothesis.

RICHARD YOUNG

Theme in Fictional Literature: A Way into Complexity

Among the most significant of recent developments in rhetoric is the reemergence of interest in the art of invention. From the early sixties on, two trends in rhetorical scholarship have become increasingly important: first, the study of the psychological processes by which the mind draws upon memory, analyzes the data of experience, and uses knowledge to go beyond what is known to new insights; and second, the design of conceptual strategies that increase the efficiency and effectiveness of these processes. The trends are exemplified in the renewed interest in classical invention, in the efforts to adapt Kenneth Burke's critical theory for use in the production of discourse, and in the numerous efforts to exploit work in the psychology of creativity, Gordon Rohman's "pre-writing" method being perhaps the most notable.[1] the significance of the trends is apparent when we recall that, historically, the strength of the discipline of rhetoric and its importance in the academic curriculum have been closely related to its ability to deal with issues of truth and inquiry.

Another of these efforts at developing a modern art of invention, the one that concerns us in this essay, is based on the principles of tagmemic linguistics, a linguistic theory developed primarily by Kenneth Pike.[2] These principles, Pike maintains, underlie all human experience as characteristic of rationality itself. For example, one such principle is that all purposive behavior comes in "chunks" or units. (Language behavior includes units such as words, sounds, stories, noun phrases, sentences.) To find and identify any unit of experience we must know its contrastive features; otherwise, we could not distinguish it from other units. We must also know how it can vary without losing its identity; otherwise, we could not recognize it again. And we must know its distribution in various systems, since all units exist in contexts, and a knowledge of such contexts is what enables us to discuss roles, make definitions, predictions, and assumptions about appropriateness of occurrence, and in general perceive systemic relationships that are part of what the unit is.

Tagmemic invention is an art of conducting original inquiries into situations that are perceived to be in some way problematic.[3] The most distinctive component of the art is a heuristic procedure that embodies, explicitly or implicitly, all of the principles of tagmemic theory. The procedure asks the inquirer to change his mode of perception of the same unit of experience, viewing it as a static, sharply defined particle, as a wave of activity, and as a field of relationships. (Any account of an experience growing out of a single mode is incomplete and reflects specific needs or intellectual biases.) In each mode the inquirer is asked to note the unit's contrastive features, variations, and distributions. In this way he is led through a set of complementary lines of inquiry that direct his attention to features of the unit he might otherwise overlook, help him bring to bear information that he already has in his memory, and identify what he does not yet know.[4] In doing so he prepares himself for intuitions of ordering principles that may resolve his problem.

The use of the art is not limited to a particular genre or subject matter, an important feature for a modern art of invention since the domain of modern rhetoric has expanded to include the production of all kinds of nonfictional discourse. If we are not to have arts of invention for each kind of discourse and for each discipline, the art must be of such a nature that it can be brought to bear usefully in all inquiries. Tagmemic invention, its developers argue, has this capacity since it is grounded in what are believed to be conceptual universals.

Although the primary purpose of tagmemic invention is to aid the writer in the act of composing, it can be brought to bear on fictional texts, where it serves as an aid in critical reading. Such a use of rhetorical art is not surprising; classical invention has served this secondary purpose for much of its history.[5] But if not surprising, it is nevertheless notable since it can be seen as a step toward the restoraton of an integrated conception of language studies, a conception we lost with the repudiation of the classical paradigm.

"The process of academic criticism," remarks Northrop Frye, "begins . . . with reading a poem [or any work of fiction] through to the end. . . . Once the end is reached, we can see the whole design of the work as a unity. It is now a simultaneous pattern radiating out from a center, not a narrative moving in time. The structure is what we call the theme, and identifying the theme is the next step. By 'identifying' a theme I do not mean spotting it: the theme is not something in the poem, much less a moral precept suggested by it, but the structural principle of the poem."[6] The semantic units that comprise the work, Frye suggests, are related paradigmatically as well as syntagmatically. In the act of reading, we relate the units temporally; we move from statement to statement, image to image. But in contemplating what has been read, we shift our attention from sequential relationships to relationships of a different sort. "In Robert Frost's 'Mending Wall'," Frye continues, "the theme is not the question whether fences do or do not make good neighbors: the theme is the identity of the 'something' with which the poem begins. We are not told definitely what it is, except that it is not elves, but whatever it is, the contrast of the two human

attitudes toward the wall and the two directions of the seasons, towards win⌐,
and towards spring, radiate from it as the center of the poem."[7] In reflecting on
the work, we reconstitute it as a nontemporal system, a semantic field that
carries a special kind of meaning.[8]

Wallace Stegner presents a similar view in a discussion of the place of
ideas in fictional discourse. "The ideas, the generalizations, ought to be implicit in the selection and arrangement of the people and places and actions. They
ought to haunt a piece of fiction."[9] Stegner's metaphor is interesting, for it
suggests the elusive nature of fictional theme. It is often difficult to perceive
and, when perceived, difficult to describe without distortion.

Every reader occasionally has the feeling that he or she "understands,"
in some sense of the word, all the parts of a work without understanding the
whole. The linguistic features—vocabulary, syntax, etc.—may be familiar; and
he or she can paraphrase it, summarize the events, describe the characters and
setting. Yet he or she may still feel that something essential remains to be
apprehended. The difficulty arises not from critical ineptitude, at least not
necessarily, but rather from the nature of the work as a complex system
functioning within the mind of a reader.

"Complex system" here refers to a unified system composed of numerous parts which interact in a non-simple way. A biological cell is a complex
system; a column of figures to be added is not. When we say that a literary work
is more than the sum of its parts, we are saying, as an eminent systems analyst
puts it, that "given the properties of the parts and the laws of their interaction, it
is not a trivial matter to infer the properties of the whole."[10] The parts often do
not seem to "add up" to a meaningful whole because they are not additive; they
relate in more subtle and elusive ways.

Understanding the theme, and in some sense the meaning of the work as
a whole, requires the apprehension of a semantic field that relates the parts to
each other and to the world beyond the work. And this is no trivial matter. As
Frye points out, the theme is not something in the work, something that might be
underlined with a pencil. The ghost may be real, but it is invisible. It is not a part
of the work or all the parts taken together; it is a relational principle that emerges
out of the reader's active involvement with the text. Since the theme is less
immediately accessible than other features of the work, apprehending it is more
difficult and more subject to misapprehensions. The reader must move beyond
the linguistic features of the text to what Roman Ingarden calls "portrayed
objectivities," and beyond these to the structural principle that relates them and
gives them meaning.[11] The movement toward the apprehension of theme is
progressively more subtle and more demanding of the reader.

But even when he does apprehend the theme of a work, the reader finds
himself in a position somewhat similar to that of the religious mystic, who

cannot adequately communicate his experience or how he achieved it. Undistorted articulation is difficult, for discursive language is unilinear, whereas what must be described is multilinear. As C. S. Lewis points out,

> Some things it [language] communicates so badly that we never attempt to communicate them by words if any other medium is available. Those who think they are testing a boy's "elementary" command of English by asking him to describe in words how one ties one's tie or what a pair of scissors is like are far astray. For precisely what language can hardly do at all, and never does well, is to inform us about complex physical shapes and movements. Hence we never in real life voluntarily use language for this purpose; we draw a diagram or go through pantomimic gestures.[12]

A semantic field, as experienced by the reader, in which, as one writer puts it, all the parts of the work "vibrate in a dynamic, charged, mutually-supportive relationship" is quite as difficult to articulate as a complex physical shape or movement.[13]

Cleanth Brooks and Robert Penn Warren provide an illustration of the difficulty in their commentary on "The Lottery," a short story by Shirley Jackson. After listing several observations about human nature suggested by events in the text, they conclude with this statement:

> If we hesitate to specify a particular "point" that the story makes, it is not because the story is vague and fuzzy, but rather because its web of observations about human nature is too subtle and too complex to be stated in one or two brief maxims.[14]

I do not mean to suggest that the theme of a work cannot be articulated once it has been apprehended, only that the task is difficult because of the nature of what is to be articulated.

There are no mechanical procedures which can lead the reader infallibly to the discovery of a theme, nothing like the rules of addition, which guide one without the aid of intuition or special ability to the correct solution of an arithmetic problem. But this does not imply that the reader's sole alternative is trial-and-error search guided only by his experience and imagination. It is possible to devise heuristic procedures, i.e., systematic discovery procedures, which enable more methodical exploration of a literary work. Although systematic, heuristic search is neither mechanical nor wholly conscious; intuitive leaps as well as step-by-step analysis are required, as are thorough familiarity with the text and relevant knowledge about the world.

The problems of discovering and articulating theme suggest the special relevance of what in tagmemics is called a "field perspective," a conceptual emphasis on multiple systems of relationships.[15] For a failure to perceive theme appears to arise from a failure to perceive the parts of the literary work as functioning in a particular kind of system. Tagmemic theory assumes that a unit's distribution in larger contexts is essential to an adequate description of the unit. More specifically, an adequate description of any unit of human behavior (systactic, lexical, phonological, social, philosophical) includes as one of its components the unit's distribution in a sequence of hierarchically ordered events, in a class, and in a network of contrastive vectors of a matrix. Unless the parts of a work are seen as functioning in larger, complementary systems, they cannot be understood. Hence the notion presented earlier that one may understand the parts of a literary work without understanding the whole seems questionable.

What I would like to argue is that a field analysis which relates semantic units in three interdependent systems (sequence, class, and matrix) not only leads one into analyses of the conventional elements of plot and motif but provides insight into theme as well.

Analyses of all three systems in Isaac Babel's "Crossing into Poland" will illustrate the method.[16] The story, told by a Red Army soldier, begins with a splendid, panoramic description of the VI Division moving from Russia into Poland. Late in the night the soldier is billeted in a ransacked house occupied by four Jews—a pregnant woman and three men, one of whom is huddled against the wall, apparently asleep. Repelled by the squalor, the soldier contemptuously orders them to clean up the room. "'What a filthy way to live!' The two Jews rose from their places and, hopping on their felt soles, cleared the mess from the floor. They skipped about noiselessly, monkey-fashion, like Japs in a circus act, their necks swelling and twisting" (p. 42). After the soldier falls asleep, he has a nightmare in which the Division Commander pursues the Brigade Commander and shoots him, shouting "Why did you turn back the brigade?" (p. 42). His threshing about and calling out in his sleep causes the woman to awaken him. And she then reveals that the man huddled against the wall was her father, who had been killed by the retreating Poles:

> "Good sir," said the Jewess, shaking up the feather bed, "the Poles cut his throat, and he begging them: 'Kill me in the yard so that my daughter shan't see me die.' But they did as suited them. He passed away in this room, thinking of me—And now I should wish to know," cried the woman with sudden and terrible violence, "I should wish to know where in the whole world you could find another father like my father?" (P. 43)

With this the story ends.

Although the story's theme is my principal concern, some discussion of plot and motif is necessary since the systems are interdependent. Plot analysis here means identifying the structure of the events—a structure that is both sequential and hierarchical. The ability to do this seems to depend in large part upon the perception of (a) an abstract underlying pattern, which may be shared by numerous literary works, and as the patterns of fairy tales described by Propp;[17] and (b) the perception of mutually reinforcing linguistic cues: sequence markers, shifts in dramatis personae (in actors, location, time, manner, instrument, etc.), shifts from direct to indirect discourse, shifts in tense, etc. The initial identification of the plot appears to be intuitive; then one may look for confirmation and refinement by a closer study of linguistic cues.

Babel's story can be segmented initially into two parts: the first, the events of the Russian advance into Poland; the second, the events that occur in the house where the officer is billeted. Although the first part can be regarded as a single, coherent episode, the second is a sequence of three loosely connected sub-parts, each of which constitutes a separate episode: (1) the description of the cluttered room and acts of the Jews who occupy it, (2) the narrator's dream, in which the Brigade Commander is shot, apparently for cowardice and (3) the woman's account of her father's execution and his concern for her at the moment of death. Each of the episodes is strongly cued by abrupt shifts in scene, time, actors, and action.

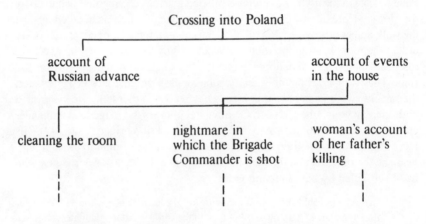

Further segmentation is, of course, possible since all the episodes are composed of isolable events. The decision to focus attention at one level of the hierarchy rather than another is always somewhat arbitrary, although not entirely so. If the total action of the story is being studied, the appropriate units for consideration are likely to be high-level ones. Certainly one test of appropriateness is pragmatic: does the analysis help one proceed with the inquiry?

The parts of the story can be redistributed in semantic classes. Fictional works are intricately patterned, highly redundant systems: units at all levels subtly echo and re-echo through the work as repetitions, contrasts, and analogies. As Gerard Manley Hopkins observed, "the artificial part of poetry, perhaps we shall be right to say all artifice, reduces itself to the principle of parallelism."[18] Units perceived as in some sense parallel can be grouped into classes, which then become conceptual entities in their own right; those with wide domains are motifs. Such classification introduces another kind of patterning—nontemporal and generic—into our conceptualization of the text. Here, however, the analyst is on uncertain ground; for as Roman Jakobson points out, artistic prose—"where parallelisms are not so strictly marked and strictly regular as 'continuous parallelism' [in verse] and where there is no dominant figure of sound—present more entangled problems for poetics."[19] Nevertheless, readers do tend to agree on what constitute parallel units in a text. Our intuitive ability often exceeds our analytic ability.

Classifying the episodes of the plot on the basis of shared features is a much simpler task than classifying units at a lower level, where one finds bewildering webs of recurrences.[20] The first two episodes can be grouped together since they present contrastive descriptions of scenes, as can the last two since the two killings constitute analogous acts. The episodes can also be reclassified on the basis of other features. The last episode can be grouped with the first since the acts of both the father and the advancing troops are presented in heroic terms, and the second and third episodes can be grouped since the acts of the two Jews and the Brigade Commander are, roughly speaking, cowardly. Furthermore, the second and last episodes can be grouped, since the principal actors in both are Jews, as can the first and third, since the principal actors are soldiers. Even when attention is focused on high-level units, the complexity of the categorical relations constantly threatens to swamp efforts to see the work clearly and whole. Nevertheless, certain relationships begin to emerge which bring the reader closer toward the apprehension of the theme of the story.

Both the sequential and class systems provide clues to a third system which is our chief concern—a network of intersecting categories of semantic units which constitutes a statement of literary theme. None of these systems is completely independent of the other. As has already been suggested, the four episodes isolated in the plot analysis can be treated as in various ways parallel and reordered into classes. Insight into one system tends to give insight into the other. And so with the third system as well. On the basis of clues provided by such analyses, the units can be reordered once again, this time in a matrix which reflects features of both the sequential and class systems. The result is a deceptively simple array whose dimensions are determined by the epistemological and axiological distinctions underlying the narrator's account of his experience and whose cells are filled by the previously isolated high-level units:

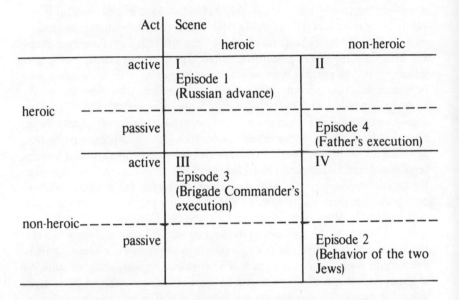

Act	Scene		
		heroic	non-heroic
heroic — active		I Episode 1 (Russian advance)	II
heroic — passive			Episode 4 (Father's execution)
non-heroic — active		III Episode 3 (Brigade Commander's execution)	IV
non-heroic — passive			Episode 2 (Behavior of the two Jews)

In spite of the numerous clues available at this stage of the analytical process, constructing a matrix usually involves some trial-and-error activity. Several matrices may be devised and discarded before devising one which seems adequate; a series of increasingly intelligent mistakes is often required to arrive at an adequate matrix. The matrix, I want to argue, is a statement of the theme, and matrix analysis is a heuristic which aids in its discovery.

Each of the rows and columns joins episodes along one dimension (scene) and contrasts them along another (act), thus providing a systematic way of displaying the pervasive likenesses and differences which were revealed earlier in the classifications. Adding another dimension to the rows by dividing them into active and passive is a way of presenting the qualitative differences between similar acts. There is a difference between cowardice and servility, just as there is a difference between the aggressive, destructive courage of a soldier and the "passive" courage of Christ or Martin Luther King. The diagonal cells also reveal significant relationships. The narrator's descriptions of the troops and the two Jews suggest a strong bias in favor of the one and against the other— Cossack and Jew occupy antithetical positions in his value system. But two experiences, represented in the other diagonal, are incompatible with this system: the first, the brigade commander's retreat, and the second, the selfless courage of the father. The values by which the narrator ordered experience at the beginning of the story are no longer adequate to account for his experiences at the end; he is being forced into a more complex image of the world.

The narrator's crossing into Poland is thus the occasion for a psychological journey. In "Defining Narrative Units" Jonathan Culler argues that "what the reader is looking for in a plot is a passage from one state to another—a passage to which he can assign thematic value."[21] The nature of the passage in Babel's story becomes clear when events of the story are viewed paradigmatically as well as syntagmatically.

I do not mean to imply that a reader actually constructs a matrix in his mind whenever he apprehends the theme of a literary work, although it is probably true that the semantic field which does evolve in his mind results from perceiving many of the same cues that are used to construct matrices. A matrix is a way of representing a subtle, more complicated and probably less sharply defined field system in the reader's mind, in much the same way that a weather map represents meteorological phenomena. But it is important to note here that matrix analysis also offers a way of encouraging the intuition of theme, of coaxing the imaginative act when it does not emerge of its own accord.

A matrix, like the other systems one constructs when analyzing a work of fiction, arises out of an interaction between reader and text; and because of this there are likely to be differences in the matrices constructed by different readers. We cannot speak of a correct matrix, as we can of a correct answer to an arithmetic problem, for a matrix is an interpretive act which is to some extent influenced by the unique knowledge, values, and biases of the reader. He inevitably adds something of himself to the data. On the other hand, we can speak of more or less reasonable matrices, for what can reasonably be said about a text is to a large extent constrained by the features of the text.

Precisely how one evaluates a matrix is not clear, but certain standards do seem appropriate. For example, a reasonable matrix ought to account in one way or another for all features of the text perceived as significant. It should also probably be consistent with other relevant information one has about the text, about other works by the author, and about the author himself. It is known, for example, that Babel experienced a conflict between the values of his Jewish heritage and those of a Communist officer in a Cossack regiment;[22] and the conflict appears in a number of his works, as in this passage from "The Rabbi's Son":

> His things were strewn about pell-mell—mandates of the propagandist and notebooks of the Jewish poet, the portraits of Lenin and Maimonides lay side by side, the knotted iron of Lenin's skull beside the dull silk of the portraits of Maimonides. A lock of woman's hair lay in a book, the Resolutions of the Party's Sixth Congress, and the margins of Communist leaflets were crowded with crooked lines of ancient Hebrew verse. They fell upon me in a mean and depressing rain—pages of the Song of Songs and revolver cartridges.[23]

Such information tends to confirm certain matrices and discourage others. A reasonable matrix also has characteristic formal features. Its structure, as we have already seen, complements the class and sequential systems by integrating the units and relationships in these systems into an array which provides another basic perspective on the text. And a really elegant matrix does this simply and without strain.

A concern for the quality of a particular matrix should not, however, obscure what is for our purposes the principal function of matrix analysis— which is to help the mind to a special sort of understanding of the text. It is the act of inquiry, not the product of that inquiry, which is of primary interest here. And even a poorly constructed matrix may trigger the desired insight. Once it has occurred, constructing a more adequate matrix is a simple task; the ability to construct a reasonable matrix can be taken as evidence that the reader has arrived at an understanding of the theme of the work.

Unusual as it is to conceive of theme in diagrammatic terms, a matrix offers a way of displaying the structural principle the reader has apprehended while avoiding at least some of the losses which inevitably accompany the use of discursive language. And it has other advantages as well. It provides an alternative to an unintegrated list of generalizations or the reduction of the work to a single maxim, a common though unsatisfactory expedient, the limitations of which have been noted in the passage by Brooks and Warren. Stating a theme in terms of a matrix is also less arbitrary since one can explain more fully how it was developed; it is thus more susceptible to criticism and evaluation.

It is possible, however, to derive a list of generalizations from a matrix, and this may at times be useful for pedagogical purposes. For instance, cells I and II of the matrix presented earlier suggest that admirable human qualities are not restricted by race or environment and that there are different kinds of courage. Cell II suggests that significant human suffering occurs unexpectedly and may not be recognized for what it is; or as Auden put it, "even the dreadful martyrdom must run its course/Anyhow in a corner, some untidy spot/Where the dogs go on with their doggy life and the torturer's horse/Scratches its innocent behind on a tree."[24] It is difficult to make an exhaustive list, for the matrix suggests lines of inquiry which can be followed for some distance. Although it is reductive, like any other analytical act, the matrix preserves some of the suggestiveness of the experienced word.

I have been suggesting that a field perspective, a mode of inquiry described in tagmemic invention, can be useful to the literary critic in the analysis of fictional works. But is may be particularly useful with certain works that resist analysis by more conventional means, such as Joyce's *Ulysses*, Pound's *Cantos*, and Eliot's *Waste Land*. As Joseph Frank has argued, these works have spatial rather than temporal form, and understanding them requires "the simultaneous perception in space of word-groups which, when read consecutively in time, have no comprehensible relation to each other."[25] In the poems by Eliot and Pound,

> syntactical sequence is given up for a structure depending on the perception of relationships between disconnected word-groups. To be properly understood, these word-groups must be juxtaposed with one another and perceived simultaneously; only when this is done can they be adequately understood; for while they follow one another in time, their meaning does not depend on this temporal relationship. The one difficulty of these poems, which no amount of textual exegesis can wholly overcome, is the internal conflict between the time-logic of language and the space-logic implicit in the modern conception of the nature of poetry.[26]

Such works, in which significant relationships among the parts are wholly paradigmatic, appear to offer especially appropriate occasions for borrowing analytical tools from a sister discipline.

ROBERT DiYANNI

The Return of Eloquence: Richard Lanham and the Teaching of Writing

The publication of *Style: An Anti-Textbook* (New Haven, CT: Yale Univ. Pr., 1974) earned Richard Lanham a national reputation as a eloquent spokesman for a rhetorical approach to teaching composition. This reputation has become solidified with Lanham's subsequent books, which taken together, testify to his continued interest in writing, rhetoric, and literacy: *The Motives of Eloquence* (New Haven, CT: Yale Univ. Pr., 1976), *Revising Prose* (New York: Scribner's, 1979), *Revising Business Prose* (New York: Scribner's, 1980), *Analyzing Prose* (New York: Scribner's, 1983) and *Literacy and the Survival of Humanism* (New Haven, CT: Yale Univ. Pr., 1983).

Perhaps the most important of these for composition is *Analyzing Prose*, Lanham's most complete argument for and sustained explanation of the pedagogical value of prose analysis. In this book Lanham establishes style as the primary domain of rhetoric and rhetoric as the primary approach to style. More specifically, he wishes to supplant the Platonic-Aristotelian philosophical approach to rhetoric with the more genuinely rhetorical stance toward language and reality espoused by the Sophists. For the traditional rhetorical goals of clarity, brevity, and sincerity, Lanham substitutes eloquence, play, and self-dramatization. In fact, in his earlier *The Motives of Eloquence*, Lanham attempted to rewrite literary history by redressing the balance accorded the serious, mimetic, moral approaches to texts that have dominated Western criticism since Plato. Defending the sophistic views attacked by both Socrates and Plato, Lanham reanimates sophistic rhetorical ideals, restoring their emphasis on play with language and thought, on the instabilities of moral positions, on the pleasure of the text—all as counters to the Platonic insistence on moral seriousness and absolute truth.

For Lanham, prose style begins not in clarity but in pleasure, the pleasure of language. In calling for a theory of composition that expresses "its pleasures as well as its duties" (*Style*, p. 13) Lanham turns to style as the source and center of verbal pleasure. He locates the roots of current problems with the teaching of writing in an obsession with clarity, and he laments the priority accorded it in many rhetoric and composition textbooks. Furthermore, he links clarity to the pragmatic impulse that sees words as tools, as pointers to denote what matters. And this, from the pragmatic standpoint, is content, not style.

In this connection Lanham also notes that our Puritan heritage has led us to see writing as joyless work rather than as joyful play. Lanham resists the double thrust of pragmatism and puritanism. Questioning the assumptions that prose ought to be all work and no play and that it ought to be seen through without being noticed, he argues that the way to improve writing is to teach style as verbal play. Moreover, he insists that we encourage our students to take pleasure in language by attending to its various manifestations and diverse uses in advertising, television and film, popular magazines, and all manner of books spanning a wide range of styles, voices, and historical periods.

Lanham's approach is rhetorical rather than linguistic. He does not attempt to study prose or teach it with the linguist's scientific method. Seeing linguistics as a regrettable influence on composition, he urges writing teachers to "woo eloquence, not mathematics" (*Style*, p. 67). His unhappiness with linguistics stems from its frequent slighting of stylistic surface in a search for the deep structures of language. In its emphasis on transforming surface detail into deep structure, linguistic analysis, Lanham contends, frequently bypasses the rhetorical contexts that make style worth studying, such as its purpose and occasion, its motive and tone. Linguistic approaches to style, in short, strip it of personality by ignoring the personal self it embodies and the social context it reflects.

To these limitations of linguistics as an approach to style I would add others. From the standpoint of interpretation, linguistics limits what we can derive from texts. Its scientific animus underplays the psychological significance of texts as well as their moral and social implications. In addition, reading and writing are made out to be far more abstract and methodical acts than our experience indicates. They are art, not science, and they should be taught humanistically and rhetorically, not scientifically.

Lanham's approach to reading and writing is not subject to these strictures. In fact, he demonstrates repeatedly both in *Analyzing Prose* and *The Motives of Eloquence* how rhetorical analysis can take up where linguistic description leaves off. In highlighting the surfaces of prose along with its verbal artifice, his analyses contextualize that writing, identifying its human voice and motive. Moreover, Lanham's analyses offer lessons in how to see prose, how to look *at* it rather than *through* it. He grants prose the same respect typically accorded poetry, analyzing its structure and syntax, its rhythm and sound, to arrive at its meaning. And while there may be nothing unusual in Lanham's saying that style matters as much as content, few have written with such penetration about the way prose style achieves meaning. But Lanham's vigorous argument for the serious study of prose tells us more than that all prose reveals the writer, that any utterance transcends its strict information quotient. His argument also clarifies the ways in which a study of prose style takes on the coloration of epistemology. Lanham suggests that our active and recreative seeing of the world, combined with incessant and inevitable role playing, make notions of a central self and a stable reality untenable. "To perceive the world," he reminds us, "is to compose it. . . . To write is to compose the world as well as view it." (*Analyzing Prose*, p. 3). If indeed what is out there is inseparable from our perception of it, then, as Lanham suggests, a theory of style founded upon a stable reality and an unchanging self is dangerously misleading—hence Lanham's revisionist reading of Western rhetoric and literature, emphasizing the quarrel between the Aristotelian-Platonic central self characterized by stability, morality, and high seriousness and the sophistic social self with its shifting roles, its dramatic emphasis on performance, and its ludic concern for the pleasures of social engagement and the play of language. And hence, too, his insistence that prose style is not a mere matter of words. "Prose style," he notes, "models human motive. Every statement about style is, if we know how to interpret it, a statement about behavior" (*Analyzing Prose*, p. 9).

Lanham's emphasis on style, however, ignores the other two elements of the rhetorical triad: invention and arrangement. This is understandable perhaps, given both the revisionist nature of his work and its strong analytical impulse. It becomes more understandable in light of his insistence that "composition should not be asked to do too much. Its natural subject is style." (*Style*, p. 14). Why its natural subject is style, how invention and arrangement are, as he argues, "implicit in a study of style," and how they "emerge naturally only from a concentration on it" (*Style*, p. 14) he does not say. Nor does he offer much hope of teaching invention and arrangement. Instead, he dismisses them by suggesting that students who cannot think logically, who cannot invent arguments and arrange them, ought not to study composition. In effect, he would limit the study of composition to those who are ready for work on style, primarily analysis and imitation.

But this argument is not convincing. If Lanham is right about the centrality of style in the rhetorical triad, and if indeed invention and arrangement emerge from its teaching, then any student should be able to learn how to write by attending primarily to style. And if he is not right, then his approach to style needs to be supplemented with an equally intelligent and rigorous approach to invention and arrangement. Such an approach would acknowledge how writing requires thinking through a subject, and how thinking runs along with writing, language, and thought emerging together. Such an approach would also acknowledge how, as Lanham reminds us, "none of us knows what he thinks till he sees what he writes. We surrender ourselves to language, and not once but over and over; we oscillate between language and concept, from draft to draft" (*Motives of Eloquence*, p. 23).

To supplement Lanham's lucid and ludic approach to style, we need a philosophy of composition, one that stresses the connection between thinking and writing, and between seeing and thinking, and one that recognizes the importance of feeling and imagination. Such a philosophy, not surprisingly, is implicit in Romantic poetic theory, especially in Wordsworth's "Preface to the *Literary Ballads*" and in Coleridge's essays on method from *The Friend*. Moreover, the compositional implications of Coleridge's theory of imagination are made explicit in the pedagogy lucidly articulated in Ann E. Berthoff's *Forming/Thinking/Writing* and *The Making of Meaning*.[1] The two books together provide the best philosophy of composition available. Moreover, they share the epistemological orientation of Lanham to a strong degree, particularly in their reliance on the thinking of E. H. Gombrich, Rudolf Arnheim, and Kenneth Burke.[2]

Without suggesting that composing can be neatly segregated into a series of stages—inventing, drafting, revising for example—we should also note that Lanham's approach to composition needs a stronger conception of revision. Much of what he describes as revising in both *Revising Prose* and *Revising Business Prose* is really editing. Eliminating wordiness, avoiding ambiguity, using active voice verbs, choosing words and phrases with an eye to their shape and an ear to their sound—these and other useful bits of advice are stylistic editing procedures. And on these Lanham's advice illuminates. But as full-scale revision strategies to rethink and restructure discourse, his guidelines are inadequate.

More helpful, perhaps, is the following comment from *Analyzing Prose*: "Writing and revising are, for most of us, two different kinds of acts. When you write, you are writing for 'content,' trying to shape and fix an argument. When you revise you reverse this process, look At rather than Through. The whole act of writing is an oscillation of these two kinds of vision, Through and At" (p. 220). But even these remarks require qualification. Some of us would say that writing and editing (not revising) are two different acts. We would argue that writing is essentially revising, and that our revisions do more than merely polish diction and adjust syntax to fit meaning. Revision is a repeated attempt to discover what we mean and to find forms that fit those meanings. The act of revising, then, extends to invention and arrangement as well as to style.

What of the pedagogical implications of Lanham's work for the teaching of writing and reading? First of all, suggests Lanham, teach the figures of sound and the forms of sentence arrangement, along with the vocabulary of rhetoric. Lanham includes chapters in *Analyzing Prose* on periodic and running style, parataxis and hypotaxis, voiced and unvoiced styles, noun and verb styles. In each he manages to provide descriptive rhetorical terminology without being either intimidating or pedantic. He suggests further that we help students to see and hear the devices of sound, form, and rhythm that inform style, and that we urge students in their own writing to imitate the features of style they observe in their reading. He believes that imitating many styles and trying on stylistic identities will enable students, paradoxically, to discover their own voices. He doesn't explain how this happens, but he links the idea with his notion that adolescent writers have not yet developed a fully formed identity. Since they don't yet know who they are, they can't present an authentic self, a sincere "I" in their prose. But they can imitate the styles and inflections of other writers. In so doing they will imitate in their own ways, adapting, modifying, adjusting their prose to suit and conform to their developing selves. Their stylistic excursions, Lanham holds, will parallel their emerging identities.

In advocating a return to imitation, Lanham graphs and charts sentences to highlight their patterns of sound and sense. He does this most elaborately in *Analyzing Prose* where he diagrams a political speech of Lincoln, a letter of Eisenhower, excerpts from popular magazines and detective fiction, along with poetry by R. D. Laing and prose by John Lyly—to cite just a few of the varied works he examines. In addition to analyzing the rhetorical patterns of prose, Lanham would reintroduce reading aloud into the classroom. He attributes, in fact, many of the problems of writing—its mindlessness, monotony, gracelessness, and general blandness—to an inability to hear the sounds of words and rhythms of sentences, an inability to see the shapes of sentences and the patterns of paragraphs. And the remedy for these, Lanham argues, is more reading, especially reading aloud.

The rationale for reading aloud seems sensible enough: writers often don't see something in their own writing until they hear it. The ear catches things the eye has missed; the ear prompts the eye to see. Reading aloud enables writers to listen to their language and hear how sound shapes sense. To develop such auditory discrimination, Lanham argues, is one of the ways we can best raise our students' consciousness about their writing and about language generally. But reading aloud offers other advantages. Readers must make choices about the tempo and tone of their reading; they must choose a spirit in which to read; they must allow the rhythms of sentence and paragraph to reveal the shape of thought. Moreover, the skills that will follow such a heightened awareness of language should enhance our students' auditory imaginations. And if we think the auditory imagination as important as Lanham does, we may very well decide to follow his advice and make "every course in composition . . . a course in slow reading" (*Style*, p. 102).

Lanham is right: style should be brought back seriously into the composition classroom, and in just the way he advises—with an emphasis on the rhetorical rather than the linguistic dimensions of language. Rather than drill our students in handbook grammar exercises or sentence combining, we should, as part of our work in composition, require that they read and write imitations and variations based on a wide range of styles, and that they experiment with the sounds of words, the rhythms of sentences, and the shape of content. We need, as Lanham, suggests, to help students see and hear both their own language and the language that lives all around them. In reminding us that "our eyes tell us what the style has been saying all along" (*Analyzing Prose*, p. 90), and by encouraging readers to read prose aloud, he further strengthens our belief that prose ought to be heard as well as seen, that it ought to be both looked at and listened to. If we follow Lanham's suggestions, we surely will help our students develop the verbal tact and intuition necessary for perceptive reading and eloquent writing.

JOHN CLIFFORD

Toward Real Philosophic Laboratories

Like innovative literary critics, writing theorists have also appropriated and transformed ideas from other disciplines, often illuminating ignored or problematic aspects of the composing process. Some, like Ross Winterowd and Richard Young, have identified useful models for composing in the rigor and eloquence of linguistic analysis. Others, like Frank D'Angelo and James Kinneavy, have mined the rich ore of classical rhetoric. Recently, Linda Flower and John Hayes have imported elaborate schema of the mind across the borders of cognitive psychology and composition.[1] Ann Berthoff looks at these imports with a jaundiced eye. Scorning disciplines that she considers rule-obsessed and scientific, she looks instead to sources with a decidedly philosophical bent. Appropriately, Berthoff's own suggestions and insights about writing are redolent with epistemological significance.

As a result, both Berthoff's theoretical and her practical work challenge writing teachers to consider seriously ideas from a range of philosophers, from C. S. Pierce and William James to Alfred Whitehead and Suzanne Langer. In her writing textbook, *Forming/Thinking/Writing*, she creatively distills and modifies a wide range of theory into a practical guide to help writers form and shape meaning. She then divides *The Making of Meaning* between a dozen of her own talks and essays and brief excerpts from other thinkers: Kenneth Burke, I. A. Richards, Lev Vygotsky, and Leo Tolstoy. In her most recent work, *Reclaiming the Imagination*, she effaces herself by devoting her entire book to selections from artists, scientists, and philosophers who she hopes will both give resonance to her own essays and also provide a theoretical framework within which instructors can build an informed praxis.[2]

The publishing sequence of her three books then, as it moves from classroom exercises on "seeing relationships among paragraphs" to scholarly essays like Suzanne K. Langer's "Cassirer's Theories of Language and Myth," can be seen as a gradual unpacking of the assumptions she uses to build her pedagogical apparatus. Her work, taken as a whole, illustrates how writing and its teaching can be made intellectually exciting and productive by exploring the implications of such concepts as knowing, meaning, and thought, and their relation to language. For Berthoff, the philosophical richness of this exploration can give writing teachers guidance and vision. And in quite specific ways, she demonstrates how the theory generated from this philosophical inquiry can be brought to bear on what we do in class on Monday morning.

Indeed, Berthoff's textbook and the copious pedagogical references in her essays convincingly demonstrate that she has a lively interest in the workaday world of composition practitioners, in the pragmatics of how writers learn to form paragraphs and sentences more effectively. Throughout her writing she insists on the necessity of making theory useful. Without a solid grounding in the social and psychological complexity of classrooms, even the best theories, she believes, serve no useful purpose. Since she thinks that effective teachers are philosophically aware, she takes seriously her call to weld philosophical frames of reference to classroom techniques. *Forming/Thinking/Writing*, in fact, begins with a discussion of philosophy and pedagogy. It announces that "this book is intended for those who want to teach composition primarily and centrally. [It] will not appeal to teachers who prefer to work with manuals and guides and a rigid syllabus. This is a book about the composing process that provides continuing opportunities to put theory into practice; it does not simply line up exercises that demonstrate theoretical points" (p. 1). In other words, Berthoff's text embodies a philosophy of composition; it does not merely append exercises onto abstract discussions.

Her alternative to both recipe swapping and appositional musings on Derridean hermeneutics is to provide students with "assisted invitations." The term is borrowed from I. A. Richards and refers to instructional strategies in reading and writing that encourage students to be reflective as they look for relationships in paragraphs as diverse as those of Gertrude Stein, William Blake, and Claude Lévi-Strauss. She encourages writers to look carefully at how they respond to these readings; she wants them to look and look again at their own judging, evaluating, forming, revising, and interpreting. With the teacher as guide and exemplar, the textbook could be seen as an occasion for the creative sparks she hopes will be set off by critical reading and writing. In fact, everything that happens in the classroom is fit for this kind of scrutiny, for a continuous audit. A typical invitation would be for students to carefully observe a painting, or perhaps a forest pond, keeping track of their responses, comments and descriptions on one side of a notebook page. On the opposing side the writer annotates, interprets, and glosses the original. Berthoff somewhat melodramatically refers to this scrupulous reflexivity as understanding our understanding, knowing our knowledge, and interpreting our interpretations. In this continuous inquiry of experience, traditional distinctions between the creative and the critical invariably blur.

Berthoff believes in the dynamic interplay that double-entry notebooks encourage. The mental gymnastics needed for this kind of composing is heady and demanding, especially for inexperienced readers and writers uninitiated in the dizzying rhythms of dialectic. For the many students who lack a supportive educational history that would allow them to see themselves as capable of producing insights on insights, there must be considerable disorientation as they wonder about the value of their wondering. Berthoff is taking a calculated pedagogical risk through her optimistic leap of faith about the forming abilities of the mind. The rewards she hopes for—intellectual discovery, an increase in self-esteem, and insight into the resourcefulness of language—are impressive. One can, however, imagine considerable frustration as inexperienced writers wrestle first with the ideas of serious thinkers and then with their own judgments of the success of that encounter. There will be substantial energy demands on the sensitive and supportive instructor willing to sustain the dialectical ebb and flow of such reflexive and collaborative learning. Teachers have to be ready to be spontaneous, to think on their feet, to quickly shift from discussion to small groups to a demonstration and back to discussion. Getting college writers to think carefully is stressful. For the strong and the convinced, the rewards are apparently compelling enough to forsake the comfortable routine of traditional lecture and discussion. Instead, Berthoff's method is based on first accepting and then exploiting ambiguity and confusion. That will not appeal to instructors seduced by the schematic certainty of five-paragraph themes or comparison-and-contrast essays. On the other hand, the restless, the independent, and the adventurous on both sides of the desk will be motivated by the increased potential for intellectual growth and serious discourse. To make one's classroom into what Berthoff calls a "real philosophic laboratory" implies that an instructor must also look carefully at what she is doing and why, that she must also continually be alert to how meaning is made, how evaluations are evaluated. In a comprehensive commitment to awareness, Berthoff's ideal classroom becomes an ecosystem constituted by subtle intellectual, social, and emotional interactions.

Because Berthoff is an experienced innovator, she knows that instructional change must be prepared for, that for instructors to undergo a lasting pedagogical transformation there must be more than imaginative techniques; there must be a heightened consciousness of the complexity involved. However justified a rebellion against "the bad old ways" might be, making a dialectical classroom work involves more than enthusiasm. So she devotes her second book, *The Making of Meaning,* to both her own theoretical essays and assorted philosophical readings. In this way she presents her philosophical underpinnings, intending her text to be an "assisted invitation" to explore ever-branching avenues of theoretical inquiry so that her colleagues too can create teaching techniques resonant with philosophical thinking. By dialectically engaging theories of meaning, the nature of perception, models of process, and writing as a way of knowing and as a mode of learning, the reader of Berthoff's essays and readings is off on a journey limited only by one's capacity for imagination.

In "Towards a Pedagogy of Knowing," a seminal essay in *The Making of Meaning*, we encounter a representative essay by Berthoff that announces a recurring motif in her work: the conviction that method is not disinterested, that the relation between ends and means cannot be value free, that teachers and theorists are always situated in particular social and political realities.[3] If we think of the New Critics' retreat from a disagreeably ideological world into an autonomous text, her point seems relevant. If we examine the importance that behaviorists place on methodology, her observation is clearly appropriate. She wants to dissuade instructors from adopting the kind of innocent eclecticism that says it is fine to do sentence combining and outlining on Monday, heuristics and topic sentences on Wednesday, and freewriting and editing on Friday. Berthoff disagrees because these techniques reflect different beliefs and attitudes about the nature of writing and the way learning takes place. Each has roots in different philosophical soil, and each has been nurtured by varying presuppositions. Not to discriminate among them demonstrates, she believes, a misunderstanding of the metaphysical origins of all methods. She also makes it clear that not all techniques are equally useful. Her frequent references to the progressive educational strategies of Paulo Freire, for instance, makes it obvious that her own pedagogical ideology is neither innocent nor meant to be.[4]

In discussing the composing process in "Towards a Pedagogy of Knowing," for example, Berthoff demonstrates the ubiquitous stage model of composing found in most traditional rhetorics as an over-regularized distortion of the real dialectical nature of writing. Central to her own account of composing is the belief that language and thought are simultaneous and correlative. She does not believe that we first think of what we want to write and then write it. The discursive flow of language, its generalizing, forming power, its ability to call forth images, memories, and half-formed ideas from mysterious interiors of the mind gives it power as a speculative instrument.[5] In Berthoff's model, writers generate and revise synchronically, not stage-by-stage in an artifically regimented sequence. Revision is always possible, as emerging meanings need clarifications that invariably lead to new meanings and new clarifications. The resulting process is linear, recursive, and open-ended in its dialectical flow.

Reflexivity, then, is the mental operation that helps a writer's meaning evolve and mature. The making of meaning is not rule-governed or predictive. Rather, Berthoff holds that writers need to experience the confusion endemic to the early phases of a piece of writing. Only then will they begin to understand how the chaos of writing can lead to forms that will generate even more forms. By engaging in the process again and again, writers also come to understand how language mediates between perception and reality, how language is itself the richest heuristic. Throughout the dozen essays in *The Making of Meaning*, Berthoff again and again gives language a privileged status as the primary creative tool of the mind. If composing is chaotic, then language will eventually bring order. If order subsequently dissolves under the pressure of new perceptions, then language will again enhance the mind's self-ordering movement toward clarity. Language and the mind create discourse harmoniously, fluidly, organically.[6]

In her talks and essays, it is quite clear that the composing process is the source of Berthoff's pedagogical enthusiasm. Although she does not ignore style and form, her intelligence is drawn primarily to what happens as writers generate, shape and analyze their drafts. Instead of organizing the experience with schematic invention devices like the tagmemicists' wave, particle, and field heuristic, she hopes that writers will learn to tolerate ambiguity, that they will learn from their own invention strategies, that they will learn to navigate their own circuitous paths toward meaning. In an essay not collected in *The Making of Meaning*, Berthoff quotes I. A. Richards as support for this recursive and experiential method of learning: "Clear consciousness of what we are doing is our best means of control."[7] The algorithmic is rejected in favor of active inquiry; the prescribed gives way to trial and error. If writers are to arrive at meanings that matter, they must rely not on prescriptive map makers, but must instead chart their own course through the uncertainties of composing.

The reader of Berthoff's essays cannot help but be excited by her call for philosophical sophistication in the theory and practice of composition. Such awareness will certainly add dignity and intellectual vigor to what is often regarded as a pedestrian enterprise. By demonstrating the myriad connections that writing and its teaching have with our philosophical heritage, she raises our consciousness about the humanistic centrality of composition studies. Her emphasis on the need to wed theory and practice also helps to undo the debilitating and unprofessional myth that a serious interest in teaching undermines the credibility of scholars. Berthoff's essays take us light years from traditional obsessions with surface decorum and ceremonial theme writing. Her pedagogy of knowing challenges the inertia of comfortable routine and expedience.

Even as casual observers of working models of Freudian and Marxian theory know, sound constructs are mediated through practitioners. And classroom practitioners of writing vary greatly in their competence, background, and commitment. Since Berthoff's pedagogy of knowing is by its very nature unpredictable, neither a dialectical notebook nor a classroom dynamic guarantees that students will produce strong or personally meaningful writing. As in all strong pedagogical philosophies, so much will depend on how well the instructor can weave the contextual threads of language, authority, trust, knowledge, background, and commitment into a convincing learning experience. Since a dialectical method is not cut from typical patterns, choices abound. Instructors and students must develop a trusting, collaborative relationship. Everyone will need patience, tolerance for error and confusion, and a good deal of self-confidence. Berthoff's anthology of philosophical selections, *Reclaiming the Imagination*, attempts to build that self-esteem by broadening and deepening epistomological awareness and authority.

One of the frustrating dilemmas of trying to persuade instructors to change their teaching is the ease and regularity with which they slip back into classroom methods at variance with new insights. New techniques alone cannot withstand the psychological pressures to return to a discarded but comfortable pedagogy. To sustain a commitment to a pedagogy of knowing, for example, belief in the method's intellectual foundation must be broad and deep. In *Reclaiming the Imagination*, Berthoff has selected readings she hopes will be convincing and enduring, illuminating and sustaining. She also wants to de-mystify philosophy by demonstrating its relevance and then, through accessible selections, to help instructors explore ideas about perception, interpretation, knowing, and context. Most of the excerpts play out variations on the theme of imagination, which she sees, quoting Coleridge, as "the prime agent of all human perception."[8] If composing involves the recognition of relationships among ideas, images, and perceptions, then imagination is the mind's shaping spirit. Imagination becomes, then, a composing heuristic, intimately inter-twined with discursive language as it perceives, forms, and makes sense of reality. Imagination gives creative and critical force to the active mind making meaning in language.

One of the four major sections in *Reclaiming the Imagination*, "Inter-pretation and the Act of Knowing," contains selections from the writings of C. S. Peirce, Kenneth Burke, R. G. Collingwood, J. Robert Oppenheimer, and others. Placing such provocative thinkers side by side epitomizes Berthoff's creative reworking of I. A. Richard's notion of assisted invitations. In the preface she requests that readers keep a dialectical notebook to audit emerging meanings, concepts, and ideas. I did, curious about the implications of first absorbing the ideas of these interesting minds and then watching myself interpret my interpretations. Of course, each reader will see individual worlds in the rich and highly suggestive ideas of C. S. Peirce and Clifford Geertz, but in my early responses to excerpts on perspective and context from these two writers, I was struck by the importance of their ideas to Berthoff's thinking and by extension, to composition theory. Peirce's cogent insight that the ego is also a sign makes his relevance to discussions about language and the autonomy of the self striking. Since for Peirce the self is itself an interpretable text already embedded in an intricate social context, a reader's neutrality in interpreting or evaluating any text is seriously in doubt. Peirce offers an interesting refutation to the conundrum of whether reading is subjective or objective.

Peirce posits, as does I. A. Richards, a contextual theorem of meaning that is based neither in readers nor in texts but rather in the interpretive interaction between the two. In the following excerpt, Berthoff, with characteristic philosophical texture, plays with Peirce's notions of triadicity:

> We can follow Vygotsky's argument about why we should begin our study not with "language" or "thought" but with the nexus of the two, with the "unit of meaning." We can study Walker Percy and I. A. Richards, both of whom have demonstrated the inadequacies of the dyadic model of the sign. We can build on C. S. Peirce's formulation that one sign requires for its interpretation another sign. . . . Anything we can do to substantiate the notion that meaning does not subsist in lexical definition but requires context and prespective will help form the concept of triadicity—the idea that the meaning relationship must include the meaning-maker and the idea he thinks with, not just the sign and what it stands for.[9]

Since language mediates between us and the world, it follows that we can never know reality, but only "seek to know our knowledge of reality."[10] This view of language as the symbolization of thought is a linchpin in Berthoff's pedagogy of knowing, and one that has been the source of considerable friction between her position and those of linguists and cognitive psychologists who she feels have nothing to offer to rhetorical theory or composition pedagogy. She does not value the insights of modern linguists and psychologists because she believes they base their concepts of language and thought on a dyadic model, constituted only by Saussure's signifier and signified. Although this view of language fits the position of many psychologists, it does not adequately reflect recent thinking among leading cognitivists. Scribner and Cole's work on the cognitive consequence of literacy, for example, is influenced by humanistic perspectives, and a cognitive writing theorist like Linda Flower rejects the logical positivist's communication diagram with its senders and receivers.[11] There are significant philosophical differences among cognitivists, differences Berthoff should confront more explicitly.

Berthoff sees the positivist view of language and thought as an oversimplification of a multi-leveled dialectical interaction. For her, their formalistic models negate the interpretive force of prespective and context. She believes it is the nature of signifiers "to be unclear, multi-valent, polysemous, ambiguous, until perspective and context are clear."[12] Whereas certain linguists and cognitivists work toward predictive models, Berthoff champions ambiguities as "hinges of thought." She holds with C. S. Peirce's belief that "every reasoning involves another reasoning which in its turn involves another, and so on ad infinitum."[13] This quote could be paraphrased into "it depends," a sentiment that is soft enough to make it anathema to the hard scientific trust of recent thinking in linguistics and cognitive psychology. For Berthoff, this disparity is serious enough to warrant their exclusion from intellectual conversation in composition studies. In what she perceives as a struggle for theoretical influence over composition, she draws explicit battlelines: "They are not our allies."[14]

However, this exclusionary tendency in Berthoff's work blurs the distinction between dialectic and debate, between a philosophical search for truth and the defense of a particular epistemology, however appropriate. Having heard Ann Berthoff give papers at conferences around the country, I can attest to the intellectual vigor of her arguments and the excitement generated by her cogent questioning of many of our uninformed traditional assumptions. Nevertheless, her persistent attacks on cognitive psychologists, traditional rhetoricians, and linguists dilutre the impact of her ultimate concern—the strengthening of the profession's classroom praxis.

Dialectic is such an appealing technique because it seeks to confront and resolve oppositions, not because it dismisses contradictions as worthless. I am also disappointed with the enthusiastic reception the work of cognitivists has received recently.[15] However, their theories are serious enough for us to collectively explore the epistemological ground their elaborate structures are built on. And we will also have to confront the inevitable reality that some composition theorists will find this ground fertile and congenial enough to set up camp. I think that would be unfortunate, but disputatiousness will not prevent them from joining forces with a positivist view of composing. To be that influential only a balanced explication of the value of one's own alternative ideas will do. Fortunately, through judicious exposition Berthoff herself gives us a model of this kind of careful analysis in "I. A. Richards and the Audit of Meaning," which appeared in *New Literary History* (Autumn, 1982). It is the kind of scholarly performance our profession will benefit most from.

It seems natural that composition theorists, especially in their emerging intellectual and institutional struggles toward respectability, would look to shore up their credibility by borrowing accepted ideas and methodologies from established disciplines. Our leading theorists—from Janet Emig to Ross Winterowd—have been importing ideas from linguistics, literary theory, psychology, and philosophy for the past decade. Still, it is prudent to be wary about embracing ideas from disciplines with different perspectives on how knowledge comes about, what language is, and what role imagination and interpretation play in the life of the mind. After all, scholars are hardly neutral about these matters. To think metaphorically about language as either a garment or a melody matters greatly in how seriously you value prewriting or how systematically you stress revision. It matters if writing teachers are relying for their understanding of how meaning gets made on Aristotle instead of Heidegger, on Herbert Spencer instead of Susanne Langer.

Instructors informed by the philosophic perspectives in *Reclaiming the Imagination* would be less likely to use formalistic techniques. If you are impressed by Susanne Langer's position in *Philosophy in a New Key* that symbolic acts like writing are the essence of our humanity, you will probably not spend the semester passing on wads of information on tagmemic grids, syllogisms, or subordination. More likely your classroom will become a collaborative workshop where a community of writers read and critique each other's work.[16]

It is not difficult to sympathize with Berthoff's frustration with seemingly broad-minded theorists who refuse to see how far from shore we can drift on theoretical currents. Only in retrospect, for example, can we clearly recognize in the avowed objectivity of New Critical readings very specific social and political beliefs. Those critics were no more free of preconceptions than the more explicit Marxists. Berthoff's insistence that all theorists travel with ideological baggage is worth careful thought.

One scholar intensely aware of the influence these tacit convictions have on our ideas is Clifford Geertz, whose essay, "Thick Description: Toward an Interpretive Theory of Culture," Berthoff places after the brief C. S. Peirce excerpt on semiotics in *Reclaiming the Imagination*. Like Peirce, this semiotic ethnographer believes that knowing is not the discovery of an existing truth, but an interpretation of our selective perceptions. We are, Geertz observes, "suspended in webs of significance" that we ourselves have spun. Berthoff hopes Geertz's method will be seen as an exciting alternative to traditional research studies of the composing process. In his work Geertz rejects the strict codes of structural analysis and instead looks below the surface of events to unearth the highly contextual and imaginative universes we have created for ourselves. Although he tries to clarify, he is ever mindful of the complexity of culture. To analyze social discourse, the ethnographer places critical signifiers within an intelligent frame, not to arrive at objective certainty but to sustain professional discussion and maintain interest in symbolic forms. For Geertz, as for Berthoff, interpretation is a powerful force in our attempts to understand cultures, texts, or classrooms.

Reading Geertz in relation to Peirce is as illuminating as it is mind boggling, and that's just what Berthoff hopes a dialectical notebook will foster—a free exploration of connections, an inner dialogue between mind and perception, between the self and the world. This is also the kind of refinement of debate needed in composition studies, especially now as our profession becomes more sophisticated and more diverse with maturity. Geertz and Peirce's ideas also demonstrate how stimulating it is to read outside one's own discipline. If we are to grow strong in an accepted field, writing specialists need this kind of cross-fertilization.

There are dozens of other fascinating groupings in *Reclaiming the Imagination*, for example, Vygotsky, Whitehead, and Auden on "The Unit of Meaning" and Coleridge, Klee, and Bergman on "Artists at Work." Reading through this collection using a dialectical notebook is a demanding and energizing experience. The selections were so rich in practical implication that connections, ideas, and insights seem to tumble onto my notebook.

I wish that Berthoff included selections from other thinkers—say, Nietzsche, Heidegger, or even John Dewey—but she makes no inclusive claims. She has gathered together an original and engaging anthology of creative minds. And there is no doubt that if we drink deep, our own thinking about the potential and importance of writing will be enriched.

Beyond its obvious practical implications, *Reclaiming the Imagination*, like Berthoff's work in general, gives us the opportunity to question our epistemological assumptions, to examine the intricate ways our own pedagogy and theory are intertwined. We are also reminded that our classroom attempts to produce writing that has the snap and substance of authentic commitment are intimately bound up with the vigor and freshness of our own ideas and spirits. An open, informed, and enthusiastic dialectic can renew our intellectual energy and help us sustain the current renaissance in writing theory that Ann Berthoff so enlivens.

PATRICIA BIZZELL AND BRUCE HERZBERG

Writing across the Curriculum: A Bibliographic Essay

"Writing across the curriculum" has come to mean three things to writing teachers in America. It denotes, first, a theory of the function of writing in learning; second, a pedagogy to encourage particular uses of writing in learning; and third, a program that applies the pedagogy in a particular school. American interest in the theoretical, pedagogical, and institutional aspects of writing across the curriculum has been growing rapidly in recent years, in part as a response to perceived declines in students' writing ability. Harvey Wiener, president of the Council of Writing Program Administrators, estimates that there are now about four hundred college-level writing-across-the-curriculum programs.[1] Most American scholarship in the field is also recent, appearing after 1975.

The concept of writing across the curriculum was introduced in the 1960s by James Britton and his colleagues at the University of London Institute of Education. They studied language in secondary-level classrooms and found that most speaking, reading, and writing is used to convey information (Barnes et al., *Language*). In the London group's seminal work, *The Development of Writing Abilities (11-18)*, Britton and his colleagues found that the overwhelming majority of student writing is "transactional," that is, writing used to convey information to a relatively distant and impersonal audience, usually the teacher in the role of examiner. Britton and his colleagues contrasted transactional writing with two other kinds, "poetic" and "expressive." Poetic writing allows the student to step back from the role of active participant in the world, to contemplate and speculate, and to share his or her thoughts with an intimate audience, for example, the teacher in the role of trusted adult. Expressive writing also allows students to explore ideas informally, but in expository modes such as the class journal rather than in fiction or poetry. (For summaries of the London group's work, see Applebee, "London Projects"; Rosen, "Interview"; Shafer, "British Proposal.")

The London group's studies in developmental psychology and the philosophy of language suggest that adolescents, like younger children, need to use language in personal, exploratory ways, with the support of a friendly audience, in order to learn (Britton, *Language*). In other words, they need more opportunities for poetic and expressive writing. This need is particularly great for students whose social origins put them at a comparatively greater remove from school conventions of language use. Students need to be able to make connections in their own vernacular between school knowledge and their own interests and values before they can be expected to master transactional writing.

Out of this understanding of the function of the language in learning grew the London group's Writing across the Curriculum Project, headed by Nancy Martin. The Writing across the Curriculum Project published a series of pamphlets demonstrating, with many examples of expressive and poetic writing and talking, the academic benefits of allowing students to use language in the full range of ways. The pamphlets (*Information*; *Why Write?*; *Talking*; *Science*; *Options*) also suggest assignments for expressive and poetic writing in a variety of disciplines (see also Nancy Martin et al., *Writing and Learning*).

A Language for Life, the report of the Bullock Commission, on which Britton served, advocates similar changes in language instruction across the curriculum. (See Brunetti, "Bullock Report.") This commission was appointed by then Secretary of State for Education and Science Margaret Thatcher to respond to Britain's version of the "back-to-basics" furor. Britton wrote the Bullock Report's chapters on early language development and collaborated on chapters dealing with writing instruction and language across the curriculum.

Britton and his colleagues were influenced by James Moffett's curriculum for *Teaching the Universe of Discourse* on the elementary and secondary levels, a curriculum recently detailed, with suggestions for college use, in Moffett's *Active Voice*. Moffett sorts language along a continuum from private, oral, concrete uses to public, written, abstract uses. Students will more easily master the full range of uses if they are encouraged to begin with those closest to their own speech. These beginning forms of language use are what Britton would call expressive—such as dialogues and letters—and poetic—such as plays and fictional autobiographies. Like Britton, Moffett does not aim to replace all transactional writing with expressive and poetic writing, but rather to help students feel comfortable with the full range of ways to use language to explore and communicate ideas.

Janet Emig was one of the first American theorists to make use of Britton's work. In *The Composing Processes of Twelfth Graders*, she revises Britton's classification of language uses. Her "reflexive" resembles his expressive, and her "extensive" resembles his transactional. Like Britton, she finds that when secondary-level students are given more opportunities to write reflexively, they engage in a more thoughtful writing process, write better and feel better about what they write, and learn more. Emig's argument for the importance of reflexive or expressive writing, however, differs from Britton's. In her seminal essay, "Writing as a Mode of Learning," Emig looks more to cognitive than to developmental psychology for evidence of the importance of all ways to use writing in learning. Whereas the London group emphasizes the continuity between speech and writing, Emig emphasizes the unique cognitive advantages conferred by writing. Writing requires imagining the audience and reinforces learning by involving hand, eye, and brain. The written text facilitates reflecting on and reformulating ideas. Writing thus becomes a central means to constitute and propagate knowledge.

Emig agrees with Britton that students must be given more opportunities to write reflexively (expressively) in all disciplines. Several studies have confirmed her finding that American students on the secondary and college levels do not have such opportunities now, because the great majority of the writing they do is transactional (Donlan, "Teaching Writing'" Tighe and Koziol, "Practices"; Eblen, "A Survey"). The most comprehensive of these studies is Arthur N. Applebee's *Writing in the Secondary Schools: English and the Content Areas.* American interest in writing across the curriculum has been strengthened by the conjunction of findings that most student writing is transactional, and of widespread feelings that student writing ability is declining. Suspecting a causal relationship, many composition administrators have argued for a program to inform college faculty in all disciplines of the need for expressive and poetic writing, as well as the usual transactional assignments.

In addition to encouraging cross-disciplinary uses of expressive and poetic writing, some work on writing across the curriculum explores uses of language peculiar to the academy. The aim of this work is to reform freshman composition pedagogy as well as writing instruction in courses outside the English department. Elaine Maimon has argued that this new freshman composition pedagogy should teach academic discourse (*Instructor's Manual*). She explains that each academic discipline has its own way of making sense of experience, which is embodied in the discourse conventions of the discipline. Moreover, some discourse conventions are shared by all academic disciplines— that is, there is an academic discourse as well as disciplinary discourses. A. D. Van Nostrand argues ("Writing and Knowledge") that studying academic discourse teaches students how to find—or create—significant relationships between facts, rather than simply to report facts. The freshman composition course, where students learn what ways of relating facts are significant in the academy, is the place where they are initiated into academic discourse (Bizzell, "Initiation").

Writing program administrators have been eagerly exchanging ideas on how to implement the various aims of writing across the curriculum. A national network of writing-across-the-curriculum programs has been formed; several newsletters circulate. College-level writing-across-the-curriculum programs typically take one of two forms, Laurence Peters has found ("Across the U.S."). One common kind of program is centered in an interdisciplinary freshman composition course. The other is centered in upper-level writing-intensive courses in various disciplines.

The most complete account of an interdisciplinary freshman composition course can be found in *Writing in the Arts and Sciences*, a textbook by Elaine Maimon and several of her colleagues from other departments at Beaver College. The book begins with the section "Writing to Learn," which discusses cross-disciplinary uses of expressive writing, heuristics, and informal academic writing, such as class notes and library work. The second major section, "Learning to Write," comprises chapters on discipline-specific discourse such as the humanities research paper, the social science case study, and the natural science laboratory report. A few other textbooks for writing across the curriculum have appeared, and more are likely to come out in the near future (Behrens, "Meditations"; Bizzel and Herzberg, "Textbooks"). Another model for the interdisciplinary course has been developed by David Hamilton ("Interdisciplinary Writing"): students practice "serious parodies" of disciplinary discourse in order to grasp the underlying conceptual activities specific to each discipline. (See also Rose, "Remedial Writing.")

Writing-across-the-curriculum programs based in upper-level writing-intensive courses frequently stress the importance of expressive writing in all disciplines. Toby Fulwiler has shown how journals can be used both to explore academic content and to relate knowledge to one's own values ("Journals"). With Art Young, he has also edited a collection of essays on the teaching of poetic, expressive, and transactional writing in the Michigan Technological University writing-across-the-curriculum program (*Language Connections*). On the other hand, in collections such as those edited by C. William Griffin (*Teaching Writing*) and by Christopher Thaiss (*Writing to Learn*), the assumption is not necessarily that expressive writing needs to be increased. Rather, teachers in all disciplines should use writing for learning in ways particularly useful in their disciplines. (See also Odell, "Process.")

Faculty development has become an important aspect of writing across the curriculum. Professors who have not been trained to teach writing, whether they teach literature or other academic disciplines, often have too narrow a notion of "good" writing as grammatically correct writing. If they do not see themselves as writers, experiencing the complexities of the composing process, they often do not appreciate students' need for guidance through this process. They may be reluctant to take on the extra work of teaching writing, or fear that it will take time away from essential course content. They may be wary of the writing program administrator's expanded influence in college affairs.

This need for faculty development has prompted much work on how to start a writing-across-the-curriculum program and conduct writing workshops for faculty from all disciplines. Elaine Maimon has given practical advice on coping with intracampus politics ("Cinderella"; "Getting Started"). Some workshops, such as those conducted by Anne Herrington ("Writing to Learn") and Ann Raimes ("Writing and Learning"), seek to sensitize faculty to the ways they are teaching academic discourse and to make their assignment design and essay evaluation more effective through discussion of examples from their own courses (see also Rose, "Faculty Talk"; Walvoord, *Helping Students*). Another kind of workshop aims to develop faculty's view of themselves as writers by asking them to write expressively and to critique each other's work. Toby Fulwriter has been an influential proponent of such workshops ("Showing, not Telling"). (See also Bergman, "Inclusive Literacy"; Freisinger, "Cross-Disciplinary Workshops.")

This American work on pedagogical and institutional concerns has relied for its theoretical underpinnings on the scholarship by Britton—by far the most frequently cited authority—Emig, and Moffett. Their work has helped us to understand the function of writing in the intellectual development of the individual student. But Britton, Emig, and Moffett have done most of their work on the elementary and secondary level. We are only now beginning to realize that new American theoretical work in writing across the curriculum is needed, work which addresses concerns particular to American, college-level writing instruction. This new theoretical work is beginning to take shape around the question of whether all students should be required to learn academic discourse. Mina Shaughnessy has diagnosed basic writers' fundamental problem as ignorance of academic discourse conventions ("Needed Research").

In exploring this question, theorists are reexamining the importance of expressive writing in writing-across-the-curriculum programs. Expressive writing plays a part in most programs. It can be regarded as one important stage in a writing process which will issue eventually in finished pieces of academic writing. But C. H. Knoblauch and Lil Brannon have argued that keeping up a student-teacher dialogue through expressive writing should be the main goal of writing across the curriculum, because it is through such dialogue that inquiry methods are learned ("Writing as Learning"). They see the teaching of academic discourse as drill in "formal shells," leading to nothing more than "grammar across the curriculum." They fear that students whose home languages are at a relatively greater remove from academic discourse will be unduly penalized by a policy which requires all students to master academic discourse. These students will spend so much time on superficial aspects of academic discourse, such as Standard English usage, that they will have little time left for substantive learning.

Other theorists argue that learning and discourse conventions cannot be separated in the academy. Students must be able eventually to use academic discourse if they are to master the full complexities of academic thinking. The notion of dialogue or conversation as a mode of learning here is redefined to mean not a face-to-face encounter, but a sustained communal enterprise. Charles Bazerman ("Conversation Model") has explained that learning how to enter this ongoing conversation means learning how the academic community talks and writes about what it does. As Elaine Maimon has argued, this is a matter of "Talking to Strangers" for students unfamiliar with the academic discourse community. But if students are not required to learn this discourse, they risk not participating fully in college intellectual life. To help them, we need more study of how this community develops and transmits its discourse conventions, a study in which scholars trained in literary criticism may be particularly well suited to engage (Maimon, "Maps and Genres").

Such study would help to return rhetoric to its eminent place in the curriculum. James Raymond has argued that rhetoric is the least reductive, most interdisciplinary methodology in the liberal arts ("Rhetoric"). Taking a similar position, James Kinneavy has observed that increased attention to rhetoric helps faculty in all disciplines to communicate better with each other about the intellectual problems upon which they are working. They are thus better prepared to train their students not only to develop complex arguments within the disciplines but also to explain their areas of expertise cogently to a general audience. Kinneavy hopes that the spread of writing-across-the-curriculum programs will eventually revivify informed public discourse in our democracy, since citizens will be better able to sift evidence and evaluate debates on complex issues ("Writing across the Curriculum").

The study of "rhetoric across the curriculum," to coin a phrase, is becoming the study of how the academic community constitutes and legitimates its knowledge through its discourse. We are learning, as Kenneth Bruffee has shown, that knowledge is a "social entity," always collaboratively produced ("Structure of Knowledge"). From such study, too, we learn how other communities similarly constitute themselves in language. Because this is becoming the focus of rhetoric, literary critics have recently been studying it together with composition specialists. In one such fruitful exchange (Horner, *Bridging the Gap*), eminent scholars agree that the establishment of English departments was justified by a false distinction between literary discourse and discourse that conveys information. This distinction lead to a separation between reading instruction, which focuses upon interpreting literary texts, and writing instruction, which focuses upon producing expository texts. Because this separation not only devalues composition studies but also impoverishes literary theory, it is now ending. A new kind of English department is emerging, united under a rhetorical paradigm, and well suited to study all kinds of discourse, not just fiction and poetry, and to foster rhetoric across the curriculum.

Bibliography

Applebee, Arthur N. "Writing Across the Curriculum: The London Projects." *English Journal*, 66 (1977), 81-85.

_____. *Writing in the Secondary School: English and the Content Areas.* Urbana, IL: National Council of Teachers of English, 1981.
    Eighty-two percent of teachers surveyed agree that writing instruction is the responsibility of all faculty. But only 3 percent of lesson time is spent on writing of paragraph length or more. Very little attention is given to the writing process. Virtually all writing is informational (transactional), for an audience of teacher-as-examiner.

Barnes, Douglas, James Britton, and Harold Rosen. *Language, the Learner, and the School.* Harmondsworth, England: Penguin, 1969.

Bazerman, Charles. "A Relationship between Reading and Writing: The Conversation Model." *College English*, 41 (1980), 656–61.

Behrens, Laurence. "Meditations, Reminiscences, Polemics: Composition Readers and the Service Course." *College English*, 41 (1980), 561–70.
    Surveying composition readers, Behrens finds that almost all selections are meditations, reminiscences, or polemics. Most of the writing that students do in other courses, however, seeks to convey information, and students are better at conveying information than they are at writing meditations, reminiscences, and polemics. A new kind of reader is needed to "serve" students by teaching the kinds of writing they do in other courses.

Bergman, Charles A. "An Inclusive Literacy: U. S. Schools Are Teaching and Writing in All the Subject Disciplines." *AAHE Bulletin* (December 1982), pp. 3–5.
    Bergman argues for writing across the curriculum as a way of demystifying the conventions of academic discourse, and describes the "conversation experience" of faculty at his university after a workshop with Kenneth Bruffee in which they learned to see themselves as writers.

_____. "Writing Across the Curriculum: An Annotated Bibliography." *AAHE Bulletin* (1983–84), pp. 33–38.
    Bergman selects forty-one entries, citing some important theoretical

works and a number of articles that describe writing-across-the-curriculum programs at specific schools.

Bizzell, Patricia. "College Composition: Initiation into the Academic Discourse Community." *Curriculum Inquiry*, 12 (1982), 191–207.

Bizzel argues that students' unequal distance from school discourse is a function of social class, that access to academic discourse is a prerequisite for social power, and that linguistically disenfranchised students can be helped by a writing-across-the-curriculum approach that seeks to demystify the conventions of academic discourse.

Bizzell, Patricia, and Bruce Herzberg. "Writing-across-the-Curriculum Textbooks: A Bibliographic Essay." *Rhetoric Review*, forthcoming.

Britton, James. *Language and Learning*. Harmondsworth, England: Penguin, 1970.

Britton develops the theory that we construct our understanding of the world through language, an individual task shaped by social interaction.

Britton, James, et al. *The Development of Writing Abilities (11-18)*. London: Macmillan Education, 1975; rpt. Urbana, IL: National Council of Teachers of English, 1977.

Bruffee, Kenneth. "The Structure of Knowledge and the Future of Liberal Education." *Liberal Education*, 67 (1981), 177–86.

We have assumed that knowledge is determined by external reality and should be attained by individual effort in a hierarchical educational system. But the work of Einstein, Heisenberg, and Gödel suggests that knowledge is created and promulgated through social activity. Hence education should be restructured for collaborative work, as in peer-tutoring workshops and writing-across-the-curriculum programs.

Brunetti, Gerald J. "The Bullock Report: Some Implications for American Teachers and Parents." *English Journal*, 67 (1978), 58–64.

Bullock Commission. *A Language for Life*. London: H.M.S.O., 1975.

Donlan, Dan. "Teaching Writing in the Content Areas: Eleven Hypotheses from a Teacher Survey." *Research in the Teaching of English*, 8 (1974), 250–62.

Dunn, Robert F. "A Response to Two Views." *AAHE Bulletin*, (December 1982), pp. 7–8.

Eblen, Charlene. "Writing Across-the-Curriculum: A Survey of A University Faculty's Views and Classroom Practices." *Research in the Teaching of English*, 17 (1983), 343–48.

Emig, Janet. *The Composing Processes of Twelfth Graders*. Urbana, IL: National Council of Teachers of English, 1971.

_____. "Writing as a Mode of Learning." *College Composition and Communication*, 28 (1977), 122–28. Rpt. in *The Writing Teacher's Sourcebook*. Ed. Gary Tate and E. P. J. Corbett. New York: Oxford Univ. Pr., 1981, pp. 69–78.

Freisinger, Randall R. "Cross-Disciplinary Writing Workshops: Theory and Practice." *College English*, 42 (1980), 154–56, 161–66.
    Following Britton, Freisinger strongly defends the use of expressive writing in all disciplines, in spite of faculty resistance to this notion. He uses Piaget to argue that the absence of expressive writing retards cognitive development in college-age students.

Fulwiler, Toby. "Journals across the Disciplines." *English Journal*, 69 (1980), 14–19.
    Fulwiler cites Britton and Emig on the need for expressive writing across the curriculum, and argues that journals have served this end well. He describes both the "academic journal," which focuses on course content, and the "personal journal," which focuses on ethical responses to course content.

_____. "Showing, not Telling, at a Writing Workshop." *College English*, 43 (1981), 55–63.
    A good account of Fulwiler's methods in faculty workshops. He details five strategies and recommends conducting the workshop like a retreat.

Fulwiler, Toby, and Art Young, ed. *Language Connections: Writing and Reading across the Curriculum*. Urbana, IL: National Council of Teachers of English, 1982.
    Twelve essays from the Michigan Tech writing-across-the-curriculum program, written by professors of literature, rhetoric, and reading. Essays address the interdisciplinary teaching of poetic, expressive, and transactional writing. The book includes three essays on reading, two on peer critiquing, and a selected bibliography.

Griffin, C. Williams, ed. *Teaching Writing in All Disciplines*. San Francisco: Jossey-Bass, 1982.
    Ten essays on writing-across-the-curriculum theory and practice, including John C. Bean, Dean Drenk, and F. D. Lee, "Microtheme Strategies for Developing Cognitive Skills"; Toby Fulwiler, "Writing: An Act of Cognition"; Elaine Maimon, "Writing across the Curriculum: Past, Present, and Future"; Chris Thaiss, "The Virginia Consortium of Faculty Writing Programs: A Variety of Practices"; Barbara Fassler Walvoord and Hoke L. Smith, "Coaching the Process of Writing."

Hamilton, David. "Interdisciplinary Writing." *College English*, 41 (1980), 780–90, 795–96.

Hamilton describes the Iowa Institute on Writing for writing program administrators, which developed an interdisciplinary freshman composition course using "serious parodies" of discourse modes of various disciplines, with the aim of teaching transferable processes of conceptualization. The article also analyzes the limitations of other interdisciplinary writing courses, such as those that ask students to write about their areas of expertise for a lay audience.

Herrington, Anne J. "Writing to Learn: Writing across the Disciplines." *College English*, 43 (1981), 379–87.

Following a defense of writing across the curriculum that draws on the work of Emig and Lee Odell, Herrington describes her workshops to help faculty design writing-intensive courses in their own disciplines. She describes good assignments in economics, sociology, and psychology.

Horner, Winifred, ed. *Composition and Literature: Bridging the Gap*. Chicago: Univ. of Chicago Pr., 1983.

Twelve essays by eminent literary critics and composition specialists, including Wayne Booth, E. P. J. Corbett, E. D. Hisch, Jr., Richard Lanham, Elaine Maimon. and J. Hillis Miller.

Kinneavy, James L. "Writing across the Curriculum." *ADE Bulletin*. 76 (1983): 14–21. Rpt. in *Profession 83*. Ed. Richard Brod and Phyllis Franklin. New York: Modern Language Association, 1983, pp. 13–20.

Knoblauch, C. H., and Lil Brannon. "Writing as Learning through the Curriculum." *College English*, 45 (1983), 465–74.

Maimon, Elaine. "Cinderella to Hercules: Demythologizing Writing across the Curriculum." *Journal of Basic Writing*, 2 (1980), 3–11.

Maimon describes and debunks several "myths" that obstruct writing-across-the-curriculum programs, such as the Myth of the Simple Rules, which leads misguided college deans to think that writing across the curriculum is simply a matter of enforcing a few grammar guidelines; the Myth of Cinderella, which casts writing teachers in a menial role; the Myth of Hercules, which envisions an effective program being launched by the writing program administrator alone; and more. This issue of *JBW* includes seven other essays on writing across the curriculum.

_____. "Maps and Genres." In *Composition and Literature: Bridging the Gap*. Ed. Winifred Horner. Chicago: Univ. of Chicago Pr., 1983, pp. 110–25.

_____. "Talking to Strangers." *College Composition and Communication*, 30 (1979), 364–69.

_____. "Writing in All the Arts and Sciences: Getting Started and Gaining Momentum." *Writing Program Administration*, 4 (1981), 9–13.

Maimon discusses administrative problems of launching writing-across-the-curriculum programs; how to deal with resistance within the English department; general curriculum guidelines. This issue of *WPA* also includes Toby Fulwiler, "Writing across the Curriculum at Michigan Tech," an account of his successful faculty seminars there; and a response to both Fulwiler and Maimon by Ann Raimes.

_____. *Instructor's Manual: Writing in the Arts and Sciences*. Cambridge, MA: Winthrop Publishers, 1981.

Maimon, Elaine P., and Gerald L. Belcher, Gail W. Hearn, Barbara F. Nodine, Finbarr W. O'Connor. *Writing in the Arts and Sciences*. Cambridge, MA: Winthrop Publishers, 1981.

Martin, Nancy, et al. *Writing and Learning Across the Curriculum 11–16*. London: Ward Lock, 1976.

Moffett, James. *Active Voice: A Writing Program across the Curriculum*. Montclair, NJ: Boynton-Cook, 1981.

_____. *Teaching the Universe of Discourse*. Boston: Houghton Mifflin, 1969.

Odell, Lee. "The Process of Writing and the Process of Learning." *College Composition and Communication*, 31 (1980), 42–50.

In faculty writing workshops, Odell discovered that writing in different disciplines requires a wide variety of conceptual activities; the inability to perform them is the chief cause of bad student writing. Workshops should not, therefore, seek to persuade faculty to teach any one heuristic method. Elements from a few powerful heuristics, however, can be combined to provide an invention method useful across the disciplines.

Peters, Laurence. "Writing Across the Curriculum: Across the U.S." In *Writing to Learn: Essays and Reflections by College Teachers across the Curriculum*. Ed. Christopher Thaiss. Fairfax, VA: George Mason University Faculty Writing Program, 1982, pp. 4–19.

Raimes, Ann. "Writing and Learning across the Curriculum: The Experience of a Faculty Seminar." *College English*, 41 (1980), 797–801.

To attend a seminar led by Raimes and Charles Persky, faculty in several disciplines received released time during the semester so that they could work on writing assignments and use student writing from current courses as the principal "text." Discussions focussed on assignment design and essay evaluation.

Raymond, James C. "Rhetoric: The Methodology of the Humanities." *College English*, 44 (1982), 778–83.

Rose, Mike. "Remedial Writing Courses: A Critique and a Proposal." *College English*, 45 (1983), 109-28.

Rose argues against the focus on personal writing common to many remedial composition programs, and for an interdisciplinary course that introduces developmental students immediately to college-level reading, writing, and thinking tasks.

———. "When Faculty Talk about Writing." *College English*, 41 (1979), 272–79.

A cross-disciplinary group of faculty, teaching assistants, and student counsellors met to discuss their perceptions of student writing problems and agreed on some action—give professional recognition for composition teaching and research; teach academic discourse in freshman composition; and move university-wide standards for evaluating writing beyond a narrow focus on grammar.

Rosen, Lois, interviewer. "An Interview with James Britton, Tony Burgess, and Harold Rosen: Closeup: The Teaching of Writing in Great Britain." *English Journal*, 67 (1978), 50-58.

Shafer, Robert E. "A British Proposal for Improving Literacy." *Educational Forum*, 46 (1981), 81-96.

Shafer summarizes work of Britton and his colleagues, giving particular attention to theory. He discusses Britton's spectator/participant distinction; the work of Barnes and Rosen on the chasm between academic discourse and the students' own language; the influence of Sapir, Kelly, and Vygotsky; and the relation between speaking and writing.

Shaughnessy, Mina. "Some Needed Research on Writing." *College Composition and Communication*, 28 (1977), 317–21.

Shaughessy argues that basic writers are those "unskilled in the rituals and ways of winning arguments in academe." To help them, we need a taxonomy of academic discourse conventions.

Thaiss, Christopher, ed. *Writing to Learn: Essays and Reflections by College Teachers across the Curriculum*. Fairfax, VA: George Mason University Faculty Writing Program, 1982.

Sixteen essays by professors of accounting, education, English, finance, mathematics, nursing, physical education, and psychology. They argue for value of writing across the curriculum while describing classroom ideas that have worked well.

Tighe, M. A., and S. M. Koziol, Jr. "Practices in the Teaching of Writing by Teachers of English, Social Studies, and Science." *English Education*, 4 (1982), 76–85.

Van Nostrand, A. D. "Writing and the Generation of Knowledge." *Social Education*, 43 (1979), 178–80.

    This article heads a special section, "Writing to Learn in Social Studies," edited by Barry K. Beyer and Anita Brostoff, and aimed at secondary-level teachers.

Walvoord, Barbara E. Fassler. *Helping Students Write Well: A Guide for Teachers in All Disciplines*. New York: Modern Language Association, 1982.

    A good book for faculty who have not yet thought about how they teach writing. Walvoord concentrates on ways to respond effectively to student writing above the developmental level. Many specific examples of assignments and student papers.

Writing Across the Curriculum Project. *From Information to Understanding: What Children Do with New Ideas*. London: Ward Lock, 1973; rpt. Montclair, NJ: Boynton-Cook, 1983.

_____. *Why Write?* London: Ward Lock, 1973; rpt. Montclair, NJ: Boynton-Cook, 1983.

    Children should be encouraged to write about knowledge important to them, rather than forced to learn particular essay forms.

_____. *From Talking to Writing*. London: Ward Lock, 1973; rpt. Montclair, NJ: Boynton-Cook, 1983.

    This pamphlet argues for expressive talk, but also argues that some kinds of thinking can only be accomplished in writing, because writing facilitates reflection and reformulation. Writing assignments should call on these unique powers rather than simply asking for a report on what has been learned.

_____. *Writing in Science: Papers from a Seminar with Science Teachers*. London: Ward Lock, 1973.

_____. *Keeping Options Open: Writing in the Humanities*. London: Ward Lock, 1973; rpt. Montclair, NJ: Boynton-Cook, 1983.

Notes

Notes on Contributors

Notes

Grammar in American College Composition: An Historical Overview

1. Rollo L. Lyman, *English Grammar in American Schools before 1850* (Washington, D.C.: Govt. Printing Office, 1922), p. 5.

2. Charles C. Fries, "Linguistic Science and the Teaching of English," in *Perspectives in English*, ed. Robert C. Pooley (New York: Appleton-Century-Crofts, 1960), p. 152.

3. Lindley Murray, *An English Grammar*, 7th ed. (New York: Thomas Wilson, 1842), p. 333.

4. For an informative discussion of this phenomenon, see Edward Finegan, *Attitudes toward English Usage: The History of a War of Words* (New York: Teachers' College Press, 1980), pp. 30–60.

5. Samuel S. Greene, *Greene's Analysis*, (Philadelphia: Thomas, Cowperthwaite, 1847), p. 79.

6. William H. Wells, "Methods of Teaching English Grammar," *Barnard's American Journal of Education*, 5 (1865), 148–49.

7. F. A. Barbour, "History of English Grammar Teaching," *Educational Review*, 12 (1896), 487–507.

8. George P. Marsh, *Lectures on the English Language*, (New York: Scribner's, 1860), pp. 87–88.

9. C. Homer Bean, "How English Grammar has Been Taught in America," *Education*, 34 (1913–14), 311.

10. Alonzo Reed and Brainerd Kellogg, *Higher Lessons in English* (New York: Clark and Maynard, 1877), p. 3.

11. See especially Buck's "Make-Believe Grammar," *School Review*, 17 (1909), 21–33.

12. See, for instance, C. R. Rounds, "The Varying Systems of Nomenclature in Use in Our Texts in English Grammar," *Educational Review*, 40 (1910), 82–88.

13. George Campbell, *The Philosophy of Rhetoric* (London: William Tegg, 1850), p. 35.

14. Hugh Blair, *Lectures on Rhetoric and Belles-Lettres* (Philadelphia: Troutman and Hayes, 1853), p. 78.

15. Blair, *Lectures*, p. 101.

16. Samuel P. Newman, *A Practical System of Rhetoric* (New York: Mark H. Newman, 1843), p. 136.

17. For more information on this debate, see my essay "Mechanical Correctness in Composition Instruction," forthcoming in *College Composition and Communication*, and Finegan, *Attitudes toward English Usage*, pp. 62–75.

18. Wells, "Methods of Teaching English Grammar," p. 149.

19. For more on this examination, see A. S. Hill, "An Answer to the Cry for More English," in *Twenty Years of School and College English* (Cambridge: Harvard Univ. Pr., 1896), pp. 6–16.

20. Joseph H. Gilmore, *Outlines of the Art of Expression* (Boston: Ginn, 1876), p. 3.

21. Edwin A. Abbott, *How to Write Clearly* (Boston: Roberts Bros., 1875), p. 7.

22. Some texts did incorporate grammar, but they were rare. C. W. Bardeen's *A System of Rhetoric* of 1884, for instance, included 139 pages of straight grammar—numbered with Roman numerals and called an "Introduction"—but it also utilized a more pragmatic organizational system than most popular texts and did not sell well.

23. John F. Genung, *The Practical Elements of Rhetoric* (Boston: Ginn, 1886), p. 109.

24. E. L. Godkin, "The Illiteracy of American Boys," *Educational Review*, 13 (1897), 7.

25. Edwin C. Woolley, *Handbook of Composition: A Compendium of Rules* (Boston: D. C. Heath, 1907), p. iv.

26. See my essay, "Handbooks: History of a Genre," *Rhetoric Society Quarterly*, 13 (1983), 87–98.

27. Frank W. Scott, "Composition and the Rest of the Curriculum," *English Journal*, 7 (1918), 515.

28. For instance, Edward A. Allen in 1887: "But our grammarians, refusing to study their language in its marvelous process of development for the last thousand years, have been content either to create rules for the use of it . . . or to borrow the rules of those languages which have a differently developed system of grammar. . . . No student should be deluded into the belief that he can become a grammarian by the study of the grammar alone" ("English Grammar Viewed from All Sides," *Education*, 7 [1887], 466–69.

29. Thomas Lounsbury, *The Standard of Usage in English* (New York: Harper, 1908), p. 71.

30. George Krapp, *Modern English: Its Growth and Present Use* (New York: Scribner's, 1909), p. 330.

31. "The Call for the Organization Meeting," *Language*, 1 (1925), 6.

32. Leonard Bloomfield, "Why a Linguistic Society?" *Language*, 1 (1925), 5.

33. Sterling A. Leonard, " 'Old Purist Junk,' " *English Journal*, 7 (1918), 296. See also his *Current English Usage* (Chicago: Inland Press, 1932).

34. These studies are mentioned and evaluated by James F. Hosic in "The Essentials of Composition and Grammar," *School and Society*, 1 (1915), 581–587.

35. William Asker, "Does Knowledge of Formal Grammar Function?" *School and Society*, 17 (1923), 109–11.

36. Charles C. Fries, "Preface," *The Teaching of the English Language* (New York: Thomas Nelson, 1927).

37. Leon Mones, "A Word on Formal Grammar," *Education*, 44 (1923–24), 234.

38. See, for instance, C. R. Rounds, "Is Grammar Useful?" *Education*, 46 (1925–26), 551–559.

39. Wilbur Hatfield et al., *An Experience Curriculum in English*, (New York: Appleton-Century, 1935), p. 228.

40. See Harold B. Allen, "From Prairies to Mountains: Linguistics and Composition," *College English*, 26 (1965), 266.

41. Two good historical sources are John P. Hughes, *The Science of Language: An Introduction to Linguistics* (New York: Random House, 1962), and John Lyons, *Introduction to Theoretical Linguistics* (Cambridge: Cambridge Univ. Pr., 1968).

42. Charles C. Fries, *American English Grammar* (New York: Appleton-Century, 1940), p. vii.

43. Fries was not, of course, the only or even the most important contributor to the terms "structural grammar" or "structural linguistics." The terms had existed since the thirties, and in linguistics such books as Zellig Harris' *Methods in Structural Linguistics* (1951) and George Trager and Lee Smith's *Outline of English Structures* (1951) were much better known than Fries'. Fries, however, brought the terms to popular use in English and was almost certainly responsible for such later titles as A. A. Hill's *Introduction to Linguistic Structure* (1958) and W. Nelson Francis' *Structure of American English* (1958).

44. W. Nelson Francis, "Our Responsibility to the English Language," *College English*, 14 Language," *College English*, 14 (1953), 329.

45. W. Ross Winterowd, "Linguistics and Composition," in *Teaching Composition: Ten Bibliographical Essays*, ed. Gary Tate (Fort Worth: Texas Christian Univ. Pr., 1976), pp. 197–221.

46. Charlton Laird, "The Parts, or Vestigial Remnants, of Speech," *College English*, 18 (1957), 337.

47. Wilbur W. Hatfield, "Will Structural Grammar Help?" *English Journal*, 47 (1958), 570–72.

48. Harry R. Warfel, "Structural Linguistics and Composition," *College English*, 20 (1959), 205.

49. Samuel R. Levin, "Comparing Traditional and Structural Grammar," *College English,* 21 (1960), 260–65.

50. Allain Renoir, "Traditional Grammar or Structural Linguistics," *College English,* 22 (1961), 484.

51. Charles C. Fries, "Advances in Linguistics," *College English,* 23 (1961), 37. See also his essay, "Linguistic Science and the Teaching of English."

52. James Sledd, "A Plea for Pluralism," *College English,* 23 (1961), 16.

53. Again, James Sledd has an apposite comment on structural linguistics: "That version of modernity is now quite rejected and forgotten, having been succeeded by several other abiding truths; but despite the confusion of the shifting doctrines, a clear result has certainly been attained— namely, a state of utter confusion among school teachers and blank ignorance among their pupils. We have taught the teachers to despise our one established grammatical tradition; we have given them nothing stable to put in its place; and consequently the average student in our colleges and universities today knows nothing of any grammatical system whatsoever and is totally at a loss when in any of his classes strange vocables like *noun* and *verb* are uttered." ("What Are We Going to Do About It Now That We're Number One?" *American Speech,* 53 [1978], 184.)

54. Richard Braddock, Richard Lloyd-Jones, and Lowell Schoer, *Research in Written Composition* (Campaign, IL: NCTE, 1963), pp. 37–38.

Teaching Style

1. T. W. Baldwin, *William Shakespere's Small Latine & Lesse Greeke,* 2 vols. (Urbana, IL: Univ. of Illinois Pr., 1944); Sister Miriam Joseph, *Shakespeare's Use of the Arts of Language* (New York: Columbia Univ. Pr., 1947); Donald L. Clark, *John Milton at St. Paul's School: A Study of Ancient Rhetoric in English Renaissance Education* (New York: Columbia Univ. Pr., 1948).

2. Martin Joos, *The Five Clocks,* (New York: Harcourt, Brace, and World, Harbinger Books, 1962), p. 11.

3. Edward P. J. Corbett, "Style," in *Classical Rhetoric for the Modern Student,* 2d ed. (New York: Oxford Univ. Pr., 1971), pp. 414–593; Edward P. J. Corbett, "A Method of Analyzing Prose Style, with a Demonstration Analysis of Swift's *A Modest Proposal,*" in *The Writing Teacher's Sourcebook,* ed. Gary Tate and Edward P. J. Corbett (New York: Oxford Univ. Pr., 1981), pp. 333–52.

4. Richard Ohmann, *Shaw, the Style and the Man* (Middletown, CT: Wesleyan Univ. Pr., 1962).

5. Edwin H. Lewis, *History of the English Paragraph* (Chicago: Univ. of Chicago Pr., 1894); L. A. Sherman, *Some Observations upon Sentence-Length in English Prose* (Lincoln, NB: Univ. of Nebraska Pr., 1892).

6. See Wilbur Samuel Howell, "The British Elocutionary Movement," in his *Eighteenth-Century British Logic and Rhetoric* (Princeton, NJ: Princeton Univ. Pr., 1971), pp. 145–256.

7. George Saintsbury, *A History of Prose Rhythm* (London, 1912; reissued Bloomington, IN: Indiana Univ. Pr., 1965).

8. Thomas S. Kane, " 'The Shape and Ring of Sentences,' " *College Composition and Communication,* 28 (February 1977), 38–42.

9. Paul C. Rodgers, Jr., "Alexander Bain and the Rise of the Organic Paragraph," *Quarterly Journal of Speech,* 50 (December 1965), 399–408.

10. Francis Christensen, "A Generative Rhetoric of the Paragraph," in his *Notes Toward a New Rhetoric* (New York: Harper and Row, 1967), pp. 74–103; Alton L. Becker, "A Tagmemic Approach to Paragraph Analysis," *College Composition and Communication,* 16 (December 1965), 237–42; Paul C. Rodgers, Jr., "A Discourse-Centered Rhetoric of the Paragraph," *College Composition and Communication,* 17 (February 1966), 2–11; Frank D'Angelo, "Style as Structure," *Style,* 8 (Spring 1974), 322–64.

11. Edward P. J. Corbett, "Style," in *Classical Rhetoric,* pp. 414–593; Edward P. J. Corbett, "Expressing What You Have Discovered, Selected, and Arranged," in *The Little Rhetoric and*

Handbook, 2d ed. (Glenview, IL: Scott, Foresman, 1982), pp. 70–120; Francis Christensen, "A Generative Rhetoric of the Sentence," in his *Notes Toward a New Rhetoric* pp. 23–44; John C. Mellon, *Transformational Sentence-Combining: A Method for Enhancing the Development of Syntactic Fluency* (Urbana, IL: National Council of Teachers of English, 1969); Frank O'Hare, *Sentence-Combining: Improving Student Writing Without Formal Grammar Instruction* (Urbana, IL: National Council of Teachers of English, 1973); Walker Gibson, *Tough, Sweet, and Stuffy* (Bloomington, IN: Indiana Univ. Pr., 1966); Winston Weathers and Otis Wincheser, *Copy and Compose: A Guide to Prose Style* (Englewood Cliffs, NJ: Prentice-Hall, 1969); Joseph Williams, *Style: Ten Lessons in Clarity and Grace,* 2d ed. (Glenview, IL: Scott, Foresman, 1984); Thomas Whissen, *A Way with Words: A Guide for Writers* (New York: Oxford Univ. Pr., 1982).

Brain, Rhetoric, and Style

1. A brief and lucid account of this history is Steven Rose, "The Development of the Brain Sciences," in *The Conscious Brain* (New York: Vintage, 1976), pp. 21–48.

2. A. R. Luria, *The Working Brain: An Introduction to Neuropsychology,* trans. Basil Haigh (New York: Basic Books, 1973), pp. 306–7.

3. Morris Moscovitch, "On the Representation of Language in the Right Hemisphere of Right-Handed People," Brain and Language, 3 (January 1976), 47-71.

4. Maureen Dennis and Harry A. Whitaker, "Language Acquisition Following Hemidecortication: Linguistic Superiority of the Left over the Right Hemisphere of Right-Handed People," *Brain and Language,* 3 (July, 1976), 404-33.

5. J. E. Bogen, "Some Educational Aspects of Hemispheric Specialization," *UCLA Educator,* 17 (Spring, 1975), 27. An expanded version of this issue of the *UCLA Educator* is now available: M. C. Wittrock and others, *The Human Brain* (Englewood Cliffs, NJ: Prentice-Hall, 1977).

6. Bogen, 27.

7. Michael S. Gazzaniga, "Review of the Split Brain," *UCLA Educator,* 17 (Spring 1975), 9–12.

8. Robert D. Nebes, "Man's So-Called 'Minor' Hemisphere," *UCLA Educator,* 17 (Spring 1975), 13–16.

9. Stephen D. Krashen, "The Left Hemisphere," *UCLA Educator,* 17 (Spring 1975), 17–23.

10. Luria, p. 306.

11. Luria, p. 78.

12. "Letter to Jacques Hadamard," *The Creative Process,* ed. Brewster Ghiselin (New York: New American Library, n.d.), p. 43.

13. Nebes, p. 16.

14. Brendan A. Maher, "The Shattered Language of Schizophrenia," *Psychology Today,* 2 (Nov., 1968), pp. 30–33. See also S. R. Rochester, J. R. Martin, and S. Thurson, "Thought-Process Disorder in Schizophrenia: The Listener's Task," *Brain and Language,* 4 (Jan. 1977), 95–114.

15. To use the foregrounded style is "to present phenomena in a fully externalized form, visible and palpable in all their parts, and completely fixed in spatial and temporal relations." "On the other hand [in the backgrounded style], the externalization of only so much of the phenomena as is necessary for the purposes of the narrative, all else left in obscurity; the decisive points of the narrative alone are emphasized, what lies between is nonexistent; time and place are undefined and call for interpretation; thoughts and feelings remain unexpressed, are only suggested by the silence and the fragmentary speakers; the whole, permeated with the most unrelieved suspense and directed toward a single goal (and to that extent far more of a unity) remains mysterious and 'fraught with background.'" Erich Auerbach, *Mimesis: The Representation of Reality in Western Literature,* trans. Willard R. Trask (Princeton: Princeton Univ. Pr., 1968), pp. 6, 11–12.

16. See the section on presence in this essay.

17. Luria, pp. 78–79.

18. Adam F. Wechsler, "Crossed Aphasia in an Illiterate Dextral," *Brain and Language,* 3 (April 1976), 164–72.

19. Much of that work is assembled in *Contemporary Rhetoric: A Conceptual Background with Readings*, ed. W. Ross Winterowd (New York: Harcourt Brace Jovanovich, 1975).

20. Richard E. Young and Alton L. Becker, "Toward a Modern Theory of Rhetoric: A Tagmemic Contribution," and Francis Christensen, "A Generative Rhetoric of the Paragraph," in *Contemporary Rhetoric*, pp. 123–43.

21. Carl R. Rogers, "Toward a Theory of Creativity," *Creativity and Its Cultivation*, ed. Harold H. Anderson (New York: Harper and Row, 1959), p. 71.

22. Rogers, pp. 78–80.

23. Arthur Koestler, *The Act of Creation* (New York: Dell, 1967).

24. James L. Adams, *Conceptual Blockbusting: A Guide to Better Ideas* (San Francisco: W. H. Freeman, 1974).

25. John Crowe Ransom, "Poetry: A Note in Ontology," in *Critical Theory since Plato*, ed. Hazard Adams (New York: Harcourt Brace Jovanovich, 1971), p. 880.

26. "The Apprehension of Metaphor," *Language and Style*, 14 (Winter 1981), 20–33.

27. Christine Brooke-Rose, *A Grammar of Metaphor* (Atlantic Highlands, NJ: Hillary House, 1958).

28. Laurence Perrine, "Four Forms of Metaphor," in *Contemporary Rhetoric*, pp. 319–37.

29. In *Collected Earlier Poems*. Copyright 1938 by William Carlos Williams. Reprinted by permission of New Directions Publishing Corporation.

30. In *Collected Poems 1909–1962*. Copyright 1936 by Harcourt Brace Jovanovich, Inc. Reprinted by permission of the publisher.

31. I found this quotation written in the margin of my copy of Yeats, probably dating from about 1959. Apparently as long as twenty-five years ago, I had begun to have intuitions about metaphor and image.

32. Alfonso Caramazza, Joel Gordon, Edgar B. Ziff, and David de Luca, "Right Hemispheric Damage and Verbal Problem Solving Behavior," *Brain and Language*, 3 (January 1976), 41–46.

33. Frank Smith, "On Making Sense," in *Comprehension and Learning* (New York: Holt, Rinehart and Winston, 1975), pp. 9–48.

34. John C. Eccles, *Facing Reality* (Heidelberg and Berlin: Springer-Verlag, 1970), p. 57.

35. Roman Jakobson, "The Metaphoric and Metonymic Poles," in *Critical Theory since Plato*, pp. 1113–16.

36. Harry J. Jerison, "Evolution of the Brain," *UCLA Educator*, 17 (Spring 1975), 1–8.

37. This is much the same point that Keith Fort makes in his excellent essay "Form, Authority, and the Critical Essay," *College English*, 32 (March 1971), 629-39.

38. For an overview of reading theory, I suggest Frank Smith, *Understanding Reading*, 3d ed. (New York: Holt, Rinehart and Winston, 1982).

39. John T. Irwin, *Doubling and Incest/Repetition and Revenge: A Speculative Reading of Faulkner* (Baltimore: Johns Hopkins, 1975), pp. 6–7.

40. Smith, *Understanding Reading*, pp. 35–38.

41. This idea occurs again and again in Frye. See, for instance, "Nature and Homer," in *Fables of Identity* (New York: Harcourt Brace Jovanovich, 1963).

42. Northrop Frye, "Myth, Fiction, and Displacement," in *Fables of Identity*, p. 36.

43. Frye, p. 23.

44. Kenneth Burke, *Counter-Statement* (Los Altos, CA: Hermes Press, 1953), p. 124.

45. See W. Ross Winterowd, "Beyond Style," *Philosophy and Rhetoric*, 5 (Spring 1972), 88–110.

46. Robert E. Ornstein, *The Psychology of Consciousness* (New York: Penguin, 1975), p. 61.

47. Luria, p. 258.

48. Luria, p. 262.

49. Rose, p. 200.

50. I have encountered such an interpretation, though I cannot cite the source. The point is not so much that such an interpretation was made, but that it *might well be made*.

51. Ornstein discusses the problem of hemispherical dominance in whole societies as do Warren D. Ten Houten and Charles D. Kaplan, *Science and Its Mirror Image* (New York: Harper and Row, 1973).

52. Nebes, p. 15.

53. Eccles, pp. 52–53.

54. Robert Lowell, *Lord Weary's Castle and the Mills of the Kavanaughs* (New York: Harcourt Brace Jovanovich, 1951), p. 11. Reprinted by permission of the publisher.

55. Eccles, pp. 57–58.

56. Trans. John Wilkinson and Purcell Weaver (Notre Dame: Notre Dame University, 1969).

57. Perelman and Olbrechts-Tyteca, pp. 116–18.

58. Perelman and Olbrechts-Tyteca, pp. 65–114.

59. Earl Miner, "That Literature Is a Kind of Knowledge," *Critical Inquiry,* 2 (Spring 1976), 505.

60. Julian Jaynes, *The Origin of Consciousness in the Breakdown of the Bicameral Mind* (Boston: Houghton Mifflin, 1976).

Released into Language: Errors, Expectations, and the Legacy of Mina Shaughnessy

1. Adrienne Rich, "Teaching Language in Open Admissions (1972)," in *On Lies Secrets and Silence* (New York: Norton, 1979), pp. 51–68.

2. The preparation of this essay was supported by the Learning Research and Development Center at the University of Pittsburgh which is supported in part by the National Institute of Education. I am also grateful to Glynda Hull for her advice and assistance.

3. This talk was reprinted in *College Composition and Communication,* 27 (October 1976), 234–39. Further references to this essay will be cited in the text.

4. Mina Shaughnessy, *Errors and Expectations: A Guide for Teachers of Basic Writing* (New York: Oxford Univ. Pr., 1977). Further references to this work will be cited in the text.

5. See, for example, Barry Kroll and John Schafer, "Error Analysis and the Teaching of Composition," *College Composition and Communication,* 29 (October 1978), 243–48; Donald C. Freeman, "Linguistics and Error Analysis: On Agency," *Linguistics, Stylistics and the Teaching of Composition,* ed. Donald McQuade (Akron, OH: L & S Books, 1979), pp. 143-151, and reprinted in this volume; Kenneth A. Bruffee, "Getting Started," in *Linguistics, Stylistics and the Teaching of Composition,* pp. 52-61, and reprinted in this volume; Elaine Maimon and Barbara Nodine, "Words Enough and Time: Syntax and Error One Year After," in *Sentence Combining and the Teaching of Writing,* ed. Donald Daiker, Andrew Kerek, and Max Morenberg (Conway, AR: L & S Books, 1979), pp. 101-9; David Bartholomae, "The Study of Error," *College Composition and Communication,* 31 (October 1980), 253-69; D. M. Kagan, "Run-on and Fragment Sentences: An Error Analysis," *Research in the Teaching of English,* 14 (1980, 127–38; M. Harris, "Mending the Fragmented Free Modifier," *College Composition and Communication,* 32 (May 1981), 175–82; Donald C. Freeman, "Phenomenal Nominals," *College Composition and Communication,* 32 (May 1981), 183–205; Joseph Williams, "The Phenomenology of Error," *College Composition and Communication,* 32 (May 1981), 139–52; F. Kress and R. J. Bracewell, "Taught but Not Learned: Reasons for Grammatical Errors and Implications for Instruction," in *Teaching Writing,* ed. I Pringle and A. Freedman (Ottawa: Canadian Council of Teachers of English, 1981); Elaine Lees, "An Analysis of Sentence-Boundary Errors in Novice and Expert Writers," paper presented at Composition Conference, University of Pittsburgh, 1981; M. Hystrand, "An Analysis of Errors in Written Communication," in *What Writers Know,* ed. M. Nystrand (New York: Academic Press 1982), pp. 57–74; and Elaine Lees, "Error Analysis and the Editing Behavior of Basic Writing Students," paper presented at the Conference on College Composition and Communication, 1984.

6. Edward Said, *Beginnings: Intention and Method* (Baltimore: The Johns Hopkins Univ. Pr., 1975), p. 8

7. For articles on writing across the curriculum, see Elaine Maimon, "Talking To Strangers," *College Composition and Communication,* 30 (December 1979), 364–69; Toby Fulwiler and Art Young, *Language Connections: Writing and Reading Across the Curriculum* (Urbana, IL: NCTE, 1982); C. H. Knoblauch and Lil Brannon, "Writing as Learning Through the Curriculum," *College English,* (September 1983), 465–74; Patricia Bizzell, "College Composition: Initiation into the Academic Discourse Community," *Curriculum Inquiry,* 12 (1982), 191–207; Patricia Bizzell, "The Ethos of Academic Discourse," *College Composition and Communication,* 29 (December 1978), 351–55. See also Patricia Bizzell's and Bruce Herzberg's annotated bibliography on writing across the curriculum in this volume.

8. See Ann Berthoff's essay, "Abstraction as a Speculative Instrument," in this volume, and also, *The Making of Meaning* (Montclair, NJ: Boynton/Cook, 1981).

9. For examples with direct bearing on basic writing, see, Sondra Perl, "The Composing Processes of Unskilled College Writers, *Research in the Teaching of English,* 13 (1979), 317–36; Sondra Perl, "A Look at Basic Writers in the Process of Composing," in *Basic Writing: Essays for Teachers, Researchers, and Administrators,* ed. Lawrence Kasden and Daniel Hoeber (Urbana, IL: NCTE, 1980), pp. 13–32; Mike Rose, "Rigid Rules, Inflexible Plans, and the Stifling of Language: A Cognitivist Analysis of Writer's Block," *College Composition and Communication,* 31 (1980), 389–401; Linda Flower, "Revising Writer-Based Prose," *Journal of Basic Writing,* 3 (Fall/Winter 1981), 62–74; C. A. Daiute, "Psycholinguistic Foundations of the Writing Process," *Research in the Teaching of English,* 15 (1981), 5–22; Patricia Bizzell, "Cognition, Convention and Certainty: What We Need to Know about Writing," *PRE/TEXT,* 3 (Fall 1982), 213–244; Susan Wall, "Revision in a Rhetorical Context: Case Studies of First Year College Writers," Diss. University of Pittsburgh, 1982; Glynda Hull, "The Editing Process in Writing: A Performance Study of Experts and Novices," Diss. University Pittsburgh, 1983; Mike Rose, *Writer's Block: The Cognitive Dimension* (Carbondale and Edwardsville: Southern Illinois Univ. Pr., 1984); Mary Epes, "Tracing Errors to Their Sources: A Study of the Encoding Processes of Adult Basic Writers," unpublished ms.

10. I am not a trained linguist, so my reading in error analysis may seem idiosyncratic to a specialist. Some essays I would recommend are: S. P. Corder, "The Significance of Learner's Errors," *IRAL* 5 (November 1967), 162–69; S. P. Corder, "Idiosyncratic Dialects and Error Analysis," *IRAL,* 9 (May 1971), 148–51; and Wolfgang Zydatiss, "A 'Kiss of Life' for the Notion of Error," *IRAL* 9 (August 1974), 231–37. There is an excellent collection of essays I would recommend to composition teachers: Jack C. Richards, ed., *Error Analysis: Perspectives on Second Language Acquisition* (London: Longman, 1974). It contains the two essays by Corder listed above.

11. See S. P. Corder, "Idiosyncratic Dialects and Error Analysis," in Richards, pp. 158–71.

12. See L. Selinker, "Interlanguage," in Richards, pp. 31–54, and William Nemser, "Approximate Systems of Foreign Language Learners," in Richards, pp. 55–63.

13. See Patrick Hartwell, "Dialect Interference in Writing: A Critical View," *Research in the Teaching of English,* 14 (1980), 101–18.

14. For an excellent discussion of this problem and some suggested exercises, see Patricia Laurence, "Error's Endless Train: Why Students Don't Perceive Errors," *Journal of Basic Writing,* 1 (Spring 1975), 23–43. See also Glynda Hull, "Can Stray Dogs be Mermaids? (An Attempt to Categorize Error)," unpublished ms., and Elaine O. Lees, "Proofreading as Reading, Errors and Embarrassments," unpublished ms.

15. Glynda Hull, "The Editing Process in Writing: A Performance Study of Experts and Novices"; see also Glynda Hull, "Consulting, Intuiting, and Comprehending," paper presented at the Conference on College Composition and Communication, 1984.

16. See M. P. Jain, "Error Analysis: Source, Cause and Significance," in Richards, pp. 189–215, and Elaine Lees, "How Teachers Teach Students to Make Sentence-Boundary Errors," unpublished ms.

17. Geoffrey Hartman, "The Culture of Criticism," *PMLA,* 99 (May 1984), 371.

18. Lynn Buncher Shelly discusses this point in "The Writer and the Text: Deconstruction and Composition," Diss., University of Pittsburgh, 1984.

19. Richard Hoggart, *The Uses of Literacy* (Boston: Beacon, 1961), and *Speaking to Each Other*, vol. 1 (London: Chatto and Windus, 1970). See also Richard Rodriquez' use of Hoggart in chapter 2 of *Hunger of Memory: The Education of Richard Rodriquez* (New York: Bantam Books, 1983).

20. For examples of what I have in mind by "real work" for students, see David Bartholomae, "Teaching Basic Writing: An Alternative to Basic Skills," *Journal of Basic Writing*, 2 (Spring/Summer 1979), 85–109; and David Bartholomae, "Writing Assignments: Where Writing Begins," in *Fforum*, ed. Patricia Stock (Montclair, NJ: Boynton/Cook, 1983), pp. 300–312.

21. Richard A. Lanham, *Literacy and the Survival of Humanism* (New Haven: Yale Univ. Pr., 1983), pp. 140, 141. See, in particular, "Post-Darwinian Humanism" and "Composition, Literature and the Core Curriculum: The UCLA Writing Programs." See also Robert Di Yanni's essay on Lanham in this volume.

22. See Mike Rose, "Remedial Writing Courses: A Critique and a Proposal," *College English*, 45 (February 1983), 109–28, and Mike Rose, "The Freshman Writing Program: A Descriptive Report," an unpublished document from the UCLA Freshman Writing Program.

23. E. D. Hirsch, Jr., "Culture and Literacy," *Journal of Basic Writing* 3 (1980), 27–47. See also "Cultural Literacy," in *American Scholar*, 11 (1983), 159–69; and "Reading, Writing, and Cultural Literacy," in *Composition and Literature: Bridging the Gap*, ed. W. B. Horner (Chicago: Univ. of Chicago Pr., 1983), pp. 141–48.

24. For examples of courses, or calls for courses, that attempt to allow students to participate in adult intellectual or academic work, see David Bartholomae, "Teaching Basic Writing"; Kyle Fiore and Nan Elsasser, " 'Strangers No More': A Liberatory Literacy Curriculum," *College English*, 44 (1982), 115–28; Ira Schor, *Critical Teaching and Everyday Life* (Boston: South End Press, 1980); Mariolina Salvatori, "Reading and Writing a Text: Correlations between Reading and Writing," *College English*, 45 (1983), 657–66; and Mike Rose, "Remedial Writing Courses."

25. Mina Shaughnessy, "Basic Writing," in *Teaching Composition: Ten Bibliographic Essays*, ed. Gary Tate (Fort Worth: Texas Christian Univ. Pr., 1976), p. 152.

Knowledge, Acknowledgment, and Writing across the Curriculum: Toward an Educated Community

1. An essay with this title would not make sense without the addition of my own acknowledgements to colleagues who read and commented on this work-in-progress. James Kinneavy read two drafts of the essay and sustained me in my belief that writing across the curriculum should be the central theme. Donald McQuade, the editor of this volume, taught me to practice what I preach about revision as a creative activity. His detailed, pithy comments and questions, written in a painstakingly tiny, but always legible script, taught me more than I had ever previously learned about the editor— and by analogy the writing teacher—as intellectual catalyst. I intend to photocopy my four drafts and Don's incisive and encouraging commentary to share with my students. Don McQuade is one of the most generous—and demanding—members of our interpretive community.

2. Stanley Fish, *Is There A Text in This Class?* Cambridge, MA: Harvard Univ. Pr., 1980, p. 14.

3. See the following pages in *Errors and Expectations* for specific citations to the works of these scholars: pp. 17, 237: William Labov, *Language in the Inner City: Studies in the Black English Vernacular* (Philadelphia: Univ. of Pennsylvania Pr., 1972); p. 110: Charles Fries, *The Structure of English* (New York: Harcourt, 1952); p. 188: Otto Jesperson, *Growth and Structure of the English Language* (Garden City, NY: Doubleday, 1955); p. 189: Edward Sapir, *Language* (New York: Harcourt Brace, 1949); p. 191: Stephen Ullmann, *Semantics: An Introduction to the Science of Meaning* (New York: Oxford Univ. Pr., 1970); p. 191: Karl Reisman, "Cultural and Linguistic Ambiguity in a West Indian Village," in *Afro-American Anthropology*, ed. Norman E. Whitten, Jr. and John Szwed (New York: Free Press, 1970); p. 208: I. A. Richards, *Practical Criticism* (New York: Harcourt Brace, 1956); p. 125: R. C. Gardner and W. E. Lambert, *Attitudes and Motivation in Second-Language Learning* (Rowley, MA: Newbury House, 1972).

4. Mina Shaughnessy, *Errors and Expectations* (New York: Oxford Univ. Pr., 1977), p. vii. Further references to this volume will be cited in the text.

5. "Paradigms and Problems," in *Research on Composing,* ed. Charles Cooper and Lee Odell (Urbana, IL: National Council of the Teachers of English, 1974), p. 31.

6. Fish, *Is There A Text in This Class?*, p. 303.

7. For a further exploration of students' estrangement from academic discourse, see David Bartholomae's "Released Into Language: Errors, Expectations, and the Legacy of Mina Shaughnessy" in this volume.

8. "Inventing the University," in *Writing Blocks,* ed. Mike Rose (New York: Guilford Press, forthcoming).

9. We have a growing body of theoretical and practical material on collaborative learning. See especially Kenneth A. Bruffee, "Collaborative Learning," in *A Short Course in Writing,* 2d ed. (Boston: Little Brown, 1980); Kenneth A. Bruffee, "Liberal Education and the Social Justification of Belief," *Liberal Education,* 68 (1982), 95–114; Clark Bouton and Russell Y. Garth, eds., *Learning in Groups, New Directions for Teaching and Learning* (San Francisco: Jossey-Bass, 1983); Elaine Maimon, Gerald Belcher, Gail Hearn, Barbara Nodine, and Finbarr O'Connor, *Writing in the Arts and Sciences* (and accompanying *Instructor's Manual*) (Boston: Little Brown, 1981); Elaine Maimon, Gerald Belcher, Gail Hearn, Barbara Nodine, and Finbarr O'Connor, *Readings in the Arts and Sciences* (and accompanying *Instructor's Manual*) (Boston: Little Brown, 1984).

10. Elaine Maimon, Gerald Belcher, Gail Hearn, Barbara Nodine, and Finbarr O'Connor, *Readings in the Arts and Sciences* (Boston: Little Brown, 1984), p. 180.

11. C. H. Knoblauch and Lil Brannon, "Writing as Learning through the Curriculum," *College English,* 45 (September 1983), 470.

12. James Kinneavy, "Writing across the Curriculum," *Profession 83,* (1983), 20.

13. Hannah Arendt, *Between Past and Future* (New York: Viking, 1961), p. 196.

Getting Started

1. See *Change Magazine,* July, 1976, pp. 30–33.

2. Noam Chomsky, *Syntactic Structures* (The Hague: Mouton, 1957), p. 48.

3. John Lyons, *Chomsky* (London: Fontana, 1970), p. 42.

4. See Judith Greene, *Psycholinguistics: Chomsky and Psychology* (Harmondsworth, England: Penguin, 1972).

5. (New Haven: Yale Univ. Pr., 1967). See also, Paul Hernadi, *Beyond Genre* (Ithaca, NY: Cornell Univ. Pr., 1972).

6. Mina Shaughnessy, *Errors and Expectations* (New York: Oxford Univ. Pr., 1977).

Topoi and Form in Composition

1. This paper originally appeared in a different form under the title "Paradigms as Structural Counterparts of *Topoi* " in *Linguistics, Stylistics and the Teaching of Composition,* ed. Donald McQuade (Akron, OH: L & S Books, 1979), pp. 41–51.

2. Edward P. J. Corbett, "A Survey of Rhetoric," in *Classical Rhetoric for the Modern Student,* 2d ed. (New York: Oxford Univ. Pr., 1971), p. 626; Richard C. Jebb, "Rhetoric," in *Encyclopaedia Britannica,* 11th ed., XXIII, p. 236.

3. See, for example, the following texts: Sara E. H. Lockwood and Mary Alice Emerson, *Composition and Rhetoric for High Schools* (Boston: Ginn and Co., 1902), pp. 244–51; Charles Swain Thomas et al., *Composition and Rhetoric,* new ed. (New York: Longmans, Green, and Co., 1908), pp. 58–75; Fred N. Scott and Joseph V. Denney, *The New Composition-Rhetoric* (Boston and Chicago: Allyn and Bacon, 1911), pp. 64–108; Stratton D. Brooks, *English Composition: Book One—Enlarged* (New York: American Book Co., 1912), pp. 45–64; William M. Tanner, *Composition and Rhetoric* (Boston: Ginn and Co., 1922), pp. 140–46.

4. Bertrand Russell, "Prologue, 'What I Have Lived For,'" *The Autobiography of Bertrand Russell* (Boston: Little, Brown 1951), pp. 3–4.

The Problem of Topic in Texts

1. 16 (October 1965), 144–56.

2. 16 (December 1965), 237–42.

3. 17 (February 1966), 2–11.

4. "Symposium on the Paragraph," 17 (May 1966), 60–87.

5. "Symposium," 77.

6. Robert E. Longacre has advanced a paragraph theory which is conceptually similar to Rodgers'. He calls his unit a paragraph but allows for nonconformity to orthographic paragraph divisions. Longacre also uses some of the same tagmemic concepts as Becker. See "The Paragraph as a Grammatical Unit," in *Discourse and Syntax,* Vol. XII of *Syntax and Semantics,* ed. Talmy Givon (New York: Acdemic Press, 1979), pp. 115–34.

7. Subsequent work on paragraph structure is reviewed in Richard L. Larson, "Structure and Form in Non-Fiction Prose," in *Teaching Composition: Ten Bibliographical Essays,* ed. Gary Tate (Urbana, IL: National Council of Teachers of English, 1976), pp. 45–71.

8. *English Composition and Rhetoric* (London: Longmans, Green, 1866).

9. *The Working Principles of Rhetoric Examined in Their Literary Relations and Illustrated with Examples* (Boston: Ginn and Company, 1900), p. 359.

10. The Frequency and Placement of Topic Sentences in Expository Prose," *Research in the Teaching of English,* 8 (Winter 1974), 301. William F. Irmscher mentions that his students found the average percentage of paragraphs with identifiable topic sentences to be closer to forty or fifty. See *Teaching Expository Writing* (New York: Holt, Rinehart, & Winston, 1979), p. 98, note 4.

11. See *A Functional Analysis of Present Day English on a General Linguistic Basis,* ed. Josef Vachek (Prague: Academia, 1975). William J. Vande Kopple claims that Mathesius drew upon work published in the nineteenth century; see "Functional Sentence Perspective, Composition, and Reading," *College Composition and Communication,* 33 (February 1982), 50–63.

12. "One Instance of Prague School Methodology: Functional Analysis of Utterance of Text," in *Method and Theory in Linguistics,* ed. Paul L. Garvin (The Hague: Mouton, 1970), pp. 132–46; *Papers on Functional Sentence Perspective* (Prague: Academia, 1975).

13. Other Czechoslovakian linguists such as Jan Firbas make a similar distinction: "On Defining Theme in Functional Sentence Analysis," in *Travaux Linguistiques de Prague* (1964; rpt. University: Univ. of Alabama Pr., 1966), I, 267–80. Firbas, like Daneš, defines theme as the element possessing the least *communicative dynamism,* while the rheme has the highest communicative dynamism. *Communicative dynamism* is in turn defined as the element that "pushes the communication forward" (240).

14. Passages about Vietnam were adapted from Ray Bonds, ed., *The Vietnam War* (New York: Crown, 1979).

15. Stephen P. Witte, "Topical Structure and Revision: An Exploratory Study," *College Composition and Communication,* 34 (1983), 313–41.

16. Lester Faigley and Stephen Witte, "Topical Focus in Technical Writing," in *New Essays in Technical Writing and Communication,* ed. Paul Anderson, John Brockmann, and Carolyn Miller (Farmingdale, NY: Baywood, 1982), pp. 59–68.

17. M. A. K. Halliday and Ruqaiya Hasan, *Cohesion in English* (London: Longman, 1976), pp. 284–88.

18. Speakers interpret what is "given" and "new" by placing primary phonological stress on "new" information. See M. A. K. Halliday, "Notes on Transitivity and Theme in English," *Journal of Linguistics,* 3 (1967), 117–274.

19. Prince mentions in a footnote that "the Old/New Information Workshop held at Urbana, Summer 1978, was quickly and quite appropriately dubbed the 'Mushy Information Workshop' " ("Toward a Taxonomy of Given-New Information," in *Radical Pragmatics,* ed. Peter Cole [New York: Academic Press, 1981], p. 225).

20. See John R. Anderson and Gordon H. Bower, *Human Associative Memory* (Washington, DC:

Winston, 1973); Walter Kintsch, *The Representation of Meaning in Memory* (Hillsdale, NJ: Erlbaum, 1974); Bonnie J. F. Meyer, *The Organization of Prose and Its Effect upon Memory* (Amsterdam: North Holland, 1975); Donald A. Norman and David E. Rumelhart, *Explorations in Cognition* (San Francisco: Freeman, 1975).

21. Walter Kintsch and Douglas Vipond, "Reading Comprehension and Readability in Educational Practice and Psychological Theory," in *Perspectives on Memory Research,* ed. Lars-Goran Nilsson (Hillsdale, NJ: Lawrence Erlbaum, 1979), pp. 329–65.

22. Kintsch, *The Representation of Meaning in Memory;* Meyer, *The Organization of Prose;* Perry W. Thorndyke, "Cognitive Structures in Comprehension and Memory of Narrative Discourse," *Cognitive Psychology,* 9 (January 1977), 77–110.

23. Van Dijk first advanced the possibility of systematically describing macrostructures in *Some Aspects of Text Grammars* (The Hague: Mouton, 1972). He elaborates that notion in *Macrostructures: An Interdisciplinary Study of Global Structures in Discourse, Interaction, and Cognition* (Hillsdale, NJ: Lawrence Erlbaum, 1980).

24. "Toward a Model of Text Comprehension and Production," *Psychological Review,* 85 (September 1978), 363–94.

25. See Douglas Vipond, "Micro- and Macroprocesses in Text Comprehension," *Journal of Verbal Learning and Verbal Behavior,* 19 (June 1980), 276–96.

26. *Strategies of Discourse Comprehension* (New York: Academic Press, 1983).

27. Richard C. Anderson, Ralph E. Reynolds, Dianne L. Schallert, and Ernest T. Goetz, *Frameworks for Comprehending Discourse,* Technical Report No. 12 (Urbana, IL: Center for the Study of Reading, 1976), ERIC Document Reproduction Service No. ED 134 935.

28. See, for example, James F. Voss, Gregg T. Vesonder, and George J. Spilich, "Text Generation and Recall by High-Knowledge and Low-Knowledge Individuals," *Journal of Verbal Learning and Verbal Behavior,* 19 (December 1980), 651–67.

29. Cambridge: Cambridge Univ. Pr., 1932.

30. Several important papers were published in 1975, among them Marvin Minsky's essay on frames ("A Framework for Representing Knowledge," *The Psychology of Computer Vision,* ed. Patrick H. Winston [New York: McGraw-Hill, 1975]), Roger Schank and Robert Abelson's essay on scripts ("Scripts, Plans, and Knowledge," in *Advance Papers of the Fourth International Joint Conference on Artificial Intelligence* [Tbilisi, Georgia, USSR, 1975], rpt. in *Thinking: Readings in Cognitive Science,* ed. Philip N. Johnson-Laird and Peter C. Wason [Cambridge: Cambridge University Press, 1977], pp. 421–32), and Daniel Bobrow and Donald Norman's essay on schemata ("Some Principles of Memory Schemata," in *Representation and Understanding: Studies in Cognitive Science,* ed. Daniel G. Bobrow and Allan M. Collins [New York: Academic Press, 1975], pp. 131–50). Although researchers have meant different things by *frames, scripts,* and *schemata,* they employ these terms in reference to the same phenomenon—the configurations of knowledge that people use in understanding the world.

31. David Rumelhart, "Schemata: The Building Blocks of Cognition," in *Theoretical Issues in Reading Comprehension,* ed. Rand J. Spiro, Bertram C. Bruce, and William F. Brewer (Hillsdale, NJ: Lawrence Erlbaum, 1980), p. 48.

32. Walter H. Taylor, *Four Years with General Lee* (New York: D. Appleton & Co., 1878), p. 190.

33. *Signs, Language, and Behavior* (Englewood Cliffs, NJ: Prentice-Hall, 1946).

34. *How to Do Things with Words* (Oxford: Oxford Univ. Pr., 1962).

35. *Speech Acts* (New York: Cambridge Univ. Pr., 1969).

36. E. D. Hirsch describes the writer's degree of success in conveying intentions as *rhetorical efficiency.* See *The Philosophy of Composition* (Chicago: Univ. of Chicago Pr., 1977), p. 75.

37. See Robert de Beaugrande, *Text, Discourse, and Process* (Norwood, NJ: Ablex, 1980), p. 181.

38. In *Speech Acts,* Vol. III of *Syntax and Semantics,* ed. Peter Cole and Jerry Morgan (New York: Academic Press, 1975), pp. 41–58.

39. See Martin Steinmann, "Speech-Act Theory and Writing," in *What Writers Know: The Language, Process and Structure of Written Discourse*, ed. Martin Nystrand (New York: Academic, 1982), pp. 307–10.

40. "Focusing and Discourse," *Discourse Processes*, 6 (1983), 115.

41. Charles Bazerman explores differences among scholarly articles in biochemistry, sociology, and literary criticism in the use of previous literature, in meeting the expectations of readers, and in the presentation of the author. See "What Written Knowledge Does," *Philosophy of the Social Sciences*, 11 (1981), 361–87.

The Effects of Intensive Sentence Combining on the Writing Ability of College Freshmen

1. J. Stephen Sherwin, *Four Problems in Teaching English: A Critique of Research* (Scranton, PA: International Textbook Co., 1969), p. 155. Sherwin cites the following three studies: Donna Kay Raub, *The Audio-Lingual Drill Technique: An Approach to Teaching Composition*, Master's thesis, George Peabody College for Teachers, 1966; James W. Ney, "Applied Linguistics in the Seventh Grade," *English Journal*, 55 (October 1966), 895–97, 902; John C. Mellon, *Transformational Sentence-Combining: A Method for Enhancing the Development of Syntactic Fluency in English Composition*, United States Office of Education Cooperative Research Project No. 5-8418 (Cambridge, MA: Graduate School of Education, Harvard University, 1967). Mellon's study subsequently appeared as NCTE Research Report No. 10 (Urbana, IL, 1969).

2. Barbara D. Miller and James W. Ney, "The Effect of Systematic Oral Exercises on the Writing of Fourth-Grade Students," *Research in the Teaching of English*, (1968), 44–61; Kellogg W. Hunt and Roy O'Donnell, *An Elementary School Curriculum to Develop Better Writing Skills*, United States Office of Education Project No. 8-9093 (Tallahassee, FL: Florida State University, 1970); M. R. Vitale, F. J. King, D. W. Shontz, and G. M. Huntley, "Effect of Sentence-Combining Exercises Upon Several Restricted Written Composition Tasks," *Journal of Educational Psychology*, 62 (1971), 521–25; Anne Obenchain, *Effectiveness of the Precise Essay Question in Programming the Sequential Development of Written Composition Skills and the Simultaneous Development of Critical Reading Skills*, Master's thesis, George Washington University, 1971; Frank O'Hare, *Sentence Combining: Improving Student Writing without Formal Grammar Instruction* (Urbana, IL: National Council of Teachers of English, 1973); Kenneth David Fischer, *An Investigation to Determine if Selected Exercises in Sentence-Combining Can Improve Reading and Writing*, Diss. Indiana University, 1973; David Perron, *An Exploratory Approach to Extending the Syntactic Development of Fourth-Grade Students Through the Use of Sentence-Combining Methods*, Diss. Indiana University, 1974; Warren E. Combs, *Some Further Effects and Implications of Sentence-Combining Exercises for the Secondary Language Arts Curriculum*, Diss. University of Minnesota, 1975, and "Further Effects of Sentence-Combining Practice on Writing Ability," *Research in the Teaching of English*, 10 (Fall 1976), 137–49; Elray L. Pedersen, *Improving Syntactic and Conceptual Fluency in the Writing of Language Arts Students Through Extended Practice in Sentence-Combining*, Diss. University of Minnesota, 1976.

3. Kellogg W. Hunt, *Grammatical Structures Written at Three Grade Levels* (Champaign, IL: National Council of Teachers of English, 1965), esp. p. 56, and *Syntactic Maturity in Schoolchildren and Adults* (Chicago: Society for Research in Child Development, 1970), esp. p. 20.

4. Roy C. O'Donnell, William J. Griffin, and Raymond C. Norris, *Syntax of Kindergarten and Elementary School Children: A Transformational Analysis* (Champaign, IL: National Council of Teachers of English, 1967).

5. For reports on unsuccessful attempts to demonstrate such a correspondence, see Mellon, *Transformational Sentence Combining*, p. 69; and Perron, *An Exploratory Approach*, p. 158.

6. *Sentence Combining*, pp. 62–66.

7. "Further Effects," 144–46.

8. *Improving Syntactic and Conceptual Fluency*, pp. 73–83.

9. "Experimental Study in Transformational Sentence Combining" at Miami University, Oxford, Ohio, codirected by the present writers. We gratefully acknowledge the generous financial support of the EXXON Education Foundation, which made the project possible.

10. See note 3 above. Hunt pointed out that "if the average high school graduate is ever to write like a skilled adult, he has nearly as much yet to learn about how to embed more clauses as he learned in all of his public school years" (*Syntactic Maturity*, p. 20).

11. For example, Strong has argued that "In no sense, then, is sentence combining a comprehensive writing program in and of itself. It can be *a part* of a well-articulated program, but common sense suggests that it can't be the one and only instructional strategy. That would be sheer lunacy" ("Sentence Combining: Back to Basics and Beyond," *English Journal*, 65 [February 1976], 61).

12. Hunt and O'Donnell's students spent about one hour per week on SC, for nine months (*An Elementary School Curriculum*, p. 7); Mellon's, about two to two and one-half hours per week, including out-of-class study, for nine months (*Transformational Sentence Combining*, pp. 36–39); O'Hare's, about two hours and a quarter, including homework, for eight weeks (*Sentence Combining*, pp. 42–43); Combs, roughly the same as O'Hare's but within a much shorter time span ("Further Effects," 139); Ney's, in an unsuccessful experiment, thirty minutes per week for eleven weeks (James W. Ney, "The Hazards of the Course: Sentence Combining in Freshman English," *The English Record* [Summer/Autumn 1976], 71).

13. William Strong, *Sentence Combining: A Composing Book* (New York: Random House, 1973).

14. Francis Christensen, *The Christensen Rhetoric Program: The Sentence and the Paragraph* (New York: Harper and Row, 1968).

15. For a defense of this claim, see O'Hare, *Sentence Combining*, pp. 26–32; also cf. Miller and Ney, "The Effect of Systematic Oral Exercises."

16. Sandra L. Stotsky, "Sentence Combining as a Curricular Activity: Its Effect on Written Language Development and Reading Comprehension," *Research in the Teaching of English*, 9 (1975), 30–71; Courtney B. Cazden, *Child Language and Education* (New York: Holt, 1972), p. 141; Marilyn S. Sternglass, "Composition Teacher as Reading Teacher," *College Composition and Communication*, 27 (December 1976), 378–82.

17. We shall not include detailed results of the reading test here (STEP II, Form A). The posttest scores showed consistent but statistically not significant gains for the experimental group, both in vocabulary and reading comprehension, as well as in the total score. However, there was a whopping difference in favor of sentence combiners in the number of test items completed, suggesting a relationship between sentence-combining practice and reading speed.

18. A score of 25 + in English or 26 + on the composite part of ACT places a student in an upper track of freshman English at Miami University. Such students were excluded from the study population.

19. Guesses of an "adequate sample" for syntactic analysis vary. For fourth graders, Hunt and O'Donnell established 476 words as ideal but could elicit only 300 (p. 12); the same number, equal to about 35 T-units, was used by Perron (p. 95). For seventh graders, Mellon aimed for 90 T-units (which, however, "many of the students . . . failed to achieve," p. 40), Combs only for one-third of that size, while O'Hare settled for 50 T-units, hoping for a 500-word sample (p. 46). For students just past twelfth grade, a 600–700 word sample seemed reasonable.

20. Richard Braddock, Richard Lloyd-Jones, and Lowell Schoer, *Research in Written Composition* (Urbana: National Council of Teachers of English, 1963), p. 17; Christine San Jose, *Grammatical Structures in Four Modes of Writing at Fourth-Grade Level*, Diss., Syracuse University, 1972.

21. The criteria and procedures established by Hunt in *Grammatical Structures and Syntactic Maturity* have been widely adopted in recent SC research, cited in note 2, above; for a convenient recent summary, see Perron, *An Exploratory Approach*, pp. 104–8. The only relatively unfamiliar term used in this paper is *T-unit*, which can be defined as a main clause together with all its modifiers, restrictive or nonrestrictive.

22. For a critique of the forced-choice design used by O'Hare, see Robert J. Marzano, "The Sentence-Combining Myth," *English Journal*, 65 (February 1976), 57–59. The other approaches are discussed, with further references given, in Braddock et al., *Research in Written Composition*, pp. 12–14.

23. The hypotheses were tested for significance at the .05 level of confidence by an analysis of covariance. The posttest score for each quantitative and qualitative variable was separately analyzed, with the corresponding pretest as a covariate in each analysis. This type of analysis makes it possible to control statistically any initial differences that might have been present between the experimental and control groups.

24. *Grammatical Structures*, p. 57.

25. According to Hunt's synopsis, fourth graders' average clause length of 6.6 words increases to twelfth graders' 8.6 words (*Grammatical Structures*, p. 56).

26. *The Christensen Rhetoric Program*, p. vi.

27. *Sentence Combining*, p. 72.

28. Francis Christensen, "The Problem of Defining a Mature Style," *English Journal*, 57 (April 1968), 572–79; James Moffett, *Teaching the Universe of Discourse* (New York: Houghton-Mifflin, 1968), esp. chapter 5, "Grammar and the Sentence," pp. 155–87. (For Moffett's rebuttal of some of Christensen's criticisms of SC, however, see pp. 171–74; in the same vein, Sabina T. Johnson, "Some Tentative Strictures on Generative Rhetoric," *College English*, 31 [November 1969], 157–65).

29. Marzano, "The Sentence-Combining Myth," p. 59.

30. *Grammatical Structures*, p. 157.

31. Sherwin, *Four Problems*, p. 150.

32. *Four Problems*, p. 155.

33. Sherwin, *Four Problems*, p. 155.

34. "Back to the Basics and Beyond."

Postscript

The 1977 conference paper on which this article was based represented the first of a series of reports on the study described here. Subsequent published reports by the same authors include "Sentence Combining and Syntactic Maturity in Freshman English," *College Composition and Communication*, 29 (1978), 36–41; "Sentence Combining at the College Level: An Experimental Study," *Research in the Teaching of English*, 12 (1978), 245–56; and "Sentence Combining and College Composition," *Perceptual and Motor Skills*, 51 (1980), 1059–157; Monograph Supplement 1–V51. The instructional methodology and representative materials that developed out of this experiment have been described and demonstrated in Donald A. Daiker, Andrew Kerek, and Max Morenberg, "Using 'Open' Sentence-Combining Exercises in the College Composition Class-room," in *Sentence Combining and the Teaching of Writing* (Akron, OH: L & S Books, 1979), rpt. in Richard Graves, ed., *Rhetoric and Composition: A Sourcebook for Teachers and Writers*, 2d ed. (Montclair, NJ: Boynton/Cook, 1983); "Building Writing Competence with Sentence Combining," *Curriculum Review*, 18 (1979), 401–404; "Using Sentence Combining: A Sample Exercise," *Arizona English Bulletin*, 21 (1979), 16–22; as well as the textbook *The Writer's Options* (New York: Harper and Row, 1979; 2d ed., 1982; 3d ed., 1985).

Syntactic Complexity and Writing Quality

1. Kellog W. Hunt, *Differences in Grammatical Structures Written at Three Grade Levels, the Structures to be Analyzed by Transformational Methods*, Technical Report, Cooperative Research Project No. 1998 (Tallahassee: Florida State University, 1964), ERIC Document 003 322; *Grammatical Structures Written at Three Grade Levels*, NCTE Research Report No. 3 (Urbana, IL:

National Council of Teachers of English, 1965); *Syntactic Maturity in School Children and Adults,* Monographs of the Society for Research in Child Development, 35 (1, serial no. 134); "Early and Late Blooming Syntactic Structures," in *Evaluating Writing: Describing, Measuring, Judging,* ed. Charles R. Cooper and Lee Odell (Urbana, IL: National Council of Teachers of English, 1977).

2. Cf. *Differences in Grammatical Structures.*

3. Roy C. O'Donnell, W. J. Griffin, and R. C. Norris, *Syntax of Kindergarten and Elementary School Children: A Transformational Analysis.* NCTE Research Report No. 8 (Urbana, IL: National Council of Teachers of English, 1967); Murray F. Stewart, "Freshman Sentence Combining: A Canadian Project," *Research in the Teaching of English,* 12 (1978), 257–68.

4. John C. Mellon, *Transformational Sentence-Combining: A Method for Enhancing the Development of Syntactic Complexity in English Composition,* NCTE Research Report No. 10 (Urbana, IL: National Council of Teachers of English, 1969); Frank O'Hare, *Sentence Combining: Improving Student Writing Without Formal Grammar Instruction,* NCTE Research Report No. 15 (Urbana, IL: National Council of Teachers of English, 1973); J. E. M. Mulder, C. Braun, and W. G. Holliday, "Effects of Sentence-Combining Practice on Linguistic Maturity Levels of Adult Students," *Adult Education,* 28 (1978), 111–20; Murray F. Stewart, "Syntactic Maturity from High School to University: A First Look," *Research in the Teaching of English,* 12 (1978), 37–46; Max Morenberg, Donald A. Daiker, and Andrew Kerek, "Sentence Combining at the College Level: An Experimental Study," *Research in the Teaching of English,* 12 (1978), 245–56; Lester L. Faigley, "Generative Rhetoric as a Way of Increasing Syntactic Fluency," *College Composition and Communication,* 30 (1979), 176–81; Faigley, "The Influence of Generative Rhetoric on the Syntactic Maturity and Writing Effectiveness of College Freshmen," *Research in the Teaching of English,* 13 (1979), 197–206.

5. Stewart, "Freshman Sentence Combining."

6. Ellen Nold and Sarah W. Freedman, "An Analysis of Readers' Responses to Student Writing," *Research in the Teaching of English,* 11 (1977), 164–74; Faigley, "Influence"; Stephen P. Witte and Lester Faigley, *A Comparative Evaluation of Analytic and Synthetic Approaches to the Teaching of Writing,* Texas Writing Research Group Technical Report No. 1 (Austin: University of Texas, 1981), ERIC Document 209 677.

7. Francis Christensen, "A Generative Rhetoric of the Sentence," in his *Notes Toward a New Rhetoric: Six Essays for Teachers* (New York: Harper and Row, 1968), pp. 23–44.

8. Morenberg et al., "Sentence Combining at the College Level"; Donald A. Daiker, Andrew Kerek, and Max Morenberg, "Sentence-Combining and Syntactic Maturity in Freshman English," *College Composition and Communication,* 29 (1978), 36–41; Andrew Kerek, Donald A. Daiker, and Max Morenberg, "Sentence Combining and College Composition," *Perceptual and Motor Skills,* 51 (1980), Monograph Supplement No. 1.

9. *Grammatical Structures Written at Three Grade Levels.*

10. The "aluminum" task is reproduced in *Measures for Research and Evaluation in the English Language Arts.,* ed. W. Fagan, C. R. Cooper, and J. Jensen (Urbana, IL: National Council of Teachers of English, 1975).

11. Kerek et al., "Sentence Combining and College Composition."

12. B. Winer, *Statistical Principles in Experimental Design* (New York: McGraw-Hill, 1971).

13. Faigley, "Generative Rhetoric" and "Influence"; Morenberg et al., "Sentence Combining at the College Level"; Daiker et al., "Sentence Combining and Syntactic Maturity"; Kerek et al., "Sentence Combining and College Composition."

14. See note 6 above.

Linguistics and Error Analysis: On Agency

1. Insights, that is, somewhat deeper than the following, gleaned from a handbook proposal that I reviewed for a publisher a few years ago: "A sentence is a complete thought."

2. See Mina Shaughnessy, *Errors and Expectations* (New York: Oxford Univ. Pr., 1977), and E.

D. Hirsch, Jr., *The Philosophy of Composition* (Chicago: Univ. of Chicago Pr., 1978). I have outlined my reasons for preferring Shaughnessy's approach to Hirsch's in a review of *The Philosophy of Composition*, "Toward Relative Readability," *Chronical of Higher Education* (April 3, 1978), p. 18.

3. That is, the theoretical position put forward in Noam Chomsky, *Aspects of the Theory of Syntax* (Cambridge, MA: MIT Press, 1965), which I have adapted to my purposes here.

4. The rule is called Velar Softening in Noam Chomsky and Morris Halle, *The Sound Pattern of English* (New York: Harper and Row, 1968).

5. See Chomsky, *Cartesian Linguistics* (New York: Harper and Row, 1966), p. 33.

6. I hold no brief for the elegance of these revisions, only for their slight superiority to the originals.

7. In later developments of the theoretical position of Chomsky's *Aspects*, *-ion* nominals like *"correction"* were shown to be present in the lexicon, not derived by transformation. But that refinement does not affect the points at issue here.

8. At Temple University these opportunities are called "garden paths."

9. Justine T. Stillings and Muffy E. A. Siegel, "Teaching Grammar: Some Linguistic Predictions," unpublished ms., Temple University, Department of English.

10. The only reasonably full transformationally based scholarly grammar of English is Robert P. Stockwell, Paul Schachter, and Barbara Hall Partee, *The Major Syntactic Structures of English* (New York: Holt, Rinehart, and Winston, 1973).

11. This essay was first delivered as a talk at the Delaware Valley Writing Council's conference on evaluating writing in October 1978. For discussion and criticism I am grateful to Muffy E. A. Siegel, Justine T. Stillings, William Labov, Jill Carrier, and, in particular, Kenneth G. Schaefer.

Non-Linguistic Linguistics and the Teaching of Style

1. The bibliography is very large. The following are themselves significant studies and contain extensive bibliographies. William Labov, *Language in the Inner City: Studies in the Black English Vernacular* (Philadelphia: University of Pennsylvania Pr., 1972); Walt Wolfram and Ralph Fasold, *The Study of Social Dialects in American English* (Englewood Cliffs, NJ: Prentice-Hall, 1974).

2. Richard E. Young, Alton Becker, and Kenneth Pike, *Rhetoric: Discovery and Change* (New York: 1970); Frank D'Angelo, *A Conceptual Theory of Rhetoric* (Cambridge, MA: Winthrop, 1975).

3. Noam Chomsky, *Syntactic Structures* (The Hague: Mouton, 1965).

4. *Aspects of the Theory of Syntax* (Cambridge: M.I.T. Pr., 1965).

5. Donald Bateman and Frank Zidonis, *The Effect of a Study of Transformational Grammar on the Writing of 9th and 10th Graders* (Champaign, IL: NCTE, 1966); John Mellon, *Transformational Sentence Combining* (Champaign, IL: NCTE, 1969); Frank O'Hare, *Sentence Combining* (Champaign, IL: NCTE, 1973).

6. O'Hare, p. 22.

7. H. L. Mencken, *Prejudices*, Fifth Series (New York: Octagon, 1966), pp. 196–97.

8. The growing literature on text grammars requires a bibliography of its own. One of the more useful recent publications, particularly in regard to its extensive bibliography on the subject is M. A. K. Halliday and Ruqaiya Hasan, *Cohesion in English* (London: Longman, 1976).

9. A. A. Hill, *Introduction to Linguistic Structures* (New York: 1958).

10. Noam Chomsky and Morris Halle, *The Sound Patterns of English* (New York: Harper and Row, 1968).

11. Kellogg Hunt, "Syntactic Maturity in Schoolchildren and Adults," *Monographs for the Society of Researchers in Child Development* (February 1970); Roy C. O'Donnell, "A Critique of Some Indices of Syntactic Maturity," *Research in the Teaching of English*, (Spring 1977), 49–53.

12. See the Afterword, below. The preliminary report is available on request.

13. E. B. Coleman, "The Comprehensibility of Several Grammatical Transformations," *Journal of Psychology*, (September 1964), 186–90.

14. Hunt, "Syntactic Maturity."

15. A fuller version of this description appears in "Literary Style: A Personal Voice," in *Style and Variables in English,* ed. Timothy Shopen and Joseph M. Williams (Cambridge, MA: Winthrop, 1980).

Composition via Stylistics

1. In my most recent freshman English class, the median number of compositions claimed to be written in high school was 10 and the range 0–75. On the same questionnaire, the television viewing was conceded to be 10½ hours a week (median), with a range of 0–28. It is probable that 1½ hours of television each day is a minimum and exceeds the amount of time spent on reading. Asked what book they had recently read for pleasure, 7 cited a non-fiction work, 6 named books made known by television or film, 2 books read in high school, 5 none and 11 (about one-third) works that could be included within the broadest category of leisure fiction (3 by Tolkien). It is probable that these figures give a slightly more optimistic view of the reading habits of this group than is actually the case.

2. This is the subject of an interesting chapter in E. D. Hirsch's fascinating and insightful but impractical *Philosophy of Composition* (Chicago: Univ. of Chicago Pr., 1977), pp. 175–91.

3. Mina Shaughnessy's *Errors and Expectations* (New York: Oxford Univ. Pr., 1977) is, as the title suggests, almost entirely taken up with the classification of errors.

4. My specific reference here is to the two-quarter freshman English course given at Cleveland State University, but my concern is with any such course and the theory on which it rests.

5. See his *English Grammars and English Grammar* (New York: Scribners, 1972).

6. J. Marouzeau, *Traité de stylistique latine* (Paris: Societé d'edition "Les Belles Lettres", 1962); Charles Bally, *Traité de stylistique française,* 3d ed. (Genève: Georg & cie., 1951); Henri J. G. Godin, *Les Resources stylistiques du Français contemporain* (Oxford: Blackwell, 1948). Needless to say, none of these is anywhere near complete.

7. Louis T. Milic, *Stylists on Style* (New York: Scribners, 1969), pp. 30–21; also William S. Chisholm and Louis T. Milic, *The English Language: Form and Use* (New York: 1974), pp. 469–79.

8. I find upon re-reading the introduction to the first edition of Francis Christensen's *Notes Toward a New Rhetoric,* 2d ed. (New York: Harper and Row, 1978), that our views coincide, though they are carried out differently. Things were not quite so desperate when Christensen was writing.

9. Shaughnessy, p. 75 (one error corrected).

Style through Control: The Pleasures of the Beginning Writer

1. E. D. Hirsch, Jr., *The Philosophy of Composition* (Chicago: Univ. of Chicago Pr., 1977), p. 141, summarizing Milic's position in "Theories of Style and Their Implications for the Teaching of Composition," *College Composition and Communication,* 16 (1965), 2–6.

2. Louis T. Milic, "Rhetorical Choice and Stylistic Option," *Literary Style: A Symposium,* ed. Seymour Chatman (New York: Oxford Univ. Pr., 1971), p. 84.

3. Milic, p. 83.

4. Milic, p. 85.

5. "Suicide Notes are Dull," *Science Digest,* November 1974 (based on the work of Edwin S. Schneidman as reported in *Human Behavior*).

6. Charles E. Osgood, "Some Effects of Motivation on Style of Encoding," in *Style in Language,* ed. Thomas A. Sebeok (Cambridge, MA: Technology Press of M.I.T., 1960), pp. 293–306.

7. Richard A. Lanham, *Style: An Anti-Textbook* (New Haven: Yale Univ. Pr., 1974), p. 116.

8. Sandra Schor and Judith Fishman, "The Writing Cycle," in *The Random House Guide to Writing,* 3d ed. (New York: Random House, 1981).

9. Norman N. Holland, "Identity: An Interrogation at the Border of Psychology," *Language and Style,* 10 (Fall 1977), 199–209; Lanham, *Style,* p. 124.

10. Lanham, *Style,* p. 118.

11. Excellent assignments with concealed structures are included in the important work of Marie Ponsot and Rosemary Deen of the Queens College English Department, in *Beat Not the Poor Desk: Writing: What to Teach, How to Teach It and Why* (Montclair: Boynton/Cook, 1982).

12. A. E. Hotchner, "Hemingway Talks to American Youth," *This Week* (Oct. 18, 1959), p. 11, as quoted in Milic, "Rhetorical Choice."

13. Milic, "Rhetorical Choice," p. 82.

14. Scott Fields of the Queens College Composition Staff.

Language Studies and Composing Processes

1. See "A Cognitive Process Theory of Writing," *College Composition and Communication* (hereafter cited as *CCC*), 32 (December 1981), 365–87.

2. As discussed, for example, in Peter Elbow, *Writing without Teachers* (New York: Oxford Univ. Pr., 1973).

3. Champaign, IL: National Council of Teachers of English, 1963.

4. *Research in Written Composition,* pp. 37–38.

5. J. Stephen Sherwin, *Four Problems in the Teaching of English: A Critique of Research* (Scranton, PA: International Textbook Company, 1969), especially, pp. 116–35.

6. Elaine Chaika, "Who Can Be Taught?" *College English,* 35 (February 1974), 144–52.

7. Martha Kolln, "Closing the Books on Alchemy," *CCC,* 32 (May 1981), 139–51.

8. Ronald Shook, "Counterstatement: Response to Martha Kolln, 'Closing the Books on Alchemy,' " *CCC,* 34 (December 1983), 491–95.

9. "Reply by Martha Kolln," *CCC,* 34 (December 1983), 500.

10. Marilyn Goldberg, "Intuitive Knowledge and Conscious Knowledge," *CCC,* forthcoming.

11. See Richard Ohmann, "Generative Grammars and the Concept of Literary Style," *Word,* 20 (December 1964), 423–39; Kellogg Hunt, *Grammatical Structures Written at Three Grade Levels* (Champaign, IL: National Council of Teachers of English, 1965).

12. Mark Lester, "The Value of Transformational Grammar in Teaching Composition," *CCC,* 18 (December 1967), 227–31.

13. W. B. Elley et al., "The Role of Grammar in a Secondary School Curriculum," *Research in the Teaching of English,* 10 (Spring 1976), 5–21.

14. Roy O'Donnell, William Griffin, and Raymond Norris, *The Syntax of Kindergarten and Elementary School Children: A Transformational Analysis* (Champaign, IL: National Council of Teachers of English, 1969).

15. John Mellon, *Transformational Sentence-Combining: A Method for Enhancing the Development of Syntactic Fluency in English Composition* (Champaign, IL: National Council of Teachers of English, 1969).

16. Urbana, IL: National Council of Teachers of English, 1973.

17. "Sentence Combining and Syntactic Maturity in Freshman English," *CCC,* 29 (February 1978), 40.

18. New York: Random House, 1973.

19. New York: Harper and Row, 1980.

20. Lester Faigley, "Names in Search of a Concept: Maturity, Fluency, Complexity, and Growth in Written Syntax," *CCC,* 31 (October 1980), 291–300.

21. Susan Peck McDonald, "Interpreting Growth in Writing," *CCC,* 31 (October 1980), 301–10.

22. Professor Williams has raised the question at numerous professional conferences and seminars.

23. Michael Holzman, "Scientism and Sentence Combining," *CCC,* 34 (February 1983), 73–79.

24. London: Longman, 1976.

25. *CCC,* 34 (December 1983), 400–416.

26. *CCC,* 34 (December 1983), 417–29.

27. *CCC*, 34 (December 1983), 430–46.

28. *CCC*, 33 (February 1982), 50–63.

29. *CCC*, forthcoming.

30. *CCC*, 34 (October 1983), 313–41.

31. New York: Harcourt, Brace and World, 1970.

32. Richard Young and Frank Koen, *The Tagmemic Discovery Procedure: An Evaluation of Its Uses in the Teaching of Rhetoric*, Final Report, NEH Grant No. OEO-5238-71-116 (Ann Arbor: University of Michigan, Department of Humanities, College of Engineering, 1973).

33. Kenneth L. Pike, "A Linguistic Contribution to Composition," *CCC*, 15 (May 1964), 82–88.

34. Pike, "A Linguistic Contribution," 82.

35. Pike, "A Linguistic Contribution," 83–85.

36. Pike, "A Linguistic Contribution," 87–88.

37. Pike, "A Linguistic Contribution," 88.

38. For a short exposition of Rogerian rhetoric, see Maxine Hairston, "Carl Rogers' Alternative to Traditional Rhetoric," *CCC*, 27 (December 1976), 373–77. For a longer explanation, see *Rhetoric: Discovery and Change,* chapter 12.

39. *CCC*, 15 (October 1964), 129–35.

40. *CCC*, 15 (October 1964), 136–40.

41. For Flower, see note 1 above. See also Janet Emig, *The Composing Processes of Twelfth-Graders* (Champaign, IL: National Council of Teachers of English, 1971); Donald Graves, "An Examination of the Writing Processes of Seven-Year-Old Children," *Research in the Teaching of English,* 9 (Winter 1975), 227–41; Carol Berkenkotter, "Decisions and Revisions: The Planning Strategies of a Publishing Writer," *CCC*, 34 (May 1983), 156–69; Sondra Perl, "Understanding Composing," *CCC*, 31 (December 1980), 363–69.

Abstraction as a Speculative Instrument

1. *Speculative Instruments* (New York: Harcourt, 1968), pp. 115–16. I have discussed this phrase and the understanding of mediation it implies in several places: "I. A. Richards and the Philosophy of Rhetoric," *Rhetoric Society Quarterly,* 10 (Fall 1980), 211–30; "I. A. Richards and the Audit of Meaning," *New Literary History,* 13 (Fall 1982), 63–79; "Speculative Instruments," in *The Making of Meaning: Metaphors, Models and Maxims for Writing Teachers* (Rochelle Park, NY: Boynton/Cook, 1982), pp. 113–26.

2. "On a New Definition of 'Symbol,'" in *Philosophical Sketches* (Baltimore: Johns Hopkins Press, 1962), p. 62; "Abstraction in Science and Abstraction in Art," in *Problems of Art* (New York: Scribner's, 1957), p. 162.

3. Langer, *Problems,* p. 163.

4. For a succinct explanation of "mythic ideation," see Ernst Cassirer, *Language and Myth,* (New York: Harper, 1946). Silvano Arieti explains "paleologic" in *Creativity: The Magic Synthesis* (New York: Basic Books, 1976). Freud explains "primary process" in *The Interpretation of Dreams.* The most important form is art. Since verbal art is *discourse,* there is a terminological problem; Susanne K. Langer recognized and solved it, I think, by introducing the word *virtual.* See *Feeling and Form* (New York: Scribner's, 1953).

The chief reason for avoiding the terms "conscious" and "unconscious" as names for the two kinds of abstraction I mean to differentiate is that depending on them forestalls the attempt to understand how consciousness and symbolization are "simultaneous and correlative," as Owen Barfield puts it. We need, I think, to make all phases of composing conscious in this sense; we need to teach ways to *represent* developing intuitions and intentions and to differentiate that process of consciousness from *self-consciousness.*

5. Coleridge makes this fundamental point in the fifth of his Philosophical Lectures.

6. Lev Vygotsky, *Thought and Language* (Cambridge, MA: MIT Pr., 1962), p.80.

7. Rudolf Arnheim, *Art and Visual Perception* (Berkeley: Univ. of California Pr., 1954), pp. 166–67.

8. Ernst Cassirer, *Philosophy of Symbolic Forms* (New Haven: Yale Univ. Pr., 1953), 319. For an excellent survey and critique of a similar illogical pairing of concrete/abstract, see Ruldolf Arnheim, *Visual Thinking* (Berkeley: Univ. of California Pr., 1969) in a chapter called "What Abstraction is Not."

9. "Writing in the College Years: Some Indices of Growth," *College Composition and Communication,* 31 (October 1980), 311–24.

10. *The Philosophy of Rhetoric* (New York: Oxford Univ. Pr., 1965), p. 23.

11. J. Robert Oppenheimer, *The Open Mind* (New York: Simon and Schuster, 1949), p. 24.

States of Mind, Acts of Mind, Forms of Discourse: Toward a Provisional Pragmatic Framework

1. James Britton et al., *The Developmental of Writing Abilities (11–18),* London: Macmillan, 1975.

2. Nancy Martin et al., *Writing and Learning Across the Curriculum 11–16,* London: Ward Lock Educational, 1976.

3. This term is inherently problematical. Its most likely meaning is: students in this course at this moment in this classroom.

4. One example will suffice: compare the student text on Josiah Wedgwood (*Writing and Learning,* p. 64) with the student text on nineteenth-century workhouses (Ibid., p. 87). One represents the encyclopedist-student-of-history merely replicating a body of information; the second, on the other hand, *enters* the historical situation, through the action of the imagination on the knowledge, and writes from within it. One is handled externally; the second is apprehended "feelingly": the information has not only been read; it has been interpreted and criticized. One is virtuously slavish; the second operates powerfully within constraints which are used as enabling frames; one is a (rather alienated) spectator-text; the other is an expressive participant-spectator text, which is also impressive for the amount of sheer information it has subsumed.

5. See Erving Goffman, *Frame Analysis* (New York: Harper and Row, 1974).

6. On Harding, see James Britton, *Prospect and Retrospect* (Montclair, NJ: Boynton/Cook, 1982), pp. 46–67; and D. W. Harding, *Experience into Words* (Cambridge: Cambridge Univ. Pr., 1963), pp. 175–97.

7. Edith Bone, *Seven Years Solitary* (London: Hamish Hamilton, 1957). From 1949, Bone was held in solitary confinement in a Hungarian prison; found guilty of espionage, she lived under a threat of execution until she was released without warning in 1956 as a result of the uprising. Jacobo Timerman, *Prisoner without a Cell, Cell without a Number* (New York: Alfred Knopf, 1981).

8. One of the best accounts of this is to be found in Marguerite Yourcenar, *Memoirs of Hadrian* (New York: Farrar, Straus and Giroux, 1981), pp. 55–56. Keats's *Letters* provide one of the best examples of a writer exploring the complexities of the relationship between "self," identity, and writing: Keats, to the best of our knowledge, never uses the term "role," but it was clearly for him a rich and richly speculative question.

9. For a fuller account of this, see our *Frames of Mind: A Course in Composition* (New York: Random House, forthcoming), and *Acts of Mind, Forms of Discourse: A Theory of Composition* (New York: Random House, forthcoming).

10. A useful analysis of paratactic/hypotactic structures is offered by Thomas Farrell in "I.Q. and Standard English," *CCC,* 24, (December 1983), 470–84. Two of the best discussions of parataxis/hypotaxis not mentioned by Farrell are offered by Eric Auerbach in *Mimesis* (Princeton: Princeton Univ. Pr., 1968), and G. W. Turner, *Stylistics* (Harmondsworth, England: Penguin Books, 1973). A *paratactic* text is one in which all parts are presented as equivalent (e.g., A.B.C.D., or A and B and C and D); a *hypotactic* text is one in which various kinds of embeddings and subordinations, foregroundings and backgroundings, take place. The general consensus is that paratactic texts are closer in structure to utterance than are hypotactic texts.

11. James A. Notopoulos, "Parataxis in Homer," *Transactions of the American Philological Association,* 80 (1949), 1–23, quoted in Farrell, "I.Q. and Standard English," 11.

12. William Labov defines *evaluation* as "the means used by the narrator to indicate the point of the narrative, its raison d'etre: why it was told, and what the narrator is getting at." See Labov, *Language in the Inner City* (Philadelphia: Univ. of Pennsylvania Pr., 1972), p. 366.

13. *Daily Times,* May 10, 1983, Sec. A., p. 10.

14. George Kelly, *A Theory of Personality* (New York: Norton, 1963), pp. 8–9.

15. See Lev Vygotsky, *Thought and Language* (Cambridge, MA: MIT Press, 1962), p. 45.

The Process of Creative Discovery: Theory, Research, and Implications for Teaching

1. Readers may note similarities between our approach and others that have been articulated in the literature on rhetorical theory, most notably the work on heuristics by Richard Young. There are, as well, similarities that may be drawn between the classroom practices we advocate and the techniques introduced by William Coles, Peter Elbow, and Ken Macrorie. In this essay we will not discuss how our work either differs from or is congruent with other contributions to the field of composition. Nor will we attempt here to place our discussion with respect to the vast literatures dealing with thought, reflection, creativity, or problem-solving. Ours is another task. It is to present a few of the major implications of a new line of philosophical inquiry for pedagogical theories and practices. We make no claim to having the final word on this or related topics. In fact, in concentrating on the act we call creative discovery, we recognize that much else of vital concern for teachers and students must be left out.

2. Plato, *Meno* (Baltimore: Penguin, 1975), p. 128, 1.80D.

3. Plato, *Meno,* p. 128, 1.80C.

4. Jurgen Habermas, *Knowledge and Human Interests,* trans. Jeremy J. Shapiro (Boston: Beacon Press, 1971), pp. 214, 228, 234.

5. Eugene Gendlin et al., "Focusing Ability in Psychotherapy, Personality and Creativity," in *Research in Psychotherapy,* ed. George Shlein (Washington: American Psychological Association, 1968), pp. 116–28.

6. Ludwig Wittgenstein, *Philosophical Investigations,* trans. G. E. M. Anscombe (New York: Macmillan, 1968).

7. Martin Heidegger, *What Is a Thing?,* trans. W. B. Barton, Jr. and Vera Deutsch (Chicago: Henry Regnery, 1967).

8. Eugene Gendlin, *Experiencing and the Creation of Meaning* (New York: Free Press, 1962); "A Theory of Personality Change," in *Personality Change,* ed. Philip Worchel and Donn Byrne (New York: John Wiley, 1964); "What are the grounds of Explication?", *The Monist,* 49 (1965), 137–64; "Experiential Explication and Truth," *Journal of Existentialism,* 6 (1966), 131–46; "Experiential Phenomenology," in *Phenomenology and the Social Sciences,* ed. E. Natanson (Evanston, IL: Northwestern University Press, 1973).

9. The reader familiar with William James' description of the "stream of consciousness" in his *Psychology* will recognize the similarity between what we are referring to in this paragraph and James's famous observations. If we do not credit James as a major inspiration it is due to his not having used this observation to build a systematic experiential theory.

10. These examples—direct reference, metaphor, recognition—are only three of the seven relations that Gendlin analyzes at length in his *Experiencing and the Creation of Meaning.* The full account has served as the basis for numerous theoretical extensions, from the description of a radically empirical phenomenology ("Experiential Phenomenology," in *Phenomenology and the Social Sciences,* 1973), to a process theory of personality ("A Theory of Personality Change," in *Personality Change,* 1964), to the specification of the grounds on which truth may be located within the unfolding of explication ("Experiential Explication and Truth," in *Journal of Existentialism,* 6 [1966]), to a fuller application to conceptual difficulties that range from relativity theory in physics

to problems in ethology, biology, evolutionary theory, and the study of consciousness (work in progress).

11. Sondra Perl, "Five Writers Writing: Case Studies of the Composing Processes of Unskilled College Writers," Diss. New York University, 1978.

12. Heidegger, *What Is a Thing?*

13. Flower and Hayes demonstrate the usefulness of the "writer-based" and "reader-based" distinction in the analysis of written products. In the study referred to in this essay these terms are used to denote experientially identifiable processes present in varying degrees whenever writing occurs. See L. S. Flower, and J. R. Hayes, "Problem-Solving Strategies and the Writing Process," *College English,* 39 (1977), 449–61.

14. Unlike dialectical models (Kosok, 1966) this model is not at a loss to say what lies between stages of reflection—*felt* meaning—and is capable of apprehending a "beginning" that is no more than a vague, implicit, bodily sense. Let us call it a "knowing-but-not-knowing" (KBNK) sense. KBNK may come at any and all states of a creative process, from "knowing-but-not-knowing" how to begin, to the sense one cannot yet articulate of how to make the final revisions. It is the attending through direct reference to KBNK that constitutes the first interactive moment and through which KBNK differentiates itself into (a) a new version of the experiential aspect to which KBNK formerly referred, and (b) a new direct referent, which may be no more than a dawning sense that with further attending, this aspect may yield another differentiated sense. This new dawning sense that comes may be schematizable as the sense that "something-of-interest-may-be-discovered-here" (SOIMBDH). SOIMBDH involves an anticaptory implying of what next may be discovered, and constitutes a context, which Gendlin equates with what is commonly called a "positive mental set," for bringing attention to the new version of the experiential aspect to which SOIMBDH refers. It is this bringing of an aspect of experiencing into a context that implies the further differentiating of it that engenders new steps toward creative discovery. To state this another way, a forward-reaching anticipatory sense allows for a fresh reaching back to the inchoate feel of what, in the presense of an implying of further differentiations of it, yields a new grasp on itself. (See M. Kosok, "The Formalization of Hegel's Dialectical Logic," *International Philosophical Quarterly,* 6 (1966), 262–76.

In a work in progress one of the authors (Egendorf) describes in detail how this model may be seen to address some of the major shortcomings of dialectic, and to answer Broughton's call for the specification of "broader, qualitatively different, and more reflective domains of cognitive-affective development" that lie "beyond formal operations" as schematized by Piaget. (See J. Broughton, "Beyond Formal Operations: Theoretical Thought in Adolescence," *Teachers College Record,* 79 (1977), 87–97.

15. The IOFI principle allows us to understand theoretically how self-reflection resolves the quandary of self-expression. The reflexivity of self-reflection is the way in which experiencing may instance itself in symbolization. Self-reflection means attending to one's own experiencing so as to provide a context for it to instance itself (further differentiate itself). Thus, it is reflecting on one's sense of knowing-but-not-knowing that may resolve the quandary of self-expression through providing possibilities for that very sense—which "comprises," first implicitly, far more than may be brought to either the subject's or the observer's mind by the direct referent "knowing-but-not-knowing"—to begin instancing (explicating) itself in symbols.

16. See Gendlin "The Experiential Response," in *Use of Interpretation in Treatment,* ed. Richard Hammer (New York: Grune and Stratton, 1968); "Experiential Psychotherapy," in *Current Psychotherapies,* ed. Robert Corsini (Ithaca, IL: Peacock, 1973): and "Focusing," *Psychotherapy: Theory Research, and Practice,* 6 (Winter 1969); see also Arthur Egendorf, "Psychotherapy with Vietnam Veterans," in *Stress Disorders among Vietnam Veterans, ed.* Charles F. Figley (New York: Brunner/Mazel, 1968).

17. Eugene Gendlin, "Focusing," pp.4–15.

18. Plato, p. 139, 1.86C.

19. Martin Heidegger, *What Is Called Thinking?*, trans. by J. Glenn Gray (New York: Harper and Row, 1968), p. 15.

20. Heidegger, *What Is Called Thinking?*, p. 15.

21. Heidegger, *What Is Called Thinking?*, p. 15.

Alternatives to Mad-Hatterism

1. Lewis Carroll, *The Annotated Alice: Alice's Adventures in Wonderland,* ed. Martin Gardner (Middlesex, England: Penguin Books, 1970), p. 95.

2. Leonard Bloomfield, *Language* (London: Allen and Unwin, 1935), p. 21.

3. Francis Christensen, "A Generative Rhetoric of the Sentence," *College English,* 14 (October 1963); rpt. in *The Sentence and the Paragraph* (Urbana, IL: National Council of Teachers of English, 1966).

4. In particular, similar models are advanced in two unpublished papers written for the National Institute of Education, 1977: Linda Flower and Richard Hayes, "Plans and Cognitive Process of Writing," and Bertram Bruce, Allan Collins, and Ann Rubin, "A Cognitive Science Approach to Writing."

5. Eve V. Clark and Herbert H. Clark, *Psychology and Language* (New York: Harcourt, 1977), pp. 273–92.

6. Flower and Hayes, "Plans and the Cognitive Process of Writing."

7. Walter Kintsch, *The Representation of Meaning in Memory* (Hillsdale, NJ: Laurence Erlbaum, 1974), pp. 251–56.

8. Ellen W. Nold and Sarah W. Freedman, "An Analysis of Readers' Responses to Essays," *Research in the Teaching of English,* 2 (Fall 1977), 164–74; Sarah Warshauer Freedman, "Influences on the Evaluators of Student Writing," Diss. Stanford University, 1977.

9. Frank Smith's *Psycholinguistics and Reading* (New York: Holt, Rinehart and Winston, 1973) is an especially helpful source book, explaining these and other reading problems.

10. A. D. Van Nostrand, *Functional Writing* (Boston: Houghton, Mifflin, 1978).

11. See James Coomber's "Perceiving the Structure of Written Materials," *Research in the Teaching of English,* 9 (Winter 1975) for a concise discussion of this problem.

12. Kenneth Burke, *A Grammar of Motives* (New York: Prentice-Hall, 1945).

13. W. Ross Winterowd, "The Grammar of Coherence," *College English,* 31 (May 1970), 828–36.

14. Kenneth L. Pike, *Language in Relation to a Unified Theory of Human Behavior* (The Hague: Mouton, 1967).

15. Richard Young, Alton Becker, and Kenneth Pike, *Rhetoric: Discovery and Change* (New York: Harcourt, 1970).

16. John Mellon, *Transformational Sentence Combining: A Method of Enhancing the Development of Syntactic Fluency in English Composition* (Urbana, IL: National Council of Teachers of English, 1969); Frank O'Hare, *Sentence Combining: Improving Student Writing without Formal Grammar Instruction* (Urbana, IL: National Council of Teachers of English, 1973).

17. Warren E. Combs' article, "Further Effects of Sentence Combining Practice on Writing Ability," *Research in the Teaching of English,* 10 (Fall 1976), provides the most thorough and concise review and extension of the research.

18. Freedman, "Influences on Evaluators of Student Writing."

19. Fred I. Godshalk, Frances Swineford, and William E. Coffin, *The Measurement of Writing Ability* (New York: College Entrance Examination Board, 1966).

20. Sara E. Saunders and John H. Littlefield, "Perhaps Test Essays Can Reflect Significant Improvement in Freshman Composition," *Research in the Teaching of English,* 9 (Fall 1975), 145–53.

Composition in the Mimetic Mode: *Imitatio* and *Exercitatio*

1. Robert M. Pirsig, *Zen and the Art of Motorcycle Maintenance* (New York: Bantam, 1974), p. 170.

2. Allan A. Glatthorn and Harold Fleming, *Models for Composition* (New York: Harcourt, Brace, Jovanovich, 1967), p. v.

3. Glatthorn and Fleming, *Models for Composition 2* (New York: Harcourt, Brace, Jovanovich, 1968), p. vii.

4. Marcus Fabius Quintilianus, *De Institutione Oratoria*, Vol. IV, Book X, trans. H. E. Butler (Cambridge: Harvard Univ. Pr., 1958), p. 75.

5. Johann Wolfgang Von Goethe, *Conversations with Eckermann* (Washington: M. W. Dunne, 1901), p. 149.

6. *Timber: or Discoveries*, in *Ben Jonson: The Complete Poems,* ed. George Parfit (Baltimore: Penguin, 1975), p. 448.

7. "A College Magazine," in *Essays by Robert Louis Stevenson* (New York: Scribner's, 1918), pp. 286–87.

8. Ed. Russel B. Nye (Boston: Houghton Mifflin, 1958), pp. 12–13.

9. In a letter to me, March 12, 1969.

10. In a letter to me, March, 1969.

11. In a letter to me, March 25, 1969.

12. In a letter to me, March, 1969.

13. In a letter to me, April, 1969. Subsequent references to this source shall appear in the text.

14. In a letter to me, June 25, 1969.

15. In a letter to me, April 3, 1969.

16. In a letter to me, May, 1969.

17. In a letter to me, March, 1969.

18. In a letter to me, March, 1969. Subsequent references to this source shall appear in the text.

20. In a letter to me, June 27, 1969.

21. In a letter to me, March 17, 1969.

22. *The Lichtenberg Reader: Selected Writings of Georg Christoph Lichtenberg*, trans. and ed. Franz H. Mautner and Henry Hatfield (Boston: Beacon Press, 1959), p. 62.

23. Samuel Taylor Coleridge, "On Poesy or Art," in *Biographical Essays of My Literary Life and Opinions* (London: Rest Fenner, 1907), II, 255–60.

24. Jonson, p. 425.

25. See "A Generative Rhetoric of the Sentence," *College Composition and Communication,* 14 (October 1963), 155–61; and "A Generative Rhetoric of the Paragraph," *College Composition and Communication,* 16 (October 1965), 144–56. Both are included in Christensen's *Notes Toward a New Rhetoric: Six Essays for Teachers* (New York: Harper and Row, 1967).

26. *American Composition and Rhetoric* (New York: Scribner's, 1968), p. 203.

27. Winifred Bryan Horner, ed., *Composition and Literature: Bridging the Gap* (Chicago: University of Chicago Press, 1983, 104–109.

The Relation of the Whole to the Part in Interpretation Theory and in the Composing Process

1. See Ingrid Strom, "Research in Grammar and Usage and Its Implications for Teaching Writing," *Bulletin of the School of Education, Indiana University* (1960), pp. 1–21. Also see Richard Braddock et al., *Research in Written Composition* (Champaign, IL: NCTE, 1963), p. 34; Frank O'Hare, *Sentence Combining: Improving Student Writing without Formal Grammar Instruction,* Research Report No. 15 (Urbana, IL: National Council of Teachers of English, 1971). For a British view see Andrew Wilkinson, *The Foundations of Language* (New York: Oxford Univ. Pr., 1971), pp. 32–34.

2. Patricia Senn Brievik, "Effects of Library-Based Instruction in the Academic Success of

Disadvantaged Undergraduates," in H. B. Rader, ed., *Academic Library Instruction: Objectives, Program and Faculty Involvement* (Ann Arbor, MI: Pierian Press, 1975), pp. 45–55.

3. L. Ray Carry and J. Fred Weaver, *Patterns of Mathematics Achievement in Grades 4, 5, and 6: X-Population* (Palo Alto, CA: Stanford University School Mathematics Study Group, 1969); see especially chapter 6 and appendixes B and D, pp. 167 ff. and 201 ff.

4. See James L. Kinneavy, John Q. Cope, and J. W. Campbell, *Writing—Basic Modes of Organization* (Dubuque, IA: Kendall/Hunt, 1976), pp. 30–34 for a use of the Piaget model in teaching description. See Eugene C. Luschei, *The Logical Systems of Lesniewski* (Amsterdam: North Holland, 1962), pp. 151 ff., for a summary of Lesniewski's theory of mereology. The defect in Piaget's model, for my purposes, is that his three matrix structures do not seem to include some obvious non-mathematical structures, such as plot. The drawback in Lesniewski's theory, for my purposes, is that he reduces parts of a whole to subsets of a set. But the part-whole relationship is often not that of a subset-set relationship; that is, a door-room relationship is not that of a kind of a room to a room.

5. Richard E. Palmer, *Hermeneutics: Interpretation Theory in Schleiermacher, Dilthey, Heidegger, and Gadamer* (Evanston, IL: Northwestern University Press, 1969), p. 87.

6. Hans-Georg Gadamer, *Truth and Method,* tr. G. Barden and J. Cumming. (New York: The Seabury Press, 1969), p. 154.

7. See John C. Maraldo, *Der Hermeneutische Zirkel* (Munich: Verlag Karl Alber, 1974), p. 13; Gadamer, pp. 154 ff.; Emilio Betti, *Allgemeine Auslegungslehre als Methodik der Geisteswissenschaften* (Tübingen: J. C. B. Mohr, 1976), pp. 219–20.

8. Gadamer, p. 167.

9. See Betti, comparing the *iter geneticum* with the *iter hermeneuticum,* pp. 179 ff., 222; Gadamer, 19 ff.; for more lengthy considerations on the relation between rhetoric and hermeneutics, see Hans-Georg Gadamer, *Philosophical Hermeneutics,* tr. and ed. David E. Linge (Berkely, CA: Univ. of California Pr., 1977), pp. 20–26; see further Klaus Dockhorn, "Gelehrten-Anzeigen," *Gottingen,* 213, Heft 3/4 (1966), 169–206.

10. Hans-Georg Gadamer, in a talk at Gustavus Adolphus College, St. Peter's Minnesota, Dec. 2, 1977, mentioned that Melanchthon, starting a book on rhetoric, ended up writing one on the interpretation of written texts. I assume he refers to *Loci communes rerum theologicarum seu hypotoposes theologicae,* Luther's (and Protestantism's) first important theological treatise. The rhetorical origin is obvious in the first two words of the title—the abbreviated form by which the works is usually known.

11. See Betti, pp. 220, 221, 222, 224.

12. See Gadamer, p. 167, discussing Droysen; pp. 236, 237, 268 ff., discussing the concept of horizon, especially p. 273.

13. See Gadamer, p. 163; Maraldo, pp. 33-50; and the two volumes *Hermeneutik und Dialektik,* ed. Rudiger Bubner, Konrad Cramer, and Reiner Wiehl (Tübingen: J. C. B. Mohr, 1970), especially I, 167 ff. and II, 273 ff.

14. See Maraldo, explaining Schleiermacher, p. 31; Betti, p. 224.

15. See Malcolm Cowley, ed., *Writers at Work: The Paris Review Interviews* (New York: Viking, 1958). There are additional volumes in the series.

16. For applications of these concepts at various levels, see Kenneth Pike, *Language in Relation to a Unified Theory of Human Behavior,* 3 vols., (Glendale, CA: Summer Institute of Linguistics, 1960); for the discourse level, see Richard Young, Samuel Becker, and Kenneth Pike, *Rhetoric: Discovery and Change* (New York: Harcourt, Brace and World, 1970); for the paragraph level, see below.

17. E. D. Hirsch, Jr., *The Aims of Interpretation* (Chicago: Univ. of Chicago Pr., 1976), p. 66.

18. Jacques Derrida, *Of Grammatology,* tr. G. Spivak (Baltimore: The Johns Hopkins Univ. Pr., 1976), p. 29, his italics.

19. Claude Lévi-Strauss, *Structural Anthropology,* tr. Claire Jacobson and Brooke Grundfest Schoepf (New York: Doubleday, Anchor Books, 1967), p. 33.

20. Lévi-Strauss, p. 208.

21. Paul Ricoeur, *Le Conflit des interpretations* (Paris: Editions du Seuil, 1969), p. 81.

22. Ricoeur, p. 81.

23. Paul Ricoeur, "Qu'est-ce qu'un texte?" in Bubner, *Hermeneutik*, II, 190.

24. Ricoeur, "Qu'est-ce qu'un texte?" p. 191, p. 196.

25. Ricoeur, "Qu'est-ce qu'un texte?" p. 196.

26. Gérard Genette, *Figures III* (Paris: Editions du Seuil, 1972), p. 75.

27. Genette, p. 76.

28. Genette, p. 76.

29. Genette, p. 80, p. 81, pp. 84–5.

30. Lévi-Strauss, p. 206.

31. Lévi-Strauss, p. 207, his italics.

32. John R. Searle, *Speech Acts: An Essay in the Philosophy of Language* (Cambridge: Cambridge Univ. Pr., 1969), pp. 17–19.

33. Paul Valéry, *Variété, III* (Paris: Gallimard, 1936), p. 158.

34. Searle, pp. 62–63.

35. See pp. 84, 85, 86, 90, 91, especially p. 92; on p. 94 the context becomes part of the formula; see also pp. 116, 117, 142, 143, 144, 145, 146, 147, 149, 152, 186.

36. See Searle, p. 152.

37. D. Terence Langendoen, *The London School of Linguistics: A Study of B. Malinowski and J. R. Firth* (Cambridge, MA: M.I.T. Press, 1968), p. 19, note 1.

38. Mary Louise Pratt, *Toward a Speech Act Theory of Literary Discourse* (Bloomington, IN: Indiana Univ. Pr., 1977), pp. 85–86.

39. Pratt, p. 141.

40. Pratt, pp. 141–42.

41. C. E. Bazell, *Linguistic Form* (Istanbul: Istanbul Press, 1953).

42. Bazell, p. 88 ff.

43. Donald Daiker, Andrew Kerek, Max Morenberg, "Sentence Combining and Syntactic Maturity in Freshman English," *College Composition and Communication*, 19 (February 1978), 36–41.

44. Daiker, p. 14, in the manuscript version. See also their essay in this volume.

45. O'Hare, pp. 69, 76.

46. John C. Mellon, *Transformational Sentence Combining: A Method for Enhancing the Development of Syntactic Fluency in English Composition*, Research Report No. 10 (Champaign, IL: National Council of Teachers of English, 1969), p. 2; Kellogg Hunt, *Grammatical Structures Written at Three Grade Levels*, Research Report No. 3 (Champaign, IL: National Council of Teachers of English, 1965), p. 151.

47. A. L. Becker, "Symposium on the Paragraph," *College Composition and Communication*, 17 (May 1966), 71.

48. Paul C. Rodgers, Jr., "Symposium on the Paragraph," *College Composition and Communication*, 17 (May 1966), 73.

49. Rodgers, 73.

50. Gadamer, p. 153.

51. Gadamer, p. 154.

52. Quoted in Rhys Roberts, ed., *Dionysius of Halicarnassus*, tr. Rhys Roberts, *On Literary Composition* (London: Macmillan, 1919), p. 304. He refers to S. H. Butcher, *Harvard Lectures on Greek Subjects*, pp. 117–20.

53. Mario Untersteiner, *The Sophists*, tr. Kathleen Freeman (Oxford: Basil Blackwell, 1954), quoting Gino Funaioli, *Studi de letteratura antica*, (Bologna, 1946), I, 176; Untersteiner, p. 197.

54. W. K. C. Guthrie, *A History of Greek Philosophy* (Cambridge: At the University Press, 1969), III, 272, n. 4.

55. Untersteiner, p. 41.

56. Untersteiner, p. 47, pp. 52–53.

57. Untersteiner, p. 29.

58. *Philosophy and Rhetoric*, 7 (1975), 175–86.

59. Eduard Zeller, *History of Greek Philosophy,* tr. S. F. Alleyne (London: Longmans, Green, and Co., 1881), II, 485n.

60. Untersteiner, pp. 116 ff.

61. Untersteiner, p. 161.

62. Untersteiner, p. 161.

63. Guthrie, p. 431.

64. Plato, *Phaedrus,* tr. W. C. Helmbold and W. G. Rabinowitz (Indianapolis: Bobbs-Merrill, 1958), 271 E ff.; the italics under the several occurrences of this are the translators' and the other italics are mine.

66. See Herman Bonitz, *Index Aristotelicus* (Berlin: Akademische Druck. U. Verlangsantalt, 1955), p. 358a.

67. See H. H. Joachim, *Aristotle: The Nicomachean Ethics,* ed. S. A. Rees (Oxford: At the Clarendon Press, 1951), pp. 2, 14–18.

68. *Nich. Ethics,* 1104a, 8–9.

69. *On Literary Composition,* tr. W. Rhys Roberts (London: Macmillan, 1910), pp. 12, 84.

70. The number depends on the concordance consulted. This figure is from J. B. Smith, *Greek-English Concordance to the New Testament* (Scottdale, PA: Herald Press, 1955), p. 187; George Wigram, *The Englishman's Greek Concordance to the New Testament,* 9th ed., (Grand Rapids, MI: Zondervan Publishing House, 1971), pp. 398–399, gives 83. At any rate, the number is high.

71. Paul Tillich, "Kairos and Logos," *Philosophie und Schicksal: Schriften zur Erkenntnislehre und Existenzphilosophie,* in *Gesammelte Werke,* IV, 46; cf. also "Kairos I," *Der Widerstreit von Raum und Zeit: Schriften Zur Geschichtsphilosophie,* in *Gesammelte Werke,* VI, 10. For further lengthy statements of Tillich on *kairos,* see "Kairos II, Ideen zur Geisteslage der Gegenwart," 29–41, "Kairos und Utopie," 149–56, both in *Gessammelte Werke,* VI; and "Kairos and Karoi," *Systematic Theology,* (Chicago, IL: Univ. of Chicago Pr., 1963), III, 369–72.

72. "Christian Root-Terms: *Kerygma, Mysterium, Kairos, Oikonomia,*" in Thomas A. O'Meara, O. P., and Celestin D. Weisser, O. P., eds., *Paul Tillich in Catholic Thought* (Dubuque, IA: Priority Press, 1964), 202–4, quoted in Carl J. Armbruster, S.J., *The Vision of Paul Tillich* (New York: Sheed and Ward), 1967, p. 270.

73. See Max Pohlenz, "To Prepon," *Kleine Schriften,* II, ed. Heinrich Dorrie (Hildsheim: G. Olms, 1965), pp. 100–139.

74. Pohlenz, 109.

75. *De Inventione,* I, 6, 8. Different terms are used by different authors for these concepts. Yon believes that Cicero may have repudiated the position of the *Inventione* in the *De Oratore,* I, 31, 138 and II, 24, 104 and in the *Orator,* XIV, 45, 46. See Albert Yon, ed., *Cicero, L'Orateur, Du Meilleur genre d'orateurs* (Paris: Les Belles Lettres, 1974), pp. xlvii–xlviii.

76. Lloyd F. Bitzer, "The Rhetorical Situation," *Philosophy and Rhetoric,* I (1968), 1–14; Edwin Black, *Rhetorical Criticism: A Study in Method* (New York: Macmillan, 1965).

77. Tr. H. Richard Niebuhr (New York: Meridian Books, 1956).

78. Tillich, *Systematic Theology,* III, 371.

79. Sigmund Freud, *The Interpretation of Dreams,* tr. A. A. Brill, in *The Major Works of Sigmund Freud,* ed. Robert Maynard Hutchins and Mortimer J. Adler (Chicago:IL, Encyclopedia Britannica, Inc., 1952), p. 285.

80. See pp. 180, 181, 182, 200, 201, 202, 205, 206, 209, 210, 211, 212, 237, 240, 332, 336, 338; on the dangers of interpretation of fictional dreams of poets and novelists, see p. 327.

81. See Gadamer, pp. 167, 174, 190, for Dilthey and Droysen; see Maraldo, p. 74.

Theme in Fictional Literature: A Way into Complexity

1. A discussion and documentation of these trends can be found in Richard Young, "Invention: A Topographical Survey," in *Teaching Composition: Ten Bibliographical Essays,* ed., Gary Tate (Forth Worth: Texas Christian University Press, 1976), pp. 1–43.

2. A brief summary of these principles can be found in Kenneth Pike,"Beyond the Sentence," *College Composition and Communication,* 15 (Oct. 1964), 129–35. For additional citations, see Young, "Topographical Survey," pp. 21–22.

3. For an extended explanation of tagmemic invention, see Richard E. Young, Alton L. Becker, and Kenneth L. Pike, *Rhetoric: Discovery and Change* (New York: Harcourt, Brace and World, 1970), pp. 25–169.

4. For an explanation and illusrations, see Young, Becker, and Pike, *Rhetoric,* pp. 119–54, especially p. 127.

5. Edward P. J. Corbett's "Introduction" in *Rhetorical Analyses of Literary Works* (New York: Oxford Univ. Pr., 1969) provides a brief discussion of the tradition.

6. Northrop Frye, "Literary Criticism," in *The Aims and Methods of Scholarship in Modern Languages and Literature,* ed. James Thorpe (New York: Modern Language Association, 1963), p. 65.

7. Frye, "Literary Criticism", p. 75.

8. The term as used here refers to one kind of system within a particular literary work and not, as in Jost Trier's work, to "closely-knit sectors of the vocabulary, in which a particular sphere is divided up, classified and organized in such a way that each element helps to delimit its neighbors and is delimited by them." Stephen Ullmann, *Semantics: An Introduction to the Science of Meaning* (New York: Barnes and Noble, 1964), p. 245.

9. Wallace Stegner, "Fiction: A Lens on Life," *Saturday Review of Literature,* April 22, 1950, 9–10.

10. Herbert A. Simon, "The Architecture of Complexity," *Proceedings of the American Philosophical Society,* 106 (1962), 468.

11. Roman Ingarden, *The Cognition of the Literary Work of Art,* trans. Ruth Ann Crowley and Kenneth R. Olson (Evanston, IL: Northwestern Univ. Pr., 1973), pp. 37–41.

12. C. S. Lewis, *Studies in Words* (London: Cambridge Univ. Pr., 1960), p. 214.

13. William Holtz, "Spatial Form in Modern Literature: A Reconsideration." *Critical Inquiry,* 4 (Winter 1977), 278.

14. Cleanth Brooks and Robert Penn Warren, *Understanding Fiction,* 2d ed. (New York: Appleton-Century Crofts, 1959), p. 75.

15. Young, Becker, and Pike, *Rhetoric,* pp. 122–30. For a more extensive discussion of field perspective, see Kenneth L. Pike, "Language as Particle, Wave and Field," *Texas Quarterly,* 2 (Summer 1954), 37–54.

16. Page references following the quotations are to Isaac Babel, *The Collected Stories,* ed. and trans. Walter Morison (Cleveland, OH: World, 1960).

17. Vladimir Propp, *Morphology of the Folktale,* trans. Laurence Scott; rev. and ed. Louis A. Wagner, AFS Memoir Series, Vol. 9 (Austin: Univ. of Texas Pr., 1968).

18. Quoted in Roman Jakobson, "Closing Statement: Linguistics and Poetics," in *Style in Language,* ed. Thomas A. Sebeok (Cambridge, MA: MIT Press, 1960), p. 368.

19. Jakobson, "Closing Statement," p. 374.

20. For an illustration of classification of low-level units, see Mark Schorer, "Fiction and the 'Analogical Matrix,' " in *Critiques and Essays on Modern Fiction: 1920–1951,* ed. John W. Aldridge (New York: Ronald Press, 1952), pp. 83–98.

21. Jonathan Culler, "Defining Narrative Units," in *Style and Structure in Literature: Essays on the New Stylistics,* ed. Roger Fowler (Ithaca, NY: Cornell Univ. Pr., 1975), p. 139.

22. For discussions of this conflict see Frank O'Connor, *The Lonely Voice: A Study of the Short Story* (Cleveland, OH: World, 1963), pp. 187–201; and Lionel Trilling, "Introduction" to Babel, *Collected Stories,* pp. 93–137.

23. Babel, *Collected Stories*, pp. 192–93.

24. W. H. Auden, "Musée des Beaux Arts," in *The Collected Poetry of W. H. Auden* (New York: Random House, 1945).

25. Joseph Frank, "Spatial Form in Modern Literature," in *Critiques and Essays in Criticism: 1920–1948*, ed. Robert Wooster Stallman (New York: Ronald Press, 1949), p. 321. William Holtz suggested extending tagmemic field theory to the works discussed by Frank in "Field Theory and Literature," *Centennial Review*, 2 (Fall 1967), 532–48.

26. Frank, "Spatial Form," p. 321.

The Return of Eloquence: Richard Lanham and the Teaching of Writing

1. Both are published by Boynton/Cook Publishers, Montclair, NJ, 1979 and 1981 respectively. See, in addition, Berthoff's essay in this volume, "Abstraction as Speculative Instrument," pp. 227–37.

2. E. H. Gombrich, *Art and Illusion* (Princeton: Princeton Univ. Pr., 1960); Rudolf Arnheim, *Art and Visual Perception* (Berkeley: Univ. of California Pr., 1964); Kenneth Burke, *Counterstatement* (Berkeley: Univ. of California Pr., 1930).

Toward Real Philosophic Laboratories: Ann Berthoff on Writing Theory and Practice

1. Some representative works: W. Ross Winterowd, "The Grammar of Coherence," *College English*, 31 (May 1970), 328–35; Richard Young, Alton Becker, and Kenneth Pike, *Rhetoric: Discovery and Change* (New York: Harcourt, Brace and World, 1970); Frank D'Angelo, *A Conceptual Theory of Rhetoric* (Cambridge, MA: Winthrop, 1975); James Kinneavy, *A Theory of Discourse* (Englewood Cliffs, NJ: Prentice-Hall, 1971, rpt. New York: Norton, 1980); Linda Flower and John R. Hayes, "A Cognitive Process Theory of Writing," *College Composition and Communication*, 32 (December 1981), 365–87. Essays by the first four authors also appear in this volume.

2. *Forming/Thinking/Writing: The Composing Imagination* (Rochelle Park, NJ: Hayden Book Company, 1978); *The Making of Meaning: Metaphors, Models and Maxims for Writing Teachers* (Monclair, NJ: Boynton/Cook Publishers, 1981); *Reclaiming the Imagination, Philosophical Perspective for Writers and Teachers of Writing* (Upper Montclair, NJ: Boynton/Cook Publishers, Inc., 1984).

3. Perhaps the most obvious source for this view is Thomas Kuhn, *The Structure of Scientific Revolutions*, 2d ed. (Chicago: Univ. of Chicago Pr., 1970).

4. See Paulo Freire, *Educational for Critical Consciousness* (New York: Seabury Press, 1973), and *Pedagogy of the Oppressed*, trans. M. B. Ramos (New York: Herder and Herder, 1972).

5. For an illuminating essay on this Heideggerian view of language, see Paul Kameen, "Rewording the Rhetoric of Composition," *Pre/Text* 1 (Spring-Fall 1980), 73–94. See also Berthoff's new essay in the present volume, "Abstraction As a Speculative Instrument."

6. This optimistic view of language is, of course, not universally held. Ross Winterowd, for example, examines Derrida's darker perspective of language in "Post-Structuralism and Composition," *Pre/Text* 4 (Spring 1983), 79–92, and in "Black Holes, Indeterminacy and Paulo Freire," *Rhetoric Review*, 2 (September 1983), 28–35.

7. "I. A. Richards and the Philosophy of Rhetoric," *Rhetoric Society Quarterly*, 10 (Fall 1980), 195–219.

8. *The Making of Meaning*, p. 15.

9. "Thinking about Language," in *The Making of Meaning*, p. 109.

10. "Thinking about Language," p. 108.

11. Michael Cole and Sylvia Scribner, *The Psychology of Literacy* (Cambridge, MA: Harvard Univ. Pr., 1981). See also Linda Flower, "Response to Anthony Petrosky," *College Composition and Communication*, (February 1984), 96–7.

12. "Learning the Uses of Chaos," in *The Making of Meaning,* p. 71.

13. *Reclaiming the Imagination,* p. 226.

14. "The Teacher as Researcher," in *The Making of Meaning,* p. 31.

15. For two assessments of cognitive psychology and writing theory, see Patricia Bizzell, "Cognition, Convention, and Certainty: What We Need to Know About Writing," *Pre/Text* 3 (Fall 1982), 213–43, and John Clifford, "Cognitive Psychology and Writing: A Critique," *Freshman English News,* 13 (Spring 1984), 16–18.

16. The specifics of this kind of writing workshop and its theoretical assumptions are cogently unpacked in C. H. Knoblauch and Lil Brannon, *Rhetorical Traditions and the Teaching of Writing* (Upper Montclair, NJ: Boynton/Cook Publishers, 1984), pp. 98–150.

Writing across the Curriculum: A Bibliographic Essay

1. As quoted in Robert F. Dunn, "A Response to Two Views," *AAHE Bulletin* (December 1982), p. 7. Subsequent references to works cited are included in parentheses in the text.

Notes on Contributors

David Bartholomae is Associate Professor of English and Director of Composition at the University of Pittsburgh. He is a member of the Executive Committee of the Conference on College Composition and Communication and has served on the Board of Directors of the Council of Writing Program Administrators. He has published several essays on composition theory and teaching. In 1981 he won the Braddock Award for his essay "The Study of Error," which appeared originally in *College Composition and Communication*.

Ann E. Berthoff is Professor of English at the University of Massachusetts at Boston. She has served on the National Council of Teachers of English Commission on Composition and the Executive Committee of the Modern Language Association Division of Teaching of Writing. She has taught in the Bread Loaf School of English Program in Writing and in 1980 directed an NEH Summer Seminar, Philosophy and the Composing Process. Her publications include *The Resolved Soul: A Study of Marvell's Major Poems* and three books on writing, *Forming/Thinking/Writing, The Making of Meaning,* and *Reclaiming the Imagination.*

Patricia Bizzell and Bruce Herzberg direct writing-across-the-curriculum programs at their respective schools, Holy Cross and Bentley College. Bizzell's recent publications include a review-essay in *PrelText* on the work of Flower and Hayes, and Herzberg's a primer on word processing for *Writing Program Administration*. Bizzell and Herzberg frequently collaborate, most recently on the *Bedford Bibliography for Teachers of Writing* and on a bibliographic essay concerning writing-across-the-curriculum textbooks for *Rhetoric Review*. They live in Worcester, Massachusetts, with their two daughters.

Kenneth Bruffee is Professor of English at Brooklyn College, City University of New York. He is the former chair of the Modern Language Association Teaching of Writing Division, editor of *WPA*, the journal of the Council of Writing Program Administrators, and director of a national institute on peer tutoring and collaborative learning. He has published widely on innovation in postsecondary education and on modern British fiction. His books include *A Short Course in Writing* and *Elegiac Romance: Cultural Change and Loss of the Hero in Modern Fiction.*

John Clifford is Associate Professor of English and Director of Writing at the University of North Carolina at Wilmington. He has published three writing texts, most recently *Writing, Reading and Research*. His essays and reviews have appeared in *Freshman*

English News, Research in the Teaching of English, and *College Composition and Communication.*

Robert J. Connors is Professor of English at the University of New Hampshire, Durham. He has published articles in *College English, College Composition and Communication, Rhetoric Society Quarterly, Freshman English News, Journal of Technical Writing and Communication,* and *Rhetoric Review.* He is coeditor, with Lisa S. Ede and Andrea Lunsford, of *Essays on Classical Rhetoric and Modern Discourse* (Southern Illinois University Press, 1984), which received the MLA Mina P. Shaughnessy Award for 1985.

Edward P. J. Corbett is Professor of English at Ohio State University. His publications include *Classical Rhetoric for the Modern Student, The Little Rhetoric and Handbook,* and *The Writing Teacher's Sourcebook.*

Donald A. Daiker, Andrew Kerek, and Max Morenberg: Professors of English at Miami University, the authors have collaborated on numerous books and articles, including *The Writer's Options, Sentence Combining and the Teaching of Writing, Sentence Combining and College Composition,* and *Sentence Combining: A Rhetorical Perspective.* Donald A. Daiker, Director of Miami's Center for the Study of Writing, has published on American literature and coauthored *Literature: Options for Reading and Writing.* Andrew Kerek is Associate Dean of the College of Arts and Science, with a publishing record in linguistics. Max Morenberg is Director of the Linguistics Program at Miami and Co-Director of the Ohio Writing Project.

Frank J. D'Angelo directs the doctoral program in rhetoric and composition at Arizona State University. A former chair of the Conference on College Composition and Communication and member of the Executive Committee of the National Council of Teachers of English, he currently serves on the Executive Committee of the Modern Language Association, the Board of Directors of the Rhetoric Society of America, and the Publications Committee of the CCCC. He has published widely in professional journals.

Robert DiYanni is Associate Professor of English at Pace University, where he teaches composition and English and American literature. He is coeditor, with John Clifford, of *Modern American Prose: A Reader for Writers,* author of *Connections: Reading/Writing/ Thinking,* and editor of *Reading Literature: An Introduction to Fiction, Poetry, Drama, and Essay.*

Lester Faigley is a member of the English department at the University of Texas, Austin, where he teaches courses on discourse analysis and theories of composing in the graduate rhetoric program. He is the coauthor, with Stephen Witte, of *Evaluating College Writing Programs* (Southern Illinois University Press, 1983) and the principal author of *Assessing Writers' Knowledge and Processes of Composing* (Ablex).

Donald C. Freeman, formerly Professor of English at Temple University and the University of Massachusetts, is author of *Linguistics and Literary Style, Essays in Modern Stylistics,* and numerous articles on English stylistics, metrics, and the teaching of writing. He is currently Director of Professional Development with the international law firm of Baker & McKenzie.

D. G. Kehl is Professor of English at Arizona State University, Tempe. He is author of "The Chiaroscuro World of Par Graffitist Lagerkvist" (*Modern Fiction Studies*, 1969), "The Belletrist and the Graffitist" (*CEA Critic*, 1978), "The Doublespeak of Academia" (*National Forum*, 1980), and *Control Yourself: Practicing the Art of Self-Discipline*. His research interests include literature and theology, rhetoric, and popular culture.

James Kinneavy is Jane and Roland Blumberg Centennial Professor of English at the University of Texas, Austin where he directs the graduate rhetoric program. He has published widely on rhetoric and composition and has written several studies, including *A Theory of Discourse, Three Contemporary Theories of the Lyric*, and most recently, *Did Christian Faith Derive from Greek Rhetoric?*

Richard L. Larson is Professor of English and Director of the Institute for the Study of Literacy at Herbert Lehman College, City University of New York. Professor Larson has published essays in *College English, Rhetoric Society Quarterly, English Leaflet, College Composition and Communication*, and in numerous collections.

Donald A. McQuade is Professor of English and Director of the freshman composition program at the University of California, Berkeley. His publications include *Popular Writing in America: The Interaction of Style and Audience* (edited with Robert Atwan), *Edsels, Luckies, and Frigidaires: Advertising the American Way* (coauthored with Robert Atwan and John Wright), *Writing Productively*, and *The Harper American Literature* (general editor.)

Elaine Maimon is Professor of English and Associate Vice President of Beaver College, where she also directs the writing-across-the-curriculum program. With four colleagues representing a variety of disciplines, she has written two composition textbooks, *Writing in the Arts and Sciences* and *Readings in the Arts and Sciences*. As a member of the NEH National Board of Consultants, she has advised many colleges and universities on writing and the humanities.

Louis T. Milic is Professor of English at Cleveland State University. He is author of "Theories of Style and Their Implications for the Teaching of Composition" (*College Composition and Communication*, 1966), and *A Quantitative Approach to the Style of Jonathan Swift* and editor of *Stylists on Style*. His research interests include rhetoric, eighteenth-century English literature, and computer-assisted literary research.

For the past five years, Ellen Nold has been battling Mad Hatterism in industry as a manager at Apple Computer. She maintains her ties with academia by attending professional meetings. Her research interests include revision and computers and the writing process.

Sondra Perl and Arthur Egendorf: Sondra Perl is Associate Professor of English at Herbert H. Lehman College, City University of New York, and Director of the New York City Writing Project. She is coauthor, with Nancy Wilson, of *Through Teachers' Eyes: Portraits of Writing Teachers at Work* and author of many articles on writing research and theory. She was recipient of a Guggenheim Fellowship for 1984–85. Arthur Egendorf practices and teaches psychotherapy in New York. A member of the President's Commission on Mental Health, he has written numerous articles and was one of the principal authors of the congressional study *Legacies of Vietnam*. His latest book is *Healing from the War: Trauma and Transformation after Vietnam*.

Sandra Schor is Assistant Professor of English at Queens College of the City University of New York, where she has been Director of Composition and Director of the Queens English Project. Named a "Master Teacher" in the CUNY Faculty Development program, she is currently training colleagues from other disciplines in the teaching of basic writing. She has published poems, short stories, and articles and is author, with Judith Fishman Summerfield, of *The Random House Guide to Writing* and, with Frederick Crews, of *The Borzoi Handbook for Writers*.

Judith Fishman Summerfield teaches at Queens College, CUNY. She has served on the Executive Committee of the Conference on College Composition and Communication and has taught graduate workshops on narratology at various universities. She is coauthor, with Sandra Schor, of *The Random House Guide to Writing* and author of *Responding to Prose*. Geoffrey Summerfield has taught at the University of York, England, the University of California at Berkeley, New York University, Utah State University, the University of Nebraska, and City University of New York. He participated in the Dartmouth Seminar and the Sydney International Conference. His recent books include *Welcome* (selected poems), *Four Seasons,* and *Fantasy and Reason: Children, Culture, and Literature 1695-1815*. He now lives in New York, working as a writer, consultant, and adjunct professor.

Joseph M. Williams is Professor of English and Linguistics at the University of Chicago. He is the author of *The New English, The Origins of the English Language*, and *Style*. He is coeditor, with Timothy Shopen, of *Standards and Dialects* and *Style and Variables*. With a colleague, Gregory Colomb, he has recently completed *Discourse Structure*.

W. Ross Winterowd is the Bruce R. McElderry Professor of English at the University of Southern California, where he founded the graduate program in rhetoric, linguistics, and literature. He has published widely in composition, rhetoric, and other fields. His most recent book is *Composition/Rhetoric:A Synthesis* (Southern Illinois University Press, 1986).

Stephen P. Witte, John A. Daly, and Roger Cherry: Stephen P. Witte, formerly Assistant Professor of English at the University of Texas, Austin, now works for Information Transfer Services. He has published on research in composition and is coauthor, with Lester Faigley, of *Evaluating College Writing Programs* (Southern Illinois University Press, 1983). John A. Daly is Associate Professor, College of Communication, University of Texas, Austin. Editor of the journal *Communication Education* and coeditor of *Written Communication*, he has published many articles and edited two books, *Avoiding Communication: Shyness, Reticence, and Communication Apprehension* and *Personality and Interpersonal Communication*. Roger D. Cherry is Assistant Professor of English at New Mexico State University. He is coauthor, with Lester Faigley, David

Jolliffe, and Anna Skinner, of *Assessing Writers' Knowledge and Processes of Composing*.

Richard Young is Professor of English and Rhetoric and Head of the English Department at Carnegie-Mellon University, where he has been developing graduate programs in rhetorical studies. He received his Ph.D. in English Language and Literature from the University of Michigan in 1964. From 1964 to 1978 he was a member of the Department of Humanities at Michigan and, for five years, Chairman of the Department. While at Michigan he was also a Research Associate in the Center for Research on Language and Language Behavior, working on problems in rhetoric—particularly on problems associated with discourse structures larger than the sentence and with modern theories of rhetorical invention.